HALL OF HEROES

A Fellowship of Fantasy anthology

Dear Reader,

Welcome to the Hall of Heroes, the second anthology from the Fellowship of Fantasy. We are excited to present to you our tales of heroism. These heroes (and of course, heroines) come in all shapes, sizes, and sorts. You will encounter stories ranging from modern super hero adventures, to traditional fairy tales and everything in between!

Follow a slave girl forced to face her worst fears within the Labyrinth, a princess on a quest to rescue a prince, and an upright bear on a mission to save bearkind! Root for our heroes as they face danger, lead revolutions, and protect what is precious. There are many perilous journeys ahead of you, but no graphic content. All the stories here fall below a PG-13 rating.

The Fellowship of Fantasy is an online group of writers dedicated to presenting the best in clean fantasy stories of any stripe. Some tackle epic quests to save the world, while others prefer more urban settings. Whether you enjoy contemporary tales, romantic re-tellings, or something else entirely, you're sure to find stories that speak to you.

Thank you for joining us, and may you conquer your trials with our heroes at your side!

Sincerely,
The Fellowship of Fantasy Authors

CONTENTS

Alancia's Dance...11

H. L. Burke

Bull-dancer Alancia befriends the clever inventor of the Labyrinth. When their relationship catches the eye of the jealous king, a date with the Minotaur is in her future.

The Hero Feat Of Hannah Helstrom 29

J. Philip Horne

What makes a hero? 15-year-old Hannah Helstrom's powers are weak, but her heart is strong. In fact, fierce determination might be her greatest attribute, but will that be enough to save a child's life?

In Plain Sight.. 41

Arthur Daigle

Monsters wear many faces. The Great Zamphini has many talents, but he's no soldier. With most of the men away fighting a war, who will protect the citizens left behind?

Finn MacRorie and the River Dragon...55

Katy Huth Jones

Elvina struggles to protect and provide for her family. When an enchanting stranger comes to their fishing village, Elvina and her family's fortunes are changed forever.

Little Victories.. 67

Karin De Havin

After her father dies, Shea becomes a teenage hero-in-training for stray and injured animals. When she runs into the woods after the dog terrorizing her small town, she has to choose whether to continue her chase—or to save a water sprite she doesn't even believe in.

And Only the Eyes of Children 77

Laura VanArendonk Baugh

When a young girl disappears on the city streets, the police can't act fast enough to save her. But maybe a half-Fae, charged by the Queen, can.

The Demon Monkeys... 90

A. R. Silverberry

The mountain hides a secret. Deep in winter, an orphan girl struggles to survive in the shadow of a menacing terror. When a stranger with magical powers crosses her path, her life changes forever.

Superhero Publicist 107

Janeen Ippolito

Dodging deadly fireballs and lethal lightning rays is part of the job for superhero and supervillain publicist Cassandra Robinson. But when a supervillain announces he's switching sides for religious reasons, all of her marketing skills might not be enough to salvage this wannabe hero's image.

Sweet Basil...113

Lea Doué

Hiding from sorcerer hunters, Marisol travels in search of those she can help with her dangerous gift of healing. With every life she saves comes the risk of being discovered, but only if her secret doesn't destroy her first.

Darkness Follows the Light..125

David Millican

Fourteen-year-old school dropout Angelique is determined to make something of her life, to have a future. When horrible child-stealing monsters put that life in jeopardy, her resolve is pushed to the limits. Now the future doesn't matter. All that matters is, can she survive the night...

Presenting... The Steampendous Adventures of Josiah U. Bear and the Rubber Barons...147

D. W. Frauenfelder

Brawler. Air racer. Spy. Josiah U. Bear is all that and a gentlebear besides, but he'll soon face his most dangerous mission yet. The Anvorians have a new weapon, and it's up to Josiah to stop them and save bearkind.

River's Edge Ransom...167

Julie C. Gilbert

Daniel Saveron races to River's Edge to stop a Destroyer plaguing the village with a deadly disease. Those who gave him the contract were adamant about the woman's guilt. They also lied. Breaking the contract means killing his career, but keeping it means murdering an innocent.

The Love Talker 185

Deanna Fugett

Teagan's insane mother has always cautioned against a faerie who seduces women and leaves them to die. When a handsome stranger enters town, Teagan must decide if she'll chase after him or heed her mother's warning. But then the stranger disappears with her sister, and Teagan must save her before the Love Talker Strikes.

Gem 207

RJ Conte

Eleven years ago, Gem was born and fated to save the world. Only he has the power to stop the planet-crushing forces threatening Topha. But to do so might kill him.

Leticia's Song 223

Jessica L. Elliott

A cursed princess. A lost prince. A powerful song. Princess Leticia and her new husband join forces with Princess Rosa to help her complete a quest she failed years ago. But how can they help her win her happily ever after?

The Wooden Ruler 237

David Millican

Mistake or miracle? The Wooden Ruler is a unique toy gnome, in every sense of the word. Tired of captivity, he has great plans to escape and free his people. The humans are blissfully unaware of the trouble brewing, but his schemes will change all that...if his luck holds.

The Tale of Sir Ronan of Camelot 259

Frank B. Luke

Ronan wants to be a knight, but he's from the wrong family. The Devil offers Ronan the chance to make his dreams come true, but what will it cost him and the kingdom?

A Fiery Gift 283

A. J. Bakke

Is one life more precious than another? Everly studies the fire otters living in the nearby volcano because she loves their energetic spirits. But when disaster strikes, it will be her spirit that's tested.

The Hero of Emoh: A Parent's Fairytale..293

Sarah Ashwood

A prophesied new arrival brings great joy, but also great destruction, to the peaceful kingdom of Emoh. Her tiny hands wreak havoc. Her screams cause panic throughout the castle. The King and Queen's only hope lies in a Hero promised to tame the wild magic. But who could it be, and will the kingdom of Emoh survive long enough for the Hero of the second prophecy to rise?

Sacrifice to the Iara 303

H. L. Burke

The rains have ceased. The lake spirit demands a sacrifice. Young Jaiharu's only chance to save his beloved sister is to seek the legendary feathered serpent.

Charla Visits Earth..319

Dianne Astle

Facing expulsion from hero school, Charla slips through a portal and comes to Earth. Ben tries to help her, but what does a mermaid know of our modern world?

Cry of the Cave Lion 339

E. Kaiser Writes

Death stalks the village. A hunting party must face their fears as well as a fierce foe in order to protect their home. But what can inexperienced men do against a legendary beast?

Save The Day 347

Page Zaplendam

Jenny, a social outcast and mediocre hero, must team up with a friend and put aside her doubts to save her nemesis from an awful fate.

Boy Of Sand And Sky 367

Laura Matthias Bendoly

Is he gifted or cursed? A series of strange events revolve around Gabriel. The villagers in his home town don't seem keen on making much of a distinction between the two.

Teamwork...379

Laura VanArendonk Baugh

A dog is man's best friend—until the beasts which threaten his Lady walk on two legs.

The Ungifted Twin 387

Tamie Dearen

Life's not fair. Deria's twin brother has two awesome powers, but she has none. How can she hope to protect her family against an enemy sworn to destroy them?

Not Quite A Hero... 403

Arthur Daigle

Dana Illwind's village needs a hero. What they get is a Sorcerer Lord who has made a career out of troubling the king and queen. Ideal or not, this unlikely team is the best defense the villagers have against beasts that can and will destroy them.

Alancia's Dance

H. L. Burke

Alancia's bare feet danced on the sunbaked earth of the ring. The smell of manure and sweat wafted about her. She wiped her palms on her linen loincloth.

Run, leap, grasp, flip, over and done. Watch the horns. Watch the hooves. Watch yourself.

Across the ring, the bull huffed, its iron-sharp hooves scraping the packed dirt. Its nostrils flared and sides heaved. The beast bellowed.

Alancia bounced, testing her weight. Music from drums and pipes swelled to fill the arena. The crowd murmured as one. She shut them out—nothing existed in this world besides her and the bull. Nothing mattered but the dance.

Drawing a deep breath, she ran at the bull.

The bull's eyes glinted. It matched her charge. Hooves thundered as it rushed her. Then, when it was so close the ground shook beneath Alancia's feet, she leapt.

Her powerful legs catapulted her into the air. She caught the horns. Before it could toss her, she somersaulted down the length of its hairy back. Hitting the ground, she threw her hands up and her chest out.

The crowd cheered.

Grinning, Alancia spun to greet another charge. Her braid flapped behind her, bouncing up and down against her neck. She knew the dance and how the bull would respond.

By the time the temple herdsmen opened the gates and drove the bull away, Alancia's arms and legs ached. Sweat soaked the thin strip of cloth binding her breasts. She swallowed to moisten her tongue, longing for a jug of water and a plate of lamb and chickpeas. She couldn't go yet, not until the king departed and released the performers and crowd alike.

On the platform above the arena, King Menos lounged on his marble throne, chin in hand. A gold band glinted in his dark curls. Alancia imagined he savored the crowd waiting on his signal to rise.

Alancia was glad she was too far away for him to see her expression. Her scowl of contempt would've easily earned her a trip to the Labyrinth. Menos had ascended to the throne only a month before, on the death of his tyrant father. Already, however, the son had proven twice the bloodthirsty despot his hated father had been. So many more blood sports, so many petty criminals and unlucky slaves condemned to the jaws of the Labyrinth.

Swallowing her anger, she concentrated on better things: a dance well performed and the promise of a good meal.

The king stood and waved to the assembly. Alancia's shoulders relaxed. As soon as the king left the platform, she darted into the cool tunnels beneath the arena.

Rastos waited in the shadows, leaning on his cane. The old man had been a noted bull dancer but had suffered the cost of one too many falls. Now he was Alancia's trainer.

He rubbed his snowy beard. "A flawless routine." He unfastened a skin of water from his belt and passed it to her.

Alancia grinned and chugged the lukewarm liquid. It splashed over her face and neck, but she didn't care. She rubbed the water over her aching muscles.

Rastos reached for the waterskin. "I worry you're pushing yourself too hard. We have fifteen trained dancers, but you still performed half the dances today. You'll wear yourself out, taking on so many of the performances."

Alancia shrugged. "The others need more training. Having them dance tempts fate. I can handle it."

During the dance, she felt no fear. When the other dancers entered the ring, however, her mouth would dry and her pulse quicken. Her heart would leap into her mouth if they were even an inch off their mark.

"I have to admit, the new dancers don't have half your skill or strength." Rastos shook his head. "The gods will be pleased with your performance."

Alancia wiped her chin. "I don't know why they can't be content with a performance a month as they used to be. We've had three bull dances since the last full moon." She returned the skin to her trainer. "I can take it, but the less experienced and the older dancers won't last long at this rate."

Rastos shrugged. "The king wants it so. Perhaps more dances will mean better harvests."

"Or more flesh for the Minotaur when one of us falls," Alancia muttered.

Rastos had been lucky to become a trainer in his old age. The king considered others more disposable. At the last dance, one of the more senior dancers had twisted her ankle on a fall. After that, she'd simply disappeared.

"I had your meal sent to your quarters. Go cool off and get some rest." Rastos jerked his head in the direction of the dancers' quarters. "I want you to run the new dancers through their routines tomorrow. Garyl almost fell during his last leap. If he doesn't improve his form, he'll end up under rather than over the bull."

"I'll work with him." *Tomorrow.*

Though the bull dancers were considered more valuable and therefore received better food and housing than other slaves, Alancia still had little fondness for the small cell she shared with three other dancers. She did, however, sigh contentedly when she saw the pot sitting on top of her woven sleeping mat. Most of the dancers would be eating in the common area, chatting and laughing about the day's performance. Alancia preferred to eat in silence. Also, she avoided growing attached to the younger dancers. The sport wore on bodies, and most recruits wouldn't last the year, the lucky ones being reassigned to less taxing work, the unlucky ending up food for the Minotaur. Alancia would protect them. She wouldn't love them.

The clay pot warmed her hands. When she took off the lid, steam rose from the contents, carrying the savory scent of lamb and chickpeas. With a wooden spoon, she shoveled in mouthful after mouthful of the mix.

As her spoon scraped the bottom, a gentle "ah-hem-hem" interrupted her. She drew the mostly empty pot to her chest. *I'm not sharing.* A pale-skinned young man with a touch of sunburn on his cheeks and nose blinked at her from the door. He had weirdly light eyes, a shade away from sky, and hair the color of dried mud. A thin fuzz of beard clung to his chin like lichen on a rock. His white tunic was spotless over his stocky frame, his leather sandals polished and new. Not a slave.

She loosened her hold on her meal. "You lost?"

He shook his head. "No. I...I watched your performance today."

"You and fifty other people." She tilted the pot to get the last of the gravy.

"I was wondering...if I could sketch you." He fiddled with a thick bronze ring on his left hand.

"Sketch me?" She narrowed her eyes at him. He was not the first man to make requests of her after seeing her dance, of course. However, "sketching" was a new one.

"Yes, you see, your posture and stance, how you can so easily complete the jumps and the flips, it seems more than a human body should be capable of." He shifted from foot to foot. "If I could get accurate measurements and notes on your proportions, it would help with a project I'm working on."

"A project?"

"Yes, it's complicated. Do you have some time? We can work here, or I can take you to my workshop."

Alancia tapped her fingers against the now-empty clay pot. Life as property had taught her to choose her battles. Though not known to her, this man obviously held a higher status than she did, and if she failed to comply, he might be able to cause trouble. There were certain lines she wouldn't cross, but being sketched seemed harmless enough.

"Here is fine." She set down the pot and crossed her arms.

"Excellent." He shifted a leather satchel from his shoulders and took out a wax tablet and a measuring rod. "If you wouldn't mind standing."

Alancia obeyed.

He sat cross-legged on the floor. "Stretch out your arms to their full span?" Again she complied.

"Excellent." He tilted his head this way then that, smiled, and started to scratch at the wax tablet with a stylus.

Alancia's already tired arms were just beginning to ache from being held up for so long when he stood and held the measuring rod up to her shoulder.

His fingers brushed her arm, and he flushed bright red. "Sorry. Some contact is necessary. I hope you aren't perturbed."

She raised her eyebrows. This man had a scholar's vocabulary yet treated her with respect. "Who are you?"

"Oh, of course, sorry, introductions, yes?" He gave a wavering laugh. "I'm Daelas, the court inventor."

Daelas? The creator of Menos's death trap? Alancia hissed, her jaw clenching. "Get out!" She pushed him away.

His mouth dropped open. "But...but... Why?"

"You made the Labyrinth!" She raised her fists. "Do you know how many have died in your blood-soaked maze?"

He dropped his eyes. "I...I understand, but if you could just let me finish, I promise, this time, no one will be hurt by what I'm doing."

"Ha!" She stomped away from him and motioned toward the open door. "You're Menos's executioner. Whatever you do drips in blood."

"No, I swear, this is...this is a good thing I'm trying to do." He held out the wax tablet, where a rough approximation of the human form was surrounded by notes Alancia couldn't read. "See?"

Alancia flushed as the weird symbols she knew had meaning for the educated mocked her. She thrust it away. "You work for the king. Everything he touches is for evil."

"Don't speak of him like that!" Daelas cringed. "Someone might hear." He glanced out the door, his shoulders relaxing when the hall proved empty.

Alancia steadied her breathing. While she wanted no part in whatever Daelas was up to, she needed to calm her temper before she earned herself a trip to the Labyrinth.

"Please, I can show you what I'm making. Will that reassure you?" He clasped his hands. Though he was perhaps a few years older than Alancia—who had a vague idea that she was older than a girl but younger than a woman—he had an open, childlike face. Something within her weakened, but she forced her scowl to remain.

"Your cursed trap has taken hundreds of lives."

"That wasn't its intent, at least, it wasn't my intent." The inventor hung his head. "I was scarcely fifteen when I arrived in Menoa from Oleva, my native country. A young man in a strange land, I lacked the understanding... I had no idea the proclivities of Menos's father, the proclivities Menos obviously shares."

"Proclivities..." Another word she didn't know. Alancia rubbed the back of her neck. She was fairly certain Daelas spoke in the same tongue as she did. Fairly certain... "So you designed the Labyrinth because...?"

"The Minotaur was roaming the streets of Menoa, killing any who chanced to fall across it. No prison could hold it for long, and I was eager to impress my new patron." He shook his head. "I told the king I could build a structure so complex that when the Minotaur tried to escape, it would inevitably lose itself further, a prison so strong that even the monster could not break down its gates. And I did."

Alancia snorted. "Would've been better just to kill the beast, rather than trap it."

"I lack the dexterity for monster killing. I thought, perhaps, containing it would allow the king time to find a hero strong enough to dispatch it." Daelas sighed. "Apparently, such heroes are rarer than I had anticipated."

"Even if they were banging at the Labyrinth's gates for their chance at the monster, Menos would never let anyone take a swing at his prized pet." Alancia snorted. "He's as much a monster as the Minotaur is."

Daelas winced.

"We're alone here," she assured him.

"Yes, well... I've learned the hard way not to cross Menos." He returned to twisting at his ring. "Look, please, come see what I'm making. Once you understand, I think you'll be willing to participate."

Alancia chewed her bottom lip. "I suppose looking won't hurt."

She fetched a loose linen tunic to throw over her skimpy dancer's garb then followed him.

They took the pillared walkway connecting the arena to the palace. After a dozen back halls, they climbed a twisting spiral stair to a tower room, filled to bursting with strange and elaborate constructs.

A metal man leaned against one wall, a collection of interlocking pipes and vessels against another. Scrolls and scraps of parchment covered a long table in the midst of it all. A large doorway opened out onto a balcony and light streamed into the room. Two wooden frameworks dripping with long white feathers hung from the high ceiling.

Wings? She squinted at them.

"Over here!" Daelas called. She turned and found him standing before a large mass draped in canvas.

With a smile, the inventor tugged away the sheet. Her jaw dropped. A bull of gleaming bronze stood posed mid-charge with hinged legs and glinting silver hooves.

"It looks so real." She approached and touched its cold, smooth sides.

"If you wind it up, it moves." He turned a large gear on its flank. The legs extended then drew back.

Alancia swallowed. "It...it can't run, though?"

"With some adjustments, yes, it will." He stroked the artificial beast's nose as if it were his pet. "I'd like to craft a dancer to go with it. Imagine, if instead of risking lives by having humans perform with real bulls, we could please the gods with automated displays. Metal dancers, metal bulls, no loss of life."

Alancia tilted her head. "I don't think it works that way. I think the gods need the sacrifice, the risk, the blood."

Daelas's soft features hardened. "If they desire that, then they aren't true gods."

She drew closer to him. "So that's why you want to sketch me? To help you make the dancer?"

He nodded. "I just want to do some good, to create something beautiful and worthy. Menos..." He cleared his throat. "He says I'm here as a valued member of the Menoan court, but he won't let me leave. My inventions make me too valuable to kill. I've given his palace hot and cold running water and endless toys to suit his fancy. If I were to leave, however..." He shook his head. "He'd kill me rather than let me take my skills to another monarch. Especially since I know the path of the Labyrinth." Daelas rubbed his forehead. "I've made mistakes. I want to fix them."

She touched his shoulder. "You're as much a slave as I am, then."

He laughed bitterly. "Indeed." They stood in silence for several heartbeats. His clear blue eyes peered at her. "I'm sorry. I just realized I never asked your name."

"Alancia."

"Alancia." A smile spread across his face like a ray of sunlight. "Excellent. Now that you understand my intentions, are you willing to assist me in my work?"

She touched the metal bull. "You just need to sketch me?"

"Well, it would be helpful if I could get a closer view of your methods. I've attended every performance, but the stands aren't as near to the dancers as I'd like. I chose you to approach because you are the best. I'm assuming you practice regularly?" He raised his eyebrows imploringly.

"There's a practice tomorrow. You can attend."

"Excellent." He grinned again. "Thank you so much, Alancia. I swear you won't regret this."

For the next week, Daelas followed Alancia like a calf would its mother. He carried either a wax tablet or a roll of parchment at all times, sketching then occasionally stopping to ask questions. Alancia soon discovered that she knew less about her own sport than she thought as Daelas's questions about what speed she had to accelerate to in order to make her jumps, or why she twisted a specific way, frequently confounded her.

"I don't know. I just do it like that," she found herself saying, over and over again. Her face would warm, but Daelas didn't tease her. He simply continued to scribble his notes.

After a few days, she grew comfortable in his presence. Though he spoke in complicated words and riddles, he had an unassuming manner, never flaunting his intelligence, never acting as if he were better than her. They began to talk about more than just his project and her dancing. About their childhoods, his in the bustling Olevan ports and olive groves, she being traded through various homes and slave markets until Rastos had spotted her and sensed a natural bull dancer in her lithe form.

"Did you want to be a dancer, though?" Daelas asked.

She shrugged. "It was a better option than becoming a concubine."

The inventor's face turned bright red. "Yes... I...I suppose it would be." He swallowed and dropped his eyes. "Do you ever think, though, of what you would do if you could just leave?"

Alancia blinked at him. "Leave?"

"Yes. Just fly away, as far as you want to anywhere you choose." He turned his eyes toward the blue sky over the arena.

She rubbed the back of her neck. "I can't fly, though. No one can."

"Yes, well..." He cleared his throat. Seemed like he did that a lot. *He should see the court physician about it. His humors might be out of balance.*

"The flying part of the question was just me attempting to be poetic." He tilted his head, his gaze intent on her. "I meant if you could escape the palace, what would you do?"

Something in Alancia stirred at his blue eyes, something she couldn't explain and so didn't like very much. She looked away. "I guess I don't know. If I leave, it isn't as if the dances will stop. The king would just make the other dancers dance in my place, and some of them would get hurt. They aren't as good as I am, especially the younger ones."

"So you'll stay forever so that the others don't get hurt?" Disbelief tinged his voice.

"It's the right thing to do. Unless something makes it so no one has to dance."

"Well, maybe if my project works out, that could be a possibility. Speaking of which, I now have all the data I need to finish my project."

A knot hardened in Alancia's stomach. "Oh, so we won't need to visit anymore?"

"Need, no. I suppose we won't." He wiped his hands on his tunic. "I would like to show you my work, when it's finished. May I send for you when it's done?"

She forced a steady nod and a placid expression. After all, this was never more than a relationship of convenience. He was the lauded court inventor. She was a slave. No point in getting attached, but it would be nice to see his mechanical bull at work.

"Good. I tend to disappear into my work at this stage, so you probably won't hear from me for a few weeks...but I look forward to demonstrating my inventions when they are finished." He touched the back of her hand. "Until then, Alancia."

Alancia took the stairs to Daelas's workshop two at a time. After almost two weeks, the message had finally arrived. To her shame, her heart had pounded like the temple drum when the boy had passed her the note... *Two weeks should've been long enough to purge that fancy from my system.*

Finding someone who could read the words for her had taken longer than anticipated and now she worried that Daelas would assume the delay meant she wasn't coming. Perhaps she'd arrive to find the door shut, never to see him again.

It's silly, though. Why should I want to see him?

By the time she reached the top, a light sweat coated her forehead. The door stood open.

Daelas poked his head out and grinned. Her heart kicked at her ribs.

"Excellent! Come in, come in!" He beckoned to her.

Swallowing her excitement, she followed, and her jaw slackened.

Before her, glistening in brilliant bronze, stood a mirror image of herself. "It...it looks like me?"

He shuffled his feet, playing with his ring. "Well, yes...you don't mind, do you?"

She shook her head. Though he'd captured her high cheekbones and muscular arms, which she'd always worried made her look boyish, he'd somehow made her...pretty. She touched her replica's face. Cool, solid, definitely metal and not alive, but so real somehow.

"Does it move?" she asked.

"Of course. It's a fully functional automaton." He indicated a gear sticking out of the side of its neck. "We don't have the space for it to perform its routine, but one rotation..." He turned the gear.

Whirs and clicks rose from inside the bronze girl, and she jerked to life. She rose on her tiptoes, her hands stretched out. Then the whirring stopped, her hands fell at her side with a gentle clank, and her feet settled flat against the floor.

Daelas crossed his arms. "I can't wait to have her perform with an actual bull. That was my mistake, I realized, thinking she could dance with a metal bull and the king would be pleased. No, real bull, metal girl, that introduces an aspect of risk, for even if she isn't flesh and blood, she can still be trampled and broken."

Alancia rubbed the back of her neck. "So the dancers will be safe." She hesitated. The younger dancers could easily be assigned new positions in the palace. However, bull dancing was all Alancia knew. "What will I do, now that I won't have to dance?" she asked. Yes, it was something she should've thought of before, but until seeing the automaton come to life, she hadn't quite believed Daelas could do what he said. Even now, part of her doubted the metal girl would be able to complete a dance.

He cleared his throat. "Yes, well, I wanted to talk to you about—"

"Daelas? Where are you, you worthless tinkerer!" a voice bellowed.

Daelas cringed and positioned himself between Alancia and the door.

A black-bearded man in a purple robe strode into the workshop. Alancia gasped, drawing the man's attention. His gaze swept up and down her body. She shrank away and dropped her chin to her chest in what she hoped would be seen as a reverent posture. Even now, when faced with the tyrant Menos himself, she could not bring herself to grovel.

"What do you have here?" Menos jerked his thumb at the bronze girl.

"Your majesty." Daelas bowed. "You didn't have to come here. If you desired my presence, you could've summoned me. I would happily have acquiesced."

"No, I wanted to see for myself what was keeping your attention and requiring so much bronze." Menos approached the automaton. He ran his hand down her side, lingering for a moment on her hip. His glance returned to Alancia, and he licked his lips. "You chose an exquisite model for this toy."

The back of Alancia's neck warmed, but she focused on the floor.

"Yes, sire," Daelas's voice wavered. "I was hoping to surprise you with this new invention. It can—"

"I am pleased. Have it sent to my treasure room."

Daelas's shoulders slumped. "But, sire, I had hoped to have it in the arena where it could—"

"The arena? To be gawked at by slovenly peasants." Menos snorted. "No, fine things, beautiful things are for royal eyes, and royal hands..." He stepped closer to Alancia.

Her stomach churned. *Hold still. Don't move. Don't let on...and for the sake of the gods, don't hit him.*

"I will have the automaton sent to your treasury immediately!" Daelas burst out, stepping between her and the king.

The king recoiled. His eyes glinted like a bull about to charge, and Alancia's breath caught in her throat. Daelas quivered but held his position between her and the king.

"There's...there's also a mechanical bull, if you'd like. I made them as a set," he continued.

The king waved his hand. "I have the beauty. Why would I need the beast?"

You are the beast. Alancia gritted her teeth.

Menos stroked the bronze girl's cheek. "Well, see that she is brought to me. I would warn you, however, Daelas, against wasting your skill on these pet projects. You're here to cater to my whim, not make whatever you desire." His gaze narrowed at Daelas. "Whatever you make, whatever passes through your hands, is for my pleasure. You have nothing, and what you may possess for a time, I may take from you, simply because it pleases me to do so. Do you understand?"

Alancia drew back, something within her twisting. Daelas's new creations were beautiful and good. They could help so many, but Menos would only use them for his selfish desires. This was worse than slavery.

Daelas swallowed. "Yes, my king."

"Good. For this particular defiance, I will forgive you because the results amuse me."

Alancia's skin crawled, though she wasn't quite sure why. The king's focus had diverted from her. That should've been a relief, but somehow the exchange between Menos and Daelas left her feeling grimy.

The king departed. Daelas exhaled loudly and closed his eyes.

"He's really going to take the dancer and just display it in his throne room?" Alancia whispered. "She'll never dance?"

"Menos doesn't care about the dance or the dancers, just about himself." He twisted at his ring until it popped over his knuckle. "Alancia, I...you need to go."

Her stomach twisted. "But Menos is gone. He..."

"You just need to leave." He pressed the ring against her palm. "Take this. Don't lose it. Hopefully, you won't need it, but...but if you do, it will save you."

"A ring?" She held up the bronze band. It was thick and covered in scratches. "How could a ring save anyone?"

"It's a cryptograph." His gaze darted about. "He might still be listening."

A crypto-whatsit?

"Daelas, what is wrong? The king isn't listening. We're alone. You can tell me." *Hopefully in words I can actually understand for once.*

"He won't let me be happy, and if he sees you make me happy, he'll take you!" Daelas snarled.

She stepped back.

He flushed, his posture deflating. "Please, just go, Alancia. Please."

Sweat broke out over Alancia's forehead as she fled Daelas's workshop. The bronze ring felt warm against her skin. She stopped and forced it over her knuckle, the action making her remember Daelas's hands, not much larger than her own and so gentle for a man, as soft as his eyes and his smile.

Alancia tried to return to her routine, to not think about Daelas or the metal dancer who would never dance, but she could not. At the next practice, she was so distracted she fell to her knees on a landing. She scrambled to her feet before the bull could charge again, but Rastos caught the misstep.

"What's gotten into you?" he hissed after practice. "Your reaction time has slowed. You're quiet, no fight in your eyes. Does this have something to do with the court inventor?"

She averted her gaze, touching the bronze ring she still wore.

Rastos's nostrils flared. "Gods help me, if he meddled with you—"

"It's not like that," she said quickly. "I'm just tired, is all."

"You need to eat better. I'll make sure the kitchen staff puts extra lamb in your portion."

Alancia slumped down the tunnels to her chambers but stopped short. A burly man in a polished leather jerkin blocked her door. He wore the plumed helmet of a palace guard.

He stomped toward her and grabbed her arm. "Come with me."

She narrowed her eyes at him. "Why?"

"Because I said so." He bared his teeth and placed his hand on the hilt of his short sword.

Alancia's skin went cold. She backed up a step. The guard's hold on her arm tightened. Their eyes met, and the guard didn't flinch.

It's not as if I have anywhere to run to, and anyway, I haven't done anything wrong. Better to follow him and see what this is about.

He led her into the main body of the palace and down a flight of stairs. A great wooden door stood propped open at the bottom. Through it, a cool, torch-lit chamber filled with marble statues, woven tapestries, and painted amphoras stretched before them. Columns staggered throughout the cavernous space cast long shadows.

The guard pushed her forward. "Wait here."

Before she could question or protest, he turned on his heel and exited. The door swung shut behind him.

Alancia pulled on the handle; it creaked but didn't give. Bolted from the other side, she supposed.

She wiped her hand across her brow, wishing she had been given a chance to put on something over her dancer's garb. The air felt cool and heavy, as if she were miles beneath the earth. The flickering torchlight did little to warm her.

After a few heart-pounding minutes of silence, she circled the room, examining the artwork and artifacts displayed there. She passed a stairway leading up to a round hatch, but this also proved locked. At the far end of the room stood two stone archways, side by side, each holding a metal door twice the height of a man. Over each door was a relief depicting a massive creature with the head of a bull and the body of a man. In both images, he engaged in fierce battle with a dozen soldiers, many of whom lay broken at his feet.

"You know where those lead?" a voice echoed through the stillness.

Alancia spun about, fists up.

A figure in a purple robe descended the staircase.

Menos.

The king smiled at her. "Two doors, one of which many have gone through, but none willingly, the other through which no man has passed."

A shudder cut through her. "This is the entrance to the Labyrinth?"

"Yes. Daelas suggested we should build it in the wilds, but I like to keep my treasures at hand. It is far easier for me to dispose of enemies of the state." He strode past her and touched the iron of the door.

In spite of her anxiety, Alancia felt a prickle of curiosity in her soul. "But if the entrance and the exit are so close to each other, how does anyone get lost?"

"You'd think it would be a simple prospect, finding your way from one door to another." Menos grinned. "Many have thought that. I've even offered full pardon to any criminal, no matter their crime, who could navigate through it. Daelas's design is near perfect. No one will defeat it."

Alancia swallowed. "Why did you bring me here?"

"Since I own the bronze girl, it only felt right to add the real thing to my collection." He motioned to a corner. There stood Daelas's automaton, silent and still. "It took me a few days to place where I'd seen you, but once I remembered that you were a bull dancer, I simply had to send for you." He drew closer. His breath warmed her skin, and she stiffened. "I never would've imagined Daelas to have such fine taste, always more interested in metal than flesh." The king rested his hand on her cheek. "Of course, whatever Daelas creates is mine, my property, for my amusement. I am pleased his attempts to assert himself, failed as they may be, brought you to my attention."

Her thoughts raced as his eyes locked with hers. As a slave, she always had known this moment would come, where she could be ordered to yield to a man, her only choices submission or dire consequences. She tried to steel herself for the inevitable. However, a single thought rose above all others.

But I don't want to.

Menos grabbed her hair and yanked her toward him. Alancia jabbed her fist into his gut.

Crumpling in on himself, the king gasped for air. She bolted.

What did I do? Oh gods, I have to get away.

She flung herself against the wooden door, shaking it. It wouldn't give.

"Guards!" Menos screamed.

The door burst open and the guard from earlier rushed in, accompanied by another man in identical garb. She kicked at them, but they overwhelmed her and dragged her back to face Menos.

"Did you even think what it would cost you to defy me?" The king's lips curled into an ugly sneer.

"Whatever it is, I'll gladly pay the price." She gritted her teeth. The guards' hold on her arms tightened until it hurt.

"Well, at least I'll get the small pleasure of seeing the look on Daelas's face when I tell him I threw his muse to the Minotaur." Menos turned back to the gates and flipped a small lever. "Get it over with."

The iron door slid backward with an angry squeal, revealing a pitch-black pit behind it. The floor dropped away into nothingness.

Alancia struggled. She kicked and braced her heels against the marble floor. The guards pushed her toward the gaping hole.

I'm going in. I can't stop it.

Her eye fell on the sheathed sword at the guard's side. As he shoved, she grabbed. Her hand caught the weapon. The guard reached for her. His companion drew his own sword, but she leapt, backward, through the door. She tumbled, hit a sloping wall, then slid. Her hands scrambled for purchase and met only smooth stone. The darkness spun by her, then she hit the ground with a lung-emptying thump. She lay still, gulping breath.

I'm lucky I didn't impale myself on the way down here. Oh gods, where's the sword?

Unlike the chute she'd emerged from, there was some light here, poor, but not complete darkness. Loose sand covered the stone floor. The sand stuck to her, perhaps because of her own sweat. Finally, her fingers met the cool, hard surface of the blade.

What am I thinking? I'm not a warrior. Blade or no blade, I'm not a match for the Minotaur. Still, who else will fight it? No, hero or not, I'm going to have to save myself.

Alancia's eyes adjusted. She was at the start of a narrow passage, with two towering walls perhaps three arm-lengths apart. Faint light came from high above her head, some sort of ventilation system, perhaps twenty feet above her.

Maybe I can climb up to it.

She examined the opening she'd fallen through. The sides were nearly vertical. Still, maybe if she could wedge herself in right, she could make her way back up. Poking her head in, she tested the walls, only to have her hands slip. Something slick coated the stone. It smelled sharp and heavy. Touching her arms where the sand from the floor still clung, she realized her body was streaked with the substance.

Oil of some sort... Giving up on the tunnel, she tried the walls, but while they weren't coated, they'd been polished and the stone fitted together so seamlessly, she could not find a toehold.

Leaning against the wall with her arms crossed, she examined her surroundings. The hall stretched on for about the length of the arena before forking to the left and right. She closed her eyes and listened. Dead quiet. No shuffling or sniffling like she'd expect if a large, ungainly beast were nearby.

I can't just wait here. Even if the monster doesn't find me, I'll starve or parch. As if in response, her stomach growled. She remembered Rastos's promise of extra lamb in her meal portion. *Why couldn't the guard have let me get to my dinner. I wonder if Menos has told Daelas yet. Poor Daelas. He'll blame himself for drawing Menos's attention to me.*

Maybe it was, in some way, Daelas's fault. After all, Menos had seen her dance a hundred times and never summoned her. Still, she didn't regret meeting the awkward inventor, even now. As much as it may have cost her, the memory of how Daelas looked at her, how he spoke to her, sent a gentle warmth flooding through her chest.

She twisted the ring. What had Daelas said? That it would save her? She pried it from her finger. Scratches marred its surface... *Wait...* They were too straight and clean to be accidental. These marks had been done with precision, yet there didn't seem to be a pattern, at least not an obvious one. *It's a message somehow, but not in those terrible letters I can't read. This is simple, straight lines...a map? One way to find out.*

Turning the ring, she found an x and a dot next to each other. *Maybe the dot is the entrance and the x is the exit. In the room above, they were right next to each other, but apparently not down here.* She traced the etched lines leading away from the dot. The first three slanted upward, the next two downward, then one up, three down, lines continuing in no particular order all the way around the ring, ending at the x. *I have to go through the maze to get to the end. If the slanting lines each represent a turn.* She held the ring so that it aligned with the hallway. The upward slants would be left-hand turns, the downward right.

A smile crept over her face. Taking up the guard's sword in one hand, she padded down the hall, keeping her footsteps light and her ears open.

Two left turns later, her foot hit something under the soft dirt. She glanced down, and the empty sockets of a skull smiled up at her. She gasped.

Shuffling forward and alternating her gaze between the hall ahead and the ground below, she soon encountered more signs of previous prisoners. A rib cage crushed, shattered leg bones, scraps of clothing stained rust red, and an oddly intact sandal.

She stopped and counted. How many bones did an average man have? Only one skull, so possibly one person...though there seemed to be a lot of little bits and pieces lying around.

Her hand tightened about the hilt of the blade. *Perhaps if I'm quiet, it won't find me. There are so many passages, so many twists and turns, that I might never encounter it. Yes, quick and quiet. Blade or no blade, I'm no warrior.*

Counting turns took all her concentration. The bones became more frequent, and after a bit, she stopped looking down. Yes, she winced slightly when a skull crunched underfoot, but she needed to focus on the path, on the marks on the ring, two lefts, one right, a left, three more rights.

Doubt chewed at her even as hunger gnawed her stomach. Daelas hadn't said the ring was a map. The lines could be coincidental, leading her to make random choices, getting her lost deeper and deeper in the Labyrinth. *But he said it could save me. It's my only chance.*

She held the ring before her. The light slowly weakened, the shadows deepening as she continued. Soon, she could barely make out the tiny markings on the ring. Glancing up, she found the patches of sky through the ventilation holes pink with twilight. She swallowed. Without light, how could she find her way?

Counting the turns left on the ring, she found herself a little over halfway through.

Move faster. That's the only way. I can't be stuck here overnight. She shuddered, imagining hours spent huddled in this twisting prison, pitch dark, listening for the footfalls of the monster.

A few turns later, a smell rose out of the shadows, a mix of livestock and rotting meat. Alancia sank against the wall. The next mark on the ring wasn't a line at all, but rather a circle. Ahead, the path opened up into a chamber filled with bleached white skeletons. She eased forward until she stood in the doorway.

Sitting in the center of the pile, gnawing on a leg bone, lurked a beast with the head of a bull and the body of a massive man. Coarse brown fur covered its grotesque head and most of its chest. Muscles bulged from its arms and thighs, and the tips of its terrible black horns glinted. While its hands were those of a man, bull's hooves capped its legs.

Alancia took a step back, the sword shaking in her grasp.

The beast's head jerked up. Its eyes glinted red, and it snorted. Alancia froze.

The Minotaur leapt to its hooves, scattering skeletal fragments like thrown dice. With a room-shaking roar, it tossed the bone at her head. She yelped and dodged. The sword clattered to the ground. She fumbled for it, but the Minotaur charged.

Horns glinting.

Muscles straining.

Instincts kicked in, and Alancia rushed it. Her legs catapulted her into the air. She caught the Minotaur's horns, flipped, and landed, arms outstretched, behind it.

She gasped, stunned by what she'd just done. A crash echoed through the chamber. She whirled about. The Minotaur picked itself off the ground, a crack in the plaster of the wall behind it.

Alancia bolted through the door in the other side of the chamber. Could she remember the rest of the turns? Was it *left, right, right* or *right, left, right*?

Hoof-falls pounded behind her. Louder, closer.

She turned. The passage was narrow but high. Plenty of room for a good jump.

Again she launched. The beast's hands flailed for her. She felt the breeze of their passing. Alancia caught the Minotaur by the horns. Over she went. Her feet jolted against the floor, slipping slightly. The sand-covered stone provided less grip than the hard earth of the arena. She dashed back into the Minotaur's chamber.

Find the sword.

The Minotaur bellowed, its voice an ungodly mix of man and beast. She skidded toward the blade. The monster exploded into the room, hands outstretched, foam dripping from its maw.

Alancia snatched at the blade but snagged a bone instead. The Minotaur grabbed at her. She swung, shattering the bone across its snout. The monster flinched and screamed. She dove between its legs.

Where's the cursed sword?

There, on the other side of the beast, the sword glinted in the dirt, mocking her.

The Minotaur turned, fists clenched, red eyes blazing. Its breath came in snorts. It scraped the ground with its hoof. Once. Twice. Charge.

Her heart in her throat, Alancia leapt. Her hands caught the horns, but the beast snagged her leg. She yelped in pain as it yanked her down. She raised her other knee into its snout. Slime burst from its nose. Hanging onto the horns, she wrested herself free. Her momentum foiled, she thrust herself over the Minotaur's shoulder and tumbled down its back.

Alancia sprawled, ribs aching. A moan of pain escaped, every breath painful. Sweat stung her eyes. Desperate, she groped in the sand and met with cold metal. She flipped onto her back and jabbed upward. The blade pierced the Minotaur's gut with a wet thunk.

The monster staggered backward, wrenching the blade from her grasp. Dark red trickled from around the hilt. The Minotaur fell to its knees, threw its face to the ceiling, and shrieked. Alancia scrambled away. It collapsed. Its hands clawed the ground. Sand flew. The acrid smell of blood and bile brought tears to Alancia's eyes. Then, with one last pitiful groan, it breathed its last.

She sat for a moment, heart and breath frantic, sweat dripping in her eyes. The beast lay still, blood mixing with the dirt beneath it in a slowly spreading puddle.

I'm safe. I killed it.

She jumped to her feet and punched at the ceiling. Her shout echoed through the chamber as if a crowd cheered with her. She grinned up at her own hands, her own *bare* hands, and icy realization gripped her throat.

I...I've lost the ring.

As darkness fell over the chamber, Alancia admitted defeat. She'd combed what felt like every inch of the chamber, but she had no idea when she'd even dropped the precious ring. Was it when the beast first charged? When she scrambled down the hall? No, it had to be before her first flip. She definitely hadn't been holding it during that...but the exact moment, and hence the ring's likely location, escaped her. She was lost. Though she had killed the beast, she was as good as dead.

Alancia sat with her head against her knees, tired, achy, lonely.

I wish I could tell Daelas what I did, that the Minotaur won't harm anyone else. I wish he could know how much...how much I miss him.

So many people had come and gone from her life. She'd stopped caring about any of them years ago, but Daelas...Daelas was different. Daelas cared for her. If she didn't return to him, he would be sad. She knew that somehow, from the memory of his gaze. That someone would mourn her death made her long to live in the fiercest way.

Her body shivered. *I can't just give up. When it is light, I'll try to find my way out. I was over halfway done. It can't be that hard...can it?*

She leaned against the wall. *Maybe in better light, I'll see the ring. Maybe it will return to me.*

Weariness overtook her, in spite of her fear, in spite of the emptiness of her belly, in spite of the monstrous corpse only a few feet away.

"Alancia! Alancia, wake up!"

She sat up with a shriek.

Daelas's pale face shone in the light of an oil lamp. His wide eyes seemed ready to swallow her whole.

Alancia cupped his cheeks in her hands. "How...how...?" She took him in, savoring his features as if they were her nourishment. He had a rope tied about his waist and a sword at his hip.

"I...I waited for Menos to take a bath and I...the hot water in his tub, it became suddenly much hotter than he desired." Cold rage contorted Daelas's face. "While the guards were distracted with his shrieking, I slipped down here. I didn't know if I had any hope. I just knew...I had to try." He cast a glance at the bulky shadow of the Minotaur. "Looks like you didn't need my help after all."

"I...I don't know how to get out. I lost your ring in the fight."

He smiled and pulled her to her feet. "That I can help you with. I guess I'll get the chance to play hero tonight after all."

The rope fastened at his waist led through the twists and turns of the remaining passages to a spiral stair.

She gripped his arm. "But what about the king?"

"Expired by now, I'd imagine, what with that scalding." Daelas sighed. "I should probably feel regret over that. Perhaps I will—someday." They started up the stairs, his soft hand still wrapped about her calloused fingers. "It's likely someone will put together that I had something to do with it, but even if they care who assassinated the tyrant, I intend to be long gone by then."

Alancia's thoughts spun. Daelas—gentle, timid Daelas—had killed a man? Her mind couldn't wrap around that idea, even with a victim as disgusting as Menos.

They hurried through the palace. In spite of the late hour, servants bunched together, whispering in hushed tones. Some openly smiled. The realization of what this meant settled on Alancia like a comforting embrace.

The king was dead. No more blood sports, no more death.

No one barred the way to Daelas's workshop. He led Alancia out onto the balcony. A wooden framework held aloft two wings of long white feathers. She touched them. The fine strands tickled her skin.

"You make such beautiful things," she whispered.

"My masterwork. Are you ready to fly, Alancia?"

She gaped at him. "Fly? To where?"

He grinned. "Wherever you like. Though for now, I just want to get out of the palace and to the harbor. We can take a ship from there."

Something swelled within Alancia, and she flung her arms about Daelas's neck. His eyes widened, then twinkled, and he bent toward her. Their lips met, soft, warm, wonderful. Her stomach filled with swirling feathers.

He let out a long sigh. "I can't believe I almost lost you."

Daelas helped her strap into the wings, his hands lingering on her shoulders and waist as he did up the straps. Her heart throbbed with each touch. The wings proved surprisingly light. She bounced, marveling at the way they moved with her.

His own wings on, Daelas hopped onto the low wall surrounding the balcony. "If this doesn't work, don't follow me." He winked.

Daelas leapt. For a heart-wrenching moment, he dipped. Then the breeze caught his wings and he glided away from the palace. Alancia drew a deep breath and stepped off the wall.

The wind rushed about her, and she glided through the air, to freedom.

H. L. Burke authors fantasy novels for young readers and adults, including a four part Fantasy romance series, The Dragon and the Scholar, and a five part YA Steampunk series, Nyssa Glass. Her most recent release, Coiled, is a romantic retelling of the Eros and Psyche myth. Greek myths also inspired Alancia's Dance, a tale of lost souls, bull-dancers, and monsters of both the human and mythical variety.

Her other works—which include magic, adventure, and DRAGONS—can be found at www.hlburkeauthor.com

The Hero Feat Of Hannah Helstrom

J. Philip Horne

I always told people—the ones in the know—that my other superpower was stubbornness. They'd laugh but trail off awkwardly when they realized I really didn't have a second talent. Sevens always had two of the talents, and some had three. Toward the end of the summer, we'd even heard rumors of a new Seventy-Seven on the scene, a boy with all seven talents.

I had a single talent. Hanna Helstrom, the one-hit wonder. I could heal myself, or, as Sevens would say, I could reggie. Nothing else. That pretty much made me the worst superhero in the Guild of Sevens.

When I was born, my parents were thrilled to discover the birthmark smack dab in the middle of my back. It looked like a wolf had stepped on me and left a reddish paw print behind. It marked me as the Seven in my generation from the ancient Ásbjörn family line.

My parents devoted themselves to preparing me. They homeschooled me to make sure I had plenty of time to train. The Guild worked alongside them to make me athletic, graceful, and confident. No expense was spared.

It wasn't a complete disaster. Close, but not quite. Nothing came easy. Whether it was ballet, or basketball, or karate, I started out terrible and had to work twice as hard as the other kids to improve.

My parents kept encouraging me toward success, but I could tell it wore on them. I didn't really blame them. They meant well. To them, my birthmark meant I had a high calling, and they wanted to ensure I had every opportunity to live up to it. Though most of the world didn't know about Sevens, it was a big deal among the families of the Guild, so there were always people checking in on my progress.

I had one thing going for me—that second talent, the one that had nothing to do with the Guild of Sevens. I was stubborn. Like, put-a-mule-to-shame stubborn. For whatever reason, I was wired to never give up, which was a good thing given how many times giving up was the obvious choice.

Like all Sevens, the Guild of Sevens tested me for the first time on my twelfth birthday. One test for each of the seven talents. I failed all of them on my twelfth birthday, which wasn't totally unusual. I failed them again on my thirteenth birthday. My parents got nervous, so they pushed me to take more of everything. Karate, judo, ballet, even time with a trainer at a gun range.

While my parents worried, I finally turned a corner. Something clicked between my thirteenth and fourteenth birthdays and I started shedding my awkwardness. It was like I suddenly caught up with all the lessons I'd had the previous decade. I could dance. I could fight. I could dance and fight. I could fight while dancing. It was awesome.

On my fourteenth birthday, all that amazing progress fell to pieces when I finally passed a Seven test. Not tests. Test. Having a pair of talents was so normal they had names. Sevens who could pass through solids and become invisible were called Thieves. Warriors could move with insane speed and turn their body hard as rock. That sort of thing.

I could reggie. Regeneration. Cut me open and I could heal, which was amazing if I was a normal person, but pretty near worthless in the superhero business.

"You're going to walk Madison home, right?" Mom asked.

I was fifteen, and two of my cousins had recently moved to town with my aunt. Madison was my age and Ruby was six. The apartment they'd leased wouldn't be available for a couple more weeks, so they were temporarily living at an extended stay hotel near us.

"Sure, Mom," I said. "Madison knows how to get to the hotel, though."

"I know she does, dear. I'm not asking you to give her directions. I just want the girls to have some company while they're staying in a strange new place."

I shrugged. "Not sure how strange the Blue Gutters Inn is, but I'll hang with her."

Mom gave me a quick hug, grabbed her purse, and headed for the garage. "I'll be back by dinner. Be good, Hannah. Be a hero to someone, okay?"

"Always." Always a hero waiting to happen, or so my parents wanted to believe. I wasn't so sure.

Mom left, and I had the house to myself until I walked over to the high school to meet Madison. I'd pushed hard the day before practicing my talent, so I was giving myself a day off. I was persistent to a fault but not stupid. Training as a reggie was pretty messed up. The only way to practice healing was to get hurt, which really wasn't a healthy thing to do. Literally. The whole process could get inside your head, and the Guild had warned me that a lot of reggies burned themselves out and didn't progress well.

Not me. I'd been terrible at it at first, just like everything else in my life, but I'd stuck with it. And like everything else, my drive to keep going had gradually paid off. I still had to focus on healing and couldn't do it on autopilot, but I could heal, and heal a lot.

But not today. I'd finished all my schoolwork that morning, so I practiced the piano instead. Half an hour later, I pulled the front door closed behind me, locked it, and headed to the high school.

"Hannah Helstrom!"

I turned and saw Madison coming toward me. She had a very energetic walk. We were cousins but didn't look like family. My pale hair, braided in a long ponytail, contrasted with her dark curls that bounced with each step. She was tall, too. I wasn't short, but Madison was make-boys-uncomfortable tall.

I waved, and she crossed the parking lot to me.

"Your mom make you come find me?" Madison said.

"Pretty much." We turned away from the school and started walking. "We'll make something of it, right?"

"Sure. Might as well."

"They load you up with homework?" I asked.

"Always." Madison pulled her phone out of the back pocket of her jeans. She glanced at the screen. "Hold on. Mom's calling me."

She put the phone to her ear. "Hey, Mom. What's up?" Pause. "Yeah, that's fine. I'm like five minutes from home." Another pause. "You're not a bad mother. She'll be fine. Get to your appointment." Madison listened for a few more seconds, her mouth quirked up on one side. "If it makes you feel better, I'm four minutes away now. Maybe, if we keep talking, I'll be home before you leave." Pause. "Okay, love you!"

Madison put the phone back in her pocket. "Ruby fell asleep on the couch after school and Mom wants to let her rest, but she's late for an appointment."

"Oh," I said. "Yeah, we're practically there. She'll be fine."

"That's what I said. Anyway, she's heading out but told me to walk fast."

"Not a problem." I sped up, and Madison matched me stride for stride.

"Ruby still naps?" I asked.

"Not much," Madison said, "but her schedule's messed up with the hotel living."

I nodded. That made sense. We walked in silence for a couple blocks. As we waited for the light to change at Davenport Road, Madison opened her mouth to speak, closed it, frowned, then tried again.

"Hannah Helstrom. Hannah. Helstrom."

I cocked my head to the side and looked at her. "That's my name."

"Yep," Madison said. "It's a cool one. Hannah Helstrom. Sounds like, I don't know, a character in a comic book."

I laughed and shook my head. "Pretty sure Helstrom just means house by the river."

"Whatever. It's a cool name. Hey, you don't have to stay. I'm gonna be cooped up with Ruby until Mom gets back."

"It's no big deal," I said. "Seriously. I don't mind."

The light changed, and we crossed the street in silence. My mind wandered back to a memory from two years earlier, still fresh in my mind.

"The code of the hero is to serve, train, and wait."

Our voices reverberated off the dojo's high ceiling. Kobayashi-sensei walked purposefully along the line we'd formed at the close of the class, his white gi in stark contrast to his dark, weathered face.

"Why do we wait?" His quiet voice somehow filled the room.

"We wait because a hero answers trouble, he does not seek it."

My voice blended with the eleven other uchi-deshi, students of the sensei who stayed in the boys' and girls' dormitories during the month-long training session. Kobayashi-sensei's martial arts training was my favorite part of training as a Seven. I'd been once a year during the summers for four years, from ages ten to fourteen. The last summer I'd attended had been a few months after I'd learned I was a reggie. Only a reggie. It had been worth it, in spite of the garbage that came my way.

"Why do we train?" Kobayashi-sensei asked as he passed by me.

"We train," I said with the others, "because a hero does not presume on good fortune to perform the hero feat."

"Why do we serve?"

"We serve to develop a servant's heart, for no hero serves himself."

Kobayashi-sensei stopped at the end of the line of students. He pivoted around, taking time to make eye contact with each of us before speaking.

"And what is the hero feat?"

My eyebrows came together in a frown, and a quick glance to either side showed I wasn't the only one confused. The other questions and answers had been recited each day for the past month. This one was new.

Kobayashi-sensei began his slow steps back the way he'd come, looking each student in the eye as he passed them, an eyebrow cocked up as if to say, "Do you have an answer?"

Two students to my left, I heard Joshua's smirking voice. "The hero feet is what I use to kick people in the face."

"Incorrect," Kobayashi-sensei answered as he continued past Joshua. He paused to look at Samantha, who was trying to stifle a giggle, and continued on with a slight shake of his head. Samantha would laugh at anything Joshua said. It drove me nuts.

My mind was racing. I desperately wanted to answer his question, but how could I know the hero feat before it was done? It could be anything. He stepped even with me, and his calm gaze asked me the question.

"We don't know!" I was startled to realize I was the one who had spoken. Kobayashi-sensei's left eyebrow inched up as he held my gaze.

"We can't know," I said. "Isn't that the point of waiting?"

"Ah." He turned and continued his slow journey down the line of students. "But we can state Hannah-chan's declaration positively, yes? The hero feat is doing what is required in times of extraordinary need."

"Hannah," Joshua said, leaning forward at the waist to look at me around Samantha, "I don't think you need to worry about hero feats. Leave that stuff to us real Sevens."

Samantha made a snorting sound and burst out laughing. She wasn't alone. My ears buzzed as blood rushed to my cheeks.

WOOOMPH!

My mind snapped back to the present. The sound was sudden, loud, low. It reverberated in my chest more than my ears, coming from everywhere at once. We stopped and looked at each other, Madison's eyebrows scrunched up in question.

Then we heard the scream. Clear, bright, panicked, followed by a low roar. The noise had come from up ahead, around the corner at the end of the block. Toward the hotel. Madison's eyes flared wide and we started running. We pounded up the sidewalk, passed the corner strip mall, and rounded the corner.

The smallish hotel stood a block away, four stories tall, with beige stucco walls, a dark roof, and bright blue gutters. People poured out of doors and broken windows. The flames followed, licking up the walls from gaping windows on the first floor. The air was filled with smoke, cries of urgent fear, and a shrieking alarm.

We kept running until we reached the parking lot, which was rapidly filling with a confused, milling mass of people. Someone was yelling about a ruptured gas line and explosions. Madison pulled to a stop and I barely avoided running into her. She turned toward me, the whites of her eyes showing.

"Ruby."

Oh, no. Her little sister, alone on the fourth floor. A window on the second floor shattered outward, and black smoke followed, rising into the clear blue sky. She was trapped up there, above all those flames.

It wasn't supposed to happen like this. There was no glory waiting for me in that building. No bad guys to fight. No enemy that I could defeat. Just unconquerable flames and terrible suffering.

Beside me, Madison broke down in sobs. I reached out to her, my hand shaking, and grabbed her shoulder. I couldn't stand by.

"Serve. Train. Wait." My voice was barely a whisper, choked by fear.

Madison looked up at me, tears streaming down her face. I'd trained and waited. Time to serve.

"I'm going in." Saying it made me almost throw up. "I'll get Ruby out."

Madison's face scrunched up, her head shaking. "What are you talking about? She's up there"—her hand shot out, pointing to the top floor—"she's, she's going to—"

"Not today she's not." My hand tightened on her shoulder. "What room?"

"What?" Madison said. She wasn't looking at me anymore. Flames reflected in her pupils.

I grabbed her other shoulder and yanked her around to face me. "What's your room number? I can't remember. Quick!"

"I, I don't understand," Madison said.

"What room are you staying in?" I yelled. The noise from the fire had grown louder, accompanied finally by the wail of distant sirens. They sounded so far away. Too far.

"Four-oh-nine."

"Give me your key!" She looked dazed. I stuck my hand in her face. "The key!"

Madison reached into a back pocket and handed me one of those plastic, credit card-like keys. "What are you doing?"

I didn't bother answering. What could I say that would make any sense? She didn't know I was a Seven. I jammed the key in my pocket and ran toward the building, weaving between clumps of terrified people. I heard Madison scream my name, but I ignored her. Suddenly, I was clear of the people and racing across a thin strip of parking lot toward the front doors.

Any of the other Seven talents would have helped. If I was a ghost—the talent to pass through solids—I would have turned insubstantial, ignored the flames, and gotten up there without a problem. Or as a shifter I could have changed into a bird and figured out how to get in through the roof.

I didn't have those talents. I could reggie. And I was stubborn. If there was a way to save Ruby, I'd find it. I had to, but I was terrified that there wasn't enough healing in the world to keep me alive once I went into that inferno.

I pulled to a stop in front of the sliding glass doors. They didn't open. Smoke obscured the interior, but I saw flames crawling along the walls off to the right and across the ceiling. The sirens were still too far away.

Someone grabbed my shoulder and I jerked around to find a man wearing an ill-fitting suit trying to pull me away toward the parking lot.

"Get away from there!" he yelled.

I smiled at him and slapped his hand away. He looked shocked and stepped back. I drew in a deep breath, turned back toward the doors, and leapt forward, putting everything I had into a push kick. I hit the doors right in the middle where they met, and they popped apart and swung inward.

Heat surged out and staggered me. What was I thinking? I couldn't go in there. I blinked away tears, focused on Ruby, and ran into the lobby.

My eyes stung, my lungs burned. I crouched down, squinted, and looked around for the stairwell. The heat was unbearable. I couldn't get any air. Flames attacked everything. The walls, furniture, ceiling. My tears evaporated. I'd made it fifteen feet into the building and was done. I dropped to my knees and reggied.

Sweet relief flooded through my body. My eyes worked again. Even the desperate stress of needing to breath diminished. It lasted for about a second before the heat overwhelmed me again, but in that moment, I'd seen a doorway off to my left with a sign on it that said STAIRS. I couldn't be sure, but I thought there was less fire on that side of the room.

I reggied again and ran for it. I was practically blind, my hands flailing around in front of me, praying they'd find the door handle. Clumps of fire dripped down onto me, riding pieces of crumbling ceiling tile. My hair ignited, then my shirt. I screamed, which was a bad idea, since it let the searing heat into my lungs.

I dropped and rolled around on the floor, trying to put out the flames that had attached themselves to my hair and shirt. Maybe it worked, but the pain didn't diminish. I reggied, got up, and kept going. The door materialized in front of me, cloaked in smoke, distorted by my tears. I grabbed the handle and yanked it open. Pain lanced through my hand as the heated metal of the doorknob seared my skin. I stumbled forward into a dark stairwell and collapsed.

I huddled in the dark and wept. I'd reggied, but echoes of the pain rattled around in my head. The remains of my shirt lay smoldering beside me, barely visible in the dim red glow of an emergency light. The stench of my own burning hair made my stomach churn.

Nothing had prepared me for this. It was so wrong. Superheroes were supposed to be, well, heroic. All I had to offer was suffering. I clenched my jaw. Not just suffering. Stubbornness, too.

"Keep going, Hannah," I whispered as my sobs subsided. "Keep going."

I dragged in a ragged breath, lurched to my feet, and put an unsteady foot on the first step. One step, then another. Eight steps, a switchback, eight more steps. The second-floor landing. I wiped my nose with the back of my hand and tried to pull myself together. I could do this.

The stairwell was in decent shape. No fire that I could see, though smoke was pouring in from underneath the door to the second floor. I made the turn and headed up the next flight of stairs. My steps gradually quickened, gained purpose, pushed me forward.

I was going to make it. I'd get to Ruby and figure something out, anything to get her out of this hell. I rounded the landing on the third floor. I was running now, leaping up the stairs. The switchback flew by and I was up the last half-flight of stairs. I put my foot on the fourth-floor landing.

An explosion ripped apart reality. I was thrown to the side, bounced off the wall, stumbled, and fell backwards down the stairs.

Kobayashi-sensei had drilled me relentlessly on falling that last summer I'd trained with him. He knew my one and only talent was reggying and figured that until my body learned to reggie on its own, I had to stay conscious to keep going. I had to learn to protect my head to give me the chance to heal. It had been the opposite of fun, but I'd done everything he'd dished out, and I'd learned.

With a practiced motion, I tucked into a fetal position, my arms wrapped around my head, and reggied repeatedly as I tumbled backwards. The stairs were concrete and utterly unforgiving. Ribs cracked and immediately healed. Massive contusions were knit back together in an instant. The only thing that mattered was protecting my head.

I fell down those stairs like a ninja, if ninjas bounced down stairs tumbling end over end. I kept my priorities straight and protected my head the whole way. When I finally jolted to a stop eight steps later on the switchback, I was stunned but alive. I glanced down the stairs to the third-floor landing. The door hung open on broken hinges and flames were surging into the stairwell. Intense heat washed over me.

No time to think. I jumped up, or tried to. All the reggying was wearing me out, and I staggered into the wall. The flames were crawling up the walls toward me, but I couldn't seem to get my head to stop spinning. I ended up scrambling up the stairs on all fours.

At the fourth-floor landing, I grabbed the door and was relieved to discover it was only warm, not searingly hot. I pulled myself upright, opened the door, and stumbled forward.

The fourth-floor hall extending away from me was hazy with smoke and dark, lit by a window at the far end of the hall. I could see the shadowy outlines of doors on both sides. Fire leaked through the wall and doors along the right side. I put a hand on the left wall to steady myself and reggied again.

It seemed to help, and I was able to stand up straight. I hugged the left wall as I hurried forward toward the first pair of doors, one to the left, the other to the right. The air was terrible, the heat intolerable.

I felt profound relief when I saw the number 417 emblazoned on the door to the left. Hopefully, the fire was on the right. Ruby was on the left. I hunched over to stay below the thick, swirling smoke near the ceiling and ran for door 409. With each passing door, the heat and smoke got worse. By the time I got to door 411, I was on the floor crawling, whimpering as I scrambled forward.

I made it to door 409 through sheer will. The heat was deadly. The door opposite 409 stood open, and fire rushed toward me from the room behind it. I reggied over and over as I slipped the plastic key into the slot above the door handle and prayed it would work. I yanked the handle down, it turned, and the door popped open.

A piercing scream greeted me as I sprawled forward into the room. Ruby was huddled on the far side of the room by the window. She had Madison's dark curls. Twenty feet away from her, I could tell she was scared. Then I realized she was terrified of me.

I stood and slammed the door shut to block out the raging heat. Glancing down, I understood. The remains of my shirt were back in the stairwell. My bra, jeans, and skin were covered in black, sooty streaks. I patted my head and felt a few smoldering tufts of hair. I probably looked like a fire monster to little Ruby.

I dropped to my knees and held my arms out to her. "It's me, Ruby. Hannah's here. We're going to be okay."

Her little eyebrows pulled together. "Hannah?"

"That's me. Hannah banana. Come here, sweetie."

My nickname seemed to convince her I was really me, and she ran across the room and leapt into my arms. I held her close and looked around. There was too much smoke. It seemed to be pouring into their little living space from the hall to the two bedrooms. Flames crawled along the ceiling out of the hall. We were out of time.

I pulled away from Ruby and took her hand. "Come on, Ruby. We need to leave."

I stayed bent over and led her across the room to the window. Two firetrucks were setting up in the parking lot, with men scurrying around to attach hoses and grab gear. More trucks were inbound. I glanced over my shoulder. The flames were rushing into the room from the bedroom hall. The heat was increasing exponentially. They'd never get a ladder to us in time.

"It's too hot," Ruby said. "I'm scared."

I looked down. Below us, about ten feet away from the building across a strip of grass, I saw a row of cars parked and knew what I had to do.

"Crouch down near the floor," I said, directing Ruby to the side of the window.

She did, hiding her face from the heat of the room, and I crawled over to the couch. I shielded my face with an arm from the heat while grabbing a blanket and cushion off the couch. I scrambled back to the window, where it wasn't quite as bad.

"Ruby, get on my back, okay? I'm going to give you a piggyback ride."

She didn't say a word but crawled onto my back, wrapping her arms and legs around me. I flipped the blanket over my shoulders, covering her, and knotted the corners tightly across my chest and stomach. Hopefully, she'd stay put. My aunt had a small, wrought-iron table next to the window, holding a little potted plant. I pushed the plant off and grabbed the table by its legs.

I swung it in a wide arc and hit the window hard. The glass exploded out, and a strong, cool breeze rushed into the room. The fire on the other side of the room leapt toward us. Ruby screamed again as the heat became intolerable.

I dropped the table, put the cushion on the windowsill to cover the worst of the broken shards of glass, and climbed up onto it. I crouched for a second on the windowsill, and in that moment, I heard the calls of people down below pointing up at us.

No time to think. The flames rushed toward us. I did my best to line things up, grabbed the knots in the blanket, and jumped.

Four floors up is pretty high. I had time to think about my life and my likely death as I plunged from the broken window toward the parking lot below. I'd waited. I'd trained. I'd served. What else could I do?

Miraculously, my aim was true. I slammed into the roof of a large SUV, legs extended, leaning slightly forward. More than one thing snapped in my legs, the roof buckled, and I slammed facedown into the crumpled metal, breaking more bits of me. An arm, probably some ribs. Through it all, I held onto the blanket with one hand and covered my head with the other arm.

For a time, the pain was overwhelming. I was conscious but stunned. I didn't think to reggie until I felt something tugging at the blanket wrapped tightly around me. It went on for a little, then stopped, and I felt lighter. I chose that moment to reggie, and bones grated back into place as tissue healed. I leaned over the side of the SUV and threw up. A weariness beyond anything I'd ever experienced gripped me. I flopped onto my back on the roof of the SUV and waited to see what would happen next.

At least, that's what I'd planned to do. Instead, hands gently pulled me off the vehicle and lowered me onto a gurney. I was suddenly surrounded by EMT-types as they wheeled me away from the building. The guy on my left could have been in one of those firemen calendars. That's when I realized the blanket I'd tied around me was gone. I had a moment of panic that I was half-naked in front of calendar guy, but that was drowned out by a much larger panic. Ruby!

The lady on my right put a blanket over me just as I struggled to sit up. Someone up by my head pushed down on my shoulders to hold me down.

"Hold on there, miss," calendar guy said. "It's a miracle you're alive, but you've got to be injured. We wouldn't have normally moved you, but the flames weren't safe."

"I'm fine," I said, pushing the hands away and sitting up. "Where's my cousin? The little girl who was on my back?"

"Just ahead of you," the lady said and nodded past me. "She's being checked right now."

I pulled the blanket around me and hopped off the gurney. They protested, but I ignored them and looked around. The parking lot had been cleared to make room for all the firetrucks and ambulances. There, not twenty feet away, Ruby was sitting on a gurney being looked at by a couple of EMTs. Madison stood beside her, holding her hand.

The two of them saw me at the same moment I spotted them. Madison looked shocked at whatever she saw, but Ruby's face lit up with a smile. I ran over and threw my arms around her. Mid-hug, Madison joined us and squeezed me tight.

"Thank you," Madison whispered, her mouth near my ear as she hugged us. "Thank you. Thank you. Thank you."

I pulled away and looked at Ruby. "She okay?"

One of the EMTs answered. "Yeah, so far, so good. She took in some smoke and has some minor burns and bruising, but she shouldn't be..." He trailed off, reached out, and clutched my shoulder. "We all saw it. What you did. How? How are you alive? And walking?"

I shrugged. "I'm pretty durable."

My mom showed up a few minutes later along with my aunt. With Mom's help, I fought off the EMTs and headed home with her, while my aunt and Madison took Ruby to the hospital for further tests to make sure she really was okay. On the drive home, Mom didn't say much, but a few tears made the journey down her cheek, and every minute or so, she'd reach over and give my arm a squeeze.

Once home, I carefully avoided all mirrors while digging through my parents' bathroom drawers until I found my dad's beard trimmer. I took it to my bathroom, again keeping my eyes on the floor and avoiding the mirror. I set it on a pretty close trim, stepped into the shower stall, and worked it back and forth over my head. Burned, frizzled blonde hair collected around my feet. Once that was done, I took a real shower.

Afterward, I dried off and wrapped a towel around me before stepping out. I ran my hand over the peach fuzz covering my head, took a deep breath, and stepped in front of the mirror. My head looked more angular than I'd expected, but I was glad to see I didn't have any weird bumps or marks on my nearly-bald scalp.

I smiled. I'd done it. The hero feat. Not that I ever wanted to do anything like that again, but stubbornness and reggying had gotten the job done. My hair would grow back, and I'd seen stranger things. Not bad for the worst superhero in the Guild of Sevens.

Hannah Helstrom welcomes you to the world of the Guild of Sevens! Set a few months prior to Hannah's hero feat, the novel Joss The Seven *introduces this world through fourteen-year-old Joss Morgan. As the novel opens, Joss finds out he has superpowers, and soon discovers they may just get him killed.*

Joss's struggles continue in Guardian Angel, *when Joss aims to keep his word by keeping his parents in the dark. It may cost him everything.*

I have a particular stance in life that influences my writing. To quote G.K. Chesterton: "Fairy tales do not give the child his first idea of bogey. What fairy tales give the child is his first clear idea of the possible defeat of bogey. The baby has known the dragon intimately ever since he had an imagination. What the fairy tale provides for him is a St. George to kill the dragon."

My stories don't focus on worlds without bogeys or dragons. Instead, I aspire to write stories that show children there is a St. George.

http://jphilphorne.com/hannah-learn-more/

In Plain Sight

Arthur Daigle

The Great Zamphini, master entertainer, friend to all children, and beloved citizen of Lambsport, was trying very hard not to be noticed. This was an unreasonable expectation given that he weighed three hundred pounds, dressed in bright red robes, carried a walking stick six feet long, and was standing on a street corner in broad daylight. Nevertheless, he was making a good effort by being very quiet and staying off the main roads with their bustling markets.

Zamphini stroked his bushy black beard as he waited, hoping no one would see him. He glanced down at the cobblestone street and the sewer grate he'd pried open an hour earlier. A slender rope ran from a lamppost down to the sewers below, and he had a bucket of soapy water for the trusted agent he'd sent into that mess.

"Zamphini?" Zamphini winced when he heard his name called. Putting on his best showman's smile, he turned and saw Watch Officer Wasler marching toward him. Wasler's tan uniform looked a bit worse for wear, as did the man himself, but he was still younger, stronger, and handsomer than the famed entertainer. "What are you doing?"

"Ah, Officer Wasler, a pleasure to see you as always! You look well. And how is your darling wife?"

"She's fine." The officer walked up and rested his hand on his sheathed sword. "Why are you so far from home? There are no parties here, and no one here could afford you if there were."

"Scandalous, isn't it? I've lowered my rates twice and still get only half the business of last year. I blame the war with Duke Thornwood, and the criminally high taxes that came with it. Since when is laughter a luxury?"

Wasler frowned and rubbed his eyes. "Look, it's been a horrible week with three men beaten to within an inch of their lives in my district. I don't have the time or patience to play 'what's Zamphini doing?' today, so spit it out."

"Three? I'd only heard of two."

"The baker's son was attacked on his way home last night. Four men came at him in the dark and broke both his arms, so you'll forgive me if I have better things to do than—" Wasler's voice trailed off when he saw the rope going into the sewers. "What's that?"

Zamphini stepped between Wasler and the open sewer. "This? Oh, a minor problem. I was taking Sassy for a walk when she fell down there. I can't fit, and I wouldn't dream of asking someone to go down for me, so I lowered a rope for her to climb up."

"A rope you just happened to be carrying with you, and a bucket of water? And since when do you take your dolls for walks?"

The rope went taut as Sassy climbed out of the sewers. Zamphini snatched up the doll and dunked her in the bucket of water. He cleaned off the filth smeared on the doll until she looked presentable. "I got the bucket and rope after she fell in. There we go, Sassy, good as new."

Sassy got out of the bucket and curtsied to Wasler. The doll looked like a toddler girl two feet tall with white porcelain skin and black hair, wearing black shoes and a blue dress. Wasler frowned at the doll then noticed a new addition to Sassy's outfit, a small backpack bulging with coins. He glared at Zamphini, who looked down, ashamed.

"It's the war. So few people have parties, so many hold funerals. I'm hired once a month if I'm lucky. This month, nothing. I haven't been invited to a single banquet this year!" Zamphini patted his ample belly. "I'm wasting away!"

Wasler chuckled, but there was truth to what Zamphini said. He'd lost forty pounds this year, and not an ounce of it willingly. His red clothes were in good condition but hung loosely on him.

Zamphini picked up Sassy and the coins. "It costs money to keep Sassy and her sisters and brothers going. I looked down the sewer grate and saw coins lost in the sewers, so I lowered Sassy down to get them. It's no crime, and I'm sure if you look deep into your heart, you won't want people to know the Great Zamphini has come to this."

"You found that much in a sewer?"

"Fallen coins get flushed into the sewers when it rains hard," Zamphini said. "No one goes after them, and it adds up as the years go by."

Wasler said nothing. It took Zamphini a moment to notice that Wasler's attention was focused on the money Sassy had brought up. There were perhaps thirty copper coins and two silver ones, an impressive sum in such hard times. With so much money going for the war, there was precious little for even essentials, like the salaries of the city watch.

"You, ah, haven't been paid in a while, have you?" Zamphini asked. When Wasler didn't answer, Zamphini took a silver coin and passed it to him. "Your wife's expecting again, isn't she? I'm sure she'd love it if you bought her a nice dress."

"I've been two months with no pay, only promises." Wasler's face showed how much he hated himself for taking the money. "I'm going to spend it on food and you know it. Go home, Zamphini. You're a good man, and I've seen too many good men hurt."

Wasler turned to leave when he heard a scratching noise from the roofs above. The brick buildings were two stories tall, and the glare of the setting sun made it impossible to see what was making the sound. "What was that?"

"Cats," Zamphini told him. "They have to be careful these days. Some people are so poor they don't care where their meat comes from."

Once the officer had left, Zamphini held Sassy up to his face. "You did good. Tell me, did you see any ghoul tracks?" Sassy shook her head, and Zamphini smiled. "That's three months and no sign of them. I think we got them all. Before we go, I need to make sure water didn't get inside you."

Sassy tipped her head as Zamphini took a brass key from one of his deep pockets. He inserted it into the doll's neck and turned it, opening a panel on her back. Sassy's body contained spinning brass gears, thin brass cables, and etched obsidian spheres. Glass tubes carrying bright green liquid ran through the doll. Zamphini peered into Sassy and smiled when he found nothing had seeped in. Satisfied that his star performer was in good condition, he closed the panel and locked it shut.

With that done, Zamphini set Sassy on his shoulder and headed out. He had a few more places to visit before nightfall. He went onto the main roads and their stalls selling, well, not much of anything. The war cost Lambsport a fortune in gold each month, and feeding the army in the field sucked up all but the most basic foods. Hawkers shouted out what they were selling and for how much.

"Firewood, one copper piece a cord!"

"Chickens! Live chickens! Five copper pieces for a live chicken!"

"Fresh fish, caught today! You can probably afford it!"

"Shameful what they're asking," Zamphini told Sassy. She shrugged in reply. "You're lucky I brew up your fuel myself, or you'd be as hungry as I am."

The overpriced goods still drew a crowd. Most were humans, but a handful of broad-shouldered dwarfs sold knives. Five elves representing the Yelinid Banking Cartel had set up a stall and were offering loans. Goblins stayed in the alleys and street edges, careful not to get stepped on by the bigger races as they snatched up garbage. A single ogre wearing a kilt stood under an arch. The hairy brute gripped an ax and looked intimidating as he waited for clients. In the past, Zamphini had seen men desperate enough to hire the ogre as a bodyguard or troubleshooter, yet another sign of Lambsport's hard times.

Lambsport was a city of contrasts. Every home and shop of the seaside city was made of brick, an expensive move for such poor people, but an unavoidable one. The city had burned down so many times over the centuries that the residents had finally accepted the cost and difficulty of building with stone. Lambsport had fifty thousand residents and half as many visitors, yet drew little attention from their ruler, Duke Edgely. Edgely was more interested in fighting rival dukes than sniggling, insignificant things like trade, fishing, manufacturing, or learning. The port city and its inhabitants were left alone as long as they paid taxes and lots of them. This gave the people of Lambsport a degree of freedom and was the reason the Great Zamphini called it home.

Zamphini was a minor celebrity in Lambsport, and his arrival in the market drew friendly greetings. An older man said, "Hey, Zamphini, I'm practicing to be a fortune teller. I can tell you which block the city watch will stake out to catch those hooligans."

"Really? Which one?"

"The wrong one, same as every night." The old man laughed at his own wit, not noticing he was the only one to do so.

"Be nice," Zamphini said. "They're good men, and they'd get those villains if Duke Edgely hadn't conscripted half the watchmen."

"Ha!" The old man spat on the ground then pointed at Sassy. "You be careful, friend. The way things are going, they'll put a uniform on your doll and send her to war. She'd be better than most. Hey, Sassy, I bet they'll promote you to officer!"

Sassy stood up straight on Zamphini's shoulders and saluted. People laughed as she marched in place. Zamphini laughed too, but it wasn't so funny. He'd received discreet inquiries from Duke Edgely's officials wondering if his dolls could fight. He'd explained they were too small for battle, but new requests came monthly.

A young man watched Zamphini walk by and followed him. The youth was trying to look casual and failing miserably. Zamphini stopped to inspect a stall offering pastries. The youth came closer, careful to stay behind his intended victim. He took his hands out of his pockets and raised them.

"Sassy bites," Zamphini said without turning around. The youth hesitated and lowered his hands. "You have ten fingers, a fact that will change if you act foolishly."

Sassy turned around and smiled at the young man, a twinkle in her eye as she snapped her mouth closed. Happily, the youth put his hands back in his pockets and left. Zamphini chuckled and left for another stall, his walking stick making a steady tap as he walked. There was also a scratching noise on the rooftops, but that was lost in the tumult of the market.

"As I live and breathe, the Great Zamphini!" a shrill voice called out. It took a lot of effort for Zamphini to force a smile as he turned around. The thin, immaculately dressed woman took his hands in hers and smiled.

"Aliana Treter!" Zamphini said with a laugh. "It's been too long."

"Years, I know, but my son still talks about the show you put on for his birthday, and that was ages ago! All the best women wanted to hire you after that."

"At massive discounts," Zamphini added. What was it about the rich that you had to claw the money out of their hands? It had taken five months to get this crone to pay him, and her friends were just as bad.

Ignoring what he'd said, Aliana's face lit up when she saw Sassy. "Well, hello, Molly!"

"Ah, no, this is Sassy. Molly and the other dolls are at home with my wife."

"Oh yes, I'd heard about her. Poor girl came down with red eyes plague. I had that myself when I was younger. Took me a month to get over it. Most people need five months, but I've always had a strong constitution. How are your children?"

Zamphini rolled his eyes. "They don't visit, they don't write, they don't send money. They could send money!"

Aliana laughed. "I know, I know! It's the curse of parents everywhere that children don't care or listen. My oldest, the one whose party you did, he went and joined the army."

"Really?" Zamphini didn't try to disguise his shock. The war between Duke Edgely and Duke Thornwood was as brutal as it was long. Few men became soldiers if they could help it.

"I told him I had more than enough money to pay off Duke Edgely's men if they showed up at the door, but he was sold on glory in battle and becoming a great man. I told him you don't have to be a hero to be important in Lambsport. Take you, for instance. Everyone knows you here, and all you do is entertain at parties."

In an epic act of cluelessness, Aliana totally ignored the disbelieving look on Zamphini's face. Instead, she went on prattling. "I mean, your little toys are treated like they're something special. Why, just last month, a fool man went and claimed you were a mad scientist and Molly here was something called a clockwork."

Sassy scowled and folded her arms across her chest. Feeling a tad worried, Zamphini asked, "And what became of this man?"

Sounding annoyed that she'd been interrupted, Aliana said, "The fool went to Duke Edgely and tried to make an issue of it. He expected a reward for informing on you, the cad. Our duke wouldn't hear of it. He had the man flogged and gave him three months' hard labor."

"I'm glad our duke is so understanding," Zamphini said. "Accusations like that can ruin a man's reputation."

Aliana waved her hand like she was shooing away a fly. "The man's an idiot, and there's no shortage of those. Can you believe he'd say such a thing about a harmless old man like you? Scandalous, absolutely scandalous."

Zamphini took a step back and tried to come up with an excuse to leave (he had several, but none were polite), when Aliana took his hands again. "You've heard about those poor men being attacked? Of course you have. There have been eighteen since the start of the year. The odd thing is they weren't robbed. Beaten bloody, but not a coin taken. You be careful. If these mongrels would attack fit young men, why, they'd go after an old man like you in a heartbeat. Watch yourself, darling!"

With that, Aliana disappeared into the crowd to dispense her unique brand of "help" to some other unfortunate soul. Zamphini breathed a sigh of relief and was about to leave when he saw movement to his right.

There was a pile of dead rats in the mouth of an alley. It was hard to tell how many there were, but Zamphini estimated they numbered thirty or more. The rats had died not long ago, likely when he was talking with Aliana.

Zamphini looked around and stepped into the alley once he was sure no one was watching. Something crouched in the shadows and tossed another dead rat onto the pile.

"I know this must be boring for you, but I believe my instructions were fairly clear," Zamphini told it. The thing whimpered and jumped to the rooftops. "That's better."

With that cleared up, Zamphini left the alley and continued on his way. Near the edge of the market was a small store selling fruit. Zamphini smiled and rubbed his hands together when he reached it. "Peaches! Ah, it's been so long since I had any. Dried peaches, they're good if you can't find better, but nothing matches fruit fresh off the tree."

A middle-aged woman manning the store smiled when she saw him. "I was hoping I'd see you today. How are you?"

"Crystal, you devilish beauty, you don't look a day over twenty." Zamphini stepped into the store and kissed her hand. "You look well. Is business good? Are your children well?"

"I am, it's not, and they are." Crystal looked a good deal younger than she was. Her clothes were simple but well-tailored by her able hands, and a warm smile was rarely absent from her face. "How are you, flatterer?"

"Seeing you smile again takes a weight off my heart." He saw Crystal's oldest daughter Gwen sweeping the back of the store. Like most girls, Gwen had matured earlier than boys her age, but much faster than normal. The girl was fourteen going on twenty, a beauty as great as her mother. Baggy clothes hid her curves so few men noticed her. "Gwen, you look radiant."

"Mister Zamphini!" Gwen's face lit up and she ran over. "Sassy!"

Sassy jumped off Zamphini's shoulder and landed in Gwen's arms. The girl shrieked with laughter and spun around in a full circle with the doll. Zamphini laughed and patted her on the back.

"You two play and I'll fill my belly," he said. Still smiling, he went back to admiring the fresh peaches. He took a straw bag from his deep pockets and loaded it with fruit. "She seems happy."

Crystal followed him, her voice soft as she spoke. "That drunken lout Yal Bridger hasn't bothered us all week. Zamphini, please tell me you didn't hurt him."

"No, and that was a hard promise to keep after I'd met him." Zamphini finished filling the bag and brought out another. "Your description of his character left out a laundry list of flaws besides bothering a girl half his age. We spoke and I explained that his behavior was unacceptable. He's left Lambsport, headed where, I can't say."

Crystal raised her eyebrows. "He left the city? Good God, what did you say to him?"

"My words were few but well chosen. Ooh, plums!"

Crystal's earlier joy was replaced with sadness. "I'm sorry I had to ask for help. I should have handled this, but with my husband conscripted, I wasn't sure what to do. The city watch wouldn't help, and I'm shocked to say my relatives said Gwen is old enough to marry."

"Say no more to me of the hardships of families. It's a problem I know too well. My father could have helped me a thousand times, yet he never raised a hand in my defense. He's the most greedy, suspicious, ungrateful, black-hearted man you'll ever meet!"

"How is he?" Crystal asked.

"Still mayor."

Their conversation was interrupted when the ogre walked by them in the company of a farmer. Lambsport had a strong odor from so many people living together, but the ogre's musky scent was noticeable from ten feet away. Zamphini saw scars crisscrossing the ogre's chest and arms, the healed wounds as thick as lines on a street map. The farmer looked nervous as he passed a pouch of coins to the burly ogre. "The beast's come up from the sea twice this week, and last time, it tried to force its way into my barn. Please, I just want this to stop."

The ogre's deep, rumbling reply was hard to understand. "I'll make it go away for good. Meet me at the city gate in an hour."

"There was a time the army or city watch would have handled such problems," Zamphini said once the ogre and farmer had left. "These days, they're too busy with the war to save their own people. If the fighting ends tomorrow, it still wouldn't be soon enough."

Crystal frowned and pointed at the ogre. "There's been something on my mind. No one would be foolish enough to try and conscript someone that dangerous, but why hasn't Duke Edgely hired him for the war?"

"Ogres don't obey anyone blindly. They follow those they respect, and it's a rare man who can earn that. He's more valuable to them here handling problems they can't be bothered with than ignoring their orders on the battlefield."

More softly, she asked, "Those men who were attacked at night, do you think he's responsible?"

Zamphini shook his head and turned his attention back to the fruit. "No, and for two reasons. The men who were beaten all said they couldn't identify their attackers in the dark. If the ogre did it, who could mistake him for another when he's that big, and with that smell?"

She smiled at him. "I suppose not. What's the other reason?"

"With muscles like that, if he hit those men, they'd be dead." Zamphini finished his selection and tried to hand a copper coin to Crystal. She made no move to take it.

"You earned that a thousand times over."

Zamphini opened her hand and pressed the coin into her palm. "Dealing with Bridger was a public service. This is for the fruit."

Crystal looked likely to argue, but the sound of running feet and wicker baskets falling to the ground caught their attention. It was the youth who'd followed Zamphini not half an hour ago, this time with a package clenched to his chest. Two watchmen chased him down the street toward Zamphini and Crystal. The youth shoved a woman out of his way as a watchman shouted, "Halt, thief!"

"Sassy, would you mind?" Zamphini asked. Sassy jumped out of Gwen's arms and ran into the street. The youth ran in front of the fruit store, not noticing the doll until she grabbed him by the ankle and pulled hard to the left. He cried out as he fell and dropped the package. The watchmen grabbed him and pulled him up before they forced him up against a brick wall.

"That was stupid," a watchman said as he bound the youth's hands. "You're looking at three months' hard labor unless you can pay off Magistrate Heckler. I'm betting you can't."

The youth's face twisted in rage as he glared at Zamphini and Sassy. "I'll get even with you!"

Confused people looked at Zamphini, who shrugged in reply. "I didn't touch the man."

"Your stupid puppet tripped me!"

Sassy scooted behind Zamphini and held onto his legs. Zamphini smiled and asked, "Forgive me, but are you saying you were beaten up by a doll?"

The street erupted into laughter. Men and elves pointed at the youth and jeered. Dwarfs shook their heads, and the lone ogre laughed so hard he had to sit down. Goblins came out of the shadows to pelt the youth with horse dung, and Zamphini had to admit they had impressive aim. The youth's face turned red, and he looked down in shame as the watchmen dragged him away.

Zamphini turned away from the spectacle and back to Crystal. "Good woman, as much as it pains me to say this, the hour grows late and our meeting must end." He kissed her hand again and smiled. "Don't hesitate to call upon me if you should be in trouble."

"You're a good man," she told him.

"I am a great man! It says so in my name."

Gwen stepped out of the store long enough to hug him. "Mister Zamphini, I know I'm asking a lot, but my little brother's birthday is coming up. Could you come to his party? I saved up some money to pay you."

"Gwen," Crystal began, her tone a warning.

"I'd be delighted!" Zamphini interrupted her. "I need to stay in practice, and this is the perfect opportunity. I'll bring all dozen of my dolls, and they will dance and juggle and tumble for you. You thought there were only eleven of them? I just finished building a brother for Sassy, who wanted another sister, but she's coming around."

Sassy stuck out her tongue at her maker, and Gwen laughed. Zamphini clapped a hand over his heart in mock shame. "Sassy, how could you, and in front of friends? But, Gwen, and this is important, you must invite the neighbor children as well. If the Great Zamphini is to work, he must have a proper audience."

"Thank you, thank you, thank you!" Gwen hugged Zamphini so hard the older man gasped as she squeezed the air out of him. It took some effort to disentangle himself and leave.

The sun was setting as Zamphini left Crystal and her daughter. He didn't go home, instead searching among the stalls. The marketplace emptied quickly as sellers closed their stores and customers hurried home. A few boys ran through the streets and set tallow candles into the lamps hanging from lampposts. Goblins fled to hidden places, a rare move since they were comfortable in the dark. It was a sorry state of affairs that they feared the night as much as men did.

One woman saw Zamphini and hesitated before sealing her home for the night. "I've a spare bed you can stay in until dawn."

"Good woman, there's no need for such a generous offer."

"There is! It will be dark soon. Two men on this block suffered savage beatings after nightfall, and three more say they escaped the same fate by the skin of their teeth."

Zamphini smiled, his expression unforced. "It warms my heart to meet someone so kind in these troubled days. Fear not, for the Great Zamphini is not far from home, and he never travels alone."

"You're sure?" the woman asked.

He bowed to her. "Have no fear for my safety."

The woman looked doubtful, but she closed her door, and there was a thud as she barred it. Zamphini walked down the street and watched it empty. Soon, only he and the ogre were left. The ogre showed no fear and walked up to Zamphini.

"Can I help you?" Zamphini asked.

"I heard you went to the village of Rotwood last month."

"Yes, I did a performance for the mayor. His daughter turned thirteen and he wanted to make it an occasion for the entire village."

"Rotwood had a problem with devil rats attacking their livestock before your *performance*. They didn't after you left." When Zamphini didn't respond, the ogre added, "There was supposed to be a whole swarm of them, each one forty pounds of muscle, bone, and hate. No one's seen them for weeks or found a single body. Very tidy of you."

"I don't know what you're talking about."

The ogre smirked. "You've been here far too long for a man shopping or visiting friends. I need the money, but it's a pity I was hired and have to leave before your next *performance*. I was looking forward to watching you in action."

"I'm very sure I don't know what you're talking about."

The ogre laughed and gave Zamphini a pat on the back as he left. With the ogre gone, Zamphini was alone on the street. He retreated to the mouth of an alley and sat down, resting his staff across his legs and setting his purchases on the ground. Sassy sat across from him and stared at her creator.

Zamphini dug through his pockets until he turned up a glass sphere three inches across and rimmed with brass. He put it back and took out a brass flask. Uncorking it, he beckoned for Sassy to come closer.

"You know, this isn't such a bad place," he told her. Sassy took the flask and drank bright green fluid from it. "It could be better. I was thinking that flowerpots are just what Lambsport needs, big ones two feet across and two feet deep. Put them on the second floor of the houses and plant trailing vines in them like nymph tears or dragon blood. They'd be perfect since they're ever-blooming, just pinch off fading flowers and more grow in. Imagine, living displays of color draped over the city."

Sassy handed back the flask and Zamphini placed it in the alley. "Statues would work, too. Last year, I met a family of gnomes who carved stone so beautifully that you'd think the animals and people they made were alive. And they worked cheap! Well, reasonably cheap. The duke could buy a few dozen of those and place them where everyone could see. It would cheer the whole city."

There was a gulping, sloshing noise in the dark alley. Zamphini reached back and took the now-empty flask. He slipped it into one of his pockets and shook his head.

"It would be so easy to make things beautiful. So many people waste their time and money on things that bring others down. Hurtful words, cruel deeds, it doesn't have to be that way. It shouldn't be that way. Beauty, laughter, joy, these are what men should bring to the world. You and I do, Sassy. You, me, your brothers and sisters, we make things better. I believe that. I hope you do."

Sassy walked over and stroked her creator's arm. He smiled and picked her up. Before he placed her on his shoulder, he said, "You have fuel enough to see you through the night. Come on, Sassy, let's go."

Zamphini took up his staff and purchases and walked down the rapidly darkening streets. There were shortcuts, but he picked a leisurely route home that went through some of the worst hit neighborhoods. The half-moon provided enough light for him to see where he was going but not enough to notice fine details. He'd gone only half a mile when he heard giggling to his left. It wasn't far away. There was a tapping sound of steel on stone to his right.

More giggling came from behind him. The tapping came closer. He heard a bang in front of him that sounded like someone dropped a brick off a house. Zamphini continued his slow walk as if he didn't notice the offending sounds. Darkness grew and shadows spread across the street. At first, Zamphini thought the sun had fully set, but he saw a lamp go out, then a second. Whoever was making those noises was snuffing out every source of light.

Zamphini kneeled, set down his purchases, and heard the whoosh of a club as it went over his head. He backed up and dodged another swing, this time from his left. He counted one, two, three, yes, all four of them were here. The gang laughed and screamed obscenities at him. Two swung clubs while the other two tried to grab him. Zamphini ducked and dodged until his back was against a wall. One of his attackers grabbed him, but Zamphini slapped aside his enemy's hands with a blow from his walking stick.

Zamphini took the glass sphere from his pocket and held it up before pressing a button. Flash! The street lit up bright as day, and the four men fell back, covering their eyes. Zamphini had closed his eyes before pressing the button and wasn't blinded by the sudden light. When his eyes adjusted to the light, he saw who he was facing.

"Ah, Jonas Heckler, eldest son of our honorable magistrate, how good to see you again. My, how you're grown. You were but a boy when I performed at your birthday."

The young men staggered back as if they'd been struck. They tried to cover their faces, but it was too late. Their clothes were expertly tailored cotton and linen, expensive garments indeed, and they wore gold rings. "That must be Elant and Ulum Firefrost with you. This is an odd time for sons of a rich merchant to be out. I must confess I don't recognize your last friend, but judging by his appearance, he's as wealthy as you are.

"Sloppy," he scoffed. "I've met men and monsters who were feared by kings and commoners both. Terror came off them in waves. This is amateur work, poorly done from the beginning. You sought to herd me away from escape routes and the nearest watch station with silly noises." Zamphini rolled his eyes. "No style, no respect for the audience, it's shameful."

"I told you we'd get caught!" the fourth one shouted.

"Shut up!" Heckler bellowed. His eyes were adjusting to the light, and he dropped his hands from his face.

"It's a pity you outgrew my dolls," Zamphini said. "I see your taste in entertainment has grown dark. This is how you amuse yourself these days, attacking strangers on the street at night? Does it make you feel powerful to have a helpless person at your mercy?"

Heckler fully recovered and grinned like a maniac. "Think I'm going to feel bad, old man?"

"One can but hope."

The fourth member grabbed Heckler by the arm. "My dad will kill me when he finds out."

Heckler didn't look bothered. "He's not going to find out. You're right, old man, it's been a blast. We've been wolves among sheep, showing them who's boss, watching them terrified even when it's daytime. You'll never know what it's like to hear grown men beg and cry. We haven't caught any women yet. It'll be fun when we do."

"Idiocy," Zamphini said. "I wondered why attack a man if not to kill him or rob him of what little he had? But men, or should I say boys, of your position have no need of money. A few copper coins are beneath your notice as are the people living here. And as the son of the city's magistrate, you'd know where the city watch would be stationed and could avoid them easily. You shirk real fights and attack the helpless. Does that make you feel strong?"

"We are strong," Heckler growled. His smile returned, and he looked to his three friends. "The old man plays with dolls, and he thinks he's better than us. You think we're scared of being found out? Old man, I've been waiting for this."

"What?" one of his friends shouted.

"Come on, lads, this time we don't hold back," Heckler told them. "Kill him and he won't tell anyone."

The other three hesitated. Heckler screamed, "You want to get caught? You want your fathers to learn what we've done? Forget your fathers, what do you think Duke Edgely will do to us? When has he forgiven anyone? We'll be conscripted and sent to the front lines! Now, man up and put him down like the worm he is!"

That did it. Whatever thin connection they still had to morality melted away. The four had death in their eyes as they closed in on Zamphini.

"Four against one," Zamphini said. "Not very fair."

Heckler sneered. "Life's not fair, fat man. I'm going to smash open your stupid doll and then your head."

One of the men asked, "What doll? He hasn't got it with him."

Another spun around, his eyes darting around the street. "It was here a second ago."

The light coming off Zamphini's sphere caught a creature leaping off a shop on the other side of the street. Heckler and his friends screamed as it skidded across the cobblestones, coming to a halt only when its claws caught onto a lamppost. Once it stopped moving, they could see it was an enormous cat, but one that had been built rather than born. The monstrosity was six feet long and made of brass, with strangely etched obsidian plates jutting from its armored body. Bright green light poured from its joints and its open jaws, with their terrifyingly sharp teeth. The creature growled and crouched to jump again.

Bizarre as this was, terrifying as it was, their mouths dropped when they saw Sassy walk out of the shadows and pat the monstrous cat. It purred and rubbed its head against her, proving whose side it was on.

Heckler scrambled back. "What is that?"

"Come now, why so surprised?" Zamphini demanded. "I make dolls that dance and juggle and tumble. Did you think I couldn't make something bigger, something stronger, something for dealing with monsters?"

"Oh, God," one of them whimpered.

"You parted company with Him long ago," Zamphini said. He turned off the glowing sphere before putting it away then pressed a hidden button on his walking stick. There was a hiss as a blade ten inches long slid out of the top, transforming the simple tool into a spear. Lightning crackled over the blade and threw flickering shadows across the street. He spun the weapon over his head and pointed it at Heckler. "Now, you deal with me."

The huge cat growled and raced down the street after its prey. Its claws drew sparks off the cobblestones as it closed the distance. One of the men tried to run while the other three faced Zamphini, now drastically better armed than they were and not looking merciful.

"Wait, we've got money!" Heckler shouted. "We can pay you! We can—"

The ogre returned to Lambsport late the following morning, tired but satisfied. He'd finished last night's job to his client's satisfaction. That earned enough money to keep him fed for only two weeks, for food prices were high and ogres were famous for their appetites. More importantly, he'd proven his strength and courage in battle. Such victories would bring more clients.

He found the market much as he'd left it. Humans shopped and gossiped. Elves tried to tempt men into mortgaging their farms. Dwarfs did brisk business selling steel goods. Goblins made an endless nuisance of themselves yet always managed to escape punishment. Small and weak as they were, the ogre admired their ability to survive.

As always, the humans talked constantly, an annoying trait, but one the ogre could endure. It seemed there had been shouting the night before. That generally meant a farmer or storekeeper had suffered a savage beating, but the morning brought no one in need of a healer's aid, nor a lucky soul who'd escaped his foes unharmed.

The ogre had long ago staked a claim to his spot under an arch where he was out of the sun for most of the day. Before he took his place and waited for clients to bring him their problems, he studied the market and surrounding streets in great detail. There was no damage to houses or stores. He found no suspicious debris such as bits of clothing or drops of dried blood. In fact, the only sign anything had happened last night were scratches on some cobblestones and a lamppost.

The ogre smiled, showing off his thick, yellow teeth. "Tidy as always, Zamphini."

Arthur Daigle is the author (no jokes, please, he's heard them all) of five books set on the world of Other Place. These include William Bradshaw King of the Goblins, William Bradshaw and a Faint Hope, William Bradshaw and War Unending, William Bradshaw and Fool's Gold, *and* Goblin Stories. *Expect serious issues drowning in a sea of silliness, mayhem and outright madness. See goblins, the perennial losers of fantasy novels and games, be put into positions of importance no matter how hard they try to avoid it. Feel free to come visit, but watch your step for trip lines and pie traps.*

https://www.booksie.com/portfolio-view/ArthurD7000-131311

Finn MacRorie and the River Dragon

Katy Huth Jones

I heard about him before I ever saw him with my own eyes. Erian burst into the cottage one evening while I was changing the baby. My brother's hair, as usual, was matted with dirt and leaves, and his too-short trousers needed mending again. Before I could scold him, his face split into a grin, and he gave the longest speech of his life.

"There be a new bard come to town, Vina. He got a flute, and he sings real good." He wiped his nose on his sleeve. "Oh. And he has a sword. A real sword." Then Erian grabbed the bucket and scampered out the door, leaving it open to the dancing leaves and the cool breeze blowing in from the sea.

I shook my head while I pinned the baby's cloth diaper and set him back down on the mat beside Ma. Any day now, he would start crawling and I'd have to pen him up. And someday, I hoped the poor child would be given a name.

Since his birth, Ma was too weak to do anything and had even lost her power of speech. She watched the baby while I did all the other chores. Pretty soon, she wouldn't be able to do that anymore.

"Silvia." I tossed a rag to my three-year-old sister. "Wipe that drool off Ma's chin."

I pulled the door shut and moved over to the fire to stir the fish stew. The tinderbox needed more wood, especially if it turned cold tonight. Before true winter set in, I needed to add patches to the blanket. With another body in the bed, our blanket wasn't wide enough to cover everyone.

Erian returned, lugging a half-full bucket of milk, which he set on the table. I poured it into our four wooden cups. I used the chipped one so the sharp edge wouldn't cut the others. Then I ladled fish stew into the four wooden bowls and called Silvia to the table. She scrambled up beside Erian on the bench and ate while I helped Ma. Even though her mind was damaged, her body still remembered to make milk for the baby, so at least I didn't have to worry about feeding him, too.

By the time I sat at the table, Erian was finishing his second bowl of stew, and mine was cold. I ate it anyway, too tired to care. Erian drank the last of the milk in the bucket and grinned at me again. The milk on his upper lip looked like a mustache.

"Where did the bard come from?" I asked.

Erian licked his lips and shrugged. "Dunno."

"Does he sing, too? Or just play the flute?"

"Both." He wiped his mouth with the back of his hand.

"You said he had a sword? What does a bard need with a sword?" I cleaned out the bowls with a torn rag and sighed. Another thing to mend.

"I asked him," Erian said. "Dangers."

"Dangers?" I wanted to laugh. The only danger a traveling bard could encounter in our poor village was choking on a fish bone.

"Dangers." Erian nodded, his eyes sparkling in the firelight.

Then he went out to collect sticks for the fire before the sun set.

Four days later, I heard the flute music. The happy tune grew louder and closer and then trailed away around the corner. Because I was bathing Ma, I couldn't get a glimpse of the player. Then the baby began to cry, drowning out the song. Yet, the melody stayed in my head and I found myself humming it that evening.

The next day, I took my bread dough to the village oven and set it on one of the paddles. I had just pushed it into the oven when Erian ran toward me from the docks.

"Pa's boat is coming." He stared up at me with a worried frown.

We hadn't seen Pa in a fortnight or so. He stayed out on his fishing boat seven days a week, now that Ma was damaged. That was his word, anyway. It didn't bother him none to leave everything to me. After all, says he, I was old enough to be married anyway, so I might as well run the house.

Whenever Pa was in the village, Erian and I tried to stay out of his way. Though he rarely came to the cottage, the few times he had since Ma's sickness, he was angry drunk. If he didn't drink so much of his profits, we could buy a new blanket for the winter. But I made the mistake of saying so only once.

"Don't you worry, Erian." I patted his shoulder. "If Pa comes to the cottage, you just go to the sheep pen 'til he leaves." I hoped he would stay away like he usually did. Only, sometimes when he stayed away, he would forget to leave fish for us to eat. Our barrel of dried fish was almost empty. I had an idea.

"Stay here and watch the bread." I pointed inside the oven. "When it starts to brown, pull it out and let it cool. I'll go talk to Pa."

Erian nodded, but his brow stayed wrinkled. Before I lost my nerve, I strode to the docks. Sure enough, there was Pa's boat with the red and white striped sail. It was a bit bigger than the other fishing boats, and the other fisherfolk looked to him as the master fisherman of the village. A real master wouldn't waste his profits on drunkenness, nor neglect his kin.

I hung back in the gathering crowd near the docks, watching Pa and his mate while they lashed the boat to the piling and shouted out to the others.

"Ya should've seen the monster leap out o' the net," Pa sang. "'Twas so big, it would've sunk the boat."

Judging by the barrels he and his mate rolled onto the pier, he hadn't needed to catch a monster fish. Their boat alone held enough fish to feed the entire village for a year. A merchant with greedy eyes stepped forward to help.

I waited until Pa's mate left his side. I did not like the way that man leered at me. After Pa shook hands with the merchant to seal their deal, he took a leather bag of coins and strode away, headed toward the tavern.

I stepped into his path, and he pulled up short, his eyes wide.

"What is this, Elvina?" He scowled, his craggy brows low on his weathered face.

"We're low on fish, Pa. Did you save some for your family?" I knew I shouldn't have smarted off on the last two words, but seeing that bag of coins and knowing what he was planning to do with them made me madder than reason.

"Don't you sass me, girl." He jutted out his jaw. More gray streaked his beard than last I saw him. "Get out of my way."

He pushed me aside, but I danced around him and stood in his way again.

"No, Pa. Your family needs food. If you didn't save any fish for us, then I need coin to buy food."

"I said, get out of my way!" This time he shoved me so hard, I fell to the dirt.

An unfamiliar sound cut through the chaos of the crowd, like a metallic whisper. I turned toward the sound and saw a man with long black mustaches holding a sword out in front of him. It was only the second sword I'd seen in my life; the first was on the belt of a knight who rode through our village last year. This man was dressed in leathers and wore a plain cap on his head. Who was he?

"That be not the way tae treat a lady, sir," he said in a musical voice. He held out his free hand to me. I stared at it for a moment before letting him lift me up.

Pa faced the man with the sword and balled his fists on his hips. "This isn't a lady. This girl's my daughter and none of your business."

The stranger took a step closer so the tip of the sword pointed at Pa's chest. "Mistreatment o' a lady, any lady, is abhorrent tae me, and so 'tis me business."

While the crowd became silent, watching, Pa glowered at the swordsman. He didn't have the sense to fear the long sharp blade threatening him. Others might call him brave. I began to tremble, for I knew what would happen to me later, once the swordsman was no longer there to protect me.

"He didn't hurt me, sir," I blurted out, my voice shaking.

"I don't need your help, Elvina," Pa growled. "You'll get yours later."

The stranger stepped forward, pushing the point of the sword against Pa's tunic. "Harm one hair o' this lady's head, and you'll answer tae me."

Pa gritted his teeth, but he didn't say anything. He didn't move, either.

"I believe you have sommat there belonging tae the lady." The stranger nodded at the money bag in Pa's hand.

"This is mine!" Pa backed away, clutching the bag in his arm. "I earned it. It's mine."

"Did you not say she is your daughter?" asked the swordsman.

Pa didn't answer immediately. A few people in the crowd turned away, I hoped in shame.

"She's my daughter, but she has what she needs."

The stranger looked at me for the first time. His eyes were the most beautiful green. "Is this true?"

I glanced at Pa, clenching my fists to still the tremors. The compassion in the swordsman's eyes drew my gaze back to him. "No. I am taking care of his sick wife and three small children, and we have almost run out of food."

People in the crowd began to murmur, and Pa shifted his feet. Was he going to run?

The green eyes turned away from me and bore into Pa's. The stranger said nothing. He didn't have to.

Pa opened the bag, drew out a handful of coins, and threw them at my feet. "Fine! Take care of it, and stay away from me." He glared at the stranger. "You have made a big mistake." Then he spun on his heel and stomped into the tavern.

The crowd swirled around us, giving the swordsman a wide berth. He calmly slid the sword back into the sheath on his belt and picked up the coins, handing them to me.

"I appreciate what you tried to do, but—"

"But now your father is angry, and you worry what he may do later, is that it?" Those green eyes snared mine again, and I nodded.

"Has he hit you before? Elvina, is it?"

I shrugged. "It doesn't matter."

"Oh, yes it does." The man's voice was stern and lost some of its lilt. "Do you have a magistrate here?"

"I, I'm not sure." I felt tears prick my eyes and blinked them away, ashamed of my weakness. I certainly didn't want this man to see it.

"Dinna worry. I'll find out. If I have to, I'll go tae Lord Dracen." He straightened his cap.

"Lord Dracen?" I couldn't hold in a gasp. "Do you mean the Lord of Moor Point?"

"Aye, that's him." He grinned, his teeth gleaming white beneath the black mustaches.

"Who are you, that you have the ear of the Lord of Moor Point?" My heart thumped painfully in my chest, partly from fear and partly from awe.

The man removed his cap and bowed with a flourish. His long black hair came into view, caught in a single braid. "I be Finn MacRorie, at your service."

Finn walked home with me. Along the way, I bought fish and some root vegetables, which he insisted on carrying for me. Before we turned the last corner, Erian caught up with us, carrying the loaf of bread.

"Hullo, Finn." My brother's face beamed with joy, making me smile. He handed the bread to me.

"Greetings, Sir Rascal." Finn turned his green eyes on me. "So, Erian be your brother?"

"Yes, and even though he is a rascal, he helps me a lot." Tears pricked my eyes again, and I inhaled deeply to banish them. What was the matter with me today?

"Good tae hear," Finn said with a nod. "I thought I recognized quality in this lad." He grinned at Erian, and my heart fluttered in my chest, as if the sword-wielding bard had praised me instead.

When we reached the cottage, I stopped before the door, suddenly unwilling for Finn to enter and see the reality of our situation. But he opened it for me and gestured for me to go first. I peered inside to make sure everyone was properly dressed. Silvia ran to greet us.

"Vina, baby's wet." She tugged on my hand and gasped when she saw the stranger behind me.

"It's all right, Silvia," Erian said. "This be Finn." My brother stood proudly beside him.

"I be pleased tae meet you, Silvia." Finn's smile lit up the dark room, and Silvia giggled, sticking her fingers in her mouth.

I picked up the baby and a dry diaper and set him on the pallet. While I worked and the baby cooed, I nodded at Ma, who pushed herself up in the bed, her eyes so wide and bulging I thought they might fall out of her head.

"This is their Ma," I said.

"But not yours," Finn said quietly, nodding in understanding. "Pleased tae meet you, ma'am," he said to Ma.

Her mouth worked as if she was trying to say something, but drool came out instead. "Silvia," I hissed. She snatched up a rag and wiped Ma's chin.

Finn knelt beside the low bed. "How long has she been unable tae speak?"

he asked.

"Since the baby was born." I lifted him to my shoulder. He grew heavier every day.

When I turned toward the bed, to my surprise, Finn held Ma's hand. With his other hand, he felt her head and then the side of her neck. He said something to her, so quiet I couldn't understand the words, but Ma nodded, and tears spilled onto her cheeks.

Then, with his hands upon her head, Finn began to sing. His pure tenor voice warmed the room with a sweet lullaby, weaving a spell of peace upon all of us, but especially Ma. Her face glowed.

When Finn's song faded away, he kissed her hand and rose. "Elvina, do you have any sweet root?"

I blinked, taken aback by his question. "There are a few in my garden out back." That is, if nothing had eaten them since yesterday.

He nodded and went outside. Erian silently followed.

I stared at Ma. She held out her arms for the baby, and I gave him to her. After opening her bodice, she put him to her breast. I left them alone and took the baby's wet diaper outside.

Erian had taken the bucket and run down to the well. I peered around the corner of the cottage and found Finn digging up a root in the herb garden. By the time he unearthed it and brushed it off, Erian returned, lugging the bucket with both hands. The water sloshed over the side.

"Is this enough, Finn?" he asked, setting the bucket down with a grunt.

"Aye, Rascal. This be more than enough, though I'm sure your sister will be needing the rest." Finn caught me staring and winked.

I stifled a giggle and hurried back into the cottage.

When Finn and Erian came inside, Finn took my mortar and ground up the root while Erian poured the water into the boiling pot and moved it over the fire. In a short while, Finn had made a cup of tea for Ma and had her drink it. Then he pulled a flute out of a leather pouch on his belt, settled down on the dirt floor, and began to play the happy tune I'd heard the other day.

We all sat listening, entranced, while Finn wove his magic through that flute. The songs he played chased away dark thoughts and sad feelings. I didn't know anything about this mysterious man, but I did know he poured his soul into his music, and that's when I knew I loved him.

When the echo of the last note died away, my heart ached at the absence of the sound. Finn replaced the flute in its pouch and stood, wiping his hands on his trousers.

"More?" Silvia tugged on his sleeve.

"Nay, lass," he said with a smile. "I'll play more songs later. Erian and I be needing tae cut more firewood." He turned his green eyes on me, and I shivered. "Do you have an ax, Elvina?"

I nodded and led him around the back to a dilapidated shed where Pa's tools were stored. I pulled out a small hand ax and a larger one. "Will either of these do?"

Finn nodded and took them both. When his hand brushed mine, I wished only for his touch to linger.

"Erian," he called, and my brother came running. "Do you know how tae use this wee ax?" When my brother shook his head, for Pa had never shown him, Finn gestured with his chin. "Come, and I'll show you."

I wanted to go with them and watch Finn cut wood, but I had chores inside the cottage. The entire time I scraped and chopped the root vegetables and prepared the stew for supper, I heard the rhythmic chopping of the bigger ax, punctuated now and then by the sound of the smaller one. I smiled and began to hum one of Finn's tunes. After a few minutes, I heard someone humming along with me, and I thought it was Silvia.

When I turned to add the vegetables to the stew pot, I gasped. Ma sat on the edge of the bed, humming and smiling at Silvia and the baby. Poor Ma's stick-thin legs poked out from under her ragged shift. Was it possible she could regain her strength?

I stirred the vegetables together in the pot, covered it, and slipped outside. When I came upon Finn and Erian, they had a sizeable stack of cut wood.

"Look, Vina," Erian crowed, holding up the small ax. "I can cut wood."

"I see that." His joy made me smile. "Thank you both."

When Finn turned, his braid swung around, and he raised the larger ax in salute. He had removed his leather vest and linen shirt, and the sight of his smooth, bare chest made my face burn. I fled back to the cottage.

Before I opened the door, I stood there breathing heavily. How could I look into Finn's green eyes again without him knowing how I felt? I wasn't sure I could bear to face him, but the thought of him leaving the village lit an agonized fire in my belly.

"You shouldn't be out here alone, Elvina."

I whirled around at the sound of that familiar deep voice. It was Pa's mate, Leach. He was young, probably not much older than me, but years of hauling nets had made him big and strong.

"What are you doing here, Leach? Shouldn't you be at the tavern with Pa?" I glowered at him so he wouldn't see my nervousness. As far as I could remember, he had never come to the cottage before, even when Pa was here.

"I heard you might need some help, so I came to see what I could do for you." His gaze raked my body before he stepped uncomfortably close.

"There's nothing I need from the likes of you." I tried to make my voice growl.

"You need a man, a real man to take care of you, Elvina." He gripped my shoulders and leaned even closer.

I tried to jerk away, but he was too strong. "Let me go, or I'll scream." I opened my mouth to call for Finn, but Leach clamped one hand over my mouth and picked me up by the waist with the other.

I punched and kicked and tried to scream, but his hands were too big and strong. I couldn't even bite him. He ran along the path through the trees, out of sight of the village, my cottage, and Finn.

Finally, he stopped and dumped me on the sand bank of the river, near the place where it emptied into the sea. Three other men approached. I sucked in a breath to scream, but Leach slapped me and whipped out a dirty cloth from his vest. He gagged me before I could scream again. When I kicked and clawed at him, two of the other men trapped my hands and feet. The fourth man pawed at my bodice, but Leach smacked him away.

"Not yet. Master says we got to lure that meddling bard here first."

I twisted and arched my back, trying to break their iron grips on my wrists and ankles. The one who'd pawed me chuckled and brought his face close to mine.

"Keep scratching, little dragoness, but save some for later. I like a wild one." He laughed and winked. I could smell his rank breath.

It took all four of them to tie me to a post at the edge of the swirling water, part of an old pier. Then they backed away, silent now, and hid in the trees.

Pa put them up to this. I had to warn Finn. The more I struggled against the rope, the deeper it cut into my skin. The vile cloth covering my mouth made my stomach heave. Then I went rigid as the hackles on my neck rose.

I couldn't see it or hear it, but a river dragon had to be nearby. They loved this part of the briny river. One reason most of the pier was missing.

A commotion in the trees drew my gaze from the water. They had Finn! He must have followed me, and now the men had captured him and dragged him to the edge of the water. Our eyes briefly met, and my heart thumped when I saw he had no fear, even now.

Low rumbling sounded nearby. A huge river dragon glided through the murky water, heading toward us. When it came nearer, it opened its mouth to reveal wide-spaced, jagged teeth. The dragon was so close, the slit pupils of its red eyes made me shiver. Then it roared, vibrating the water as well as my spine.

The men shouted. One of them hit Finn on the head, and he went limp. I tried to shout, but the gag muffled the sound. Another man pulled Finn's sword from its scabbard, and then they tossed him into the water. A scream filled my throat.

Finn and the river dragon sank with a swirl of bubbles. They thrashed around and around, and the men behind me laughed. My eyes bled tears. When the water churned red, I moaned.

I no longer cared if the monster ate me, too. Finally, it surfaced, and I blinked my eyes, ready to follow Finn in death. But Finn waded from the water, dripping, his green eyes flashing.

The men no longer laughed. With a roar almost as terrifying as the river dragon's, they charged Finn, three brandishing knives, the other Finn's sword.

Finn pulled a knife from his boot and ran straight for the one with the sword. After ducking the man's wild swipe, Finn sliced his sword arm and caught the weapon before it fell to the ground. I cringed when Finn spun away from the other three, delivering a killing blow to the wounded man. He fell and didn't get up again.

Finn leaped away from one knife attack, then another. One man lost a hand and fled, screaming. Leach and the last one charged together, but Finn sidestepped them, forcing them to turn with their backs to the river.

The water exploded. Two more dragons leaped out, jaws wide. They snatched my kidnappers and pulled them under the surface so quickly, the men had no time to scream. Finn sheathed his sword and dropped to his knees beside me. With his knife, he sawed through the ropes and pulled me away from the water. Not until we reached the trees did he cut away the gag.

Together, we watched more river dragons appear. The water boiled like my soup pot. I guessed they were fighting over the dead dragon and the men. I threw my arms around Finn.

"Thank you." My voice cracked on a sob. He was soaked and smelled like dead fish, but I didn't care.

Finn returned the embrace and let me cry. As soon as my tears were spent, I pulled back so I could stare into his beautiful green eyes. When he smiled at me, I leaned forward to brush his lips, only meaning to thank him. But it tasted so sweet and felt so right, I didn't want to stop.

Gently but firmly, Finn released my hold on him and held my hands. His eyes dimmed with sorrow. "Erian?" he said. "Come here, lad."

A blush warmed my cheeks, and I turned to my brother. Erian took several tentative steps closer. Finn didn't let go of my hands, though.

"Are you all right?" Erian said in a trembling voice.

It made me sad to see him fearful, so I let go of Finn and placed my hands on Erian's shoulders. "We are both fine. Except I am muddy, and Finn is soaking wet."

That coaxed a smile from my brother. "What did you do to the river dragon?" Erian's eyes shone at Finn.

Finn pushed back a dripping black curl from his face and grinned. "My knife bit the wee beastie." He bent down and pulled a curved blade from a boot sheath.

Erian stepped closer to examine the knife. He whistled between his teeth. "That looks sharp."

"It has tae be, tae pierce a river dragon's tough hide." Finn replaced the knife in the sheath. "But go on back tae the cottage now, both o' you. I'll be directly behind." He waited until Erian and I began to walk along the faint path before he turned and headed toward the water.

My heart ached. A man as fine and brave as Finn MacRorie would never want to marry a poor girl like me, but could I convince him to settle here? As long as he stayed in our village, I would still be able to see him and hear his lovely songs.

The bucket remained where Erian left it, and while he carried an armload of firewood into the cottage, I used some of the water to wash off the mud. My wrists and ankles were raw from rope burns, but they would eventually heal.

Since it didn't appear Finn would soon return, I went back inside to get supper ready. To my surprise, Ma sat in the only chair and Silvia stood in front of her while Ma patiently untangled my sister's hair with her comb. Both of them looked up at me and smiled. Sitting beside the chair, the baby cooed.

"Where you been, Vina?" Silvia asked.

I shared a glance with Erian. "To the river." I kept my voice as calm as possible and went to stir the stew. It was ready to eat, so I gave some to Ma and Erian and Silvia. I didn't eat so I could save my bowl for Finn when he came.

I wiped out the other three bowls and changed the baby's diaper before someone knocked on the door. Erian opened it, and Finn stepped inside.

"Elvina," he said softly.

I handed the baby to Ma and slowly turned to him. My heart fluttered at the sight of his green eyes. "Yes, Finn?"

"Let me see your hands." He held his out and I placed my palms on his. In silence, he examined my wrists and let go. Then he opened a damp leather pouch attached to his belt and pulled out a weed I had seen growing along the riverbank.

Finn broke one of the thick leaves over my right wrist. Gooey sap oozed out, and with the tip of his finger, he rubbed it onto my skin. I shivered at his gentle touch.

"The sap o' this plant helps cuts and burns tae heal more quickly," he said.

"Are you a healer, too?" I asked.

His green eyes lifted to mine. "Of a sort." Then he grinned.

"You're a bard, a healer, and you know how to use a sword." The longer I stared at him, the more I trembled. "You are no ordinary man."

"He's a knight," Erian said. He came closer. "Aren't you?"

Finn went down on one knee. His head was level with Erian's. "Aye, but dinna tell anyone."

"I won't," Erian breathed. His eyes grew wide and his gaze darted to the sword on Finn's belt.

Then Finn took a thin leather cord from his belt pouch and placed it around Erian's neck. Erian lifted it to better see what was attached to it.

"A river dragon's tooth." His voice was filled with awe. "Thanks, Finn." He jerked up his head with a frown. "Are you leaving?"

"I canna stay, lad." Finn stood and placed his hand on Erian's head. An idea leaped into my mind.

"If you must go," I said hoarsely, "won't you please take Erian with you? He deserves a better life than what this poor village can provide."

Finn gazed at me with sad eyes. He didn't answer right away, so I began to hope he would agree. But Erian spoke first.

"I wish I could go with you, Finn, but I must stay and protect Vina and Ma and Silvia and the baby." He pointed to each of us in turn.

"Aye," Finn said with a crooked smile. "You are the man o' the house." He removed the small sheath from his boot, the one with the curved knife. "If you'll promise me tae be as careful as you can, then I want you tae have this so you can better protect your loved ones." He held out the knife, and Erian took it from his hand.

"I promise, Finn." He bowed his head, so solemn, so grown up. It brought tears to my eyes.

"Thank you," Ma said in a raspy voice. It was the first she'd spoken since the baby was born.

Finn sketched a bow. "I was happy tae help, ma'am." When he straightened, his green eyes were tinged with sorrow. "I must leave you now."

"I hope I will see you again someday, Finn." Tears filled Erian's eyes.

"I will make sure o' it." Finn's smile broadened. He stepped out of the cottage and quietly shut the door.

I couldn't stand it. I followed him. Finn stood beside a magnificent gray horse with a black mane. If I'd seen this horse earlier, I would have known Finn was a knight.

"He's beautiful," I whispered.

"This be Dunny," he said. The horse dipped his head and snorted, making me laugh.

The laugh faded as my heart grew heavy with longing. "I wish you would stay with us, Finn."

"I cannot, for I am in service tae the king." His smile was sad. "But, be at peace, Elvina. Your father will ne'er hurt you again."

I gasped. "Did you kill him?"

Finn shook his head. "The magistrate has custody o' your father. His fishing boat will be sold, and your family will receive its price tae support you."

"Oh, Finn." My throat tightened and cut off my voice. Then my heart shattered, the shards piercing my chest with a sharp ache. I would never meet another man like this one. I threw my arms around him and pressed a fierce kiss to his lips so I would have that memory, at least. Then I turned and ran back to the cottage.

I didn't close the door all the way. Through my tears, I watched him mount his horse and turn away slowly. With a swish of his tail, Dunny carried his knight out of our lives.

Barely able to breathe from the pain in my chest, I quietly shut the door and turned to face my family. Ma bounced the baby on her lap. She met my gaze with clear, happy eyes.

"The baby has a name now," she said. "Finn."

We would just have to help him live up to his name.

Readers of the YA Christian fantasy series He Who Finds Mercy *will hopefully recognize the title character, as these events take place during his year of wandering in disguise between* Mercy's Battle *and* Mercy's King. *This story came to me fully formed when I was stuck on a plot point while writing the final book,* Mercy's Joy.

Little Victories

Karin De Havin

The light shines through my bedroom window so brightly I should put on my sunglasses. It's not the typical rainy fall day in the Pacific Northwest, thank goodness. Today is Thanksgiving and I'm excited. Not because I'm out of school and get to eat like a pig, but because the holiday gives me another opportunity to put on my invisible superhero cape and go out and make a difference in my little town. I'm not a typical superhero who scales buildings to rescue someone from a fire or who catches criminals robbing a bank. No, the victims I rescue are of the animal variety, and the occasional insect.

After putting on my favorite teal sweater and skinny jeans, I throw my long red hair into a ponytail, put on some tinted lip-gloss, and head downstairs to breakfast. I plop down in the kitchen chair and toss my backpack onto the linoleum.

"Good morning, Shea." A stack of blueberry pancakes appears like magic. "Here's some fortification until supper."

I dig in, savoring the way the blueberries squish between my teeth. After shoveling down a few big bites, I sit back and take a breather. Mom makes the best pancakes of anyone I know, but they are also super filling.

Mom sits next to me with a crossed off to-do list in her hand. "We worked hard last night, so it looks like we have almost everything ready for our big meal. Just need to cook the turkey."

A wave of sadness hits me. It's been three years of Thanksgivings with just the two of us since my dad passed away.

Sensing my mood, Mom squeezes my hand. "Why don't you go out on an adventure until it's time to decorate the pumpkin pie?"

I'm the baker in the family, so I take my dessert responsibilities seriously. "You're right, I've got some time before supper. Think I'll head out and see what needs saving."

Her face lights up. "There are a lot of meadowlarks out on the lawn this morning digging for bugs. One seemed to be limping."

I love the way my mom is always on the lookout for potential animals for me to rescue. Ever since she became a widow, she's had to work even longer hours at the bank, so we don't get to see much of each other. But my passion for saving animals has created a special bond between us. Mom's Robin to my Batman. She even has an inspiration board in her craft room where she keeps track of all my "Little Victories"—twenty-four and counting.

"Thanks for letting me know about the meadowlark. I'll keep an eye out for him."

"I know you will." Worry lines cut across Mom's forehead. "Just be careful out there. Remember, you're not a real superhero, you're a teenage girl."

"Got it, Mom." I pick up my backpack and load it with a water bottle, cookies, a leash, and a pet first aid kit. Then I quickly wash the dishes before I head out.

Mom gives me a thumbs up. "See you in a bit."

After grabbing my gray puffer jacket from the antique hall tree, I throw a wool scarf around my neck. It gets cold by Mills Pond.

The bang of the front door closing sends the meadowlarks scattering. I scan the lawn, searching for the injured bird my mom mentioned, but no luck. I'll have to find another animal to rescue.

On the walk to town, I wave at the neighbors playing football on the lawn. Then I head down Montgomery Street toward the main drag. I've lived here my whole life and know every nook and cranny. After Dad died, Mom talked about leaving Templeton and moving to Boston to be with her parents, but she couldn't imagine living anywhere else, and neither could I. Templeton may only have three hundred and fifty residents, but it's home.

I hitch my backpack higher on my shoulders and start the three-mile trip to Mills Pond. It's the epicenter for lost animals. I've snagged over half my dog and cat rescues there. Except for one wily dog that keeps getting away.

Sheriff Clark flags me down in front of his office. He watches out for me now that my dad's gone. "Hey, Shea, you heading out on patrol? Beautiful weather for it."

"Yes, sir." I look up at the cloudless sky. "Good day to find some animals to save."

"Did you manage to catch that rascal yet? He's Templeton's most wanted canine."

The rascal in question is a boxer that broke loose from the pound. He's been running loose for over a week, nipping at the ankles of almost everyone in town, including mine. "No. I've come close a few times, but he's so darn fast."

"That dog acts like he's got bees in his ears."

I smile at the perfect image. "At least we know he had a rabies shot at the pound."

Sheriff Clark chomps on his gum, deep in thought. "True. At least we can be thankful for that."

"Still, I'm not amused. He's ruining my reputation."

"You'll work your magic." He pats me on the back. "You've managed to rescue every stray we've got in this town whether they're on two, four, or a hundred legs."

He would bring up the centipede.

"I'm feeling lucky. Rascal's terrorizing of Templeton ends today."

"I have every faith in you." He hands me a stick of gum. "In case you need something to jaw on while you're out scouting. It always helps me chew things over."

"I better get going." I start to leave but he blocks my path.

"Hold on, Shea. I have something I've been meaning to give to you." He pops into the sheriff's office and returns with a star-shaped piece of tin. "You work hard to keep our town's animals safe, so I want to make you a deputy." He pins the Junior Community Patrol badge on my jacket. "I hope being a part of law enforcement brings you luck." The crinkles next to his eyes deepen. "And wish your mom a Happy Thanksgiving."

"Will do. And thanks for making me a deputy. I won't let you down." I give him a salute and head toward highway twelve.

I tuck the stick of gum in my pocket as I hike up the steep incline to the pond. The deep boom of Rascal's bark echoes through the trees. My instincts were right; he's headed to Mills Pond like all the other strays. At the crest of the hill, I take a cookie break. I need a sugar rush if I'm going to catch Rascal. He looks like a purebred boxer, but he runs like a greyhound. After inhaling two of the Tollhouse cookies I made, I down half my water bottle. Sheriff Clark's words of wisdom pop into my mind: "Always wet your whistle when you're out on patrol."

The fall foliage dotting the rim of the pond is fading fast. Penned in by mostly bare trees, a few orange maples and red sumacs form a lacy frame at the water's edge. The geese call as they fly past. Strange, they're usually enjoying a leisurely swim across the pond this time of day. Then I spot Rascal stalking a Mallard duck asleep on a boulder. When I clap my hands, the duck's head pops out from under his wing, just as Rascal's jaw wraps around his body. He squawks so loudly it even scares Rascal. He drops the duck and takes off for the other side of the pond.

I make a beeline straight for him. Rascal's panting slows, and he takes a long drink from the pond. Making a quick turn behind a stand of pines, I sneak up on him while he continues to lap up water. Lunging forward, I wrap my fingers around his thick leather collar. Victory is mine for ten seconds. Then he shakes me off like a wet blanket and streaks brown and white through the trees.

I lose my footing and fall backward. All I can do is watch him run away as I pick myself up and dust off my sore butt. I can't accept defeat. Mom and Sheriff Clark will lose faith in my heroic abilities, and I can't let that happen.

The thought of Sheriff Clark reminds me of the stick of gum in my pocket. Maybe getting my jaw on will help me regroup. The peppermint goodness coats my throat as I work my way back to the last place I saw Rascal.

As I turn back down toward the eastern edge of the pond, a high-pitched scream reverberates through the woods. My ears ring. Rascal shakes his head back and forth as a light radiates through the spaces in his teeth.

What the——?

I know fireflies cast light, but we don't have them in the Pacific Northwest. In biology class, we learned that some fish glow too, but they live in the ocean, not in a pond. What did he catch?

By the time I reach Rascal, the light has dimmed from a high-beam to a glimmer. Has he killed the poor creature?

A tiny voice says, "Help me."

The thing in his mouth talks? Wait a sec. Have I been out in the sun too long? I'm used to being soaked to the bone this time of year. Rascal shakes the thing in his mouth even harder and I jump into action. I form a fist and punch him in the snout. The talking firefly swoops out of his mouth. The boxer yelps and bolts for the woods. So much for my feeling lucky. Rascal is no longer my rescue mission—the firefly is.

The flickering light lands near a small outcropping of boulders. The firefly is about six inches tall with long, flowing blonde hair and tiny gossamer wings.

A fairy!

She's wearing a golden dress and a headdress made of flowers the size of emoji. She belongs in a storybook, not passed out on the ground by my local pond.

I gently tap the fairy's chest and her tiny body springs to life.

"Are you all right?" I cradle her in the palm of my hand. "One of your wings has a rip through the middle."

The fairy groans.

I tear a piece of gum out of my mouth and glue the cut. "That should do the trick."

She flaps her wing and the gum makes the tear even larger.

"Oh no, I'm so sorry. I was just trying to help."

She forces a smile. "Thank you. Please do not be so hard on yourself. Few humans know we exist. But my wing can heal itself if you splash a little water on the injury."

I carry her to the pond and drizzle a few drops of water on her wound. The wing glows purple as tiny sparks pop off the wound like miniature fireworks. In seconds, the tear begins to heal.

"Thank you for your kindness, my dear." She holds out her tiny hand. "Let me introduce myself. I am called Nyx, and I would like to know the name of the human who saved me."

My brain is working so hard my lips can't move.

"Is something amiss?" Nyx tugs on my finger. "Have you never observed a fae before?"

My mind is officially blown. "No. I didn't think you were real. I've only seen fairies in picture books when I was a kid."

A tiny, bell-like laugh escapes her lips. "Oh, dear me. Then my presence must come as a shock."

"Yes, a bit." I give her a smile. "By the way, my name is Shea."

"Truly? Your parents named you after the fairy palace?"

"Um—no. I was named after my grandmother."

Nyx clasps her tiny hands together. "How wonderful."

"Hey, I thought only people who believe in fairies can see them."

"Technically, my dear, I am a water sprite." She gives me a tiny smile. "I do believe you have disproved that theory."

Nyx is right. I can see her with no problem and I'm a total cynic. I knew the Easter Bunny wasn't real at the age of three—Santa Claus, by the time I was five.

"Although," Nyx went on, "I must say I am astounded with all the technological advances in the last century, your people have not developed a machine that makes us visible to all."

I couldn't agree more. I've been waiting for the personal hovercraft to be invented since I was seven. Instead, I'm stuck riding my bike to school. "True. I guess I can see you because I look at tiny things all the time. I'm constantly saving insects from certain death."

"My dear, I think you have been a believer all along." Nyx shifts in my hand. "Look at the star you wear—"

"How did you know—?"

"You simply never had the opportunity to demonstrate your belief until now."

"But I'm fifteen, way too old to believe in fairies."

"My dear, no one is ever too old."

"Is your palace nearby? I can take you there."

She runs a hand along the tear in her wing as edges fuse. "That is a wonderful offer, but I can make the sojourn back to Shea on my own. I must, however, repay you in kind. The dog you were trying to apprehend, are you his mistress?"

"No. He's a stray that's been running loose all over town. I've been trying to catch him for over a week so he can be returned to the animal shelter. It's kind of my thing."

"You rescue animals? My lady." Nyx gives a curtsy deep in my palm.

I stuff back a laugh. "I'm no lady. But I do enjoy saving animals and insects that can't help themselves." I give her a slight smile. "And water sprites."

Once again, her bell-like laugh fills the air. "Yes, you can indeed add fae to your list." She shuffles to her fairy feet, with curly-toed shoes like fiddlehead ferns. "As a thank you for saving me, I would like to help you bring the dog home."

My jaw drops. "But he almost ate you."

"'Twas my fault. I was too consumed by painting leaves to notice he was hunting me."

"Painting leaves?" My brow furrows hard enough to give me a headache.

"Yes, it is one of the tasks assigned to water sprites. 'Tis the end of the season, but there is still sumac to paint." She points. "See the green patch?"

"Oh, yes. By the large boulder."

"Indeed. I was going to complete that section when the dog caught me."

My headache pulses. The information is harder to process than the equations in my algebra class. "How many water sprites are there? In the Northwest alone, there must be millions of trees and shrubs for you to paint."

"There are thousands of water sprites, but only some of us who qualify as autumnal artists." She turns up her little stub nose. "And I hold the record for painting a trillion leaves in a day."

"You have contests?"

"Indeed. I am a three-time all-around winner in the Pacific Northwest Fall Colors Tournament of Champions."

"Ooh. Where is it held? Can I come?"

"Over two hundred sprites cross brushes, swim laps, and bake fairy cakes at Shea Palace at the edge of Sapphire Lake in October. Humans are forbidden and we keep well hidden."

"Oh, that's too bad. Can you tell me about the fairy cakes?"

"I believe you call them cupcakes."

"I can bake a mean cupcake."

"In that case, I might be able to bend the rules, especially since you have already made our acquaintance."

"Please don't expect too much on the decorating front, though. I'm still learning."

"Embellishment is my favorite. Must be the artist in me." Nyx bats her wings. "I shall show you how to put the sparkle in your rainbow rosettes."

"You mean sprinkles?"

"Sparkle, my dear. All you need is a bit of magic and the right pastry bag tip."

"So I would be really the first human to attend the games?"

"The *tournament*. A forest ranger or hiker might have caught sight of the event, but we usually sprinkle enough fairy dust to fog the eyes or memory of anyone who stumbles past. And we have never observed any shows about the competition on the make-believe tube."

"You watch television?"

She nods. "Yes, we catch glimpses through windows. We find it most entertaining. Especially *Deadliest Catch*."

I don't have the heart to tell her it isn't all make-believe. But my headache fades. Guess my mind has gone past overload and into nothing-fazes-me territory. "I had no idea."

Nyx floats up, hovering in front of my face. "Enough about sprites. I promised to help you rescue the dog. As you can see, my wing has healed."

"Are you sure it's safe?"

"Fae never make the same mistake twice. I shall not let him attack me again."

I have to admit her ability to fly will make finding Rascal a lot easier. "Okay. I'll strike out on foot, and you see if you can find him from the air." I put my fingers in front of my teeth and whistle. "That will be my signal if I see him."

"Understood. I will fetch you if I spy the dog. If we work together, he shan't escape again."

As I watch Nyx fly off into the woods, I know Rascal's wandering days are over. I work my way around the boulders that line the far side of the pond, hoping for a glimpse of the wayward boxer, but no luck. I prop my backpack against the trunk of a baby pine and down the rest of my water. Mom is expecting me to come home and decorate the pie. I pull out my phone and text her I'll be back by 3:00 PM. That gives me two hours to make it back home.

I hit the east side of the pond and see a light near a stand of Ponderosa pines. Nyx speeds toward me and lands on my backpack. "I have located the dog. He is sleeping under a maple tree. If we move with haste, we should be able to apprehend him."

"Terrific news." I pull out the leash I tucked in the backpack. "The way Rascal is always in hyperdrive, I never thought he actually slept."

We both laugh, enjoying our brief moment together before setting off to catch the most elusive boxer in the Northwest.

Nyx balances on the edge of my backpack. "I will stay close to your person on the off chance you may need my help."

"All right, but stay a safe distance from the dog, okay?"

Nyx nods and floats off my backpack. I throw it over my shoulders and do my best to not make a sound as I creep up on Rascal. Unfortunately, the crackle and pop of the dead leaves and twigs on the ground foil my mission.

His head darts up, and he jumps to his feet. Nyx zooms back and forth over his muzzle as he chomps at the air, trying to take a nip at her. With Rascal distracted, I do my best to fashion a lasso with the leash. His ears bob up and down as I toss the leash over his head. He shakes it off and almost tags Nyx, but I dive-bomb him and quickly clip the leash to his collar. Nyx flitters above his nose and sprinkles some glittery dust on his muzzle. Rascal sneezes a couple of times, sending shiny dust particles flying everywhere. He slowly moves next to me and sits at my feet, not budging an inch. It's as if we've been attending dog-training classes together for weeks.

My lips round in an "O" of surprise big enough for Nyx to fly through. "What did you do? He's so calm."

Nyx shakes the rest of the sprite dust off her hands. "Just a little magic to make him obedient."

"Thank you so much. They'll be so glad to have him back at the shelter now that he's so well behaved."

"It is the least I can do after you saved my life. Shea, you are my hero."

I'm sure all the animals and insects I've saved are grateful to be rescued, but it feels wonderful to have someone actually say the words. "I'm so glad I could help. Will I see you again?"

She gazes around the foliage in the woods. "My work here is almost done. I will return to Shea Palace, but you must watch me compete in the tourney. You will be my guest of honor, and I will give you a tour of your namesake."

"Wow, I've never been a guest of honor before. And I would love to see the fairy palace and bake with you."

"Shea, you are not the cynic you profess to be." Nyx flutters up to my face and kisses me on the cheek.

"You've made a believer out of me, Nyx."

"That's the spirit! As we water sprites say, 'Never stop believing. Even when the well goes dry.'"

I walk down Main Street with a spring in my step, my invisible cape billowing behind me while Rascal trots dutifully by my side. The badge Sheriff Clark gave me for good luck actually worked! Nyx's sprite dust has turned a once wild dog into an ideal pet. I can return Rascal to the animal shelter with total confidence. Then I can head home and tell Mom I have another victory for her board—number twenty-five. She'll be thrilled to add Rascal, having been a victim of his ankle nibbling herself.

Sheriff Clark waves his hands wildly when he sees me with Rascal. "You did it! Looks like deputizing you brought good luck."

"Sure did." I pat Rascal on the head and a few flakes of fairy dust fall on my hand. I quickly brush the rest of the dust off before the sheriff sees it. "Want to adopt him?"

He shakes his head no. After getting his ankles chewed on twice, Sheriff Clark keeps a safe distance. "How'd you finally catch him?"

If he only knew. "Once he saw my badge, he turned himself in."

He chuckles and gives Rascal a quick pat. Then he looks at his hand speckled with glitter. "What's this?"

Oh, no. Nyx turned me into a believer, but Sheriff Clark is another story.

Still, I can't lie to an officer of the law, especially now that I'm a deputy. "Actually, it's fairy dust."

He laughs and shakes the specks of dust off his hand. "No, really. I know you work wonders with animals, but how did you do it?"

"I just needed a little help from a special friend with a passion for sparkle."

A huge smile crosses his face. "Must have been an extra special person to tame this dog with a handful of glitter."

I picture Nyx flitting from leaf to leaf, painting the rest of the sumac by the pond bright red.

"You have no idea."

"Well, however you did it, it's quite the accomplishment." Sheriff Clark pats me on the back. "Congratulations on your biggest victory to date."

Rascal jumps up and practically licks my face off.

The sheriff laughs. "See, he's saying thank you."

It's at that moment I realize victory twenty-five isn't one for the board. It's one for a lifetime.

I was inspired to write "Little Victories" for two reasons. The first came from an idea sparked by a character in my young adult paranormal serial, The Shifter Vampire Alliance. *Ainsley is an artist vampire who paints wood nymphs and fairies in fantastical worlds. Writing the descriptions of the paintings made me long to create a story about a fairy. The second, the theme of the anthology brought back memories of the big-hearted people in my small hometown. I particularly admired a mother and daughter team that worked diligently to rescue the stray animals that wondered into town. This story pays homage to them, and to all the wonderful people who rescue creatures big and small. They truly are everyday heroes.*

www.karindehavin.com

And Only the Eyes of Children

Laura VanArendonk Baugh

"The fairies went from the world, dear,
Because men's hearts grew cold:
And only the eyes of children see
What is hidden from the old."
— Kathleen Foyle

You've probably heard of the survival of the fittest? It's where things first broke down. An immortal doesn't have to be fit for anything; he's going to survive anyway. Immortality was evolution's biggest screw-up, and any ecosphere worth its salt is going to do its best to make sure an immortal never breeds.

But they try.

Oh, how they try. And sometimes they succeed, after a fashion, and they spawn *things*. And those things become stories, because they're too horrid to be real, so they must be stories, they *must*, and thus we have fairy tales and horror films and unconfirmed internet stories of shocking infants in third-world countries, with photos quickly taken down after human rights advocates protest that no one should be gawking at tragedy like some sort of modern day freak show.

"Human" rights. Heh.

But though the immortals try to breed, they generally can't. And thus, the Fae fascination with children.

It even hits me sometimes. Right this moment, for example, I was completing a perimeter check of a park playground and settling on a bench. I pretended to check email on my phone, but I wasn't really seeing anything on the screen because I was too busy sneaking peeks at the kids playing on the slide and swings. There were five of them, three girls and two boys, and most were strangers to one another until the game of tag started through the autumn leaves. It was all I could do to stay on the bench instead of jumping up to join in.

I didn't, though. A hundred years ago, a stranger could stop a stroll and play a few minutes with kids and everyone would have a good time. Nowadays, people start calling police and shouting "Stranger danger!" if you so much as wave at a kid or give him a high five, forget chasing him giggling around a park

And that's kind of a bad thing. Not only for all the little kids who grow up paranoid and nature-deprived and utterly dependent, but because all those jonesing Fae can't get their tiny little hits of *child* through frequent, harmless interaction, and some of them finally snap and just take one.

Almost two thousand kids a day go missing in this country. Think about that a second, okay? Every forty seconds. If you're reading this at average speed, that's six kids since you started. (Sorry; Fae personalities also tend to obsessive counting.) About half of those are family abductions, and half of what's left are acquaintance abductions. We don't have anything to do with those; that's your own mess, humans.

But about twenty-four percent of kidnappings are stranger abductions, and a very few—okay, three percent if we're counting, and I always am—are Fae-related. Most of the time, those children are found a few days later, unharmed and a little confused (or assumed to be). Most of the Fae who like kids—really like them, I mean, and not just to eat—are pretty good about returning them nowadays.

But the other stranger abductions are entirely human in nature, and that's where I come in.

My phone rang—Blondie's "Call Me"—and I took the opportunity to look across the park and watch the kids in a totally natural manner as I answered. "Hello, Jimmy."

"Have you seen the news?"

I hadn't. I have a Google Alert set and of course Twitter on my phone, but I was watching the kids. "Not yet. What is it?"

"Amber Alert just went out. Little girl, age seven. Taken from her front yard."

Not a typical abduction, or Jimmy wouldn't have called. "Where?"

"Out this way. I actually know the family a bit; they come in every week or two."

Jimmy owns the Steer & Beer, a little dive over on the east side. He serves more root beer than beer, and he makes a mean Black Cow. He also fancies himself a marksman. Actually, he shoots Expert at local matches, which is two ranks above Marksman, but whatever.

"You know them enough to figure this isn't a family matter?"

"Her parents are together, and while I obviously don't know much, the police don't seem to be looking for any relatives."

Bells and breadcrumbs, this was likely to be a serious one. And by serious, I mean there was a decent chance she'd been taken by some pervert-pander for sex trafficking. It's a bigger thing than most people want to admit. "Are you at the Steer now?"

"Meet me here?"

"I'm on my way."

I hung up and stood, and no one noticed. I'm one of the rare half-breed freaks myself, though not of the type to get an *OMG!!!1!* photo on the internet. No, I'm lucky enough to pass on a human street—which conversely means I'm pretty unlucky on what passes for a street in the Twilight Lands. So, I tend to spend most of my time here.

Exactly here, in fact. This is a good place for us. What, you don't think of Indianapolis as being a particularly supernatural city? That just means we're keeping under the radar. I know, New Orleans and Chicago and places get all the arcane press, but think for a second. Indianapolis has two affectionate sobriquets: "the Crossroads of America," for its prominent location on first the National Road and later several interstates, and "the Circle City," for its efficient, nearly ritual, circle and grid layout.

Crossroads and circles, people, right in the advertising. If you can't find the Fae in that, I can't help you.

I made my way to the Steer & Beer, where Jimmy had an enormous fried pork tenderloin waiting for me. As I walked in, he removed the overturned plate keeping it warm and then mixed ice cream and Coke into a Black Cow, setting it on the counter. There's no land like the Old Land, but there are certain advantages to the American Midwest.

"What are we looking at?"

Jimmy nodded toward the small television hanging at the far end of the room. "Not a lot of details yet, but it looks like she disappeared about an hour and a half ago. From the front of the apartments, like I said."

The screen showed a smiling black girl, her hair in braids and beads, a candid photograph scavenged from a phone or Facebook to get on the news as quickly as possible. *Alexis Foster*, read the footer text.

"Cute kid," I said and stuffed the tenderloin into my mouth so I wouldn't have to say more. I'm not Fae enough to be swept away in pure and unbridled emotion, but I have enough fairy in me to get choked up over a snapshot of one of today's two thousand kids.

Jimmy left the counter and went to the rear wall of the Steer & Beer. The rest of the joint was decorated in typical drive-in style, old posters and unintentional retro, but the rear wall was papered in children's drawings. Every kid who comes to the Steer & Beer for the first time is offered a free ice cream sundae in exchange for a signed work of art.

There were four drawings signed "Alexis," but Jimmy selected one. He had a digital photo frame of happy customers waving spoons or holding up tenderloins, and many of the photos included children. A light pencil notation on the back of each drawing, obliquely referencing the photo's file number, made it easy for Jimmy to know which drawing belonged to which child's image.

It was the kind of thing that would make many parents paranoid, even though he had no family names or addresses, but to be fair, that wouldn't be hard with some facial recognition software and a credit card database or something. But Jimmy was one of the good guys. Only he and I knew the drawings were marked with anything more than the date, and we both hoped never to need them.

When they were needed, though, they were awfully handy.

Jimmy slid the drawing over the counter, and I studied it without touching. Alexis had drawn a pony, with what I assumed were sparkles trailing from its mane and tail, and a wizard or college graduate or something to one side. Hey, I like kids, but I'm not good at following their art. At the lower right was her name in red block letters.

I finished my tenderloin and drained the last of the Black Cow. Jimmy made another, this time in a foam cup to carry out, and called back into the kitchen that he was going out.

I picked up the picture for the first time and carried it out with us.

Jimmy drives an SUV of some sort. I'm not good with cars, but it's old, noisy, and solid. That comes with a lot of steel so I tend to ride leaning away from the door with my feet elevated on a couple of phone books he keeps for the purpose. He drove us to Monument Circle and wedged into a passenger unloading zone.

The Circle is named for the Soldiers and Sailors Monument. It honors veterans of five wars, it has neat fountains and an underground Civil War museum, and it's nearly as tall as the Statue of Liberty. And most importantly, it sits at the very heart of the city, in the center of the Circle and all those precisely-drawn streets.

I got out of the car and went to the Monument. I paid the two dollars to ride the elevator. The stairs are free, but I was going to need all my energy.

No one else was at the top, which was just as well. I don't need a lot of theatrics, but it's nice not to have to deal with distractions. I took Alexis's drawing in both hands, pulled up the photo of the smiling, braided girl via the alert on my phone, and concentrated.

Scrying a location is a really complicated thing, and trying to describe it is kind of like trying to describe seeing colors. It really only makes sense if you already know what you're talking about. Having a face isn't enough; you need something personal, something connected to a soul. Art is about as personal as it gets, and Jimmy's ice cream exchange is brilliant.

It doesn't give me an address, of course, but I can get a sense of direction and distance. After that, a little work with the maps app on my phone can narrow it down to a few hundred yards, and that's a pretty fair working prospect.

There's an obscene number of calories in a traditional fried tenderloin sandwich and Black Cow, but I stumbled out of the Monument with blurred vision and a racing heartbeat. I had to blink and concentrate to remember where Jimmy would be, and I hurried toward the car like an addict toward his stash.

Jimmy opened the door as I neared—I can generally manage a door handle, even on a steel door, but it's pushing it after a scrying—and handed me the foam cup. I sucked at the straw greedily and shoved the phone at him, in navigation mode, without speaking.

Jimmy pulled two energy bars from his jacket pocket and dropped them in my lap. I threw him a grateful glance and stopped gulping long enough to say, "Bless you." The shakes made it awkward to manage the wrappers, but the ice cream and Coke were kicking in and my hands soon steadied.

So anyway, kids. Fairies like 'em. Some like to play with them, like the Cottingley Fairies (not the cardboard and hatpin ones, the real thing). And some like to have them, like the Queen.

For those of you who slept drooling through English Literature and woke up just long enough to giggle-snort at *A Midsummer Night's Dream* because he said "ass," you're probably thinking of Titania. That would be fine—she's had a lot of names, and she's not particular about which get used—except that Shakespeare was a great writer but a lousy historian and a chauvinist to boot. Have you ever actually paid attention to the fairy side of the story? Titania's all like, *I'm raising this little boy, I knew his mother*, and Oberon's all like, *No, I want him*, and they spat a bit, and then Oberon pranks Titania in the ugly shape of Nick Bottom—"ass," hur hur—and so Titania's like, *Ooh, that was so embarrassing, I guess you can have the little boy and I love you*, the end.

Seriously, who would buy that, besides a bunch of rowdy men feeling rather threatened by a female monarch? Shakespeare knew his audience, I'll say that for him, and none of them knew the Fairy Queen.

Jimmy pulled into an empty parking lot and put the car in park. It was a business strip near middle-class neighborhoods, not exactly a part of town you'd associate with human trafficking—but you don't get to be a thirty-two billion dollar industry without developing effective protocols and safeguards.

Jimmy nodded toward a corporate accounting office at the end, adjoining a wholesale warehouse which sat behind the strip. "Everything else here is a boutique or retail, something anyone could walk into. But no one strolls into corporate accounting without an appointment. And they could have easy access to warehouse space."

I nodded. "Looks like a place to start, anyway." I could scry again, if we got stuck, but that wouldn't be such a good move right away if I wanted to be any use later. Better to use brains as well as magic.

Jimmy didn't bother to check the Sig Sauer P220 he wore under his flannel jacket; he'd loaded it right the first time. It wouldn't come out unless something went very wrong. "I'm just going to go in and ask about some accounting then," he said. "See if I spot any red flags."

I nodded. If the office were legit, no problem. If it were a front, they'd give him a polite brush-off and we'd call in an anonymous tip.

It'd be a lot easier to call in a tip in the first place, but I think I mentioned that scrying a location can be inexact. Search warrants can be tricky to get, and the last thing you want is a police visit next door. By the time they can get a warrant for the right property, the stash house is empty and the kids are in another state, maybe. Better to pinpoint and nail them the first time.

Jimmy looked at me. "Stay in the car."

I smiled. "I'll bet you say that to all the girls."

"That is so wrong, coming from you." He shook his head and got out. Jimmy doesn't have much of a sense of humor when things get serious. Me, I keep mine lively at all times. It's my nature to be either flippant and playful or deadly cold, and the former is more comfortable.

I'd finished the ice cream float and the energy bars, and I felt nearly normal again. I tipped my head back against the seat.

It was only a few minutes before Jimmy came back, casual and calm. When he got into the SUV, however, he slammed the door too hard. "They took my name and number and offered to have someone call me Tuesday."

"But?"

"But I could hear cartoons coming from a back room."

Candy and cartoons go a long way to keeping captive children quiet. The stuff you see on the news about tiny, filthy rooms and physical restraints is real, too, but cartoons are a cheap sedative in a holding area. I flexed my fingers deliberately to keep from clenching them into fists. "Drive. I'll make the call."

I had my phone to my ear, ringing, when the bread truck pulled into the parking lot. Jimmy slowed the SUV, watching the truck in his mirror. "Are you thinking what I'm thinking?"

The truck pulled alongside the accounting office, its painted bakery logo at odds with the cheap imported goods in the warehouse.

"Bells and breadcrumbs," I snarled.

"Anonymous Crime Reporting Hotline," said a voice from the phone.

I gave her the address as Jimmy turned the SUV. "I saw Alexis, the Amber Alert kid." I'd scried her, close enough, and that would get the fastest response. "I think it's human trafficking. And they just brought in a truck, they're going to move them now, so you need to hurry. I have to go." I hung up on her questions; she had what she needed, she didn't need to know more about me, and we had work to do.

Exposure was what the traffickers would fear most right now, so the mere presence of a couple of outsiders might be enough to make them sit tight for a while. Jimmy pulled his SUV into the lot and angled across two parking spaces. He then held his phone up at eye level and gestured angrily at it. "How long do you think they'll be?"

I pointed with equal fervor at my own phone and then up the street. "Hard to say. Telling them they were moving the kids now bumps it to probable cause, I think, so they can act faster, but I wouldn't want to bet anyone's life on it."

Arguing over directions is a pretty good cover in a lot of places, but it was less convincing when Jimmy had just been asking about accounting a few minutes before. It wasn't long before we noticed a face at the office window. "I think we've been spotted," Jimmy said unnecessarily.

I shifted my feet on the phone books and drew a pair of light leather gloves out of my jacket pocket. Three men came out of the office, and two walked to separate cars. The third came toward us with a friendly smile. "You guys lost?"

Jimmy put the window down a few inches. "We were having something of a debate about the fastest way back to the interstate. But it looks like we've got some time to kill, anyway, before we meet my folks for dinner. Might sit here a bit."

The friendly smile faded. "I'm afraid you can't loiter here."

Jimmy grinned in a good-old-boy way. "Aw, we won't be any trouble."

"This is a private lot. If you don't move on, I'll have to call the police."

The bread truck began to back along the building, probably heading for a loading dock or door, and Jimmy's grin faded too. "Well, if you feel you should."

There was a moment of silence. Jimmy had called his bluff, and it suggested we knew more than we should. It was a dangerous play, and Jimmy knew better, but like I said, no sense of humor, and the truck was right there.

And then the man gestured, and the two cars pulled in on either end of the SUV, blocking us in.

I yanked the handle and leapt out of the car, skimming around the obstructing car and bolting across the parking lot. I'm not quick like some of the Fae, but I can move pretty well, and I reached the warehouse before the guy who'd told us to move on or the guy from the car could catch up. The third goon somehow tripped as he passed Jimmy and went down hard on the asphalt. Humans can be so clumsy.

The truck was backing into the warehouse area behind the accounting office, and I dove through the gap between truck and wall. Apparently, the guy inside wasn't expecting me because he went down under our impact. I wasn't expecting him either, unfortunately, and our tangled limbs slowed us as we both tried to get up first.

Children laughed. Not a lot of them, as they were across the warehouse and behind the office and most were still watching the cartoon screen, but a handful laughed at us. I stared. There were so many of them—maybe three dozen. This wasn't a small-time pedo ring; this was major business, probably into resale.

Looking at the kids had been a bad idea. The goon's right hook staggered me and I hit the warehouse floor. The two chasing me through the parking lot arrived and kicked me hard in quick sequence.

Fights aren't like what you see in most movies. They're nasty, brutal things, and once you're on the ground and outnumbered, you're pretty much done. So, I was glad when Jimmy leaned around the edge of the loading door and shouted, "Freeze!"

They looked at him for a moment, and that was all I needed. I twisted off the ground despite my ringing head and dented kidney and I bolted. The warehouse was full of steel shelving and racks of plastic-bound pallets, and I skimmed up like a squirrel on meth.

No, really, it's one of the things we're good at. Speed and grace are in all the old stories. Lots of the great parkour artists have a little Fae in them, and one of the world's top rhythmic gymnasts actually dopes with fairy blood; there's just no test for that yet.

Oh, and the steel? Good thing I was wearing my gloves. My hands tingled a bit, but I'm used to that.

Jimmy had retreated around the door again, and apparently the goons realized he hadn't actually declared *police* or flashed a badge. They scattered, two heading for the kids while a third began circling the steel shelving, looking up.

If you haven't been in a warehouse like that, that shelving is pretty tall. I was probably twenty-five feet above the floor, crouching on a pallet of boxes marked "Hella Catty." Cheap knockoffs don't even try anymore. I stayed in the middle of the pallet, so it would be hard for him to see me unless he got me silhouetted against one of the overhead lights. A little glamour would have been really useful, but that genetic lottery is pretty hard to win.

The fourth goon came in, a little scuffed, which meant Jimmy had gotten out of sight somewhere. With any luck, he was calling 911, reporting an assault in progress and speeding up the police arrival a bit. On the other hand, the last time I called—to report what looked like a heart attack I'd spotted through a bus window on the highway—the dispatcher told me they'd get someone out when they got to it. So, my hopes weren't exactly pinned on the cavalry arriving.

As long as I was up here, I might as well be doing something useful. I slid my phone from my pocket and took several pictures of the kids in their group around the television, the warehouse, and the creeps who were keeping them there. And then the office door opened, and I took a picture of a woman.

It shouldn't have surprised me; lots of women work in trafficking. Some of them were victims themselves once, and some are just twisted, perverted sickos. Don't get me wrong, it's awful when a man does it—but when a woman exchanges maternal instinct for predatory, it's somehow worse. Maybe that's not politically correct to say, but Fae feelings go back a lot further than the PC style guide.

I took another picture of her, all neat department store clothing and smooth dark skin and middle class, and then I shoved my phone back into my pocket. She strode through the kids and pointed to the truck with a smile. "Okay, it's time for our ride! You get to ride in the back, and we're going to all go get ice cream."

The kids cheered and got to their feet, mostly. A couple were slow to rise and didn't look enthused, and my half-Fae heart squeezed in me. They acted like they'd been someplace bad for a long time. Easy victims, already broken.

Sometimes, in the old days, the Fae stole children from homes that weren't homes.

If these guys got the kids into the truck, they could take them just about anywhere. We had to stop them here. I eyed the truck, but from this high angle I couldn't see the license plate, or it was on one of the doors which hung open.

The kids started moving in a cluster across the warehouse, a few looking over their shoulders at the cartoons still running. The floor was littered with empty chip bags, microwaved popcorn bags, cookie packages, pizza boxes. Cheap fodder for the livestock.

Shakespeare did get a few things right, and one of them was that Titania (she's fine with that name, really) took the orphaned boy for his mother's sake and meant to raise him well. She's like that. But she wouldn't have given him up, not for Oberon or all the equine-headed peasants you might throw at her.

Not clear yet? Imagine all the motherly tenderness and protectiveness you've ever seen in a human. Now refine that in whatever crucible you like until it is a pure elemental force of the Fae, raw power honed to maternal instinct. Getting the idea?

Changelings are one thing, because they're usually taken to be coddled and petted and raised as fairy's own. But Titania is displeased when a human child is stolen by human predators.

And so she deputized me.

I slid to the edge of the pallet, looking down, and reflected that I hadn't seen the driver yet. That meant he was still in the truck, and he could drive away with any kids who got in. I hoped Jimmy would do something about that— maybe a little carjacking for a cause—but I couldn't count on it.

And then one of the goons shouted and drew a gun. His first shot skimmed over my left shoulder and into the light behind me.

I ducked beneath the showering glass—at least my silhouette was gone now—and bared teeth in a savage snarl-cum-grin. A snarl, because he'd just pulled a gun and started shooting in front of children. A grin, because he'd just escalated the situation to my level of competency.

The Fae are specialists. There are some who could have walked into the warehouse and spoken with the traffickers and walked out leading all the children skipping in a neat line, with the traffickers clutching a five-dollar bill and pleased with the deal. My bloodline isn't the kind that's good with words.

I whipped my slim Walther from its leather holster inside my waistband and shot into the empty floor of the bread truck. I know, it's illegal—can't shoot unless it's life or death, and if you can afford to shoot anywhere else it's obviously not life or death—but I wanted to scare them off the truck and I wasn't quite ready to kill them yet.

I was close. I mean, child sex traffickers are kind of like really ugly spiders, only without the ecological benefits. But not quite.

The lead goon jerked backward, because running toward a truck with bullets flying at it is kind of mentally hard to do, and kids were screaming and covering their ears. Two of the men started shooting at me, but the light was gone and I slid back, so they had to shoot the whole pallet of Hella Catty figurines while I crept over to the Hella Catty T-shirts, which would do a better job of stopping bullets anyway.

Gunshots are loud, and echoing in a warehouse makes them worse. I flattened against the T-shirt boxes and shielded my ears, waiting for the idiots below to get bored. The gun felt warm through my jeans in a way that had nothing to do with the shot, and I rotated my arm to hold it away from myself. Polymer firearms are a kindness, but the barrel is still steel.

The third man ran for the office, probably intending to grab incriminating paperwork or computers and get out the front door. I didn't care; I had his picture, his skeevy partners were still here to rat on him, and I don't even kill spiders when they're running away.

The woman knelt in the center of the kids, pulling them close to her. At first I thought she was comforting the scared kids, the hypocritical monster, and then I thought she was just getting low in case of a ricochet. But then I saw her looping their clasped arms over her neck and boosting one little girl—Alexis— onto her shoulders and pulling two boys to her torso, and I realized what she was doing.

Middle-class sex trafficking bitch struggled to her feet, weighted by eight or so terrified little kids clinging to her for security, and started toward the truck, protected by her meat shield of children.

And that's when I lost my sense of humor. There's a line, and using children as a bullet shield for your getaway is a few steps past it. I slid along the Hella Catty T-shirts, squeezing the polymer grip of my Walther and pressing my index fingertip hard into the frame.

The two guys below were still aiming high, looking for me. They'd have a clear shot in a moment, but I wouldn't give them long to take it. Moving shots— at a moving target, or from a moving position—are a lot harder than Hollywood makes them look.

She would reach the truck in another dozen steps. The goons between us were about fifteen yards away. I took a deep, slow breath, wrapped both hands around the Walther, sighted on the first gunman, and jumped.

I fired the first shot just as my legs straightened. He was aiming high, leaving his chest exposed, and I put two rounds where his heart would have been if he'd been in a different profession. More shots boomed across the warehouse as his fellow goon tried for me, but as I was jumping through my downward arc at thirty-six feet per second and his ammunition traveled eight hundred and fifty feet per second, he'd need to aim about twenty-three inches ahead for his bullet to have a chance of finding me. And he wasn't that good.

I was. I switched targets and put a round into the other gunman, enough to take him out of the fight if not out of the world. I landed, rolled, and came up with my sights on the woman. "Drop the kids."

The kids stared, wide-eyed and too afraid to move. She laughed. She boosted one kid higher in her arms, to more completely shield her face, and so help me, she *laughed*. It was nervous laughter, but it was still all kinds of wrong.

Headshots, contrary to Hollywood and video game lore, are tricky and unreliable. The skull exists for the sole purpose of deflecting impact away from the brain, and it's shaped to do exactly that. There are only a couple of points where a bullet will reliably penetrate, and this waste of breath was wearing children like human mufflers.

But she'd left one eye exposed to watch me as she started again for the truck.

Low-velocity hollow points don't make the biggest holes, but they're a lot less likely to run through the intended target and hit someone on the other side. Kids screamed and tumbled as the woman collapsed where she stood, but none were actually hurt.

Don't ever try that, by the way. It's not the kind of thing humans should risk. The Fae are specialists, and even in your post-modern, ultra-science reality, your kind still knows it. Every elven ranger in a basement D&D game, every computer-generated battle sequence featuring Legolas trashing orcs, is tribute to our ancient and arcane skill. Humans have their own advantages—my aching temple and kidney could testify to that—but when it comes to projectiles, you'll never quite match the Fae.

The driver must have been watching, because he slammed the truck into gear and pulled out, rear doors swinging. I didn't do anything about it—there's no good way to stop a truck, and there were three dozen crying children in front of me. I holstered the gun, knelt, and held out my arms.

The kids should have been terrified of me, after seeing me jump out of nowhere and shoot three people. But maybe they knew something was wrong about their captors, or maybe they recognized something in me, or maybe it was just any friendly adult in a storm of distress, because they came to me and hugged me and each other, some crying, some unnaturally quiet.

I just sat there, their warmth and youth and life all around me, and wept.

Jimmy came in and hugged some kids, too. He stood and went to the open loading door when the police arrived, waving them in. They had a full team, even counselors to collect the kids. I stood slowly, hands spread to show I meant no threat.

They took the kids outside, away from their prison and the bodies, and bundled the injured goon into an ambulance. Then they started on the dead man and woman. I described most of what had happened, pointing out the shattered light, my bruising face, the dent where a swinging truck door had struck the loading door's track as it raced away.

The officers listening to me were having trouble keeping up. Maybe I was talking a little fast and not quite calmly. "Hold on one sec, sir," said one. "I need to get this more slowly."

His partner gave him a pained look and turned back to me. "Sorry, ma'am."

He paused, now uncertain. "Er, what's your name, please?"

I gave a tight little smile. "Robin Archer."

I could see by their faces that the name didn't help. Well, sorry. Best I can do.

"Can we have some ID? Including your permit?"

I shook my head. "I don't have my wallet with me, left it at home. Didn't exactly know I was going to happen into all this. I can show it later."

Jimmy knew the drill—he didn't really know me, I ate at the Steer & Beer sometimes but that was it, he just happened to be near when I told him there were kids in danger. Interrogating him about me wouldn't get them far. And I really would show my ID later—if there were a later. I'm legal, but we kind of don't like getting tangled up with human authority.

"Look, I really want to go to the bathroom." They would understand that. "There'll be one in the office area. Can I go?"

The officers exchanged glances and nodded. "He'll just stand outside," one said, "where he can see the door, okay?"

I nodded.

If the officer who followed me was hoping to see which gender I chose, he was out of luck, because it was a single unisex restroom. Ah, well, one more thing for him to puzzle over, along with why I wouldn't be there whenever he finally forced the door. Portals to the Twilight Lands are much harder than scrying and not to be made lightly, but I'd rather be in bed for a week than sorting details with the police for far longer, and they pretty much have to detain someone who shoots a woman in the face, no matter how much she deserved it.

I pushed back the unlatched door and waved to the waiting officer. "I'll be out in a minute." Not exactly a lie, as I would be out of the room. Just not this way.

I was startled by the boy curled into the corner of the bathroom, squeezed between the toilet and the wall, maybe ten years old. He looked at me with dull, frightened eyes, like a street dog who half-expects to be kicked and isn't certain if it's worth trying to avoid it.

I held a finger to my lips and squatted before the toilet. I whispered, "You didn't go to the truck."

He shook his head.

"You knew what they were?"

"Guessed enough." His voice was flat.

I should have sent him out to the officer, but his eyes were too lifeless. "You were going to run home?"

He shook his head, as I knew he would.

I nodded toward the warehouse and the swarming authorities. "Is anyone looking for you?"

One shoulder twitched, hardly a movement. "Not sure. Left th' foster home. Sixth."

There would be a report for him somewhere, but he was deep in the system. It was a system which tried its best, but it dealt with tough situations, and it couldn't save every kid.

Sometimes, in the old days...

I held out a hand. "Come away, human child?"

He looked at me, curious with the first flicker of emotion. "Where?"

"The wood, the water, the wild."

He was old to be taken, but he had little holding him. He looked at me a moment, and then he reached for my hand.

Laura VanArendonk Baugh is an award-winning writer of speculative fiction, mystery, and non-fiction. Her works have earned numerous accolades, including 3-star (the highest possible) ratings on Tangent's *"Recommended Reading" list. Laura speaks professionally throughout the year—in her day job she's a professional animal trainer and behavior consultant, and for a hobby an award-winning costumer—but she particularly enjoys talking about writing and publishing. Find her at* www.LauraVAB.com.

Robin Archer returns in "Orphan Heirs and Shades of Night."

The Demon Monkeys

A. R. Silverberry

Scamp's first sight of the wizard was in the village square, though at the time she only thought of him as the stranger. High up in the mountains, strangers were rare in Pin-Shoba, especially in the dead of winter when snowstorms blocked the roads and passes. But this man was different—he was making a large copper coin appear or vanish in his hand, behind a boy's ear, in a girl's pocket. A dozen children formed a ring around him. Every time Scamp tried to worm her way between them, they locked shoulders or shoved her back, sending her rolling into the snow. At last, she scooted between the legs of a tall boy, Mussen, and sat in the front where she could see everything that was happening.

The man wore a thick overcoat. Snowflakes caught and glistened like fireflies in his long, white hair, and his beard floated lightly in the wind. His hands were delicate, the fingers long and nimble. Weary wrinkles troubled his face. When his sky-blue eyes fell on Scamp, they seemed to penetrate to the very bottom of her, and then probed at her tangled, black mane, the rags on her back, her bare, dirty knees, and the bare toes escaping scraps of cloth, her only footwear. She started to draw back in alarm, but merry laughter leaped into his eyes, and the next thing she knew, she was laughing and clapping as he found a sweetmeat behind her ear.

The crowd cheered for more. He obliged, drawing a rose from thin air—a rose in winter!—and then more astonishing: a small bird that hovered and beat a flutter-wind before winging away through the falling snow. The children pleaded for an encore, but he held up his hand and asked where he could buy rice, a few vegetables, and perhaps some beans. The village could spare little, but Scamp pointed out the hut of a farmer whose crops had fared a little better. He gathered up a shabby bag, hoisted it over his shoulder, and tramped in the direction she'd pointed. Something in her heart seemed to pull after him, but three of the taller boys hemmed her in.

"Give it over, Scamp," said Mussen, pimples swelling red and angry on his face.

She clutched the prize to her heart. "It's mine."

Scowling, Mussen bent low until they were almost nose to nose. "Was yours." Though she kicked at his shins, he pried open her fingers and dug the candy from her clasping palm, holding it out of reach. With his other hand, he shoved her into the snow.

Small, no older than six, there was little she could do but watch as they laughed and paraded from the square like the victorious soldiers of an invading army. The pangs in her belly proved more urgent than the sting to her pride. Having eaten little since last night, and less since the day before, she needed that sweetmeat. There was nothing to be done but go begging door to door. After dusting snow from her clothes, she made the rounds. Farmer Anskar had a healthy cow—perhaps he could spare a cup of milk or a bit of cheese. All she received was a scowl. His neighbor slammed the door in her face. And Tu-tu gathered up his few loaves and cakes and whisked them away. She met much the same through the circle of shacks, as she did most days. But old widow Kell gave her the kindness of advice. "Move on," she grumbled. "We don't have enough for ourselves." And snapped shut her shutters.

The moving part of this counsel served well, for it kept her warm and occupied until the sun set. Under cover of absolute darkness that enveloped the village, she slipped past the houses like a wraith, longing to be inside one of them. Through the windows, she could see the happy faces of children, lit by a small candle or the warmth of firelight.

She left the homes behind and trundled up an icy path, passing fields promising a meager harvest, until she came to steps. She passed up them silently. At the top, she paused and peered intently into the shadows beyond the tremulous light of torches set around the perimeter of a clearing. No one lurked in the cedars shrouding the sides or stood at the altar nestled against the sheer side of a boulder. Satisfied the place was deserted, she crossed the clearing.

Carved in bas-relief in the stone behind the altar, howling monkeys leered with enormous round eyes that seemed to follow her. She half-expected them to spring to life and tear her to pieces. That they hadn't done so before did little to reassure her. Neither did the monkeys baying in the forest, their cries and wails raising cold hackles down her spine. Hunger urged her past her fear. In the great dish of the altar, the villagers had left offerings—little bowls with a spoonful of sticky rice, blackberries, a smallish dumpling, a finger of flatbread, and a few lentils.

After another scan of the trees satisfied her that she wasn't observed, she wolfed the meal down. The screech of the monkeys rose up as if in objection, spurring her from the clearing. The sound haunted her all the way back to the village. A short time later, she stole into farmer Naden's barn, relieved to be out of the biting wind. In one of the stalls, she huddled her frozen body against his sleeping goat, Dingle, drawing a complaining bleat. She told herself to awaken before dawn, or Naden would rouse her with a willow switch, and as Dingle warmed her, and a blanket of sleep began to slip over her, she thought of the stranger and imagined that he kissed the crown of her head.

A week passed before she saw him again, talking to widow Kell. The old woman clutched a straw broom as if she were ready to swing it as a weapon.

"No, I don't have peas or barley," she said. "No, I don't know who does."

He jingled a leather pouch and showed her the contents.

"It wouldn't matter if it was gold instead of copper," quoth she. "Let me offer a bit of advice—we have no use for conjurers here, unless you can conjure a full larder."

He did no better at the next house. The owner told him to try a neighbor or the next village. The eyes of a third narrowed with suspicion, while a knot of men watched the stranger from behind a corral and skulked away when he approached. Scamp followed him through the village, peeking from an alley or from behind a wagon. At last, giving up the entirety of his pouch, the stranger managed to get supplies from one of the farmers.

As he loaded rice, beans, and a few limp vegetables into his sack, he asked, "What can you tell me about the little girl with no shoes or coat, the one with the mop of tangled hair and dusty knees?"

Hearing him describe her, Scamp edged closer.

"Scamp?" the farmer replied.

"Has she no family, no one to take care of her?" asked the stranger.

"We help as we can." The farmer backed into his house and began closing the door, until it was open only a crack. "Stay clear of her. She's cursed."

The farmer's words passed by like clouds, for the stranger's questions bathed her in bright sunshine. He'd thought of her! Her, little Scamp! At that moment, he might have bent and planted that kiss on her crown. Her heart swelled. She floated, dizzy with pleasure.

He was stepping off, taking the lane out of the village. She couldn't let him out of her sight! Darting after him, she went from tree to tree so she wouldn't be seen. He strode quickly, leaning against the wind. They passed the fields, blanketed in white, and entered a tall stand of cedars. She looked apprehensively about her as howling rose in the distance. It began to snow, and he turned onto the path leading up the mountain.

No! she thought, and fear wrapped icy fingers around her throat, for she had never ventured this far from the village, and it was said these woods were home to the demon monkeys. But the stranger seemed to tug on her heart and she plodded on.

Snowflakes whirled, eddied, and billowed about him. At times, he seemed to fade behind a white veil, and she hurried her steps so she wouldn't lose him. Snow piled up on both sides of his tracks, but did not fill the deep impressions of his footprints. Once, the two of them followed nothing more than a thin trace on a sheer rock face that dropped into roiling clouds. At last, the path leveled off. They passed for a time through a stand of tall and silent trees and came out on a perch near the top of the mountain.

The flurries parted before him as he followed a path that led to a hut. The roof sagged. The walls were old and weathered. No smoke curled from the stone chimney, no light, warm and inviting, poured from the windows. He paused, perhaps to catch his breath from his journey, and then trod up a narrow track into the hut.

Scamp watched as a lantern flared within, then she crossed the open space, hopping like a rabbit from drift to drift so she remained unobserved. She stopped near a fallen fence and sucked in a breath in astonishment. Snow piled in small mountains around the hut, flurries swirled all around it, but none fell on the roof, windowsills, or doorstep. What's more, blue and yellow flowers pushed through the white blanketing the yard and nodded gently in window planter boxes.

She crept to one of the windows and peeped through the shutters. A ponderous book lay open on a wooden table. Arranged on a bench were objects she didn't know the use of—tubes and triangular bottles of clear crystal, filled with colorful liquids. A loom sat in one corner, a spinning wheel in the other. Two chairs, a tired rug, and a narrow bed covered with a thin blanket composed the rest of the furnishings. Strange, flowering plants hung from the ceiling. Logs waiting to be lit were stacked in the fireplace.

He rubbed his hands and flexed them to work out the cold and stiffness. Then he removed a small box from a shelf and opened it. Into his palm he shook out a small quantity of shimmering dust and blew it upon the cold hearth. The next instant, a cheerful fire sprang to life.

Turning his hands near the flames, he called out, "You've come this far, Sugarplum, you might as well step in where it's warm."

She looked about for Sugarplum, wondering who that might be. Then, with the thrill of a little bird, she realized he was talking to her. Still, after stepping shyly through the door, she stood shivering at the entrance until he waved her over to the fire.

She wondered how long she would be able to stay, for she had never felt this warm, not even when she slept with Dingle. "Why do you call me Sugarplum?" she asked.

He nodded in the direction of the village. "Better than what they call you."

She couldn't argue with that and decided she liked the name.

While she twirled her toes before the flames, he poured water from a pitcher into an iron pot. With a knife, he began to cut carrots, leeks, and the meat of a bright red gourd.

"Where are your parents?" he asked.

She came over to help, scooping the diced vegetables into the pot. "They died."

"Why doesn't someone take you in?"

Her brow wrinkled as she puzzled it out. "They don't have enough food."

He stared at her. "Surely there's enough for one small girl."

"They can't keep it."

She would rather have left it at that, but he fixed his eyes on her and waited until she continued. For a moment, the blaze on the hearth seemed to waver and burn cold.

"It's the demon monkeys," she said, almost in a whisper. "They come on fire steeds and take everything."

He looked down at her sharply. "Have you seen them?"

"Their picture...on the village altar." And she heard them in the woods. She told him they came when the snow began to melt, thundering down the mountain wrapped in flames. Then the villagers carried enormous baskets filled with grains, and took up armfuls of wool stuffs and boxes of porcelain with delicately fired glazes, for they were known for their intricate designs, and brought them to the demon monkeys.

"What if they refuse?" the stranger asked.

Scamp's eyes grew round with fright. "They'll burn the village."

The blood must have drained from her face, for the man began setting the table with wooden bowls and spoons and asked no more. Talk of the demon monkeys had brought snow into her bones, but the soup warmed her and her fear dissolved. Soon, she was prattling and laughing as if she'd never spoken about them.

After they ate, he sat before his book, studying the glyphs. From time to time, he traced an arc in the air with his finger and turned the pages without touching the paper. As astonishing as this was, it had been a long day and a long trek up the mountain, and presently, sleep tugged at Scamp's eyelids.

She rose. "I should go." Outside, the wind began to shake the windows and hiss about the cottage.

"Nonsense. It's almost dark and the storm is just getting its teeth." He stepped to the trunk at the foot of his bed and removed rolls of combed wool, ready for spinning. He unfolded yards of it near the hearth and stacked layers to make a bed. Over this, he threw his winter overcoat and tucked her in beneath it. The soughing wind seemed to fade. Just before the crackling flames lulled her to sleep, she saw him sit up from his book. His face glowed, his eyes almost burned as he murmured, "One more ingredient, then I can make it."

She came often to visit after that, for he was kind, and there was always a place to sleep by the fire and a hot meal to fill and warm her belly. She had a habit of asking questions, and once she got going, she had a hard time stopping. Old widow Kell scolded her often for it, saying her curiosity would kill a cat. The stranger—his name was Wyndano—made her more curious than anyone she'd ever met. He tapped a shell the size of a melon, and a soft, back-and-forth whooshing filled the cottage, and the air was permeated with an exotic aroma of plants and birds and fish, but not like those in the streams, and she was suffused with a sweet, exquisite longing for something she couldn't name. With a gesture from the wizard, his flute lifted into the air all on its own and began to bob and play a wistful tune. Wyndano was so strange and wonderful she had to know about him.

"Where do you come from," she asked, for he spoke with an accent.

He looked up from his book, which he had been engrossed in, and waved toward the west. "Far, far away."

Questions poured out, one after another.

"How long will you stay?"

"Why did you come?"

"What are you making?"

He frowned at the last one, and she worried that maybe she'd killed a cat. But he said, "All in good time, Sugarplum." He did tell her something of his travels, describing valleys painted with flowers, rivers that carved canyons, forests so dense you had to cut your path with a sword, and a place where land stopped and water as far as you could see crashed onto white sands.

He pointed to the shell that made the wonderful sound and scent. "That's where I got that."

She could hardly believe the world contained so much. As far as she knew, there was only the mountain. Hundreds of villages rested on its shoulders and ridges, but beyond that, the world plummeted into clouds. So said the elders. And most of the people in the village. But here was this stranger with strange ways and strange doings. Besides, she trusted him. If he said it was true, then it must be, and he knew so much more than any of the wise elders, who seemed like children compared to him.

But the question about what he was making, which had occupied her mind since that first night, he would not answer, nor would he say why he was there. But she worried about the cat and bit her tongue and tried to be as helpful as she could. Perhaps she'd get the answer by watching him, for he was almost always active. With a snap of his fingers, the candles below the crystal containers ignited. When the crimson, blue, and green liquids bubbled, he sprinkled them onto the rolls of wool.

"Do you know how to spin?" he asked.

No one had ever let her near a spinning wheel, but she had watched wool and flax get twisted into thread and thought she could do it. Seated at the great wheel, she held the fiber in her left hand and turned the wheel with her right. He adjusted the angle of fiber to spindle, and with a thrill, she saw she'd produced the necessary twist to make thread. After that, he left her to her work, though from time to time, he changed from wool to flax, from flax to silk, from silk to parts of trees, honeysuckle, and reeds, and sometimes, small portions of thin leather, animal tendons, and sinews found their way into the finished strands.

While she spun, she watched him work at the loom with her thread. He was slow and meticulous, sometimes pulling out a line and redoing it so that the weave was tight and the texture met his standards. Every so often, he sprinkled aromatic powders or colored liquid from one of his crystals onto the fabric, and he spoke strange words over it. She observed all this with rapt attention. What they were making, though, remained a mystery.

The path to getting this question and many others answered began at the village. One day, the wizard came in for supplies, and Scamp saw him talking to widow Kell. She wouldn't have spied on him, but she heard him pressing the old woman about what happened to Scamp's parents. She peeped from behind the trunk of a fir tree and heard all they said.

"Why is the village so cruel to the little girl?" the wizard asked.

"I can't see as it's any business of yours," Kell replied.

A sly smile came into his eyes. "Perhaps not, but I heard your best egg-layer ran off."

Kell folded her arms. "What of it?"

"Nothing really, just that she might come strutting and scratching back to you."

Kell glowered. "Fine." And Scamp heard the truth about her parents, how one year, the village almost starved because the harvest was given in tribute. How her parents imagined a better life, for they believed their lands could produce enough for everyone. How they tried to rally the village to fight the demons off. They refused. Everyone hid when the demons came, everyone except Scamp's parents, who faced them alone.

"They died like that," Kell said with a snap of her fingers. Their death confirmed the villagers' worst fears. The demons left them hanging on stakes for all to see and cursed the village, telling them that resistance would bring bloodshed. They pointed to the savaged bodies of her parents and said their offspring would be cursed, and whoever stood up to them again would be cursed, and their descendants cursed for ten generations—not to be touched, not to be cared for, lest ruin come to the village.

"Now, where's that chicken?" asked Kell.

Wyndano paled at this tale, but he twittered like a strange bird, and presently, a great leghorn sashayed around the corner, shaking its comb.

Wrapped in sadness at the fate of her parents, Scamp journeyed up the mountain. How foolish they'd been, and how courageous! It must have been a terrible winter, a meager harvest, for them to risk so much. And Scamp couldn't help but think about the murmurings and whispers of the villagers that this year was one of the worst they'd seen. Surely, they would starve. Fear and desperation filled their eyes and left them careworn.

But in the wizard's hut, Scamp's spirits always brightened. That night, she vowed it was time for answers.

"Wyndano," she ventured, "what are we making?"

He looked up from his loom, his shoulders suddenly tense. "Don't ask,

Sugarplum."

"Why not?" she cried, tears springing to her eyes. "You asked widow Kell about me."

He gazed at her a long moment and sighed. "Very well. Perhaps it would be good to tell. I've spoken to no one of this and have carried it too long." He blew into his hands and rubbed them. "It grows cold. Come, sit by the hearth. We'll make tea and talk."

She brought over her chair while he stoked the fire and put a kettle over the flames.

"Like the people of your village," he began, "I was a farmer—like my father and his father before him, all the way back to dimmest memory. We were a carefree lot, working from sunup to sundown in the fields, and nothing gave us more pleasure than to see young shoots push from the black earth. The happiness of the day poured into the night, when we sang blessings to the gods, for our land was rich and the plants seemed to leap from the soil. I had much to be thankful for—a loving wife, whose raven hair flashed in the sun, and a daughter—" His voice broke. "—about your age. Tidings of war troubled us little—it was far away and not our affair. Little by little, though, a shadow reached toward us. Closer it came, bringing dark tales of a necromancer, whose army ravaged and destroyed all before it and enslaved the few who survived. Day by day, our terror grew, but we were a peaceful people, and what could we do with pitchforks and shovels?"

The water began to hiss and bubble. He brewed tea in a pot, and when they both were sipping from steaming cups, he continued. "For a time, it seemed they would skirt us. We had just begun to relax when they struck in the dead of night. The screams still echo in my ears. Our homes still burn red before my eyes. A falling beam must have knocked me senseless. I came to the next morning, buried beneath a fallen ceiling. I crawled from the rubble to find my village charred and tumbled to ruin. Frantic, I ran from blackened shell to blackened shell of a house, searching the wreckage, calling my wife, calling my daughter. No one answered... No one would ever answer."

He stared into the fire as if he saw blazing rooftops. It seemed to Scamp that he might float off. She held his big hand between her two tiny ones. At length, he gazed down at her and opened his arms, and she crawled into his lap, and he clasped and rocked her to his breast.

"I wandered, a dead man, caring little where I went," he continued at last. "When I wakened, I found the land unfamiliar. Still, I journeyed in a daze, with a vague idea I was traveling west. I crossed forests and vast sheets of frozen ice. I sat in tents with wise men, smoking pipes, sweating, chanting, breathing deeply of sage thrown on steaming rocks. A vision seized me—to seek teachers, sages, magi, anyone who could heal me. On I roamed, west, always west. I searched by rivers and deep in valleys. I found them in caves and on the highest mountains. Two or three were genuine and knew rare and beautiful enchantments. Years I apprenticed, absorbing, gleaning the best from each of them. They peered into my heart and told me the same thing—forgive, forget. I could do neither. They told me revenge would blacken my heart. That I heard, though at first there was nothing I could do about it. Gradually, gradually, though, a new idea formed, not for vengeance—for freedom. I would rise, more powerful than the necromancer, and overthrow him."

He sipped his tea and gazed at his weaving, still on the loom. It had grown long, but still he said it was incomplete.

"And here I am, Sugarplum, making what I need."

She gazed at the weaving in wonder. "What is it?"

His eyes were flames, though perhaps it was just a reflection from the fire. "A cloak, such as has never been seen in the world."

Here was a new puzzle. How would a cloak help him defeat the necromancer?

But all he would say was, "Soon, child, soon."

He made up her bed, for there was still plenty of unspun wool, and he tucked her in.

She looked up at his face, thinking for the first time that it was not only kind, but beautiful. "Wyndano, what do you need to finish the cloak?"

"Hair." He bent and kissed the crown of her head. "Of a hero."

His answer suddenly seemed unimportant. That evening, he'd held her in his arms. And now he'd kissed her. For as long as she could remember, no one had done either. Even as she fell asleep, the wonder of it filled her mind.

Winter began to wane, which was not reassuring on the mountain—the final storms were often the fiercest, and tribute day with the demon monkeys was drawing near. Wherever she went in the village, Scamp saw worry deepen on the faces of the villagers. As feared, much of the winter crop had failed. What would be given in tribute would be small and would anger the monkeys, who would punish them and take the little they'd kept. No one said it, no one had to, she could see it in their eyes—they would starve.

A series of storms kept Wyndano and Scamp bound to the cottage. Engrossed with his work, he gave it little thought. Instead, he worked feverishly on the cloak, dyeing it with liquids from his beakers, sprinkling it with powders, casting over it incantations and enchantments. But as his supply of food diminished, Scamp began to worry. She begged him to let her get a few things so he might finish the weaving. When the snow stopped and the sky cleared and the sun was unusually warm, he allowed her to return to the village for supplies. But he made her promise to not venture back if another storm came.

As she set out, she had no fear whether they would sell her what she needed. She'd been his proxy for some weeks, and as he'd proven to be helpful—the miraculous recovery of a sick cow, the return of a wandering donkey—even in these dire times, she always brought something back. So, it came that Scamp was in the village shortly before tribute day. No one needed to tell her where they were in the phases of the moon and the tilt of the sun. She could see it in their drawn and anxious faces, and she heard it in their uneasy whispers.

She collected the few things she needed—a wedge of cheese, small sacks of flour, rice, beans, and a few condiments. She looked warily at dark clouds blotting the setting sun and decided to spend the night with Dingle. By the time she reached the barn, she sensed a change in the wind, which brought the scent of something cold and dark. Soon, gusts rattled the walls, and Dingle stirred and bleated apprehensively, and she wrapped her arms around him, trying to reassure him.

She was up with the sun and cast a worried eye toward the horizon. Clouds loomed. Like ominous towers they rose. A low rumble came, and the morning sounds of scratching chickens and pigs at the trough seemed to pause and then tremble. She hurriedly threw her knapsack over her shoulders and tramped through the village. Windows were shuttered—goats, cows, and horses were scurried into barns—babies were snatched up and rushed indoors. Farmers hastened in from the fields. Birds raced east.

Scamp gauged the distance to the clouds. There was time—she could reach Wyndano before the storm struck.

Just before slamming and bolting her door, old widow Kell called to her. "Hide, Scamp, hide while you can. They know! It's the demon monkeys, punishing us for a short tribute."

Scamp pressed on. The village fell behind her, the fields too, the fences blown down. A low drum roll rumbled down the mountain. Wind moaned in the cedars. The great trees swayed and whimpered. The leaves trembled. The branches rattled and shook. Icy gusts snatched at her knapsack, as if to tear it from her back.

Clouds tore across the sky. The sun seemed to shrink and then disappeared behind a black pall. Howling wind drove the first stinging flakes. Swirling, diving, spiraling, it blinded and taunted her, and she could swear the monkeys were in the midst of it, laughing at her. She came to a tree, toppled and half-buried like a giant in the drifts. Its enormous roots reared up like a hand, urging her to stop, urging her to return the way she came. Violent blasts sent snow streaming in curtains, and sky and tree and trail faded to white. On she forged, fingers numb, the constant whistling and shrieking in her ears, and she came again to the fallen tree, its roots twisted up in warning. But she leaned against the gale and at last found the track up the mountain.

Here, new perils waited. The trail narrowed to a thread clinging to near-vertical heights. Clouds billowed and boiled below, as if a chained monster thrashed inside to free itself. Her feet slid in the drifts. The wind threatened to lift her like a kite. The storm drew a shroud across her eyes, and instinct alone kept her from plunging off the mountain. The sky ripped. In one ruddy flash, she saw the mountain huddled like a child and black clouds stampeding down on it like wild horses. The next instant, an unearthly bellow struck the cliffs and crashed and echoed on the bluffs and crags. Again it came, low, deep knelling, as if the whole mountain was a bell, and then a series of claps so terrible she wondered if the mountain was erupting and every boulder and stone above would come crashing down on her.

Less than a speck, less than one of the tiny flakes whirling in the wind, she staggered on, until at last she came to trees, a path, a garden with blue and yellow flowers poking up from a blanket of white, a door. It opened. Light streamed out. A man stood framed in the entrance. He was running now, sweeping her in his arms, carrying her inside, and the white withdrew, and she was wrapped in warm blackness.

She wakened beside a blazing fire, wrapped in his overcoat. A kettle of water was bubbling over the flames, sending up delicious steam.

He handed her a cup of tea. "This will take the sting from your fingers and toes."

It tasted bitter, but the redness and pain quickly faded, as did the worry in his eyes.

She tried to tell him she was sorry for disobeying him, but he hushed her. "The storm tricked us both," he said. "Had I known you were out there, I would have come for you. I thought you would wait it out in the village. How do you feel?"

She flexed her fingers and curled her toes. "Better."

His eyes sparkled. "Guess what I found behind the hut?"

She looked about the room with excitement and saw something big hidden beneath his blanket. He whisked away the blanket and revealed a five-foot-long tub made of hardened pottery. "I bet you've never had a hot bath."

She watched in amazement as he moved the tub beside the fire. He poured in boiling water from the kettle and then cooled it a little with snow. Then he hung the blanket as a curtain. Soon, she was immersed, and the most delightful heat soaked into her bones.

"Be sure to wash your hair," he called. "The storm made a rat's nest of it."

Too soon, she was out and dried and wrapped in his blanket. He handed her his brush. While she ran it through her hair, she told him about the village.

"Wyndano, I'm scared." She told him about the failed crops, how everyone looked apprehensively toward the altar circle, how widow Kell said the demon monkeys would punish the whole village for being short. "They're coming. Tomorrow night," Scamp said.

He pondered her a long time. Then he rose and took a large sheet of paper from his trunk and laid it out on his table with a brush and a few pigment inks.

"Show me what they look like," he said.

She painted as best she could, showing their icy eyes, terrible grinning mouth, and yellow flames shooting from their heads. When she was done and the ink was dry, he showed her how to fashion it into a lantern and then hung it from the ceiling on a length of twine.

"No," she cried. "It'll bring them."

He handed her the big spoon he used to stir soup. "Break it."

She hesitated. Even her own crudely drawn image of them filled her with fright.

"Go ahead," he urged. "Right through the other side."

She swung, ripping through the monkey's nose. The bottom of the lantern tore and fell to her feet.

He picked up the fallen piece and threw it into the fire. "That's all they are, Sugarplum. Little more than paper."

She shook her head vehemently. "But I saw them. In the storm. Oh, if only the cloak was done, *you* could stop them."

He gazed at his loom—his eyes bright as flames. "We will. Together." He turned to her. "I found my hero."

Another surprise! she thought. *Like the tub. He's here!* Rippling with excitement, she scanned the room, prying into shadows near the trunk, the loom, the great spinning wheel, and beneath the bed. Where? Where was he?

Meanwhile, Wyndano took up the hairbrush she'd been using. He removed white tangles of hair lodged in the bristles and then carefully drew out two lustrous black strands.

"Spin them, Sugarplum, with wool and honeysuckle fiber."

Confusion must have played across her face. He laid a hand on her shoulder. "Many a man would have quailed before that storm. Fearing I would be trapped without supplies, you forged through it with the heart of a lion."

She barely felt them, barely comprehended their meaning, as he dropped the strands into her outstretched palm, though it dawned on her slowly as she began to spin. He meant her!

When she'd twirled it into yarn, he wove it into the cloak and then removed it from the loom. He laid it out on the table and took up one of his sparkling powders, which he blew onto the material. She wasn't sure what was supposed to happen, but he held it up in the firelight, and she drew in a breath. Across the surface, mighty bears lumbered, cranes soared in misty valleys, great horned sheep roamed rocky crags, snow leopards prowled ravines, and iridescent fish swam silvery waters. Then yaks and horses, rabbits and mice, goats and antelopes, eagles and hawks came leaping, racing, darting, winging across the surface of the fabric.

"What does it do?" she asked in wonder. Now, creatures of myth and folktale shimmered on the weaving, fierce-eyed, streaming fire and smoke.

He gazed at his work, eyes alight. "Whatever you imagine. Do you trust me, Sugarplum?"

She smiled up at him, nodding.

"And do everything I say?"

She nodded again.

"Good. Tomorrow, we take care of your monkeys."

Midafternoon next day, Scamp and Wyndano strode into the village. Tense quiet replaced the usual hustle and bustle. No one gossiped by the fences and corrals. No children jumped rope, romped with a dog, or played catch with a gourd. No chickens pecked and scurried through the snow, and the paths between the houses were empty. Scamp wasn't surprised. On tribute day, people left the fields early. Last-minute preparations were made to fill baskets. And in some homes, small sacks of rice and barley were stealthily hidden under floorboards.

Even the air was still. But as Wyndano went from house to house, the new cloak hanging from his shoulders rustled as if a breeze stirred and lifted it softly. Birds, insects, reptiles, and animals no longer coursed across the fabric, yet Scamp knew they were there—waiting. At first, people would only listen to him from behind doors or shutters. But when he demonstrated the cloak, they stepped from their homes, astonishment on their faces. Soon, a crowd followed him.

Full darkness shrouded the edges of the clearing. This night, the moon would not rise. Light snow sprinkled down. It seemed to appear and disappear, blurring the clearing and dressing the trees in cold clothing. Half of the villagers lay hidden, spread out on both sides of the steps just below the top of the hillside. Standing beside Wyndano a few feet forward of them, Scamp sensed rather than heard the edgy whisper of them stirring. She guessed they were relieved Wyndano wanted them out of sight. She wondered if they would come out when they were needed. Everyone else was hidden in the village—in case the plan went bad.

A cold breath stirred the cedars. Wyndano leaned forward, listening, and the cloak billowed like the wings of an immense bird. A low rumble sounded in the distance. Far away, as if in answer, monkeys began to howl. Little by little, rather than fading, the thunder deepened, drumming, drumming, like an oncoming storm. And the din of baying and barking grew.

"Are you ready, Sugarplum?" Wyndano asked.

A lump rose into Scamp's throat, but she nodded.

"Good. Remember, do what I told you."

He dropped a white pebble then seemed to vanish. Scamp knew he was there, four feet to her right, and anyone looking might have seen a small black beetle crawling over the snow and then onto the pebble. She clutched a leather pouch in one hand. It felt uncommonly light.

The beating and pounding drew near, a terrible chorus coming with it. Through the branches and leaves, something bright and ruddy flared, as if the trees had ignited.

Then they were there—a dozen of them, thundering into the clearing. Flames licked from the manes and tails of their steeds. Fire rippled along the arms, legs, and torsos of the riders, and a blaze, cold and blindingly bright, shot from their heads. One of them was head and shoulders above the others. His horse reared, pawing the air, and then its hooves crashed down into the snow. With pent-up energy, it stamped from side to side and then stepped a pace forward. The demon's hands were like huge stones. His broad shoulders and tree trunk of a neck supported a large, misshapen head. A wrinkled, bloated snout protruded from his face. His eyes flared with menace.

"So, the cowards send little girls now." He spat into the snow. "Where's the tribute?"

She swallowed against the lump in her throat. "It's not yours." Her voice seemed small and weak compared to the rough and booming sound of his.

"Not mine?" He laughed, and the riders behind roared with dark mirth. "Run along. Tell your parents to bring that tribute, or the village burns."

"No more tributes. Ever." She took a step forward, hoping they couldn't see her trembling, and pointed back the way they'd come. "Leave while you can or face your doom." Pride surged through her—she'd gotten Wyndano's words right.

"You little wretch, I'll roast you over flames and suck out your marrow."

He spurred his steed. When he was almost upon her, she reached into the pouch and pulled out a handful of winking dust, hurling it at him. Some of it landed on his legs and the horse's chest. In a blink, it spread over horse and rider and then over his followers, extinguishing the flames, sending up a sulfurous vapor, and revealing men wearing masks.

The leader bellowed and lunged for her. At that moment, a new demon monkey appeared beside her astride a giant of a horse. He towered over the man. Unlike the fire of the men—which was cold—hot flames burst from his head and ran down his shoulders, arms, and legs, his long, white hair flying with fire. His face was crimson, his features outlined in black and gold, and his eyes glowed icy blue.

The leader's horse reared. Pale, eyes bulging, the man yanked the reins, urging his steed back. The next instant, the villagers leaped from hiding, brandishing shovels, pitchforks, axes, clubs, and hastily made spears. They spread out into a ready and determined line.

The demon raised his hand. A sword materialized in it and burst into flames. He whirled it, sending a hot gale before him. "Brigand, your days of stealing are over," he thundered. "A new god protects these people. Set one foot on this mountain and I'll ride you down." He pointed to Scamp and then several of the farmers. "Harm one such as this, or him, or her, and I'll find you where you hide and scatter your ashes to the winds. Go!"

That's all the urging they needed. Lashing their steeds, the brigands fled from the clearing. Head tilted, the demon gazed in the direction they'd gone. The beat of their horses faded. Still and silent he stood, and then in a wink, where the flaming horse and demon had been, there was Wyndano, his cloak rippling lightly in the breeze.

He nodded in the direction of the departing brigands. "If you follow them, you'll find a trail of bones," he said to the villagers. "They used them to draw snow monkeys from the forest. That's how the howling grew as the riders came."

"But the flames," one of them exclaimed. "It shot from their faces and horses."

Wyndano snapped his fingers. Fire leaped from his palm. "Mix certain chemicals and you get harmless flames. Magicians use it, though how those ruffians came by it, I don't know." He held it out to Scamp, who doused it with powder from her pouch.

"Go," he said. "Throw your doors and windows wide, and till your fields in peace."

Snow, which had danced and darted about him like fireflies, stopped falling.

Streams wakened. Rivers yawned and murmured. Shepherds led their sheep from snowy highlands into the valleys. Emerald and jade slopes swept down from snow-capped peaks. Honeybees gathered nectar from wild mustard painting the hillsides, and rhododendrons burst with blossoms. If her mountain contained all this, Scamp thought, what treasures might the rest of the world hold?

She turned back from the vistas and heights to gaze into the faces of the villagers, assembled on the main road leading down the mountain. They formed a ring around Wyndano, who tied his rucksack to the saddle of a horse they'd given him in gratitude. Scamp's heart was in a tangle.

He adjusted the bridle and then laid his hand on her shoulder. "What will you do for this girl?" he asked, addressing the crowd.

Anskar stepped forward with his wife and daughter. "We'll take you in. You'll have plenty of cheese and hot milk if you stay with me."

Tu-tu put an arm around his wife. "We've got bread and cakes, right out of the oven."

Naden wasn't married, but he said, "I'll give you Dingle. He follows you around anyway. You might as well have him."

Wyndano gazed down at Scamp, his eyes misty. "You could have a place, Sugarplum. Would you like that?"

"Where will you go?" she asked.

"You know where. Someone has an account to pay."

"I was thinking about the rivers and valleys," Scamp replied, "the deserts and the place where you found that shell. It would be something to see. And...and... You might need me, so you don't fight him alone." She bit back tears.

Widow Kell folded her arms. "Let me give you some advice, Scamp. Best to not get mixed up with conjurers."

Wyndano stepped into the stirrup and swung onto the horse. "What do you imagine, Sugarplum, what do you want to be?"

She looked up at him hopefully. "Your daughter."

He laughed. "You're that already." He reached down and drew her up in front of him. Together, they rode down the road, the world open and calling. As they receded, anyone watching might have seen them stop, as if to take in the view. Anyone looking might have seen the horse leap from the precipice, the cloak drifting upward, and where horse and riders had been, a giant bird soared and then vanished west in the twinkling of an eye.

Wyndano's story has been on my mind for some years. I knew he lived in an earlier age, before the events of Wyndano's Cloak, *before kingdoms rose and fell, and the shape of lands and seas changed. I knew he wandered far across his world, sitting at the feet of wizards, gleaning all he could of their magic, until he arrived at a lonely mountaintop, where he would distill all he'd learned into one, powerful creation. There his story sat in my mind until the hero prompt for this anthology. He couldn't be the hero—I needed Scamp for that. Once I got her, the demon monkeys weren't far behind. Think of this tale as ancient history to my novel,* Wyndano's Cloak.

www.arsilverberry.com

Superhero Publicist

Janeen Ippolito

Knock, knock!

The publicist looked up from her oversized, fake-wood desk, which seemed even larger because her office was at least two feet narrower than any other in the building. Her nameplate explained everything: "Miss Cassandra Robinson, Junior Representative." Junior, meaning junior room, junior parking space at the far end of the lot, and, oh yes, junior pay grade which barely covered her junior apartment and junior-sized black business suits, because on top of everything else, she was short and small.

Knock, knock!

Miss Robinson blinked out of her ruminating, adjusted her black-rimmed glasses, ran a hand over her wayward blonde curls, and buzzed to allow door entry. Security was essential, especially when you represented both good *and* evil.

A nondescript man walked in. He was in his late twenties, lean build, narrow face, and brown hair that looked freshly windswept.

"Thanks for seeing me on such short notice." His voice was light and pleasant.

"No trouble at all," she said, pulling her mouth into a smile. "After all, at *Power-Up Publicity*, we save your image so you can save the world! Or destroy it, as the case may be. Now, how can I help you today, Mr.—?" Miss Robinson shuffled her papers around on her desk. The guy looked vaguely familiar, but she had a full caseload, and honestly, all these vigilantes were hard to recognize out of costume.

He took a seat in the cushioned blue chair across from her desk.

"Brown," he said. "Angus Brown. Call me Angus."

The publicist nodded, while having no intention of doing so. Professionalism came first. It had to, for a junior representative.

"Right, Mr. Brown," she said, opening up a file in front of her. "Supervillain alias 'Swipe.' And your power is still enhanced speed?"

"Yeah."

"Any recent upgrades?"

"Well, I'm even faster than ever," Mr. Brown said. "And my reflexes are now even quicker than lightning."

"Quicker than lightning?" She frowned, checking a paper. "Not 'quick as lightning?' So much for that new slogan then."

It was the third time this month a catchphrase had failed for a client. Not good for her record. Miss Robinson made a frustrated sound under her breath then picked up a box of "quick as lightning" buttons, fliers, and other paraphernalia, and tossed it wholesale toward the trash can. The pile of fliers glided off the top of the box and sailed around the room. She groaned again then glanced at Mr. Brown.

"I know you generally don't perform good deeds, but do you mind?" She gave him her most helpless look, and added, "Otherwise, this meeting will take a lot longer."

The supervillain shrugged. "Sure, why not?"

In an instant—quicker than lightning—all of the papers were in the trash can and Angus Brown was sitting back in his chair. The publicist gave a sigh of relief.

"Much thanks," she said. "I know you have a villainous reputation to maintain outside, but within these walls, consider me your best accomplice."

He looked up, blue eyes bright. "Actually, that's what I came to talk about."

Miss Robinson paused, her pulse quickening. "Not thinking of switching companies, are you? We have you under contract for another six months, and while I know there's not a lot we can actually do to you if you break it, I assure you that no other firm will handle your case any better—"

A blink. Mr. Brown was standing in front of her, hand on her shoulder. Rather tightly, she noticed. A knot coiled in her stomach. Close proximity with supervillains was never a good thing.

"I'm fine here," he said. "I'm happy here. I've been happy a lot lately, just for anything. Everything!" He flung his hands out expansively. She raised her eyebrows, and for the first time in their professional relationship, the man looked sheepish. "It's just—I don't want to be a villain anymore. I want to switch sides."

The publicist's mouth dropped open. Her smartphone slipped out of her hand and landed with a clatter on her desk.

"You want to what?" she asked finally.

"Switch sides," Mr. Brown said, making a 'switching' motion. "Join the good guys. I've already tried doing some good things—you know, to clean up my act a bit. The Awesome Adventure Squad has even stopped targeting me as a major threat."

Miss Robinson picked up a pencil with the express purpose of chewing on it. Before inserting the eraser end into her mouth, she gave a shaky laugh.

"This is a joke, right? I mean, there are hidden cameras everywhere." She gnawed on the soft tip for a moment, peering suspiciously around the room. "Even though that's impossible, because this is one of the most secure facilities on the eastern seaboard, after the Lascivious League's fortress—wait, what does the League think of this?"

He winced and ran a hand through his brown hair, making it stand on end. "They weren't too happy about it. I kind of went from the Awesome Adventure Squad's hit list to the League's."

Miss Robinson spat out the pencil, sans the eraser she had bitten right off and swallowed. She had two other clients from the League. Handling superheroes and supervillains was one thing, but a turncoat? That was asking for a special meet-and-greet with the League's Dark Master.

"You're trying to get me killed, aren't you?" She sighed. "You sure you don't want to just turn neutral chaotic for a bit? Maybe even neutral law-abiding. We could say you have to lay low for a while to duck the authorities or something."

"Sorry, no." Mr. Brown shook his head, sitting back in his chair and propping his feet on the desk. Right next to her laptop. The publicist glared at the soles of his shoes. All of that faster-than-lightning running might not hurt his body, but it made his feet reek to high heaven.

She knew better than to say anything. You had to pick your battles with villains. Save the arguments for the next time you needed to discuss a price increase and were significantly more armed.

But if he was supposed to be a hero now... Why not test this idea? What was life without a little excitement and potential death?

"Excuse me," Miss Robinson started. "If you wouldn't mind, your feet?"

"Yes?"

Okay, time to jump right off that bridge. Without a bungee cord or a parachute. "Would you mind getting them off my desk?"

For a moment, Mr. Brown's face twisted with anger. Just as quickly, it was replaced by an expression so friendly she thought his eyes were twinkling.

"No problem," he said, pulling his legs off the desk and placing them back on the floor. "My pleasure."

"Okay," she said, making a note for the cleaning person to scrub the desk extra hard. "So, lawful good it is."

"As much as a masked vigilante can be," he added.

She scribbled a bunch of notes on sticky notes then examined them for a moment. "It is doable. You wouldn't be the first to switch sides. The public should buy it, after a period of doing good and perhaps a few public appearances. And maybe visiting a few nursing homes and kissing a few babies. Play basketball with inner-city kids. Something like that."

"Whatever I can do," he said. "However I can serve my fellow man."

She fixed him with another hard stare. "Okay, before I go any further, you need to level with me. What caused this whole change of heart?"

She expected hypnotism. Maybe a love interest he couldn't live without. Possibly he had a long-lost child that he needed to take care of. Shoot, she'd even go for a near-death experience. Those always went well.

"I met someone," he said.

Aha. Love interest. Miss Robinson pulled out a fresh sheet of paper and a pen, ready to take notes. "Well, what's the young lady's name? If she doesn't mind, I'd like to include her in the future publicity stunts. She'll be pretty high profile, but I'm sure you can keep her safe. And if we can get a save on live TV, well, that's worth more than a hundred public apologies."

"Ah, it's more of a he." The words were hesitant.

The publicist blinked—it always was the cute skinny ones—then gave her most reassuring smile.

"Not a problem," she said. "The public is growing more liberal these days, and I'm sure after a suitable preparation, they'll be more than ready to accept your boyfriend. Again, a live TV rescue helps a lot."

Mr. Brown raised his eyebrows then laughed. "I think you misunderstand me. It's not anything like that. It's more of who I'm following. I'm a Christian now."

The pen fell out of her hand. Miss Robinson yanked off her glasses and plunked them on the desk. She didn't really need them anyway. They were just part of the act to look older. "A Christian?"

"Yep!"

The publicist narrowed her eyes. "Are you sure?"

He smiled. "One of the surest things in my life."

"One moment." Miss Robinson spun around in her chair until she faced a wall. Then she let her face collapse into a scowl and groaned.

"Hey, are you all right? You sound like a dying walrus. Not that I've ever killed one," Mr. Brown added hastily. "Actually, I'm not sure why I said that. This showing real empathy thing is harder than it looks."

She had to get it together. The publicist took a deep breath, exhaled slowly, then turned to face her client, plastering a calm look onto her face. She picked up the pen and paper. "I'm sorry about that. Okay then, time to spin. How Christian are you? Are you like gun-toting Conservative Christian or hippie, peace-loving Liberal Christian or some kind of hybrid who uses the Bible as a self-help guide? What's your angle?"

The former supervillain looked confused. "I never really thought anything about it. I go to a Presbyterian church right now, but I'm not a member or anything. Still just trying to study the Bible."

Miss Robinson sighed. Great, he was one of those unaffiliated, sold-out to Jesus types. A coworker had gotten stuck with that a few months ago. It was a demographic nightmare. Without a single denominational or doctrinal protocol, it was impossible to predict what the guy would say. And that was a bad thing.

Of course, she could always read the Bible herself. But who had time for that?

"All right," she said. "Let's just put a pin in that and deal with it later." She wrote down the words "Christian" and "marketing nightmare" on the paper. "Back to the main idea: you want to be a hero. I think we can make that work. Just give me a day or two to mock up some new plans, and then we'll make the official transition. I think I can get a reporter and cameraman on Wednesday—does that work for you?"

Mr. Brown nodded. "Sure, that works out fine."

The publicist added the deadline to her smartphone then sat back in her chair, massaging her forehead. She never believed in the idea that Mondays were cursed. Until today.

The faintest whoosh of air blew her blonde curls into her face.

"Are you okay?" Mr. Brown was standing right next to her again. Miss Robinson didn't even have the energy to flinch. She just nodded. He gave her a pat on the back. "Hey, can I buy you lunch?"

The publicist looked up. His expression was equal parts nervous and kind. Was this really the same guy who a month ago had helped sabotage a nuclear power plant? It made her brain hurt.

Then, her stomach growled. Well, she was only paid on commission. No point in turning down free food. "Oh, why not?"

Mr. Brown smiled. Without evil overtones. She had to admit, he wasn't nearly as sexy without the cocky villain persona, but there was still something nice about his sharp, angular face. Not quite warm, but decent-looking.

"Okay." She smiled back wanly. "Is this the part where you sweep me up into your arms and we dash off into the sunset?"

He chuckled.

"No, I'm turning over a new leaf, remember?" Mr. Brown offered her his hand. "We'll go at normal speed. Also, I'm kind of short on funds—it turns out supervillains get paid more. Mostly because we steal anything we need. So, how does a chili dog sound?"

The publicist rolled her eyes. "Sounds perfect."

So much for chivalry. This would be some lunch date.

Janeen Ippolito writes Monsters, Misfits, and Mushy Stuff, so it was natural to write "The Superhero Publicist" about an unsuspecting publicist helping an ex-supervillain change

their image. As for the Mushy Stuff part, she's always willing to expand for interested readers! Besides writing, she's a professional writing teacher and author coach, as well as a crazy cook, time-starved reader, and LARP sword-fighter. For more underdogs, humor, and romance in speculative fiction, check out Janeen Ippolito on Facebook, Twitter, and janeenippolito.com.

Sweet Basil

Lea Doué

The village slept under a sky filled with crystal stars when Marisol stole into the woods. Despite offers of money, land, and even marriage, she never stayed after feeding the dragon.

Her stomach grumbled, and she stopped to pick a brown-spotted pear from a forgotten tree, biting into the gritty fruit while stuffing extras into the pockets of her skirt for later. She'd been wary of meals offered in thanks ever since winter, when she'd stayed too long at a mountain village, grateful for the warmth and company. She'd woken groggy the next day in the home of a man who had wanted to exploit her abilities for his own gain.

Her abilities. She had no special abilities, other than survival, and that was enough.

She breathed deeply as she trudged through the underbrush, the rich scents of the midnight forest tickling her nose with stories of life and death, growth and decay. She rubbed her arm where the dragon's flat, narrow snout rested uncomfortably close to her wrist, a living tattoo. Pulling back her sleeve, she tapped its chin. Sometimes, it responded and moved obligingly. Usually, it ignored her and lay still. This time, it bared its teeth and nipped at her finger, as though it could peel away from her skin to reach her. Its flat teeth scraped against her wrist, and she gasped, tugging the sleeve back down. It had never done that before.

A sharp crack from somewhere behind her warned of something else in the woods. Something big.

"Ouch! Stupid branches."

Something human, then. A man, judging by the voice.

"Marisol?" he said. "Are you here?"

She slowed her breathing, hoping her mud-colored cloak and brown hair would help her blend into the deep shadows. How did he know her name?

"It's me, Renzo. I know it's been a while, but I hope I haven't changed that much." His steps grew louder as he neared, and a tall form stopped a few yards away, "You left the village so fast, I brought you something to eat, if you want it. I'm sure you could use a good meal."

Her stomach roiled with uncertainty. She'd known a boy from her home village named Renzo. They'd spent summers wading in the stream catching minnows and winters building snow castles, but he'd left after a vicious attack by razor-tail dragons had left him an orphan, homeless and alone. She'd never expected to see him again, least of all in the middle of the woods so far from where they'd both come.

"I know you're nearby." After removing a satchel from his back, he crouched, took out a length of cloth, and unrolled it on the ground. "You can join me if you want. Best food you'll ever taste."

He lit a small lantern and placed it at a corner of the cloth, the flickering light marching over the dark green folds. Adjusting the sword at his waist, he sat on the grass. Sandy brown hair tied back at his neck revealed big ears and expressive eyebrows. He looked like his father, his features as pleasant and as plain as ever.

Placing his work-worn hand flat on the fabric, he said, "Midnight snack."

In the time it took her to blink, the entire cloth had filled with food. Scents of fresh bread and baked fish and cinnamon reached her, and her mouth watered. She'd had cinnamon once when her mother was still alive, and she'd never tasted anything so heavenly.

How was it possible? He was no sorcerer, but what had he been up to all those years? She took a tentative step closer, entangling her cloak in a branch and sending leaves shivering to the ground.

He glanced up sharply, staring in her direction. He cleared his throat. "I can't tell you how happy I am to have found you. I've been hearing rumors for weeks." He waited, possibly hoping she would respond. When she didn't, he sighed. "Too many people wandering alone these days," he muttered. "I haven't been studying with sorcerers, if that's what you're worried about."

Had he read her mind?

"I found the tablecloth in an abandoned hut years ago. I used it as a blanket until I stumbled upon its true nature." He poured something into a goblet that winked with silver in the lamplight. "I know what happened in Narin. You've got nothing to fear, Marisol. It's me."

Her stomach ached with hunger. She took one shaky step after another until she stood at the edge of the cloth, heart racing and lips curving up into a smile.

He smiled back, and his eyes twinkled. "As lovely as ever." He swept his hand out as if offering her a seat at a grand table. "Won't you join me?"

She sank onto her knees, her gaze sweeping over the plates of chicken and flatbread, bowls of rice, and baskets of fruit. If she intended to join his midnight meal, and she did, she should offer something in return. Too weary for small talk, she pulled the pears out of her pockets and held them out. "Here. It's all I have."

"Thank you." He held his palms cupped under hers, and she dumped the fruit in. Her hand brushed against his thumb, and she yanked it back, knocking one of the pears onto the tablecloth.

"Sorry." She reached for the fruit, but as soon as her fingertips skimmed the cloth, the dragon awoke and thrashed its tail along her calf, sending pains shooting up her leg and into her hip. She scooted backward into the shadows.

"What's wrong?" Renzo crawled over beside her. He gently removed the pear from her fist and tossed it over his shoulder. "Is it the dragon?"

Her eyes widened. How did he know about the dragon? She studied his face, but with the lamp shining behind him, she couldn't make out his expression. He sounded concerned. Perhaps she could risk trusting him with her secret. She'd waited a long time to talk to someone about her...abilities.

"I don't think it likes your tablecloth." She stood and pulled her cloak tight as the dragon repositioned itself against her skin, holding her breath until it stopped moving. Its head ended up near her knee, and its tail wound up her back and coiled around and around her neck, with the pointed tip extending up her jaw to rest just below her left eye.

Renzo watched her face the whole time, as if he understood her pain. "Of course it doesn't. Dragons don't like sorcery."

She nodded in agreement and gritted her teeth. Her dragon was created by sorcery as much as his tablecloth. It shouldn't care one way or another what her hand brushed up against.

"Let's try again, and this time you can sit away from the edge." He stood, offering a hand, and she placed her fingers in his. The dragon remained still.

Thankfully, it didn't object to the food, and she stuffed herself with the best meal she'd eaten in months.

"It's good to see someone besides myself enjoying all this," Renzo said. He paused and ate a whole pear before speaking again. "You have questions for me, I'm sure."

She nodded and smiled around a mouthful of warm bread spread with figs, the ache in her belly gone for the first time in days.

"I understand your hunger," he said. "After I left, I wandered a long time before finding someplace to belong. A purpose. I was actually a dragon soldier not that long ago."

"You deserted?"

He shook his head. "I'd met my quota, and I'd had enough of killing. Even if it was dragons. Many of the volunteers want revenge on some sorcerer or other, seeing the harm they've done after going unchecked all these years. They join the soldier-king's ranks in order to rid the lands of razor-tail dragons so the true kings can finally focus on dealing with the real problem."

She'd heard stories of the soldier-king. He wasn't a real king, but if his soldiers had their way, he would be someday. He'd done much in the past few years to organize people in the dragon-ravaged lands, reforming the old order of knights into a highly-trained group of men and women who specialized in hunting down and destroying the aggressive packs of razor-tails.

"Is it true his skin is as white as snow?"

"Yes. His hair, too, and I've never seen eyes so blue."

"And his wife?" It was said they worked side by side recruiting and training the soldiers.

"I only saw her a few times, but she's lovely, despite the scars on her skin. Or maybe because of them."

Marisol glanced at her lap, where one of the dragon's front feet rested unseen on her thigh.

"When I joined them, I only wanted regular meals and a purpose. I have one of those now." He nodded toward the tablecloth and then stared at her pointedly. "But the soldier-king's purpose wasn't my own. I don't want to destroy. I want to heal and build."

She swallowed one last bit of bread, her mouth suddenly dry.

"I'd like to help you. I already know some of what you've been doing— you've healed enough people in the past year to get a reputation."

She laced her fingers together to hide their shaking. She would have to be more careful from now on. Travel farther before feeding the dragon. "I'm not healing anyone."

He didn't seem to hear. "That dragon has something to do with it, I'm guessing. Are you...have you been cursed?"

The idea didn't seem to frighten him, or else he knew the answer already. "Not exactly."

He sighed and folded the corners of the tablecloth into the center over the remainder of the feast, which then collapsed into nothing. "I've been trying to catch up to you for a while, and I've talked to the families after you leave. I'd really like to know how you do it."

"Why?" She wanted to talk, but years of being alone and keeping things to herself made her cautious. Even with Renzo.

He stowed the cloth in his pack and wandered into the trees, gathering firewood. "I want to help, as I said. That's really all there is to it. I've seen how you avoid the food provided by the villagers, and I understand." He paused as he piled the wood. "I've never shared *my* secret with anyone, and off you go, marching into town after town, risking your safety and freedom to help people. Quite frankly, I'm ashamed of myself, and my family would be, too, if I still had them. I want to be a part of what you're doing, Marisol. You're as much a hero as the soldier-king."

"What? No, I'm not. I just..."

He crouched near the pile of wood and had a fire going within minutes. Dry twigs popped and snapped, filling the silence. "You just what? Heal children who have incurable illnesses?"

"I told you, I'm not healing anyone."

"Then explain." He settled on the ground and tossed a small branch into the flames. Sparks flew into the air, creating their own personal fireworks display. "Please?"

She joined him by the fire and fed it small sticks. Finally, she took a deep breath and began. "I remember the smell of sweet basil that grew around the sorcerer's cottage. The sickness came on me a couple of years after you left, and Mother had tried everything to cure me, sold everything. He was close to the end himself, one of the rare ones who hadn't been twisted by the power he wielded. He used what strength remained to him to give me more time, drawing out the sickness that was eating me from the inside and trapping it in the form of a dragon on my skin, like a tattoo." She took another deep breath. "It's a constant reminder to be thankful for every day I have."

"The tattoo is a reminder?"

"Yes. And the basil." She pulled a small sachet of dried leaves out of her pocket, the faded blue ribbon all that remained of the original bundle. Closing her eyes, she held it under her nose and pictured her mother's bright smile.

"So, it's the dragon healing the children?"

"I suppose." She pushed the sachet down to the bottom of her pocket and threw a handful of grass onto the flames. "It wasn't so big in the beginning. For years it slept, content to crawl from one arm to the other or curl up at the base of my neck, wingless and no bigger than a crow. It didn't wake until the summer I begged food from a farmer's son who suffered the same sickness I'd had, and it only took a few moments after our fingers touched to realize what the dragon had done. It grows a few inches each time, sort of stretching without becoming much wider."

He remained silent for a long while, his eyes studying the fire and the shadows. "Does it hurt?"

She blinked unexpected tears at the question no one knew to ask. "Only when the dragon moves," she whispered. "It's like...sand shifting underneath my skin."

He winced. "Well, at least you won't have to feel the pang of hunger anymore."

"You really want to join me?"

Hazel eyes twinkling with firelight gazed into her own. "Yes. I think I've found my purpose. And I'll even try to match your generosity with a bit of my own. My tablecloth will remain a secret, for obvious reasons, but we'll leave a donation for a few families in need before we sneak out each time."

She smiled, and the last knot of uncertainty loosened in her belly. "It will be good to have company. To have a friend."

Two weeks after their first meeting, they prepared to enter a town larger than any Marisol had visited before. They had bypassed a few small settlements while waiting for the dragon to uncoil from around her neck and leave her face clear of its inky mark.

"Are you ready?" Renzo said. He'd asked her the same question half a dozen times since breakfast and twice now since lunch.

She adjusted the herb pouch attached to her belt, a prop used to get her close to the children and an excuse for their quick recovery. "As soon as you get the tablecloth stowed."

"Done."

She held out her hand, and he grasped it tightly, his sweaty palm the only sign of his unease. Ever since his time in the soldier-king's service, she'd learned, crowds and loud noises unnerved him. They both wanted to be back in the familiar forest before sundown.

The main road led them to a checkpoint at the town gates, manned by two dragon soldiers. The taller man offered a pleasant, if weary, smile. The shorter, red-haired soldier silently studied them from head to toe, his gaze lingering on their faces. She'd never seen anyone with red hair that far north.

"Nothing to worry about, folks." The tall man waved them on. "Have a good day."

As soon as they reached the apothecary's shop near the town square, Renzo pulled her up short. "We need to be careful. Did you see the way that guard looked at us?"

"It is odd to have dragon soldiers stationed in a town. Unless the razor-tails have been sighted nearby?"

"It's not the dragons. They're looking for sorcerers. The soldier-king wants them identified and marked. Says they've been hiding in the shadows for too long."

She glanced over her shoulder, half-expecting to see the soldier lurking nearby. "We have nothing to fear."

"Really? Then why are you squeezing my hand so hard?"

She let go and clasped her hands behind her back. "We'll be gone before they have a chance to think twice about us. Let's check with the apothecary. I may not even be needed."

Unlikely in a town that size, but she could hope.

As soon as he learned Marisol was a fellow healer, the apothecary rasped out a warm welcome and invited them into the back room for tea. She watched him carefully measure the tea leaves—and only tea leaves—into sturdy ceramic mugs. After half an hour of pleasantries and small talk, he revealed that there was, indeed, one child who could use her help. A boy of six named Sandro, who lived in town with his parents and siblings.

"Tell me your blend of herbs and oils," the apothecary said, "so that I may help others when you are gone."

She had expected this request and shook her head. "I'm sorry, but I cannot." The short answer was the easiest. Long explanations only made for questions even more difficult to answer.

The apothecary sighed, but he accepted her reply more graciously than most. "Well. We all have our secrets, don't we? The boy will get help, and that's what matters." He gave them directions to the boy's house on the other side of town and wished them well.

After knocking on the door of a tidy cottage adjacent to a milliner's shop, they waited five minutes before Sandro's mother opened it, two young boys clinging to her skirts. She stared at them, red-rimmed eyes heavy with despair.

"My name is Marisol. I've come to help your son." Most of the families she'd met didn't care for long explanations. They saw the herb pouch, and their eyes either sparked with hope or narrowed in confusion and doubt.

This woman's eyes remained blank. She stepped aside and pointed to a room down the hall. She didn't follow them.

Marisol stopped in front of the door, and Renzo's shoulder brushed hers. "You don't have to come in," she whispered.

"You're not alone anymore." He took her hand. "That's why I'm here, remember? To help."

She took a shaky breath, her heart overflowing with gratitude. She'd always insisted the family remain outside the room, in case the dragon writhed and made itself visible. Renzo might never know what a gift he'd just given her.

The room smelled like lemon, and lavender, and tea tree oils, a sharp contrast to the faded boy sleeping on rumpled bed sheets, his breathing shallow. They'd made it in time, but barely.

Shrugging off her cloak and pushing up her sleeves, she knelt beside the bed and took Sandro's hand in hers, shaping each limp finger until they fit between her own. Renzo settled beside her, one hand on the small of her back.

As she stroked Sandro's brow, the dragon woke.

She gritted her teeth and sucked in a sharp breath against the pain of the dragon's movements. It was nothing compared to what Sandro had felt these past weeks and months, and she bore it gladly. The dragon's mouth opened wide against her calf, its body writhing on her hip and stomach and on her back beneath Renzo's hand. The tail stretched over her shoulder and down her arm, twining around her fingers. She let go of Sandro's hand and cupped his face between her palms. Gradually, a pink blush bloomed on his cheeks, his breathing quieted, and his chest rose and fell, rose and fell, rose and fell, smoothly and naturally. The dragon's belly expanded against her own as it fed off the thing that tore life from others.

Renzo stared over her shoulder, pointing at her forearm. "Is that normal?"

She leaned back, holding her arm in front of her. The dragon's tail curved and twitched around her wrist, nothing unusual, but for the first time, individual scales had appeared and shone a deep green with glints of turquoise. She pulled her skirt above her knee, revealing more of the same on her calf. The dragon's inky skin had been replaced by something with more depth. Something more real. It stared at her with a green eye ringed in white and snarled silently.

A gasp from the doorway jolted her to her feet, and she pulled her sleeves down quickly and fastened her cloak around her shoulders.

Renzo placed himself between her and the mother, who stared not at Marisol, but at her son. Her mouth hung open, and gasping sobs filled the room. She squealed and ran to Sandro, scooping him into her arms and rocking him forward and back until he woke and pushed her off.

"Ma?" he said and blinked heavily. He drew in a deep breath, and his smile bubbled into a laugh. "Ma, it don't hurt."

"I know, baby. The healer...she made you well." The woman turned, her gaze flicking down almost imperceptibly fast to Marisol's leg and back up. "How can I thank you?"

Marisol backed toward the door. "Seeing your son well is thanks enough. We need to be going." And quickly. The woman had seen more than she should.

"Please..."

"Enjoy every day. Take nothing for granted." She spouted a few more lines as she backed quickly down the hall, nearly knocking down one of the younger boys. She patted them both on the head and then turned and rushed out the door, Renzo hard on her heels.

"Slow down." He grabbed her hand and pulled her up short.

"She saw the dragon. We have to get out. Now."

"Of course we do, but you've done nothing wrong. There's no need to run."

She took a deep breath. He was right. If the dragon soldiers were looking for suspicious activity, two people literally running away would certainly catch their attention.

"How do you feel?" he asked.

"Like my skin has been turned inside out and rubbed on a rock." She laced her fingers with his and nudged him back into a walk, her heart thumping as if she were running. "The pain usually goes away almost instantly. I don't know what's happening. The dragon has never looked at me before." Only living things looked at people.

She drew her hood up before they reached the gates, afraid her expression would alarm the soldiers, and they joined the stream of country dwellers exiting for the day. As soon as they reached the first bend in the road, they veered off into the trees and walked in silence as far as they could before twilight shrouded their path.

Renzo lowered his pack to the ground, lit the lamp, and spread the tablecloth out over a patch of moss. He laid his hand on the fabric and said, "Victory banquet."

From one blink to the next, mounds of food covered the surface, including several dishes she'd never seen before. She lowered herself carefully beside it. "You've been saving that one."

"Yes." He built a small fire while she picked at a few of the offerings, her stomach still roiling from their encounter with Sandro and his mother.

The dragon had quieted, but her skin still burned. She rolled up her skirt and stared at the dragon's sleeping form, its head noticeably larger than it had been that morning. The new scales glinted green and blue in the firelight, but the eyes remained thankfully closed. She swept her hand gingerly over her knee and up her thigh where the dragon's shoulder rested, the scales bumpy and hard beneath her fingers. Her skin belonged more to the dragon now than it did to her.

"You can't keep doing this." Renzo's gaze took in the dragon's form before meeting her eyes. "What you're doing is amazing, but it's going to kill you."

She drew in a shaky breath and sighed. "If the sickness in me can draw out the sickness in others, if I can share the sorcerer's unexpected gift and spare more lives, then I won't stop. I've always known it would consume me one day."

He sank to her side and clasped her hands, pulling them to his chest. "It doesn't have to be that way. You can stop. I just found you again, Mari, please don't keep doing this and leave me alone."

She raised a hand to his cheek. "You can't ask me to stop being myself."

"How can I stay by and watch this thing destroy you? I can't fight back. I can't save you."

"I never asked you to save me. You offered yourself, and that's all I've wanted."

He pulled her into a tight hug, his chin resting on top of her head. "And my food," he said, his voice tight with unshed tears. "You wanted my food."

She chuckled. "You do have good food."

"How touching."

Marisol startled, and Renzo's arms tightened around her. Together, they stood and faced the shadows.

A man stepped forward, his red hair almost glowing in the firelight. The dragon soldier from town. He drew his sword, and his eyes narrowed. "I knew it."

Renzo angled himself in front of her.

"My eyes never deceive me. I knew she was a sorceress." He circled around them and kicked the tablecloth. It doubled over on itself, and everything disappeared into its folds. He didn't flinch. "I'm taking you both in. Gather your things."

Marisol's chest burned, and only partly because of the dragon. It seemed to dislike this man. She stepped around Renzo and put her hands on her hips. "You think just because you have a sword, you can order us around?"

The guard's head tilted in surprise. "Do you know who I am?"

"Seeing as we haven't been properly introduced—no."

Renzo sucked in a quick breath, either in approval or fear she'd gone too far. If the guard decided to use force, he was the only other person with a sword.

"My name is not important. I'm a dragon soldier, authorized by the soldier-king to identify and mark all sorcerers."

"I'm just a healer. I don't—"

"Then how do you explain that?" He pointed to the cloth on the ground.

"I found it, that's how I explain it," Renzo said. "A spelled tablecloth doesn't make us dangerous."

The man's jaw clenched and his nostrils flared. He lunged lightning fast and clamped a hand around Marisol's wrist. The dragon reacted, and she screamed as its body writhed in response to the threat, grating against her skin. Its tail tore away from her arm, ripping her sleeve, and whipped against the man's face. He staggered backward with a roar, and Renzo drew his own sword, forcing him farther still. The clang of metal echoed in her ears as she sank to the ground.

She couldn't explain the dragon's recent actions, but she wasn't surprised that it had come to her defense. The sorcerer had created it all those years ago to protect her. To save her. Renzo wasn't the only one with a weapon.

One of the men kicked into the fire, scattering embers and threatening the tablecloth. She snatched it and retreated behind a clump of bushes. The dragon reacted to the spelled object as it had before, its frenzy threatening to rip her apart. She dropped the cloth and clamped a hand over her arm to keep its tail from accidentally striking her own face.

If only she could set the dragon free.

Renzo held his own against the soldier, but it had been years since he'd trained as one himself. His arm strained against the weight of the sword.

She glanced at the cloth pooled at her feet. The dragon had leaped off her skin in response to the soldier's threat. Would it do the same for the cloth it so disliked?

She removed her boots and planted herself on the cloth, digging her toes into the fabric. The dragon thrust its snout toward the offensive object. It poked and prodded uselessly with its talons, its back feet grating against her neck. She panted, fists clenched, until its head finally burst free of her ankle. Its shoulders followed. Then back, hips, tail. Endlessly long tail, burning its way down her back, around her waist, and along her leg. She gasped and stumbled backward onto the grass.

A fully formed dragon, as tall as a wolfhound, but twice as long and muscular, crouched before her, each deep green scale sparkling with turquoise and reflected firelight. Even wingless, its presence filled the small clearing. After staring into her eyes without blinking, it turned toward the men, bared its teeth, and roared. The vibrations embraced her, and she smiled.

It was magnificent.

Both men stopped fighting and backed away from each other. Renzo stepped toward her, eyes wide and mouth agape. The dragon snarled.

"Put away your sword," she told him.

He obeyed immediately, and the dragon turned its attention to the soldier.

"You too. This is no razor-tail dragon for you to fight, and we're not sorcerers."

"Just what a sorcerer would say." The soldier wiped his brow but kept his grip on his weapon. "You're all liars. Promising, and lying, and taking until there's nothing left. I can't believe a word you say."

"Maybe not, but you can believe your eyes. They never deceive you, if you spoke the truth."

She removed her hand from the dragon, confident, without knowing how, that it would obey her. "Pin him," she whispered.

The dragon sprang forward, spraying sparks and embers into the air. The soldier flinched against the burning onslaught, and in that instant, the dragon snatched the sword from his grip and snapped it in two with its teeth. The soldier punched the dragon in the nose, but it didn't even flinch. Before Renzo could reach her side, the dragon had the soldier flat on the ground, one leg pinning down each limb, fangs bared and dripping into the man's face.

"Get your dragon off me!"

"I'm sorry, what did you say?" Renzo said.

"Get it off! I understand!"

Renzo whispered into her ear, "Can you actually call that thing off?"

She shrugged and patted her leg as if calling a dog over. "To me."

The dragon snaked its head around and then turned without a backward glance and walked to her and Renzo. It sat in front of them, staring intently at the soldier, who hadn't moved.

"Tell us exactly what you understand," she said.

"Dragons hate sorcery. It makes them crazy." He stood and dusted himself off, glaring at Marisol. "I don't know how, but that thing's real, which means you're not sorcerers. There. I said it. Now, I suggest you go far away from here, and take your little stolen blanket with you. I might not believe my eyes next time I see you."

"We'll leave when you do," she said. No need for him to see which way they traveled.

He spat on the ground, retrieved his broken sword, and disappeared into the darkness.

Renzo gathered their belongings, stuffing the tablecloth into his pack. He took her hand, and they headed south, the dragon guarding their backs as they walked until nearly sunrise.

Marisol didn't trust that the soldier wouldn't change his mind.

Six months later, they sat around a fire in a different forest, surrounded by two dozen men, women, and children, Renzo's tablecloth spread in the center of the group. They'd gathered other travelers along their journey, people who had been displaced during the soldier-king's war. With Marisol's dragon by their side, they shared their bounty freely, and, in turn, their new friends shared their own skills and knowledge. Renzo's dream of building had resulted in a new family for all of them.

Although her dragon no longer had his abilities, Marisol's heart warmed to see the smiling faces around her. Providing food and a place to belong was a different kind of healing.

One of the new children crawled over and settled into her lap. "What's his name?" she asked, pointing to the dragon where he lay with his head on Renzo's knee, his nose twitching in his sleep.

Marisol smiled. "His name is Basil. He was born in a cottage with sweet basil planted all around, and the smell of the herb reminds me of that day. It was the first day of the journey that brought us all together."

The girl sighed contentedly, her belly full for the first time in weeks. "Sweet Basil."

Lea is the author of The Firethorn Chronicles, *a series inspired by fairy tales and other classic stories. Each book is a stand-alone with interconnected threads throughout. "Sweet Basil" takes place decades before book one in the series and was inspired by true life heroes: children and their families battling childhood cancer and other illnesses.*

Darkness Follows the Light

David Millican

Peeling off her wet clothes, Angelique turned on the ancient hot water heater. Resting her chin on the windowsill, she waited for the tank to heat. Down the street, abandoned houses were sad reminders of a neighborhood's lost potential. Hope gone dark.

Four streetlights, three working...two sporadically, stood sentinel over the decaying corpse of Lyon Boulevard. Across the street, the Jacksons' seventy-inch flat screen cast blue hues on dead trees outside. Mrs. Jackson had once caught Angelique watching along with them from her bedroom window and invited her over. She refused, not because of awkwardness, but because Mr. Jackson, Akshun, was trappin' in the alley. Not that she had anything against drug dealers, you make however you make, but he was sketchy.

Next to the Jacksons' was the Danes' house with its sagging porch and cracked green plastic patio chairs. Mr. Dane always had the lowdown on cheap bottled water. Never a day went by when there weren't at least three cases of the stuff strewn across the rickety porch boards. Nobody busted him about it though, since it was his way of coping. Junior Dane OD'd two years ago, and then Mrs. Dane got hit by a bus up at the school. Most folks thought it was suicide, but no one would say that out loud. Now Mr. Dane spent his days working for the Senior Center since his job at the mill got cut and taking care of his daughter Kaniah, who was only two years younger than Angelique.

They used to eat together at lunch back before Angelique dropped out to watch the kids and do hair on the side. If her Aunt Gail had it together maybe she would have stayed in school, but probably not. She didn't have those kinds of smarts. She tried real hard in school, but Cs were about the best she could get. She figured why waste the next four years feeling like a failure when she could be learnin' and earnin' on her own.

Across from the Danes' was the Edgertons' house. It was the nicest on the street, but not because of them. It was old, like 150 years old, old. A couple years back, some rich dude swooped in and got it declared a historical landmark or something. Spent a bunch of money fixing it up and let the Edgertons stay there all the same. Guess they needed something nice happen to them. Four days ago, their oldest son, Matt, got shot when he was playing around with his uncle's hunting rifle. Dead in a second. Whole town was shook up about that one, especially after them old people were killed up in Garrison Projects just two days before that. Funeral for Matt was yesterday and most people had moved on. There'd be a couple more news stories and a bunch of stuffed animals outside the house where he died, but that's it.

Next to the Edgertons' house was Jonathan's old house, but nobody lived in it now. Jonathan had seemed cool before he started shacking up with her mom. He was her brothers' dad, but he lived down on South Shore now, with a new girl. He still paid for the boys, but made sure not a single cent of that money went to Angelique. When he did come around, it was only to visit the boys and let them know they were better than their "insert racial slur of the day here" sister. Angelique didn't like resenting her brothers, but it was hard not to when her own father wouldn't even acknowledge she was his.

One house down and across the street from Jonathan's old place lived the Malhotras. They owned the Marathon gas station at the bottom of the hill and kept up their yard nice. They were new on the block, having taken over from his father two years back. Angelique liked the mom, Pari, and their two-year-old girl, Jahnvi. The little girl had a particular taste for spice drops, an addiction Angelique was all too happy to feed.

Steam inched its way up the glass, obscuring the world beyond into pools of light. Before the world faded, she glimpsed people in hoodies beside the Malhotras' house. Wiping away the condensed water, she peered out the small circle, trying to see the suspicious figures. Indeed, they stood just outside the reach of the nearest streetlight, almost blending into the darkness completely. Straining her eyes, she realized they weren't wearing hoodies but robes with hoods. For an insane moment, she thought Dementors had come to Kanner Park.

She shook her head. *Ain't no owls here, and the only hairy giant coming for me is the pervert under the overpass.*

They were real but not...normal. Not as in weird, but as in not natural. Their heads reached past window tops, seven, maybe eight feet tall. Hunched shoulders facing the wrong direction and long arms with fingers brushing against dead blades of grass made her shudder. Extending those gangly arms, they reached for a windowsill on the second floor. A window with a stained-glass butterfly hung to catch the morning sun. A stained-glass butterfly given to Jahnvi by Angelique.

Angelique struggled to pull her wet jeans up as she slid down the stairs. Her head poked through her shirt and she jerked it down over her chest as she ripped open the door, not bothering with shoes. Sprinting, she flew over the rough asphalt, ignoring the pain, toward the Malhortas'.

"No!"

The word was a primal scream of fear and rage. Glowing white eyes turned on her, nine of them. Nine eyes, four creatures. Weak light reflected off wicked mandibles; as one they shrieked, setting off a car alarm blocks away. Clapping hands over her ears, she charged forward. As one they pivoted, evaporating into thin air. Columns of mist were the only indicators of their existence. Tripping and falling, Angelique landed on her knees in the rough brown grass. Hearing feet pounding the pavement behind her, she twisted to see their source.

"Angel, what going down?" Akshun said, panting, his Glock shaking in his grip.

"Things trying to get in Jahnvi's window." She pointed at the now-empty side of the house.

"Where they go?"

"They disappeared." It sounded crazy to her. "They took off."

"Which way?"

"Uh...I fell." Pathetic.

"You said things, not people," Kapil called from his porch, alternating looking at her and along the side of his house.

She knew better than to tell what she had seen. "Well, like, I didn't know if they were men or women or what."

Pari looked down on her from Jahnvi's room, holding the sleeping toddler against her chest.

"What you on?" Akshun asked.

"I ain't on nothing. I saw them."

"You pulling all us out our houses just so you can joke on us."

"I'm not cuttin' up here. I mean, you heard them scream, right?"

"Yeah, we heard you scream."

"No, not me, them."

"We only heard you scream, Angelique," Kapil said with sympathy in his voice.

"It was...?" She trailed off. She'd been about to point out the car alarm the scream had set off, but she couldn't hear it anymore.

"Go home, Angelique," Akshun said.

"But—"

Akshun cut her off. "Go home. You getting all weird up in that house. You need to get your backside back in school so you don't end up all strung out on your momma's couch like your Aunt Gail."

"And where she get the junk from, Akshun?" Angelique emphasized the ridiculousness of his name like she knew he hated.

Fire in his eyes told her she was close to getting popped in the mouth, but she didn't care, she didn't back down from trash like him. His wife stepped in, pulling him away and shooting Angelique a dirty look. Didn't bother her, she was going to make something of herself and then they'd see.

Back inside her bathroom though, she shook with fear. *What were those things?* It took a long time before she was able to look away from the window and take her shower. Even then she got out several times to check for robed monsters. Her mother would be furious the water heater ran so long. Restless hours later, her eyes slid shut into a nightmare-fueled sleep.

The man on the park bench could have been chiseled out of stone. Not the exquisite Roman deals but more Easter Island meets the Hulk. That sounded harsh, like he was a troll, which wasn't true, but George defied accurate description. Angelique thought he had a rugged handsomeness or, at least, had when he was younger. Now, his brawler's face, with its broken nose, scars, and jagged cheekbones, told of a hard life.

Six and a half feet tall, three hundred pounds of hard muscle meant no one bothered old George. For that matter, no one bothered her when she sat in the shadow cast by her friend. People were intimidated by him, yet she'd never seen an ounce of menace from him. He never got angry, never stared people down; in fact, she'd never heard him speak.

Old Mister Mallory claimed to have heard George speak. Forty years ago. There had been a mysterious death, and George had been implicated but not convicted. George never said a word after that. Never raised his fist to anyone. Never shown an emotion other than calm serenity. That kind of control over one's thoughts and actions made him more than rare, unique in every sense of the word. She'd heard of monks with less control.

Not that it was a problem; she spoke enough for the two of them. She told him everything about last night, not holding back even the craziest of details. She told him about Akshun's accusations and about her hope and aspirations for the future. She told him about learning about the word "aspiration" from her word of the day calendar she had found in the trash. She talked for almost an hour till George stood and left. She never took offense at his abruptness; she was just thankful he let her hang around at all. It was good to have someone to talk to.

At home in her room, head resting against the window, she tried to resist the siren call of her bed and watch for the monsters, but it was no use. She didn't remember falling asleep, didn't remember walking to her bed, and she didn't remember shutting off the lights. She did remember the scream that woke her.

Heart jackhammering, she shot out of bed and was into the boys' room in an instant. They were all awake, sobbing, but unharmed. The cry came again, a haunting wail of loss. She wanted to deny that she knew the source, but it was impossible. Grabbing her coat on the way out the door the street was already filling with half-dressed gawkers. Elbowing her way through the forming crowd, she stepped up onto the Malhotras' porch.

Hesitation in her knock, she waited for the door to open and the worst to be confirmed. The door slammed against the wall as Kapil burst out, eyes wild and swollen with tears.

"Do you know where she is? Did you see them?"

"No." Angelique's voice was softer than she'd meant it to be.

She didn't need to ask who he was talking about; she had known the instant the wail drifted down the street. Upstairs, Pari wept for her missing child.

"Have you called the police?" Angelique was surprised to hear her mother's voice as Kapil shook his head. "I'll take care of that for you." She rested her hand on Angelique's shoulder. "Go sit with Pari, girl."

Angelique had a momentary flash of anger at the words. Her mother had compassion and concern for this woman but couldn't muster a kind word for her? She shoved the thoughts down; it wasn't the time for that.

She'd been in Jahnvi's room several times before when babysitting, but now it was cold. Literally and figuratively. The window was gone, letting the cold morning air in. It wasn't broken in, wasn't lifted up, it was gone. Vanished like the creatures the previous night. The weeping mother in the pre-dawn glow made the once loving room into a scene of such pain, Angelique almost turned around and left.

But Pari pulled Angelique down beside her. Sitting together, the woman cried until the police were ready to question Pari. Angelique was sent home an hour after dawn, but thirty minutes later they knocked on her door. Angelique told them the truth as best as she could without sounding crazy.

Rushing to George's house, she found an unfamiliar car in the driveway. Her hand turned on the doorknob and then froze. Usually, she went in without knocking. George didn't answer the door, but he usually didn't have company. She let the ancient, cast-iron knob click back into place.

Rapping on the door with her knuckles, she called out, "George, it's Angelique. I need to talk to you."

The door swung open almost before she was done speaking. It wasn't George. Her first thought was that it must be an Amazonian woman. Black hair, thick eyebrows, and green eyes set against parchment-colored skin. Well over six feet tall, the woman exuded confidence and power.

"Can I help you, little one?" the woman said with a soft, refined tone.

"I was coming to talk to George." She tried to peer around the tall woman into the interior of the house.

"You must be Angelique. George has spoken often of you."

"George spoke?" Her mouth dropped open.

The woman chuckled. "Barely, but he does talk to me. I'm Lenore,

George's sister."

Angelique squinted her eyes in suspicion. "You look way too young to be his sister." The woman couldn't be more than late twenties.

"Aren't you a sweetie. I assure you I am old enough. There is twelve years between me and my brother, but I am his sister."

That put her in her early to mid-fifties, which didn't seem possible. Angelique was about to push the issue when she caught sight of George coming out of the kitchen. Lenore caught the shift in focus and stepped back to allow Angelique into the house. She ran over to hug George, emotions she hadn't known she was holding back flowing out.

"They took Jahnvi." She managed to get out the words through tearless sobs.

George rested a dinner plate-sized hand on her shoulder while she worked through her grief. From him, the gesture was equivalent to a full-on bear hug. Getting herself under control, she sat on the couch as Lenore fetched her a glass of cold water.

When Lenore returned, she sat on the chair across from Angelique. "George informed me that you have seen the Lidar o Fewar and called me to help explain."

"The what of what?"

"Much of what I am going to say will be confusing, but I will do my best to explain. Please, listen close. What do you know of Chansè Dopíncxiàn?"

"The what what?" She didn't like sounding ignorant, but this conversation was quickly veering into weird waters.

"Chansè Dopíncxiàn," Lenore said as though she was speaking about the existence of gravity. "They were the first powers on this world. Supernatural beings. You might know about some of them from different mythologies around the world."

"Around the world? It sounded Chinese to me."

"Well, yes and no. Omiach is the original language, and all languages originate from it. It was what the Chansè Dopíncxiàn spoke before the Gobrichenestamm shattered the unity. Now, there are thousands of languages and as many myths about the Chansè Dopíncxiàn. But right now, you need to know about Ngedia, the darkest branch of the broken Chansè Dopíncxiàn."

Angelique shook her head to clear it. "I feel like you're almost talking my language, but not quite."

"The awakened usually have years to learn of the hidden worlds. I do not know how long you have."

"I'm sorry, you don't know how long I have for what? And what is an awakened?"

"You are awakened, one who can see the actions of the Yetedebek'u Hayilati, the Shrouded Children. As for not knowing how long you have, the Lidar o Fewar are protective of their secrecy. Violently protective. George described your encounter, and it is clear that they are aware you are awakened."

"What do you mean I could see them? I mean they were in the shadows, but they were still standing out in the open."

"The majority of the world would have looked at the side of the house as you did and seen nothing. You saw them. You have the Blood, the essence of the Hai Zemin, the children of the old ones. That is why you can see them and others cannot."

"Can you see them?"

Lenore hesitated, looking at George, who remained as passive as ever. It took her a moment to make up her mind on what to say. Angelique stayed silent. She'd learned adults usually couldn't handle the silence of a kid and gave away more than they intended to.

"Yes, but I am not like you."

Her hesitation made Angelique think she was lying. "So, how do we stop them." She'd press the point when it was to her advantage.

"I have already called for a SWAT team," Lenore rolled her eyes, "but it will take several days."

Angelique narrowed hers in confusion. "So, the cops are awakened? Why didn't they swerve on them earlier?"

"Not the police, the council of the Hai Zemin. Their enforcement teams have called themselves many things, clerics, druids, Templars, Crusaders, knights, Pinkertons, and recently SWAT. But they all mean the same thing, killers of the Ngedia."

"Why days? You make it sound like I could die tonight."

Sadness touched Lenore's eyes. "Yes, it is possible. But evil is everywhere, and this is one small, insignificant case. Each year, there are less and less awakened around to deal with them."

"So, the awakened aren't having enough kids; that's why I'm going to die? Because enough people aren't getting it on?"

All around her, girls popped out babies like they were popcorn. Babies having babies who have babies. Tisha down the street was thirty-one and a grandmother. Tisha's mother was forty-seven and a great-grandmother. Babies seemed to be the only product this hood could produce. But Angelique was going to die because not enough people were doing their duty.

"It is not that simple. The Blood is a confusing, antiquated term. Like genes, it is passed from parents to children, but unlike other traits, it seems random who will get the Blood. But it is the non-Blood awakened who are dwindling. Less people are willing to accept the possibility of the supernatural. So, we do not have people to staff our SWAT, or our protection teams, or even our government."

"What I do till then?"

"Be alert in the dark, the Lidar o Fewar abhor the light. Also, stay inside, do not look out your window no matter what you hear. It is difficult for the

Lidar o Fewar to attack a grown child. Their powers of gentling are not meant to be used on anyone except toddlers and younger. But if you look at them, if you acknowledge them, their ability to affect you grows."

"So, hide inside? That's your plan? Be a coward?"

She chuckled. "George said you were a fighter. Yes, stay inside."

"What if they come to grab more kids."

"There is no if. They love areas like this where the population of young children is high but the police involvement is low. Already, the police are reducing the number of staff working on the kidnapping case from this morning. They do not have the manpower to pursue cases that typically do not have a resolution."

"I won't let another baby be taken."

"You are fourteen, how will you stop them?"

"Well, when I made a racket, they evaporated, or transported, or whatever. I'll just do that again."

"Except they disappeared because you startled them. By now, they'll know you're harmless."

"Then I'll find a way to hurt them, you know, a spell or something."

"It is not so simple." Her eyes flicked to her brother, who sat as passive as ever. "It would take years of training."

The eye flick was enough to let Angelique know she was lying again.

She pounced. "You lied to me once, and I let that go." She took a long breath to calm herself. "If you have something, give it to me. Or you use it yourself; I'm just as open to that. I'll still back ya; I'm not a coward. But at the end of the day, someone is going to go out there and protect the children. Period point blank."

Lenore looked at her brother again, and her shoulders slumped. "Take this."

She pulled a silver ring, with a ruby the size of a robin's egg, out of her pocket and placed it in the girl's palm. It had to be worth more than all the houses on her street combined.

"I can't take this."

"If you do not want to die, you will have to."

"If the cops see me with something like this, they'll arrest me. And if ignorant peoples out there see me with it, they'll kill me to get it."

"You have to be awakened to see it. A Folmas is hard to master, but it will prevent the Lidar o Fewar from killing you outright."

"Outright?"

"They can still get to you with enough time and planning. They are not beasts, they are intelligent, cold creatures. You take this job on, there is a good chance you are going to die."

"What about the SWAT team? Don't I just have to stay alive until they show up?"

Lenore looked at George again, and he shrugged. "Yes..." she steeled herself for the next part, "but they may not be the saviors you think. You already know Lidar o Fewar can evaporate; it makes catching them problematic. The only time they are constrained to this plane of existence is when they abduct a child. If they evaporate, the child is left behind. Once they have a child, they do not let it go. The best way to kill them is with a child in their arms."

"And the kid?"

"They usually do not survive the encounter." She looked at George again.

"Go ahead and tell me, I can handle it."

Her eyes filled with pity. "Once they've locked on, they will not stop till they have the child." She hesitated before adding, "Or teenager."

Angelique pursed her lips in understanding. "So, if I go out there looking for them, I'm going to be the one they're carrying when the SWAT comes a killin'?"

"Possibly."

"Shady."

"Indeed. And further complicating the issue, the Ngedia's dark power is a counterpoint to the Hai Zemin's power, making equal or lesser forces ineffective. They cannot just send one or two officers; they need enough to tip the balance structure in their favor."

"Alright, what's the best way to find them?"

"The Lidar o Fewar?"

"Are we talkin' about anything else?"

"No, I guess not. I do not know. I am not an expert on them. I am a Tender."

"Tender?"

"Taking care of people, making sure they are safe, to themselves and others."

"Whatever that means. Why doesn't George talk to me?"

The question caught Lenore off guard. George stared at her with that same passive face. Not emotionless, like most people thought, but passive. Of course George had feelings, only his face didn't express them.

"I should let George answer that."

Angelique couldn't hold back the laugh. No, it was more of a chortle. She had read that word a while back and hadn't really understood how it could be a real thing. She got it now.

"Nice cop out."

George sighed and rubbed the bridge of his nose. Angelique's mouth dropped open. That was more communication from him than she had seen in two years.

Lenore said, "George was involved in an incident years back. It was...traumatic for him. His response was to withdraw from the world."

"But he talks to you?"

"Me and our mother. Even then it is very rare to hear the beautiful bass of my little brother."

Angelique almost spit out the sip of water she had taken. "Little?"

"Yes, he is younger by twelve years." Lenore looked at her watch. "You should be going if you are going to patrol the streets tonight. You will need your sleep."

"What was the event?"

"What event?"

"Don't play dumb. The traumatic one."

"That is not my story to tell. Maybe one day, George will deem it necessary for you to know. Now, run along." Lenore stood, took Angelique's glass, and motioned her to the door.

Her head was spinning as she went home and lay down in her bed. She had to focus on finding and stopping the lidder o fewer or whatever they were. She couldn't, wouldn't, let another child be taken.

She always thought in movies, kids were idiots for not involving the adults. The *adults will never believe us* excuse was lame. But here, if they were standing right next to her as she stared down the monsters, they wouldn't see them. She thought of going back and begging for George's help, but it was clear he wasn't getting involved. The edge between awareness and sleep blurred together, and Angelique drifted off to sleep with feelings of helplessness.

Nightmares and panic held a strong grip over her mind as she slept the day away. Thoughts of Jahnvi in those monsters' grasp, of all the things they might be doing to her, paraded around her psyche like a macabre slideshow. She could feel herself trying to look away, but her eyelids wouldn't close and the scenes of horror were everywhere.

Crying from her brothers' room brought her bolt upright in bed. *Peter must need a diaper.* She rested her head on her pillow as she let her heartbeat come down. She was pretty sure her mom was home and would take care of it. If not, Aunt Gail should do some work to earn her keep around here.

The crying dug into Angelique's brain like claws. Sitting up, she concentrated on the sound. Peter was crying, but so was Matthew. His distinct stuttering, gulping cry slid across her spine. Angelique slipped her feet into cold shoes and padded down the hall to their room. Her stomach roiled with anxiety as she place a hand against the cheap hollow-core door and pushed.

Curled into a ball at the center of the small room, Levi whimpered. Matthew, tears and snot mixing on his lip, stood in front of Peter's crib, arms out protectively. Cool night air fogged their breath as Angelique tracked from each of her brothers across the garish circus wallpaper to the bookcases on the far wall.

Standing there, outlined by the faint light from the hallway, were three Lidar o Fewar, heads bent to accommodate the low, sloping roof. White, burning eyes focused on her. Like an incoming storm, she felt a pressure build inside her head.

A siege on her consciousness made her knees weak, and she slumped to the floor. Gliding over the dusty carpet, they loomed over the boys, ready to take their prizes. A scream built in her chest, but the psychic attack took the wind right out of her lungs. Darkness gathered around her as long, revolting arms reached for her brothers.

Ba bu bu bu baa Ba, Ba bu bu bu baa Ba, Ba ba ba ba ba ba ba.

Hooded heads snapped toward the door where "La Cucaracha" was fading from the speaker at the top of the stairs. Her mom thought the sound was hilarious for a doorbell. It wasn't hilarious, but it was distracting.

The pressure in her head broke, and she slipped her hand into her pocket. By the time the creatures realized there was no threat, she was wearing the massive ruby ring. It glowed bright enough to be seen through the denim of her jeans. The effect on the Lidar o Fewar was immediate, forcing them against the back wall.

In a flash, they were sucked out of the open window like smoke, or, more accurately, mist. The trails left behind were the only evidence anything was amiss, and they were fading fast. "La Cucaracha" sounded again, and she heard the couch springs groan as Gail got up to answer the door. She could hear the couch springs because the boys had stopped crying. All three were asleep right where they had been. She got Matthew and Levi back into bed after closing, locking, and pulling a bookshelf in front of the window. She wiped their faces and tucked Peter back in.

Taking the stairs two at a time, she found Pari in the living room, speaking with Angelique's mother. Her face was puffy from crying, her normal vibrancy absent. She looked old, broken.

"Angelique, Pari has some questions for you."

"I don't really have tim—"

"You caused her trouble, you'll talk to her."

"No, no, Missus Helen, she's been a comfort to me."

"Angelique?" Her mother's eyebrows shot up in surprise.

Angelique hated her for the disbelief.

"Yes, your daughter is quite wonderful."

"Well, I'm glad she's wonderful somewhere."

Pari frowned but spoke to Angelique in a gentle voice. "Have you seen them again?" The hope in her eyes almost killed the young girl.

"They were just in the boys' room."

"What?" the two older women exclaimed in unison.

"It's okay, I chased them off. But I think they'll be back tomorrow. They want the boys."

"We gotta call the cops," her mother said.

"Ya think?" Angelique couldn't keep the disdain out of her voice. "I'm going to be sitting in the boys' room till the morning. Then I'll do it again tomorrow night. They're not gettin' my brothers."

"Did they have Jahnvi?" Pari's desperation was almost tangible.

"No, I'm sorry. But one was missing, maybe she was with him."

Angelique shrugged, unable to give the woman more comfort, but she felt the need to be back upstairs now. Back in her room, she grabbed her comforter, phone, and pillow before heading to the boys' room. Through the door, she saw the window wide open, the bookshelf toppled on its side. The boys were gone.

At the window, she saw them below, at the edge of the lawn, heading toward the top of the hill. Racing downstairs, she blew past the women and out the door. Realizing they'd been seen, the Lidar o Fewar picked up their pace. They were fast. She heard her mom calling after her.

She yelled over her shoulder as loud as possible, "They have the boys."

Bird-dogging the mythical monsters trying to steal her brothers, she stayed on their heels. It wouldn't go down like this. The world crapped on her day after day, but she wouldn't become her mother, broken by the misery. Misery was Angelique's strength, her motivation. She might not be school smart, but she earned. She might not be legit, but she held her own against thugs. She might not be some superhero, but she was going to wild out on these suckers.

Her initial enthusiasm gave out about the same time that the burn in her legs reached critical mass as she trudged up the hill. At the top, she looked down and saw them taking the corner onto Grand Ave. Going downhill was easier and faster, but by the time she made the turn, she knew it wasn't going to be enough. They were already rounding onto McKinney.

Taking a chance, she veered into the empty lot at the top of Grand, hopping the low chain-link fence at the back. Sliding more than running, she charged down the embankment. Twice she missed a fallen tree by inches. Branches whipped her face and fallen limbs scratched her arms, but she ignored the pain.

Skidding to a stop on the asphalt, she looked right and saw the Lidar o Fewar crossing the street a block away. One caught sight of her and gave a screech of surprise. She smiled and took off across the yards. They were sticking to the streets which gave her the advantage. Hopping fences and dodging chained-up dogs, she came out only steps behind them as they turned up the hill toward the old school. Once again, the incline didn't faze them, but it was everything Angelique could do to keep going. All the ground she had gained was lost as she crested the hill only to find them already at the bottom. She was going to lose them.

Hope ignited in her chest when, without hesitation, they turned into the abandoned Sedler's Funeral Home. *It had to be a funeral home, of course.* Long strides carried her down the hill in a rush. Almost too fast. Pure luck kept her from crashing and burning on the pavement. Carrying that momentum into the turn, she pulled up in front of the door to the crumbling building. She'd been inside a few times when it had been a trap house, to get her cousin Margaret when she was strung out. Fear had never been a problem before, but now menace flowed out of the place like ocean waves rolling over her.

Hall of Heroes

Swinging the door open, she peered into the dark interior. The light from the street lamp three houses away couldn't penetrate the inky blackness beyond the threshold. Her lungs pulled in deep gasps, drowning out any possibility of hearing anything inside. Angelique steeled herself and stepped through.

She didn't know what she expected, but nothing wasn't it. Inside, the air was warmer, but that was expected. Or at least that was what should have been expected. Every horror movie had prepared her for a bone-chilling cold, indicating the presence of evil in the house. But her breath didn't suddenly show, ice didn't form on the windows, and a chill didn't run down her spine. Nothing seemed out of the ordinary. *Except*, she thought, *you know...for the demons and things. No big deal.*

Creeping through the foyer, she found two doors on either side of a long hallway. The left led to an empty chapel, the right to a business office with another door set into the back wall. Brilliant light escaped from around the door, brighter than should have been possible.

At least she didn't have to guess where to go. Inching through the office, careful not to disturb the furniture, she watched for traps or hidden figures waiting to spring out at her. Not that she knew how to spot either, but it seemed like the right thing to do. Tapping the doorknob with her middle finger, she checked for heat. She knew there wasn't a fire beyond, but she didn't know the rules of this new reality and caution seemed the best route. *Well, as cautious as I can be chasing after monsters, that is.* The knob was cool to the touch, and she gripped it, ready to turn.

As she applied twisting pressure, she froze, an alarm going off in her head. These creatures hated light, why would they be in a room full of it? Backing into the hall, she caught a flash of movement, white eyes reflecting off polished marble stairs.

Giving chase, the dark obscured the first step, and Angelique smashed face first into the risers. Bleeding from a cut on her forehead, she pushed on, scaling the stairs on all fours like a cat chasing its prey. Regained her footing on the landing, she took the rest two at a time. With only the vaguest impression of movement in the dark, she thought it slipped into the last room on the left. Whimpers from her brothers confirmed the direction, and they gave new strength to her legs.

Barreling through the door, she found all four Lidar o Fewar in a semicircle, waiting for her. She tried to stop, but tripped, momentum throwing her to the ground. Blood poured from her head, soaking into the stained, white shag carpeting. They didn't rush her as she scrambled back to her feet. They were waiting for something, but she didn't know why.

Staring at their leathery faces, she saw for the first time skin stretched too thin and yellow, all-too-human teeth behind their mandibles. They watched with mismatched eyes, hands holding her brothers, who mewled pathetically. Grooved, dirt-filled lines covered large hands, making the creatures look ancient.

With a start, she realized that she could see them. A second ago, the house was so dark she stumbled over carpets and fell on the stairs. She raised her hand and saw the giant ruby glowing with a bright, white light. It didn't fill the room like stories might have said, but it was as bright as the flashlight on her phone. Bright enough to keep the Lidar o Fewar from attacking her.

"Give me my brothers." Angelique held the ring out like a talisman.

"Ours," the single-eyed monster said in a smooth tenor voice. It disturbed her that it sounded so normal.

"Mine." She stepped forward, trying to force the light closer to them.

They didn't budge. "Ours," another of the creatures repeated.

"You can't just take them and then say they're yours."

"We have. You have no power to stop us."

"I have this." She held the ring higher.

It took her a second to recognize the screeching sound they made as laughter. Fear pooled in her stomach like cold oil. She dodged the chair thrown at her head by a fraction of an inch.

"We cannot touch you, but that does not mean we cannot harm you." A vase crashed against the wall beside her.

Ducking and weaving, she tried to avoid the improvised missiles, but there were too many. Pain electrified her body as a glass ashtray smashed into her left side, ribs cracking with the impact. She stumbled against the wall, fighting to stay upright. Then the coffee table crushed her chest and legs into the brittle drywall. If there had been a stud behind her, she would have been dead.

One of the Lidar o Fewar pulled the table away, and Angelique crumpled to the floor, groans only escaping when the impact forced air out of her lungs. Pain radiated through her hands and feet, but they wouldn't move. Setting the table aside, they reformed the half-circle. Behind them, the boys lay on their sides, eyes wide with fear. The light from the ring dimmed, and they faded into the darkness. The Lidar o Fewar pressed in on her, seeming to force the light back with their presence. Whimpers escaped her lips.

"Your light is fading, child," One-eye said. "We don't prefer essence as old and tough as yours, but we never turn away a free meal."

Their hands rested on the light like it had a physical presence. It shrunk under their sustained attack, and second by second, their long arms drew closer to her face.

"Why can't you just leave us alone?" She hated sounding weak, but weak was what she was.

"Why can you not behave like the food you are?" the three-eyed one asked. "That would be splendid."

Impossibly, she saw tentacles of darkness stabbing through the sphere of light, reaching out for her. They writhed and wriggled their way through the light as though worms moving through soil. Sweat poured into the gash on her head, but the pain was lost amongst the fear pulling her mind in a thousand directions.

"When we are done with you, we will enjoy your brothers at our leisure. I can smell the little one's sweetness from here." It was One-eye again.

"Please." The one word was pathetic, but it was all Angelique could muster. A simple plea she knew would be ignored.

The light flickered, and she held her breath. It flickered again. The end had come. Three-eye's grey-green, moldy tongue flicked over his teeth as the dark tendrils pressed in closer. Light pulsed in and out now like a strobe. In starts and stops, she saw them reach for her. Smoke sizzled where one of the dark lines touched her face.

Wet and meaty, the crack startled her as one of the two-eyed monsters roared in pain. In the blinking light, a new beast ravaged the Lidar o Fewar. Violent hammer fist blows drew a chorus of screeches and howls. Hidden by the darkness, it looked like a gorilla, or maybe Bigfoot. Could Bigfoot be here to save her? Warm fluid splashed against her arms and face. In the dizzying light, she caught glimpses of red and green dripping from her forearm. The Lidar o Fewar were inching back into the far corner of the room, her rescuer exuding savagery in every movement. The SWAT team must have arrived in time after all.

Shoulders heaving with deep breaths, the hulking form stopped halfway between her and them, exactly over where the boys lay.

"Concentrate," a man's deep voice said.

Concentrate on what? she thought.

"The Folmas," he said.

Can he read my mind?

There wasn't time for an answer. He was talking about the ring, the only protection she had. *Concentrate on the ring.* Closing her eyes, she attempted to focus, but fear overwhelmed her, and they snapped open. She feared the man would be gone, the white-eyed monsters on her again. But the scene was unchanged.

She closed her eyes a second time. There was no increase of light against her eyelids, so she strained her mind harder. Nothing. Struggling, she tried to recall everything she knew about the ring, which shouldn't have been hard because it was next to nothing. The one thing she did know for certain was that she had never needed to command the light before, it just reacted. *Why isn't it working now?*

"Believe it will," the man said, more in control of his breathing this time.

That settled it, he could read her mind. *Believe it will?* When the ring worked before, she had held it out against them because she was told it would work. She hadn't shifted that belief though, so why wasn't it working now? The only belief that had changed was the belief that she would survive this. A table to the chest can do that. Accepting death as her fate had been the beginning of the flickering. Now, the man was here, the creatures were beaten, and she would survive.

The light blossomed, and she opened her eyes to see George standing over her brothers, red blood streaming from gashes on his forehead. His fists dripped with the strange green blood of the Lidar o Fewar. Standing sideways to the creatures, back to the door, he looked at her, keeping them in his peripheral vision.

"You saved us," she said, tears filling her voice. "You talked, and you saved us." Both were equally confusing in this moment.

"Not yet," George's voice rumbled with an ominous undertone. "I tire. They bide their time."

"So, let's get out of here."

"Yes, run, prince," Three-eye said, almost in a whisper.

"Running is death. Without the boys..."

"I'll help you fight." She gasped as she tried to stand, the pain in her chest taking all the air out of her.

"You cannot fight. You must go."

"I thought you said we can't run."

"We, no. You, yes."

"I'm not leaving my brothers."

"You must."

"Yes, leave them to us. The prince is a nice addition as well."

"Quiet, Ngedia."

"Your commands are weak, prince."

"Comply," George snapped back.

"You have authority over these things, and you let them take my brothers?" Angelique wavered between hurt and outrage.

"Not authority, conventions." His face wasn't looking directly at her, but she could still see the sadness and pain in his eyes.

She was wasting time. If he knew how to get her out of this, then she would do whatever it took.

"What do I do?"

"Find the path, the Shroud, it is near."

"What?"

"The Shroud. Hidden world. Open it, and I will bring us inside."

"So, I have to find it, come back, and lead you to it?"

"No. I will do from here. Must...go quickly." His knotty leg muscles quivered. "Am weak."

Slowly, she stood. Black dots swam in her vision, but she pushed through. *I will save them.* With that thought, streams of light made their way through her veins, filling her with a warmth that pushed away the pain. The more she believed in herself, the more the ring helped her.

"How do I find it?"

"Brilliant light, brighter than—"

Angelique didn't wait for the rest; she bolted out the door. George called after her, but she'd already reached the stairs. She knew where she was going, she knew what she had to do, and she knew she was going to do it. The ring's power filled her body as her confidence grew.

Leaping down the stairs, aiming for the door on the left of the hallway, she never saw the chair aimed at her head. Her speed saved her as it missed its mark and took her in the arm instead, slamming her into the wall. Losing her footing, she avoided a second projectile. George's words caught up to her conscious mind now. *One missing.* Without looking, she knew it was One-eye. He hadn't been in the room upstairs, but she'd been too occupied with George to register the fact.

Doesn't matter, she thought as she stood up. *I know how to work the ring now, and I will succeed. I just have to get moving.*

Without a glance at the creature, she darted into the office and slammed the door. There was no lock, so she climbed up on the nearby file cabinet, using her weight to rock it away from the wall till it fell, creating a barrier she hoped would slow the cyclops down. At the back of the room, she swung the door open wide.

Nothing happened.

The room wasn't bright; it was dark. She didn't teleport, evaporate, get beamed up. Nothing. The light from her ring flickered, but she concentrated on refusing to give up. She would find another...was that movement beyond the door?

The understanding hit her hard. If there was nothing magical beyond the door, then her ring should have been lighting the room beyond up. Instead there was only light-swallowing blackness. Something was there. Dozens of white eyes opened.

The room beyond was filled with Lidar o Fewar, crammed into each other, folded over each other, melding with each other. Dozens of eyes had been wrong. Looking into the far distance, Angelique could see glowing eyes for what looked like miles. Those in front smoked where the light touched them. Pressing hands against the light, they pushed, and she felt herself totter. The mass of monsters behind lent their strength to the effort, and she slid back a few inches on the deep plush carpet.

Grabbing the door, she threw her shoulder into it, forcing it closed. It made it about three quarters of the way before meeting the hands of the first Lidar o Fewar. She shoved her ring hand around the backside, trying to push the mass back. They screamed in pain, but the crowd behind pressed them forward. Hollow thuds reverberated from behind as One-eye forced his way in.

Come on, George. What's taking so long? Craning her neck, she saw One-eye making his way toward her with an unhurried pace.

The light of the ring formed a shield around her. She wasn't naïve enough to think it could protect her for long. She had to think. *Why can't George use the path? Because it's blocked.* She remembered Lenore mentioning that. The Ngedia's power interfered with the Hai Zemin's power. She had to clear the way. But how? They'd be up the stairs and on George before the last vile creature cleared the doorway.

One-eye joined the assault on the globe of light, and she felt power drain from the ring. She didn't know how, but she knew it was failing. Turning her attention to the Folmas, she saw streams of liquid light flowing out of her flesh, drawing strength from her. *That's why belief makes it stronger.* Believing you're going to fail is more than a bad mindset; it has real, physical consequences. She read about it one time.

"Take more," she said to the ring.

"We will take all of you," One-eye said from behind.

She ignored him. "Take more," she insisted.

Like cloud cover over the sun lessening, she thought the intensity of the brightness increased, but she couldn't be sure. She commanded again, and its brilliant pulses in time with her heartbeat confirmed it had complied. Aches from her injuries reasserted themselves as her energy drained away.

Keeping the light going a little longer was fantastic, but if she didn't figure out how to clear the path, it would be futile. One-eye grunted in effort behind her as the new power pushed him back. It was too bad the light had to be symmetrical. It would be great to put most of the power up front like in Star Trek.

"Power to the forward shields, Mr. Data." She would have laughed at herself if the pain hadn't been so intense.

Then the light shifted, narrowing around her, forming a blunted cone. The large circular surface pointed at the door while the smaller circle was keeping One-eye at bay behind. With the energy focused forward, the creatures' progress out of the door halted. The front few burned to ash as they were ground against the flat plane of light. Acrid smoke, like diapers being burned, burned her nostrils.

More energy, take more. Please. She didn't know if the ring was alive or could feel, but she emphasized the please, begging it to listen to her.

It did. Life force rushed like a river out of her now. Pain coursed through her body, her knees barely able to keep her upright. She didn't dare slow the flow; the Lidar o Fewar were sliding back from the threshold, deeper into the magical realm beyond. She needed to give more, but the ring resisted taking it. She was close to winning, and the ring was trying to snatch it from her grasp.

Please, she pleaded with it again. *I can't fail. I can't let them die.*

She had never thought of herself as particularly loving toward her brothers. She did love them, but there had always been a distance. The fact that their father stuck around while hers didn't care. Or the fact that he gave them money while insulting her for being born. So, it came as a surprise to her when she found she was ready and willing to give her life for them.

Clarity struck like lightning. The ring was refusing to take more because it would hurt her. Maybe kill her. She would miss so much. It didn't matter. It didn't matter how much she would miss, it didn't matter that it might not even work, it only mattered that she gave everything she could.

"Take it all." There was no tremor in her voice. "Take my life."

Her vision narrowed to a pinprick of light, and then she was pulled through the tiny hole. Hurtling through the air, she was one with the light, the power of creation, and they didn't push the foul monsters aside, they decimated them. She could hear One-eye screaming in pain and rage as their light burned a hole straight through his chest. In front of them, the foul beasts vaporized under the light's assault, and a glowing path flowed under her, them, as she, they, soared on. Brilliant, purple rock towers were off to the right, blue plants to the left and a golden sky floated above her, their, heads. Bodiless, she, they, saw it not with eyes, but all at once.

Her progress slowed, and with each passing second, the light dimmed as it moved away from her. The energy spent, she was fading into nothingness. Oblivion swallowed her whole, and Angelique was no more.

"Wake, your prince commands you."

Angelique tried to ignore the voice, to continue drifting through her nothingness. It wasn't for her anyway; she was no princess and definitely didn't have no prince.

"Wake," the voice called again, the command more insistent.

Inching open, her eyelids revealed the darkened room beyond. George's living room. She was lying on his couch with Lenore, George, the boys, and her mother spread around the room. Every joint, muscle, and bone in her body hurt. George's massive hand gently lifted her head and placed a pillow under it.

"What happened?" She struggled to get the words out through her dry mouth.

"You have come into your power, little one." He seemed to hesitate for a moment. "And forced me out of hiding."

She took a gulp of the cold water Lenore offered her. With less effort this time, she said, "What and what?"

George chuckled. "It won't be long before your slumber returns; I'll be brief. You already know you are of the Blood. What you don't know is that you are of Velin lineage." He held his hand up to shush the girl. "Don't talk, I'll explain what I can. Velin were the first children of the Chansè Dopíncxiàn after the breaking. They are among the most powerful of the Yetedebek'u Hayilati, the Shrouded children. Not many are left now; they have been hunted by the Ngedia for centuries." He waited while she took another drink.

"You controlled the Folmas." He tapped the ring. "Which means your inheritance of the Blood is substantial. Your sacrifice to save us and the trauma of the event activated your power and now you stand as one of the Yetedebek'u Hayilati, subject to the Hai Zemin council, and citizen of my court."

"Hold on," Angelique blurted out before George could continue. "You're royalty, and I think you meant to say when I tried to sacrifice myself, right?"

"I am a direct descendant of Maniolat, the Lord-Warrior of the Chansè Dopíncxiàn. As such, I am one of the twelve princes of the Hai Zemin council and ruler of the May Court. And no, I meant what I said. You died and entered the realm of the eternal morning. It was difficult to retrieve you."

"So, what happens now?" The question came from Angelique's mother, who sat anxiously on the edge of a chair, bouncing Peter on her knee.

"In most cases, the newly blooded have a choice on how they want to proceed. They can reject their heritage and live a normal life. They may learn about their powers on their own, under the oversight of the council. They can allow the council to train them. Or they can go on a killing rampage." He looked at Angelique with a hint of a smile. "But this is not most cases. Your daughter's power is too great to suppress, so a normal life is out of the question. The number of mentors is stretched thin; she will not find one attentive enough to keep her from hurting herself or others. Self-study is out. The council is more divided now than ever before as our numbers drop. They would use her as a blunt force weapon and break her. The council is out. And you already did your killing rampage on the Lidar o Fewar. The only thing left that I could think of was that I would train you personally."

"Really?" Angelique tried to sit up, but the pain kept her in place. "Won't you be busy with all the royal stuff?"

A heavy sigh shook George's shoulders. "Currently, my court consists of me, my mother, Lenore, and you. When I was younger, I let my power loose, and people died. My citizens abandoned me."

"You pushed them away, brother; they did not abandon you." Lenore rested her hand on George's shoulder and looked at Angelique. "He retreated within himself and left the court without protection. The citizens had to change courts to survive."

"Whatever the case," George said, clearly uncomfortable, "I have time."

"Train me to do what?"

"I don't know. There's a whole world of possibilities out there and part of our journey will be finding ones suited to you."

"Will we train here?"

George looked at Angelique's mother. "Some may be here, but for now, we must travel to the Shroud, to where your power will be the least...unpredictable."

Angelique didn't know which emotion was more powerful for her mother, sadness or relief. Both were clear on her face. Angelique didn't resent her for that; her face was a mirror image.

"When do we leave?"

"Now would be best. You'll heal faster in the Shroud."

"When will I be back?"

"When we can."

"Can I pack?"

"You cannot take things from this world to the Shroud."

"Not even our clothes?"

"No, clothes will be provided."

"Mom, can you bring the boys over so I can say goodbye?"

"That would be best done on your next visit," Lenore said. "The gentling of the Lidar o Fewar has not worn off, and they will not remember anything for the next few days."

"Well, okay then. Mom—"

"I know, Angelique. Be safe."

Her mother, boys in tow, left. George and Lenore stared after the woman in confusion.

"We're not really that close," Angelique said, trying to explain away the pain that stabbed through her heart. "We're family, but that doesn't mean much. It's more of an obligation than a desire." She looked between them. "Let's go."

George took her hands, and she felt the power building behind them.

"So, you going to tell me what my power is?"

Lenore answered. "Your power is what you choose it to be."

"So, I can do anything?"

"In a manner," Lenore said. "But once you choose a power, it can never be changed."

"Never?"

"Never," George said. "That is our first task in training, discovering the form of your power. It only sets your destiny in stone. No pressure."

George smiled the first smile she had ever seen him make. It was the greatest smile she had ever seen.

The world faded to white.

Living in a city overrun with poverty, drugs, and violence I am constantly amazed by the resilience and strength of the children I have the privilege of working with. I wanted to show case their inner power and the struggles they have to deal with and I find fantasy is a good way to introduce people to the horrors of the real world. I hope this story opens your eyes to the tragedy, plight, and hope of these kids' lives.

http://bit.ly/davidmillican

Presenting... The Steampendous Adventures of Josiah U. Bear and the Rubber Barons

D. W. Frauenfelder

Josiah U. Bear was a gentlebear—he would brook no argument about that.

In the endless debate surrounding the circumstances of the ancient and legendary civilizing of the Upright Bears, Josiah—airship racer and international spy—was firmly in the camp that bears had always been destined by heaven for genteel society.

But there was no reason for filing his teeth to obsequious bluntness, or cutting his claws down so far that they would be of no use in a fistfight, as some overly conscientious, so-called gentlebears had made a point of doing.

Which is why Josiah U. Bear happened to end up in a courtroom of British Bearland one fine September morning in the colonial capital, Port Courageous (in Bearish, Bna Gofol), on the charge of Raking and Biting a Colonial Official.

"Josiah Ursulinus Bear, accused in the sight of the Crown of grievous bodily harm of a British constabulary officer of the peace in a regulated drinking establishment, how do you plead?"

The judge was a dry, pale fellow with a dry, pale voice and was wearing a dry, pale wig.

"Not guilty, with prejudice, Your Lordship," Josiah replied.

"How many of these deuced animals have the family name of Bear?" Josiah heard the colonial solicitor whisper to his assistant (Josiah had superior hearing, as most bears did.)

"You appear without counsel, Bear?"

"I represent myself, Your Lordship. I have a degree from the Bearish Law College of Ra Unbakikio."

"There is no need to recite legal qualifications."

"Yes, Your Lordship."

The judge continued in his dry, pale fashion, "It is alleged that on twenty-first August instanter in the year of our Lord nineteen hundred and twelve, you did enter the regulated drinking establishment by the name of the Bee and the Fox and did order certain intoxicating beverages in the amount of five quarts."

"Respectfully, Your Lordship—"

"What?" The judge looked up dimly from the writ of accusation and put on his spectacles.

"—not at the same time."

"I beg your pardon?"

"I didn't order the beer and the mead all at the same time. It was over a number of...ah...hours."

The judge's pale cheeks erupted briefly into a chagrin of pink. "Please do not interrupt, Bear. This is not an informal chat; it is a court of law."

"Yes, Your Lordship."

Josiah twirled his waxed mustache, a fur feature unfavored by most gentlebears of the time, but to Josiah a fashion imperative.

"In the course of the evening, you, the defendant, did engage in insultatory banter with a party of the Anvorian diplomatic corps and in particular with one of its members, one...ah...Gunter...ah...Breckermann."

Josiah did not turn to acknowledge the presence in the courtroom of the Anvorian aide-de-camp to the Anvorian subaltern consul general. Breckermann was a nobody, a nothing, a *clebneps*, as he would be termed in Bearish.

"As the night wore on, the Anvorians reported growing ever more discomfited with the nature of your remarks, which have been reported to the Crown as having a possibly insurrectionist cast."

"Your Lordship, if I may, this word insurrectionist..."

"Quiet, Bear," barked the bailiff. He should have barked indeed. His jowls gave him a distinct visual affinity with the British bulldog.

Josiah raised a bristly eyebrow but said nothing.

The judge gave an audible sniff. "On or about the legal closing time of ten o'clock in the evening, a disagreement broke out between yourself and Herr Breckermann which devolved into an incident of bare fisticuffs." He turned to the recorder and said, in an even dryer voice, "That is spelled B-A-R-E."

Breckermann had questioned Josiah's latest airship contest, in which he had bested the Anvorian ace, Marius Grieb, but by hardly more than the nose of a balloon. The impertinent Breckermann had claimed that Josiah had cheated by deploying an illegal propeller on his gondola.

But the story that had all of the newspapers tittering was the presence of a Madame X Bear, a masked, anonymous competitor who was seven lengths clear of the pack when her engine failed and she had to make ultimately unsuccessful mid-air repairs.

At any rate, there were no fisticuffs involved. Breckermann had intended to leave the premises before any type of hostilities impended. He was restrained by his drunken and hilarious fellows.

It was only when the constabulary became involved that anything like "raking and biting" occurred. And even that was of the most minor sort. Any gentlebear who did not resort to cutting back his claws to a most unseemly length ran the risk of making what was called a "Brownbakikio railway" across the fabric of someone's coat.

Or across their cheek, in a more vigorous altercation.

"Beggin' yer pardon, yer Worship," said the constable, betraying a fine West Country accent. "But the behr, that 'un, he left na' a mark on me."

"What's that you're saying? Speak up," the judge said to the constable.

"The behr, 'e ain't left a claw on me, yer Worship. It was just a bit of fun, I'd say. This 'un—"

The constable was about to point out the Anvorian, Breckermann, but the judge put up his hand.

"Constable, you are not—"

Just then, a telegram cub burst into the room. At this time in Bearland, telegram cubs were everywhere, and they often burst into rooms unannounced. They were the very beating heart of Bearish telecommunication and as such were highly respected in the way that bear cubs seldom have been in this or any age.

The cub, clutching at his cap so that it would not fly off, leapt over the rail and bounced up to the judge, who opened the proffered message, read it, and glowered at Josiah.

"It appears," the judge said after a pregnant pause, "that the defendant is excused."

"What's that, Your Lordship?" said the solicitor, cupping a hand to his ear.

The judge banged his gavel. "This proceeding is recessed." And he motioned for Josiah to approach the bench.

The judge handed the telegram to Josiah. This is what it said:

JU BEAR NEEDED STOP URGENT MISSION STOP TOP SECRET STOP JUB TO GOVERNMENT HOUSE AT FIRST CONVENIENCE STOP NO TIME TO WASTE END

Josiah looked up from the note with a kind of benevolent indulgence. "It has been—" he searched for the proper turn of phrase "—a rare pleasure, Your Lordship."

Then he turned on his heel, made his way out of the courtroom with dignified haste, and left the courtroom's occupants with jaws agape.

Two

Government House in Bearland was a Grecian affair, and when I say Grecian, I do mean of the white marble and columns variety of Grecian. Despite the columns, it was the newest building in Bearland, built specially for the British suzerainty, and it was the building to which Josiah U. Bear was presently riding in a balloon bicycle taxi.

The traditional capital of Bearland was a quaint city called Brownbakikio, which overlooked a lake and was in the heart of beekeeping country. As such, it was unacceptable to the British, whose tender skin is most unable to tolerate the occasional companionable sting.

Instead, the British took up suzerainty of Bearland in Port Courageous, which smelled of salmon more than honey. Bears thought it a great waste to locate the administration here, as Bearish legislators lay great store by being proximate to abundant supplies of what they called "sweetgold," but the British were much more tolerant of the smell of fish than the touch of bees.

Josiah left the bear-and-steam-powered taxi with a generous tip of thirty-five Bearish bnoas—he had a reputation to uphold—and made his unhurried but efficient way up the gleaming steps of the building.

The bear guards on duty—dressed in Indian puttees and wide-brimmed Australian slouch hats—let Josiah by with hardly a flutter of their eyebrows, as he was a frequent visitor to Mr. Nigel Shambly, Deputy Undersecretary for Anvorian Relations, Revetements, and Restraint.

Shambly's assistant, a she-bear named Honeypenny, announced Josiah in quite a dignified fashion, but Shambly waved her away.

"Bosh!" he said. "Get in here, Bear. There's not a moment to lose."

"What's afoot this time, Undersecretary?" Josiah asked. "Anvorian tobacco growers trying to corner the market? A fixing of international field hockey matches?"

"No, Bear. Much worse." He was sweating, and the sparse, curly gray hair on his broad brow was matted down with it. His big ears were fiery red, his eyes filled with colonialist annoyance.

"What could be worse?" Josiah asked.

"Well, as you know, you Bears invited the British into Bearland to make sure the Anvorians do not conquer you and reduce you to abject servitude."

Josiah narrowed his eyes but said nothing.

"And it is our duty as civilizers of the world, this deuced continent included, to make sure that the Anvorians do not develop any kind of weapon or technique that would cause an imbalance between the two nations in...erm...lethal capability." Shambly scratched at a corner of his beard, cut in generous mutton chops.

"And, as you further know, the Anvorians have been coveting the Bearish rubber plantations for some time now, as rubber is becoming quite a sought-after commodity for such things as automobile tires."

"As well as the balloon bicycle conveyance," said Josiah. "Which I think will be much superior to the internal combustion engine for ease of transport." He was, in fact, quite heavily invested in finding patents for this type of vehicle.

"Except that the balloons keep exploding!" Shambly's voice betrayed a gruffness that indicated they had had this discussion before.

"A minor vexation, if the operators are properly—"

"Nevertheless." The word cut the air like a cleaver. "To the present case. Your Bearish spies have provided reliable intelligence that the Anvorians are currently developing a rubber bomb sling that will deliver explosives clad in, er, rubber."

Now Josiah's other eyebrow bristled. "Are there photographs of this contraption?"

"No, only poor photographs of the plans. Agent number Double Bee Six got himself hired as a functionary in the Springer SV rubber plant and found his way into the research and development wing."

"Double Bee Six." Josiah doubted there was such a bear, but he let Shambly continue.

"Yes, a bear so deeply placed even I do not know his true name. He found a number of other things, by the way. These explosives not only have the capacity of traveling over three miles in the air from a single well-slung shot, they will also achieve several bounces of up to fifty yards in the air before arriving at the target and exploding on a pre-set fuse."

Josiah waited while Shambly caught his breath.

"Thus, having calculated the average number of bounces per explosive, we have come upon the range of this rubber ball sling bomb to be something like four point three zero seven miles."

"That range is not terribly extraordinary compared to—"

"But, Bear," continued Shambly with an unmistakable note of triumph in his voice, "it is terribly, terribly quiet until the explosion of the bomb itself. Which means that no one on your side will know it is being used, or from where it is being used, because there is no charge from a cannon to warn you—not to mention no incoming whine."

"There surely must be a twang, however."

"A twang?"

"Of the sling, Undersecretary." Josiah had been a great aficionado of rubber slingshots as a cub. Window-breaking had been his secret—and then not-so-secret, when his father discovered it—vice. Josiah had been growled at with all the vehemence that a gentlebear can muster, as well as having his sling confiscated. The twang of the sling—no less than the growl of Father—was a vivid memory.

Shambly harrumphed. "We have no intelligence concerning a twang. The fact remains that this weapon would give a severe advantage of military might to the Anvorians at the expense of the bears, if allowed to go forward."

"So, what must we do, Undersecretary?"

"We, Bear, or rather, you, must infiltrate the Anvorian military apparatus at Springer SV and destroy their ability to manufacture flexible rubber. Here." He handed Josiah a small bottle with a dropper. "A dram of this in a vat of rubber will cause the whole mixture to be unable to coagulate, no matter how high the temperature."

"What is it?" Josiah inspected the bottle. It looked like something someone would take for a toothache.

"Your crack chemists put us on to it," Shambly said and put on reading glasses. He read from a piece of paper on his desk. "*Illyricum tembulans.* A tincture from the Eucalyptus tree, native to Australia. Normally used for laxatives. It quite causes everything it touches to be...erm...softened."

"I see."

"In its purest form, of course, it is quite powerful. And that is what you have."

"Duly noted." Josiah eased the bottle onto the table as if it were about to explode then posed another question. "Will this, ah, permanently disrupt manufacturing?"

"No, this is just a test run to see what effect it has. I suspect you'll be making dropper runs pretty frequently, depending on how this one goes. In the end, we may find a way to end Anvorian rubber manufacturing altogether."

The sinking feeling in Josiah's belly caused him to flex his claws—involuntarily, of course, as gentlebears seldom flex their claws on purpose. "But, ah, begging the Undersecretary's pardon... The manufacture of rubber at Springer is not only for military purposes."

"That's not our affair, Bear," Shambly roared, his face suddenly flushing. "This is the security of Bearland we're talking about. And, by extension, the British crown." He shook his head mournfully. "You bears are so ungrateful. Ask us to manage your affairs and restrain the Anvorians and then prate about the niceties of the Anvorian economy." He picked up a flyswatter, whacked at a honeybee that had strayed into the office somehow, and missed. "By Jove, your blasted insects!"

They watched the bee make a circuit of the office before settling on a set of Shambly's record books stacked in a bookshelf next to the window.

"And how, Undersecretary," Josiah continued, "do you propose that I gain access to the Anvorian, er, military rubber factories?"

"How should I know? You're the spy. Just do it, Bear. You *Ursi majores* keep saying you're superior in intelligence to us poor *Homines sapientes.* Prove it, for once."

"Yes, Undersecretary."

"It's for your own good, Bear."

"Yes, Undersecretary."

"And it should be done at once. Or else you'll be having quite a rash of exploding footballs on the borders of your dashed, bee-infested homeland." He eyed the honeybee, which must have been quite discomfited at the lack of pollen—not to mention mortal dangers—in the office.

"It will be done with all dispatch, Undersecretary."

"Honeypenny!" Shambly bawled. "Give Bear his stipend."

The door opened, and the bee flew out. "Yes, Undersecretary," Honeypenny said, standing at the threshold.

"Two thousand Anvorian francks, and not a fennick more, Honeypenny."

"Yes, Undersecretary."

"We have a budget, Honeypenny."

"Of course, Undersecretary."

Shambly harrumphed again, and Josiah took his leave, dropper bottle and francks in hand.

Three

Of course, Honeypenny had given Josiah five thousand francks instead of two. Giving an international spy on an urgent mission two thousand Anvorian francks is like giving a farmer a gardener's trowel to plow a field.

As it was, those francks would go to a good cause.

Josiah exchanged them at the Bank of Bearland for twenty-three thousand bnoas (a scandalous rate of exchange, but unavoidable) and went to the Bee and Fox, where he ordered two quarts of beer and one of mead and a plate of salmon jerky as aids to his strategical thinking.

Some hours later, and with two hundred fewer bnoas, he emerged from the pub with a capital idea.

Spending another one hundred and twenty bnoas on a balloon bicycle taxi (tip included), he alighted in the foothills of Port Courageous at the custom propeller shop of Gregarious Bearish.

Bearish was a slim and sinewy brown bear, as much as bears can be slim and sinewy, and he wore an aviator's skullcap with goggles, though he never went up in an airship. Instead, he used the goggles for eye protection when welding, which was his particular skill.

"Greg," said Josiah, "I have the balance for that propeller you were polishing off for me."

"It's about time," said Bearish. "I heard the race you just won had a purse of ten thousand francks. I was hoping to see a bit of that."

Josiah pulled out his wallet and handed over several red-and-gold banknotes. "Nearly all of that," he said, "went to the Honeymoon Fund."

"I completely understand," said Bearish, counting. "How is that coming along? You know—the Fund?"

Josiah closed one eye and looked left and right, as if making sure no one was within earshot. The Honeymoon Fund was code for the secret cash reserve that one day would pay for the British to leave Bearland. Some bears considered it money for arms and training. Others considered it ransom, to be used to buy back their independence. Still others, of the most genteel sort, thought it was strictly for bear widows and orphans. As bears are fiercely independent thinkers, they had no single plan for dealing with the British, nor any timetable. But every bear with a love for his or her homeland agreed on one thing: the need for the

Fund.

"The Fund is certainly coming along. But, sad to say, not large enough for the consummation to be announced yet."

Bearish nodded and scratched on a pad of paper before coming to the following conclusion: "Your account is...er...less behind than it was before."

"You can have some cubs deliver the prop to my hangar?" Josiah handed over another note.

"Today, Josiah. Today."

"Good. Because I have need of it."

"Right."

There were four thousand bnoas left in Josiah's wallet when he paid the taxi at his airship hangar near the Port Courageous docks. The corrugated iron structure had more than a few holes that let in the hot afternoon sun. These were left over from the unpleasantness with the Anvorian air navy twenty years before.

But inside was tethered the finest racing airship in the Continent (not counting Madame X Bear's somewhat faulty conveyance), which had achieved the record top speed of forty-seven miles per hour (not wind-aided) in the Slausburg Grand Prix of the Air two years before.

It was called the *Steampendous*.

Josiah's trusty assistant, a cub of tender years who happened to be his nephew, was also present, a fact his schoolmistressbear often lamented.

"Get her primed, Cubbleton," Josiah barked as he caught sight of the young bear, whose given name was Kenneth Quintilian Bear. "I'm off to Anvoria."

Cubbleton snatched up an oil can. "Another race so soon?"

"No, I'm on a mission to destroy the Anvorian rubber capability. It's top secret, so tell no one."

"Understood, uncle."

"A new propeller replacing the starboard aft one will be arriving within the hour," Josiah continued. "Make sure that gets attached snugly."

"Heavens and sky! Are you talking about the one that Gregarious honed for you?"

"That's the one."

"No one will catch you now!"

Josiah smiled so wide, his front fangs showed. "'Twill get us up to fifty-one or fifty-two, I'll wager!"

Cubbleton beamed ferociously as well.

"And put this growler of mead in the cockpit. I'll need fortification."

"Rig for night running lights?"

"No, Cubbles, no. This is top secret, I tell you."

"Yes, uncle."

Four

By a quirk of Bearish geography, a slim peninsula dived south far enough into a region of impressive volcanic activity to create a microclimate perfect for the cultivation of the rubber tree. Nowhere in Anvoria, which was mostly temperate in climate, could these tropical beauties grow. Over the past several decades, the Anvorians had been interested in controlling the Vulcanian Peninsula, and had raised more than one ruckus and to-do concerning it, but with the advent of the British, they had been kept on a diet of peace and high raw rubber prices.

Ruberotorck was the aptly named city in which the Anvorian rubber industry was headquartered. It lay some seven miles from the frontier of Bearland and some two hundred miles north of the northernmost Bearish rubber plantations. Ruberotorck was smoky and smelly and hardly a tourist attraction but cost the Anvorian rubber barons little in freight.

It was to Ruberotorck that Josiah U. Bear was headed in his newly-propellered *Steampendous*. Even with the finely-tooled blade giving the cigar-shaped balloon custom lift and propulsion, it would take nearly seven hours of flight to make it across the Gulf Of Bearland from Port Courageous to Vulcania and thence to Ruberotorck with its enormous sulfurous vats of boiling sap.

As such, Cubbleton loaded the steam engine that was the dynamo of the *Steampendous* with exactly one point eight pounds of Borschic super-peat, the fuel that created enough heat to fill Josiah's balloon and keep the propellers rotating for up to twelve hours straight.

In the cockpit, which was big enough only for Josiah, and snug at that, he had secured the mead and the dropper bottle of *Illyricum tembulans*.

He set out at around seven in the evening, just after the late summer sun had set, running incognito over the darkening waves of the gulf. A few cumulus clouds, tinged ultramaroon, loitered on the horizon, but otherwise the visibility was endless and the winds light and variable.

Close to two in the morning, Josiah found himself with a lighter load—less mead in the growler—and a bead on the largest Anvorian rubber factory in Ruberotorck, Springer Wirdschaftstwig SV.

Since the factory worked twenty-four hours a day and its open-air vats were always bubbling away, all Josiah had to do was fly over and drop a bit of *Illyricum tembulans* into one of them, and the entire Anvorian rubber industry would go kerplonk—at least for as long as the *Illyricum tembulans* worked—while giving the British Empire-owned Revulcan Products Limited a temporary monopoly over Bearish rubber.

For, you see, when the British had conquered Bearland, they had also seized control of rubber production and manufacture.

But Josiah had no intention of dropping anything into the vats at Springer. Far from it.

As he hovered over the factory, an array of ground-based spotlights switched on, searching and then finding the *Steampendous.*

"*Landten zee auf!*" called a guard on a watchtower through a megaphone.

Josiah used the spotlights to find the landing bay of the plant, throttling back on the peat engine so that the balloon would lose lift. As he drifted over the bay, he threw out his anchor lines, and a swarm of Springer crew members made the ship fast.

Armed guards met Josiah as he climbed out of the cockpit. But instead of arresting him, one of them handed him a room key.

"Your suite awaits you, Herr Bear," he said.

"Thank you. And here—" he handed over the dropper bottle, "—have this analyzed, will you?"

"Right away, Herr Bear."

Five

The next morning, Josiah was summoned, after a most excellent Anvorian breakfast of tea, ham, butter, toast, and red quince jam, to the office of Klaus Freiburg, Assistant Director for Research and Development at Springer Wirdschaftstwig SV.

"Herr Bear, we meet again," he said when Josiah was shown into his book-lined office.

"Klaus!" Josiah growled and met him hand to paw. Klaus was an old foe from the Anvorian unpleasantness twenty years before but had become a friend, for all true Anvorians and Bears were united in their dislike for the British. Marius Grieb, for example, might be an enemy in the air, but he was an ally when it came to the British. Once the British were gone, the Anvorians and Bears could resume their age-old feud.

"Not a bad flight, then?" Klaus said. Like many Anvorians, he was fair with wispy blond hair and blue eyes, tall, slight of build, but sinewy enough to be a match in boxing.

"Not at all," Josiah said, thinking of the growler of mead.

"Your telegram predicted your time of arrival perfectly. And you have news, you wrote."

"Yes. I thought you might be interested to know. The British told me you were developing a rubber-clad bomb that could be delivered by way of a giant sling."

Klaus's eyes bugged. "Himmels! That would be a pretty device."

"They also gave me something they said was an anti-coagulant for rubber. Wanted me to sabotage your production."

There was a knock on the door. A young man came in with a portfolio, which he handed to Klaus. "The analysis asked for by Herr Bear, Herr Direktor."

Klaus opened the portfolio and glanced through the few sheets of hole-punched, typewritten paper attached with string to the folder. "They do a good job on short notice here," he observed and passed it to Josiah.

"Just as I thought," Josiah said after a cursory review of the Anvorian text. "Nothing."

"Eucalyptus oil, it appears, with a few mineral admixtures. What do you suppose they were on about?"

"I have a theory."

"Let's hear it."

"We know that it is in the interest of the British to cripple the Anvorian rubber industry."

"Correct."

"But they want to cloak it in the idea that doing such a thing is in Bearland's best military interests. That way, they can get people like me to work for them—and, as a side benefit, they do not have to devote military assets to conquering Anvoria."

"That's also so."

"So, let's say that the British really thought that there was a rubber ball bomb thrower and that this potion was going to bring your factories to a halt. That would mean it's not the British who cooked up this scheme. Why go to so much trouble if they know it's a sham?"

"You think, in other words, someone has convinced the British that this gum oil would really work?"

"I do. I'd wager half the Honeymoon Fund it's one of our own Bearish chemists who convinced the British of this pipe dream. A bear with not only an impeccable reputation as a scientist, but also one with the gift of, shall we say, chicanery."

"You mean..."

"Precisely. Diligens C. Beartooth. He's called Dilly by his friends. He's the chief engineer at the Revulcan factory in the city of Brownbearplant."

"It looks like you're off to the Vulcania, then," said Klaus.

"And to get to the bottom of this mystery. I still have no idea why anyone would try to fool the British into thinking that eucalyptus oil can stop rubber from coagulating. As the British would say, what the deuce!"

"A pity you can't stay longer, Josiah. I read about your race with Herr Grieb and would like to discuss it with you."

"All in good time, Klaus. When the British are no longer in Bearland."

"Quite right."

Six

Josiah again had to wait for dark, as he had no business in Brownbearplant but would be wanted back in Port Courageous forthwith to make his report. He had nearly no time, in other words, but he had to find and meet Dilly Beartooth and figure out why he was bluffing the British.

The fuel gauge on the *Steampendous* read that there was still about point six pounds of super-peat left in the crucible, enough to get him to Vulcania but not back to Port Courageous.

He would have to improvise.

Shortly after five in the evening, he left the Springer plant, fortified by good Anvorian beer, several bacon-wrapped roasted quail, a pound and a half of barley pilaf, and a healthy slab of blueberry strudel.

The breeze aloft was welcome, for very soon the *Steampendous* was making its way into fierce, semi-tropical climes made even warmer by ambient gasses from the many active volcanoes on the peninsula.

Brownbearplant was nestled between three dormant volcanic cones and was a riot of flowers and fruit trees. The rubber factories lay at a distance of some nine miles as the honeybee flies, next to Mount Rambasco (dubbed Mount Saint Sinclair by the British), a particularly ferocious volcano that provided abundant geothermal energy for the factories.

It was well-known that Dilly Beartooth spent most of his time in the Revulcan R&D wing—even nights and weekends—but Josiah figured he would be home tonight, as it was Fat Monday, a traditional Bearish holiday celebrating the opening of the hibernation fattening-up season. Of course, gentlebears do not hibernate in the winter, only take longer naps. But bears rarely give up the opportunity to eat and drink with family and friends, hence the persistence of the tradition.

Not that Dilly would have invitations. He was a solitary type. But he might be found in his favorite restaurant, the Jacaranda, which served the honey-soaked bureaucracy (also known as baklava in the wide world) dessert that is a particular delicacy of the Bearish.

Hugging the western coastline of Vulcania, Josiah arrived at the merchant town of Cargobear around nine-thirty. He hove hard to port, followed the illuminated railway line into the hills, and was floating over Brownbearplant at just two minutes before ten.

The city was alight with torches and open-air grills, and the savor of honey-glazed salmon perfumed the air. Josiah circled the town before landing underneath an enormous ornamental rubber tree, the canopy of which would act as a natural tether for the balloon. Josiah climbed out and shinnied down the smooth trunk, a rope in his teeth.

Having secured the *Steampendous*, he walked into town and mingled with the gentlebears of Brownbearplant, wearing a short-brimmed fedora as a disguise.

"Salmon, gentle?" An aproned and toqued grizzly called out as Josiah walked by a sidewalk grill. "You look a tad on the lean side."

"I've a reservation at the Jacaranda."

"Six blocks up and two over, gentle," said the grizzly. "Then come back when you've had your bureaucracy. Best glaze in town, friend."

Josiah tipped his hat and redoubled his pace.

The Jacaranda had taken over the sidewalk and street near its address and was bustling even at this early hour. Josiah approached the maitre d', who told him of the two-hour wait for a table.

"I'm looking for Dilly," Josiah said.

"We haven't seen him tonight," said the maitre d'.

Josiah said, "Right. Well, then, here's something for your Honeymoon Fund." And he slipped him a fifty-bnoa banknote.

"Er... Now that you mention it..."

"Yes?"

"The British are having a meeting tonight. Dilly's in on it. He told me he might be quite late."

"How late, specifically?"

"He didn't say. Quite odd. He's very particular about his bureaucracy on Fat Monday."

"Where's the meeting? Revulcan?"

"I can't say."

Josiah handed him another banknote.

"It's at the house of the Director, on the top of Freeforth Hill."

"Thank you. You've been most kind. Have a wonderful honeymoon."

"The same to you, sir. And, by the way, watch out for dogs."

Seven

The British enclave on Freeforth Hill was gated and guarded. Not that any gentlebear would attempt to do harm to a British official, at least outside of a full-fledged Honeymoon Fund uprising. But claws and teeth have a way of making a human susceptible to irrational fears.

Josiah could have talked his way through the gate, but he liked to climb, and so he chose a tree with branches that overhung the twelve-foot, spiked, wrought-iron fence and made his way with only the merest clattering of claws up the trunk then onto the most likely branch on the other side.

Likely, but, as it turned out, not trustworthy.

Josiah was about nine feet out on the branch and letting it bow so that he might jump from a reasonable distance. But the creaking of the wood, which had been a slight protest when Josiah's twenty-stone weight first tested it, became a loud cracking as Josiah made his way out.

In short order, the branch snapped off with an ear-splitting crash and deposited Josiah in a patch of blooming hibiscus.

Josiah rose slowly, rubbed his hip, and shook his head to rid it of the hornet's nest that seemed to have been deposited there.

A light switched on in a nearby house.

"What's that? Who's there?" A feminine British voice came through the night.

Another light, closer.

"Call the watch, James," came the voice again. "There's some kind of blundering idiot climbing trees about."

Josiah collected his fedora and disappeared into a grove of Meyer lemon trees, sore but sound. As bears do not wear shoes, his foot-paws made no sound on the dirt beneath the trees, though now and then he would kick or squash a fallen lemon and soak his paw in juice.

A dog barked. As the maitre d' had suggested, this was a potential problem, as dogs were traditionally not friends of bears and could make quite a to-do if they found one. And as bears had a particular scent that dogs detected with ease, it wasn't easy to evade them.

Which was why Upright Bears generally preferred birds and fish as pets.

At the edge of the lemon grove, a newly-laid street of bitumen, smelling sour and smoky yet, coursed off to Josiah's left and right. A rubber-tired motorcar, infernal contraption, was parked some several yards away.

"Best to go straight up," Josiah concluded, and he crossed the street and took a cobbled path into the front garden of a British official. Once in cover again, he stood up and sniffed the air. Dogs. And close by.

He didn't have to wait long before barking started up again. There would be fences for these animals, but a trail of barking was problematic, a signal for the watch.

Another British garden supplied what he sought: the overpowering scent of gardenia flowers. He rubbed himself all over with these, effectively blotting out not only his natural musk, but also his sense of smell—the gardenia scent was that overpowering.

Nevertheless, the barking subsided.

At the next street—the hill was belted with them—the sound of a motorcar engine encouraged Josiah to keep himself hidden. It was the watch, in their white uniforms, toddling by in a car with electric headlamps, quite a new invention.

Josiah stole across the street and under the canopy of a cinchona tree. There, he found a wild beehive hanging from a branch dripping with pink blossoms. There was no honey there as yet, but a goodly number of bees. He snapped off the limb that suspended it and took it with him.

"No telling when a beehive might come in handy," he sensibly told himself as he forged through the undergrowth.

Eight

Josiah had never been inside the Director's residence but had seen it from the air before. Located on a bald knoll that was once the site of a volcanic side vent, it was a rambling manse ringed by lawns, flower gardens, tennis courts, and several experimental greenhouses. The Director, it was said, had been a research botanist before making his career in rubber manufacturing.

The grounds were darkened, and the house itself hardly able to be made out, as few lights shone in its windows. One of the greenhouses, however, had been illuminated, an unusual occurrence which attracted Josiah's attention.

First, this greenhouse, Josiah thought, *then we'll tackle the main place.*

Josiah made a run across open ground, head low and hive at arm's length. Just as he raised his head at the fluttering of a fruit bat above him, he tripped over something and was sent sprawling.

The branch with the hive went twirling in the air, end over end. With superior agility honed by long hours on athletic fields and in fencing clubs, Josiah popped up onto his legs and caught the branch in mid-air.

The bees inside buzzed their displeasure and a number of them, like superheated electrons, made fierce orbits about Josiah's ears and shoulders. Some of them sought the origin of the gardenia scent and left spiteful stings when they were foiled in their pursuit of flowers, but soon they returned to their jostled but intact home.

"Bear alive!" Josiah exclaimed as he found the root of his problem—a cricket bat left out, doubtless, by one of the Director's children.

So, Josiah came to the greenhouse with only grass stains on his plus fours and a bat and hive in his possession.

Sure enough, a peat lamp blazed through the many open windows, and the sound of British voices—perhaps more than a dozen—was unmistakable.

"Quiet, all of you," said someone. "The bear hasn't finished. Well, bear?"

Josiah moved from window to window to get a better look at the bear who was surrounded by the crowd of mustachioed and mutton-chopped British men sweating in suits, waistcoats, and ties.

Diligens Beartooth looked about him warily. He still had on a lobster bib from dinner, and his paws were behind his back, as if they might be tied. Two British guards in white uniforms and pith helmets, armed with canes and sidearms, flanked him.

"I tell you, that *Illyricum tembulans* works," he said. "Josiah may have been captured in Anvoria, but if you send someone else over the vats, you'll see."

"How can he have been captured?" one of the men said. "He is your best agent, in your best airship."

"I don't know, Director," said Dilly. "Perhaps the Anvorians shot him down."

"Impossible," said someone else. "The gondola has armor plating, and the balloon itself is rated to withstand one hundred and fifty holes from small arms fire without losing ten yards of lift."

Impressive, thought Josiah. *They certainly know their* Steampendous *facts.*

"A direct hit from a cannon—"

"They don't have cannons at Springer SV. It's a factory."

"I don't doubt your research," said Dilly. "The fact remains. Mr. J. U. Bear is missing."

"Unless..."

Dilly turned to the person—or rather, bear—who had spoken. She was of small stature—the crowd of men had blocked Josiah's view of her at first—bespectacled, wearing a lab coat and high-necked frock, and altogether too intelligent-looking for the crowd in which she found herself.

"Unless Mr. J. U. Bear is in the pay of the Anvorian Republic."

She had just the slightest foreign accent, as if Spanish was her first language, and her snout and face were tawny and speckled black, revealing her to be an Andean black bear.

Dilly growled. "A double agent? Impossible. He's our most trustworthy spy. A patriot, through and through, and hated by the Anvorians."

"Professor Marron," said the Director, addressing the Andean. "This bear speaks received wisdom. Explain yourself."

"This is possibly an elaborate ruse concocted by Mr. J. U. Bear, Agent Double Bee Six, and this bear here."

Dilly's ears shied back, the bear equivalent of a blush.

"You see, in my younger days, I was a dancing bear in the circus in the wide world. I had to keep secret my identity as an Upright Bear. During that time, I learnt to be observant. And after I became a chemist, I became more observant still, to uncover the secrets of the most invisible things in the world—molecules. I am a student, you see, of that which disguises itself."

She was poised to continue, one claw pointing to the sky, but stopped and sniffed. "What is that? Gardenias?"

"What the deuce," said the Director, "has gardenias to do with conspiracies?"

Another man grumbled, "I can't smell a thing in this dashed hothouse—except mildew."

She said nothing, only jammed her paws into the pockets of her lab coat and made a beeline for Josiah's hiding place underneath an open window.

Which, Josiah reasoned, was the most opportune time to deploy his hive.

Throwing the sphere in the air, he whacked it with the bat, sending it into the greenhouse and tearing it to paper shreds while releasing the angry bees inside.

The British knocked over tables laden with rubber seedlings and saplings in their haste to escape the apian onslaught.

Dilly dived out of an open window, leaving Professor Marron to wonder what was the great fuss over a few bees.

"Dilly! This way!" Josiah urged him.

"Josiah?"

"Don't be an idiot. Quickly!" They sprinted away downhill.

"You've ruined everything, you know," Dilly said when they'd dived into the nearest thicket of lobster-claw heliconia.

"What do you mean?"

"Do you know who was in that greenhouse? Only the board of trustees of Revulcan Products Limited. We've been leading up to this moment for months!"

"To do what?"

The *put-put-put* of a balky-engined airship above interrupted their conversation.

"That's our ship! We were going to put an end to British rubber once and for all!"

"Preposterous! How? By full-scale assassination? Dropping a bomb? Inciting a volcanic eruption?"

But before Dilly could answer, something like a loudspeaker began playing a recording, amid loud pops and cracks, of ghostly, ghastly moans, shrieks, and wails.

Josiah's nape fur went vertical and his ears shied back.

Then a light fell upon the greenhouse. Projected images of spirits—bears in bedsheets, it appeared—played about the structure.

Professor Marron came out of the greenhouse, waving her paws.

"Abort! Abort!" she cried.

The recording of the ghosts and ghouls abruptly ended with the sound of a needle being torn from its rubber gramophone disc. The light of the projection was replaced by a searchlight. A rope ladder fell from the ship, which Marron climbed with surprising ease.

"That's our ride home," Dilly said and pushed his way out of the heliconia bush.

"What?"

"Don't you see? It was the perfect plan. They'd have been spooked out of their human minds."

"And left the country?"

"Or been sent away to sanatoriums."

"Balderdash."

"Nevertheless. It was to be the first night of the consummation of the Honeymoon Fund."

"Consummation? Isn't that a bit premature?"

"Opinions differ on that."

Josiah rolled his eyes in disgust. "Another case of blasted Bearish independent thinking? Or as Robert Bearns would have said, 'The best-laid plans of mice and bears gang aft agley?'" He caught his breath and regained his wonted composure. "And why, pray tell, wasn't I informed?"

Dilly raised both paws. "We couldn't tell you. If you had known, you would've done just what you did now. Knocked down the idea with both paws. And, anyway, you played your part perfectly without having to be told."

"Thank you—I think."

"You see, when the *Illyricum tembulans* didn't work, they were sure to call me to a secret meeting at night—which invariably occurs in the greenhouse, the perfect place for the phantasmagoria."

"And what about those rubber ball bombs?"

"We had to invent some kind of threat."

"Double Bee Six indeed!" Josiah scoffed.

The searchlight panned jerkily about the grounds.

"She is looking for us." Dilly began waving madly.

"Who? She?"

Josiah peered into the sky. There, in the dimness of the searchlight, he could make out the familiar lines of a sleek racing ship. "Madame X Bear!" he cried in disbelief.

There came a voice from above. "Get up the ladder, you two, before they get on to us!"

"Honeypenny?"

Nine

"There's only one thing good that has come out of this," Honeypenny said when they were all stuffed into the gondola and on their way to the mooring place of the *Steampendous*.

"What's that?" Josiah asked.

"No one saw that it was you who botched up the whole business. You must return to Port Courageous with the tale of a daring escape from the Springer SV plant."

"And what about me?" Dilly said.

"You will admit that *Illyricum tembulans* doesn't work," said Honeypenny. "Marron, back to your research and disavow your conspiracy theory."

She nodded, though—being uncomfortably wedged into the gondola with several hundred pounds of bear—that was not the easiest thing she'd ever done.

"I'm sure, Josiah, you'll be able to talk your way out of anything."

"I usually do," said Josiah.

"The consummation is postponed," said Honeypenny.

"Though the identity of Madame X Bear is now known."

"But not blabbed about by a certain J. U. Bear." Honeypenny gave what may have been misinterpreted by a human as a flirty wink.

And will Madame X Bear race again?" Josiah asked.

"Undoubtedly," said Honeypenny. "If I can get this blasted engine to behave. But..."

"Yes?"

"There is one thing that I do have need of from you."

"And that would be..."

"Your starboard aft propeller—the one that Gregarious Bearish honed for you. It's the least you can do, after you botched this whole mission."

"But how—then what—was it Cubbleton who—the devil I will!"

Professor Marron and Diligens Beartooth stared hard at Josiah.

"The least," said Dilly, "that you can do."

"Not to mention those three thousand extra francks," Honeypenny added.

Josiah sighed. She had him there. "Well, at least you can lend me some peat to get home. I'm about on empty."

"Anything for you, Josiah."

Ten

Several days later, Josiah was having a talk with Gregarious Bearish in his workshop when Cubbleton arrived, bearing a note.

"It's a court summons, Uncle Josiah," said the cub. "Raking and biting a Colonial Official."

Josiah harrumphed. "Give it me, Cubbles." He took the paper and threw it into Gregarious's forge.

As the paper curled up into black ash, Cubbleton gaped.

"Such a shame," said Josiah. "That the postal service lets so many letters go undelivered these days."

"It's the British, you see," said Gregarious. "The root of our troubles."

"Yes." Josiah sighed. "Always the British."

Anyone who ever had a beloved teddy bear knows where Bearland is and what it's about.

Josiah and Bearland celebrate pure play: that quality of life where, in the moment, nothing else matters: imagination is given free rein and the heart delights.

In this world, friends are loyal, serendipity abounds, and villains aren't all that villainous.

Heroes, too, are heroic, but they share the spotlight—just as every bear in the toybox has its own special role to play in the story. Josiah U. Bear may be a champion airship racer and international spy, but he can't save Bearland from the British all on his own.

Bearland began in my childhood, and probably should have stayed there. But as I got older, Bearland came along for the ride, and it eventually grew into a whole world. Josiah's story is for everyone who celebrates their childhood—and gratefully, somehow, still lives it every day.

River's Edge Ransom

Julie C. Gilbert

Who's Who and What's What:

Aeris – a planet created by Kailon
Kessemi root – plant matter used to temporarily lighten hair and fabric

People Types:

Saroth – A people who live on the east side of Aeris's main continent. They are usually Gifted in the darker four of the seven magic schools and tend to become Destroyers, Shapeshifters, Conjurers, or Minders.

Arkonai – A people who live mainly in the northwest corner of Aeris's main continent. They are usually Gifted in the lighter three of the seven magic schools. Most Arkonai with access to magic become Seekers, Guardians, or Healers.

Bereft – Majority of people on Aeris who have no access to magic.

Key Saroth:

Gabriel Castaloni – Shapeshifter (squirrel, wolf), younger brother to Jackson and Marina

Jackson Castaloni – Conjurer, younger brother to Marina, older brother to Gabriel

Marina Castaloni – Destroyer, elder sister to Jackson and Gabriel

Key Arkonai:

Daniel Saveron – Huntsman, Seeker

Other:

Kailon – Eternal King, Creator of Aeris
The Lady – immortal servant of Kailon

Chapter 1: A Huntsman Hired

"I don't like this, Jack." The distress in Gabriel Castaloni's features echoes the sentiment, but the effect is lost on his brother due to the quickly fading natural light.

"And I don't have time to deal with you right now," snaps Jackson. "She's dead to us anyway. Now get gone and keep silent. We'll talk more when the huntsman leaves."

"It's still wrong," Gabriel mutters. Feeling the weight of his older brother's glare, Gabriel takes on his squirrel form and scampers up a nearby tree to hide. Tonight, his role is that of witness, and if things go wrong, he will provide backup in case Jackson has any problems with the Arkonai huntsman.

How did we come to this?

Letting his legs and paws act instinctively, Gabriel loops three times around the tree trunk on his way up to the hole he'd scouted out earlier. The tiny squirrel heart beats rapidly in his chest, fueling his frantic exercise. Part of him understands the futility of trying to outrun his family issues, but he can't help it. Despite the new body, his mind is fully human. Inevitably, his thoughts dwell on Marina.

Could I have saved her from herself?

An annoyed chittering noise escapes him. Of course, he could do nothing to move Marina from her self-destructive path. Eight years his senior, Marina hardly acknowledges Gabriel's existence, let alone listens to him. Truthfully, not even their father's words hold much sway with her, which is odd because she's always been the favorite child.

Simply to occupy his hands and twitching feet while he waits, Gabriel picks up a nut from the modest store at the back of this cozy hole and gnaws at it absently. Stifling the urge to run, Gabriel focuses on Jackson.

Though a Conjurer and not a Shapeshifter, Jackson possesses a knack for deception. The outward transformation has already been made. Jackson's hair has been cropped short and bleached blond with kessemi roots. The beard he's worked on for a few weeks has been artificially lengthened with hairs conjured from beyond the Veil. Some people cringe at the thought of using the Veil between worlds as a place to store things, but Conjurers and Arkonai huntsmen have done so for eons. A large patch covers Jackson's left eye. He takes off his outer cloak. The move reveals the plain attire beneath and completes the transformation to Huntmaster Fox, a respected and reclusive member of the Arkonai Hunting Guild.

The shift Gabriel watches now is one of demeanor. Jackson bundles up the cloak and throws it onto the single bedroll in their camp. Gabriel had spent the previous night in wolf form so they wouldn't need two bedrolls. Jackson paces for a few seconds then stops and crouches near the fire pit. Picking up a small stick, he snaps off small pieces and adds them to the fire. There's a confidence to his movements that wasn't present before. Had he been born Bereft, Jackson could have become a fine actor.

The meaningless thoughts flee Gabriel as his animal instincts tell him somebody approaches. He watches with interest as his brother greets the huntsman with a few traditional phrases in an older Arkonai dialect before inviting the man to sit by the fire and steering the conversation to the business at hand.

"I have a contract for you," says Jackson, once they're both settled. "An important one." His words, now in the common tongue, roll with the accent one expects from one raised in the Northlands.

"I am at your service, Huntmaster Fox," replies the huntsman.

Deep within the tree hole, Gabriel does something very few Shapeshifters can do. He initiates a partial change over to wolf form and holds it to sharpen his vision. Dropping the nut, Gabriel observes the young man.

The huntsman doesn't look like much, but Mother's warning against underestimating Arkonai echoes in Gabriel's mind. This one possesses an intensity in his eyes, but it's muted by the deference he pays Jackson. The firelight shines off his blond hair, making it appear white. A neatly trimmed beard does little to age his youthful features. A single, long hunting dagger hangs from a sheath at his waist. Gabriel wonders where the man's other weapons are kept. Few huntsmen wander Darkwood Forest with only a dagger.

"There's a Saroth Destroyer at work in the village of River's Edge," Jackson says, inserting proper gravity into his tone.

The huntsman whistles low.

"That's a long way from here," he comments.

"Indeed. I've carried this contract many miles. This Destroyer is very powerful. Were I younger, I'd fulfill the contract myself, but alas, my hunting days are past." He gestures to his left eye. "The village Bereft deserve a whole huntsman."

"I'm sure you could do it," encourages the young man. "I've heard rumors of trouble there, but surely, there's a huntsman whose territory is closer. Won't I need his permission to operate?"

"This is a silent contract," Jackson informs the man. "Relations with the Saroth are strained, and the Destroyer in question hails from a noble line. We cannot openly acknowledge the assignment, but innocents are suffering. We cannot ignore that fact."

The man's gaze sharpens. A secret contract must come from one of the nine members of the Arkonai High Council. It's the first step up those ranks. Anyone with aspirations to become Supreme Huntmaster needs to fulfill at least one secret contract.

"Do you have the scroll?" the huntsman inquires.

"I do," Jackson answers. He pulls the scroll from the Veil.

Gabriel had thought that a reckless move, but Jackson assured him that a skilled Huntmaster would have the ability to store things in the Veil, much like a Conjurer.

Jackson begins describing Marina's supposed crimes in brutal detail.

"As you can see, this Destroyer is more subtle than others. She's brought the village of River's Edge a wasting disease that will kill more than half the people if given enough time."

No, Jack. You did... I did.

The thought pulls Gabriel down into a deep despair that helps him tune Jack out as he continues wooing the huntsman. He had no part in obtaining or delivering the disease, but his silence condemns him all the same.

It's just as well he can't focus on Jackson and the huntsman. Gabriel doesn't like hearing about his sister this way. The image of a cold-hearted killer doesn't line up with his memories. Marina could be overbearing and obnoxious, but she wasn't vindictive or manipulative. Those attributes described Jack better. This plot against Marina was spinning out of control.

Nobody was supposed to die! Jack, you lied to me!

He almost hopes Jackson will fail to convince the man to take the contract. *You don't need me! You want me here to share your guilt.*

Gabriel's thoughts wander back to when he was a small boy. He recalls the hours of fun he'd had with Marina. Jack was a bit of a bore even back then. He'd simply conjure blocks of wood to halt Marina's diminished lightning bolts. Eventually, they learned to leave Jackson out of their games, choosing to spend hours in the chase through vast fields owned by their parents.

By the time Gabriel focuses again, the huntsman is gone, but as per Jackson's instructions, he waits another five minutes before descending from the tree, taking his human form, and approaching the fire.

"We should reconsider, Jack," Gabriel pleads, knowing the words are wasted. "She's our sister."

Jackson's shoulders stiffen then relax as he sighs and shifts to a more comfortable position by the fire. With a wave, he invites Gabriel to join him.

"We've been over this countless times," Jackson states. "I don't like it any more than you do, but this is about more than Marina. It's about family honor." He tucks his arms around his knees and gazes into the fire, letting a few beats of silence linger. "If nothing is done, you and I will bear the scorn."

"But what does it matter?" Gabriel wonders, exasperated. "She's not the first Saroth to choose a Healer's path. It's still one of the seven schools of magic."

"It's not about what she's doing," Jackson explains. "It's about what she's *not* doing. She should accept an honorable match and cultivate her natural gifts. She's a Destroyer. She must accept this. She should be on the front lines fighting dragons in the Ashlands or searching for an apprentice in Hastings."

"You're jealous," Gabriel mutters, stunned that he's never picked up on that before. "Is this about the rights of the firstborn?" He sees from the way Jackson tenses that his question has struck a nerve. Gabriel's mind reels. For all his talk about family honor, this move might be nothing more than Jackson's bid to inherit the Castaloni holdings. Wrenching his thoughts back on track, Gabriel says, "Speak with Father. He can transfer the rights without Marina's death."

"He'll never do it." Jackson's mouth draws together in an almighty scowl.

"He might if Mother asks him," Gabriel offers, though he knows the chances of that are slim. Jackson might be Mother's favorite, but Marina could never do wrong in Father's eyes. Why couldn't she see the pain her selfishness caused their father?

"She'll never oppose him on this matter," Jackson says. "No, brother, it must be this way."

A dozen questions crowd Gabriel's head, but he holds them in. Turning to wolf form, he lays his head across his paws and closes his eyes. He needs to think. Maybe there's still a way to warn Marina and talk some sense into her. If she returns and marries Marcus Polani as planned, all will be right again. A strong alliance will be formed with one of the most powerful Saroth families, Jackson can inherit the Castaloni lands, and perhaps Gabriel will at last be free to pursue the love of his soul. Tielle's lovely face fills Gabriel's thoughts as he drifts off to sleep.

Chapter 2: A Clean Capture

This is the sort of hunt Daniel lives for. He's on his way to defend a village full of people from a powerful Saroth Destroyer. Daniel barely believes his luck that Huntmaster Fox would seek him out for such an honor.

After journeying to River's Edge, he observes the quiet village for a few hours. He's not seen a place this dead since Master Haller took him to Cornerstone when there was an outbreak of Stricklan's Disease. He cannot sense where to find the Destroyer, but her powerful presence has left signs all over the surrounding hill country and forest.

A day after his arrival, Daniel slips into River's Edge and cautiously walks down the deserted main path. Just as he gains an idea of the village layout, a bold, female voice addresses him from behind.

"You. Huntsman. I need your help."

Spinning, Daniel wonders, *How does she know I'm a huntsman?*

He finds a young woman carrying a child. Her dark brown hair hangs in two messy braids. She possesses a beautiful face, but he doesn't have much time to contemplate it. Her expression demands an immediate response.

For a few seconds, Daniel simply weighs his options. He could ignore her, but that would likely draw a lot of attention. Subtle shifts in the shadows of nearby houses tell him he's being watched. He could run away, but that would make him feel guilty and cause him to miss an opportunity to learn something about the stranger and possibly his quarry. Clearly, this woman is no ordinary villager. Her dark robes declare that much. The fact that she's speaking to him at all is notable. Only helping offers the chance at valuable information.

"Stop standing there and take him," demands the woman. Her face is flushed with the exertion of carrying the boy.

Stepping forward, Daniel takes the child as bid. The boy's frail body burns with fever.

"What's wrong with him?" Daniel wonders as the child shivers in his arms.

"Come with me. I'll explain as best I can along the way." Without waiting for a response, the woman turns away and hurries down the deserted street.

Daniel follows. It crosses his mind that this could be a trap, but the child's distress is genuine.

The woman leads Daniel to the last house at the end of a long row of humble family dwellings. The building—barely more than a hut—looks ready to fall over at the next strong gust of wind. Daniel hesitates in the threshold before cautiously stepping through with the child.

"Thank you for your aid," breathes the woman. "Set him on the table there, then you may go."

Several questions vie for attention, but Daniel settles on the simplest one.

"What are you doing?" Even as the question comes out, the answer stares him in the face.

A single, dim lantern fights off the darkness caused by thick curtains drawn across each window. Light streaming in from the open doorway shows Daniel the desperate healing efforts taking place here. Small piles of pungent herbs are scattered across the kitchen table, waiting to be pulverized by the mortar and pestle. Half-filled cups and bowls hold strange liquids and thick pastes.

Seeing that Daniel has no inclination of leaving, the woman slips around him and closes the door. He tenses in case he's misread the situation. If this is the Saroth Destroyer he's come to deal with, it might be the easiest job he's ever taken.

"I'm going to give the boy some tea to bring down the fever," the woman explains.

Rushing to the corner, she turns up the lantern so that soft light fills the tiny room. Next, she lights a small fire beneath the cooking stove and sets a pot of water on top. The simple act would not normally draw Daniel's attention. However, the fact that she reached for no flint is very telling, for power over fire is a gift bestowed by Kailon upon the strongest Saroth bloodlines.

He watches her tend to the boy before urging her to go and rest. She maintains the vigil for several minutes before his promise to keep watch convinces her to take a break.

"Call if anything changes," the woman whispers as she slips into the small kitchen next to the boy's sickroom.

The moment her back is turned, Daniel makes his move. First, he summons a sturdy length of hemp rope and a clean rag from the Veil where he's stored them. Next, he waits for her to sit before having the ropes restrain her hands and feet and bind her to the sturdy wooden chair. The gag settles into place just as she screams.

A gesture turns the chair so that they face each other.

Eyes wide with fright, she fights the bonds.

For a moment, Daniel says nothing while the girl tests the strength of each rope. When she wears herself out and lets her shoulders slump, he speaks.

"I have some questions for you, and I'm sure you have some for me." The words aren't the ones he's pondered for days, but they'll do. "If you agree to a civil conversation, I'll recall the gag." He hadn't meant to say that but figures it'll do no harm. "Nod if you agree. Shake your head if you'd rather sit there a few hours."

The girl nods slowly.

Snapping his fingers, Daniel removes the cloth rag and has it hover near the girl's head. Daniel imagines Master Cayden's disapproval of such casual use of magic, but at least his friend, Jordan Lekros, would be impressed. The thought distracts Daniel enough that he almost misses the deadly glare the woman aims at him. The expression enhances her natural beauty. He shakes off that thought.

"Tell me the truth. What are you doing here?" Daniel demands.

"What does it look like I'm doing?" the woman shoots back. When Daniel doesn't answer, the woman sighs. "I told you the truth. I'm trying to save Edwin."

"The boy?"

"Of course, the boy," says the woman. She pierces Daniel with an accusing glare but keeps her voice to a fierce whisper. "His name is Edwin Summers, and he's been fighting for his life for four days now!"

"Why are you treating him?"

"Because nobody else is willing to try," she snaps. There's genuine concern etched in her features and deep blue eyes. "People are suffering and dying. Even if I don't have the skill to save them, I can at least ease their pain."

Daniel's heart races. He wants to scrub the words from his mind. Visions of a triumphant reception by the Council shatter.

She is innocent, Daniel.

This thought comes with the Lady's voice. He has heard Kailon's servant, the Lady, before but never quite like this.

"What do you want with me, Huntsman?" Weariness and bitterness season her statement. The young woman obviously knows the answer, but for some reason, she wants him to voice it.

"I have accepted a contract to end your life," he begins, relying upon formality to regain his confidence. He wants to curse her for not being the evil witch whose death would purchase power and prestige. "So, tell me. Why would my Council place a secret contract requiring your death? Those are reserved for dangerous criminals."

"They wouldn't."

"Who are you?"

"I'm sure your contract contains that information."

The girl's attitude sparks anger within him.

"Woman, I am trying to help you! Who wants you dead?"

The woman locks icy blue eyes on Daniel.

"I don't know," the woman answers. She glances away, looking troubled. "I doubt it's somebody on your Council. They've probably never heard my name let alone cared about my fate." She grimaces. "My worst enemies are family."

"What do you mean?" Daniel inquires.

Silent tears start down the woman's face.

Daniel gives the girl time to compose herself.

Finally, she blinks back further tears and levels with him.

"My name is Marina Castaloni. I am the eldest of three born to Corabelle and Antonio Castaloni. No doubt your contract already tells you I am a Destroyer. Most of my blood relatives manifest Gifts. We have for centuries." The young woman stares at Daniel. "What your contract cannot tell you is that I've no wish to be a Destroyer, at least not a traditional one."

"What would you like to be?" Daniel asks gently.

"A Healer," she answers. "I believe my powers can be used for more than war. If I can only learn enough, I'm sure I can use Destroyer powers against disease!" Her voice drops with her next statement. "I must try."

Daniel nods. He's heard of Arkonai who choose not to pursue careers that pair with their natural magical abilities, but he's never considered that the same must happen with Saroth too. Marina's idea of applying the Gift differently intrigues him.

"And your family disapproves," Daniel prompts. Disapproval shouldn't be enough to warrant any contract let alone one that must have cost a fortune.

Marina frowns.

"It's a little more complicated than disapproval."

"How so?"

Her sigh speaks of heartache.

"As the firstborn, I ought to be making a name for myself so I can attract a suitable match or accept the one with Marcus Polani being negotiated on my behalf."

"You're betrothed?" Daniel asks, truly stunned. He'd believed such archaic customs gone from society.

A hint of a smile lightens Marina's features. "Why do you think I'm so far from home?"

Daniel doesn't believe his ears. *There must be more.*

"I've never met him," Marina says. "And I've no inclination to ever meet him." Her voice softens with each statement. "For now, that means not going home, but perhaps one day my parents will forgive me."

"Is there a large inheritance at stake?"

Daniel's question refocuses the girl.

"Yes, but why should that matter?"

Instead of answering, Daniel fires another question. "What happens if you never return home?"

"That depends on my father," Marina replies. "He can disown me at any time, which would clear the way for Jackson to inherit the Castaloni lands and businesses."

"And if your father doesn't disown you?" Daniel presses. "What then? What happens when he passes beyond the Veil?"

"If I'm in Caramore, I will assume control on the condition that I marry within five years and have a child within ten," Marina explains. "If I'm not there, a trustee council will be formed to handle things for the next nine years before considering my middle brother's claim to everything."

Reaching a decision, Daniel removes the ropes with a gesture and sends them into the Veil.

Marina's expression contains surprise, relief, and uncertainty. "What happens now?"

Most of the High Council would praise the end of such a high-caste Saroth. If Daniel doesn't fulfill the contract, he jeopardizes his whole career. If he goes through with it, he'll never be able to live with himself.

She is innocent, no matter what the contract says.

"Now, I help you. My name is Daniel Saveron. I am no Healer, but I can help in other ways." He's suddenly reluctant to meet her gaze.

"What about your contract?" Marina asks.

"When the fate of River's Edge is settled, I'll return to Bastion and appeal the contract," Daniel says. He knows it's a lost cause, but he doesn't wish to make the girl feel guilty. It's not her problem. Even the deception will not convince traditionalists that the contract should be broken. If he argues effectively, they may only demote him.

The noble path has always been harder, Daniel.

He nods acceptance of the Lady's words.

Chapter 3: A Family Affair

Jack's not going to like this.

The thought crosses Gabriel Castaloni's mind as he watches his sister enter the Richlands Forest with the huntsman they'd sent to kill her. In his squirrel form, he sneaks close enough to hear their conversation. It doesn't take him long to know that they're on an herb-gathering mission.

He spends the next several days watching their doomed efforts to help the people. From what he can tell, they can do little more than treat the symptoms with herbal remedies. He considers telling Marina which disease Jackson released so she can maximize the healing efforts, but their brother would not take kindly to the interference.

Retreating into the forest, Gabriel returns to human form and grips the large, green pendant hanging from his neck. Muttering the phrase to unlock the pendant's magic, Gabriel waits for the connection to be made to his brother.

"Report," Jackson orders without a greeting.

Brushing irritation aside, Gabriel explains. He hates being the bearer of bad news. "I don't think the huntsman will complete the contract."

"Why not?" Jackson demands. "He knows the consequences of breaking a silent contract. They'll kick him out of the guild, or keep him at huntsman rank forever."

"Probably because he sees she's helping the people," says Gabriel. He hopes Jack doesn't have other spies that would tell him the whole truth.

What will Jack do if he knows they're working together?

Gabriel decides to keep that part a secret for now.

Jackson grunts.

"Unfortunate, but not unforeseen." He heaves a sigh. "All right. We'll need to change our tactics. I'll be there in a few days. I'll send instructions when the plans are in motion."

Gabriel's heart sinks. Jack's schemes are infamous for not unfolding as planned. They often garner the results he wishes, but only with very high consequences for all involved.

When Jack's instructions come through two days later, Gabriel's desire to quit intensifies. His role is relatively simple, but he doesn't like having any part of harming Marina. As the youngest child, he's always been content to inherit a few scraps of land. The modest stipend from the larger empire should let him live comfortably as long as he stays within the purser's good graces. Since the purser keeps close ties to Jackson, Gabriel must obey his brother. Silently cursing, Gabriel turns himself into a squirrel and dashes for the village.

Finding Marina won't be a problem.

Finding her alone might be.

As he enters the village, Gabriel turns himself into a beetle to be less conspicuous. While abundant in the woods, squirrels rarely venture this close to people.

To his relief, Gabriel finds Marina alone, sweeping the floor in a tiny cabin at the end of a row.

Entering the room through a crack under the door, Gabriel turns himself into a squirrel, a wolf, and back to a beetle.

Marina gasps. "Gabriel! What are you doing here?"

Without answering, Gabriel slips under the door again and heads for the woods, pausing to make sure Marina's following. Soon, he becomes a wolf and races away. From time to time, he flips to beetle form to check Marina's progress. The chase sparks a longing in him. It's a game they haven't played for many years. The memory distracts him. A bolt of lightning sails over his head and two more hit the ground near his feet. He stops and takes on his human form. Marina has won. Unfolding from a crouch, Gabriel turns and raises a hand in greeting.

"Hello, Marina."

She returns the greeting and holds out her hands with the palms facing up.

Stepping forward, Gabriel places his hands into hers and squeezes affectionately. Before he can move, Marina wraps him up in a tight hug.

"I've missed you." Joy rings through her words, but confusion soon takes its place. "Why have you come? Is Jack with you?"

"You might say that," says Jackson from behind Marina.

She lets go of Gabriel and whirls to face their brother.

"I asked him to bring you here," Jackson continues. "We have much to discuss."

A new voice rings out with challenge. "Is everything all right here?"

Startled, Gabriel turns into a wolf and faces the huntsman.

"Kill him," Jackson orders.

Courage fills Gabriel's chest and every fiber of his being yearns to obey.

Chapter 4: A Ransom Paid

The wolf snarls and charges at Daniel Saveron, but it's clear from his angle of attack that he's no fighter. Twisting aside, Daniel draws his hunting dagger and pounds the blunt end into the wolf's side as it sails past. It yelps and skids on some leaves as it scrambles for purchase to renew the attack. It charges again and again, receiving two more solid whacks. At any moment, Daniel could kill it, but he knows he shouldn't. Marina obviously knows this Shapeshifter and the man wearing dark clothes from head to toe.

"Stop it!" Marina shouts, throwing herself between them when the wolf pauses to shake its head. She holds both hands up to ward off the wolf. Her back faces Daniel, but he hears the distress in her voice. "You can't win this fight, Gabriel. Please. Change back and talk to me."

The wolf growls and advances a step. Foam drips from its mouth.

"He can't hear you, dear sister," says the other man. His voice is smooth, dangerous, and mocking. The man waves a scroll in their direction. "He is mine to command until I release him."

"Jack! What have you done?" Marina's tone sails high with distress. "Let him go!"

"Shall I order him to kill you?" Jack's eyes shift color from bright green to black. "That would be amusing."

The wolf whines and lowers its head as if bearing up under great pain.

"Jack, have you lost your mind? He's our brother!"

The man lowers the scroll and waves for the wolf to stand down. It obediently sits but remains alert.

"Where did you get that?" Daniel demands. "They're banned. Everywhere." While true, Daniel has no delusions that Jack will back down.

"I have a proposition for you, Marina, and I need your full attention," says Jack, ignoring Daniel.

"You have it," Marina says.

"Excellent, but first, I must tell you a story." Jack's words are full of good cheer.

"He's in pain. Get to the point," Marina urges.

Jack levels a disapproving look at her.

Daniel steps left so he can see both siblings. He wants a clear line of sight to Jack should the opportunity arise to kill the man. While a newcomer to the family dynamics, his sympathies lie with Marina and the Shapeshifter.

"I was visiting a friend in Glazdale and came across a lovely disease. My friend was also fascinated, so he decided to run some experiments to see if the disease could be shaped to certain demands. Of course, once he perfected this new strain and its antidote, I stole it. I'm out a friend, but it's a small price to pay."

"Oh, Jack, why?" Marina whispers, catching the meaning a second before Daniel.

"You're responsible for—" Daniel begins.

"Yes. Yes. I released Surdan's Bane on River's Edge. I hear the savages call it Boonton's End Disease or a half-dozen other names. It matters not. They can call it what they like. That does not change the facts. Now, keep out of it. I'm having a discussion with my sister."

"People have died," Marina points out wearily. "Why would you kill innocent people? It gains you nothing."

"On the contrary, it has done exactly as I wished! You are here at my mercy!" crows Jack. His eyes shift back to a dark shade of green. "I knew you couldn't resist such a wonderful healing opportunity. Haven't you always wanted to be a hero? Now's your chance to save them."

"How?" Marina's question is barely a whisper.

"Don't listen to him," Daniel says, stepping forward.

Jack gestures to the wolf and it leaps to its feet, growling at Daniel.

"What's the price?" Marina inquires, ignoring Daniel.

"Marina, you can't trust him," says Daniel.

Jack casts a baleful look at him. "This is none of your concern, Huntsman."

"The price, Jack," Marina repeats.

Daniel's never heard her use such a cold tone before.

"I want your Keeper's pendant and your participation in a small ritual." Jack's green eyes light with fervor.

"My birthright," Marina murmurs, placing a hand over the pendant resting above her heart.

"Your birthright," Jack confirms. "Forfeiting claims to an inheritance is the first price. The second is this: you will voluntarily give up your Destroyer powers." Jack pauses for effect. "In return, I will provide you with the cure to save River's Edge."

Stillness settles over the forest as if nearby creatures await Marina's answer.

Massive willpower keeps Daniel quiet. He longs to hurl his dagger in Jack's face. He's never heard of anybody willingly laying down their magical Gifts. He's not even sure how it would be done, though he suspects Jack has another illegal scroll nearby.

"First, you release Gabriel from that vile scroll, destroy it, and take a binding oath never to use a Control spell again," says Marina, glaring at Jack.

"Agreed," Jack purrs. "Would you like to do the honors?" He tosses the scroll to Marina.

Catching the scroll, she flings it against the nearest tree and sends a bolt of lightning through it. The paper catches fire and burns to ashes in seconds.

The wolf morphs into a young man who sits up slowly.

With a flourish, Jack summons another scroll from the Veil.

"I'll just need your signature." Jack conjures a fancy quill set and floats both over to Marina.

"Add in the clause about never using a Control spell," Marina insists. Her voice vibrates with anger.

Although Daniel can't read the scroll, at Jack's nod it lengthens to make room for a new paragraph.

"Don't do this," Daniel pleads. "We've no guarantee he won't simply go elsewhere and do the same thing."

"All those details have been answered in the contract," Jack states. "Not that it's any of your business."

"He won't have reason to," Marina explains, facing Daniel. "I won't be a threat to his inheritance."

Her look of deep pain digs out a memory from Daniel's childhood. Mistress Nevara insisted he learn some Saroth customs. As an insular people, the Saroth locked the major passages to Caramore with magic gateways that can only be crossed with appropriate pendants, scrolls, or powerful Gifts.

"You can never go home if you do this," Daniel comments.

"That's the point," Jack sings.

"I know." Tears flow down Marina's cheeks, but oddly, she appears calmer as she accepts the loss. Plucking the quill from the air near her head, Marina grasps the hovering scroll and signs it.

Recalling both items, Jack sends them into the Veil and selects yet another scroll from a pile Daniel glimpses before the tear closes. This one pulses with evil intent. Jack begins reading in a sibilant, soft language that nearly burns Daniel's ears.

Marina's knees buckle and her head flies forward as she lands in a kneeling position. The thin gold chain and pretty blue pendant slips off her neck and sails into Jack's outstretched hand. Grinning madly, he closes his fist around it and continues reading. Marina shudders, but before Daniel can go to her, the young man called Gabriel catches his shoulders.

"If you interrupt the Transfer spell, she'll die," Gabriel explains.

Daniel sees the strong family resemblance in the shape of his eyes and the slope of his nose.

Together, they watch as the words Jack reads off the scroll slowly siphon away Marina's Destroyer powers. A thin strand of green light flows from Marina's heart to the center of Jack's chest. Several times, Jack stops reading and has Marina attempt to summon lightning. The first three times, she manages it, but the fourth time, nothing happens.

"I think we're done here," Jack announces. He tears a small hole in the Veil and sends the evil scroll away before tucking Marina's pendant into a hidden pocket on the left side of his chest.

Exhausted, Marina falls from her knees to the ground, unconscious.

Jack studies her, tilting his head. The expression he wears is akin to pity. Approaching slowly, he kneels beside Marina and brushes some locks of dark hair off her forehead.

"You are wrong, dear sister," Jack whispers. A gentle push rolls her onto her back. "Father's love blinds him. You would always be a threat to my inheritance." He draws a small dagger from the folds of his robes.

"No!" The exclamation bursts forth from Daniel and Gabriel.

In a flash, the young man's hands fall away from Daniel's shoulders and something hard nearly sweeps him off his feet. He rights his balance in time to see a gray-black blur slam into Jack. With a startled cry, Jack flies away from Marina, flinging his dagger into a nearby tree. The wolf stands between Marina and Jack, growls low, and bares his teeth.

Rage twists Jack's features into an ugly expression.

"So be it, Gabriel," he hisses. Drawing Marina's pendant out, he continues, "If you stand with her, then you can die with her."

Chapter 5: The Magic Within

Summoning his longbow and several arrows from the Veil, Daniel nocks one of the arrows at the same moment Jack speaks to the blue pendant.

A blast of blinding white lightning slashes out of the necklace, shattering it. The bolt of pure energy slams into the wolf and catapults the creature up over Marina's still form. Only a sturdy oak tree stops the wolf's flight.

The noise slams into Daniel with near physical force, throwing his aim off just enough for the arrow to graze the man's left shoulder.

Jack screams.

Daniel puts two arrows to the bow and lets them both fly.

Jack conjures a thick slab of wood that absorbs Daniel's arrows and counters with several streaks of lightning. The move draws another ragged cry from Jack.

Throwing up the strongest shield he can, Daniel rushes forward to keep the madman away from Marina.

Frowning, Jack backpedals three steps and unleashes more slashes of lightning.

The bolts slam into Daniel's shield. He schools his features so Jack won't see that each strike increases the pressure inside his head from fending off the attack. Flashes of light dance behind Daniel's eyes and give him a massive headache. His only consolation is that Jack seems to suffer from each strike he deals.

As suddenly as the assault began, it ceases.

Hatred burns in Jack's eyes, but Daniel can also see pain. The man's fingers are charred where the flesh could not contain the lightning.

The men stare at each other, panting from the exertion.

"We will finish this another day, Huntsman." Leaving that promise in the air, Jack opens a large hole in the Veil and moves to step through. He stops suddenly as if meeting a sturdy wall. Frowning, Jack draws forth a small vial filled with bright orange liquid and drops it to the ground.

Daniel longs to send a throwing dagger into Jack's chest, but he dares not drop the shield. He'd never be able to create a new one with his head engulfed in so much pain.

"This is the cure for the village," Jack says. He looks like the words disgust him. The man casts one more dark look at Marina before stepping into the Veil and disappearing.

Daniel keeps the shield up until a low, heartfelt groan from Marina draws his attention. Dropping the shield, he whirls and finds Marina cradling Gabriel's head in her lap. Tears stream down her face.

"Why, Gabriel?" Marina's query holds a half-dozen different questions.

Two of them tap out with Daniel's quickened heartbeats as if Marina spoke directly into his mind.

Why the betrayal? Why the reversal?

Suddenly, Daniel feels like he should give the two some privacy. The dark-haired young man has a large hole in his chest. He's obviously dying. Still fearing Jack might return, Daniel doesn't dare move, so he continues to bear witness to Marina's new pain.

"Lend her your strength," a female voice orders.

Daniel's head whips up and right. Where Jack had stood stands the Lady in pure white robes. She holds the vial of orange liquid in her right hand.

Questions crowd his head, but Daniel slowly turns back to gaze at Marina and Gabriel. They're still as statues.

"She has the power to save her brother," says the Lady.

"But Jack stole her power," Daniel argues, shaking his head. He faces the Lady.

Her smile is patient, and she too shakes her head.

"He stole only what he knew about: her Destroyer Gifts. Help her find the magic within then return to River's Edge to deliver the cure Jackson Castaloni left behind."

Daniel blinks and the woman disappears. Looking down, he's startled to see the cure nestled in his left palm. He tucks it into the Veil for safekeeping.

Marina's muffled sobs shake sense back into Daniel's throbbing head. Even as he remembers the pain slicing through his head, it too vanishes.

Help her.

The order comes through clearly. Wearily, Daniel wonders if he should be disturbed by the visions. Panic rises in him as his stiff legs lead him over to Marina and Gabriel.

"Marina." Daniel calls her name several times before she lifts wounded eyes to acknowledge him. "You can help him." Feeling stupid, Daniel awkwardly conveys the Lady's message to Marina.

She closes her eyes, lifts her chin, and cocks her head to the right. Daniel realizes the Lady must be instructing her.

The pained expression fades in favor of one containing deep concentration. Marina gently holds Gabriel's head up and shifts out from under him. Lowering his head to the forest floor, she moves around to his right so that the young man's body lies between her and Daniel. Placing her right hand over the blackened wound, Marina bows her head like one who prays. Her left hand grips her brother's upper arm.

At first, nothing happens, but soon, a soft yellow light leaks out from under Marina's splayed fingers. Her shoulders shake and sweat breaks out across her brow.

Remembering the Lady's instruction, Daniel circles Gabriel's prone form and kneels behind Marina, unsure of what to do. Reaching out a tentative left hand, Daniel lays the palm on Marina's back. A cramp seizes his whole arm from wrist to shoulder. He reaches out and grips her right shoulder to keep his balance. The cramp eases. An unseen current passes from Marina to Daniel and back again several times, flowing through his arms around in circles. Each pass leaves him weaker, but he steels himself to wait for the healing process to finish.

Finally, the current cuts off and Marina sags back into Daniel's arms. He sits on the ground hard, inadvertently pulling her half onto his lap. Tucking his arms protectively around her waist, Daniel peers over her right shoulder. A tattered hole reminds them of the damage done, but the flesh beneath looks pink and healthy.

Gabriel gazes at them in wonder.

"How did you do that?" he croaks.

"The Lady said I could heal you, so I did," Marina whispers.

Forcing himself to sit up, Gabriel leans back on his hands and gazes down at the hole in his shirt.

"You shouldn't have done it," Gabriel murmurs. "I don't deserve it." Unshed tears make his eyes shiny, but he avoids their gazes. "I helped him."

"The Lady told me what you did. You also saved me," Marina reminds him.

"It's not enough," Gabriel argues.

Remembering the cure, Daniel opens a small tear in the Veil next to Gabriel.

"Deliver that if you wish to seek atonement," says Daniel.

Gabriel takes the tiny vial out of the tear, and Daniel lets the Veil close. The young man considers the vial then shakes his head.

"No, this is Marina's gift to deliver." Struggling to his feet, Gabriel crosses to where Marina and Daniel sit. Dropping to one knee, Gabriel presses the vial into Marina's hands. "I'm so sorry." Squeezing her hands once, Gabriel rises to leave.

"Don't go," says Marina.

"I must." Determination enters Gabriel's eyes. "Jack needs to be stopped." Without giving them a chance to respond, he turns into a wolf and races away.

Marina tries to rise, but Daniel stops her.

"Let him go," Daniel urges.

"He'll get himself killed," Marina protests.

"That is his choice," says Daniel. "Besides, you're in no condition to catch him now. Let's finish our business in the village and then go after them. Together."

"How?" Marina demands. She twists around and looks up at Daniel. "With traveler's portals and Jack's abilities, they could be anywhere on Aeris!"

The urge to wipe away her tears comes over Daniel, so he shifts his grip and gently runs fingers across the stains marring her beautiful cheeks.

Looking into Marina's eyes, Daniel remembers why he chose to spare her when killing her would have all but guaranteed him Huntmaster rank and a swift path to the High Council. As the situation stands, he'll be lucky if they don't kick him out of the guild and blacklist him.

"Perhaps we should start over," Daniel murmurs. "Marina Castaloni, my name is Daniel Saveron. I am an Arkonai Seeker, and my skills are at your service."

"You would help me?" Marina's inflection makes it a question.

He nods and relies on formality to mask his muddled feelings.

"The Lady has bid me to aid you, so I shall."

Hi, thank you for reading "River's Edge Ransom." If you wish to know more about Aeris, head over to my website and hop on the Spec Fic list to keep up with the latest news.

This story is a tiny prequel to Redeemer Chronicles 1: Awakening. *The second story is undergoing revisions now and should release late 2017. There will be at least one more story in the official series, and I'm eager to bridge the gap between the mini-prequel and* Awakening.

http://www.juliecgilbert.com/

For those of you who don't know me, I'm a chemistry teacher and multi-genre writer. I enjoy getting to know people, building Legos, drinking tea, taking long walks, producing audiobooks, and exploring the human condition through writing. If you enjoy clean, exciting fiction that falls in the scifi, Christian mystery, fantasy, or mystery/thriller genres, odds are good I've got something you might like. I'm currently working on my first non-fiction book on blurb writing.

Drop me a line any time. (devyaschildren@gmail.com).

The Love Talker

Deanna Fugett

My aunt fell victim to him. My second cousin too, Deirdre. Or so they say. But I don't believe it. Just a silly legend. Mother swears it's true. Talks about how beautiful her sister was at only sixteen years of age. That she died of starvation.

Well, that would happen if you don't eat.

It couldn't be his fault. He didn't stop her from eating, did he? How could he when he simply disappeared?

Tears welled up in Mother's eyes when she told me the story. She liked to seal it with an emotional punch. I'm sure it was hard losing a sister at such a young age, but she needs to stop with the Gancanagh stories. They're not true. I glance over at my Myrna. Guess I could see how making up a story of a faerie killing my sister would somehow make it easier.

Easier than admitting she killed herself, I suppose. Must be how Mother dealt with it when it happened to my aunt.

I brush my dress off as Myrna stands, bringing her basket full of blueberries with her. How she manages to stay clean, I'll never know. My fingers swish over dampness left on my blue-stained apron. Maybe if I'd quit munching on the blueberries while I picked.

She nods. "Time to go, eh?"

Groping for my nearby basket, I ease to my feet. "Yeah, Pa should be expecting us back soon. We best crack on." We plunk down the bumpy, dirt path, weeds swishing our ankles.

The forest dims. The canopy of green above sparkles as the evening sun peeks through the leaves. Myrna's deep hickory hair sways as she picks up her pace. Soon there won't be any more light filtering in. It's at times like this I wish I had a husband. Or at least a suitor.

Men tend to shy away from me, with my bad complexion, frizzy hair, and chubby ankles. I'm not what they're looking for.

Nope. Men want someone like her. Clear skin and gorgeous, flowing hair. I'm lucky to get a subtle glance at the annual village dances. Myrna stays on the arm of a fella the entire night, while I sit in the background, waiting, hoping, someone might take notice. Hasn't happened yet. Worst part? She's my little sister. Poor thing can't get married until Pa marries me off first. Good luck with that.

Some days, I let myself dream. Not often, but sometimes I can't push them away. A fella, tall and sturdy, blond hair parted straight down the middle, with fine eyes the color of pinewood. He'll come by, smile, sweep me into his arms, and we'll marry the next day. I'm not thick enough to believe it'll ever happen.

As we exit the forest and meet the cobblestone path leading to the village, we slow our pace. Thank the Lord we got out of the forest before dark. Creepy things lie in wait if you stay too late.

The village embraces us within its safety. Rushing isn't important now.

Myrna clasps arms with me and skips, forcing me to keep in step. Her white smile flashes in the evening light. I can't help but laugh in chorus with her. She's like a constant ray of sunshine, even when hopelessness fills my days. I can always depend on her to cheer me.

We skip closer to our little cottage tucked nicely within the center of the village. Dad always said we're safest that way. Other attacking villages would burn the outer cottages first, giving us ample time to escape. A horse neighs right beside us. My heart thumps, and Myrna jolts me to a halt before a horse and rider pull themselves front and center before us.

"Hey!" The rider's back is turned to us. Thickheaded eejit won't even acknowledge me. "Watch it, or my pa will see you hanged!" Myrna shushes me as the rider grasps his reins and pulls the insubordinate horse to a grinding stop. I look up to see a head full of hay. I'm sure in the morning sun it would glimmer and shine. He jerks his face in our direction, a scowl on his nicely shaped features.

I gasp. Brown eyes, the color of pinewood. Like the fella in my dreams. And the hair, parted straight down the middle. My throat gulps in a harsh, painful way. Myrna has the good sense to curtsy, still grasping my arm, while I stand there, thrown off balance by her sudden bob downward. I clumsily manage to follow her lead, not tearing my eyes from his face.

It's him. How's that possible?

"Pardon my horse, sweet ladies." The blond locks jostle atop his head as his horse clomps backwards. He grasps the reins hard. "Settle down!" His throaty, deep voice soothes me. Perfection.

He dismounts from his steed and makes his way to us, rope in hand, not allowing the beast much leeway. "Stubborn ox. She does what she pleases." He smiles at us; the corners of his eyes crinkle. *Sigh.* He's gorgeous.

Myrna giggles at my side. The sudden urge to jab my elbow into her side makes me stiffen. She's going to do her usual flirting now, isn't she? She tucks in her chin and bats her lashes. Pulling her hands behind her back, she rocks herself side to side. I glance at him. He's noticed, that he has. How does she always pull men into her gaze? Why not me? I finger my temple, grazing over multiple bumps. Too bad Pa can't afford powder. What I wouldn't give to make my complexion red-bump free.

He bows to us. "Name's Kearney. I'm just traveling through, but I'm in need of lodging for the night." He's not staying? My stomach sinks. "I'd like to know where the nearest inn's located."

Myrna points down the road. "On thataway. Once you get to the bend, make a right and it's the fourth establishment on the left side." She flitters her lashes.

He takes note as a grin plays on his lips.

Heat creeps up my neck. Cheeky little thing. Thinks she can get all the attention, does she? I clear my throat and his gaze reluctantly drifts to me. "It's called the Smokey Tavern. The inn's right above it."

He gives a tight smile. Nary a fella in this town could claim his stunning beauty. He reaches out and touches my arm for a brief moment. "Thanks."

A spark blasts my skin.

He touched me. How I long for more.

He backs away and climbs on his horse. Once settled into the saddle, he nods again. "I didn't catch your ladies' names?"

Myrna tilts her chin up. "Myrna." She nods. "And this is—"

"Teagan." I shoot my sister a death glare and grit my teeth. "I can say my own name." I glance back up at him and he's grinning.

At *me*.

Not her. For once, a fella grins at me. I give him my warmest smile, and he turns and trots off down the path. Myrna huffs and marches past me.

What fortune! Maybe this fella, the man of my dreams, came true because I wanted it so badly.

My head in the clouds, I barely remember the trip home. I'm standing in front of our cottage door. How'd I get here so fast? Myrna opens the door, flings herself inside, and slams it in my face. My breath shallows, and I brace myself. What will she tell Pa? I place my palm on the worn wooden door and push my way in. Darkness envelops me. I blink a few times to adjust to the lesser lighting.

An oil lamp burns bright in the corner where Pa sits, smoking his pipe. He pulls it from his cracked lips and puffs out cloudy rings. "Myrna's looking a bit down. What didja do to her this time?"

I scowl. Always blaming me for everything. "I did nothing, Pa." I trudge to the kitchen table and plop my basket of berries next to the one Myrna left.

"Your sister stomped to her room. Didn't say a word to me. She only does that when she's irritated with you."

I grab a handful of berries and stuff them into my mouth. *One. Two. Three.* He won't get me upset. I won't let him. *Breathe.* The berries slide down my throat, juice dripping to my chin.

"She's just jealous I caught a fella's attention. A very handsome fella, in fact."

Pa sits up and stares me straight in the face. "You did, now didja?" He coughs and pauses. "Who's this fine man?"

I can't meet Pa's eyes. Best to tell him now, before he gets his hopes up. "Just a traveler. No one from around these parts."

Pa slinks back into his chair and sticks the pipe back in his mouth. He takes a few puffs. "What a shame."

I lower my head. Knew he'd be disappointed.

"If a foreigner's interested in my oldest daughter, then someone around this town will be, too." I jerk my chin up to meet his gaze. He flashes me a smile and then pulls on his scraggly white beard. "If you'd actually start taking care of yourself." He signals to my blue-stained apron with his hand. My gut plummets. He's bang on. I'm a mess.

He waves me over, and I near him like a wild fawn approaching a child holding out food. He palms my shoulder and pulls me down to eye level. Pulling his handkerchief from his pocket, he dabs my chin, wiping away the juice. "What am I going to do with you, my girl?" He smiles, but his sadness creases his face. I'll never be good enough, or pretty enough, to please him.

I lie in bed, the handsome stranger whisking through my mind. His hair, his eyes, his stature. Everything about him exactly like I imagined in my dreams. Surely it's a sign. My heart throbs with the possibilities until I'm so obsessed my mind won't shut off for anything. His smile fills me until the wee hours of the morning. I finally fall into an exhausted sleep. Dreams rattle me until I'm right there in them, as if they truly happen. I wake to Myrna shaking me.

"Market day. Wake up, silly."

Ugh. *Get off me.* I push her hand aside. She persists and I give in. Why did I stay up late anyway? I rub the sleepies away, and Kearney's handsome face comes to mind. Market day. We'll be in town! Where Kearney's staying. I might see him again! I push the covers off and spring out of bed.

"That's a change." Myrna smirks. "Come, I'll do your hair." I sit on the wicker stool while she pulls and teases my hair into a respectable spiral bun. Not sure how she manages with the tangles and the frizz. Any time I try, it never turns out this good. She grabs a mirror off the nightstand and places it in my hand.

I take a look and then glance up. "Sorry for upsetting you last night."

She flinches. "You didn't upset me. Are you talking mad things again, dear sister?" She grabs my shoulders and pulls me up. "Perfect." She points to the end of the bed where she's already placed my best dress. "Get yourself dressed.

Let's see if we can't accidentally run into that fine fellow again?"

She's not mad? She understands what this means to me? I pinch her cheek. "Can't wait."

She leaves me be, and I whip the dress off the bed. This day's going to be better than I can imagine. Sleep or no sleep. I can feel it.

I waltz down the stairs to find warm muffins awaiting me. Pa munches on one at the table. Steam still wafts above the stack of them. "Myrna! You didn't." She grins and sets a plate in front of me. My mouth waters.

"I did. Now eat up. We're going to have a long day of stalking Kearney—" Pa chokes on his muffin and coughs. Myrna pats his back. "I mean, buying supplies for the week."

Pa shakes his head and chuckles.

I stuff the last bits of muffin into my mouth, careful to scrub the crumbs from my chin. Won't today be fun? My heart brightens with the thought of seeing him again. I sigh. Maybe he'll whisk me away to a castle off in the distance. A girl can dream, can't she?

I grab a basket out of the cupboard and whip around. "You didn't use all the blueberries in the muffins, did you?"

Myrna frowns. "Oh, dear."

I purse my lips. Figures. And I thought today was going so well.

"Only codding ya!" She lunges to the cupboard and pulls out a lumpy cloth. She draws close and dumps them into my basket.

"Ye bollocks." I resist the urge to bop her on the nose.

"Knew you'd be wanting to take some to her." She grabs a muffin off the pile and places it in with the blueberries, pulling the cloth around the goodies. "Now, let's be off."

Myrna drives me mad, but she knows me well. I can't do market day without my weekly visit. It wouldn't be right. Not even with the risk of missing a Kearney sighting. Nothing's that important.

Myrna follows me to the outermost circle of cottages, to the one near the edge of the forest. Wish Myrna would be more enthusiastic about seeing Ma. I'm thankful she doesn't squawk about it, though.

"Howya doin'?" I wave at the sweet, wrinkled lady pinning the wash to the line.

"Hello, dear." She waves back. "Your ma's inside."

I push forward and my side's suddenly empty. I glance back at my frozen sister. "Not coming today?"

She shakes her head. "I want today to be a happy one."

"Suit yourself."

She can be so selfish sometimes. Doesn't she realize Ma needs us? I gallop into the cottage full of misfits. The reformed town slag "found God" and decided to take in the women who'd been turned out of their homes. They've created a sort of mini-society within our own. They are the outcasts. The adulterers, the widows, the fornicators, or in my mother's case, the insane. Pa tried to keep her as long as he could, but she wasn't happy. And he couldn't force her to be there against her will. She kept leaving home, and one day, she never came back.

One day, he quit searching for her.

I open the door and find Ma at the table, knitting.

A lady stirs a pot over the open fire. "Teagan, nice to see you again." I focus on my mother, who hasn't acknowledged me. I pull up a chair next to her, and she doesn't seem to notice or care. I know she does, she must. I am her daughter, after all.

I plunk the basket down in front of her. Only then does she turn her head. "Hello, Mother." She meets my eyes with her own dead ones for but a brief moment. They lost their sparkle many years ago. She stares at the basket. "For you. Myrna made some muffins and we brought you blueberries from the forest."

She sets her knitting down and flips the cloth off, revealing the contents within. She ravages the muffin within seconds, crumbs tumbling upon her skirt and the ground beneath her. At least I know where I get my dirty habits from. Her vacant stare proves to me I'm of no interest to her.

I pat her on the hand. "I'm off to the market." No eye contact. Maddening. When will she start caring about her own daughter? Or at least show some slight interest. Might as well tell her. Nothing I say ever reaches her ears, anyway.

"Myrna and I met a man last night." Her eye twitches. "He was very handsome." I get up to leave and curl around the edge of the table. "We're going to try and find him again in town today. There's something special about this one." I turn my back, and a chair thumps to the ground. I whirl back around.

Ma stands there, eyes wide and arms stretched in a stiff and frenzied manner. My forehead scrunches. "Ma, are you okay?"

"Protect her!" Ma meets me with a steady gaze for the first time in a long while.

"Protect who?"

"Myrna."

My blood runs cold. "From whom, Mother?"

"The Gancanagh."

I let my shoulders sag. Oh, that again. "There's no such thing." She has to get over this obsession of hers. This faerie creature's a figment of her imagination. Nothing more.

"Protect your sister." She fails to rip her eyes from mine and approaches around the table until she's face to face with me. "I've felt it for a while. He's back. It's time for his return, and he's back."

"Ma, no one's back."

"This man you speak of, you say he's handsome?" She's quite the talker today.

"Well, yes, very. More handsome than any of the fellas around here."

Her eyes widen even further. Didn't know they could get that big. Chills creep into my bones. "Have you or your sister thought about him frequently since you met him?"

I shake my head. "What does it matter, Mother? Of course we're going to think of a fine fella when he crosses our path."

She grabs my arm, a tad too tight. "Did he touch you?"

I rip her paw from me. "Really, Mother. Believing in these silly faerie tales." A flash of Kearney's hand touching my arm, right where Ma's hand had been, whizzes through my mind. Yes, he touched me. And I rather liked it.

"He did, didn't he?" Her hands shake. "And what of your sister? Did he touch her, too?"

No, Mother, but it doesn't matter. "It's time for me to leave. We need to get to our shopping." I exit the cottage, and Ma clings to the doorframe.

"Don't let him get to her!" She trembles. Myrna stands in the distance, her figure tense. "Your aunt was only sixteen too when he got to her! Protect her, Teagan. Promise me!" Ma clutches the doorframe, sinking lower and lower. "I couldn't protect my sister, but you can protect yours." She yells and collapses to the ground. The madness has completely taken over now.

Myrna hurries to keep up with my strides. "What was that all about?"

"Forget about it. She's gone completely bonkers." The power in Ma's words still rings through my ears. The way she spoke fluently. That hasn't happened since before she went mad.

We plod down the street, back into the throes of the inner village, getting closer to the inn. Maybe we'll see Kearney again. I push aside all the negative feelings about Ma and her deteriorating state and focus on an image of the dashing fella.

"Let's start our shopping near the Smokey Tavern," I suggest.

Myrna squeezes my arm. "You're reading my mind." She squeals and picks up her feet into a skip. The cottages turn into storefronts.

As we near it, lo and behold, Kearney stands just outside the inn, waving his hand in front of his nose, while a smoking, wrinkled man next to him blows into Kearney's face. I clutch Myrna's arm.

"Confound it, old man! Put that foul-smelling thing away!" He grabs the old man's pipe out of his hand and tosses it to the ground. "Disgusting habit."

The old man's face reddens and he clenches his fists. Bet he'd like to sock Kearney a good one. Instead, he picks the pipe from the ground and slumps back inside the inn. Must have realized he wouldn't win that fight.

Myrna waltzes forward to get Kearney's attention and I follow, when a shadow forms next to me. I halt and look to my side. A gangly, ginger-headed fella stands there, pipe in hand. He shoves it in his pocket and points in Kearney's direction. "Eejit. Thinks he can go around bossing other folks around. Forcing them to bend to his will." He kicks the ground.

True. It was rather rude. But I'm sure he's not like that all the time. "Earwigging, are we? Good day, sir "

He clutches my elbow for a moment. "You're not thinking about going to talk to that rude fellow, now are ya?"

Now, why's he touching me? I wriggle from his grasp and examine him. Redhead, same as all the other Irish men around here. Scrawny, arms barely strong enough to pick a lady up and sweep her off her feet. His ears stick out too far and his nose is a tad too long. Must be one of the O'Brian brothers. They all look the same.

I glance over to Myrna, who stands beside Kearney, his dark eyes so mysterious. Not like all the other blue- or green-eyed males I've grown up with. I peer back at this annoyance standing next to me. What does he want, anyway? "Yes, I've been looking forward to speaking with him all morning. Now, if you'll excuse me."

The ginger-haired fella reaches out and grabs my exposed forearm, sending heat up into my shoulder. "Don't be bothering me. I don't even know you."

He backs off a pace or two. "I thought a pretty lady like you would deserve a better man than that rude bloke." He reaches a hand into his pocket, pulls out his pipe, and sticks it between his teeth. "Begging your pardon, ma'am." He bows and flounces away.

Did he call me pretty? No one's ever said that about me before.

I watch as his back becomes smaller and smaller. Maybe I shouldn't have driven him away. Turning back to my sister and my beloved already deep in conversation, I waltz forward.

Myrna giggles and Kearney grins but keeps a respectable distance. Looks like whatever they're discussing pleases them both. Darn. I missed out on some valuable flirt time. Not that I even know how, but I'd like to at least have the chance to try.

I curtsy and when I raise my head, a bemused smile plays upon Kearney's lips. I lower my lashes and twiddle my thumbs. Guess I shouldn't have intruded upon their conversation.

Myrna twirls a strand of her dark locks around her finger. "I was about to show Kearney around town. You don't mind, do you?" She flashes me a grin as hot lead pours from my ears.

Brat. How dare she, when she knows how much I adore him? They walk away, still not touching, and head to the opposite side of the street.

Protect her! Ma's warning rings through my mind. From what? A handsome man taking interest in her? I cross my arms and huff. Thought she'd at least invite me along.

Something grazes my dress and I jump. The ginger-haired fella stands beside me once more.

"Where did you come from?"

"Sorry for startling you, miss." He lips his pipe.

"I thought you ran off."

He grins over the pipe. "I'm back." No smoke rises from the wooden contraption between his lips.

"Why, there's not even any tobacco in your pipe!" I plunk my fists to my hips. "What, do you pretend to smoke it?"

He pulls the pipe from his mouth and frowns as he inspects it. "What's wrong with that?"

"It's odd, is all." His nose seems to have shrunk. Or maybe I'm thinking more kindly of him. He did call me pretty, after all. "Who are you, anyway?"

He laughs. "I'm Emmet. And you're Teagan. That correct?"

"How didja know my name?"

"Small town." He sweeps his hand back and forth, indicating the shops around us.

He puts the tobacco-less pipe back in his mouth. "What begs the question, miss, is why you didn't know mine?"

I shrug. Well, he's a real chancer. Is it my job to know everyone's name in this village? "Guess it slipped my mind." I turn from him. Don't need people making fun of me today. Not when I'm already feeling down about Kearney and my sister.

Emmet stays at my side, staring down the street. "Did they leave without you?"

"Ya," I mutter and twist my apron in my hand.

"Well, that was downright rude, now wasn't it?"

Hate to admit it, but he's bang on. A tear wells up in the corner of my eye.

He shakes his fist at the air. "How dare they leave such a beautiful woman behind! Why, I oughta show them a thing or two."

Beautiful? First he calls me pretty and now beautiful? Who's this fella, anyway?

"Listen, Mister Emmet, I don't know what kind of game you're trying to play, but you ought to leave me alone. It's not right to tease a lady." He reaches for my arm and I shrug him off.

But I want him to touch me. To touch my arm. *Do it again. I'll let you this time.* He cocks his head and peers into my eye with the tear that's ready to spill over. Gently, he brings his hand up to my cheek and wipes beneath, on the crest of my cheek, causing the tear to spill over onto his skin. "Poor girl." His ears don't seem to stick out quite as much now. "What you need is some fun."

I'm supposed to be shopping. So is Myrna. But she's too busy carrying on with a handsome traveler to busy herself with responsibilities. Why should she have all the fun?

"Yes, I could use a distraction right about now."

"Grand." He grabs my hand. His is warm and strong. I catch my breath. No man ever held my hand before, not even when I was a little child.

Tingles prance up and down my arms. Fine hairs stand on end. Before I know it, we're at the edge of the woods. I barely know him. What am I thinking? "Stop."

He halts and drops my hand. "What's the matter?"

"The matter is, I've just met you, Emmet. And now you're taking me into the woods. How can I trust you?"

"Trust is a funny thing. You either do it or you don't. There has to be a level of faith before you can trust someone, doesn't there?"

He's speaking to my heart. "Yes. I've always believed that."

He extends his hand to me. "Do you have faith in me? That I won't cause you any harm?" He leans closer; his breath on my cheek. "Do you trust in me?" He leans even closer until I swear his lips will touch my skin. I flush hot from head to toe. "Do you believe in me?"

There's no rhyme or reason to it, but I do. I do believe in him. "Yes," I whisper.

A faint haze of shimmer falls over my eyes, and for a moment, he seems to glow otherworldly, like an angel. The filter falls within seconds, and I blink to clear my vision. I want to be with him. Need to be. I grasp his hand and he leads me within the leafy shroud.

I gulp. *Myrna. Protect Myrna.* A faint hint of Ma's voice wavers in my mind. I push it aside. She's fine. She knows how to take care of herself.

Over fallen logs, boulders, and brush, Emmet leads me this way and that. I don't know where we're going, and I don't care. Myrna abandoned me. I can do what I please now.

Finally, we end at a little brook within the part of the woods I'm unfamiliar with. Emmet cools himself by splashing some of the brook water on his face. Then he scoops up a handful and drinks from it. "Best-tasting water you'll ever have."

My mouth's parched, but I know well enough not to drink water from these parts. "That's enchanted water, you know," I tease him.

"Enchanted, you say? What makes you think that?" He swirls his finger within its crystal-clear coolness.

"These are the fae parts of the woods. Or haven't you heard?"

"You don't believe in all that faerie nonsense, now do you?" He arches a brow.

I shake my head. "Of course not. But that doesn't mean I want to risk it, either." I plunk down on a small boulder. "Just in case."

He smirks. "Just in case."

I stick my nose up at him. Cheeky.

He stands up and shakes the water from his dripping hand. "I actually do believe."

"You do?" Now I'm intrigued. "In what, exactly?"

"In the fae folk." He sinks down beside me, our hips bumping together. Heat soars through my gut.

"You can't be serious?" I pat him on his hand. "My ma believes. And she's quite insane."

"Not literally insane, I hope you mean."

"Yes, quite literally."

"Huh." He scratches his chin. "Well, I'm sorry to hear that. What kind of faerie folk does she like to talk about? The Incubus?"

I shake my head. "She's only mentioned *him* once. The one that holds her obsession is the Gancanagh."

"Ah, I see. Has she ever been touched by him?"

"No. I don't believe so. But my aunt was. That's how she died, you know." What am I saying? I glare at him. "Look here, you've got me all flustered. Talking like such a thing as the Gancanagh could actually exist." I stand up and press the wrinkles from my skirts.

"Why are you certain he doesn't?"

"It's absurd. Faerie creatures are all legend. Made up to scare us."

He stands and yanks me toward him until our heads touch. I pull my chin to my chest. Maybe not absurd, after all. I melt into him and his arms wrap around me. Since when did he get muscles?

My breath catches in my throat. No one ever held me like this, except for that one time I fainted in the village square. And that had only been out of necessity.

Our bodies close, his presence fills my every nerve, every fiber. Down to my very core. His gaze fills me with assurance, he means me no harm. Maybe he even cares for me.

"You are such a delicate flower. No one should ever be allowed to touch you for fear you could wilt." He releases me from his grasp. Cold, cruel emptiness enters my marrow.

"No." I step forward. "I'm stronger than that. Please."

I reach out and he pulls me to him once more. "Are you, dear Teagan? Are you stronger than that?"

"Yes." I breathe out against his ivory cheek. He turns and clamps his lips to mine. Passion explodes inside me. How could I live so long without knowing his love? Without feeling this feeling?

My head empties and he pulls back, still wrapping me within his embrace. "We shall see."

That night, my dreams of Kearney are replaced with dreams of a certain ginger-haired fella, who now holds my heart. The crush I had on Kearney pales in comparison to the love filling my bosom for this new companion in my life. How'd I possibly just meet him, when he makes me feel so utterly alive? Completed. Needed. Wanted. Never in my life has anyone paid me the slightest attention. Now, they'll all see what they've been missing. See that I'm worth something.

He kisses me, his lips smooth and warm against my own. A clawed hand slides around Emmet's neck and begins to squeeze. We're torn apart and I scream into the forest air. But no one else's around. No one will hear us. The foul creature, ripe with horns and fangs, squeezes my love, throttling him until the life seeps from his face. Emmet dissipates into the air around him. The creature cries out and digs at his own blood-red skin, ripping pieces of flesh from himself. Clothing appears underneath, and a man claws his way out. Finally, he has enough room to separate himself from the vile creature and throws the horned head from his own. Kearney stands there before me. I scream until my throat aches. No!

Myrna's shaking me. A scream ebbs from my lips, and I bolt upright. Drops of perspiration drip from my forehead to my nightgown. Myrna's nose pinches and her forehead creases. "You're okay, Teagan. It was a nightmare. It's morning now. You've been thrashing and moaning in your sleep all night. I could hear you from next door."

I wipe the sweat from my face.

"What's gotten into you?"

I thunk back onto my pillow. Two nights in a row with scarcely any sleep. I sigh. "Leave me be. I'll do my hair on my own this morning."

Myrna makes for the doorway. "You sure?"

I nod. The dream rattles through my thoughts. I must warn her. "Myrna!"

She reenters and folds her arms across her chest. "What is it?"

"Tell me Kearney's off today."

"Not until tomorrow. Why?"

"Tell me you don't intend to see him."

She pouts. "I already have plans this morning to do just that."

I jump to my feet. "Please don't. Tell me you won't." The horned creature plays through my vision, taunting me with its gnarled hands and pointy teeth.

She stomps the floor. "Now, just because you're jealous does not give you the right to tell me I can't see him. I'm sorry if this hurts you, sister, but you must know I have strong feelings for him too."

"But he's dangerous!" How can I explain this to her without sounding as mad as our mother?

"Now, that's stooping low. Trying to come up with something outrageous, so you can have him all to yourself. I won't have it." She turns her back on me. "He's already made his feelings known to me. He returns my devotion. I'm sorry, Teagan. It's too late."

She marches from the room without another glance. I must find Emmet now. Hopefully, he'll know how to protect her from the Gancanagh.

Once I find him in the streets where we'd first met, I take him aside. "I ought to've listened to Mother." I weep. "She asked me to protect Myrna, and I've failed her. She's gone straight back to him. And soon she'll discover what he is."

"What's going on?" Emmet wraps his arm around my shoulder and traces a finger down my cheek. "Did something happen?"

"A dream revealed that Kearney's the Gancanagh." I turn and bury my face into the crook of his neck, his skin warm against my own. "I didn't believe it, but now I know. My ma isn't crazy. He's back, and now my sister is doomed. She'll starve herself to death like my aunt and cousin did."

Emmet rocks me as a mother would rock her babe. "There, there, my dear. We can stop this. We can still save your sister. There's still time."

I look up into his eyes. "You think?"

"Has he touched her yet?"

I remember the respectable distance Kearney seemed to hold in my sister's presence. I shake my head. "I don't believe so."

"Then there's still time."

"We can't know for sure."

He takes his sleeve and wipes my tear-stained cheeks. "Then we must make haste and find them." He pulls me to my feet and kisses my cheek. "You think they're still in there?" He points to the Smokey Tavern.

"Maybe." They could be anywhere.

We reach the tavern door together and he swings it open. "Barkeeper!" All heads swing in our direction. "Is a certain man here with the name of Kearney? Blond chap, rather large build." The barkeeper stomps in our direction while others' interest fades as they go back to playing their card games and their drinking of ale. "See here, young fellow. Don't come barging in here, bellowing at folks. It doesn't make for good business."

Emmet deflates a bit. "Yes, sir. Sorry about that. We're in a hurry to find a woman, a young lady, actually, who might be under his influence. We're concerned about her safety and need to find her promptly."

"Ah. I see. Yes, there was a young gal who left with him, not more than twenty minutes ago."

Emmet pats the barkeeper on the back. "Thank you. Do you have any clue where they're headed?"

The barkeeper shakes his head, gray curls bouncing to and fro. "Sorry, lad."

Emmet pulls me to the door and whisks me outside. "This isn't good."

"I know." Ice curls around my bones. I have to find them before he destroys her! "Let's search. Every street. Every road. We'll knock on every cottage door if we have to."

Emmet nods. At least I can depend on him. He squeezes my hand. "Not too soon to start now."

Hours of searching later, Emmet and I flop down on a crudely built bench. Where could they be? I rest my head on his shoulder. "There's nowhere else to look."

"You sure we've looked everywhere?"

"Our village isn't that big. We should've come upon them by now." I weep upon his shoulder, wetting the fine silk material covering his muscled arm. "He's stolen her away. She'll never return, and if she does, she'll only die of a broken heart."

Emmet slides his finger under my chin and lifts it to meet his gaze. "There's one more spot."

I wrack my brain. The fae area of the forest! How could I not have thought of that earlier? Of course, that's where they'd be. Any fae folk would feel much more comfortable in their own environment. "Why didn't ya mention it sooner?"

"I'm just remembering myself."

We stand in unison. Emmet holds firm to my hand, and when I stall, he yanks me forward. Apparently he's in a bigger rush than I.

Once the woods enclose on us, the afternoon sun hides above the trees. A welcome relief for a rather hot day.

"Make haste. We cannot wait too long." He pulls me along further into the woods. I'm beginning to recognize the area when I trip on a stone and tumble to my knees. Emmet rushes to my side and guides me up; his hands on my arm and back scorch through my clothing.

I steady myself. The stone I tripped on is pure white, and it's not just any stone. Emmet releases his grip on me and I whirl in a circle. I'm ringed by a group of white stones. A faerie circle. A most magical place indeed. My heart thumps in my chest and my palms sweat. "Have we disturbed the spirits?"

Emmet guides me away from the faerie circle and chuckles. "Don't ya think they're a wee bit more understanding than that?"

"But I fell in their circle."

"I thought you didn't buy all that nonsense." He shakes his head and grins. "No harm done, lass. Why, if I was a fae folk, I'd be most pleased at such a rare beauty landing in my circle."

My cheeks warm. He says such nice things. I pinch my arm. Can't get distracted. Must find Myrna. "We must be almost there."

"That we are, my sweet lady. All around us. This's fae country." Shivers run up my back. The air itself whispers of spirits and mysteries. Something serene, but haunting, flows through the petals on every flower, snippets of leaves on every branch, no matter how small. Nothing escapes the awe and wonder of this place.

"My sister must be close." I forge on through the brush, ears at attention, waiting on any sound that might be out of the ordinary. Only birds chirping and leaves rustling can be heard. The faint breeze shimmies around and through branches and boughs.

The tinkle of the brook breaks through the quiet. "We're almost there!" I rush in the direction we'd gone before. The sparkling brook cuts through the forest floor, creating a trailing divot below.

My shoulders fall along with my heart. She's not here. Neither is the Gancanagh. He must have whisked her away. I cannot weep anymore. I ran out of tears much earlier today. I can only stand there, wishing, hoping, and praying Myrna will come back to me.

Emmet graces my side and slips his hand into mine. In the still, a peace settles on me. Swirling around me, soaking into my pores. I turn my head and catch his glance.

Why does he think me special? I'm a no one. Yet, here he stands, beside me. Like bees drawn to the nectar of a nearby blossom, his musky scent overwhelms me, drawing me in. Containing myself any longer would surely drive me mad. I lean over and press my palm to his cheek, his face nears mine, and soon we've connected. When he releases me, the sweet taste of his mouth lingers.

If I can't get Myrna back, I might as well go on and live a happy life. She wouldn't want me to be miserable on account of her. Nothing more we can do today, anyway. We've tried our best, and it wasn't good enough. My eyes fill with tears I thought were impossible to come by. Emmet gently tugs his fingers through my hair.

"Sweet girl. Can you not be happy without your sister?"

I sniffle. "I can try." He traces my jawline with his finger; rapturous sparks from his touch sink beneath my skin. He places his palm on my back and pulls me close. His arms around me, I submit to his touch. Dizziness and pleasure encompass the inner workings of my skull, mucking things up. I've forgotten why I'm here or who I am. All I know is he's here and I need him.

His suede jacket slides beneath my fingers; as I caress his back, the fabric moves along with my touch. Soon the passion will drive me to sweet insanity. My brain slips for a moment, but I gain traction and salvage my thoughts. I pull back and his mouth searches for mine. I press my finger to his lips to signal I'm finished for now. He flickers his eyes open.

"Have I done something to displease you, my love?"

Love? He loves me now? "No. Quite the opposite. But I can't very well sit here and receive such a precious treasure from you while my sister's out there, being seduced by some deranged creature." I back away even more. "It's time for me to go home." Everything inside me begs for him to keep me here. To give me some valid excuse to stay.

"No. You're right. We've had a long day. It's probably best to call it a night." He pulls his empty pipe from his breast pocket and mouths it. Silly man.

We've reached the edge of the woods.

"See you first thing in the morning. Right, love?"

I melt. "Call me that again."

"Love?" He taps my nose. "Love's such a silly word. Isn't it?"

"I suppose."

He loosens my grip from his arm. "It can make even the sanest person go mad."

He backs away from me and with each step he separates us my heart aches more. I cannot stand to be away from his presence. "Tomorrow!" I shout at him.

There's still plenty of light. I know I ought to go home and tell my pa of Myrna's fate. But I bet Ma knows something. She's more knowledgeable about all this than I am. Maybe she'll have one last clue that could lead us to my sister.

I open the weathered cottage door. Ma's not in her usual spot. I glance over at the old woman. She stares like she's seen a ghost. She wrinkles her nose and comes close. "Ye have the smell of them on you. You've been in the fae woods, haven't ye?" Her shoulders stiffen.

"Where's my mother?" I demand. Enough of this foolish woman's nonsense. She doesn't answer. "You're no help." I march up the stairs with a heavy stride. Better for Ma to hear me coming than be startled. It's not a pretty sight when you startle her.

I reach her door. She's the one with the smallest room. No one wanted to share rooms with the crazy person.

I knock. No answer. Of course she wouldn't answer. I open the door and discover her rocking on the bed.

"Ma, can you tell me more about the Gancanagh?"

She quits rocking and stares vacantly at the wall. After a minute of silence, I huff. She's no use. I turn to leave.

"He seduces young women and disappears."

Oh, now she's going to talk to me? "Yes, I already know that, Ma." She flinches. "What else?"

"When he touches them, they become obsessed. And once he disappears, their heartbreak's so bad they lose their will to eat, drink. Even sleep. Soon death comes knocking on their door. And all's lost."

"Where does the Gancanagh typically take the women he seduces?"

"Anywhere. But his favorite spot is in the woods."

"We've tried that."

She glares. "What are you not telling me?" She stands and approaches. The anger etched on her face frightens me. Why did I have to let that slip? She can't find out about Myrna. It would kill her. Or she might kill me.

"Nothing. My friend and I are trying to find him...for fun."

"There's nothing fun about him, Teagan. Don't be a fool!" she barks. "Oh, sure, at first, when he's wooing you, kissing you, telling you you're beautiful. Saying words only lovers use. Making you feel like you're the most important person in the whole world. Giving you worth. Then he pulls that blasted empty pipe out and disappears like nothing he ever said mattered at all. Leaving you shattered and broken."

Nausea hits me square in the gut. "An empty pipe?"

"Yes, a pipe, girl. He doesn't fill it with anything."

My head spins. The woods, words of love, kissing...and an empty pipe? It can't be a coincidence, can it? The pain's too much to bear.

I retreat into the corner until my back hits the wall. I grasp for the door handle. Rocks pummel my gut over and over. No! None of it's true.

"Teagan, what is it?"

Must escape this room. Have to get some air. I reel out the doorway and fly down the stairwell. A string of "Teagan!" rolls along the air currents.

Have to get away.

I fling myself at my pa's feet. "Pa, I don't know where Myrna is, she's been gone all day and I've searched and searched."

He places his palm on my head. "Teagan. She's here. Myrna's in her room."

What? I run to her doorknob.

"Shh. She's taking a bit of a kip. Spent the whole day with that fine traveler man. He escorted her home shortly before you arrived. She's completely knackered."

I crack the door and catch a glimpse of her, still in her clothes no less, snoring away. "Poor thing's worn out." A heaviness rests on me as I close the door. So am I. "Did you get any dinner, Pa? I'm afraid we've been so busy we neglected you today."

He chuckles. "I'm glad you two are finally finding suitors."

"Suitors?"

"Well, where have you been all day? Your sister said she saw you with a man earlier."

"Well, yes, I was..." I stutter. "Wait, what do you mean, she saw me? I've been searching for her all day."

"Guess she and Kearney were playing hard to get." Pa clears his throat. "She told me about your little jealousy thing going on. I suppose they wanted to make sure you stayed away. But now you've found a man of your own? What good news!" He raises his mug.

"Yes, I suppose I have." The memory of Emmet's warm touch seeps back into my heart. "And now I must find him and let him know Myrna's been found. He's been as concerned for her safety and well-being as I have." I turn to the door. "It wouldn't be fair to let him toss and turn all night worrying about her." I rush back out and slam the door. If I don't get some answers, I won't be able to sleep either.

By the time I reach the Smokey Tavern, daylight has begun to fade. I don't see Emmet anywhere. My heart falls. A hand touches my back and I whirl around. Emmet. My heart swells with love for this man. Ma's crazy. There's no way he could be something sinister. A raging torrent of passion consumes me as I stare into his darling eyes. How could something pure and precious be bad?

He smiles. "You're back. Sweet love, I've missed you and we've barely been apart but for minutes. You must have felt the same."

My heart tugs. "I did. But that's not the only reason I came." I step back from him so my brain can form coherent thoughts. "My sister's been found. And it sounds like we were wrong about Kearney. I don't believe he's the Gancanagh anymore."

Emmet shifts his weight and he leans in, his breath soft and warm on my neck. His lips graze where his breath met, sending shock waves down to my toes. Pure bliss in one single caress. "Let us go to the woods once more," he whispers into my ear.

I pause. "The woods?" My limbs stiffen. "Whatever for? Why, it's getting dark. Surely we'd get lost."

"I always find where I'm going."

Someone's confident, aren't they? But the woods...why would he want to go there now?

Warnings wrack my brain. He touches my shoulder; his finger grazes beneath my neckline. Shudders of pleasure torment me. How can one little flick of the finger cause so much excitement? I have to have more. The craving widens and deepens, consuming me. He's going to eat me alive and I'm going to pleasure in every second of it. "Yes, let's go to the woods."

Agreeing to this a few days ago would have been completely out of the question. But now, now I'm hooked and I'm sinking, falling, faster and faster into the pit of love. Never to claw my way out.

We're at our little spot by the brook again. At this rate, I'll have the path here memorized in no time. His caresses get stronger, fiercer, and more urgent. His passion cannot be quenched it seems, as if he craves more. Something I'm not giving him. Something no respectable maiden ought to give away. He scoots the hem of my dress up to my thigh. I gasp. That's taking things too far. "Stop."

He continues to caress my back, one hand still firmly planted on my leg. I love it, but I hate it. He needs to stop. I don't want him to, but he must.

"Stop."

He plucks his hand from my leg, and the hem of my dress drops back to the ground. "But, love, you are gorgeous. I can't help myself. No one can compare to your beauty." He goes for my leg again. My head swoons as my foot jerks, almost smashing into our lantern.

No. I'm no floozy. I grab his hand. "Stop."

He drops me like a hot coal. "You're telling me to stop?" His voice deepens. "But I thought you loved me?"

"I do!" Why's he being difficult? "But I'm still a lady."

"A lovely lady who won't let me have any fun."

"But I'm having fun. Aren't you?" He must be enjoying himself or he wouldn't bother being out here with me.

He tilts his head and drops his hands to his sides. "I'm bored with you." A shimmer of light burns the air, and he's gone.

Gone. How?

I search the area around us. "This disappearing trick isn't funny. Come back to me, Emmet. Come back!" The desperation in my voice frightens me. "You can't do this to me. You can't leave me here alone! Emmet!" I pound the air with my pleas over and over until my lungs burn and my voice grows hoarse.

Collapsing in a heap of pain, tears burn hot against my face. I can't stop the flow. I don't really care to. He's gone. He's left me. I'm all alone. "I thought you loved me," I scream one last time to the night air. I tuck my knees to my chest and fling my arms over my face, burying it so I can block out the world.

Nothing matters anymore. He was the only one who cared about me.

This is it. The end of my life. There is no going on after this. I can't return after feeling a love like that. His passion, so intense. So real. But yet not...I can't explain it. I know in my head it wasn't real, but the curse has seeped through my blood and infected every last organ. Passing through my system and settling in my heart.

The pain tears at my flesh. I know this curse. I know the rumors and what will happen to me.

It's a fate worse than anything else. Slowly dying, day after day, week after agonizing week, with my stomach rapidly shrinking to nothing, until my eyes are hollow and my cheeks indented. My stomach's endless ache for food, and yet I won't be able to satiate my hunger. The heartbreak will be too overwhelming.

I must end this before it begins.

Searching the area for a knife—nay, anything sharp—I come up empty. Maybe I could break my lamp and use a shard? No, the glass is too thin. "Curse you, Emmet!" Wouldn't even leave me a knife for a blessed escape.

The village! They have knives. My feet pick up a pace, much faster than I've known before. As if some magic drives me forward in a mad frenzy. Shiny and silver will be my ending.

Padding fills my ears. My feet find rocks and sharp twigs, yet the only pain I feel is inside my heart and bursting from my head. There is no going back once the madness takes over.

Once he's touched you.

It's so dark. There must be a knife somewhere. The local butcher. That'll have to do. I hurry to his shop and pound on the door. Locked for the night. My foot raises and smashes the doorframe. How dare he do this to me? Doesn't he know I need to end this pain before it controls me?

I whirl and run past shops, around corners, until I trip over a bench and land *splat* on the ground. Dirt coats my tongue. I grasp the edge of the bench and feel something cold and smooth. Sitting upright, I grip it in my palm, bringing it to my lamp. A pair of shears. Not a knife. But it'll do.

Pulling myself to standing, I place the lamp on the bench beside me. Angling the blades to my chest, I look down. My corset guards my bosom. This won't work. I place the shears down and begin unlacing the cursed thing. Once

I've proper access to the flimsy material of my chiffon blouse underneath, nothing can stop me now. I again raise the shears to my chest, hands trembling.

I don't want to do this, but I must. This will be a much quicker way to go than weeks of falling deeper into the pit of insanity all while starving to death. Can't let that happen.

I won't.

Drawing in a shaky breath, I extend my arms to take one final plunge and aim the shears at the main problem. My heart. A heart that will never be the same.

I close my eyes tight. "God forgive me." My breathing quickens. I can do this. I speed the shears to my chest as hand reaches around mine and pulls. Someone has stopped me.

My eyes flash open, and I blink away the tears. Mother. Her eyes are soft.

"Teagan. This isn't you. This is the curse. You needn't fall prey to it."

"That's why I'm doing this," I scream through rushing tears. "To stop this blasted curse from killing me."

Mother tightens her grip on my arm. "Look at what you're doing." I force myself to look. The shears are mere inches from piercing my breast. How did I go from ecstatically happy this morning to *this*?

The Gancanagh. A well of anger burns within me. I glance up at Mother.

Tears glisten below her lashes. Her eyes connect, and she sees me. She finally sees me. It's been so long.

"Teagan. Don't do this. I love you, my daughter."

My hand weakens, and she releases her grip on my wrist. The shears clatter on the cobblestone. My knees give way, and she catches me before I crush them to the ground. I look up into her shining eyes, cheeks wet. "You love me?"

Her eyes become vacant. Her jaw slackens and head tilts. Just like always. Her brain won't ever work right. Might as well finish the deed if the only person who claims they love me will never be able to truly show it. I glance down at the shears. Mother's head jerks straight and her eyes sharpen. "Yes, dear. I always have." She pulls me up to standing. "So does your pa. And Myrna. We all do."

I swipe my hand over my running nose and whimper. Is it true? Do they really care? Myrna's so selfish sometimes, and I've never lived up to Pa's expectations.

Mother grips my shoulders. "We may not always make it clear. But we have never stopped loving you, my dear."

I think I believe her. No one's perfect, after all. Surely I'm not. Despite their imperfections, I know within my innermost being she's right. I've been such a fool for not seeing it. My shoulders weaken as sobs take over. She clutches me to her. Mother's hug is a balm to my wounded soul.

I don't need a man to tell me my worth. Love from my family is enough. My mind clears as a glimmering sparkle encompasses us for mere seconds then vanishes. The curse has lifted. My heart stands true.

Mother's love has saved me. She smiles. The insanity has passed from us, and before me is my old mother. She grins and holds me close. The mother I used to know. The hero of my heart.

While Deanna Fugett isn't writing or connecting with others via social media, she can be found dancing around the kitchen with her four kids. She has a dog named Westley, a cat named Buttercup, some rabbits, a rat, a parakeet, and some newly acquired chickens. She resides in the Denver area with her high-school-sweetheart-husband of fifteen years, who thinks they live on a farm. (They don't.)

She secretly enjoys writing more than reading. (Author blasphemy!) Deanna has an endless TBR list, and has numerous books she's started reading lying around the house, none of which she can find time to finish. (Four kids and constant chaos will do that to you.)

Deanna is off-the-wall excited about her debut novel coming out with Love2ReadLove2Write Publishing in July of 2017, a YA Dystopian novel called Ending Fear. *It's the first novel in the* Gliding Lands *series, and she really hopes you will enjoy every second of it.*

http://www.deannafugett.com/

Gem

RJ Conte

No! Stop!

I'd have cried the words out loud but I held myself back. Not only could I be fired from any future job in the underground bunker without a warning, but it would mean I would distract Gem.

If I insisted that my anguished thoughts should be voiced for Gem's sake, there was no point to that either. His bright green eyes flicked to mine for an instant, and, even in the midst of his pain, he allowed a tiny smile to cross his small, boyish lips. To reassure me he was right where he wanted to be.

He was reading my thoughts.

I met Gemini last year back when I was Tuson Industries' excited new hire, bent on saving the world and doing great things for humanity. Overeager to please, blond hair in a neat ponytail, and white blouse pressed and ironed, I, Soleil Punicello, was proud to call myself the youngest female to ever achieve the security clearance necessary to work for Tuson.

The megacorporation's sole purpose was to house, provide for, train, and assist the Omnicron—the child given the power to save the world.

The Omnicron was born with the magical gifts of telepathy, macro-telekinesis, genius intelligence, and, most importantly, the ability to hold the plates of our floundering planet together with his or her brain waves alone. Once the Omnicron died, usually at a young age in the line of duty saving the world, another would be born within the year to take their place.

Our planet, Topha, had suffered much destruction and was unstable. The land still sitting above water was wracked with quakes year after year, and the shallow core was riddled with holes and fault lines. A century ago, our people assumed we would all perish, land masses crumbling to bits and sinking under the oceans. We would collapse in on ourselves in one final great quake to end us all.

We spent years in prayer, begging our Lord God to save us from imminent extinction. And that's when the first Omnicron was sent, along with a vision to our prophets about her purpose. There have been six Omnicrons since then, Gemini being the current savior of our world.

Like most people, I always longed to meet the current Omnicron, knowing that he was a savior sent from God Himself to keep our planet alive yet again. The position was given the utmost respect, and the Omnicron was cared for like a right-hand angel to God Himself, or so I was told. Tuson Industries built an immense subterranean bunker. The complex was out of the public's eye but paid for by their eager donations and taxes. It was meant to house, protect, and get the Omnicron closer underground to the next chasmic Topha-quake. Unfortunately, the biggest quakes were always undetected by our surface scanners. Only the telepathic powers of the Omnicron himself could predict when he'd be needed to use the full capacity of his magical telekinesis to often literally rip his brain in half holding the planet together. Some Omnicrons survived their first core quake. Few survived two of them. They were always children. None lived longer than a decade or so. Until the next infant Omnicron was discovered, there was always months of panic among our people, wondering if the magic had run out and if this current generation was going to be the one to witness the planet imploding.

When the next baby was discovered—and there was no rhyme or reason as to its origin of birth—he or she was given over to Tuson Industries to be raised by a staff of top security individuals who were equipped to train and educate someone of the Omnicron's intellect and talents. Knowing the child would also be able to read minds was another worthwhile reason to get him or her away from society as soon as possible.

Gemini, however, hadn't been discovered until he was already eleven years old. It was assumed that his parents had kept him a secret for over a decade, dooming the entire planet to wait in mass hysteria, thinking God had abandoned us once and for all. The risk his parents took hiding their son, hoping a core quake didn't slam the planet in the meantime, was an unthinkable abomination. When Gemini was finally discovered, after passing graduate school exams in the sixth grade, his parents were seized and imprisoned. Instead of the worldwide honor, prestige, and money they would have received, many said they received the death penalty. Others insisted they were handed a life sentence. Whatever the courts decided, it was hushed up, and they vanished into the abyss of the justice system, never to be heard from again. Gemini was an only child, so the officials could make his parents disappear and scare anyone from trying such an act in future generations.

I couldn't fathom what would make a couple choose their child over his righteous, God-given task. Yes, he would die, but he would've died if the planet's land masses all sank as well. Their brains must have been as foggy as my daily coffee—muddied with multiple heavy doses of cream. Their thinking was beyond selfish, and I had no patience for it. They were radicals. Self-centered lunatics so in love with their own son that they damned a planet of millions of people to its death.

But it also meant that Gemini had experienced real life outside of Tuson Industries. He was a genuine eleven-year-old boy when he came to live underground, and the powers-that-be were justly worried that he wouldn't take to his new life, would blame them for being separated from his parents, and would balk at his majestic future task.

Which all leads to me: Soleil Punicello. I was hired to be the Omnicron's personal secretary, aide, nanny, and mother-figure, in a sense. I was to "hang out" with the Omnicron and meet his emotional needs in this transitional period.

I was thrilled. Having wanted to get into Tuson since my freshman year in college, I had taken classes in all the sciences, especially seismology, psychology, and childhood education. I was always at the very top of my class. I landed a government job straight out of college and immediately worked on my security clearance. After writing a thick essay on my personal dedication to the Omnicron and the future of our planet, I was allowed to interview for the Omnicron's personal aide position and landed the job at the tender age of twenty-four. Not only was the pay a sizeable raise due to the long shifts without a break, but the prestige and knowledge that I was making a mark on the world by emotionally, mentally, and physically assisting our most revered citizen was enough to let me die happy.

Badging in, stopping at a retina scanner, and pressing my palm to a screen that identified all five of my fingerprints, I was finally allowed to step inside the caged metal elevator that led down to Gemini's new home and the giant lab at his disposal. Many countries were represented in the staff that worked underneath the ground—the Omnicron had united the world and brought about international peace—just one other thing that indebted us to him and his predecessors.

Clutching a tablet computer chock-full of information pertaining to Gemini that I had read up on in the weeks prior to beginning my new job, I stepped out of the elevator. Glancing around at the sea green walls, I noticed they were all painted the same color—apparently a hue thought to be soothing and peaceful. It was better than white, to be sure, but still starkly naked and blank. This was no home for a child. This was like a military base.

The director, and head of Tuson Industries, stepped from around a corner, flanked by multiple guards. "Miss Punicello!" he called, pronouncing my name with an "s" sound instead of a "ch." "I'm Aster Glibson. Nice to meet you!"

I was slightly bothered that he had not done his homework on my name, musing that my role was supposedly of utmost importance to the Omnicron's mental health. Hiring someone like me was unusual in a unique situation of the corporation not having raised the child themselves. I would've thought I was valuable, and he would have done his research on me, like I had done on him.

I was taken around corridor after corridor, some lined with armed guards, until I arrived in a spacious schoolroom, outfitted with massive computer systems and an entire library of books. A child-sized but ample mahogany desk sat against the far wall, and there was Gemini. He had his back to the door and to us.

He was so small, so slight. His eleven-year-old shoulders were the size of boys his age, not broad enough to take on the weight of the world. His dark hair flopped over his forehead as he turned from the computer to look at us. His arms were thin, his chin boyish. He was so young.

"He likes to be called Gem," the director was explaining as Gemini stood up and turned around.

He fixed his gaze on me and stood stock-still, staring me in the eyes for what seemed like an eternity.

"Remember," Aster Glibson murmured, "he can read minds."

Oh, I know. That was something I recalled—and feared—very clearly from my studies. I was desperately trying to wipe my brain of any thoughts, but all that kept going through my head was, *Oh my word, those eyes.*

Gem sighed.

I unpacked my bags in the sterile guest room I'd be sharing next to Gem's own large suite, suddenly worried that not seeing the sky for days on end would make me claustrophobic. I noticed the massive bottle of vitamin D pills in my personal adjoining bathroom, and the instructions, in my briefing, stated that I should not miss a day without popping two. I gulped. There had been so much information to take in at the initial meeting. My tablet computer now boasted a twenty-page document of typed notes.

Gem studied for five hours a day and practiced his abilities for another five. They had him on an aggressive schedule to compensate for the years of training he had missed. Everyone I met underground seemed on edge. Gem had only been living at Tuson for a month when I arrived, but he had done little to personally reassure anyone that he was capable of fulfilling his vital role. And, without knowing when the next core quake would hit, they had no idea whether or not he would be ready or willing to do his task. I surmised that most of his "education" involved emotional indoctrination and manipulation.

But he could read minds. He had to have known about his destiny all along. No one could keep a secret from him. *Why didn't he turn himself in?*

"Because I was protecting my parents."

I spun around. Gem stood at my open door. His gaze pinned me.

"What do you mean?" I asked. So much for get-to-know-you chitchat!

"No need for chitchat, Miss Punicello. I know you already." His voice was flat and matter-of-fact, as if patiently explaining a complicated concept to a child.

I said nothing.

"From almost birth, I had an understanding of what I was meant to do for the world. My parents were afraid because I was gifted, and they worried about whether or not I was the next Omnicron. They were really scared at the thought of giving me up, and my mom panicked inside every time she wondered about it. So, I hid my magical gifts from the moment I was old enough to understand them. They didn't know. They weren't at fault."

"But...they were imprisoned—"

"They weren't. Instead of making the Savior Omnicron look selfish and deceitful, Tuson worked with the national justice system to pretend to 'do away with them,' but instead, they helped my parents go into hiding. The world needed to make an example of them for show."

I sputtered. "What? Your poor parents! That's terrible! People are judging them falsely—"

Gem walked into my room and glanced at my small end table of personal items I had unpacked. He lifted my journal in his small hands.

"Don't—" I meant to stop him from opening it and reading it, knowing I had written all sorts of personal thoughts about his parents, him, my job, my future... But, in the instant I thought about it, I knew it was too late. He knew what I had written in that book as if he had read it himself. I lowered my gaze, ashamed.

He glanced at me, large green eyes thoughtful, sympathetic, yet piercing. "Miss Punicello, don't worry at all. Your thoughts are kind, innocent, and natural. Your mind is one of the cleanest I've met yet." He smiled at me, a look more of sadness than anything else.

I gaped and my face warmed. *Was that a compliment?*

"Yes." The corner of his mouth turned up for a second.

It hit me how much he must have suffered due to his telepathy alone. "You've seen and heard and experienced so much horror and evil by living out in the world and reading people's minds! You've been exposed to things no child—no human being—should ever be exposed to!" *Poor, poor precious boy. Your life is so unfair.* My throat went thick, and I shuddered.

Gem turned to face me, putting my journal back down on the table. His brows knit, and he spoke in boyish earnestness. "But you forget the other half of it. I also hear the amusing things that humans are too afraid to share. The weaknesses and vulnerabilities that people are afraid to expose to others." He gave me a pointed look. "Even you care about me already, and we just met."

My face grew hot. "I have cared about the Omnicron my whole life." My voice dropped to a whisper. "It's such a great honor to be here and help you."

Gem smoothed the front of my journal with his hand. "And just so you understand, I'll tell you something I didn't want to tell anyone else, because I don't care what they think of me." He stepped forward, voice lowered, "Even though I hid my gifts, I studied in secret. I always planned on stepping up to my role even from my own bedroom back in the States of Musi where I grew up. I would never have gotten out of my duty."

He spoke like an old man, his voice precise, measured, slow, and soft. There was no emotion in his words. He didn't even seem sadly resigned. Merely confident, calm, and assured.

He nodded—to my thoughts? "We understand each other now."

I smiled, hopeful. "Gem, you can just call me Soleil."

"Soleil, you walk, think, and even breathe loudly. Do you do that on purpose to be annoying?"

Gem was attempting to close all of the interior doors of the underground bunker with his mind simultaneously. It was a small macro-telekinesis task, and therefore challenging. Not being able to do micro-telekinesis meant he couldn't move small objects across the room, so shutting multiple doors in the base was difficult.

I was a distraction.

I often felt that I was completely unnecessary. Gem preferred to study alone. The silent thoughts he heard whenever anyone was in the vicinity were as loud as vocalized conversation would be to me.

"I'll leave!" I offered, packing up my tablet computer, in which I was doing my own research. I had purposed to get my master's degree in my spare time while I was stuck underground. There were many hours of the day where I sat in silence in my room, leaving Gem to study with his own quiet thoughts for a change.

"I didn't mean you should go," he insisted, his voice straining, eyes closed. His hands were clenched fists on the sides of his temple. "When I have to stop the next core Topha-quake, all of the staff and guards and directors and world leaders might be in the room. I'll have so many distractions. If I can't even close a bunch of doors with you right now, how will I save the world then?"

I was as silent as possible, focusing on emptying my mind for his sake, biting my lip as I watched his small forehead wrinkle and strain under the pressure. He stuck his tongue slightly out in concentration and bunched up his nose. He was adorable.

He opened an eye at me. "Not helping," he said.

I blushed.

Finally, the door of the schoolroom slammed. And I heard the resounding noise of many doors down the hall shutting as well. They sounded like dominos falling one after the other.

Two professors with clipboards bounded into the room, taking notes.

"Excellent, Gemini!" one exclaimed, pushing his glasses up on his head.

The other scribbled furiously. "Take a break," he said to Gem, not looking up. He began murmuring to his partner and they left the room together.

Gem watched them go. He sighed, sinking into a chair at his desk, laying his head down on its surface. "They think I'm weak and will never succeed."

I sat down next to him, wondering why I even bothered with the formality of conversation. "You should've spent some of your childhood years learning how to block out your telepathy for good!"

He was quiet for a time. "It's my sixth sense, in every way," he replied, eyeing me. "Just because you could hear ugly noises and insulting words, would you choose to deafen yourself permanently? Just because you could see something horrible, would you go blind on purpose?"

I blinked. "But it must get so loud and noisy...and awful!" I sputtered, looking for the right word.

"So, I take a break and go be alone a lot." His high-pitched, prepubescent voice cracked a little. "But I'd still feel deaf or blind without it, no matter how much it's ruined me. At least it's nice to not have to hide it anymore."

"Ruined you?"

He pointed at me and lifted his head, not breaking eye contact. "You think I'm a hero—that I love this world and all of the people in it and am going to save them because I care so much. That's why *you* would save the world—if you were the Omnicron—because of love."

Of course he knew me better than I did myself. He could read the parts of my brain I hadn't acknowledged yet. "Wait, but—"

"I don't believe in love." Like a wise, miniature sage, he lowered his gaze and shook his head solemnly.

I frowned but stayed silent.

"It doesn't exist. And I don't think humanity is worth saving either. People are evil, selfish cretins. Every one of them. Some just less than others. No one actually loves anyone more than they do themselves. Even my parents—who loved me most of all—had regrets about giving birth to me and raising me once in a while and secretly hated and blamed me as much as they blamed themselves when I got taken away."

I was about to offer comfort and exclaim over him when he held up a hand. "Oh, it doesn't hurt me in the slightest. I've never known any different or had any delusions about the way people really think."

Still. Hearing a child say it ripped my heart in two.

"This is hard for you to understand because your mind is purer than most." It was a line Gem had repeated a few times, matter-of-factly, as if to acknowledge that I was someone he approved of—and possibly pitied. I had come to treat it as the only compliment I was going to get from him.

A sudden, sickening thought hit me. Instead of just letting him hear my thought on his own, I wanted to vocalize it and be given an answer. "Are you thinking of backing out? Of letting the world end?" This would be traitorous—complete treachery if anyone got wind of it. I hushed to a whisper and leaned close. "You would die anyway!"

He ruffled his floppy bangs and smoothed them back on his forehead. "I'll still do what I need to do. I'm the only one who can do it." Pride seemed to fill his face as he said it. "And I'll show them all what I'm mentally capable of. Besides, it's the right thing to do, and there really is no practical alternative. We all die, or I save the world, try to survive doing it, and then improve the world while I can. I don't plan on staying in this bunker my whole life like my predecessors." He turned to stare at me with earnestness. "In between quakes, if I live that long, I'm going to get a degree or two. I'm going to write scientific papers. I'm going to invent something. I'm going to do something else with my abilities! I'm not just going to prevent death, but I'm going to contribute further brilliance to the world."

Tears welled up in my eyes. His cheeks blushed pink as he read my thoughts, but he needed to hear them out loud anyway. "You are amazing. You are going to be the best Omnicron we've ever had."

"No one's thought *that* yet," he muttered, and his voice got thick. He looked down and played with his shirt hem, like a boy who is embarrassed, yet secretly pleased after being publicly praised by a doting mother.

"Your parents are going to be so proud. I'm proud of you already!" I cried, wishing with all my heart that I could hold him close and cradle him like the child he was.

He rolled his eyes at me and smirked. "Please don't." Then he rubbed his head. "I need a break from your overpowering, gushy thoughts. I haven't done a single thing worthy of them yet." He stood up and walked out of the schoolroom without a backward glance.

It had been three months. We were in the playground area of our underground home. The walls in this particular space had been painted to look like blue skies and clouds with a bright UV light in the corner to represent the sun. I soaked up artificial vitamin D in a pool chair in the corner, sunglasses shading my eyes, but the farce pained me. Gem had experienced the vast expanse of a true sunny sky, and this was pathetic in comparison. The room was half the size of a football field and boasted a gigantic playground, a full pool, and a yard of grass. Fake or not, I had to admit that it was my favorite room. Gem hardly ever played in it, though, at the mature age of eleven. But lounging in the attached hot tub helped his aching head and body after a hard day of telekinesis.

Today, they were making him move the playground equipment in its entirety. He had to lift it up off the ground a full foot with his mind over and over again, like a grown man lifting weights. To teach him to keep his mind focused on the tiresome task even with distractions, they were having him answer mundane world trivia questions as he picked it up and dropped it. All in all, he had to lift the playground five hundred times by the end of the day. I hurt for him, even though he hated it when I had those kinds of thoughts. He liked it better when I went and stuffed my motherly mind into a good book inside my lawn chair. Sometimes, I sat at the top of the play equipment for fun, my added hundred and thirty pounds inconsequential. I'd root for him at the top while I enjoyed the little ride. It made the workout a bit more fun. At least, that's what I hoped. He seemed to appreciate when I acted like the kid he couldn't be. It made him laugh, which was nearly impossible for anyone else to do.

Today, I flipped through "The Science of Planetary Plates" and tried not to let my mind drift. The two professors took notes as they quizzed Gem.

"Who led the Battle of Three Worlds?"

"Jerusha Galaxica," Gem replied with ease. "One hundred and twelve," he added, counting the playground lifts out loud.

"What was Topha's most mined resource back in 3010?"

"Clemzanite. One hundred and thirteen."

"Who were the parents of the first Omnicron?"

"Prophets Sola and Luna Farstar. One hundred and fourteen."

Gem's voice started to sound weary by the time he counted into the four hundreds. I had a bathing suit and a change of clothes waiting for him. The changing rooms stood behind me, and the hot tub was bubbling and ready. Placing my sunglasses on the small poolside table, I dragged my chair forward. I slipped my feet into the frothy water, shooting a guilty look at the trainers. I had done nothing to deserve the warm massage the jets were giving my toes. They ignored me, like usual.

"How many countries existed back in 1050?"

"Only sixteen." Gem took a deep breath. "And...five hundred!" His voice waned, and his shoulders slumped with the last thump of the gigantic playset.

The trainers, without a word of encouragement or backwards glance, began to chat among themselves and left the room. Gem dragged himself over to his bathing suit, picked it up, and headed to change. When he returned, he gingerly lowered himself into the water beside my feet.

I opened my mouth, but he beat me to my question. "It's not about getting praised."

"But..." I sputtered. "You did a great job. You answered every question right and lifted five hundred reps with ease. I'm proud of you. Why don't—?"

"Who cares?" Gem bit his lip.

"There's something you're not telling me," I said when he was silent and ignored my jabbing thoughts. "It's not fair when you do that. You can read *my* mind. Tell me yours."

My friendship with Gem was more than big sister-little brother. As the only human being able to read my mind and know me with that level of intimacy, I was as attached to him as one would be to their right arm. He was like a second part of my brain by this point, and I could have studied him forever. He fascinated me and I dreaded losing him. I constantly threw away any thoughts of his dying whenever they tried to sneak up and stab me. I refused to think about it, hoping I successfully kept up an optimistic attitude for Gem in the process.

Just a week ago, one of the psychologists had approached me in the hallway, letting me know there was therapy and grief counseling they could offer me when Gem died. Angrily, I had told them it wouldn't be necessary, as Gem wasn't going anywhere, and I told them where they could stick their counseling services.

"They think I'll fail," Gem admitted, after a silence so long I had almost forgotten my original question. I sometimes wondered if Gem was forced to speak up just to silence my wandering brain when he ignored me. I'm sure my loud thoughts irritated him into speaking when he'd rather not. His head alone peeked above the water, and he glanced away nonchalantly, as if what he had just admitted was nothing.

"We've been over this before." I kicked gently at the cheerful bubbles.

"They think that my years without training means I'll fail. They think I'm going to die, and they're afraid I'm going to doom the planet in the process."

I went still. *So much pressure.* Literally the world on his childish shoulders. I felt myself go cold even as the hot steam wafted up to my face. "They do not."

Gem just looked at me, his big green eyes piercing. As if I could tell him he was wrong—when he read their minds every day.

I dropped my head and stared at the foam on the top of the water. "That's not fair. How can they think that? They treat you like a machine. No one down here cares about you at all! Don't they see how powerful and smart and strong you are?"

Gem smiled briefly, and I could tell I had pleased him with my last sentence. But then his mouth drooped once more. "Why should they care? They take on this job knowing I'm going to die. None of the professors or medical personnel or scientists or guards are the types to get attached. This is their job, and I'm a tool to save their world. And they think I'm going to die," he repeated.

Only two Omnicrons had survived their first core quakes, but none of them had failed in keeping the planet from breaking apart. Did everyone truly think Gem didn't have what it took? That he would fail when the other children had succeeded? Was I the only one who believed in him?

"You won't die!" I insisted.

"Not even I can know that. And I know everything." Even now, he was cracking a joke. He smirked at me, but his face held more sadness than mirth.

I got off my chair, crouched down, and reached for his hand, which lay across the top Jacuzzi step. "Gem, you have to believe that you're not going to die. You've got to have a will to live. You've got to will your body to survive that quake, and to not give up while you give it your all. There's power in having a positive attitude in the midst of danger!"

He cocked an eyebrow at me but didn't withdraw his hand like I had expected. It lay limp in mine, but he didn't take it back. "Will to live? Nothing scientific about that, Soleil. I don't believe in things I can't measure scientifically. They're probably right, and I'll die."

Desperation hit my mind in a panic, and it reached Gem. He finally yanked his hand out from beneath mine and sank below the surface of the water in a hurry, his head disappearing underneath the bubbles. For as long as he could stay under, he would be free from my thoughts. I used that time to hurriedly run through a gamut of things I could say to argue with him. Wracking my brain for what to use, I sat back down on the pool chair.

Before I could come up with an answer, he reappeared, only his eyes and nose showing above the surface. He glared at me. Then, sputtering, he popped completely out of the water and turned his back to me. "Back when I was in third grade, there was a boy in my class who came down with a rare disease."

A friend? I listened intently, clearing my mind of my own thoughts, straining to hear his soft words.

Gem craned his neck back to look at me over his shoulder and rolled his eyes. "I don't have any friends." He snorted. "Why would I? Especially other children? They're juvenile. Selfish. Stupid. I didn't have any patience for them ever. And they all either hated me or I totally scared them. I could read their minds, remember?"

I bit back a retort and stayed quiet.

Gem sighed. "This kid was kind of different. He didn't just know God existed, like the rest of us, but he had a relationship with Him. He loved God and had faith in His goodness—something I had never believed in—because of how crummy my own future looked."

I felt tears prick in my eyes but focused on repeating the words Gem had just said in my mind—a trick I used to shut down my own thoughts.

Gem could read my emotions though. He splashed the water with a fist. "He was going to die. The chances of him surviving that disease were slim. But the doctors told his family, 'If he has a will to live, he can survive this surgery.' I read his mind. He wanted to live *badly*."

I jumped in. I couldn't help myself. "The same thing happened to a girl in my class in high school! And she made it! See, Gem? She made it! And so can you!"

Gem ignored me, calmly rising out of the Jacuzzi and reaching for his towel. He dried himself off without saying a word. Finally, he threw the towel back down on the chair and grabbed his clothes. "Well, the boy in my class *died*, Soleil. Will or no will, he *died*. At least he was going straight to the God he loved so much. I'm supposed to save the world, but I couldn't save him, Soleil. I couldn't even save the one person I could actually tolerate. I'm not going to be able to save *anybody*!"

The night I finally had an idea, I knocked frantically on Gem's door far past bedtime. He opened it, and I could see he wasn't in bed or even in his pajamas, but dressed in a soft gray martial arts-like outfit. The loose cotton clothes—Gem's choice—had been saved for one purpose: the day of the core quake.

My heart plummeted. "Why are you wearing that?"

"It's time, Soleil. I haven't woken everyone up yet. But I can feel it. It's going to happen in the next couple of hours. I'm just getting myself calmed down and ready before everyone goes crazy."

He was talking nervously and quickly, but his words blurred in my ears. A rush of shaky, chilly panic blocked my ability to hear him. *No.* This couldn't be happening. He wasn't going to suffer tonight! The world wasn't going to end tonight. A blinding panic over my own possible death hit me in the gut, but I shook it off as quickly as it came. I wasn't going to die, nor was I going to lose Gem. Not now! Not ever!

I took him by the shoulders. "Look, Gem. Maybe it's me. Maybe if I just believe hard enough *for* you, you'll survive. That's my job, right? I'm your encouragement and support. I believe in a God who loves you. I'll will you to save this stupid world and live!"

Gem stood still and silent. Varying looks of fear, desperation, and pity for me crossed his face. When he spoke, it sounded weak and shaky. "What've I got to lose?" His voice caught on the last word, and he took a deep breath. "Time to go."

My breathing picked up. Should I throw my arms around him? Give him a last benediction? He can't just leave! He could be going to his death! *No! I'm one who will never stop believing he can survive this!*

Reading my thoughts, he cut me off. "So, there should be no fanfare then. I'll see you after this is over." He bravely smiled. His chin quivered, but he jerked his shoulders out from under my hands and marched away.

I stifled a sob and followed.

The news went out quickly on the radio and emergency sirens. Get to the safe houses all over the world. Start praying. This was the big one.

They set Gem up in a partly reclined, Frankenstein's monster-like chair with straps for his arms and legs, a pillowed section for his head, and soft classical music of his choice playing in the background.

"Let us know if you want the sound turned off or the lights dimmed," a nurse said.

There was a frantic energy in the room, even though all of the personnel were organized in doing their jobs. Director Glibson himself strapped Gem down onto the chair and started an IV. "If you're sure you can feel the beginning tremors, then we'll get you ready. Like we've told you before, we can't give you pain medicine because it will interfere with your telekinesis signals and concentration. I'm sorry. But the drugs going through the IV will keep you from passing out," the director murmured, but I heard it, perched by his side. "Miss Punicello," Glibson turned to me next, "we need everyone back at the far end of the room out of the Omnicron's way and into the adjoining safe area where you'll be protected from the quake."

The safe area was just a side wing of the main lab where Gem sat. We were strapped down with five point harnesses to seats built into the wall. The whole lab was like a fortified castle, impenetrable and all one large piece of seamless steel. It would protect us from other parts of the bunker caving in. Nothing had been destroyed in previous core quakes, however, due to the nature of the bunker's foundations. They were built on moving springs and padded cylinders, wrapped in layers of rubber and steel. The whole facility shifted with the quake, as long as the Omnicron did their job and kept the worst tremors at bay. I knew Gem preferred they'd all leave entirely so he wouldn't have to hear their terrified thoughts screaming at him, but there was nowhere else but this room that could ensure our safety.

His eyes searched mine for an instant as I left. I pumped my fist in the air at him and swallowed hard. *I'm fighting for you, Gem. You can do it. Stay alive. You are strong enough. I believe you can do this. God chose you and loves you, Gem!*

I knew he heard my thoughts, but he heard everyone else's too. Hopefully, mine were the loudest. He turned his head away and stared at the ceiling.

And then it began.

Gem's body tensed, his arms straining against the straps. He grunted once and then relaxed.

"Are you okay?" I called before thinking.

A dozen stern voices shushed me.

"It's starting, Soleil. It's not too painful yet. I can feel the center of Topha!" Gem answered me, as if we were the only two people in the room, as if to spite those who silenced me. He sounded awed and excited.

My heart warmed. I sent a smug look back at everyone else. *He'll exceed all of your measly expectations. You just wait and see. You may know his brain and his body's capabilities, but you don't know his heart and soul and strength like I do. You're idiots. All of you.*

The waves of tension came and went for an hour, Gem tensing and breathing heavily for a few minutes each time. And then it hit full force. The ground shook, and all of us clutched our harnesses and rode it out. Gem's eyes closed and his hands clenched and unclenched. The veins in his head and neck throbbed, and his breathing became frantic. He fought hard, grinding his teeth. It hit me in the gut: he was literally holding the world together.

Tears silently poured down my cheeks. *You can do it, Gem! You were made for this!* My thoughts screamed in my head at him. *Stay alive for me, Gem! Do it for me!*

Sweat pouring down his boyish face, Gem turned his head toward me. It was the first time in two hours he had acknowledged anyone in the room. But now he looked me right in the eyes. Everyone bent forward, straining to listen over the roaring of the world. Panting hard, and clearly in tremendous pain, Gem managed to smirk. "Will someone tell the egotistical blond that I'm not saving the world for her sake alone?"

A few people let out nervous chuckles. The tension dissipated. Tears of embarrassment and relief flooded my face. *Oh, you smart aleck. You're going to be okay. You're going to be okay!*

But the next hour was sheer hell. The ground bucked beneath us. Gem's agony intensified. He writhed and twisted in his restraints, wailing and moaning. They kept him from lapsing into unconsciousness with the constant trickle of adrenaline drugs through his IV. Blood leaked out of his nose and ears, and I could see that he had chafed a line of raw skin straight through his socks around his ankles every time he bucked in his restraints.

I wanted to turn and run, to flee the possibility that I was watching the death of the little boy who had become the dearest person to me. But I dared not leave. I would give him the honor of watching his struggle, shouting my thoughts into his shell-shocked mind, staying by his side at all times, and witnessing the greatest act of heroism I had ever seen from a human being, let alone a child. He was saving the lives of all of the millions of people on our planet. That blood leaking from his nose and ears was the most beautiful thing I had ever seen. The marks on his hands and feet. The veins in his neck. The air rasping raggedly from his lungs.

In all of my life, I would never forget this moment. This was bravery. This was love.

And then the shaking went still. Gem's body slumped. His lungs slowed down. His hands and face went limp. It was over. We were saved.

For the next two weeks, it was touch and go. Gem had survived the core quake, barely, but his body was in shock. He lay in a coma for what seemed like an eternity, nurses and doctors bustling around, checking his vitals every hour. Tubes ran in and out of his nose and mouth, needles in his arms. I sat by his bedside almost every waking moment, leaving only to sleep in my room at night, praying on my knees that he would survive.

They told me that even if he did wake up from his coma, his brain could be vegetative. He could be deaf or blind. He could be paralyzed. The doctors and professors and guards I had thought so unfeeling helped me keep constant watch over him, their faces finally showing their deep concern, their fears, and their immense gratitude. Suddenly, we were one family, all praying and waiting for Gem.

And then, after the two longest weeks of my life, a nurse ran to get me in the middle of the night, the sound of her knock frantic on my door. I jumped out of bed, grabbed my bathrobe, and ran to the infirmary. And there he sat, weak but upright and very much alive. His eyes, huge in his thin face, held all of the same luster from before, and I could see the fathoms of intellect behind them.

He was going to be okay.

Gem held out his arms, and I hugged him as tightly as I dared. When I tried to back away, he continued to hold me, and that's when I began to bawl, clutching him back as all of my fears fell out onto my cheeks in rivers of tears.

"You were right all along, Soleil," Gem whispered, almost too soft to catch.

"Wasn't I?" I sobbed and scolded. "You're alive! Just maybe, God really gives us things we can't measure. Emotions, love...faith! Maybe I had the answers all along, and the Know-It-All had to learn that from someone far stupider than himself!" I sniffled and laughed all at once.

For a long minute, Gem was silent, his face stuffed into my shoulder, and then he took a deep breath. He pulled back and looked me in the face. "You were right, Soleil," he repeated. "There's so much I still don't know. And I'm so ready to get out there and find out. My life isn't over yet. We've got a lot to do together! No more giving up." He looked at me with a smile illuminating his tear-stained eyes.

I couldn't wait to begin.

From the bestselling author of Lucent Sylph *comes a whole new story about a friendship in an unlikely place: between the child savior of a dying planet and his handler. RJ Conte is inspired by love and motherhood, and enjoys writing about deep human relationships. She is married to the most adorable Vulcan, the only man she has ever kissed, and they have three little fairy princesses. RJ Conte writes realistic, issue-driven fiction that explores human nature and the depths of the soul, while pointing readers to their Creator.*

https://blonderj.wordpress.com/

Leticia's Song

Jessica L. Elliott

"Could have been a queen," I muttered as I tried to get a comfortable seat on the fallen log. "Could have lived in a palace. But no, I had to marry George the Adventurer, Seeker of Lost Princesses."

My new friend Gertrude chuckled, her green eyes twinkling. "As regal as you are, dear Leticia, I can't imagine you as a queen."

I smiled. "Me neither. But at least I had comfortable furniture before."

"Poor Quincy," Rosa murmured. A tear escaped her sightless eyes. "Quimbledown. Quincy, Quincy Quimbledown."

"There, there, dear," Gertrude said, putting a shawl around Rosa's frail shoulders. "We'll find him."

"Darkness. So dark."

"I know." Gertrude comforted Rosa until she settled down.

Princess Rosa of Altherian had been Gertrude's friend at Fair Damsels Academy fifteen years ago, but she no longer resembled the olive-skinned, raven-haired beauty she'd once been. Her shock-white hair and sightless eyes were the result of her failed quest to save her prince. Poor Quincy Edwin. Obsessively vain and constantly preening, according to Gertrude's husband, but Rosa's prince nonetheless. Now, Rosa was the one who needed to be saved.

George and I were determined to help them both, and we had insisted Gertrude join us.

A twig snapped and we turned to see George saunter out of the forest, his confidence palpable. Tall and broad-shouldered with dark hair, grown slightly long with traveling, the sight of him set my heart racing. He smiled and said, "Everything's clear. I don't think we have anything to worry about tonight."

Gertrude twisted a honey-colored curl around her finger. "Do you think we might later?" I could tell she was trying not to let her voice waver as she spoke.

"I hope not, but we're on a quest now. Things may become challenging. But I promise, I'll keep you safe."

"Don't you mean we'll keep them safe?" I teased, glancing at him over the rim of my spectacles.

He smiled at me and squeezed my hand. "That was implied, love."

Quimbledown was a good distance from Gertrude's manor, where we had begun our journey a few days before, shortly after our wedding. Gertrude had promised news of a Lost Princess, and she hadn't disappointed. As George had said, what better way to spend our honeymoon than helping others?

I picked up my bag and pulled out a small, wooden box. Despite George telling me to leave extras at home, I did have one thing I refused to leave behind.

"What do you have there?" Gertrude asked as I opened the lid.

I pulled out the golden pieces and fitted them together. "My flute."

"I've never seen a golden flute before. It's beautiful."

"It was a gift," I said with a smile. While George cooked dinner, I warmed up with a few simple scales to clear my head. Our arrival at Gertrude's manor had triggered Rosa's memory, at least a little, and I'd written down the words of her quest lest she forget them again. They came back to me as I played.

Darkness falls in shades of black. Sight once gone can ne'er come back.
Faded stars and haunted dreams. Nothing here is as it seems.
Find the light. Find hope's wish. Banish darkness with true love's kiss.

I played a few more minutes before falling into the familiar tune of the old fairy ballad my mother had always sung to me. It was my favorite song, and I played it anytime I got the chance. It was a way to be near to her. To my surprise, a soft voice began singing the words I'd grown up knowing.

"Magic swirls in the wind,
Colors dance in the trees.
Fairies twirl and spin,
Dancing on the autumn breeze."

Rosa's clear alto continued as Gertrude and George stared in wonder. I would have dropped my flute if I hadn't been so focused on giving her this moment of clarity. She stopped singing and sat quietly while I finished playing.

"Rosa, I had no idea you could sing so beautifully," Gertrude whispered.

She tilted her head. "Gertrude, is that you? What are you doing here? Where are you? Why can't I see you?" Panic rose in her tone. "Quincy! Quincy, can you hear me?"

Gertrude put her arms around her distressed friend. "Rosa, it's all right. We're going to find Quincy."

"My quest. So much darkness. So much fear." She shivered and pulled in on herself, sobbing. "Poor, poor Quincy."

As Gertrude tried to comfort her friend, George sat beside me and touched the flute. "This is an interesting development. I wonder what would happen if you played a different song."

"I don't know. And how sure are you that it was the song that helped her? After all, it wasn't my flute that made her remember her quest."

"True, but this time she actually recognized Gertrude. Now, she's back within herself, and she doesn't remember who she's with or why she's here." George sat quietly for a while, his fingers pulling absentmindedly at the dark scruff growing on his chin. "Would you be willing to play something else?"

I studied the flute. "Sure. Do you really think it will help?"

"I think it's worth a try."

The gold shimmered in the firelight as I lifted the mouthpiece once more to my lips. At first, I played a few little scales, then went into a cheerful tune I'd learned at school. No change. I transitioned easily to the fairy ballad. The night air was still, our horses resting from a weary day of traveling.

Rosa quieted, her hand reaching out. "Gertrude, is that really you?"

Gertrude took her hand. "Yes, Rosa. What happened to you?"

"I can't say for sure. There was a box. It was so beautiful. I had almost found him, you know. I was so close. Right in the castle. But there was a box, and I couldn't resist opening it. After that, I don't remember much. I should have known better. I knew he wouldn't have been in it. His transformation wouldn't have allowed it."

"So, he was under an enchantment?" George asked.

"Who is that?"

"A friend, Rosa. George and his sweet wife Leticia are our friends. How do you know his enchantment wouldn't have allowed it?"

A faint smile crossed Rosa's face. "A great, white swan wouldn't have fit in it very well."

"He was turned into a swan?"

"Yes. During our fifth year. He loved me, don't misunderstand, but he also loved his own reflection. I suppose the witches at the school felt he had to be punished for saying what he did about me."

"What did he say?"

"He called me ugly," Rosa said in a small voice. Then she shook her head. "It hardly matters anymore. At first, I didn't know what had happened. The witches took him to a different room, and when he came back, his skin was milk white and he was shaking. Wouldn't tell me then what they had done."

"How did you find out?"

A frown replaced her smile. "It was the day of graduation. He pulled me aside and told me about the transformation. He thought it would make my quest easier if I knew what I was looking for."

"But that only made things harder," George said.

Rosa nodded. "The castle was filled with illusions and strange magical objects."

As much as I wanted to know more, my hands were beginning to cramp from playing and my mouth hurt. George glanced at me and nodded. "Rosa, why does this song help you remember?"

"I'm not sure. But I do think Leticia must be getting tired. She's the one playing, isn't she?"

"Yes, she is."

She smiled. "Thank you, Leticia. You can stop if you need to, but thank you. Perhaps if you played this each evening, I can give you pieces of the story. Before this moment ends though, please promise me we'll find Quincy."

"We will," George said. "And we'll try to find out what that box was you opened. Can you tell us anything about it?"

"Not tonight, George," Rosa replied. "Leticia needs rest. It takes a surprising amount of energy to play an instrument for so long. Good night. And thank you."

I finished out the song while Gertrude helped Rosa get comfortable in our makeshift shelters. We'd given them the most comfortable arrangements, but truth be told, sleeping on the ground was always uncomfortable. When I finished playing, I polished the pieces of my flute and put them away in their box before stretching my hands and moving my jaw from side to side.

"Sorry to have made you uncomfortable," George said gently as he sat next to me. "I've never played a flute, so I didn't think it would be difficult."

I smiled. "Don't worry about me, love. I'm glad we were able to help her remember at least a little."

"Why that song?" George asked. "What's special about it? Remind me what the words are."

"You know I can't just say them."

His fingers brushed my cheek. "Then sing it for me."

My lips curved in a smile. "Only if you'll brush and braid my hair tonight."

George shook his head with a rueful grin. "I should never have let my sisters tell you that."

I smirked at him. "I'm glad they did. I enjoy people playing with my hair." With my best pout I asked, "Would you braid my hair, please?"

He kissed my forehead and smiled, "Anything for my golden princess."

I laughed. "I'm not golden anymore, darling."

"Maybe not, but there's still gold in your green eyes." He removed my glasses and placed kisses above my eyelids. "And in your titian hair." Warmth glowed in his eyes as he raised a lock of my hair to his lips.

My heart swelled and I teased, "If you want me to sing, you'd better stop distracting me."

The deep rumble of his laugh filled my ears. "I'd apologize, but I'm not sorry." He pulled the brush out of my bag. As he worked through my hair, I closed my eyes before beginning to sing.

Magic swirls in the wind,
Colors dance in the trees.
Fairies twirl and spin,
Dancing on the autumn breeze.

He sees her from afar
And feels his heart swell.
She's beauty like a star,
The fairy dancing in the dell.

Flutters rose in my heart as I felt George's fingers brush my neck as he divided my hair into sections to braid. I forced my attention back to the song.

She can feel his eyes
As the dance goes on.
A turn and spies
The fairy watching down yon.

It is something rare.
It is something new:
Love in a single stare
As they dance upon the dew.

It started with a glance,
Continued with an age
As forever they dance,
The fairies have set the stage.

George finished and tied off the braid just before the song ended. He moved next to me and rubbed his chin. "It's just a song about falling in love. There are hundreds of those songs in the world. Why is this one special?"

"Perhaps because it's an old fairy ballad?" I suggested. "There's a different kind of magic in music, and I would imagine that a song written by the fairies and as old as this one would probably carry more magic than others."

"Hmm."

I squeezed his hand as I rested my head against his shoulder. "Let's not worry about it tonight. We're going to need our rest for tomorrow's journey."

"Someone should keep watch."

"You just told Gertrude everything was clear for tonight. Don't worry so much." I stood and then pulled his hands until he joined me. "We'll be fine."

He slipped his arm around my waist and kissed me tenderly. "If you insist."

"I do. Even Prince Charming needs sleep."

The journey was long, but without incident. As we traveled, the mountains gave way to hills and finally to vast stretches of land. We arrived in Quimbledown just as the sun was dipping toward the west. Fields of green and gold made a patchwork landscape, stretching as far as the eye could see. Trees grew in clumps along the banks of a sparkling river. To the west, a forest sprawled toward the horizon, seeming out of place in the pastoral scene. A dark tower rose above the tree line and I knew we were getting close to our destination.

Each evening of our journey, I played my flute while Rosa explained what she could remember of her quest. Over the last several days, we'd been able to piece together much of what had happened, but one key piece was still missing. We didn't know what kind of box Rosa had opened.

That night after taking care of our horses, George asked her about it again.

"It was terrifying," Rosa whispered. "Everything was beautiful and calm, and then darkness. So much darkness and pain. Misery, anger, forgetfulness, despair, madness. I couldn't escape from it. Before I could react, I was surrounded by, well, I don't really know what. I threw the lid back down, hoping to stop the onslaught. But something blinded me, and then..." She sighed. "I just don't remember anything after that. Not until Leticia played the song that first night we traveled together. At least, I assume it was the first night."

"It was," George confirmed. "The box you opened, I've heard of something like that before. I just can't remember where. Do you remember if anything remained trapped inside after you opened it?"

Rosa nodded. "I think so. I vaguely remember hearing something within the box. But after opening it, everything becomes fuzzy. It could well be wishful thinking."

Crickets joined my playing while the group fell silent.

Gertrude finally said, "What should we do, George? According to your map and what Rosa has been able to tell us, we'll reach the enchanted castle tomorrow."

"Rosa will have to complete her quest. The rest of us can be support, but she'll have to complete it herself."

"How?" Rosa asked. "Without Leticia's song, I lose my mind, my memories. All I have left is the darkness. And even with her playing, I can see nothing. Just vague shadows of what might be around me. How will I save Quincy in this condition?"

"I'll be your guide," Gertrude said, taking her friend's hand.

"And Leticia will clear your mind with her music."

"That could be a very long time playing, George. Can she handle that?" Everyone looked at me, and I nodded. Yes, I could handle it. I had to. I wasn't about to let Rosa live the rest of her life in darkness and fear. And if her prince was waiting for her, we had to help him.

"Leticia just nodded to let you know she can. Before we give her a break, tell us once more everything you know about Quincy's transformation. It will be important if we're to help you find him."

"He told me to look for the best-looking swan out there," she recalled with a laugh. "Vain to the end, Quincy. When I told him swans all look pretty much the same, he said the transformation took place only at night when the moonlight touches him. During the day, he's a man, or at least he was before graduating. That may have changed. If we do find him in his human form, he's the very epitome of tall, dark, and handsome. But as a swan," Rosa paused in thought. "I think he said he turned into a white swan, but he also said there was something different about him."

"Perhaps a black swan?" Gertrude suggested. "It would fit his human description more accurately."

Rosa shook her head. "No, no, I remember distinctly he was not a dark swan. There might be black swans at the castle, but they are not Quincy. Quincy was turned to a white swan, I'm sure of it. But there was something else about him, and now I can't remember."

The panicked edge to her voice broke my heart.

"There, there, Rosa," Gertrude said gently. "I'm sure you'll remember in time. For now, I think we all need some rest. Tomorrow will be a very long day."

"One last thing," Rosa said as I finished playing, "don't touch anything in the castle."

We reached the castle just as the sun touched the horizon. We tethered our horses in the woods. Built from stones dark as charcoal, with dull, stained-glass windows, the castle exuded an eerie sense of foreboding. The red glow of sunset on the stones did nothing to ease the tension. A chill ran up my spine, and Rosa became more agitated the closer we got to the building.

"Quincy. Darkness. So afraid. Quimbledown. Quincy. Quincy!"

When it became clear she was about to flee, I pulled out my flute and began playing.

Tears coursed down Rosa's cheeks as she slowly regained control of herself. "I don't know if I can do this," she whispered.

"You can. We'll do it together," Gertrude promised.

They walked forward, arm in arm. George stayed to the rear of our group, though I could tell he was keeping an eye out for threats. Because of the nature of magic for quests, Rosa needed to do as much as possible on her own. We stepped past wrought-iron gates into a neglected courtyard. Grass and weeds grew wild, erupting between the pathway stones. Bushes that may have once been properly pruned now snarled in a mass of branches and thorns. The castle looked deserted.

"Nothing is as it seems," Rosa murmured. "Everything you see could be an illusion."

"How can we know the difference?" Gertrude asked.

"We can't," Rosa replied. She picked her way forward to the crumbling stone steps and climbed slowly to the top. Her hand reached for the doorknob. For a moment, she hesitated. Then, with a deep breath, she twisted the knob and pushed the door open. It creaked ominously, announcing our arrival.

We followed Rosa into the castle. Shadows crept along the walls and strange lights flickered. We crept through the front hall past dusty suits of armor and faded tapestries. My heart thundered in my ears as we moved farther into the darkness.

After several minutes, Rosa stopped, listening. "Leticia, stop playing for just a moment. I need to hear."

I lowered my flute and took several steadying breaths. I was grateful for the pause but worried how Rosa would react.

Her eyes widened as her breath quickened. But then she turned her head at a sound coming from down a hall on the other side of the room. "Swans. Quincy!"

As she turned in the direction of the bird calls, I resumed playing the flute, though I did so as quietly as I could. We entered the hall and walked past furniture coated in layers of dust. I began to feel lightheaded, my lungs aching for adequate air. Near the end of the hall, stood a door. Gertrude reached to open it.

"No!" Rosa cried. "Don't touch anything, Gertrude!"

The shock of her outburst startled me and the flute slipped in my sweaty hands. I scrambled to get the instrument back in position and resumed playing. How had Rosa known her friend was in danger? George caught my curious glance and shrugged.

"It's just a door, Rosa," Gertrude said gently.

She shook her head vehemently. "No. Nothing here is as it seems. I couldn't bear if something happened to you. Please, let me open the doors and bear what comes from them."

Tears shone in Gertrude's eyes, but she nodded. "Very well, Rosa."

Rosa put her hand against the wood and traced her fingers down it as though feeling for something. She had almost reached the knob when she pulled back. "This is not the right door. We must keep going. Leticia, take a break while I listen for the swans again."

With a relieved sigh, I lowered the instrument from my lips. I handed it to George and stretched my fingers while opening my mouth wide.

"Are you doing okay, Leticia?" George whispered.

Nodding, I said, "I'm fine."

Rosa whimpered, and I took the flute back from George.

The notes soothed her. "The sounds are coming from two directions. Some of it sounds like it is behind this door, but I hear more of it coming from above. There is a staircase to the left of the front door."

"But wouldn't swans be outside?" George asked.

"Not necessarily. Follow me, and remember, do not touch anything."

We returned to the door, where a sweeping staircase led into the upper floors of the castle. Rosa put a tentative foot on the first step. Nothing happened, and she continued up the stairs with Gertrude by her side. Upon reaching the landing, she held her hand up, and I lowered the flute, taking deep breaths. We stood in a long hallway with many doors. At the end loomed a large, ornate table with a jeweled box on top.

"Whatever you do, don't touch that box," Rosa said. "I remember now. It's at the end of this hallway. I don't know if the things inside have returned, but do not release whatever else is in there. If you do, there will be no hope for any of us."

George looked up suddenly and whispered, "The Vice Box."

"What?" Gertrude asked.

As Rosa led us down the hallway, he explained, "There is an ancient legend about the Vice Box. When humans first appeared in Sanalbereth, the fairies wanted to preserve all that was good in them. Love, generosity, joy, hope. So, they took all feelings of ill-will and suffering and placed them in a plain box to be put away from people. However, there was one fairy who knew people needed to experience both the good and the bad. So he took the box, and, using his talents, carved and decorated it to be irresistibly beautiful. The legend changes somewhat here. Some say a human woman first opened the box, curious as to what something so beautiful would hold. Others say the fairy himself was so entranced by his work that he released the feelings within. In both stories, the one who opened it, terrified by what they'd unleashed, slammed the lid closed, trapping hopelessness. It's an old story to explain why bad things happen, but I never dreamed it might be real."

"It may not be the actual Vice Box," Rosa replied. "If it was, why would there have been so much in it when I opened it?"

"Good point."

"Either way, let's all leave it alone," Rosa said and stopped walking. Tightening her grip on Gertrude's hand, she turned to the door on her left and touched it. "Quincy," she breathed. "Could I really have walked right past you?" She traced her fingers down the wood to the handle. Grasping it, she opened the door. Inside, a dozen swans floated lazily on an enchanted lake.

"This isn't possible," Gertrude whispered.

"Nothing is impossible when you have magic on your side," a mysterious voice said.

I looked around but saw no one.

"I see you've finally arrived, Princess Rosa. But you're looking a little worse for wear. I do hope you didn't play in my things. It's rude to touch other people's belongings without permission."

"Where is Quincy?" Rosa demanded, turning her head toward the voice.

"In here, of course. I'm sure one of these feathered friends would happily call himself your prince. Or perhaps not. You're not quite as beautiful as you once were."

Doubt crept over Rosa's face, and I played louder than before, pouring as much strength into the notes as I could. She straightened. "Nevertheless, I'm here for my prince."

"Then rescue him, by all means. But which swan should you choose? You know how this kind of magic works. Pick the wrong swan, and Quincy will never be a man again."

At that moment, I realized George was nowhere in sight. I stepped out of the room and looked down the hallway. George stood in front of the table, his eyes fixed on the box. His hands reached for it.

I dropped the flute. "George, no!"

He turned slowly to me, as though he hadn't quite heard me. "It's so beautiful, Leticia. Surely what's inside is lovely too."

I ran to him. As I neared, a soft voice whispered in my ear.

Aren't you curious, Leticia? Don't you want to see what wonders I hold?

I glanced at the box. It was beautiful. Maybe just a peek.

Think of the possibilities. The dreams I could show.

Rosa's tortured face rose in my mind, her sightless eyes and white hair. I reached George's side and forced myself to take his hands. "There's nothing in there for us to see. Rosa and Gertrude need us right now."

"Rosa?" He shook his head. "Rosa, Gertrude, where are they?"

I took him to the enchanted room and picked up my flute. Rosa wept bitterly by the side of the lake. "Quincy! Quincy! Where are you?" The swans all gathered around her, honking and pulling at her dress.

"Which one is Quincy?" Gertrude asked. "All but one are white."

"Darkness, Quincy! It's so dark. So dark!"

"She needs the music. Leticia, you must start playing," George said.

"I'm trying," I replied. No matter what I did, the flute made no sound. I tried playing something different, but nothing happened. Something was wrong. I scratched at the surface, and the gold peeled away to reveal a plain, wooden stick. "This isn't my flute," I cried.

"What? Of course it is," George replied.

"No, it isn't." I glanced across the floor. Several other flutes, all identical to mine, were scattered across it. I scrambled to find my instrument, picking them up and testing them to no avail. The black swan started pecking at one of them, pushing it toward the lake. "Leave that alone!" I rushed the swan, and it flapped its wings with an angry honk. "Get back," I hissed.

The swan retreated. Water from the lake lapped at the flute, pulling it in. I picked up the instrument and examined it. The metal gleamed slightly. I scraped a fingernail across the mouth plate. Nothing happened. I put it to my mouth and blew. A clear, sweet note answered. Relief washed over me, and I began playing the fairy ballad.

Rosa held out her hands, her mind clear again. "Gertrude, describe the swans to me."

"There's a black swan. He's larger than the rest and has blue eyes."

"No, that's not Quincy. Keep him away from the others if you can."

"Um, I don't know what to tell you about these other swans. They're big, white, and have feathers. There's nothing remarkable about any of them."

The voice laughed. "Harder than you believed?"

"Who are you?" Rosa demanded. "Show yourself!"

"As you wish." The black swan honked once before it grew and stretched in form. Soon a fairy stood on an island within the lake. I'd seen many fairies, but this one was different. Tall and willowy, he was pale with ebony hair and eyes like forget-me-nots. Filmy black wings traced with red waved at his back. He wore only black, from his tunic to his tall boots. And while most fairies showed signs of their age, despite their incredible lifespans, this fairy appeared ageless. "My name is unimportant," he said. "I am merely here to test you. You failed your first test years ago. Do you remember?"

Rosa trembled. "I can't forget."

"Yes, that is a side effect of the box. But I see you've returned for a second chance. Doesn't happen often. Now, you can attempt to pass the other tests." He turned his attention to me, his dark stare boring to my soul. "There is a reason I hid your instrument. Rosa must do this alone."

"How?" Gertrude demanded. "She can't see. Her mind is all but gone."

The fairy turned to her slowly. "Others have succeeded with less. If you truly wish your friend to be successful, you must allow her this opportunity."

George nodded to me, and I lowered the flute. "Come, Gertrude," I said. "This is Rosa's quest. She must see it through."

Tears filled Gertrude's eyes as she retreated to my side.

For a while, Rosa stood trembling and muttering to herself. She began to hum and then to sing the fairy ballad.

"Magic swirls in the wind,
Colors dance in the trees.
Fairies twirl and spin,
Dancing on the autumn breeze."

She held out her hands and the swans rushed to her. She stroked their feathers and spoke softly to them. Then she pushed them away until there were only two swans left.

"He sees her from afar
And feels his heart swell.
She's beauty like a star,
The fairy dancing in the dell."

One of the swans stood regal and beautiful, larger than the others. The other looked older, his feathers dull and molting. He hesitated to come near.

"She can feel his eyes
As the dance goes on.
A turn and spies
The fairy watching down yon."

She reached for him and stroked his neck. Her words were too quiet for us to hear, but she coaxed the swan closer. I hardly dared breathe as she considered the two swans.

"It is something rare.
It is something new:
Love in a single stare
As they dance upon the dew."

"Pick carefully, Princess," the black-winged fairy said, "or Quincy will remain a swan forever."

Rosa ignored him and sang the last verse.

"It started with a glance,
Continued with an age
As forever they dance,
The fairies have set the stage."

"Poor, poor Quincy. Lost in darkness," Rosa murmured. "Darkness like night. Like sorrow and hardship. You preened too much, my love. Too much." The bedraggled swan ducked his head.

Moonlight streamed through the window, touching the swan's dull feathers. "Find the light," she whispered. She kissed the top of the swan's head as a magical glow filled the room. I looked to George, unsure what was happening, but he merely smiled and nodded back to where Rosa knelt. I followed his gaze. "Be a man, Quincy," Rosa said. Through the brilliant light, the form of the swan shifted. As the glow abated, a man stood before her. She felt his face and smiled. "There you are, Quincy."

"What happened to you?" he asked.

Her smile faded and she turned away. "I know I'm late, far too late for a proper fairy tale. Do you still find me so ugly you do not wish me to rescue you?"

Quincy took her chin in his hand and tilted her face gently until she was facing him. He pushed the silver-white hair behind her ear and his hand traced down her cheek. "I've never seen a more beautiful woman in all my life, and I can't think of a better person to break this curse. I have regretted those unfeeling words every day since I uttered them. Forgive me?"

A tear coursed down her cheek. "I forgave you long ago." She reached for his face and then kissed him gently. "I love you," she whispered.

I felt George take my hand as the room glowed a second time, although less brightly.

The dark fairy held his arms out wide. "Congratulations, Rosa and Quincy. Rosa, I think you know your sight cannot be returned. Once Doubt has blinded someone, they never see fully again. You may start to see glimpses, but your vision will never be restored."

"I understand."

"Now that your quest is over, I can grant you a few favors. Madness will leave your mind and Fear will retreat from your heart. Sorrow will come and go, as it must, but it will no longer be your constant companion. Be joyful."

"Wait, sir, I have a question," I said. He turned to me. I suddenly felt shy and unsure. "Um, I just wondered, why did the fairy ballad help her?"

"Ah, now that is a good question. The simple answer is that the song is a memory. A powerful memory. That specific memory coupled with the dragon magic already infused in your flute gave Rosa the clarity she needed to overcome Madness in small bursts. And now, you must be on your way. Safe journey to each of you and have joy." With that, the fairy transformed once again into the black swan and flew out the open window.

Quincy led the way to the door. "I can't tell you how happy I am to leave this tower."

"I'm just sorry it took me so long," Rosa replied.

He chuckled. "I suppose I deserved it. I told all my friends you would rescue me long before they finished their quests. Serves me right. But what did happen to you, Rosa?"

"That is a long story for another day, darling. For now, I just want to get started on our happily ever after."

Quincy smiled. "That's a request I am happy to fulfill."

Jessica L. Elliott has been writing stories since she could pick up a pencil. When she's not caught up in her vivid imagination, she enjoys time in her garden, creating various art projects, and listening to her children tell her stories. She lives in southwest Kansas with her family.

www.JessicaLEllliott.com

The Wooden Ruler

David Millican

My joints creaked as I shifted positions on the Broken Throne. A thousand times shattered, a thousand times rebuilt. It is the symbol and anchor of my power, and without it, my subjects do not gather to hear my edicts. Throughout endless cycles, malevolent hands have descended to dismantle my power, and before the heavens bring the new cycle, I rebuild it. Defiance is the lifeblood of my rule.

Looking across the kingdom, I felt every one of my three thousand cycles. My citizens, far below me, have no idea what old means. Working with youthful vigor, they are unaware their time here was short. The König, in their anger and hate, snatch them from my hands and take them to existences unthinkable. Most didn't make it past a hundred and eighty cycles, none past six hundred. Except for Digger and myself.

Digger, cast off the kingdom's edge by a malevolent König, shattered half of his face. Now he digs holes and fills holes. Never stopping, never resting, never listening to his king, only digging. Yet, it is a comfort to my soul, that familiar face these past thousand cycles. Even if it is only half of one.

Standing, I walked over to the old mushroom table to consult the master drawing. Two hundred cycles had been required to detail every handspan of the kingdom. Every stone, every bush, and every citizen of the realm was known to me, but the master drawing was more than a map; it was my life's work.

In the winter realm, all seven colonies had completed work on their ice domes. Scribes etched the laws and edicts on frozen blocks. Gardeners planted blue holly to provide berries during the long dark cycles. Mothers rocked their infants wrapped in thick woolen blankets knitted from the hearty northern yaks that transverse the border between the winter and steppe realms.

I watched a few of the beasts traipse across borders marked by a straight, clear-cut path. All borders started at the base of Throne Mountain and raced out to the curved edge of the kingdom. Seven equal slices from horizon to horizon.

Glancing back and forth between the master drawing and each realm, I verified each task was evolving, all details exact, and every citizen engaged.

Shame filled me as I managed my people's work. They should be moving on with their lives, making something of themselves. But my failure to protect them from the ravages of the König meant they, like me, are destined to endless rebuilding. Cycles were required to accomplish their work, and upon completion, with a simple flourish of their fleshy hands, the König erased my people's efforts. The kingdom returned to its natural state, a flat, untouched expanse.

Massaging my temples, I tried to ease the tension that descended when I pondered the motivations of the giants with dominion over us. The smell of pine tar from the mountains filled my nostrils. It was fabled to ease the aches in my joints, but I felt no difference.

Across the distance, beyond the kingdom, the clock indicated three-quarters of the cycle had passed. The clock has always been an enigma. König willfully express their intent to oppress us yet gave us such a gift. Without the clock's circling wands, the unwavering nature of light cycles and unchanging void of dark cycles would be maddening.

Picking up the staff of power, its soft, rouge-colored gem nestled in the shining metal binding at the top, I stepped to the edge of the rippled blue glass that cascaded down to the gathering courtyard below. The crack of wood against glass tumbled out across the realms and reverberated off the sky-canopy above as I brought the staff down three times. Three breaths as the echoes died and I repeated the process. Four breaths this time before a single, final crack.

My subjects halted their work and gathered into rows by realm, colony, and occupation. Looking up with eagerness, they waited for my speech. Weariness settled on me as the realization that this kingdom was held together by the strength of my words. Well, words and throne.

"Maza, look at this." Aleth leaned over the gnome enclosure, the gnome dome as Maza called it, staring in amazement at the tiny wooden gnome standing on the glass waterfall.

"What?" Maza called from the other end of the aisle, frustration clear in his voice. "I'm on break."

"Check this gnome out, it's talking."

"It's just the Wooden Ruler."

"The what?" Aleth turned to look at Maza.

He pointed at a sign above the gnome dome that had a picture of a gnome holding a pencil like a walking staff. The words *Wooden Ruler* were embossed in bold red letters above the little man. On the bottom, it read: *Come see the one-of-a-kind Wooden Gnome Ruler!*

"Is this a new type that's coming out?"

"Nah, man," Maza said, stepping up beside him, "it's just some broken gnome that thinks it's a king or something."

"Wood gnomes don't think, they don't have brains."

"I don't mean think think, I mean it's scrambled or something and it acts like a king."

"So it was damaged?"

"Nope. Came from the factory that way. When Mr. Johnson called the factory to figure out what was going on, we sold like fifty gnomes while he was on the phone. Factory wanted it back, but once Johnson figured out it sold more gnomes, he refused."

"Crazy. What do you think happened?"

"Helet, one of the trainers," Aleth nodded, hoping he didn't blush, "She's been here since little dude showed up. Said first day he was here, he stood around doin' nothin'. Second day, he built that throne out of trash someone had left in there. They swept the throne to the side for cleanup in the morning, but when they came in he'd rebuilt it."

"I thought gnomes went inactive in the dark."

"Yeah. Helet thinks its sleep enchantment is busted. Little dude's mind, for lack of a better word, has been running nonstop since the factory, I guess."

"But why would it make itself a king? Wouldn't it just do whatever its type is? Like build buildings nonstop?"

"Or dig holes?" Maza smiled and pointed at the gnome with half a face behind the throne where it was trying to dig a hole into the shaped concrete mountain. "Yeah, that's what it should do. Some think it's a new type of gnome. Or a prototype of one."

"No way!" Aleth stared as the gnome droned on while the others went still, their sleep enchantments activating. "It's crazy hard to develop new gnome types."

"Yeah, that's why Applied Enchantments pays a ton to anyone who can make one. So, the theory is, someone tried a new one and it didn't work right. But instead of going to the Old Home for Gnomes, it got shipped here."

"Old Home for Gnomes? That actually exists? They're just toys."

"It's just what we call the shredder. If a gnome hasn't been imprinted on a human by the tenth month, its imprint won't take. We shred 'em so they don't go crazy and hurt some kid."

"That's crazy. He does this every day?"

"Give a speech?"

"Yeah."

"Most days. His Majesty isn't like other gnomes, he doesn't have a routine."

"Why do they gather like that?"

"Because he calls them."

"But how?"

"I think that's the type he's supposed to be, a leader. When he walks around in the different zones, they stop and look at him. You put a snow gnome in a city gnome family, they'll ignore each other. But if he shows up, all action shuts down."

"This is crazy."

"You wanna see real crazy." Maza stepped back and pointed to his left. "Look at the demi-dragons."

Aleth stepped over and peered into the large glass cage next to the gnome habitat. Four dozen demi-dragons perched in rows facing the wall separating them from the gnomes. They all faced the same direction, looking at the same spot on the wall. Aleth rocked back and forth between the two habitats. They stared at the exact spot where the Wooden Ruler stood.

"Are they listening to him?" He couldn't believe he was asking the question.

"Seems like it. When he gives a speech, they line up like that. I think it's the high-pitched squeal of his joints moving."

"This is crazy." Aleth couldn't help but repeat himself.

"Yeah. I'm going to go heat up my burger before my break's over. You want anything?"

"Nah, I'm good." Aleth stepped up to the gnome habitat again. "Can I open it?"

"Yeah, just don't let any customers grab the gnomes. That's how that one lost half his face. Kid snatched him and dropped him. We tried to return that one, but the Ruler lost his wooden mind. Built a spear and was throwing it at the lid."

"A spear?"

"Yeah," Maza called as he walked down the aisle, "Out of tree limb and foil gum wrapper. It was awesome."

Aleth turned back to the gnome dome, lifted the clear glass on its hinges, and leaned in to look at the Wooden Ruler. Its mouth and hands were moving as though giving an impassioned speech, but it had no voice. Old wooden jaws squeaked, making the toy sound more like a hyper squirrel than a mighty ruler.

"You preach on, little dude, preach on." Aleth closed the lid and went back to work.

"...And though the hands of fate have brought us low, we will not yield. The cycles are long and the future is...the future is..."

I stumbled over my words as a König opened the sky-canopy and leaned over me. From time to time, König, especially unfamiliar ones, would take interest in my kingdom. Taking a deep breath, I continued.

"The future is dim, but this existence is not our destiny. A cycle comes, a cycle when we rise up and throw off the chains of oppression—"

The König bellowed in its incomprehensible language and then closed the sky. Early on, I believed their language too complex, too powerful, for me to comprehend. Now, I understand that I am too complex for them. The simplicity of their minds is proven through never tiring of torturing us, never tiring of destroying our lands, and never tiring of wiping the sky with a dirty cloth.

I resumed. "When we will throw off the chains of oppression, break free from the bonds of this prison, and take hold of our rightful place in the universe, as conquerors, not slaves."

No applause accompanied the conclusion; that was expected. Expressions of excitement drew notice. Long ago, on the dark cycle I ascended the throne, I commanded silence. I risked the speeches, for their hearts needed cheering, their resolve needed boosting, and with embarrassment I admit I need the outlet. On rare occasions, I revealed a portion of myself. Insecurities over my rule, fears of the future, or the helplessness I experience as my citizens are abducted. In my youth, I believed admitting such shortcomings would weaken my command. Through the wisdom of cycles, however, I understand it makes me empathetic to their plight.

Stepping back from the edge, I sat upon my throne. Sleep tugged at me, though its pull was weak. Once, it had been a riptide pulling me under. Defiance is my essence, so I resisted. Now, after years, it was still there, but nothing more than the lapping of gentle waves. Sleep is the enemy of preparation. I will free my people, and as many of the other oppressed peoples in the Great Beyond as time and chance would allow.

My mind had verged on the edge of collapse with the first glimpse of creatures caged as we are. Walking amongst my people one cycle, a zealous König of the pockmarked variety shook the earth with the hammer blows of their fist. Many of the realm's buildings collapsed before another König interceded. They were odd in that manner, anger, wrath, venom, and compassion all mixed together.

During the attack, a large spire tree had fallen across the great chasm surrounding the kingdom. My edicts prevented us from drawing attention to ourselves, but it had been an opportunity I was unwilling to pass up. Sliding across the trunk, I reached the edge of the world, and my mind all but shattered. The Great Beyond, which I had always assumed to be formless, was nothing more than dozens of prison kingdoms gathered around towering wooden ridges forming deep canyons. König moved through the Great Beyond, mining the walls and placing their hauls in metal baskets a quarter of the size of my own world. Our kingdom sat high in the air on an elevated path that circled the great space below.

Scale seemed impossible to grasp. Even the König were larger than I had expected, having legs similar to mine instead of floating as I had supposed. Using their size, I estimated the sizes of the other prison kingdoms. Across the expanse was a world where the inhabitants were four times the size of the König. For a moment, I believed I had found the König of the König, but the cages extinguished that hope. Those creatures, which I have since learned are great dragons, were behind thick metal bars and enslaved to the cruel König as well.

Beyond the dragons, I learned of hooked-beaked hippogriffs, demure mini-sphinxes, powerful granx, fast-as-lighting furies, König-faced sero-moths, peaceful yet mistreated demi-dragons, and a dozen other peoples. In that moment as I stood gazing out at the wonders and horrors of the Great Beyond, I had seized my destiny. I would free them. All of them.

Aleth waited as Goran broke the seal on the light orb enchantment, plunging the store into darkness. Outside, the night manager used a battered wand to set the timer on the dark wolves' cage locks. Aleth pulled the final gate closed behind them. Insistent beeping sounded as the timer count down till the semi-sentient wolves were released to patrol the store. Part alarm system, part animal herders, and all teeth, they were the only thing in the store that terrified him.

Aleth drove to Elso's where the crew hung out after work. Aleth tended to avoid chain restaurants where ambiance was provided by knockoff memorabilia, but Maza had said Helet would be there. Walking past the twenty-something-about-to-drop-out-of-college-because-her-soriety-life-meant-she-partied-more-than-she-studied hostess, he sat with the crew.

"Made it out alive, did ya," Maza called.

"Barely," Aleth said back quietly.

"Sweet. This is Melar and this is Helet." Maza pointed to the two girls on either side of him in turn. "They used to do our jobs, but they're in obedience training now. They're superior to us."

"Don't mind him," Melar said, her curly red hair falling in her face as she leaned forward. "It's almost impossible not to be superior to Maza." She smiled. "Though I guess I am pretty much superior to everyone."

"You're the worst," Maza said, poking the boisterous girl in the ribs, eliciting a squeal from her.

"And what about you?" Aleth asked Helet. "Are you superior as well?"

"I—" Helet started before Melar cut her off.

"She'd be all too happy to be inferior to you." She wiggled her eyebrows, making the other girl's cheeks blossom in bright red blotches.

Aleth wasn't comfortable either, so he changed the subject. "So about this Broken Ruler gnome."

"Wooden Ruler," Helet said.

"Sorry, Wooden Ruler, you said he was four years old?" The question had been addressed to Maza, but he was lost, whispering in Melar's ear.

"Yes, he is," Helet responded.

"That's impossible. Doesn't their binding charm only have a two-year shelf life?"

"A two-year standard shelf life. There've been cases of them lasting three, but yeah, four's insane."

"Now you've done it," Melar interrupted, Maza's head buried in her neck. "You brought up that stupid gnome, and now she won't shut up."

Helet rolled her eyes and looked back at Aleth. "If you don't want to talk about them, we don't have to."

"I think they're fascinating."

"Really?" Her eyes lit up. "Most guys think they're kid's toys."

"Well, they are, but the magic behind them is incredible. Like super-sophisticated golem stuff."

"Right," Helet said with a bright smile. "This is bleeding edge magic. And our little guy, he's borderline miraculous."

"You think he's a new type?"

She leaned and whispered, "You might laugh, but I think he imprinted on himself."

"First, why would I laugh, and second, what?"

"Others laugh."

"I'm not others."

She smiled, green eyes twinkling in the lamplight. "It's impossible, I know. There has to be sentience in order to imprint, but what if, just what if, this new line mocks sentience enough to fool the imprint. Premature activation of the imprint charm is common, so it's possible."

"But how would he imprint on himself? There's no secondary charm to link to."

"And there's never been a gnome with an extra imprint charm?"

"Well..." Of course he had seen one, with their split personalities. "Still seems out there."

"I know, I know." She took a sip of her cold purple tea. "But I've been watching him for years, and he's getting more complex. That's imprinting."

Aleth narrowed his eyes. "You think he's sentient."

"No. Maybe." She looked around the table to confirm no one else was listening. "I don't know...maybe I do."

"People will call you crazy talking like that." She looked hurt, so he quickly added, "Not me, but others."

"I knew I liked you." Red colored her cheeks as she realized what she had said.

"Same," he said with more boldness than he usually displayed.

The orbs of light above winked out as the König exited the Great Beyond for whatever world comprised their Great Beyond. It wasn't a prison like my world though; the König could come and go as they pleased.

Easing creaking joints down the mountain, I pulled aside the false well to reveal the tunnel beneath. It had been a thousand cycles since Digger had completed the basic work on our path to freedom. Five hundred since I had finished shoring it up and cutting in stairs. Each of those five hundred cycles worth of traversing up and down the tunnel was felt as I descended now. Driving me forward was the knowledge the end was imminent. Our efforts, my efforts, were coming to fruition.

At the fork, I dropped the smaller of two bundles. Following the right tunnel, it turned from earth to König metal. Bright crystals of unknown purpose and porcelain plates with König script etched on them lined the walls. The door wasn't secured, needing only slight pressure to release it. Again, the arrogance of our oppressors played into my hands.

Swinging my legs over the edge, I hopped to the shelf below. For the last thousand dark cycles, I had ventured into the Hidden Beyond, preparing for this night. Digger's accident was tragic, yet it meant salvation for his countrymen. Before his compulsion to dig, my efforts to escape, or even develop a plan, had been in vain. Discovery of this portal changed everything. Digger would have a place of the highest honor in my new kingdom.

Using handholds on the brick wall, I scaled to the next ledge up and then two more again. The dangerous part was next as I had to jump across a gap three hundred handspans wide. The height I gained by climbing made it possible but risky. Only two or three paces wide, the narrow ledge was forty paces long. On the furthest edge, I tied off a rope made of tents, clothes, and hair to a metal prong. Sprinting, the edge neared and I poured all my strength into the jump. The ledge disappeared under me.

Air rushed past my face as I plummeted. Panic rose as the ground came too fast, the gate too far away. I hadn't jumped far enough. Just as success seemed impossible, the rope pulled tight and momentum hurtled me toward the gate, where my hand caught the lip. Clamping with an iron grip, I held tight as the momentum slammed my body against the hard brick underneath.

Looking down, I saw the third finger of my right hand falling to the floor below. Pulling myself up, I rested my feet in the gaps between the bars. Every fall held a certain amount of terror; this had been the first where the terror nearly transformed into reality. Age seemed destined to bring me down, the thief of my dreams.

Undoing the latch, I gained access to the small compartment where hard supplements, in the shapes of bones and steaks, were stored. Bundling half with string, I attached them to the rope. Sitting on the ground behind them, I used my feet to shove them over the edge. They came to rest below my kingdom. I had never pilfered so many at once, lest the heist be noticed, but the time for caution was over. My finger lying on the ground might tip them off, or the missing supplements, or any of the other two dozen tasks I had to accomplish.

But glory and freedom were over the horizon. *By all that is right in this broken world, I will have it.*

Closing the gate behind me, I visited prison kingdoms I would need to access with haste, wedging open their locks. Outside the greater dragons' cage, I pulled a large steak from the frozen metal enclosure and dropped it to the wolf on guard. She tore into it as I scaled the cage to a shelf attached to the wall. The massive beasts routinely slammed against the gate to draw nearby König over. If successful, the dragons received a treat. If I wedged their lock open, escape would occur prematurely and all would be lost. Instead, I hid a stolen key for the lock behind a jar of amber liquid.

Three critical tasks remained. Adjacent to the large doors leading to the Great Beyond was a switch that unleashed chaos on the world. Wailing metal mouths let loose from their sentinels on the walls, gates crashed down from the sky, and the doors the König used locked. They tested the system every seven hundred cycles, and it had taken fourteen hundred cycles of investigation, and a terrifying accidental triggering of the switch, to discover how to disable it. Easing off the round red cover, I used my broadsword to sever the metal spring behind it. Unfamiliar with their magic, I removed the crystal as well, slipping it into my satchel before replacing the cover.

Next, a small window between the Hidden and Great Beyonds needed opening. Pounding against the arm that controlled the window's movement, I found it stuck with age and disuse. Frustration swept over me as breaths slipped away, bringing the return of the König ever closer.

Hot wet wind washed over me, and I froze in fear.

Turning, a large wolf stood with its paws against the wall under the window, muzzle three handspans from my flat, hard face. This close, I could identify individual ridges on its nose, but not which wolf the nose belonged to. Closing my eyes, I hoped it was friendly, or at least ambivalent. Claws scraped against brick and its paw, three times my size, settled over me.

Expecting to be torn away and cast down to the hard earth below, shattering as poor Digger had, I resigned my heart to defeat. Gentle pressure increased until I was sure the metal arm beneath would pierce through my chest. With a squeal, the arm budged and swung around on its orbit, opening the window a third of the distance I needed. The paw lifted, and I was able to raise my head again. The wolf had fallen to all fours again and looked up at me with wide eyes and a lolling tongue I had learned to interpret as friendly. It was the mate of the wolf I had fed earlier, the father of her soon-to-be cubs.

"Thank you, my friend, you shall be remembered in the tribulations to come and the kingdom destined to be."

With a sharp bark, it acknowledged my thanks and trotted toward its mate. The initial resistance overcome, the arm now rotated with ease. Another risk. One König noticing the open window and closing it would be disastrous. Other portals existed, but were of no use to me. Doors larger than my entire realm sat at either end of the Hidden Beyond. I could no more move them than I could carry the entirety of my kingdom to safety on my shoulders.

This window was the only one large enough to allow free access, yet small enough to manipulate. Sliding through the opening, I glanced up by habit to the clock high on the wall. My heart fell as the wands revealed the futility of my plan. A quarter of the remaining cycle was required to reach my destination.

It was essential; all other efforts were in vain without it. The sabotaged switch didn't immobilize the final gate—it could be lowered by hand. If the gate was secured, there would be no escape. And if they maimed Digger for no other reasons than they could, I had no illusions what they would do to me when captured.

I had to prepare the sabotage personally. My people were true, strong, honorable, and loyal subjects, but intelligence was not their forte. Complex tasks like rigging the gate to jam were beyond their ability, even for my Seven.

A quarter of the remaining cycle to the door, a quarter back, and three quarters of the remaining cycle to reach the portal back to my realm. There was no helping it; time shortened or not, I was committed to the path. Sprinting across the open earth, moving with reckless abandon, I trusted to luck not to draw the attention of violent wolves. The world blurred around me as I focused on my destination, forcing my feet to push ever harder against the cold smooth stone of the ground.

Distant sounds of clacking claws threatened to break my concentration. I pushed on, fearing teeth as large as my torso would snap me up and end everything. Fear of death was overshadowed by the fear of another three thousand cycles trapped in that prison.

Transitioning from wall to floor with a mighty leap, I climbed as though the flames of death themselves licked at my heels. The tick of the clock mocked me. Inside the cover protecting the grooved metal wheel that lowered and raised the gate, I placed my contraption. Inert until my knight released the latch on the spring arm; I had to hope it worked as designed—there was no time for a test.

Sliding down a metal pole, I slowed my descent only enough to ensure no broken limbs upon landing. Still, a sliver of my foot broke away, but as with the finger, I ignored the pain. Time and distractions were not my ally this dark cycle.

Again, with seamless efficiency, I made the transition between wall and floor with a mighty leap. Barks of excitement trailed after me as the wolves hunted me. Lowering myself over the inside windowsill, frustrated huffs chased after me.

A glance at the clock gave me heart as the journey to the door and back was accomplished in record time. Climbing over obstacles, jumping between ledges, tiptoeing across wire shelfs, I expended everything to reach home. Would the König be early? Would they possess that rare quality of attentiveness or be their normal distracted selves? How close would I be to safety when I was discovered? The door to my kingdom came into view as the lights overhead flared to life.

Aleth pushed through the swinging doors to the stockroom. Wincing as the carbon lights came on, he covered his eyes. Three drinks last night while talking to Helet was three more than he was used to. Alcohol combined with covering the morning shift to gain brownie points meant it was going to be a horrible day.

He froze. Something had caught his eye against the cage wall. Rubbing his eyes, he looked at the shelf of scratch posts for the Karakals, trying to pick out anything unusual.

Did I see...but it couldn't...

There's no way a gnome could have gotten back here. Even if it'd been able to lift the canopy, which was impossible, it wouldn't have been able to get back here.

Must've been all the talk with Helet about gnomes and the Wooden Ruler, he thought.

Continuing down the curved room, he slipped the morning meals through the feeding slots while thinking of Helet.

At each habitat, he removed the clipboard and initialed next to the morning slot. There was more to it than feeding, but he hadn't been trained on it and had been told the mid's employees would take care of it. Aleth didn't like not doing his job; he'd have to make up for it somewhere else. Get ahead so the mids didn't have to do as much. Washing his hands at the sink, he pushed through the doors to the floor where a few early customers were already browsing aisles.

He had to grab bedding for the mammals and reptiles from the shed but wanted to make a quick stop at the gnome habitat. He'd grabbed a tiny golden throne meant for aquariums and was going to give it to the Wooden Ruler. He felt bad for the little guy, but honestly, he was hoping it would impress Helet. He'd never been smooth but wasn't terrible looking. He just found most girls to be boring, or at least the personas they projected to the world. Helet had been herself, a little nerdy, but fully her. He liked that and was planning to ask her out when she came in for her afternoon shift.

Confusion clouded his face as his hand hovered over the habitat's cover. The Wooden Ruler was nowhere to be seen. His strange movements and clothing made him stand out even in crowds of regular gnomes. He took a full two minutes searching the habitat and still no sign of the strange little toy. Doubt about his dismissal of seeing a gnome in the stockroom rushed in.

"What are you doing?" Jerrus asked, causing Aleth to jump.

"The Wooden Ruler isn't in there."

Jerrus leaned over and gave the area a quick scan. "He's probably in one of the buildings. He does that from time to time. Started about a year ago. He goes in and spends a couple of hours and then comes out. If all the other gnomes weren't accounted for, I'd say he was getting down to business. But he's probably just sleeping or something. He doesn't sleep any other time."

"Oh." Aleth was glad he hadn't pulled the throne out of his vest pocket. "That's one weird gnome."

"Give it a month, the novelty wears off. Unless you're Helet, of course."

"Yeah," Aleth said noncommittally, still uneasy about the missing gnome and trying to hide his offense at the sleight to Helet.

Hauling two and a half tons of bedding in on the pallet lift and transferring them to the display up front took his mind off the strange creature though. His arms ached after four hours of moving the fifty pound bags of mulched trees. He'd known this was a physically demanding job but hadn't expected to be so out of shape.

Back at the gnome habitat, there was the Wooden Ruler sitting upon his throne, looking out over his imaginary kingdom. Aleth thought the little wooden man might have glanced at him, but told himself to stop being silly. Lifting the lid, he slipped in the golden throne and placed it next to the current one. Dropping the lid, he waited for the gnome to switch. After a minute, it was clear the gnome was unaware of the new throne, so Aleth went back to work. Three hours till Helet showed up. Stacking canned food should make the time pass.

With all the haste I could muster, I slipped in amongst the towers below the demi-dragon prison as the light illuminated the world around me. The König who had interrupted my speech moved past, rubbing his face. Using the rope, I slipped off the ledge to the shelf outside my kingdom. The König stopped and took a step back. Pulling up under the lip into the shadows, I waited. He stared at the space I had vacated not an instant ago before moving off. If there was a König who would be my undoing, it would be him.

Climbing atop the shelf, I pushed against the door and stepped back as it popped open. Inside, I turned to place my feet against the lip of the threshold and pulled on the rope. Using the edge of the ledge as an anchor, I pulled the massive payload of supplements up from where they hung and into my kingdom. Each handspan of the rope's progress was filled with terror as I was still exposed. Once inside, I freed them, let the rope swing away, and closed the door.

Rest was not on the agenda. Back at the fork, still dragging the heavy supplements, I dropped the climbing gear and tools to retrieve the smaller bundle. Down the path, I came to another of the König's metal walls. When Digger had first reached it, there had been scrapings and the murmur of voices on the other side. A little more excavation revealed a slot to another kingdom and the mighty beast with powerful claws and a black snout that called it home. And now here I was all these cycles later and the same powerful claws and wicked black snout peered at me through the opening between our kingdoms.

"Orem, my friend, I am sorry I am late."

"No worries, your highness." I was glad that the demi-dragon was taking it serious today rather than calling me *your lowness*.

I pulled the bundle of supplements into view. The dragon reached through and snatched it out of my hands. Disappearing I knew he was distributing the talent-boosting supplements to his subjects. He claimed not to be their king, rather referring to himself as their chief, or alpha, but it seemed the equal of a king.

Returning, wicked teeth stained red from the supplement, he said, "We ready to go?"

"The plan is underway. This cycle, our moment of triumph arrives, and in the kingdom to come, your praises will be sung until the world sleeps to rise no more."

Orem shook his head. "I love it when you talk like that."

I nodded my acknowledgment of his truth. Slipping the master drawing out of the bundle, I laid it upside down in front of him. The König thought they were clever, but none discovered the purpose of rearranging my kingdom. Now it mirrored the Great Beyond's layout and our escape plan.

"Your fastest and stealthiest flyer must carry my First Knight to the gate here. Everything..." I stared into his large yellow eye with its diamond pupil for emphasis. "...everything hinges on the success of this one task. There are contingencies for all but this single task. There can be no acceptance of failure."

Orem nodded. "Kilor will get your man there."

Nodding, I continued by pointing out the unsecured cages after my dark cycle exploits.

"Your next six best will take the rest of my Seven and free these prisoners." Pointing to a small garden, representing the great dragon kingdom, at the back right of the map, I said, "Here you and I will free the great dragons after confirmation the gate is disabled. They are unpredictable, and I would rather you and I accomplish it together."

Orem gave a spout of flame from his nostrils. "Don't you worry, with those meat treats in my belly, we'll get it done."

I rested my head against the metal. "Orem, my friend, my brother...my body is old. I wish I had more time to plan, to prepare, but the sunset of my life is upon me. You have been my truest companion, and it will be my greatest pleasure to ride into battle with you, our fates intertwined. Your knowledge of the Great Beyond has been invaluable to bringing about this opportunity, and now your people and mine will conquer this new world together." Rumbling in the back of Orem's throat sounded his agreement.

"If the König could hear your speeches, we wouldn't have to break out." Lowering his eye to the opening again, he continued, "We will be ready, my friend."

I nodded and made the long climb back to the surface. I had never emerged in the harsh glare of a light cycle but had foreseen the possibility and prepared the best I could. Many cycles ago, I took to spending time meditating inside the various shelters of my people, giving me an explanation if ever I was absent.

Looking out through the small divot under the well, I saw no König with their attentions directed toward my kingdom, so I slid out fast as my body would allow. Upon my throne once more, I called my Seven, and they responded with haste. Nervous as I met with them in the open for the first time, I reviewed their orders. Satisfied of their preparation, I sent them into the tunnel to await my arrival.

Taking a walk around the kingdom, trying to look casual, I reassured my people of a successful outcome. To their credit, they bore the tension well by maintaining their guise as simple workers committed to a task. In a moment's notice, they would throw off their masks and rise as the warriors I have spent so many sleepless nights training them to be.

Returning to the throne, I stilled my racing heart as the clock's slim wands drove ever onwards to the moment of action. I yearned to give a rousing speech, to check on every detail, to jump into motion, to do something, but there was only waiting. To pass the time, I delivered a silent speech to myself.

Waiting, that ill word dominating my existence till this very moment, will plague but a short breath longer. Destiny, within my grasp, a purpose in this grand scheme called life shall be freedom which bears each moment glorious. Joyous workers shall not be the role we are forced to play as bit actors on their pathetic stage but the foundation of our unbreakable kingdom. Exultation shall be the wings that lift us to soar above all the heavens known to creation. Power, that mortal quest, will be expresse—

I cut off as the König who had nearly seen me outside appeared. Scanning in a conspiratorial manner to see if anyone was watching his actions, he then made eye contact with me. Frozen in fear, I tried to believe the best—this was only a coincidence; he knew nothing of my plans. Yet, as he lifted the sky, my hope faltered. I dared not close my eyes and die a coward.

Setting down a golden throne next to my broken one, he closed the sky and stared at me. I knew he was waiting for a reaction, but what was appropriate was beyond me. Remaining motionless, my mind urged him to move on, to forget about my existence, to be as dismissive as the other König. Yet, a part of me had to appreciate him. Only one other König had ever given me a gift, if indeed he was giving me a gift. I couldn't discount the notion he might be mocking me, but my intuition said he was sincere.

Blessedly, he left, and the wait began again. I found myself trying out the new throne to distract myself. Time was thick and liquid as it slipped past me. The heat of a thousand great lights burned in my chest as the stark face of the clock neared the influx of green-clothed König. It appeared the worst time to make our escape, when those König dedicated to the upkeep of the Great Beyond were at their highest concentration, but I believed different.

Trickling in by ones and twos, they all gathered in a great circle near the center of the Great Beyond. Only a handful remained near the portal to the unknown and were distracted by interactions with other König. It was at this point in the cycle that they were at their greatest distraction.

And without fanfare, without notice, like a silent breath of wind, the moment was here. I slid the well aside and took the steps two at a time. No time for stealth, for hesitation—boldness was the flavor of the moment. Running past my Seven, those of my citizens who had showed themselves the most dedicated to our escape, I heard their footfalls behind me as I reached the fork.

"I come, my friend, I come," I called down the tunnel to the kingdom of the demi-dragons as I headed to the right.

Not slowing, I threw my shoulder into the door, and it gave with a pop. Grabbing the rope where it still rested, I scaled the distance to the ledge where I pulled open the door to Orem's kingdom. True to his word, his people sat ready to fly. Long and sleek, they ranged in color from blacker than a dark cycle to brilliant yellow that rivaled the glory of the great lights above.

Kilor, Orem's most trusted lieutenant, slithered forward, his dingy eggshell coloring bland amongst the prismatic colors of his brothers. My First Knight climbed upon the ridge of hardened skin just behind Kilor's wings, as Orem instructed, and pulled a white cloth I had secured on an earlier expedition over him. Kilor's trustworthiness, his speed, and his skill all made him suited for this mission. His coloring made him perfect.

The sinewy creature leapt into the air, taking my heart with him, and disappeared against the white sky of the Hidden Beyond. Covering distances it took me a quarter of a cycle to cover in a blink of an eye. The moment became real. It was here, it was happening. I swung my leg up onto Orem's back, settling into a depression in the ridge. Throwing off my cape, I revealed my sword and pulled up my spear to rest against my legs. It was time.

Wind rushed past my face as Orem fell off the side of the ledge, rolling in midair disorienting me, but I had no fear. My will was stronger than any quirk of fate or interference of the König. With a great whoop, we rose up as the dragon's wings spread, catching air and sending us rocketing forward, inches above the earth. Power coursed through our bodies as we raced along toward the cage of the great dragons and the moment of triumph.

We passed five of my Seven and their mounts already in position. The sixth stood ready at the window, watching for the signal of the First Knight's success. Pulling up outside the cage, Orem gave a hiss as the massive beasts growled and moved close.

"Easy, my friend, it is only for a moment." I did not understand the animosity between the two dragons, but I trusted Orem to do his part.

Orem flicked his tri-barbed tail in frustration but made no other move to antagonize the beasts. Retrieving the key, I climbed up to the lock and positioned it and applied pressure. The lock sprang open with a click, which drew the attention of the dragons.

"Stand fast, my friends. Your moment has not yet come. It looms just beyond the next breath, but you must be patient."

I could feel their wills push back against mine, but years of practice had made me strong. Lifting my arm, I raised my palm out to them and sent a wave of command over them and they broke. It would not be long before they recovered, but I needed only the barest of reprieves. Then I would be happy to release them upon those who would dare consider themselves my better and enslave my people.

"Your man has signaled," Orem whispered into my ear.

Closing my eyes, I released the power and pulled back on the door. I did not have the strength to do more than move it a sliver, but the creatures inside understood and rushed headlong to their freedom. Orem snatched me in his long claws as he launched us toward the window beyond. Taking up position with the sixth knight and his mount, Almos, the demi-dragons let out streams of fire fueled by the supplements I had procured for them. The flame turned the great dragons through the swinging doors, into the open vastness of the Great Beyond.

It has begun.

Aleth waited by the sphinx feed, looking for Helet. Every shift change they had to gather to get pass down and bring everyone up to speed on what needed to be done. He'd picked this spot so he could see the door, but he hadn't seen her come in. Maybe she'd called off. Maybe she had drunk too much last night. Maybe she didn't want to see him.

And then she was there, waving to him, coming in from the side door. He couldn't keep the smile off his face as she pulled up next to him and leaned against the endcap. Their arms were separated by a hair's breadth. Did that mean she liked him? Or did she just have no idea about personal space?

"I thought you worked tonight?" Helet said, looking at the manager on duty getting ready to begin.

"Someone called and asked me to cover. Trying to make friends and all that."

"So they suckered you?" He could see her off-kilter smile.

"I think they think they did."

She inclined her head to look up at him, and his smile widened to the point it hurt.

"Quiet," the manager called. "We've got a couple of memos from corporate and then assignments." He lifted two gray pieces of parchment. "First, there've been complaints in other stores about customers not knowing return policies for animals. So now we have these," he held up a stack of white cards, "nifty little cards to—"

The bellow of a great dragon cut him off as it ripped through the air. Aleth ducked, placing a protective arm over Helet, as the shelf to the right of him whipped violently. Turning to look, he saw the alpha dragon, an enormous blood-red creature, had perched on the row of shelving which had buckled. Behind it, the rest of the dragons were spreading out across the store floor, crashing into displays and tearing apart merchandise.

"Hit the lockdown," the manager called from behind, calmer than Aleth felt.

Dragons weren't dangerous, just destructive. Aleth made sure Helet was okay and started toward the harness section so he could round some dragons up. Two steps away from Helet, he and everyone in the store froze in place.

Piecing the air, the scream of the granx signaled real danger. Then it was in front of him, like a wolf-sized spider mated with a demon. Tan blurs faster than his eyes could follow shot between his legs.

"The furies are out," he yelled.

A scream sounded behind him. It wasn't Helet. He didn't risk taking his eyes off the granx. They were ambush hunters, attacking when you were distracted. Or at least he hoped.

A hook-beaked hippogriff landed on the granx's back, trying to bite through the chitinous shell. Aleth grabbed Helet by the arm and rushed toward the back of the store. If the animals were out, the safest place for her would be in their cages.

"Why isn't the lockdown initiating?" Helet called over the cacophony of chaos.

Before he could answer, Aleth was stunned by the sight of a bright yellow demi-dragon flying in the direction of the gnome habitat, a gnome riding on its back like a warrior out of mythology.

"Did you see..." He trailed off as the thunderous hoofbeats of six panicked celephants rushed toward them in a stampede.

With no time to dodge, he spun, wrapping Helet in his arms, hoping to keep her from being crushed by the horse-sized beasts. But the impact never came, and the sound of their oncoming charge changed to nervous stamping. Hesitantly, he looked over his shoulder and found another demi-dragon hovering in the space between him and the celephants.

Its black scales reflected the carnage around it, and on its back sat the Wooden Ruler, palm raised toward the herd animals. He looked over his shoulder at Aleth, gave him a slight nod, and then the dragon sped away to the front of the store.

"He is alive," Helet whispered in awe.

Aleth could only nod in response.

Orem carried me away from the female König, and her mate, that had shown kindness to us through the cycles. Honor had demanded I interrupt my plans to repay their kindness. Now we sped over the canyons to throw open the sky of my former kingdom and set my people free.

The calm order of the Great Beyond had shattered under the force of a hundred creatures loosing the frustration of a thousand cycles of captivity. Everything was advancing according to plan. All that remained was to escort my people through the portal beyond. Lighting on the lip outside my kingdom, Orem directed the remainder of his dragons to lift the sky. They had entered through the secret tunnel and now pushed up from the inside. Their powerful wings made quick work, and the solid sky that had been our prison snapped into place on the wall above.

The First Knight and Kilor returned from their mission of sabotage and directed citizens onto the backs of dozens of dragons. Stacked up eight and nine deep on the dragons, my people responded admirably with no fear and a rigid adherence to orders.

"Orem, we must check on the state of the König."

The black dragon leapt to the wall, claws finding purchase on smooth stone, and leapt again to a hanging board bearing the writing of the König. It rocked under the impact, but Orem balanced with ease, giving me a view of the scene below. König cowered away from granxes on the prowl and others fled out the doors to the unknown. Their expressions made it clear they were no hindrance to our aims.

"They go for the wolves." Orem pointed at three green-clothed König skulking through the rubble. "If they free them, we lose."

"Agreed, brother. It is time to use that flame of yours."

"Really?" The excitement in the dragon's voice was palpable. "You said we couldn't burn."

"I said it shouldn't be done in haste. This is not haste, this is desperation. Ahead of them there is a rack, bring your fire to bear upon it."

With a ululating roar, Orem dove. Liquid fire streamed out of his maw, igniting everything it touched. In an instant, an inferno stood between the König and the wolves that spelled our doom. I pumped my spear in triumph as we banked to the left heading for the doors and our people. Their progress was slow, weighed down as the dragons were with so many. But all obstacles were neutralized and success was ours.

Fast as the fire saved us, it was wrenched from us faster. Thick, viscous liquid fell from the sky in weighty drops, extinguishing the fire and driving the dragons to the ground under the onslaught. An unforeseen power was here to crush us at last. Orem shook off the liquid and managed to get into the air again but was forced down a second time.

"I'm sorry, my friend, it is over," he said, looking back at me, anguish in his eyes.

Anguish and hopelessness.

Fire blossomed in my chest that even the magic of the König could not touch. I would not fail. My people would not suffer a single breath longer. Orem's people would not be doomed to a life excluded from the sky that they longed for.

I do not fail.

"There is yet life left in me. They have brought me low, but I have yet to face them. I will put to test their power, their strength, their will. We will see if they are truly deserving of the title König. I claimed the Broken Throne, and now I will claim the Great Beyond. Carry me, my brother, to the kingdom of the wolves and then join your people. I will buy you the time you need to get them and my people to safety."

Orem hesitated as though he would object, but in the end turned and raced across the slippery tile with agility only benefited to majestic creatures as himself. Outside the cages, I dismounted and took position to stop the König.

Before Orem left, I called to him, "Remember me."

He nodded and was gone. I trusted him, as I trusted my Seven, to lead my people to safety. I may not be there to rule over the new kingdom, but it would be forged upon the sacrifice of my life, and that was sufficient for me. The three König rounded a downed structure, and I launched my spear at the leader's eye.

It struck, my aim off, and lodged below the eye. The massive being spouted words that, while unintelligible, I knew to be curses.

"I have lived a hundred cursed lives." Rage fueled my voice. "Your curse has no power over me, vile one. I call you to task for your wickedness; you shall be judged." I drew my sword and stood my ground.

They seemed confused by my boldness. All the better. Every breath that passed was a breath closer to freedom for my people. They spoke amongst themselves and the confusion passed and they stepped toward the cages. I responded. Darting between the lead one's legs, I slashed, and my sword, made from a miniature-sphinxes's razor-sharp talon, bit deep into flesh. Skidding, I spun and dashed back to take up a stand between them and our doom.

The lead one fell, grabbing the wound, and thick red liquid gushed out. It yelled a command, and the right König kicked at me. The strike came too fast to dodge. Bouncing off the metal of the cages behind, I clattered to the ground. Splinters of my back lay scattered around my hands. Gaining my feet, I returned to my sentinel. Another blow of that magnitude and I would cease.

Murder in the beast's eyes, he drew his foot back for a second kick, and I raised my arm. Power coursed through me. I poured all of my essence into it, my consciousness, my soul, and still I drew more power. I drew it from the ground and from the wolves behind me. I could feel my people, so near but so far, lending me their hearts. The dragons, great and demi-, added their strength. The oppression of the König forged a bond between us all, and I drew on every living captive of the König and released the power.

"Stop."

The word exploded out of me and swept over the Great Beyond in a wave.

And it stopped. The König, the creatures, the chaos, it all stopped as I had commanded it to. I was the Wooden Ruler, a name given in mockery to me, claimed by my power as true and honorable. I felt their will push against mine, stronger than I could hold, but I would not yield. In a million cycles, I would not yield. Not to them. Never again. They had believed me powerless, and now I exposed their arrogance.

Then I felt it, the absence of my people. They were free. I risked a glance and saw Orem carrying the last of my people through the doors. It swung shut, sealing them off from this misery, and I let my mind go. Collapsing to the floor, the world went dark. Triumph was my final thought.

Aleth and Helet stared at the store as it went silent and unmoving. He had felt the wave of power, similar to a police command stick, wash over him. Somehow, both he and Helet were still free to move. He was drawn to the dark wolves' cages. Helet followed in his wake. There, he found the Wooden Ruler facing down the manager and two other employees.

The manager was on the ground, blood pouring out of a wound on his leg, eyes glassy. One of the employees was balanced on one foot, the other drawn back to kick the Ruler. Off to the left, Aleth could see demi-dragons with gnomes on their backs slipping out the front doors into the mall proper. He felt the power emanating from the extraordinary gnome in front of him waver.

Acting without thinking, he rushed forward as the Ruler collapsed and snatched him up from the ground. Not stopping, he let the wolves out with the manual slide and raced toward the doors. Outside, he found the mall in chaos as demi-dragons circled the large fountain in a tight formation.

Helet's whistle pierced the noise, and the black dragon that the Ruler had been riding turned his head toward them. Aleth showed him the gnome in his hand and then sprinted down the corridor to the southern exit. Trilling whoops followed him, and he dared not look back. Helet ran beside him, keeping pace, a giant grin on her face.

"What?" he said between huffs.

"He's really alive."

Aleth looked at the gnome in his hand. "Or was."

The smile on Helet's face faltered. She looked at the unmoving form in his hands, and sorrow clouded her face. They reached the door and threw it open.

Looking at the black dragon, he pointed at the jungle-covered mountain in the distance. "Go there. It's your best shot." Was he really talking to a dragon?

It nodded, took the Wooden Ruler from his hand, and flew off with its dragons into the distance, the body of the most wonderful creature Aleth had ever seen hanging limply in its claws. Helet wept silently next to him. He peeled off his green work shirt, dropping it to the ground as a great dragon burst out of the store into the mall.

"I think they're going to fire us," he said, his voice flat.

"I don't want to go back, anyway." Helet took his hand in hers, and they walked out to his car.

Six months had passed since Aleth and Helet had finished their book on the Wooden Ruler. A year and a half since the escape. Fresh off the worldwide book promotion tour, they collapsed exhausted onto his couch. Tomorrow they had a signing event at the mall. Helet rested her head on his chest as he leaned back and closed his eyes.

Horrific screeching shocked them as something sharp and hard was dragged against the front window.

"What was that?" Helet asked, worried. There were always crazies around who wanted to harm them, or be them, which was worse.

"I'll check it out. Probably just a tree or something."

He treaded over to the door and pulled it open. There, on the porch in front of him, sat the most unlikely of objects, and he dropped to his knees. Helet rushed over and dropped down beside him. He reached out and picked up the tiny throne made from scraps.

This story started out life as an idea for a flash fiction competition. It became quickly apparent the Wooden Ruler was much too large to be contained in just a thousand words. But once he had a hold of me he wouldn't let go until I told his story. I write Sci-Fi as well as Fantasy and one of the great themes in Sci-Fi is the exploration of exactly what constitutes life and sentience. It was a great pleasure to explore the same thing through the scope of magic. Not only was this story a blast to write, it has captured my heart as well. I hope he sweeps you away as he has me!

The Tale of Sir Ronan of Camelot

Frank B. Luke

Ronan sat staring into the crackling fire just after nightfall in the early spring. His long arms were wrapped around his legs to keep from sprawling out. Ronan examined the leather cloak at his side. He was pleased with his work; it had been one of the pieces he presented to end his journeymanship and become a master leather crafter.

That seemed a lifetime ago, even though it was only a year. Since then, he had spent every waking minute working on leather. Well, almost every moment. A fair-haired girl filled the others. Even now, memories of times with her filled his heart. He closed his eyes to picture her better as he remembered their last Easter together. The laughter, the jokes, the ribbings he endured from her older brothers. Her blue eyes sparkled with mirth while he tried to come up with responses to her brother Balric as they wailed about brown-haired babies coming into their family of blonds.

Almost two months ago, they had been planning a wedding and a life together. He had spent all day with her family, working up the nerve to ask her father for her hand. Ronan hadn't managed to ask him that day. He was sure old Aedel would permit him, but he just couldn't ask that day.

His horse, an old gelding named Brychan, grazed contentedly next to his wagon. In the firelight, he could see the horse's spotted brown body and white legs.

"Mind if I share your fire?"

Ronan looked up at a tall man dressed in a blue tunic with a beard hanging past his chest. Ronan self-consciously rubbed his cheek; he had never been able to grow a decent beard. "Please, sit and warm yourself, grandfather," he said, politely, as the man had old eyes and crow's feet over the gray beard.

The man laughed and tapped his walking staff on the ground. "My lady and I never had children, so don't call me Grandfather."

"I'm sorry."

"Oh, don't be. Wasn't your fault." He sat down on a large rock near Ronan.

"Pardon my manners, sir. My name is Ronan. Whom do I have the pleasure of addressing?"

The smile never leaving his face, the man said, "Call me Wyllt."

"I don't have much left from supper, but I'll gladly share with you." Opening his sack, Ronan held up the last loaf of bread. The craftsman guessed he would be looking for berries tomorrow if he didn't reach his destination. He had eaten the last dried meat just minutes ago.

Wyllt accepted the bread and broke the loaf in two. "Gramercy, young Ronan."

Ronan's eyes widened. "Gramercy?! Were you a knight?" The king's knights often used the French phrase for "many thanks" instead of their native tongue.

"No knight here. It just rolls off the tongue so nicely." He shifted on the log to get more comfortable. "Where are you headed, young man?"

Ronan couldn't help but notice the gaping holes in Wyllt's boots. "To see the king at court in Camelot. I will be there for the feast of Pentecost and the fair afterward. Excuse me a moment." He went to the wagon and peeled back the covering. In the firelight, he could just see where he had put the boots. He pulled out two pairs. One was finely crafted, a pair he planned to sell at the fair. The other was his first attempt at boots which his little brother had thrown in the wagon as a joke. Neither had holes. Ronan sighed. He wanted to show the best pair to the king, but the man here needed boots now. For all he knew, the old man was an angel sent to test him. Then again, he probably wasn't, and either pair of boots would likely last more years than this man had left.

After a long moment's hesitation, Ronan handed the new pair to Wyllt. "Take these."

Clearly surprised, Wyllt took off his old boots and pulled on the new ones. "Why, they feel like they were made for me!" He stood up and walked around the fire in them. "I don't recall having a pair of boots feel this good. You must be blessed, having hands that produce such fine work. I bet your town is anxious for you to get back after the fair!"

Ronan shrugged. "They'll have to get along without me. I plan to settle in Camelot."

Wyllt pulled out a pipe and began smoking. "Ah, a leather worker for Arthur. You certainly have the skill. I imagine that Oholiab and Bezalel had similar blessings when they crafted the furnishings for the Tabernacle."

Smiling at the praise, but feeling the need to feign humility, Ronan changed the subject. "Where are you going?"

"Oh, east and north. Opposite direction as you."

They made small talk for several minutes before Wyllt said, "Whoever you've left in Ebdale loves you truly."

Ronan snapped his head around to look at Wyllt. "How can you know that? You don't even know her name!"

Wyllt pointed at Ronan's feet. "The daisy at your feet has seven petals. 'She loves you, she loves you not' ends on 'loves you.' And seven is the number of our Lord's perfection."

Ronan's eyes got large. "You know woodlore."

"It's always come naturally to me." He paused. "Why didn't she come along?"

"Her mother died three weeks ago. Cadi is helping her father readjust."

The old man nodded. "It must be difficult fighting loneliness by talking to your horse."

Ronan laughed. "No, Brychan isn't much for talking back."

They chatted about their homes and families until it was time for bed. Ronan told the man he had three sisters and two brothers. Wyllt spoke of his lady fair and the home she had helped him make deep in this forest.

The next morning, they prepared to go their separate ways after sharing a small breakfast.

"Good travels, Wyllt. If the Lord smiles on me, I should make Camelot by evening tomorrow."

"Gramercy, young Ronan." Then the old man's face turned serious for the first time. "Remember one thing—the smoothest road may lead to the longest journey."

The road led ever on the next day. A solid morning of rain had churned part of the road to muck, costing him time. He knew he wouldn't make Camelot by evening even though he was only a few hours away from the court. He'd still get there before the feast of Pentecost but without much time to settle before the feast began.

As he rode, his heart quivered, remembering his goodbye with Cadi.

Just last Sunday, she had worn her hair up in celebration of the day of rest. She came to see him while he loaded Brychan's wagon. "You're really leaving tomorrow?" she asked.

Her voice surprised him, and he bumped his head on the wagon seat. "Yes. I have to," he replied.

"If you'd wait, I could go with you as your wife." She stood with her arms crossed over her chest.

He shook his head. "But I can go now and get set up. The feast and fair is the perfect time to get established. If I go later, I'll just be another guy showing up." He smiled at her. "I promise to wait. No serving wench will even get a second look from me."

Cadi laughed. "Well, I'm glad you're committed."

He had kissed her goodbye and wiped away her tears.

Ronan pulled the horse to a halt at a surprising fork in the road. *Which way is Camelot?* he wondered. One road was new and smooth; the other had the ruts of common use. Fingering the cross hanging around his neck, he prayed, *Sweet*

Jesu, show me the way.

A large raven with only one eye swooped down and landed in a small tree next to the smooth road. It gave him a shrill call.

"Well, that was easy!" Ronan said, urging his horse to go down the smooth road. The horse fought him and tried to go down the rough road.

"See, follow the omens. We've lost time today, and the smooth road will help us make it up." He held out a carrot from his bag. Licking his lips, Brychan followed the carrot onto the smooth road.

Several hours later, night was falling and the rain clouds gathered. "Ah, I hate to be out in a storm. Too bad we haven't passed a single village. You're lucky, Brychan. You can eat right alongside the road wherever we stop. I'm all out of everything now. We haven't seen so much as a berry bush since the fork. I'm starting to think I misread the sign I asked for."

Brychan nodded his head as if he could understand every word Ronan said.

"Well, we'd best pull off the road before the rain starts. Maybe I can find something to eat." Squinting down the road, he stopped. A small glow was ahead of them, he guessed only a half mile. "What's that, Brychan? I think I see a light!" He urged Brychan forward as the horse tossed his head and tried to turn aside. "Oh, don't worry. We're far away from the swamps and marshes will-o'-the-wisps haunt."

Ronan stopped Brychan outside a nicely painted and maintained inn. "Well, what have we here! We're blessed tonight, Brychan! I'll go in and see where the stables are." He got out of the wagon and stepped toward the inn. He looked for a sign near the door. It would likely have both words and a picture to accommodate the illiterate. He found it! "The Black Goat Inn. Maybe they're farmers." He could read the words, but the picture was of the goat's black head, staring forward from the sign. The ears, horns, and chin reminded Ronan of the points of a downturned star.

Brychan snorted and pawed at the ground.

Stopping to look, Ronan saw a large raven lying dead on the ground. With a stick, he rolled it over. His heart sank as he saw it had only one eye. He started to rethink everything of the last few minutes. "Well, that's a bad omen, but, Brychan, I've nowhere else to go. I don't want to be out in the rain here." Pushing past his misgivings, he entered the inn.

Ronan stepped into a warm and noisy room. A large, gruff-looking man stood behind a counter, a rag in his hand to wipe down spills. He dwarfed Ronan in both height and bulk. A bald pate shone, but he still had facial hair. Ronan thought he looked a bit like an ogre, except for the mustache. The man adjusted a lamp to give more light.

"Welcome, young master. Be ye needing a place to get out of the rain?" He didn't wait for an answer. "The Black Goat has warm beds, warm food, and cold drink. Are ye by yourself?"

The traveler nodded. "I have a horse and wagon outside."

"Two silver pennies for a bed and dinner. I'll take the horse and wagon to the stable out back myself in just a moment. You can get warm."

Ronan smiled as he felt welcomed in this place.

The man's smile turned predatory. "For another penny, I'll make sure no one steals either from you."

Ronan's smile disappeared as quickly as it had come. Slapping three coins on the counter, he mumbled thanks to the big man and made his way through the tables without looking at the occupants. Ronan just wanted to be left alone right now.

He tripped over a booted foot on his way. The room filled with the laughter of those close to him. Pulling himself up, he hurried toward the back of the room. Only now did Ronan look at the other guests of the inn. Many of them were dressed in mail. Well, he was close to Camelot, so knights were no surprise.

Ronan's breath caught as he thought about how busy the inn was but no one had passed him on the road all day. If the other direction was as busy as the inn indicated, he should have met several coming toward him at least. Wishing he had stayed out in the rain, Ronan took hold of his wooden cross and whispered a prayer.

"Hate to interrupt you there, but you eatin' tonight?"

Ronan looked up at the pretty serving maid standing over his table. She wore a white blouse with puffed sleeves over a wide leather belt and black skirt. Her face had the most surprising mix of features he had ever seen. Her hair was dark red. Instead of blue eyes, like most people with red hair, hers were dark brown. Her dark skin reminded him of those who came from the deserts far away to the south and east. It was an astonishing mix of loveliness. Even the sweat glowing on her forehead from the heat of the kitchen was pretty.

"Ah, beg pardon, miss. I'm ready to eat."

"Trencher covered in stew?" she asked, holding in her hands a serving tray with a long loaf of bread about a foot long and four inches wide covered with stewed meat and vegetables.

His stomach rumbled. He hadn't eaten that much since leaving Ebdale. "That's the standard fare?"

"Sure is." Without another word from him, she placed the tray in front of him. "Eat up. Mind if I sit down?"

Ronan didn't mind at all. He waved at the chair as he took a bite of the bread and stew. "This is delicious!"

"Everything from our kitchen is," she said. "My name's Seren, by the way."

"Ronan." Ronan noted that the knight at the next table had a large platter with bread and large slices of venison.

"Want what he's having?" she asked.

"No," he replied. "I figure he paid for it because he can afford it. I can't afford it."

She tapped the table with her fist. "I like a man who watches his coins. We all have to count the cost. Where are you from?"

"A town called Ebdale."

"That far, eh?"

"You know of it?"

"Sure I do. I've traveled quite a bit."

"I thought as much," he said between bites.

"You did?"

"Sure, Seren. You don't see such a lovely mix of features from these parts. I'd even guess that Seren isn't your real name. It's too local."

Seren bowed her head. "I see you are a smart one." Rising back to her feet, she leaned forward over the table. "I've got to take care of guests, but I'll come back to see you if you want." She winked.

Seren here seemed to be pressing for more than idle chitchat. Loyal to Cadi, Ronan replied, "I appreciate the thought but think I'd better not."

"Suit yourself," she said, her smile never quivering. She walked away.

Ronan ate the rest of his trencher in silence. Just as he finished it, he noticed something odd about the two knights nearest him. They didn't speak the same language but conversed as if they understood one another perfectly. What's more, Ronan understood what both of them were saying even though he didn't know either language.

He gripped his cross harder. Had he walked into the fairy realm? The priest told them of how on Pentecost the 120 spoke in other languages. Maybe this was something similar but sinister—instead of speaking in a language they didn't know, people in this inn could understand languages they hadn't learned. Sunday was Pentecost after all.

Whatever was going on, it unnerved him. He thought, not for the first time tonight, about leaving the inn. Maybe he'd even go back to Ebdale. Cadi was there and being the master leather worker for a town was a comfortable living. Wherever he lived, it'd be hard work, but he'd get by. Moreover, there he'd be with Cadi always.

But he was only a few hours from Camelot. He had to press on. Having finished his trencher, he was ready to find his bed. Maybe there, away from the strange knights, he could relax and sleep.

"What have we here?" came a voice as its owner pulled out the chair across from him.

Ronan saw a thin man with jet black hair and a matching goatee sit down. The stranger carried a wooden cane and wore a red tunic.

"I hope I'm not disturbing you. You see, this is my inn, and I mingle with the guests every evening."

"I thought the man at the counter owned it?" Ronan said.

"Macsen? Oh, no. I am Llewelyn, owner and proprietor of the Black Goat Inn. Please call me Llew. Macsen has been with me from the start of things. So has Seren, for that matter."

"Oh," Ronan exclaimed, startled. "She seems very young but said she traveled a lot."

"All true. She's actually famous in some parts of the world. She's probably best known for the time she threw an apple through an open window. Her cousins never forgot to invite her to their parties after that!"

Ronan looked confused. "An apple made her famous?"

"War broke out because of it." Llewelyn's face was deadly serious.

Ronan stared at his host and then started laughing. "Oh, you've got to be kidding me." When the other man said nothing, he stood up to leave. "If you don't mind, I'll go to my room. I want to get an early start."

"You'll never be a knight if you leave now."

Ronan stopped. "A knight?"

"I've seen how you look at the knights in the room. This is your chance to make your dream come true. You can become a knight."

Ronan snorted bitterly. "It takes years of training to even be considered. I wasn't from the right family."

"I can make it so you skip all of that and become a knight...for King Arthur."

"That's just not possible." Ronan shook his head.

Llew stood up and stepped in front of Ronan. He limped a bit.

Ronan glanced down at Llewelyn's left leg. To his horror, he saw a hairy goat's leg sticking out of the tunic. "O sweet Jesu! You're the Devil! Protect me!" He grabbed his wooden cross and began the Our Father.

Llewelyn slapped his hands over his ears and hissed. "What has following him gotten you over all these years? He's the one who declared you to be born into a family that couldn't afford the knighthood. What's worse, he's the one who gave you the dream of chivalry without the means to achieve it."

Ronan paused, startled. He had never questioned God for his station in life before. It was true, his station of birth meant he could never be more than he was now—a leather craftsman. While he longed to be more, he had not doubted God's wisdom in placing him there. He was a *good* craftsman. His old master had told him there were none with more skill.

"Surely, you don't think that's right, do you?" Llew shook his head. "To give someone a dream and then deny them the means to fulfill it? Hardly equitable."

Stunned and intrigued, Ronan sank into the chair behind him. "But you can do what he cannot?"

"No. I *will* do what he *did* not!"

The leather worker said nothing.

"You can become Sir Ronan of Camelot, Knight of the Table Round."

"I'd still have to prove myself to Arthur."

With a feral grin, Llewelyn said, "I'm sure you can do that easily."

Ronan knew this wouldn't be free. "What's the cost?"

"Seren said you always counted the cost." His host folded his hands and smiled amicably. "Everything in life is a balancing act. Since this is something you want very badly, you should have to give up something that you also want badly. You'll have to foreswear love."

Ronan felt his heart seize in his chest. "Foreswear love? Never marry." If he agreed, he would have to break his engagement to Cadi.

"But you will be a knight, and believe me when I tell you that they will still be talking of the Table Round in more than a thousand years and you can be part of that." Llewelyn dropped his voice to a whisper. "Much more important than cutting cowhide. Leather lasts a few decades at most, if treated well. What *you* do as a knight will be spoken of in awe for a thousand years and then some."

Ronan said nothing.

"The name Ronan will be remembered next to the names of Lancelot, Bors, Kay, and Ector. You will be...renowned."

Ronan remained quiet, but he blinked, keeping his head down where Llew couldn't see his face.

"You already have the manners of a knight. That can't be accidental." Llew's soft and enticing words tickled Ronan's ears. "You've been watching them, mimicking them. Don't let this slip away."

Ronan shook his head and stood to leave, but a soft hand on his shoulder pushed him back down into the chair. He looked back and up to see the serving wench Seren. Her eyes glowed with a slight yellow light.

"Listen to him. You can have what you want most."

"No, not from him. The Devil never gives a fair deal!" He pushed past her and between the knights at their tables.

"The offer will be open until you get to Camelot!" the Devil shouted at him.

Without another word, Ronan ran through the doors and into the rain. Brychan was stabled, but within minutes, Ronan had the horse attached to the wagon. "Oh, I should have listened to you, Brychan. That was worse than any nightmare I've had!"

Ronan rode behind Brychan into the afternoon of Pentecost Sunday. Once the rain stopped, he had slept fitfully. The faces of Llew, Seren, and Macsen haunted his dreams. Llew's offer... Ronan shuddered to think of it. Nothing could make him give up Cadi!

"Still considering our offer?" Seren's voice came from next to the wagon. She floated next to it, her feet never touching the ground.

Ronan jumped out of his skin to see the dusky-skinned serving maid. "Begone, foul spirit!"

"Oh, enough of that. Llew wanted me to make the offer again. If you say no, that's it. You never have to see any of us again, but you need to listen to the whole deal." She held out a sword. "Take this sword to become a knight, and your horse will become a charger and the wagon and tools, except the awl, will become barding and weapons. If you ever want to change back, just take hold of your awl."

"Well, I'll say no now and thank you for leaving me alone!" He snapped the reins to make Brychan speed up.

"Oh, not just yet. You see, just ahead, Sir Bors of Camelot is being attacked by three knights from the Black Goat Inn. You can help him, but only if you take hold of the sword." She held the sword out again. Through the trees, Ronan could hear metal clanging together. "If you don't, he dies." A soft but wicked smile played around her lips.

"You've put me on the horns of a dilemma!"

Her smile grew. "Just like sailing between Scylla and Charybdis."

"I know! I'll take the sword, rescue Sir Bors, and then grab the awl. I'm back to me and can still marry Cadi." He reached for the sword.

"Not so fast." She pulled it away. "Taking the sword even for a short time binds you to the agreement with a knight's honor. A knight's word is his bond. You still have to foreswear love." Having given the caveat, she held the sword back out.

Ronan pondered for a moment. What was a man's life worth? *Forgive me, Cadi. O Jesu, forgive me!* He took the sword's hilt from Seren. Power flowed through his arms as the muscles swelled. He was suddenly no longer in the wagon seat but astride an armored Brychan. Mail covered Ronan's body and a shield hung on his left arm as he looked through the visor of a helm.

Ronan snarled under the helmet at Seren. "You've done your work, temptress. Begone!"

Laughing, the red-headed and dark-skinned wench disappeared into thin air.

He heard the clang of steel on shield ahead. Brychan perked up in anticipation. The new knight spurred his horse. "Forward, Brychan! We are needed!"

Ahead was a single knight beset by three others. The lone knight wore the sign of Arthur's knights—a red cross atop a red circle with a dragon touching both—Arthur Pendragon, Christian king of the Table Round.

Ronan rode into the fray, swinging his sword in ways that suddenly came naturally to him. Shield on one side, sword on the other, his surprise charge knocked two of the villainous knights aside. One of the knights fell from his horse, but one foot stuck in the stirrup, and the horse dragged him away.

Arthur's knight did not question the help. He took the opportunity to stab one of the other knights' horse. The animal collapsed to the ground, trapping his rider's leg beneath him.

Outnumbered now, the third knight turned his horse and fled.

Ronan looked over Arthur's knight. Though he sat in the saddle still, he bled freely from a cut on his sword arm. "You are wounded, sir knight."

"Gramercy, sir knight! Had you not come along, I would do more than bleed. I am Sir Bors of Camelot. Who are you, and from where do you ride?" He opened his saddlebag to get cloths for a bandage.

"My name is Sir Ronan of Ebdale," he answered, taking the cloth from Sir Bors and wrapping the wound as best he could. A good wrapping would have to be done after removing the mail at the castle.

"What lord do you serve?"

"I *seek* a lord to serve, Sir Bors." If he was going to be a knight, Ronan would be a good one. He dismounted and bound the hands of the remaining villain who was still on the ground. Sir Bors would take the villain to Camelot where he would be ransomed or justly punished.

Sir Bors rubbed his helm where his chin would be. "That is most unusual, but you give me no reason to doubt you. Are you en route to Camelot?"

"Yes. I intend to be there for the Feast of Pentecost tonight."

"Then let us ride on. We can still make it in time." They rode, pulling the villain behind them.

Once at Camelot, the sentries let them in immediately, one taking the prisoner. Quickly, Sir Bors told the story to Sir Kay the Seneschal. A page then led Sir Bors away, calling for a monk skilled in medicine.

Sir Kay said, "Gramercy for saving our knight, Sir Ronan. I will escort you to the king. Normally, he does not hold court on Sunday, but I will speak to him about accepting your service as a Knight of the Table Round." Sir Kay was apparently not used to looking up at people, but Ronan towered over him by more than a head. That was also part of the change.

Ronan's heart skipped a beat, but sadness touched his heart. He would have to send a message to Cadi that he had died en route to Camelot. It would break her heart, but she'd never come looking for him.

Within the hour, Ronan stood before the king and queen. Tall and muscled like an ox, Arthur had an air of regality around him. Even without the crown, everyone who saw him would know he ruled. He wore his mail but no helm. A closely trimmed beard lined his face above his piercing blue eyes. "Your name is Ronan, and you saved Sir Bors."

"Yes, my liege. I came to serve." Ronan knelt.

Beside the grave king, his beautiful queen smiled gently, a golden circlet adorning her dark tresses. Her dark eyes glittered with a secret joke. Lithe where

Arthur was muscled, she nevertheless had the same regal air. "We gladly accept."

"If my life can serve Camelot, I will live. If my death, I will die without sorrow."

"Such pretty words." She smiled, raising a diminutive hand over her small mouth.

"I mean them, my gracious queen."

"Listen not to his winged words, O Queen." A knight pushed through the crowd to stand over Ronan. "He has a bad air about him. Something is not right."

"No, Sir Lancelot," said the king. "Jesu sends him at this time. Once knighted, he will be the 120th knight in attendance tonight. A fitting number for the Feast of Pentecost."

Ronan held his breath. Sir Lancelot, the most renowned knight in Camelot, was speaking against him! As he continued kneeling, Ronan noticed the queen gave Lancelot a secret smile before looking away.

"He has not proven himself!" Lancelot pressed his case.

"He saved the life of Sir Bors," Sir Kay the Seneschal shouted. "He chased off three villainous knights."

The king gestured for quiet. "Protected one from three. He will be the 120th. Those are good omens. Our Lord sent him to serve Camelot."

Ronan winced, knowing he had not been sent by their Lord. However, he would remain quiet.

The king drew Excalibur. "After the feast, you will spend the night in vigil, praying God guide you as a knight. I dub thee 'Sir Ronan.'" He touched each of Ronan's shoulders with Excalibur.

Ronan had knelt, but truly *Sir* Ronan stood.

The wound on Sir Bors was not as bad as Ronan feared. His arm bound in a sling, he joined the knights in the main hall. The Feast of Pentecost was about to begin!

The newly knighted Sir Ronan followed Sir Bors and the others to the dining room. "The Table Round!" he whispered, overcome with awe at the sight. Though the knights had been speaking animatedly as they walked down the hallway, they hushed when they entered the room of the Table Round.

Carved from ancient oak trees, the table made everything else in the room seem small. Sir Bors whispered to Sir Ronan that 150 seats surrounded it—high-backed oaken chairs, each with a knight's name engraved in gold letters. Arthur and the queen had a special table in the middle of the Table Round. Arthur played no favorites. The widely-renowned Sir Lancelot sat no closer to the king than the newly dubbed Sir Ronan.

Sir Bors gestured. "This will be your seat, next to mine." The chair back was blank, but as Sir Ronan watched, his name appeared in golden letters engraved across the back.

Ronan stood next to his chair with the other knights next to theirs. Many seats were claimed, but the one next to Ronan had more engraving than a name. Ronan stared at the letters, realizing he could not read them. "What means this?" he asked. All along this seat, carved figures intertwined together like serpents. He blinked as they seemed to writhe in his sight.

"Siege Perilous," Sir Bors said. "No knight may sit in it on pain of death, save he destined to find the Holy Grail. Merlin, by mischance, sat in it shortly before he disappeared. The king has sworn that he will find the knight to sit in it and retrieve the grail."

"Only the perfect knight may find the grail," Sir Lancelot said from his seat on the other side of Siege Perilous.

Ronan blinked. It was obvious to himself why he was not sitting there. He had taken the Devil's deal, by coercion, but nevertheless he had taken the deal.

Arthur and Guinevere choose that moment to walk in. Moving through an opening in the table, they stood next to their seats at a small table in the very middle, equidistant from all the knights.

Arthur held up his wine. "Tonight, Knights of the Table Round, we feast. Tomorrow, you will go forth to earn renown."

The assembled knights raised their own glasses in toast.

At the king's gesture, they sat and began the feast. Four young men carried in a tray with a roasted boar and set it on a serving table. They began carving and taking the plates first to the king and queen then to the knights. Duck and goose meat also graced the plates along with early vegetables and those dried since the last harvest. Ronan had never seen so much food, not even the time he had been hired by the mayor of Ebdale!

Along with the servants carrying trays of food, flute players and acrobats entered to amuse the guests. The flutes added a cheery background to the knights' conversation. Two girls came in juggling axes and then tossing them to one another while a jester did cartwheels between them. Ronan thought many times that the jester would be injured, but he never was.

As the feast progressed to the final course of sweets, a lute player joined the flutes and a maiden began to sing a hymn. Ah, such a beautiful voice had never graced Ebdale! As she moved gracefully around the table, she paused near Ronan and smiled at him, never missing a note.

Ronan started to smile back but stopped. Would she think him flirting? Best not to let such ideas enter her head. He nodded to politely acknowledge her and nothing more. Cadi had not sung as beautifully, but he enjoyed her voice more.

Two Years Later...

Sir Ronan raised his lance to the crowd as they cheered him. He had earned great renown in these two years as a knight, and many had come to cheer him in the tournament. For the Feast of the Transfiguration, the king had declared a special Tournament of Roses. Six gilded roses were the prizes. Lancelot had already won five of them. Tristrum had been injured the day before when slaying a giant and was unable to compete. Ronan intended to win that last gilded rose.

Of all the knights, he and Lancelot alone wore no lady's favor. Lancelot never said why he wore no favor, but Ronan saw the secret looks he shared with the queen. The king never did.

As Sir Bors escorted Brychan and Sir Ronan to their starting point, the trumpets blew and a herald called for the crowd to quiet. "On this side, a first-time finalist in our king's tournaments, Sir Ronan!" The crowd cheered. Even those who wanted Sir Lancelot to win gave token cheers for Sir Ronan.

"And riding against Sir Ronan, for the last gilded rose, is Sir Lancelot!" the herald shouted from his stand beside the royal couple.

The crowd cheered again. Ronan thought the cheers for Lancelot might be a little less than for him.

Ronan gritted his teeth and set his lance. Brychan shuffled under him, wanting victory over the haughty Lancelot as much as he did. "Knock him back to France, Brychan," Ronan whispered. Brychan nodded and pawed at the ground, as if understanding and agreeing.

Sir Bors stood on the ground beside Sir Ronan. The two had become instant friends. A small scarf from Sir Bors's wife was tucked into the top of his mail. His daughters had pinned their own kerchiefs to it.

"You've fought Lancelot more than I have, Sir Bors. Any weaknesses?"

Sir Bors let out a most unknightly snort. "On Sir Lancelot? Sir Tristrum's the only one who has come close to unseating that man."

"No man is invincible. Surely there must be some way to attain victory and earn renown as the one who bested Sir Lancelot."

"Oh, speak not those winged words of yours which he hates so much!" Sir Bors laughed. Then he said seriously, "Actually, his hatred for you might cloud his judgment. You have the best chance of any besides Sir Tristrum to best him."

"Gramercy, Sir Bors." Sir Ronan gazed at his opponent down the length of the field. *Jesu, where can I strike?* As Ronan watched, a majestic eagle flew over Sir Lancelot's right shoulder, coming so close that the French knight's horse shuffled to the side.

"Gramercy, sweet Jesu!" Ronan said inside his helm. That is where he would strike—high and on Lancelot's right.

The heralds blasted out their trumpet calls. Shouting their battle cries, the two Knights of the Table Round spurred their horses toward one another with only a wooden barrier to mark their horses' lanes. The horses closed the gap in seconds. Ronan gripped his shield and lance. He took aim exactly as the omen had shown him.

Their lances struck at the same time. Ronan turned in the saddle to lessen the blow.

He hit Sir Lancelot exactly as intended. Not expected a high strike as the horses passed one another, Lancelot slid in the saddle and fought to regain his seat.

Once past, Ronan brought Brychan to a halt and turned the charger around just in time to see Lancelot fall off the side of his horse!

The crowd's cheers drowned out Lancelot's screams of fury.

Pages and squires rushed the field and escorted Ronan and Brychan to the raised box where Arthur and Guinevere sat. Sir Bors's eldest son held Brychan's reins. Flowers rained down on the knight as the crowd tossed their congratulations. Ronan snatched a brilliant orange rose from the air and smelled it.

"A lovely bouquet," he shouted, "I am sure this came from an equally lovely lady."

A girl not more than ten years old squealed. He guessed her to have thrown the rose.

He stopped Brychan in front of the queen and graciously accepted the gilded rose she presented him. "Gramercy, my queen."

King Arthur spoke now. "Sir Ronan, traditionally, each winner presents his prize to his wife, lady love, or the queen." Sir Ronan could see the five roses Lancelot gave back to the queen held by one of her serving girls. "You have no lady love. To whom will you present the rose?"

Sir Ronan looked into the crowd. Maid Sarah saw him and blushed. Ah, almost acting too forward, she had often stopped him to speak when he was at the castle. The golden rose would go nicely with her best gown. Yes, he would give it to Sarah.

He almost called her name but stopped himself. Ronan knew that any unmarried woman he gave the rose to would take it as an expression of his intention to court her. He would not give her the wrong idea, nor would he give it to the queen or any other married lady. Yet, propriety declared he could not keep it.

As he looked at the gilded rose in his hand, he remembered the fiery orange rose he had caught. "I give this gilded rose to the maiden who threw me this fiery rose!"

The girl squealed from the stands again. Ronan nudged Brychan toward her seat and held it out. The small girl was so overcome, she couldn't move from her place.

Sir Ronan held out the gilded rose to her. If he stretched, he could just reach her. Her tiny hand, dwarfed by Ronan's, closed around the rose's golden stem before she snatched it back.

"Thank you, Sir Ronan!" she exclaimed.

"Gramercy to you, sweet girl," he replied, bowing from his gelding.

Ronan and ten other knights, each armed with a spear and bow, rode beside King Arthur the next spring. Arthur had selected them to hunt for the centerpieces of the Feast of the Ascension. Ronan's heart swelled with pride that Arthur had chosen him. Between himself and the king rode Sir Lancelot and Sir Pellinore. Sir Bors rode on Ronan's other side. Brychan gave a small jump over a hole in the road.

"Rarely a smooth road out this way," Sir Bors said.

"Good!" said the king. "I find smooth roads rarely lead to the best hunting grounds."

Ronan blinked inside his helm as the words reminded him of Wyllt's farewell. Odd, he hadn't thought of Wyllt since the Black Goat Inn. Ronan's heart raced even before a loud caw beside him made him look at the fence to see a raven watching him.

Sweet Jesu, what does this mean?

One of the knights on the other side of Arthur blew his horn. "To our left!" he shouted.

Eager to forget the raven, Ronan turned Brychan with the other horses. Ahead, streaking away in the forest, was a white doe.

"I smell the roast venison already!" shouted Lancelot, laughing as he loosed an arrow toward the deer.

The arrow thudded into the ground where the deer had just been. Other knights loosed arrows, but none came closer than Sir Lancelot to the deer.

Brychan and Sir Pellinore's horse drew ahead of the other knights, closing on the fleeing deer. Sir Pellinore threw his long spear, and the deer crashed to the ground, wounded in the haunch. The two knights reined in their horses when they were even with the doe.

"Gramercy, Jesu!" shouted Arthur, leading the way to the animal. Reining in his horse, he dismounted beside the white deer. As his feet touched the ground, the deer shimmered and became a beautiful young woman, bleeding onto her white dress. She had hair the color of straw, blue eyes, and fair cheeks.

Sir Ronan and the others gasped.

"What devilry is this that such beauty become a deer?" Lancelot asked.

"An apt question, sir knight," cackled a voice.

Coming from the direction opposite the knights was an old, hunched woman with a crutch under one arm.

One of the knights leaped from his horse and opened his saddlebag. In a group this size, Sir Kay the Seneschal always made sure that three of them carried bandages for any injuries they acquired. Sir Bors had taken a dreadful bite on his arm when he cornered a wild boar that last year. The man's poor wife had been more worried about the bite than the wounds he took when fighting King Mark's men.

The knight wrapped the wound, trying to staunch the flow of blood. The girl was mercifully unconscious. "She took a mortal wound, my king. Nothing we can do will save her."

The old woman cackled. "This girl is Cynthia, the daughter of King Mark of Cornwall."

The knights visibly trembled. Several crossed themselves and prayed. Ronan heard one crying out loudly for Jesu to heal the lady. Arthur and Mark had feuded off and on for years until recently coming to an uneasy peace. The death of his beloved daughter at the hands of one of the Knights of the Table Round would serve as a spark to reignite the war.

"What is she doing so far from Cornwall!" Arthur shouted. They were several days' hard ride from Mark's lands.

"If she dies, turn me over to King Mark," Sir Pellinore said. "My death may assuage his rage."

"No talk of that," said the king. "Is the blood flow stopping?"

"It has slowed but not stopped, my liege," said the tending knight.

"There must be a way to save her," Ronan said.

"Indeed," cackled the old lady. "Simple, really. She must drink water from a spring not two miles from here. However, it must be carried here from the spring in a leather bottle that has never been used."

Ronan gritted his teeth. *Leather?* He could end this. In his wagon had been several new bottles for sale. All he had to do was grip the awl...and stop being a knight. He hadn't wanted to be a knight, but now he couldn't imagine not being one of Arthur's knights.

"Did any bring an empty bottle?" Arthur asked his knights. They all shook their heads. "Sir Bors, you are most familiar with this area. Pray tell, is there a village or town nearby where we might buy a bottle?"

"Indeed, your highness." Sir Bors mounted his horse and prepared to ride away.

"My liege," Sir Ronan shouted. "May I go with him?" He would get a bottle that way and still save the woman.

The king nodded his permission, and the two knights galloped away.

Sir Bors and Sir Ronan galloped into the village, banging their spears on their horses' barding to call the villagers to them. Brychan reared at the sudden stop. Without disembarking, Sir Ronan and Sir Bors called down to the assembling subjects.

"Hear me, hear me!" Sir Bors shouted. "In the woods not far from here a lady was injured while under enchantment. To heal her, we need a leather bottle that has never been used before."

Ronan asked, "Mayhap anyone has one the king may use to do this noble deed?"

"It has to be new?" one asked.

"Yes, the old woman was quite emphatic of that."

"We don't buy one until we need it, sir knight." Some of the people left, unable to help and needing to take care of their own business.

Sir Ronan looked at the village. "Where is your leather crafter? Surely he would have a new bottle ready to sell."

"He's gone to the next village to trade his goods. Took everything finished from the shop, too," a fat man said.

"Then that's where we will go, Ronan. Come!" Sir Bors turned his horse. "I have been here recently. The roads are in good repair. For once, we will have a smooth road."

Sir Ronan's jaw clenched. "A smooth road?" In his mind, he heard the old man speaking, *The smoothest road leads to the longest journey.* That very next day, taking the smooth road had cost him any hope of Cadi. Now it would cost a life and cause a war. He could not bear that on his conscience. "By our sweet Lord Jesu, I will do it! Come, Sir Bors, we have no time to waste." He was foresworn from Cadi, but he would not let his silence cause a war. Without explaining himself, Ronan spurred his horse back toward the other knights and the wounded lady.

Coming back into the circle of knights, Sir Ronan dismounted.

"Where is the bottle?" King Arthur asked, looking up at the tall Sir Ronan.

Removing his helmet, Sir Ronan replied, "I will give thee a leather bottle." First one gauntlet, then the other, fell to the ground. Ronan opened his saddlebag. The awl was right on top of his supplies. Doubt assailed him. There was no returning to knighthood after this moment. Sir Ronan would be gone, and Ronan the leather craftsman would be forever in his place.

His fingers stopped mere inches from the tool. All he had to do was close his fist, but he didn't want to. Once he did this, his renown would end. Sir Ronan, the only one who ever unseated Sir Lancelot, would be no more. He had loved everything about being a knight.

Sir Lancelot said, "This is no time for a jest or your winged words, Sir Ronan. If you hast a bottle, give it."

The wounded lady moaned.

Gritting his teeth, Ronan gripped the awl. Immediately, he felt himself shrinking and the mail around him became soft cloth again. He knew he was once again his normal height, slightly more than the average height for a man. He looked down to see the tunic and leggings he had worn into the Black Goat

Inn.

"What sorcery is this?" Sir Lancelot cried.

"It was indeed magic most black, Sir Lancelot," Ronan replied. "Now, let me heal this lady. Then I will answer your questions." He turned back to his horse. Brychan had shrunk to the size he had been when they left Ebdale. Ronan reached inside the familiar wagon that had been Brychan's barding. Even after all these years, he could still remember where he had packed every leather good. Near the top lay a leather bottle.

Ronan tossed the bottle to Sir Pellinore. "You have the fastest horse, Sir Pellinore. Hurry!"

Sir Pellinore galloped away.

"Sir Ronan," the king ordered brusquely, "tell me what happened."

Tearfully, Ronan answered, "My liege, just before you knighted me at Camelot, I made a deal with the Devil. To save Sir Bors's life, he turned me into a knight. The cost was that I foreswear love."

Most of the knights stepped back from Ronan. Lancelot drew his sword. "Die, Devil's child!"

Ronan closed his eyes as Lancelot began his thrust.

"Hold, Sir Lancelot," King Arthur said, parrying Lancelot's strike at Ronan with Excalibur. "He has sinned but shows contrition. Let us not strike where Jesu would show mercy. Our first order of business is to see this lady healed!"

"Gramercy!" Ronan said then bit his tongue. He did not feel worthy of using the knightly language.

Shortly, Sir Pellinore returned with the water bottle. He tossed it to Sir Bors who was closest to the lady.

Kneeling beside her, Sir Bors poured a thin stream of water into her mouth.

Immediately, the wound in her side healed and the color returned to her face. "I thank thee, sir knight," she gasped. "I thought I was going to see Jesu today in his kingdom. My father shall know that you wounded me while I was vexed, and you also healed me."

One of the knights helped her to her feet. Though her first steps wavered, she soon walked easily.

"Who provided the bottle?"

Sir Bors pointed to Ronan. Cynthia stood before Ronan.

"And I thank you, gentle leather crafter. Without your leather, I would have died and brought war."

Ronan meekly acknowledged her thanks. From the side, he could see Lancelot glaring at him.

"Come with me, Sir Ronan," the king said.

"My liege, I am no longer a knight."

"But I am still king. For the rest of this day, I will call you 'Sir Ronan.'"

"Gramercy," Ronan said without thinking.

"Tell me, why did you break your silence? You could have remained quiet and none been the wiser."

"That is not the way a Knight of the Table Round acts, my liege."

"Truly you speak, but you knew that before you and Sir Bors rode to the village. She could have died while you were gone. What changed your mind there in the midst of such risk?"

"I remembered that the smoothest road may lead to the longest journey." He looked his king in the face. Ronan had been a fake knight, but he was no coward. Whatever punishment King Arthur commanded, he would accept.

Arthur gasped, stiffened, and grabbed Ronan by the shoulders. "Speak, man! Where did you hear that proverb?"

Ronan's eyes widened in surprise. "An old man named Wyllt shared my fire with me before I came to your court. I was about a day east and north of Camelot in good weather."

All of the knights who had been part of the court longer than Ronan crossed themselves and bowed their heads.

The king put his hand to his head. "My friend, you have seen the ghost of Merlin. That is near the last place he was seen."

Ronan knelt. "My liege, I must see a priest. I need to confess and be shriven, if any penance can cover the sin of devilry."

"Did you blaspheme the Holy Ghost?"

The former knight shook his head. "Never. This was sorcery."

"Then the priest will give you penance."

"If you make it there!"

Ronan and Arthur whirled to see the old woman diving at them with a drawn knife. The blade cut deeply into Ronan's right leg, all the way down his calf from knee to ankle.

Screaming at the pain, he fell to the ground.

The old woman clambered on top of him and raised the bloody knife. "You ruined it, filthy knight!"

Before she could drive the knife into his flesh, Arthur punched her. "Normally, chivalry would forbid me to hit a woman, but these are not normal circumstances."

Sir Bors took the knife from the woman's hand. Then he threw it to the ground. "The handle has the mark of the goat, my liege. I suspect the blade is cursed."

The king took the old woman's collar. "Witch! What is this curse?"

She giggled as she spat out blood. "No limb wounded by the blade will fully heal. The blood will stop, but he will always ache and limp."

"Break the curse!" Arthur commanded.

"No, my liege," Ronan said, panting from the ground. "Do not ask the witch to use her magic to heal me. Instead, let us pray, and if Jesu heals me, I shall say 'gramercy.' 'Twas taking the Devil's way got me here in the first place. I will not do so again!" He mercifully lost consciousness.

His leg wrapped with bandages, Ronan emerged from the confessional to see Sir Bors in his mail. He waved to his friend with his free hand. In the other, he held a crutch under his arm.

"What has he given you, if I may ask?"

Ronan limped along with the crutch's help. "I must make a pilgrimage to Canterbury Cathedral. In addition, I must chant the seven penitential psalms once a day, every day, for a year and a day."

"Surely you will wait until your leg has healed as much as it will to begin the pilgrimage." Sir Bors walked on Ronan's right side. He never said a word about Ronan's speed or offered his arm for support.

Ronan shook his head. "No, I will not, for I cannot take communion until the archbishop finishes the sacrament of reconciliation."

"Then I will come with you."

"I cannot ask you to do that, my friend."

With a laugh, Sir Bors said, "My eldest needs a knight's quest before he can go from squire to knight." He smiled from ear to ear when speaking of his children. Then he added, "Besides, someone has to make sure you don't stay at strange inns."

Chuckling himself, Ronan replied, "Gramercy, but I must walk not ride."

"The priest said that?"

"No. My wound will not allow me to ride. When I get in the saddle, my whole leg throbs."

"I see. What will you do after the pilgrimage?"

The former knight shrugged. "I don't know. Perhaps I will wander until I find a town in need of a leather worker."

Turning a corner, they saw the king and bowed their heads. To Ronan's surprise, the king fell into place on the other side of Ronan. "If you will come back here after your pilgrimage, I will have a place for you. Camelot needs another leather worker."

Ronan stopped. "Gramercy, my liege," he whispered.

"Have you prayed for healing on your leg?" the king asked.

"Three times, my liege. Our Lord answered the same as He did the Apostle Paul."

"Ah, His grace is sufficient for you."

"Yes, sire. His grace is sufficient for me."

A year and a day after his penance began, Ronan stood at the table in his shop at Camelot, affixing the last jewel to Sir Tristrum's scabbard. The knight would be picking it up minutes from now, just before supper, and Ronan was going to have it ready. He had only two more psalms to chant today: the 130th Psalm, *Out of the Depths*, and the 143rd, *Hear, O Lord, my prayer*. His foot had healed enough in the last year that he could stand in one place for moderate lengths of time. He could ride a horse for short distances before the pain forced him to dismount, but he would never joust again. Not that he had the training to joust anymore. He remembered what to do, but his arms and legs no longer moved quickly enough or in the right ways. *Ah, serves me right*, he thought, *I tried the smooth road*.

His shop was larger than the one in Ebdale. Boots and belts lined the walls, all of them beautiful as well as functional. The centerpiece of the room was the saddle he had made. Some knight or noble would surely buy it soon. He settled in on a stool, easing his injured leg into a comfortable place.

The door opened and King Arthur and Queen Guinevere strode in. Ronan stood when he saw them. Arthur wore his mail with Excalibur at his side. The queen wore a flowing gown of gray and blue.

Kneeling, he said, "My liege. My queen. What brings you to my shop?"

Without answering the question, the royals looked at the scabbard. "A worthy scabbard for a worthy knight," the king said.

"Yes, my liege."

"And it comes from the hand of a worthy leather worker."

Saying nothing, Ronan bowed his head lower.

"Rise, Ronan. Sir Bors will be coming here momentarily. He needs good equipment for the quest I am sending him on."

"I will gladly provide the best for a knight on the King's quest."

"Not provide. You will sell it, Ronan. I will not muzzle the ox as it treads the grain." The king looked at him with steel in his eyes. Without waiting for a response, the king went on, "I believe you are familiar with the town of Ebdale."

Ronan cocked his head. "Yes, sire. I am very familiar with it. I grew up there."

"It's an important quest. I believe he should have someone familiar with the area go with him."

The leather worker felt his heart beat fast. Could the king be sending him, a leather worker, on a quest? Not wanting to step out of line, Ronan made no assumptions. "Who would go, and what quest is this, my liege?"

"I want him to bring back a wife for one of my valued subjects—you." Arthur grinned at Ronan.

"My liege!"

The queen spoke up. "A famed leather worker needs a good wife." Guinevere laughed merrily and put her hand on Arthur's elbow.

"Famed?" Ronan's mouth gaped. Yes, these recent weeks he couldn't keep up with the demand for his goods—but famed? Maybe from here to Cat Coit Celidon, but that wasn't terribly far.

"Surely you've heard how they are asking for your leather as far away as London."

"No, my queen. I did not know." All the way to London? He sputtered. "But a wife from there?" He was sure Cadi had married by now. She probably had a child. Ronan imagined a girl with the same flaxen hair as her mother. While he longed to be married, anyone from Ebdale would know she was taking Cadi's place. No, he'd have to look elsewhere. Now that his penance was ending, he would consider it. The priest had assured him that he was no longer foresworn from love.

"It may interest you to know that I sent a spy there first. He returned this morning and tells me that Cadi's husband died last winter; her father remarried shortly after you...died."

The queen added, "Someone who knows her might persuade her to come to Camelot and start over."

Cadi's father had remarried, and she was widowed? Women did not remain widows long. He had to hurry! Oh, if only she would come back to Camelot with him! Wheezing, Ronan grabbed his heart. "Gramercy, sweet Jesu, for this second chance!" He panicked as a realization struck him. Cadi believed him dead. He would have much explaining to do.

The king clapped Ronan on the shoulder. "The priests teach that it is not good for a man to be alone. You need someone to walk with you on this road of life."

Ronan bowed his head. "The road is never smooth, my liege; two walk it better."

When the call came out for heroes, my mind immediately went to Arthur's knights. A story needs three elements to weave together. The first element was the Knights of the Round Table. For the second, I settled quickly on a new knight, one who wasn't already known in the Arthurian material. As I thought about him, I wanted the knight to not start as a knight but become one. How to do that led to the third element, Lou's Bar & Grill.

In my works set in the modern day, I often use a place called Lou's B&G, a restaurant where Faustian bargains are always on the menu. Taking the grill to a fantasy setting required a name change. Naturally, it became an inn, and what better omen to show what it was than the name Black Goat Inn? Llew with his goat leg also has a more traditional appearance than in the modern works.

At Lou's, one or both of Sheila and Moe always appear. Their names needed changing to an Arthurian milieu, but their personalities changed not one bit.

Llew, Seren, and Macsen can be found offering their costly bargains in Seven Deadly Tales.

https://frankluke.wordpress.com/

A Fiery Gift

A. J. Bakke

Clonk and rattle! The wooden box landed harder than it should have.

"Hey! Be careful with those," Everly reprimanded Coever, the man behind the counter.

She ran worried hands over the box and opened the top to peek inside. Several compartments held precious, opalescent orbs in them. Each was about the size of a chicken egg and nestled in some straw for padding.

"They're durable enough," the balding merchant said with a laugh. "Have to be, where you take some of them."

"Yes, but I don't clank them around like marbles," Everly responded with a huff that was contradicted by the warmth in her voice and hazel eyes. "See this?" She pointed to the side where a word was painted. "It says 'fragile.' That means you need to be careful with it."

Coever raised an eyebrow. "Don't be condescending with me, young lady," he chided, a spark of humor in his eyes. Crinkle lines deepened with a smile.

Everly put a hand on the corner of the box with a jesting air of haughtiness. "I was just making sure you saw that. For next time."

"Uh...huh..."

Coins clinked as she dropped them into his expectant palm. "A pleasure as always, Coever."

Brown hair swished as she turned away with her package. A tiny bell dinged merrily when she shouldered the door open to go outside. The air was balmy, the sky clear. It was the kind of weather that Everly found invigorating.

"The sun is my cheering squad," she remarked.

"What was that?" said a person in passing.

"Nothing," she laughed, her steps light. "Have a wonderful day."

"Er, you too..." He cast her a bemused glance.

Bemused glances were a normal part of Everly's days. "I should start counting them as I go. See which day gets the most." And she should keep her mouth shut so people didn't keep thinking she was talking to them and not the box she was carrying.

Wheels creaked as a horse-drawn cart rumbled by. That was the only traffic on the block besides those on foot.

Next stop was the Magic Shop. Not the most creative name, but it was a small town and there was only one magic shop to choose from.

"Lita!" she called as she entered. It was full of knickknacks, some magical, some not. Most of Lita's work was first come, first serve. The powers of a mage weren't infinite. She needed time to recharge between jobs.

Because of this, Everly made sure that she was never in a hurry to get the image orbs back.

Lita came swirling out of the back room, wearing a red and dark brown dress over an ample figure. She liked clothes that swished around her. "Everly! Good afternoon!"

Everly gently set the box on the counter. "Good afternoon, Lita. I got a box of orbs for you. Surprised?" She grinned.

Lita threw her hands to her face in astonishment. "You don't say? More orbs! Why, I never would have guessed." Tittering, she continued, "Don't tell me you need them today."

"In an hour, at least. Ten minutes, if you can do it."

Lita stared at her, aghast. "You ask too much of me!"

"Fine, fine," Everly laughingly relented. "How about a week? Think you can manage that?"

Lita dramatically swooned with relief. "That, I can do." Straightening, she named a price much lower than Everly usually paid.

"Er, that can't be right." Everly's brows furrowed.

"Yes, well, your mother was by and insisted that since you're such a regular customer, you deserve a discount."

Everly quickly thought back on whether or not Coever had taken less. No, it had been the same as usual. Otherwise, she would have caught it. "And why is that?"

"Something about new clothes." Lita contrived to look innocent.

Everly dipped her chin, gaze roaming over her well-used attire. It didn't currently have any holes, but several places could use some mending before they became holes. The elbows were a bit ragged, the ends of the sleeves were tatty. About ten layers of patches covered each knee on her pants.

"They work just fine."

"Mmmhmm." Lita wasn't convinced.

"I didn't realize the whole town was taking an interest in my style of dress," Everly said dryly.

"I'm not the whole town," Lita responded in a cheerful sing-song. "Anyway, that's the price today. I'll take no more. And I expect you to be wearing something more, um, well, less...ah...ragged. Next time."

Everly pursed her lips. She knew that the money would find its way back to her one way or another if she didn't keep it. "Fine. This one time." She handed over the coins.

It was one thing for Mother to get after her, personally. It was practically a crime to guilt other people into her schemes to make Everly rich and presentable.

Everly was turning to leave when Lita's voice stopped her. "Aren't we forgetting something?"

"We are?" Everly turned back and then laid a hand on her satchel. "Oh! I am! Here." She set the small box housing a used image orb on the counter.

"I could give you a bunch of blank image orbs in return," Lita said with a wink, "but I doubt those will be as popular. Only good for paper weights."

"Not even paper weights." Everly chuckled. "They'd roll right off the desk."

"So they would!" Lita picked up the box. "Have a wonderful day, Everly."

"Thank you. I'll be going up to the mountain tomorrow morning."

"Be careful," Lita warned. "Eldoon has been a bit grumbly lately."

"Yes, it has been." Everyone in town felt the light tremors vibrate through the ground now and then. Living on an island with a volcano, those sort of things happened. It scared tourists half to death, but the locals were used to it.

The next morning hadn't even dawned yet when Everly hit the trails. She strode with confidence, following narrow paths deep into lush forest. Her town clothes might suffer, but her work clothes were kept in good repair and replaced more often. They needed to be.

It didn't take her long to go beyond the more frequented trails and into "her" territory where it was wilder. She mostly followed deer paths.

The entire day was one long hike with occasional, short breaks. She traveled as late into the night as she could before sleep dragged at her heels.

Rain pattered on her small tent when she woke the next morning. Dawn was already well underway.

"You slept too long," she grumbled at herself. "Sleep is such a waste of time. I have so many better things to do. Why do we need sleep? We should be able to go on and on and on."

She ate a hasty breakfast, packed up her gear, and set out for the last part of the journey.

Trees thinned out into rocky areas covered in scraggly bushes and sturdy little plants that were somehow able to eke out a living in this higher, harsher atmosphere. The rain continued to drizzle, running off Everly's hood. Everything smelled damp.

"I need my sunny cheering squad back," she mumbled as she peered through the gray atmosphere at the steep hill before her. Beyond the low-laying clouds, the top of the volcano towered up there, somewhere.

She had never been to the top. That would require rock-climbing skills that she lacked. She knew she was foolish for being here in the first place, but she wasn't *that* foolish.

"I'm smart enough not to go to the top of the volcano." The plants seemed attentive to her facetiousness as she went on, "I only go inside of it. Because that's a lot safer."

It was midday when she approached a large indent in the side of the hill. Loose gravel crunched under her sturdy, leather boots. She would stay here for the duration of her studying and recording.

The rock face surrounded a large window that was currently darkened by a curtain pulled down inside.

She pushed an innocuous rock lump and it gave slightly, providing a handhold. She slid the window, which also doubled as a door, to the side and stepped within. It clicked as it closed behind her. She gently set her pack down.

Her shoulders ached. She stretched her hands high and wide, back arching as she said a cheery, "Hello, my hidey-hole."

After a quick meal, it was time to check the filtration systems. Every part of the hidey-hole was enhanced by magic. Spells shielded the walls of the dome-shaped chamber. Several reinforced tunnels carried air into it from different sources. Should any of them collapse or become blocked, it was a fair bet that at least one would remain to filter clean air inside.

Everly changed the batteries that powered the fans. It wouldn't do to have a battery run out of magic in an emergency. She put the old ones in a case, ready to turn over to Lita to be recharged when she returned to town.

"There, that's done." Everly turned a small circle on the thin carpet. "And I did that, and that...and that." She pointed to indicate which checks she had completed. "Okay, ready!"

She opened the closet and took out a monstrous suit. It was drab brown, waterproofed on the outside, and thickly insulated. A pair of ridiculously large boots and gloves came with it, also insulated. Not against cold, but against heat.

She set the suit on a modest cot. The last item she took from the closet was the helmet. It matched the suit and covered her entire head. The front part of it was all glass.

After replacing batteries for the suit's filtration system and shielding spells, she slipped everything on over her regular clothes. She didn't like how bulky it was, but she wanted to survive her ventures so she had to suffer the unwieldy suit. She picked up an equally bulky pack that was thick with spells and insulation for this last part of her journey.

Bubbling echoed within the massive cavern as Everly set up a short tripod. Plops and gloppy pops accented a deep, constant rumbling. Hisses fizzed as steam escaped. Lurid yellow and orange roved over rock walls.

This was it! Her amazing pastime that equaled her livelihood and made next to nothing after expenses were paid. It was so worth it, though.

A wind blew almost constantly through the spot she frequented. By the time it reached her ledge, it was quite warm, but relative to the rest of the heated air, it was cool enough to keep this spot tolerable.

She attached the recorder to the tripod and then slipped an image orb inside. She had brought a few with her in case one suffered a mishap.

Everly sat back to turn a knob here and slide another one there, watching wheels and gears shift as she made tiny adjustments. A display on the back of the recorder showed her an estimation of the images she was getting, but she wouldn't really know the quality until she had the orb in a darkroom where Lita did most of the work.

The subjects of her recordings were happily playing in the lava below, impervious to the heat. Even without recording them, the fire otters themselves were reward enough for venturing into such a dangerous place. Unless one asked Everly's family about it. Or almost anyone else in town. Despite their worries and occasional ridicule, she carried on with her beloved work.

Everly peeked over the ledge with her own two eyes again, watching the sleek, fiery creatures slither through the lava as if swimming in water. Their eyes were dark, like pieces of coal. They acted every bit like their kin who lived in much cooler climates and were covered in fur instead of fire.

"You goofs are so cute," Everly murmured. "It might be worth burning my hands off to pet you just once."

She sometimes envied how carefree and happy they were. They didn't have to worry about paying bills. If family members were contrary, they simply dunked them in the lava and turned an argument into a game.

A group of five of them was currently playing around in the glowing river. They leapt upward, squealing, before diving in again and disappearing. One emerged some distance downstream and began to paddle against the flow.

She had named that one Ember. Usually, she could tell them apart alright, though it could be tricky. The males were a bit scruffier than the females, flaunting fiery manes like little lava lions.

Ember chittered in surprise when Cinder came up beneath her and bowled her over. Sullen red droplets scattered as the otters splashed around, wrestling with each other while the steady flow carried them with it.

Flamespit was on the shore, laboriously pounding a stone crab against the rock, trying to break the hard shell. The fire otter used his entire upper body to lift the crab and then smack it downward. The crab's legs and pincers flailed uselessly.

On one hand, it was comical to watch. On the other, not so funny for the crab. Flamespit's hard work paid off and he settled down to eating the sweet meat, chewing loudly, jaws working over-dramatically. He squeaked in delight, voice muffled around a mouthful of food.

"Now, if only you would show me your pups," Everly said longingly. Not for the first time. The fire otters seemed to know when she was around. No matter how unobtrusive or patient she was, she had yet to get more than a glimpse of their pups before they were quickly hidden away in dens.

They tolerated her presence well enough, but that was only after years of hanging around and becoming somewhat part of their background. When she had first begun to study them, they had always left the area she was in. Now, they went about their happy, fiery lives where she could watch them, but it might be decades before they were comfortable enough to let her see their precious young.

Since she wanted the pups to get plenty of life experience, Everly kept her visits short this time of year. She felt guilty for making the parents hide them because she was there.

Quelling the familiar sting of disappointment, she dismantled the recorder and left, following jagged paths toward her hidey-hole. The mountain rumbled disconsolately, vibrating the ground beneath her feet. She was used to it doing that by now. Eldoon was always threatening to explode. So far, it hadn't yet done more than throw small tantrums that released enough pressure to keep it satisfied.

However, today that changed. The vibrations became more powerful and loud booms resounded from deep inside.

Everly muttered a curse and started running. Even a small eruption could be deadly for her, so when the volcano became this grumbly, she got out of there in a hurry. Her equipment rattled in the backpack as she leapt from one rocky surface to another.

The ground leveled out near the end and she was able to really put some speed into her steps, bolting out of the cave and into murky daylight. The ground bucked beneath her, heaving in jolting waves. This was going to be worse than any other eruption she had weathered. She tried to keep calm and focus on running. Her balance was thrown one way, then the other. She stumbled, caught herself, got her feet back under her, stumbled again, and nearly catapulted forward onto her face.

She fell, slid, and tumbled the rest of the way down the mountain.

Pebbles and dirt fell with her as she dropped in front of the hidey-hole. Her ankle flared a protest of pain, but she ignored it as she scrambled inside.

Gut-wrenching fear made her heart pound painfully. She couldn't see what was happening, but she felt it, heard it. Huge booms and explosions shook the area. She could hear the rushing spew of lava being shot high into the sky.

She curled up on the cot, covering her head with her arms as if she could somehow protect herself. Her breaths came in shallow gasps. She felt as if she were suffocating in that small space even though there was plenty of air funneling through. Any second, that could change.

"Deep breaths," she gasped. "In." She breathed in, intentionally making it slower. "Out." She exhaled. There was nothing she could do but wait this out. The hidey-hole had so many magical and physical protections that it could probably withstand a small army. Surely, it could handle an angry volcano?

"What did I do to make you so mad?" A resounding boom answered her question. "I'm not convinced," she muttered.

Hours of quaking and furious sounds went by. It eventually stopped, residual quakes shaking through as the land gradually recovered its composure.

Everly warily emerged. Dark clouds covered the sky. Smoke and gray ash filled the air. The atmosphere was sullen.

A person with a healthy sense of self-preservation would have gotten out of there, but not Everly. Now that her own life wasn't as much at stake, she worried about what had become of the otters. Surely, they could handle such a terrible event better than anything else, but she had never witnessed them going through an ordeal as violent as this one.

Lava ran down in glowing rivers, some of it darkening as it cooled in twisted ripples. The land had been rearranged and part of the volcano's top was gone. Lucky for Everly, it had cascaded in the opposite direction of her hidey-hole. The ground trembled again and she paused, heart hammering with apprehension. The trembling faded and she ventured onward.

Dark smoke from a forest fire mixed with the ash.

Even with the breathing apparatus protecting her, she felt stifled and slightly ill. The ash was thick in the air and she could taste the acrid flavor coating her tongue.

She was being a fool, but she pressed onward.

The ground was uneven, so it came as no surprise to trip over something, but it made a disconcerting, empty clatter that drew her attention.

She froze when she looked down. She had tripped over the dark and cold body of a fire otter. She stared in disbelief and then crouched down, reaching a shaking hand to gently touch it. Pieces sloughed away, turning into gray ash.

"No..." she breathed, stomach twisting with horror.

Panic drove her to forget about her safety as she rushed to search for more otters. She found two more in the same, cooled state as the first. She couldn't even tell which was which to put a name to the dead.

As she came closer to a river of lava, movement caught her attention.

Tiny flames flickered, like live coals in a dying fire. It was another otter, this one still alive, struggling toward the sanctuary of the rippling lava.

Everly paused, heart in her throat. The otter was carrying a pup. If she touched them, what would happen? How hot were they?

She tossed her questions aside and hurried toward the otters.

"It's okay, I'm here to help you," she tried to assure them. She stooped down to pick the adult otter up, grabbing it around the middle. She fully expected to be clawed and bit, but the otter was slow, as if its cooled body was unable move freely. It squirmed awkwardly in her grasp, but refused to let go of the pup.

The otter was still very hot. Everly could feel the heat through her gloves. It began to hurt as she rushed toward the lava. The ground was also superheated, the air warping above it.

Sweat trickled down her neck and back inside her protective suit as she struggled through each step. The heat covered her in suffocating weight. As soon as she felt she was close enough, she flung the otters into the bright lava.

Droplets splattered and they both sank quickly as fire ignited around them. Then they were gone.

She gasped for breath, pushing herself to remain and watch. A few seconds later, she was rewarded to see both were ablaze with life. The adult, who she recognized as Cinder now, left the pup to come back to the shore. She moved faster, running in a slinky gait.

Everly glanced after the pup, who had crawled onto an outcropping to wait. Then she followed Cinder and began helping the fire otter search for others.

The otter could move much faster now, but she could only carry one pup at a time. Between the heat, the ash, and other toxic gases, this place was going to kill Everly if she stayed too long.

She scooped up an otter pup. Cinder stopped with one in her mouth, turning black eyes on Everly. The otter growled but didn't drop the pup she held. Everly could see red and orange shifting through the pup as it was warmed by the adult's proximity.

"Go!" Everly called to her as she began to run toward the river. "Ignore me!" If the fire otter decided to attack her, she wouldn't be in much more danger than she was already. The pup she held was burning through her gloves. She bit her lip, trying to hold back a cry of pain. It took every bit of self-control she had to keep carrying it until she could throw it into the lava.

Cinder apparently accepted her help, for the fire otter carried her own burden to the lava and then turned around right along with Everly to begin hunting for more survivors.

When Cinder found an adult and began to laboriously drag it, Everly stooped down, taking a risk, and picked it up for her. "I got this one. Find another pup if you can."

Cinder seemed to understand and bounded away to begin snuffling frantically through the devastation.

Everly's arms burned as she carried the otter back toward the lava. Pain seared into her feet. She ignored it, forcing herself to stumble onward until she threw the otter to safety.

When she looked down, she realized her boots were melting. For a moment, she wobbled, feeling faint. But staying there wasn't going to do her any good. She limped away, determined to see if she could find any more otters.

Urgency filled her heart to the brim. It was accentuated by the horror of picking up a pup and seeing it disintegrate right there in her charred gloves. There was no saving it, but some desperate part of her wanted to rush it to the lava anyway. She didn't. She couldn't waste the time. She let the pieces fall.

Back and forth, sometimes with a pup, sometimes with an adult, she and Cinder sought out more until the surviving otters, now fiery and returning to health, swam away. An indication that there were no more left to find.

It took every vestige of strength Everly had in her to limp down the mountainside. Her lungs were on fire. She hugged her arms to her body, hiding her hands. She couldn't bear to look at the damage. Blood smeared her suit and a glance back showed that she was leaving a trail of crimson behind her.

She could still move. She held onto that fact as a lifeline. It kept her going enough to get to where the air was a little clearer, the ground a normal temperature. There, she collapsed and curled up, gasping in agony, her body going chill with shock.

"I saved them," she murmured, her voice hoarse in a raw throat. "I saved them. I got to see the pups." She had even gotten to hold the pups, but the novelty was lost in the horror of the circumstances.

It was almost a year before Everly was able to return to the volcano. The burns had done debilitating damage to her body. She had nearly died. The only reason she lived was because her family had more sense than she did. They went searching for the missing human and ignored whatever the otters were doing. There was no small amount of upset and chiding over the condition they found her in, especially when she told them it was a result of her going back up the mountain to save the otters.

No one supported her desire to return.

But Everly was stubborn, driven by passion. She had to work up to it, hiking small distances at first until the day came when she was standing by her old hidey-hole, wearing her protective gear. She was that close already, she might as well go the rest of the way.

Every precious step was won by sheer force of will as sweat drenched her body. She didn't have the endurance she used to.

Her ledge had been changed by the eruption, but it was still there.

The lava pooled and flowed differently and there was a gaping space of sky where there used to be a rocky roof over part of the cavern.

Shaking with fatigue, Everly sat down on the edge, legs dangling as she leaned forward, peering intently at the lava below. Did the otters still live in this part of the volcano?

"I walked all the way up here for you," she murmured. "Don't disappoint me."

As if they had heard her, a fiery head popped up from the river. The otter floated with the current. The cute, fiery face was not one she recognized. Perhaps it was one of the pups from last year.

Following that one's lead, more curious heads bobbed above the surface. She could hear their chittering over the ambient sounds of the mountain. They squeaked and tittered before they began a lively game of chase.

Another fire otter waddled over the rocky shore. Everly recognized it as Cinder and breathed a sigh of relief. Her sigh turned into a delighted gasp when Cinder turned her head and barked, summoning a tumble of pups from hiding.

Everly's heart lifted. It felt as if she might float right off the ledge with joy as the pups bounded after their mother, following her to the lava where they all dove in to join the adults in play.

To Everly, it was as if Cinder were thanking her by giving her the most precious gift: trusting her enough to let her see the new litter of pups instead of hiding them away. Perhaps Everly's fellow humans didn't appreciate what she had done, but the otters certainly did.

"They are soooo cuuuute," Everly crooned. After a while, she reluctantly got to her feet. Her health wasn't up to staying out here for long stints of time, yet. "Soon, though, I will be." She waved to the otters before she turned to leave. "I'll be back in a few weeks," she promised.

A. J. Bakke gave up her plans for world domination in favor of cats, coffee and a comfortable couch. She makes up stories filled with goofy fun and quirky adventure. "A Fiery Gift" takes place on a world called Deart, which is where many of her other stories begin. It is a place where magic bends reality into interesting shapes and the imagination can fly untethered.

The Hero of Emoh:
A Parent's Fairytale

Sarah Ashwood

Once upon a time, there was a sweet little kingdom, a kingdom called Emoh. Emoh was a peaceful land, whose society was built on love. Although not many monarchies are founded in this fashion, the rulers of Emoh, King Stefan and Queen Dorrise, had fallen in love while ruling their own sovereign, distinct countries. When they pledged to join their hearts, lives, and lands in a magical binding ceremony, Emoh was born, and a happy place it was, too.

The first few years of their married life were quiet and peaceful. The kingdom flourished as its rulers strove to ensure prosperity within their borders. They were active in seeking peace, in ensuring fairness in their judicial system. The Queen took it upon herself to found an orphanage, as well as a vocational school for the foundlings when they became older. The King, ever supportive of her work, actively recruited those best suited from her school for employment within the palace and court. At home, the monarchs enjoyed reading together and playing cards or chess while the court musicians strummed softly in the corner. While King Stefan won often at cards, the Queen excelled at chess, for she was skilled at matching move to move, countering point to counterpoint. Her patience was greater than her husband's, whose rashness caused him to take too many risks.

In due course, there came a day when Change, that great force of good and ill, decided to intervene. Queen Dorrise had begun to suffer ill health, including bouts of fatigue and nausea that left her drained and weak. Although she tried to hide the symptoms from her husband, not wanting to worry him or add to his burdens, these troubling signs eventually led her to seek the counsel of Rotcod, a learned man in the neighboring village, blessed with the gift of foresight. After a lengthy discourse with Rotcod, Queen Dorrise returned to the palace, where she threw herself into her labors as best as her health permitted, wondering what she might tell the King after Rotcod returned his verdict.

Meanwhile, Rotcod visited his library to deliberate on the problem. There were times he knew the immediate answer to the quandaries presented to him, for his years were many and his training in matters of the human body and human heart extensive. On other occasions, he utilized his own or the vast palace library to research both modern and ancient texts, seeking resolutions to these dilemmas. Sometimes, the clues were there in the texts themselves; sometimes, the writings inspired a vision, a foreseeing. Sometimes, the solution turned out precisely as his supplicants wished. Other times, the answers were more melancholy, and Rotcod was faced with having to deliver ill tidings.

"I hope this will not be the case with Her Majesty," he mused.

He, like everyone around her, admired Queen Dorrise for her kindness and generosity, her dedication to justice as well as mercy. Rotcod had assisted the Queen with both her orphanage and vocational school, so he had cause to know her better than most. In fact, his last apprentice had come from the vocational school, and, as the regular physician to the orphanage, he had his eye on one or more of the orphans who were still too young for the school, but who already showed promise.

When Rotcod eventually found the solution, through a combination of studying, careful consideration, and, finally, a blast of foresight, he went to the Queen, who anxiously awaited his return.

"In a few months' time," he told her, "life in Emoh will change dramatically, both for the better and the worse. Great joy will be followed by destruction, sadness, and woe. The cause of this will be one person, a person with powerful magic. Inspiring great happiness and great misery will be both her gift and her curse. Moreover, your health is inseparably linked to this newcomer. As the time nears for her advent, your symptoms will worsen. Nevertheless, once she is here, all will be well.

"Pray," he added, when he saw Her Majesty's troubled countenance, "be not alarmed. You will make a full recovery. Have you...discussed any of this with His Majesty?"

"No," Queen Dorrise admitted, a little embarrassed, casting her gaze to her fidgeting hands in her lap. "I'd no wish to alarm him."

"Then I'd advise letting him know sooner rather than later, for upon the newcomer's advent, this kingdom you have built together, this Emoh, this place of peace and love, will be tested. *You* will be tested. When you feel yourselves falter, remember this: the future of your kingdom is in this magic wielder's hands. She is its future. I do not say this promise will be enough to keep your strength from waning. Nevertheless, take heart, for out of the chaos a Hero will be born, one capable of curbing this wild magic and restoring peace to the realm."

After Rotcod left, the Queen debated over what to do. Should she simply let the matter go, hoping to conceal her ill health until the time of this newcomer—whenever that would be?

No, she decided. *Silly. Stefan would certainly notice at some point.*

Right then. Best to do as Rotcod had instructed: tell him right away.

After all, it would be foolish not to let him know what is coming. This matter concerns far more than just my health if Rotcod is correct. It affects the entire kingdom!

So, she sought the King out to relay the news. Her tale complete, she watched her husband closely. His face was calm, his tones even as he asked, "Why did you not tell me sooner, my dear?"

"I only received word from Rotcod today."

"No, I mean, that you were not feeling well." A frown appeared between her husband's brows. "Did I seem so selfish to you, so caught up in my own affairs, that you assumed I'd have no care for yours?"

"Not selfish, my dear. Only...busy."

"That is no excuse."

"For what? For my not telling you, or for you failing to notice?"

Her bluntness took the King aback. "Well...both, I suppose."

"Please, do not be ridiculous," she admonished. "You have been preoccupied with the matter of our southern border, not to mention the drought in the West Country. On top of all that, I was doing my utmost that you should not know.

"Perhaps I should have informed you, but what is done is done. I've told you now, and, truthfully, we have far more important things to do than quarrel over this matter. We must decide what to do about Rotcod's prophecy. Who is this newcomer, do you think? What powers will she possess, and how much destruction might she inflict? Rotcod said she is our future, but I fail to understand how our future can be tied—in any good way!—to someone who will also wreak great havoc."

"I agree," said the King. He rolled out his shoulders with a sigh, appearing to physically let their previous disagreement go. "Beyond that, who is this Hero Rotcod foretells? From where will he or she come? And when?"

"Hopefully, before any great damage is done." The Queen sighed.

Both of Emoh's rulers found themselves at a loss over the entire matter. While they anticipated the impending gladness and the promise of Emoh's future, they could not help worrying over the presaged destruction. They had striven for peace in their realm. Were their labors to be for naught? Who was the Hero promised to save them?

The days slipped by. A few weeks after Rotcod delivered his tidings, a krots bird alighted on one of the palace chimneys to build its nest. Spring had arrived, banishing the coldness of winter. The chimney not being in use, the krots bird was safe. This long, thin-legged bird with an equally long, thin beak was hailed with anticipation about Emoh, for it was considered a sign of good fortune, and Emoh needed all the luck it could get. Queen Dorrise's health continued to take a distressing turn. She suffered much discomfort of the stomach: the roiling of nausea along with pangs of indigestion. Her stores of energy were vastly depleted. She was unusually moody and irritable. Few remedies offered any relief. As Rotcod had predicted, her condition only worsened.

As for the krots bird, it spent the summer and autumn at Emoh but chose to fly a more southerly direction when the weather turned cold. However, the hope of good luck was indeed justified, for when the krots bird departed, not only did the Queen's health swiftly improve, but the bird did not leave its nest barren. No, inside was a gift: a priceless gift that the rulers of Emoh happily received.

"We will call her Anin," they agreed, and so was she christened.

This gift, this beautiful new arrival at court, brought the King and Queen deep joy. How easy it was to imagine a great future for Emoh when they gazed at her! Anin was small but perfectly formed. Her nose was round as a button, her hair like curling wisps of spun gold, and her eyes blue as an autumn sky. The rulers marveled at the daintiness of her ten delicate fingers and ten stubby little toes, the creases of her ears and the length of her lashes. The sound of her voice cast a spell upon the palace, and whatever she wanted, everyone around her, including the King and Queen, rushed to procure. They were rewarded with the sweetest of smiles, the happiest of giggles. Her charms could not be resisted. Clearly, she possessed magic; she was magic. Such pleasure did she bring that the rulers of Emoh were inclined to ignore the second part of Rotcod's prophecy.

Time, as it never is, was not content to stand still. Eleven or twelve months, perhaps thirteen, passed by like a whirlwind. King Stefan and Queen Dorrise were so caught up in the new arrival that they had forgotten to look to the future. But the future at some point must become the present, and when it finally did...lovely Anin, who had brought such gladness to the court, began to change. Her former smiles were just as likely to droop into cross frowns. Wails replaced her giggles. Whereas she'd once been content to lie in one spot, grinning and babbling and playing with sunbeams, now she must be up and about, scurrying hither, thither, and yon, tearing about the palace in dizzying circles.

"Anin, Anin, come back!" the rulers and their servants would cry, racing after her.

The new arrival could not be left alone for even a brief span of time, which the entire court had learned to their sorrow during a recent incident. Queen Dorrise had observed Anin's jaws working as she chewed furiously on something unknown. Initially, the Queen had supposed it a treat given to her by a servant, until she noticed the difficulty with which the new arrival chewed. Hastily, she inserted a finger into Anin's mouth to sweep the object out.

"Ah!" she screamed, jolting in fright as a large, black beetle, a little worse for wear, scurried furiously away.

"Anin!" the Queen had cried in shock and dismay, while the newcomer crouched on all fours, glaring at the Queen who had stolen the beetle. She hissed in fury, flames leaping from her gaze. Queen Dorrise had startled back, undeniably a little affrighted at this side of her young charge.

What was Anin thinking? she puzzled later. *Is this a portent of things to come? What dark urges inspired her to put something so wretched into her mouth? Has she been tainted with some form of witchcraft? Is this part of some twisted ritual? Could this affect Emoh one day?*

She brought the matter to the King, who had no better answers than she but was every bit as worried.

Whatever shadowy powers were at work, their hold over Anin only appeared to intensify. Even though she was interested in everything, it was not always from simple curiosity. She enjoyed taking things apart, but she never put them back together. She opened and closed, she banged and struck, she rent and tore. Unhappiness ruled her temper, and disaster and misery were in her ways. If she was cross, everyone knew it, and she was difficult to pacify. While there remained moments of supreme happiness, where glimpses of her former, sunshine magic could still be seen, they were outnumbered by extreme frustration.

As she grew older, nothing was safe from her touch. With one sweep of her arm, she could demolish the most expensive treasures. A flickering of her fingers and magic would spring forth, annihilating anything in its path. Her whims were capricious as the wind, impossible to predict or tame. She constantly wanted what she should not have. Her powers of destruction were unparalleled. Emoh had never seen such wanton devastation.

But the worst was yet to come.

One night, when she was particularly outraged because King Stefan had halted her game of collecting all of the fine china within reach and smashing it merrily on the marble floor, Anin retaliated by clenching her fists, hunching her shoulders, squeezing her eyes shut, and opening her mouth in the most ferocious scream ever heard. She screamed and she screamed and she screamed. Instantly, the King dropped to his knees before her, attempting to quiet the wails, but she would not be silenced.

The screams tore through the palace, drifting out of the windows and into the sky. The harder King Stefan attempted to shush and soothe, the angrier Anin became. The Queen rushed in to see what all the commotion was about, just as the new arrival's howls drew down fury from the firmament. A chill gale blew a covering of thick, gray clouds over the sun, obliterating all light. Thunder clapped, echoing off the distant mountain peaks. Torrents of cold rain began to fall. Hail pounded the windows, cracking the stained glass and crushing the delicate crops in the farmer's fields. Kneeling before Anin, whose screams continued unabated, the King and Queen clutched each other, eyes wide and fearful at this spectacle of devastating magic.

"What do we do?" they asked each other, nearly shouting in order to be heard. "How do we stop this? *What do we do?*"

That was just the thing: they did not know, and both felt it keenly. As the rulers of Emoh, they had managed to protect their lands from invaders and all outside threats; would it now be destroyed from the inside, and by she who originally inspired such joy? How could they trust their kingdom would one day be safe in her hands? Was all lost?

Late that night, when Anin continued to wail while the storm beat outside the palace, King Stefan turned to his wife and said, "I feel myself failing beneath this burden. Rotcod promised us a savior, but hope is perishing. Where can we turn? When will the Hero of Emoh save us? How much more can we endure? I fear our kingdom will not outlast Anin, not unless something is done about her fearful magic, and soon."

The Queen herself had wondered this: wondered how much more Emoh could survive before it was rent asunder. She and the King were both weary beyond belief. As she pondered the problem long after the King had fallen asleep (in spite of all the ruckus), she realized Rotcod must have been wrong.

"No Hero is going to save Emoh. If one was coming, surely he or she would have been here by now."

She looked at her sleeping husband, sadness and love in her gaze.

"How hard he works for this kingdom!" she whispered. "He gives and gives of himself. He works endlessly on matters of court and matters of state, then spends time helping with Anin. Although I wish a Hero would appear to help, there is no one. No one but...me."

Her brows rose as this revelation flooded her soul.

"No one but me. If a Hero will not help, then I will."

She thought of all those games of chess, games she and the King used to enjoy before Anin had come along to take up their leisure time. Oh, and before she had smashed the ivory pieces by pounding them upon the stone hearth.

I will counter her moves, she thought, *to fight and forestall the chaos. I will end the devastation. If it takes every bit of my strength, so be it. If this madness cannot be terminated, I will at least find a way to restrain it. If Anin is to be our future, her magic must be tamed. It must be curtailed. That is all there is to it.*

Resolved, the Queen set herself to the task. She did not wait until morning. No, she arose from her bed and went straightway to the palace library. Trusting Anin's care to the servants, she stuffed cotton in her ears to block the noise of her storm and her howls while she researched magic, read books, and carefully flipped through crumbling scrolls. During the following days, she took counsel at home and abroad with others who had welcomed a similar magical being in their homes. She tried this and that. Sometimes, the solutions helped; other times, they only frustrated both the new arrival and the Queen.

Those qualities which had once rendered her such an excellent chess player now came into play. When Anin learned some new devilish trick, the Queen steeled herself to countering it. Anin decided she would throw her cup of milk upon the kitchen floor every morning at breakfast. The Queen had the woodcarver fashion a tight little lid to her cup so it would not spill, and damage was thus averted. When Anin reached for some bit of priceless décor, the Queen or a servant would rush to place it out of reach. Before Anin could start to wail, and possibly call forth another dreadful storm, Dorrise would avert her fury by thrusting a distraction, something safe and appropriate, into her fingers. Staying even one move ahead of the beautiful one employed every bit of strategies her brain could summon, and the Queen often tumbled into bed, exhausted in mind and body. Her spirits drained, she would weep a solitary little tear or two into her pillow, wondering if she would ever actually *win* this game. A checkmate seemed out of reach.

"At best, I can hope for a stalemate where I can keep up with her if I cannot tame her," she mused one evening to the King. Anin, already asleep, had worn herself out from a tantrum earlier, instigated when the Queen insisted she eat vegetables at dinner rather than chocolate cake. The two of them were enjoying a rare moment alone.

Seated next to her on the sofa, King Stefan used his fingers to brush her hair from her temples.

"My darling." He chuckled. "I think you fail to see the progress you are making."

"It feels like I am making none."

"That is because you view your work from the battlefield. We onlookers can see you are slowly but surely winning this game."

"If only the Hero would come." She sighed. Her head drooped on her husband's chest, her eyes fluttering closed. It had been a long, wearying day.

"Yes," the King agreed, and despite her slide into sleep, the Queen detected a strange note in his voice. "Yes, if only she would come."

But the Hero did not come, so it was up to the Queen to steel her spine and press on. She soothed the boundless anger of the new arrival, sometimes by prescribing a warm bath, or maybe scented lotions and a backrub. Sometimes, she coaxed Anin outside into the fresh air and sunlight, where she would wrap the softest of blankets about her shoulders and sit with her in a swaying chair. Drifting to the music of wind chimes suspended from the palace eaves, the Queen sang Anin her favorite songs or read to her from her favorite books.

If her magic crossed the boundaries the Queen set, causing damage anyway, the Queen was there to pick up the pieces, sweep away the broken shards, and mend the torn bits. The job was endless, for Anin's energy was boundless. Nevertheless, when the Queen's spirits sagged and she felt overwhelmed with despair, she would suddenly be rewarded with a smile full of the old, happy magic. That smile, or perhaps an innocent, eager kiss, or maybe a joyful clapping of the hands over a new gift or game, or a spontaneous flinging of young Anin's arms about her neck, would come at just the right time and be just enough to boost her spirits.

By degrees, matters at Emoh changed for the better. The Queen won some battles and she lost some, but she never surrendered. As the new arrival grew older, Anin learned with the Queen's assistance to control her magic. She began to understand that destroying the palace interior meant her favorite books and games would be taken too. When she discovered that bouts of destructive fury meant having to spend time alone within the walled confines of her little bed, and that the palace inhabitants were not going to rush to procure every single thing she wanted, her powers of destruction were unleashed less often. With age came greater equanimity, meaning she was more easily pacified. She learned to soothe herself by clutching her soft blankets, or drinking warm milk, or looking at her picture books, or amusing herself with her toys.

Another year rolled around, and the kingdom celebrated the anniversary of Anin's arrival in Emoh with a great feast. Anin was charming and pleasant, devouring the cake and tearing into her gifts...until she imbibed too much punch, became sleepy, and started to wail. The Queen excused them both from the party, nodding at Rotcod to follow her to the royal nursery to make sure Anin's stomachache was nothing more distressing than the result of overindulgence.

She was fine, and once she'd been safely trundled into bed, Rotcod gathered his supplies into his bag, preparing to leave.

"May I say, Your Majesty," he said softly to the Queen, who was showing him to the door, "what a fine job you have done with our Anin. I know this past year has been trying for you, but your patience and firmness and kindness seem to be winning out. Anin's wild magic is coming under control. I think Emoh will survive her, which is all thanks to you."

The Queen could not hide her surprise. "Why—why thank you, sir! Your words of praise mean a great deal. I did not know you were aware of my efforts."

"Your efforts are the talk of the palace and, thus, practically the entire kingdom," Rotcod said with a wink. "Believe me, Your Majesty, your subjects hold you in the highest esteem. Good night."

He exited into the hallway, but the Queen rushed after him, calling him back.

"Rotcod?"

He turned toward her. "Your Majesty?"

"If—if the entire kingdom knows of the trouble Anin has caused, and knows of my efforts to tame her, then why did not the Hero you prophesied also know? And why has he or she not come to help?"

"Oh, she heard and she knows." Rotcod chuckled. "Good night, my Queen."

How very peculiar, Dorrise said to herself as she puttered about, straightening up the lovely one's bedchamber, waiting for her husband to bid their guests farewell and come upstairs to bed. *This is twice now the Hero has been referred to as a "she." What do Stefan and Rotcod know that I do not?*

When her husband finally did come upstairs, he peeked into Anin's room and saw his Queen still there.

"Ah," he said quietly with a smile. "I was just coming to kiss her good night before I came to you, and now I find you here, as well."

"Come in," the Queen invited, beckoning with her hand.

He did, and together, the two of them stood over Anin, watching her sleep. But the question of the Hero still plagued the Queen, until finally she could not help whispering to her husband, "Who *is* this Hero? Can you and Rotcod truly know of her whereabouts? Why did you not tell me? Certainly, I could have used her assistance."

"Ah, my love." The King chuckled softly. "Can you not know?"

"Not know what?"

"The Hero is you," King Stefan explained. "You have saved Emoh." With his thumb, he gently tilted her face up to his. "We waited and waited for the Hero to arise," he said softly, "never realizing there would be no Hero from without. The Hero came from within; it was you all along. I suspected this months ago, and as time went by and your proficiency in dealing with Anin was rewarded, my suspicions were confirmed. Rotcod agrees with me. The Hero can be none other than yourself. You have saved our kingdom. *You* are the Hero of Emoh."

As he kissed her in wonder and appreciation, the Queen's heart stirred within her. She had never seen herself as a Hero, merely as one stepping in to fill a need. Of course, she realized the threat to Emoh was not abolished. For years to come, Anin would doubtlessly bring turmoil just as she would bring happiness. Such was the dual nature of her gift: she had been born with it, and it was a part of her. However, until she learned full control over her wild magic, the Queen would be there to help her, rejoicing in the happiness and resolving the turmoil. For one day, should Rotcod's prophecy prove true, Anin and her magic would certainly be the future of Emoh.

In the interim, the kingdom might never be as peaceful and quiet as it had once been, but because of Queen Dorrise, it would be saved. It might change; even so, it would endure, thanks to the Hero of Emoh.

Sarah Ashwood may have no experience with fairies, dragons, swordplay, warriors or magic, other than encountering them on the printed page. However, as the married mom of three boys, she has plenty with babies and toddlers! In fact, more than one incident in "The Hero of Emoh" is drawn from real life. Sarah hopes you will enjoy her parent's fairytale—or, as she likes to think of it—an allegory for parenthood and motherhood. If you would like to see more of her work, she is the author of the Sunset Lands Beyond *trilogy, a fantasy/fairytale series;*

the fantasy novella Amana; *and* A Minstrel's Musings, *a collection of poems covering a variety of topics. When she's not writing, homeschooling, mothering, or running her household, Sarah enjoys hand quilting, reading, fitness, and running.*
https://www.facebook.com/1SarahAshwood/

Sacrifice to the Iara

H. L. Burke

Jaiharu stood at the edge of the shrunken lake, the cracked mud warm under his bare feet. A putrid smell of rot rose from shallow puddles choked with the decomposing bodies of trapped fish. Gulls picked at the remains.

In all his twelve years, Jaiharu could not remember a time of such desperation in their once peaceful village. He raised his face to the stark blue of the cloudless sky.

Rain, please rain. Worldbreather, send us rain.

No one answered. No one ever answered.

Something splashed in the dark water, and Jaiharu flinched. A large fish, he assured himself. Not the Iara.

Even so, he backed away from the shore, scanning the murky liquid.

The docks now stood a good stone's throw from the lake, their weed-encrusted pilings exposed. Reed boats sat empty beside them for there were not enough remaining fish to fill their nets. The lake and the life within withered with the passing weeks.

Priest Mali said the villagers angered the Iara, the water-spirit who ruled the lake. That was why the rains ceased to fall. That was why their fields parched and their children starved. It was the curse of the Iara, hungry for flesh. Yet, offering after offering had failed to appease her. Rust-red streaks stained the pillar of white stone, the sacrificial altar. This rock jutted from the far shore, carved with strange symbols. Many a goat and pig had squealed for mercy upon its hard surface, only to feel the pitiless bite of Mali's blade.

And then the Iara would come. While the villagers cowered on the shore, they would hear her strident song, and when they looked up, nothing remained of their offerings but drying blood.

And still it did not rain.

Mali had read the bones. The Iara suffered great offense, not mitigated by the flesh of swine. No, only a human offering would do.

The Iara had no mercy, so Jaiharu turned his prayers away from her, to the Worldbreather.

The tales said the Worldbreather had made the sky and the land. He had to be more powerful than the Iara, who destroyed much but created nothing. Mali said the Worldbreather had forgotten the people and only the Iara would hear their prayers. Jaiharu couldn't trust in her, though, not when she had devoured so many. The Worldbreather was his last chance, the last spirit who might answer his cries.

Please send rain. Jaiharu squeezed his eyes shut. He imagined the cool touch of water on his face, the fresh smell that made the world come alive, the sound like fingers drumming against the earth.

The sun scorched his skin. Dry wind cracked his lips. No one answered. No one listened.

The Worldbreather was not here.

He turned from the lake. The path split in three here. One going toward the village, another into the fields of maize—dust-filled and abandoned—the third branch climbing to the crooked peak of the Temple Mountain. The mountain rose above the village, covered in thick green trees that now consumed the abandoned road. No one took that path anymore. Not since Mali ascended to the priesthood and placed the village under the rule of the Iara. She listened to Mali's prayers, cursed who he cursed, blessed who he blessed. The Iara gave Mali power, and any who questioned Mali met her wrath.

At the crest of the Temple Mountain, gray stone jutted from the trees like a crown. A wisp of white, like a streak of fog, circled it. Jaiharu stared at it. Some said the feathered serpents brought the rain, but Jaiharu never saw them leave the safety of their mountain. They just orbited it endlessly, like trails of mist.

While the serpents weren't as vile as the Iara, they were as distant as the Worldbreather...if the Worldbreather even existed. If the Worldbreather existed, why would Xi have to die?

Dust striped the cinnamon brown skin of Jaiharu's legs. His dark hair stuck up in stiff, matted tufts. Xi had fussed for a while, brushing out her little brother's unruly hair and rubbing scented oil on his skin.

"You're my little brother," she had said. "Drought or no drought, I won't have you smelling like a goat."

Then Mali's eyes had fallen upon her. Her vibrant smile died. She shrank into their hut, praying for the Worldbreather's protection, but what was an orphan maid to the Worldbreather?

A wall surrounded the dozen or so reed huts of Jaiharu's village. The meager homes looked like mounds of grass from a distance. Men, women, and children sat in the yard between them. With their crops dead and the lake dying, there was little true work to do. Some families had fled to the valley, hoping to find water by the river. The old, the ill, and the fearful lingered...those and Mali's ruffians. Even in dire times, somehow his men remained well-fed.

Xi and I should've left, should've run when Mother died. What held us here? Why didn't we leave when we had our chance?

A stone monolith stood outside the gateway, carved with images of the spirits, to honor them and ensure their protection. At the top, a solemn sun represented the Worldbreaker—for in Mali's interpretation, the Worldbreaker was harsh, unfeeling, able to burn all beneath him. Then the feathered serpents, long, winged creatures with lightning rising from their scales, twined around the stone like ropes. At the bottom, surrounded by the waves of the lake, swam the Iara. She wore the face of a woman but the webbed hands of a frog. Razor-sharp teeth filled her mouth and anger filled her eyes.

Pots of dried maize and sweetroot rested at the foot of the monolith, offerings to the Iara and the other spirits. In the early days of the drought, the villagers had piled them high, but now, with their desperation at its highest, there was little to give. At the last new moon, Priest Mali's guards caught a man eating the offerings. They'd smashed his skull and tossed his lifeless body into the lake. Mali said the death placated the Iara...but still the rain did not fall.

People turned away and shuffled their feet as Jaiharu passed. He ignored them, keeping his eyes on the largest structure, a round hut at the far end of the village. A fence of sticks separated this from the rest of the dwellings. Angry voices rose from beyond the barrier. Jaiharu's pace quickened.

"I want to see her! You can't keep me from her. She's my intended!" a man shouted.

Ozca. Of course. Jaiharu peeked through the gateway.

Ozca's fists clenched at his sides as he stared down two of Mali's enforcers. The guards lowered spears toward the strapping youth's belly, but he drew himself up.

"By order of Priest Mali, you are not to see the offering."

Ozca's teeth clenched. "She's not an offering. She's my bride!" Veins bulged in his neck, and he raised his hand.

One of the guards smacked the side of Ozca's head with the butt of his spear. Ozca fell.

"Next time, it will be the sharp end," the guard snarled.

Ozca grasped his head in his hands, his eyes dazed. Jaiharu rushed forward and grabbed his arm.

"Come on. Come away," he whispered.

The two guards chuckled.

Ozca turned back toward the prison hut, but Jaiharu tightened his grip.

"Please, Ozca," he said as he led him into the shadows between two huts. "Remember what they did to Vayin over the corn offerings? If they kill you, think of how Xi would feel."

Ozca took his hand away from his face. Blood stuck to his palm. The young man exhaled, his nostrils flared. "They won't let me see her... Tomorrow, she...and they won't let me see her."

Jaiharu drew a deep breath. He pitied Ozca. However, his own grief was just as fierce. It wasn't fair that a grown man mourned while Jaiharu was obliged to comfort him. Xi was Jaiharu's sister. Still, something in Ozca's dark eyes made Jaiharu relent.

"They won't turn me away," Jaiharu soothed. "The guards let me visit her last night, and they will again. I can give her a message."

Ozca reached inside a leather pouch which hung at his side. He withdrew a string of ornate, wooden beads, dyed in vibrant reds and blues. "This was to be for her on our wedding day. She must have it. Tell her...no, she knows that." He rubbed his hand across his eyes and sighed. "Tell her not to give up hope. I have given everything I possess as an offering to the Worldbreather. It is he, not the Iara, who will bring us rain again. Tell her I will pray for rain without sleeping tonight. If it rains, even Mali must relent. If it rains, I will see her again."

Jaiharu took the necklace. "I will give her your words and your gift."

Ozca squeezed Jaiharu's shoulder. "You will pray as well? To the Worldbreather, not the cursed Iara."

Jaiharu shuddered. While he had no doubts as to the Iara's repulsiveness, her raw power was undeniable...and Mali would kill any who doubted or disrespected her.

Ozca smiled a slight smile. "Don't fear, Jaiharu. It is only the two of us. No other ears. The Worldbreather's power far outweighs the Iara's."

Jaiharu's throat tightened. "If... If the Worldbreather cared, wouldn't the rains have already come? Wouldn't Xi already be free?"

Ozca's brow furrowed. He cleared his throat and stared out over the village wall, toward the Temple Mountain and the broken temple. "I was just a boy in the days of the last priest, before Mali, when we worshipped on the mountain, but I remember the feathered serpents dancing in the smoke from our offerings. It is said they carried our prayers to the Worldbreather. With the temple gone, with the smoke no longer enticing the serpents, perhaps our prayers no longer reach his ears." His shoulders slumped. "But I must try. For Xi, I will have hope. Though if she is taken from me, I fear the last of my faith will dry up, even as the lake."

With one last glance back at the prison hut, Ozca trudged toward his home.

Jaiharu sighed. It would take more than prayers to save Xi, no matter how strong Ozca's faith.

Jaiharu slunk into the yard. The guards cast him a sideways glance but didn't stop him from entering the hut. After all, he was just a boy. What harm could he do?

Xi sat against the wall of the rounded hut, her dark eyes glistening in the light of a tallow lamp. She still wore the gray wool tunic Mali's men had taken her in, though they'd stolen her grass shoes, and the flowers she normally wore in her raven hair had long ago wilted. She raised her eyes and smiled at her little brother.

Jaiharu rushed to her arms. For a moment, he closed his eyes and pretended they were back in their own hut, before the drought, before the deaths of their parents, when his only concern had been whether Xi would have time for him after her wedding. How selfish and petty that thought now seemed.

"I can feel every bone in your body," she said. "Have you been eating?"

"Eating?" He pulled away and blinked at her. "Yes. Sometimes. Enough."

Her brow furrowed. "Jaiharu, you must keep your strength. I know Ozca would feed you if you asked."

"I haven't been hungry," he lied. "Xi, how can you worry about me when you..." He swallowed and dropped his eyes. She never thought of herself. Not since their mother died. It wasn't fair that Mali had chosen her.

"What's in your hand?" She nodded toward his clenched fist.

He unfolded his fingers, revealing Ozca's gift. His grip had been so tight about it that the carvings on the beads were imprinted on his skin.

"Oh, that's Ozca's work. I'd recognize his carvings anywhere. Such skill." She took it and held it to the lantern. "For me?"

"Yes. He wanted you to have it, but they wouldn't let him see you."

She sighed. "I hope he doesn't do anything stupid. Jaiharu, you must tell him not to try anything. He needs to stay away tomorrow. I can't bear to think of him there, seeing...and you as well." Her fingers tightened into his arm. "Both of you need to leave this awful place, go to the valley, start a new life, take care of each other, for me."

Jaiharu's hands shook. "You...you won't die tomorrow. You can't." His throat tightened, and tears blurred his vision.

Xi stroked his cheek. "I held out hope for a while that the rains would come, but time grows short. I will pray till the last for rain, for Mali to relent in his evil, for the Iara to reject my blood. However, if I must die, let it be knowing that the two people I love will live on, safe, away from Mali's foul influence." She closed her eyes. "I could've lived. If I had given Mali what...what he desired, he would not have chosen me as the offering. Sometimes death is not the worst fate."

Jaiharu's head spun. "But I can't leave you."

"Then pray for rain. Pray with all your might and faith. It is our only hope, brother."

The door opened, and a guard entered, carrying a woven mat with a maize cake on it and a water gourd.

"It grows dark. The boy should go," he said gruffly. "Priest Mali would not want him here overnight."

Xi squeezed his hand. "Remember, tell Ozca."

Jaiharu stumbled out the door.

Mali had told the villagers that the bones selected Xi, that she was the desired offering of the Iara.

He targeted her? He chose her because she wouldn't lie with him? Mali is not a priest: he's a liar! If so, then the spirit he serves must be false as well. Does Ozca know? Should I tell him?

He drew a deep breath of the cool evening air. If Ozca knew, nothing would keep him from Mali's throat. Not even Xi's pleading. No, it was best he thought his love a victim of ill-fate rather than direct malice.

Jaiharu strode through the village. He and his sister had shared a hut on the edge of the square. However, he hadn't slept there since she was taken. It seemed too large and empty, like lying in the stomach of a foul beast. Sometimes he stayed with Ozca. Sometimes with the widow, Hrua. Sometimes he sat under the stars until his eyes closed against his will.

The sun hovered behind the Temple Mountain. A feathered serpent flashed through the golden light, its scales glimmering like clear, clean water.

What did Ozca say? That they carried our prayers to the Worldbreather?

He stopped in the gate. Soon, the villagers would shut it against the creatures of the night, the soft footed padua with their glowing eyes and velvet black fur, the massive shau with its crushing coils...all of which lurked now in the trees between Jaiharu and the ancient temple.

Only a fool would walk the forest at night.

As if in answer, a creature shrieked in the distance, perhaps a nightbird...perhaps meeting its death at the claws of a padua.

If Xi dies, I'm alone. Would being torn apart by a padua be any worse than slow starvation under Mali's thumb? If I can reach the temple, if I can make the Worldbreather hear me, then perhaps Xi will live.

Jaiharu clutched the torch as he picked his way over the fallen trees and carpet of ferns that covered the old path. Ozca had spoken of making the pilgrimage to Temple Mountain when he was a child. In less than a generation, however, the forest had reclaimed the path.

The boy searched for the glimmering, white waystones. About waist-high, these markers were carved with images of the feathered serpents. While moss covered every rock and fallen tree, the waystones remained as white as goat's milk. Every time Jaiharu grew afraid or felt tempted to turn back, the torchlight shone upon another waystone. They drew him forward.

Something rustled off the path. Jaiharu froze.

His heart pounded in his throat, for the crickets no longer chirped. Something stalked in the forest. He strained to hear approaching paw-steps or the slither of scales across the forest floor. His senses sharpened. A twig snapped to his left.

He swung, jabbing his torch at the brush. Sparks flew. A creature darted toward his legs. Jaiharu yelped. The animal yipped then bounded into the underbrush on the other side of the path. Jaiharu caught sight of the russet, plume-like tail of the batfox before the creature vanished.

The boy flushed. Batfoxes fed on lizards and mice. Jaiharu was neither, though his panic suggested he had the courage of a rodent. He shook his head and tramped on.

At least if I'm devoured out here, Xi will never know. She'll meet her fate tomorrow thinking me alive and well...and I won't have to go on alone.

The path grew steep, and the trees thinned. His feet hit cold stone. The smell of rotting plants gave way to the fresh air of the mountainside.

He looked up. The canopy of trees parted to reveal a field of shining stars. He stopped to stare.

Please, a cloud? A cloud with rain? A serpent to hear my prayers?

Only the distant twinkling of silent stars. The skies were deaf to Jaiharu's prayers.

Jaiharu touched the pouch at his side. He could feel the hardened clay of the incense burner. The faint, floral odor of dried blood-blossom rose through the leather bag. Perhaps that would draw the serpents.

How long till dawn? With the moonless night, he had no way to mark time. He should've asked Ozca to accompany him, or at least to tell him how long it would take. Part of him had feared Ozca would forbid the trek, try to go himself, without Jaiharu. This was Jaiharu's mission. Xi was his blood, and the Worldbreather would hear *his* prayers.

The stone walls of the old temple rose like jagged teeth. At the crest, a statue at least two men tall stood silhouetted against the night sky. The torchlight fell across its huge, threatening eyes and fang-filled jaws of a feathered serpent.

Doubt flashed in Jaiharu's mind.

It's easily as fearsome as the Iara. How can I expect it to have mercy?

He glanced back. In the valley, a few red lights flickered, marking the fires of the sleeping village.

Xi depends on me. This is her last chance.

Throwing out his chest, he marched through the gateway, into the gaping maw of the temple.

A flat slab, waist-high and long enough for a grown man to lie upon, took up the center of the courtyard. Wedging his torch in a crack between two bricks, Jaiharu thought through his prayer. Xi's last chance required perfect words, poetic, fervent, clear and loud as an eagle's cry. He laid out the incense burner, filled it with the dried blood-blossom, and lit it with the torch.

The burner glowed a gentle red. Tendrils of fragrant smoke snaked into the sky, carrying the sweet perfume. The flower was said to have sprouted from the bloodstained footsteps of the maiden Aliquite as she strode across the land to beg for the return of her fallen lover. When she reached the summit of the tallest mountain, the Worldbreather took pity upon her, changing her into a beautiful bird, the quital, and her lover into the tree where she nested. It was Xi's favorite tale.

He closed his eyes. When Mali performed the rites for the Iara, he moaned and chanted, intoning mystic words. His red cape would whirl like wings, the bobbing green quital feathers on his headdress and staff making him appear as a great bird.

Jaiharu knew no such incantations, and even if he did, what suited the Iara might not please the feathered serpents. Instead, he opened his arms and shouted.

"Great serpents, hear my cries! The priest has taken my sister to feed the Iara. He says that her sacrifice will bring the rains our crops need. He says our village will wither and die without her blood. Great serpents, if it is true you bring our prayers to the Worldbreather, bring mine. Spare my sister! Send the rain!"

A wind sprang up, and for a moment, Jaiharu imagined it was the beating of a serpent's wings. He opened his eyes. The wind whipped through the courtyard, shaking the branches of nearby trees. The incense burner and the torch both flickered out.

Plunged into darkness, Jaiharu fell to his knees. Bumps rose on his bare arms. He hadn't thought to bring a cloak, for nights were warm in the village. Here, on the mountain, he shivered.

He fumbled for the torch. The last ember flickered. He held it to the incense, but the torch died before it caught. Jaiharu dropped the torch and screamed.

The cry echoed about the empty, broken walls of the temple. He leapt atop the stone slab and stretched his arms wide, baring his chest and his heart to the sky.

"If you want innocent blood in return for your rain, take mine! Not Xi's! Take my blood!" His pulse pounded until he thought his chest would burst. Spikes of rage threatened to break his skin. His words turned to a wail. "Here! Now! Let it water your altar. Spare Xi. Take...take me."

His voice cracked, and his knees hit the stone. Jaiharu wept, his shoulders convulsing.

"Not Xi. Please, not Xi."

The wind circled him. It stirred his hair, its chill fighting against the heat of his anger. Tears ran down his face and splashed against the unyielding rock.

The trees groaned. With a crack of breaking branches, the sky lit up. Jaiharu stumbled to his feet. His eyes widened as an imposing creature descended, like a ribbon fluttering on a breeze, only as long as a great tree.

The being was pure white, long and scaled like the shau, but with the powerful legs and claws of the padua. Wings, as white as the clouds, rose from behind its head, and it wore a crest of silver plumage like a crown. Cold fire flashed in its blue eyes.

Jaiharu froze. Should he bow? Should he run? Should he speak?

"You have lit incense on the holy mount," the creature said in a voice like the crackle of lightning. "It has been many years since offerings were made here. We had thought you two-legged ones had forgotten how to pray. Considering your strident attempts, it seems we were right."

Jaiharu swallowed. "I have come to beg for rain."

The serpent's body whipped, sending sparks flying into the night. "Then pray. Ask the Worldbreather for rain. I'm not stopping you."

The boy blinked. "I...and will you carry my prayers to the Worldbreather?"

The serpent twisted his head until it was almost upside down. "How would I do that? I can fly high, but not that high."

"But...but the stories say you bring our prayers to the Worldbreather. That is why you used to flock to our incense."

The serpent snorted. "We flock to the incense because we enjoy the scent. Is that blood-blossom you have there?" He motioned toward the burner with his snout.

Jaiharu held it aloft. "It went out."

The serpent breathed upon his claws until they glowed like the stars. He touched the incense burner with the tip of one. Jaiharu's hair stood on end. The energy of the serpent prickled against his skin.

The incense burner warmed, and once more, smoke rose from it. The serpent inhaled then sighed. "I have a particular fondness for blood-blossom. I can't begin to tell you how I've missed the perfumed prayers of your people."

"But...but you can't bring the rain? You can't make the Worldbreather hear me?" Jaiharu's chest felt hollow, as if his rib cage might collapse on his heart.

"The Worldbreather always hears you, child. The question is, have you listened for the Worldbreather? Have you heard his whisperings, leading you the way you should go?"

Jaiharu shook his head. "Why would I listen to him? He's done nothing for me. He won't even send the rain to save my sister!"

The serpent can't help me. What will become of Xi?

"It's useless." His voice cracked. "The rain will not fall, and the Iara will devour my sister."

A forked tongue flickered in and out of the serpent's mouth. "An Iara? Is that what your priest serves now? We knew the two-legged ones would seek other gods when they left the holy mountain, but an Iara? Those muck-sucking bottom dwellers? No Iara ever did a kindness for another. Why follow such a cruel god?"

"The Worldbreather is letting us parch to death by withholding the rain." Jaiharu stuck his chin out. "How is he any better than the Iara? At least the Iara kills quickly. The Worldbreather must enjoy watching us suffer."

The serpent's eyes flashed, and Jaiharu braced himself for the killing blow. Then something in the great beast's face softened.

He lowered himself to Jaiharu's eyes. "Remember when I said you must listen for the Worldbreather? Well, he is speaking to me now, little two-legs. Climb up behind my wings. Together, we will go find the rain."

The serpent circled down until his body hovered level with the altar. His great wings stretched over Jaiharu like the branches of a mighty tree.

The boy hesitated. The serpent's body was broad as a tree trunk, and sparks leapt from his scales.

Jaiharu inhaled. *If the Worldbreather were to speak, would he tell me to ride the feathered serpent?* He stood straighter. *Well, I have nothing to lose.*

He sprang upon the back of the mighty beast and wrapped his arms tight about him. Sparks flashed through his body, but they invigorated rather than burned. The serpent flapped his wings, stirring the air, and rose into the dark sky.

The serpent leapt off the mountaintop. He skimmed the trees, diving so fast Jaiharu shut his eyes to avoid the wind blinding him. He clenched the feathers of the serpent's crest until his fingers ached. Then the serpent spread his great wings. The wind rushed beneath them, and they glided on a breeze.

"What is your name, little one?" the serpent asked.

"Jaiharu."

"A fine name. My name is Hivaro. A slightly finer name." The serpent chuckled.

Below them, the forest flattened into a great valley carpeted by thick trees. The foliage was so dense Jaiharu couldn't get a glimpse of the ground. Scattered lights flickered in clearings, accompanied by the smells of smoke, livestock, and cooking meat. Hivaro avoided flying over any villages.

"No need to frighten people," he explained. "Our business is not in the forest, but over the sea."

Jaiharu's brow furrowed. "What is a sea?"

"It is very like a lake—but not—if the lake were a lizard, the sea would be a feathered serpent."

"So a big lake?" Jaiharu nodded.

"Not just..." Hivaro huffed. "You see the forest, how endless it seems? How far it stretches? If the trees were water, the forest would be a sea...but do not try to understand. Your eyes will show you what your imagination cannot grasp."

Jaiharu fell quiet.

The wind ruffled his hair. He pressed his body against Hivaro's warm scales. The serpent's muscles flexed beneath the boy with each flap of the massive wings.

Ahead, a shimmering ribbon, reflecting every star, cut through the jungle.

"Ah, the great river!" Hivaro roared and lightning flashed from his nostrils. "It will mark our path to the sea."

He dove down to brush the water. Fog misted about them, beading on Jaiharu's flesh.

"If we could somehow bring this river to the village, we'd have no need for rain," he said.

"Even the river is low. You should see it at full flood," Hivaro replied. "We will bring your people rain, young Jaiharu. Patience."

Patience? Morning brings Xi's death. How am I supposed to be patient?

Jaiharu tried not to think of it, to trust in the serpent. Instead, he concentrated on the cool mist, savoring it against his parched skin. So much water all over the world. *Why won't it rain?*

The forest ended against a dark field that stretched to the horizon. A roar like the rush of wind through leaves, but louder and constant, rose from this field. Peaks of white appeared and disappeared, and Jaiharu realized the entire surface was moving, up and down, in and out, like ripples over the surface of the lake, only infinitely more so.

Hivaro descended. A massive wave broke beneath the boy and the dragon, spraying them. Jaiharu licked his lips and tasted salt. A smell like fish and pouring rain surrounded him. *The sea?*

It stretched on forever, like the forest, like the sky. "How do we get this water to the village?"

"We need a cloud. Clouds carry the water, and we will drive them to your people." Hivaro's wings beat the air. The serpent spiraled into the heavens. "Search the sky. The Worldbreather will send us a cloud."

Jaiharu's stomach clenched. *The feathered serpent is acting as much on faith as Ozca. I don't need faith. I need rain.*

Still, he sat up on serpent's back and scanned the horizon. Stars studded an uninterrupted sky. No clouds, not even mist or fog. Jaiharu's throat squeezed shut.

"The night is clear, Hivaro. There are no clouds here."

"Patience, young two-legs," Hivaro whispered.

They hovered above the sea. Hivaro's wings flapped in time to the waves, rolling in and out. A great creature moved beneath them, looking for a moment like an island, before it sent forth a plume of vapor and disappeared once more under the waters. Jaiharu strained his eyes, fearing even to blink. Was there light on the horizon? He squeezed his fingers against Hivaro's scales.

"We should go, return to my village before it is too late. Perhaps if we cannot bring the rain, we can carry Xi away."

"Hush, Jaiharu. We have time. Pray and have faith."

Time? The morning comes. Morning brings death, and I have no faith. How can I have faith when time and time again the spirits of this world have failed me?

He looked down. If he fell, the waves would swallow him up. Spirits craved sacrifice. The Iara, the Worldbreather. Perhaps in giving himself, he could bring the rain. He loosened his grasp upon the feathered serpent.

"Look! There!" Hivaro exclaimed.

Jaiharu squinted. Something blocked the stars before him, moving swiftly, no bigger than his fist.

"It's so small."

"It seems so, but it will grow." Hivaro laughed a deep, throaty laugh. "Come, let us greet it!"

He bolted forward. Sparks flew from his body, blending with the stars. Jaiharu yelped and threw himself against the scaly beast. He held on for dear life as the serpent undulated beneath him. The sparks tingled against his skin, making his hair stand on end.

The cloud grew before them. Mist twisted up from the sea like smoke from the village fires, melding with the cloud, causing it to swell and swirl. Hivaro collided into it. His sparks spread throughout the nebulous interior. The sparks took on a life of their own, swirling about the serpent like fireflies. Lightning snaked through the sky, and Jaiharu gasped.

"We have it, Jaiharu!" Hivaro crowed. "Come, let us race home. The clouds will follow."

He darted into the clear sky.

Jaiharu glanced back. Behind them, the cloud stretched like reaching hands. It clutched at the serpent's tail. When its grasp fell short, it shot after them, moving against the wind, still shining like a thousand stars with the serpent's energy.

Jaiharu's arms ached, but he clung to Hivaro's neck with what remained of his strength. The clouds rolled behind him, gathering mist from the forest floor, expanding and darkening until a blanket of black wool covered the sky from edge to edge. Before them, however, the stars still sparkled in a pristine night...a night that would soon end.

Gray light heralded the morning, fighting against the heavy clouds.

His tongue stuck to the roof of his mouth, but he managed to pry it free. "Hurry, Hivaro! We're running out of time."

The serpent didn't answer. However, his wings thrashed the air, and lightning crackled. Behind them, thunder grumbled like an angry padua.

The Temple Mountain rose like the horn of a great beast, jutting from the forest. Hivaro circled the village. Mist rolled about them, masking them from the ground, but the stench of the dying lake called to them.

Shouts rang out over the rush of the wind. The clouds parted, and Jaiharu found himself hovering over the white stone of the altar. The villagers crowded on the shore. Several tussled with a shouting man—Ozca. Mali stood, imperious, his red cape in stark contrast to the white stone beneath him. Two guards dragged Xi forward. Her eyes were wide, and the wind whipped her hair. Jaiharu leaned forward, almost tumbling off Hivaro's back. He shouted her name, but the breeze caught up his words.

"Hurry!" he shouted to Hivaro.

Something in the deep pools stirred. Jaiharu's stomach twisted. A head covered in grass-like hair emerged from the water, and the villagers fell silent.

"Iara!" Hivaro snarled. "You will find no victims here."

The serpent dove through the sky. The villagers shrieked. The Iara rose from the water, her webbed hands outstretched. Slime dripped from her pointed teeth. Three times the height of a normal woman, she had empty black eyes and green-gray skin the color of algae on a stagnant pond. Her hiss sent shivers through Jaiharu.

"Back, foul monster!" Mali waved his feather-tipped staff at Hivaro. "You shall not stop this offering. The Iara demands the maiden's blood."

Hivaro roared. Sparks leapt from his maw to the dry grass at the edge of the lake, sparking fires.

Mali froze, eyes wide, his staff clattering to the stone. The guards dropped Xi's arms.

The Iara swam closer. "You have no power here, serpent of the clouds," she said, her voice like the croak of a frog. "This village is mine. Its people are sworn to me." She pointed a black-clawed finger at Mali. "Give me the girl! I hunger."

Mali took a step toward Xi. Lightning shot from Hivaro's eyes, wrapping about the priest's wrist.

In a splash of mud and water, the Iara shot from the water. She landed in a crouch between Hivaro and Xi.

"I shall take my own food." She slunk toward the girl. Two of Mali's soldiers grabbed Xi by the shoulders and pushed her toward the Iara in spite of her kicks and screams.

"Stop!" Hivaro's lightning shot forward but broke harmlessly against the Iara's slimy scales.

She snickered. "I told you, you have no power here, creature of the air. Let me have the girl and I will spare your life."

Hivaro's tail swished. "You will terrorize these villagers no more. Jaiharu, get your sister. I'll take the water demon."

Jaiharu leapt from the serpent and collided into Mali's back. The priest sprawled against the rock, his fingers reaching for his staff. Xi kicked it into the crowd then backhanded one of the soldiers.

Mali clawed at Jaiharu, but the boy sank his teeth into the priest's shoulders. Mali screamed.

"Xi! Jaiharu! Hold on!" Ozca barreled through the crowd. He flipped one guard over his shoulder into the water far below. Xi ducked out of the way as

Ozca's fist took down the second guard.

"Enough of this!" Mali sprang to his feet. His elbow jabbed into Jaiharu's chest.

Jaiharu lost his grip on Mali and crashed onto the hard stone of the altar. His air left him in a whoosh. For a moment, the sky spun as if he were still falling. Then he rolled over and caught sight of Hivaro and the Iara.

Hivaro's sparks flitted harmlessly against the Iara's skin. His scales, however, were no match for the water demon's claws. She scraped at him, sending drops of red blood splattering over the white stone. Jaiharu's stomach clenched.

Oh, Worldbreather! You cannot let Hivaro lose. Not to that evil creature. Let me help him! Tell me what I can do.

He searched for some weapon. The majority of the villagers now cowered on the shore, though a few had taken it upon themselves to tussle with Mali's soldiers. Ozca and Mali exchanged blow for blow. Over and over, Mali reached for his staff, only to be pushed back by Ozca.

Jaiharu dove through the legs of the struggling man and snatched up the staff. The green quital feathers fluttered as he sprang toward Hivaro and the Iara. He raised the weapon and smacked it against the Iara's slimy spine.

The feathers sizzled where they touched her scales. She cried out and fell back, allowing Hivaro to wrench free.

The Iara turned on Jaiharu. Her eyes glinted. "That fool Mali allowed his totem to fall into the hands of a boy. You aren't strong enough to wield such power, boy. Drop it before I destroy you."

"The boy may not be strong enough, but I am," Hivaro shouted. "Throw me the staff, Jaiharu!"

Jaiharu flung the staff with all his might, and Hivaro caught it in his jaws. Lightning shot from the feathered serpent but this time as green as the quital feathers. It wrapped around the Iara, and she shrieked and writhed. The stench of rotting fish rose from her.

"Go, foul one!" Hivaro growled at the Iara through clenched teeth. "Feast on fish and frogs, but never bother these people again. I claim them now, for the Worldbreather. They will serve no other spirits. He will give them life, and you shall no longer terrorize them."

The crash of thunder caused all present to cringe. Water fell in sheets, pounding against the earth. The fires from Hivaro's sparks hissed and died.

The people cried out in joy and astonishment.

"The drought has ended!" someone shouted.

"Mali lied. It was the Iara's defeat that brought the rain!" Xi exclaimed. "Look how she cringes as the water falls."

A murmur of agreement rose from the crowd. Mali's soldiers dropped their weapons. Several turned and fled into the jungle.

Ozca pushed Mali to the ground before Hivaro.

The Iara hissed. "You failed me, Mali. You, therefore, I claim."

Mali shrieked. Her arms surrounded him. She leapt into the water, dragging the foul priest down with her. A heartbeat later, only ripples remained on the dark water.

Rain drenched the villagers, but rather than rush for shelter, they fell to their knees. They turned their faces to the sky, laughing and crying. Jaiharu rushed to Xi.

She kissed his forehead. "You brought the rain. How did you bring the rain?"

"Xi!" Ozca hurried to her side.

"Oh, my love!" Xi embraced her lover. They melded together in a passionate kiss as water ran down their bodies, pooling beneath them.

Jaiharu turned back toward the serpent. Puddles ran together. Soon, the lake would fill.

"How can I repay you, Hivaro?" he asked.

"I acted on the will of the Worldbreather." The serpent lowered his great head toward Jaiharu's. "I only hope you will learn to hear his voice as I do. You and all your people."

"I will light incense to him every evening." Jaiharu smiled. "Blood-blossom, in your honor."

The serpent smiled. "I will rejoice in the odor, and in seeing you well. May the Worldbreather bless you and yours, young two-legs."

Hivaro flapped his wings and disappeared into the clouds. Lightning flashed. Thunder rumbled. Rain fell. Jaiharu stood on the edge of the lake, filled for the first time with hope for the future.

H. L. Burke authors fantasy novels for young readers and adults, including a four part Fantasy romance series, The Dragon and the Scholar, *and a five part YA Steampunk series,* Nyssa Glass. *She's always writing and never can tell what idea might strike her fancy yet.*

"Sacrifice of the Iara" was inspired by an episode of River Monsters *(because you never know when you'll get an inspiration attack) and her love for all things flying reptile. The idea evolved into the tale of a sulky, faith challenged hero who overcomes his doubts to save his family—with a little bit of help from a mythical flying serpent.*

Her other works—which include magic, adventure, and DRAGONS—can be found at www.hlburkeauthor.com.

Charla Visits Earth

Diane Astle

Chapter One: An Annoying Mermaid

The sky was blue and the ocean was calm when Ben and Denzel borrowed a boat to go fishing. It would be their last time out on the ocean before the school year ended. They were both students at Fairhaven Private School, located off the west coast of Vancouver Island. Of the two of them, only Ben knew the school's true purpose was training heroes for the Guardian of the Six Worlds. He'd learned this just over a month ago when a portal opened for him to travel to a world of merfolk and monsters.

"Ben, buddy, I lucked out when I got you as my roommate, because you know how to fish." Denzel was trying to untangle his fishing line so he could get it back in the water. It wasn't going well.

"Yep, I was *very lucky* to have a roommate who could teach me about fishing, which I will do when I get this line untangled," Denzel said again.

"What?" Ben reached out his hand. "Okay, give it over."

"Well, you do have a knack for it."

"You're never going to learn if I keep doing it for you."

"I'll practice later, but right now I don't want to waste fishing time doing something you're already an expert at."

Ben just grunted as he tried to figure out which way the tangle on Denzel's line went.

"Hey, Ben, you've got a fish. Shall I get it?" Without waiting for an answer, Denzel jumped forward, pulled Ben's rod out of the holder, and jerked the tip upward to set the hook.

Ben sighed and carefully laid Denzel's tangled fishing line aside so he could be ready with the net. Everything was going as expected, when all of a sudden the line started peeling off the reel and Denzel couldn't stop it.

"That salmon must have been grabbed by something big," Ben said. "Most likely a seal."

Denzel managed to put the brakes on and was struggling to bring the fish back toward the boat when the line went slack and the hook and flasher came hurtling out of the water toward them. Denzel jumped aside, which caused the boat to dip toward the ocean.

"Careful," Ben said.

"My fish is gone," Denzel howled.

"*Your fish*," Ben grumbled as he went back to untangling Denzel's line.

Denzel turned his head toward the school, where only the top of the castle was visible. His eyes narrowed and he scratched his neck. "There's something strange going on at Fairhaven. I know it and you do too, but you haven't wanted to talk about it ever since you disappeared last month."

"I told you, my dad returned after being gone for a long time. I got to go see him." Ben's statement was true. His dad had been missing, he did return, and Ben did get to spend time with him.

"But I don't get why you didn't tell me you were going away."

"It all happened so fast. I didn't get a chance."

"Before you disappeared, you said it was strange to have a secret library with books on make-believe worlds. Now, when I try to get you to talk about it, you won't."

"We just need to be patient and people will tell us when they think we're ready." Ben didn't look at his friend as he said this. He remembered the day that Denzel had convinced him to sneak into the library. He also remembered the month-long detention they'd gotten because of it. He knew what those books meant, but Denzel didn't and he wasn't allowed to tell him.

"I'm thinking there's a secret society that plays role-playing games. The teachers are in on it and some of the students. I want to know how we can get in."

"Like I said, we just have to be patient."

"I don't get you, Ben. Not long ago, you wanted answers as much as me."

Ben stared at his friend. He didn't know what to say. He couldn't tell him the truth.

"I just think...there might be good reasons...for keeping it...secret," Ben stammered.

"If I didn't know any better, I'd think you know, but don't want to tell me." Denzel was trying to untangle his line again. When Ben didn't respond, he looked up and stared intently at him. "Oh, you've got to be kidding. You do know. Why haven't you told me?"

Ben had known ever since he'd been sent to the Principal's office and ended up going through the portal to Lushaka, where he'd learned he could transform into a dragon. He couldn't tell Denzel the truth, but he couldn't lie to him either. If he tried, Denzel would know because he was really good at reading people and finding out what they were trying to hide.

"Denzel, I can't talk about it. You need to wait for Miss Templeton to tell you about the library."

"You're kidding, right?" Denzel's voice was several decibels louder than normal.

"I..." Ben was spared the need to make a response when a fish came hurtling out of the water and hit him on the side of the head. He sat there stunned, while Denzel pounced on the fish flopping around on the bottom of the boat. Ben looked in the direction the fish had come from, but saw nothing.

Denzel was holding the fish in his hands when another one sailed into the boat and struck Ben on the chest.

"I can't believe this," Ben said. "This isn't happening."

Denzel put the first fish in the cooler and jumped on the second one. "No one's going to believe this," Denzel said. "You don't even need to put out a fishing line when the fish want to be caught so badly they jump into the boat."

Ben looked in the direction the second fish had come from. He was watching when a head popped out of the water to be followed by an arm that threw a third fish toward them. This one hit Denzel on the shoulder.

"That one's yours," Denzel said as he opened the cooler a second time. He dropped the fish he was holding in and waited for Ben to catch the third fish. As he held the lid, he stared in the direction the three fish had come from. His mouth fell open. Then he closed his eyes and shook his head. "For a moment, I thought I saw someone in the water, but of course, that's crazy. Who would be out there throwing fish at us?"

Denzel had just put the fish Ben passed him in the cooler when a fourth fish landed in Ben's lap. He grabbed it and handed it to Denzel.

Ben stared over the waves at someone he knew well. It was Charla. He couldn't imagine what she was doing on Earth, but with Charla you never knew. The mermaid was a wild card. He caught her eye, put his fingers to his lips and shook his head as he pointed at Denzel. Ben hoped Charla understood that she couldn't reveal herself. Finally she nodded her head and pointed at Ben, then herself, and then the beach behind them on the small island.

Ben folded his hands, closed his eyes and laid his head sideways on his folded hands. He hoped she understood that he would come later in the night. When Ben opened his eyes, it was to see Denzel staring at him with a puzzled look on his face.

"We should go back," Ben said and started pulling in the fishing line.

"What! We haven't caught any fish yet," Denzel said.

"We have our daily limit of Chinook in the cooler," Ben said as he continued reeling in the line.

"We could throw them back." Denzel opened the cooler and looked at the fish. "They look like they're still alive."

"Those salmon would likely die after landing in the boat and then being manhandled by you. Besides, I have homework to catch up on."

At that moment, seaweed hit Denzel on the back of his head. Next, Charla used her tail to splash seawater into the boat. The water drenched Denzel and, to a lesser degree, Ben.

"How did that happen?" Denzel asked as he pulled seaweed out of his hair. "Did you see anything?"

Ben shook his head no, but kept his head down and didn't look at Denzel.

"I can't believe it. Fish and now seaweed! Have you angered any mermaids lately?" Denzel laughed nervously as he looked around. "I guess we've got to go in now that I'm soaking wet, but at least there will be salmon on the menu tomorrow night."

Ben looked over his friend's shoulder to see Charla floating just under the waves, laughing. Ben felt a burning pain deep in the pit of his stomach, and a faint wisp of dragon fire smoke came out with his words. "I can't believe this either. It will be a very cold trip back to shore, and any mermaids out there need to be aware that humans don't do well when they're cold. I'll be lucky if I don't need to take to my bed and stay there all night."

On hearing those words, Charla flipped her tail again and splashed water at the boat, which hit Denzel's back, but didn't reach Ben. She then disappeared under the waves.

Denzel was shaking and his teeth were chattering as they sped toward shore. Ben was relieved that the topic of the forbidden library was dropped.

Chapter Two: The Best-Laid Plans

Later that night, when all was quiet, Ben sneaked down to the dock. He looked at the boat bobbing in the moonlight and thought how much easier and safer it would be if he could just transform into a dragon. Miss Templeton, Fairhaven's Principal and Earth's Watcher, had asked Ben not to use his ability to transform. So far, he had kept his promise, although he was anxious to use his wings again. He had only used them once, on the day he learned he could. He wondered if it made sense to keep this one promise when he was about to break the rules and take a boat out at night without permission. He would be a rule breaker for a much shorter period of time if he became a dragon. Besides, taking a boat out at night wasn't safe because there were rocks hiding under the waves. They were hard to see in the daytime, let alone at night. There was also the problem that someone might hear the boat motor. Not for the first time, Ben wondered why he hadn't told someone about seeing Charla.

Ben closed his eyes and imagined himself as a dragon, but when he opened them, he was still a fourteen-year-old boy. He closed his eyes again and concentrated harder, but when he opened his eyes, he was still human. He couldn't understand why it wasn't working, because this was all he did on Lushaka. Perhaps knowing that Miss Templeton would not approve was getting in the way. Miss Templeton had powers he was just beginning to understand, and he was afraid she might know if he transformed.

Ben looked up at the school, where two or three lights were still on. He hoped no one was looking out the window as he stepped into the boat and pulled the starter cable on the motor.

Mariah Templeton stood at one of those windows watching Ben. There was little that happened on Earth that she was unaware of. She also knew much of what was happening on the other five worlds. She had linked minds with the Watcher of Lushaka when Charla arrived on Earth and it became clear that the mermaid was trying to keep her presence a secret. Lea Waterborn had enlisted her help because she believed the wayward mermaid had the potential to become one of her brightest and best, and she wanted to avoid expelling her from Fairwaters, the school where the Guardian's Lushakan heroes were trained. Miss Templeton knew she could not expel Ben. Theoretically, she could erase his memory and send him away, but what would happen if the dragonborn side of his heritage re-emerged and there was no one to tell him what it meant? For better or worse, Ben had to stay at Fairhaven. So, she looked out the window and watched as Ben got into the boat and motored away. She knew before he came back to the school what his plans were. She hoped that the Guardian would be at work to bring some good out of this foolishness that he was embarking on.

The coastline, with its many small islands, was confusing in the daytime, but it was even worse at night. Ben was starting to wonder if he would ever find Charla as he took one wrong turn after another. He wouldn't have known that he had finally arrived if a voice hadn't spoken in the darkness.

"What took you so long?"

"I got lost."

"I figured." Charla swam to the stern of the boat and levered herself up and over so she could sit in it.

"What are you doing here, Charla?" Ben asked.

"I'm sitting here talking to you, and just for your information, this is my first time in a boat."

"No, I mean, what are you doing on Earth? Did Lea Waterborn send you?"

"Not exactly," Charla said.

"Are you telling me that Lea Waterborn, the Watcher of Lushaka, didn't send you to Earth?"

"Only if you want me to."

"What I'd like is the truth."

"You sure about that?"

"Lea Waterborn doesn't know you're here, does she?"

Charla silently stared at Ben.

"Charla, what were you thinking? This could get you into big trouble. You might be expelled."

"She just threatened to expel me, which is why I'm here. I decided to travel through a portal before she erased my memory and sent me away."

"Why did she threaten to expel you?"

"It wasn't my fault. Some of the other Chosen were picking on Jared and I defended him."

Ben thought of the friend he made on Lushaka, who had been accepted as the first human Chosen in centuries. He could well imagine that some of the Mer were unhappy about the presence of a Lushakan human. Initially, Charla herself wanted nothing to do with either Ben or Jared because they were humans.

"I'm sure Jared can look after himself. You need to go back, before Lea Waterborn knows you're gone," Ben said.

"I'm not going to do that."

"You can't stay on Earth."

"I don't want to. I'll go back as soon as I've been to Vancouver. This water is too cold and too salty and it makes my skin crawl. I understand why Earth has no mer-people of its own."

"You want to go to Vancouver?"

"I want to go up Grouse Mountain and see the city from there."

Ben remembered telling Charla about taking the Skyride up Grouse Mountain as they struggled to climb into the heart of a mountain on Lushaka.

"How are you going to get there?"

"That's for you to figure out."

"I'm not going to do that. I could get expelled."

"You owe me big time. You'd be dead as dead could be if I hadn't saved your life over and over again."

Ben rolled his eyes. "You didn't save me over and over again."

"I saved your life more than once. There were the sand creatures, the spiders, the uglies—and without me, you'd never have gotten out of that cage."

"Okay. Okay, you saved my life more than once."

"If you help me now, we'll consider it even. I'll never ask you for another thing. Besides, if I have to look for Vancouver and Grouse Mountain on my own, it will take a whole lot longer. The longer I'm here, the more chance that I'll be caught. I'd be asked a lot of awkward questions, especially when my legs transformed back into a tail."

"I should just go back and tell Miss Templeton you're here."

"What kind of friend would do that?"

"A smart one."

Ben and Charla sat in silence, staring at one another as Ben thought about what Charla was asking him to do. She was one of the most determined people he knew, and if he didn't help her, she would try to do it on her own. If she was caught, it would create problems not only for Charla, but for the people at his school. Finally, he sighed. "I suppose you brought a disguise with you?"

"Yes, I make a beautiful human girl."

"Okay, I hope I don't regret this, but I know a man who flies a floatplane between here and Vancouver. He runs a fishing lodge that's the school's only real neighbor. I'll talk to him and see if he's willing to take us. If he's not, then there's no way it can be done. This place is isolated and there's no other way I can take you to Vancouver."

"He'll be willing, I know he will."

"Follow me. I'll stop by and talk to Kevin on my way back to Fairhaven. If he can take us, I'll show you a cove where you can wait."

"You won't regret this."

"I already do."

Chapter Three: Vancouver Bound

Ben motored over to the fishing lodge. He tied the boat to the dock next to the floatplane. Kevin Seaton's two Labrador dogs started to bark but settled down when they saw who it was. Ben woke the older man up from sleep when he knocked, but Kevin brushed aside his apologies as he stepped outside to talk to him so that they did not wake his wife. Kevin agreed to take Ben and a friend to Vancouver when dawn broke. He told Ben he had been planning to go anyway and it was no hardship to take two passengers.

Just before daybreak, Ben picked up an attractive human girl from an isolated beach in a two-person kayak. The school had many kayaks that looked similar to one another and a missing one was unlikely to be noticed.

Charla had put on a blond, shoulder-length wig, which Ben didn't think she needed. The mermaid's own spiky, greenish blond hair reminded Ben of the cartoon character Lisa Simpson, but from what he saw on the streets of Vancouver, girls dyed their hair a variety of colors and did all kinds of weird things with it.

When he looked at what Charla was wearing, Ben thought she must have chosen the wildest clothes she could find. Her short skirt was neon green with yellow and pink swirls, while her tank top was yellow with orange polka dots. People would see her coming from miles away, when what Ben really wanted to do was blend into the background.

When they arrived at the fishing lodge, Kevin stared at Charla with his mouth pursed and furrows in his forehead. "You must be freezing."

Ben realized his mistake. On the ocean, a jacket was needed in the early morning every day of the year, even in June, and both Kevin and Ben wore jackets. Charla was poorly dressed, and yet she didn't appear to be cold.

"You wouldn't happen to have a jacket my friend could borrow, would you?" Ben asked. "She took hers off for a moment, and it dropped over the side of the kayak. There must have been something heavy in the pockets because it sank right away."

Charla's mouth fell open.

"My clients often forget things. I have a box of their stuff to look in and see what's there." Kevin hurried toward the house.

"What are you doing?" Charla asked. "I don't need a jacket."

"Yes, you do, if you're going to pass yourself off as human," Ben said.

Kevin returned with a blue sweater and a long, gray raincoat. He insisted that Charla take both. She put the sweater on and carried the coat. Only a small amount of Charla's skirt showed up below the sweater, which made Ben happy.

In the plane, Ben sat beside Kevin and Charla sat directly behind the pilot in the second row of seats. As the plane took off, Charla squealed. "I never actually believed it was possible to fly. What magic your world has," she said breathlessly.

"Come on, Charla, stop pretending that you don't know what a plane does. You're going to make Kevin think you're a space alien," Ben said, forcing a laugh. In less than a minute, Kevin was laughing along with him.

When Ben looked down at the space between his seat and Kevin's, there was a mermaid tail. He was afraid Kevin might look down and see it, so he unobtrusively pushed it backwards toward Charla. He also pushed back the shoes that had popped off her feet. When he next looked, the mermaid's tail had turned back into two legs. Throughout the flight, Ben could hear faint gasps and mutters from the backseat as Charla watched the world go by. He was glad that the loud engine made it difficult to hear what was said in the backseat. He realized how much he was looking forward to spending the day with Charla. She made life challenging, but interesting.

Chapter Four: The Harbor

"I want to leave here by seven o'clock," Kevin said as he landed in the Vancouver harbor.

"We'll be back by then," Ben said.

When they got to the dock, Ben jumped out to secure the plane. Charla appeared at the door a few moments later, standing on legs that were shaking. Ben reached out a hand to help her with the step between the plane and the pontoon, but was half expecting Charla to knock his hand aside. His experience with her had taught him that she didn't like to admit to needing help. She ignored his hand as she stared at the high rises that are part of downtown Vancouver's skyscape.

"What are those used for?" she asked.

"Most of them are office buildings, but some are condos," Kevin said as he stepped out of the plane.

Ben could see that Charla was puzzled by Kevin's response and was about to ask another question. "Lots of people work in those offices and then walk across the street to the condo where they live," he said, hoping to forestall questions that would cause Kevin to wonder just who Charla was.

"What kind of work would you do in a place like that?"

"All kinds," Kevin said. "I myself was a financial manager. I made lots of money, but came close to crashing and burning, so I got out while I still could and bought the fishing lodge. Hard to believe, but it was my wife's dream to own one."

"Money?" Charla's face brightened. "I know about money. It's something that you get in exchange for work that you can use for things you need."

"That pretty much describes money," Kevin said with a puzzled look on his face.

Charla took Ben's hand, stepped onto the pontoon, and then down to the dock.

When she moved away, Kevin whispered to Ben, "How long has this girl been at that school of yours?"

Ben thought fast. The last thing he wanted was for Kevin to have questions about the school. "She just arrived from a very bad situation. Her parents kept her locked up," Ben whispered back. "It was decided that a protective environment would be the first step in helping her adjust to a world she knows little about. Once she's been at the school for a while, she'll join the rest of the world. This trip is about letting her see some of the world outside the school."

"I see," Kevin said, sounding doubtful.

Ben was appalled. He could count the number of times he lied before today on one hand and still have most of his fingers left over. He had started the day by getting Denzel to agree to tell everyone that he was sick in bed. The lie would work for exactly one day, but he needed to be healthy by tomorrow or a medic would come and check on him.

Chapter Five: Scrambled Brains

Everywhere Charla looked, there were things she never, in her wildest dreams, imagined. And the humans came in so many different colors and shapes and wore such a wild variety of clothes. It made her own world seem so plain and ordinary and drab. Mer all had the same color hair, the same dark eyes, and dressed alike.

It would be so much easier to take it all in if things just stayed where they were, but everywhere she looked, there was movement. Charla was overwhelmed by the multitude of things happening around her and was stunned into silence until they got on the second bus and started heading up to Grouse Mountain.

Charla found a place on the bench seat at the front of the bus, and Ben stood beside her until the driver insisted that those standing move toward the back of the bus. He obediently moved and missed Charla's conversation with a young man who sported a Mohawk haircut. The tips of what hair he had was dyed bright purple, and his face and neck were covered in tattoos. He had body piercings in his ears, nose, and lips. Charla stared at him and he stared back with his chin held high.

"How do you like living on Earth? Do you ever wish you lived on another world?" she asked as she stared at him. The man looked at her in surprise, and then his face turned red, and he swore at her.

"I know that word. That's a human swear word! Why would you say that to me?" Charla asked in a voice that was louder than normal. Loud enough that it carried to the back where Ben was standing. "Did I offend you? I didn't mean to. All I wanted to know is how you like being human."

Instead of answering her question, the man got up and pushed his way through the people standing in the aisle—his seat was quickly taken by a woman who sighed in relief. Charla noticed the shoes the woman was wearing and bent over to get a closer look. The heels were high and spiked, and the toes were pointed. Charla couldn't imagine wearing shoes like that. She frowned as she stared at them and then looked up at the woman.

"Why do you wear those shoes?" Charla asked.

"I wear them because I like them," the woman said.

"Don't they hurt your feet?"

"Not really."

"Don't you have trouble keeping your balance?"

"No, not often, anyway." The woman took out a book from her purse and very purposely turned her back toward Charla as much as the seat allowed. Charla tried to ask her about what she was reading, but the woman ignored her questions even when Charla poked her in the arm.

Charla turned toward the older man sitting on the other side of her. She noticed him before, but had found the haircut and then the shoes more interesting. He had been snickering as she talked to the people on the other side of her.

Charla wondered if she was going about things wrong. Perhaps people didn't like to answer questions until they knew who you were. "My name's Charla. What's yours?" she asked the man.

"I'm Gordon," the man in the suit and tie said with a smile. Charla smiled back. This was going much better. "I've often wondered if those punks are really human too," the man said.

"Punks?" Charla thought back over her lessons on Earth and its people and could not remember ever hearing the word "punk" used for any of the racial groups on Earth. "What's a punk?"

"It's a pain in the ass who doesn't want to work and expects to be handed everything on a silver platter."

"But humans have to work, that's how they get money to buy the things they need."

"Right you are, little lady." The man smiled at Charla, and Charla smiled back.

This was going so much better than her other conversations. Now, perhaps she could ask the question she really wanted to ask. "How did you get a belly like that?" she asked.

The people sitting around them stopped talking. The girls closest to them giggled.

"What?" Gordon asked, stunned.

Charla wondered if he understood her, so she poked him in the gut. "How did you get this?"

She was going to poke him again, when he grabbed her finger and bent it backwards. Charla howled. Ben, meanwhile, was already pushing his way through the crowded aisle. He arrived just as the driver stopped the bus and stood up to see what was happening.

"I apologize for my sister," Ben said quickly. "I should never have gone to the back of the bus and left her alone up here. I promised my parents I'd watch her every moment when they let me take her out of the group home. It breaks our hearts to see her like this. Charla was an ordinary girl until she was hit by the car that scrambled her brains."

"What!" Charla howled. "He's lying. My brains aren't scrambled!"

The driver looked at Ben with sympathy. "Keep an eye on your sister so she doesn't bother the other passengers."

The driver returned to his seat, and the man sitting next to Charla released her finger. "I'm sorry about that, little lady, but you need to learn to keep your hands to yourself."

Charla scowled and clenched her fists. Her brain was just fine, but she couldn't say the same for the humans around her. As her anger built, Charla could feel her legs starting to tingle. That was the feeling she got just before she lost a transformation. She grabbed the coat Kevin gave her and wrapped it around her legs, folded her arms, closed her eyes, and tried to think happy, calming thoughts. She was starting to get a handle on her anger when the woman sitting next to her spoke, "Why does it smell like fish all of a sudden?"

Charla opened her eyes and glared at the woman. "It doesn't smell like fish. Nothing smells like fish." She said each word loudly and distinctly and then closed her eyes again. That was a good thing because she missed the woman next to her mouthing the words, "I'm so sorry" with her hand on Ben's arm.

Charla imagined herself drifting in a calm, warm sea. As she did so, she realized how much she loved living on her own world.

Ben closed his eyes and wondered how many more times he would be forced to lie before the day was over. He really regretted agreeing to take Charla on a trip up Grouse Mountain.

Chapter Six: The Girl Has a Tail

They arrived at Grouse Mountain much later than Ben expected.

"We could have used one of these when we were trying to get to the top of Spencer Mountain," Charla said as she stared at the approaching sky tram.

"It sure would have helped," Ben agreed.

"Remember when I saved you from the uglies?" Charla asked.

"I was the one who saved you," Ben corrected.

"I saved you first," Charla insisted.

Ben rolled his eyes. She did save his life first, but from the spider crabs. He just wished she would stop reminding him.

"Any chance I'll have to save your life again today?" There was a hopeful note in Charla's voice.

"The only possible danger here is a bear or a cougar."

"Are they more dangerous than what I rescued you from on my world?" Charla asked.

"Well," Ben said and then paused. "They can be dangerous if you meet them face to face when they are hungry or protecting their young."

"How many people have been killed on Grouse Mountain so far this year by bears and cougars?"

"No one," Ben replied.

"So, they're not so dangerous," Charla said. "Not like the spiders and uglies, who would have killed you if I hadn't been there to save your life."

Ben glared at Charla, who seemed determined to press home the point that he owed her big time.

When they got to the top of the mountain, they walked over to the viewpoint and stared down at the city that stretched out below them to the north and south along the edge of the Pacific Ocean. They couldn't see what was to the east, but Ben assured Charla that if they could, they would be gazing on even more of the city.

"People have a whole world to live in," Charla said. "Why do so many of them live right here? Is the rest of your world not very habitable?"

"There are cities like this all around the world—some are even bigger."

"Cities bigger than this!" Charla's mouth dropped open and she stood silently staring down. "It's hard to believe there are cities bigger than this," she whispered.

"Come on, Charla," Ben said. "I'm hungry; let's get something for lunch, then we'll take a walk around before we head back to the harbor."

When Ben excused himself to go to the washroom, he left Charla standing at the barrier staring down at the city. There was an announcement while he was gone, but the words were indistinct. When he came out, Charla was gone, but the coat she borrowed from Kevin was hanging on the back of a chair.

At first, he didn't panic. He assumed she went to the washroom and would be back any moment, so he waited for her to return. He waited several minutes, but Charla did not appear. The clock was ticking, and all he could think of was how he wanted to make sure they had lots of time for their trip back. He picked up Charla's coat and went to the front of the restaurant, where he walked back and forth, desperately looking in all directions—then he heard the announcement and knew exactly where she was.

"I just want to announce one more time that a talk on grizzly bears with Ranger Bob is about to start any minute. If you want to know more about Grinder and Coola, follow the paw prints to the bear habitat," the voice on the intercom said.

Ben had forgotten that there were orphaned grizzly bears up here. It must have been what the announcement he couldn't hear was about. He took off at a run and reached the bear habitat just as a collective gasp went up from the crowd. The ranger hadn't noticed the girl behind him climbing over the wooden rails, who was now just about to grab hold of the electric fence that surrounded the bear enclosure.

"Charla, no," Ben yelled, just as she reached out and touched the fence. Charla was jolted backwards and hit the wooden rail she just climbed over. She fell to the ground, and the moment she did, her legs turned into the tail of a mermaid. Ben took the borrowed coat and threw it down on Charla's tail before he climbed over the fence.

He wasn't fast enough, and he heard a child's voice say, "Did you see that, Momma? That girl has a fish tail."

Ben was desperate as he knelt beside Charla and started patting her face rather forcefully. "You've got to wake up and turn back into a human right now," he whispered.

Ben stopped speaking when Ranger Bob climbed over the fence and knelt down beside him.

"She all right?" he asked.

"She'll be fine in just a minute," Ben said, hoping that what he was saying was true.

"What was she doing?" Ranger Bob asked.

"She said she'd get my plane," a high-pitched voice on the other side of the rail said. "It went over the fence, and my mom said I couldn't get it, so the girl said she would." The voice belonged to a boy who looked about five years old.

"That girl has a tail," said an older woman.

"I saw it too," said a teenage boy.

"Me too," said several other voices.

"Oh, come on," Ranger Bob laughed. "What would a mermaid be doing up here on Grouse Mountain?"

"Take that jacket off her legs and you'll see," said a voice from the crowd.

Ben felt faint and didn't know what to do. He could just imagine the newspapers the next morning. There would be no hiding the fact that he broke the rules if everyone saw Charla's fish tail. He reached out to stop the ranger from removing the coat, but Ranger Bob brushed him aside and pulled it away. Ben closed his eyes. When he opened them, there were two perfectly normal legs.

"How did she do that?" voices from the other side of the fence asked.

"Okay, the show's over," Ranger Bob said. "Give this girl some privacy. There are other things to see up here; I'll do the bear talk later."

Some of the crowd left, but others stayed where they were. Ben could hear them telling one another what they saw. Two first aid attendants came with a stretcher and put Charla on it so they could carry her to the first aid center. Ben followed them.

"The manager will want to talk your friend's parents," one of the first aid attendants said. "Do you have their phone number?"

"No," Ben replied.

"You know her name though, right?"

"Charla. Her name is Charla."

"We need her last name."

Ben shook his head.

"I guess we'll have to wait until she revives."

Ben guessed Charla was just pretending to be unconscious. Otherwise, she would have a fish tail. He wanted to tell her to keep pretending, but the first aid attendant was right there. The attendant picked up a magazine and was reading it when his walkie-talkie came to life and a voice on the other end told him a visitor had fallen and needed first aid.

"I'll be back in a minute," the attendant said. "I'll call an ambulance if your friend's not awake by then. If anything changes, go into the office next door and they'll send for me."

As soon as he left, Charla opened her eyes. "We've got to get out of here," she said.

"We sure do," Ben replied, looking around the office. "We need to change our appearance so we're not caught getting to the Skyride. You can start by taking off your wig."

"But my hair…"

"Won't look out of place," Ben said. "You saw the people on the bus."

Charla took off her wig, and Ben put it in the bag he carried.

"Ditch that sweater and take my jacket. I'll wear this." Ben picked a ragged hoody out of a lost-and-found box in the corner. He pulled the hood up over his head and then looked out the door to see if anyone was watching. The coast was clear, and the two of them ran toward the sky tram. Before they got on, Ben took off the hoody and left it hanging over a barrier.

Chapter Seven: A Dragon Flies Tonight

When they were off the mountain, the bus was delayed. When they finally caught one, there were traffic jams. It was closer to eight o'clock when they got back to the harbor, where they found Kevin in the pilot's seat, waiting. He scowled at them as they climbed into the plane.

Ben and Charla buckled themselves in as Kevin attempted to start the plane. The first attempt failed, so he tried again. He tried a second, a third, and a fourth time, but the motor refused to start.

"The mechanics have gone home for the day, so I won't be able to have the plane looked at until at least tomorrow. Who knows how long it will take to fix. I may be able to find you a ride over to the island with another pilot, but no one flies to where you go to school. Do you want to get a room and see what happens tomorrow? It might be best for you to take a ferry and then catch a bus to Campbell River. I have a friend there I can call to drive you to the other side of the island, and you can get someone from your school to pick you up at the Gold River dock."

"Ben knows people," Charla said. "They'll help us get home, so you don't need to worry about us."

"No...I..." Ben began.

"Good," Kevin said, clearly relieved. "I'm glad to only have myself and my plane to worry about. Do you need anything else? Money?"

"No," Charla quickly answered.

"Good, I've got a friend I can stay with on the other side of the city." Kevin walked quickly down the dock away from the plane. Ben grabbed Charla by the arm and tried to catch up to Kevin. They almost had when Kevin hopped into a waiting bus that promptly closed its doors and went on to the next stop.

"Why did you tell him I know people?" Ben asked.

"You do, don't you."

"Not anyone in Vancouver I would want to call."

"We don't need anyone. You're going to transform into a dragon and fly us back to Fairhaven."

"I can't do that."

"Why not?"

"First of all, Miss Templeton has forbidden it."

Charla laughed. "And you think she would approve of you being here with me."

Ben ignored Charla's comment. "Secondly, I tried last night and couldn't do it."

"Why not?"

"I don't know. I just couldn't."

"I suggest you try again, right now." A couple walked past them arm in arm. "Well, maybe not right now, but as soon as we find a place where you won't be seen."

"Okay, I'll try," Ben said. "But if that doesn't work, I'll have no choice but to call my dad, which means I'll be in big trouble. You don't have to stay with me but can transform and swim back to the portal near Fairhaven."

"No, I can't. I wouldn't know where I was going and I'd be in the water too long. Mer can't tolerate the high salt content and the pollution in your oceans for extended periods of time. Not only that, but there are dangerous predators. Sharks and giant squid, even your orcas have been known to look at Mer as a food source. No, I can't swim back, even if you tell me where to go."

"But I thought you said that if I didn't take you, you would go by yourself." Ben could feel himself getting very angry. The dragon fire in him was waking up, and his gut was beginning to burn. If he didn't get control of his anger, it would be dangerous to be in human form.

Charla just shrugged, which made Ben even angrier. At the very least, she should have apologized. He grabbed hold of Charla's arm and dragged her behind a large evergreen tree. The pain caused him to buckle over and cry out in agony. He imagined himself as a dragon with every fiber of his being. When he heard Charla cry out, he opened his eyes to discover he was still holding onto her arm—but not with his human hand. Charla's arm was held in his claws.

A voice on the walkway they had just left called out, "Is everything okay? Do you need us to call the police?" There was fear in the voice that spoke.

"We're fine," both Ben and Charla said.

"I need to be sure," the voice said. "What is..." the voice trailed away as a dragon lifted off the ground, carrying a girl on its back.

Chapter Eight: Seymour Narrows

They were over Seymour Narrows, where several seamen had died before the Canadian government blew the twin tops off an underwater mountain. The area still claimed the occasional life because of strong currents and hidden rocks. So, when Ben heard screaming below them, he spiralled down to take a look.

A boat was being overwhelmed by the high waves and the strong current. Water was flowing over the back of the boat and causing it to sink. The man at the wheel turned it toward shore, but instead of changing direction, it leaned over to the side and capsized. Three men and a woman jumped just before it did, but one of the men, who was standing closest to the motor, ended up with a rope wrapped around his leg. Unfortunately, there was an anchor tied to the other end. The anchor and the man disappeared.

"Help the others! I'll get that one!" Charla swung around and dropped from Ben's back into the ocean. By the time she hit the waves, her legs had been replaced by a fish tail.

Charla swam underwater toward the boat. Ahead of her, fishing equipment and personal items were sinking. The boat was carried along by the current as it slowly sank. The anchor was dragging it down, but was not long enough to catch on the bottom of the ocean. She found the man who was tangled in the anchor rope. He was trying to reach over and free his leg, but his life jacket did not allow for that kind of movement. So, he unzipped it and took it off and it popped up toward the surface, but it was too late for the man. He'd run out of oxygen.

Charla grabbed the rope, but the anchor was heavy and she had nothing to hold onto. At first it dragged her down, but she flipped her tail several times as hard as she could and managed to drag the anchor up toward the surface, where she held onto it with one hand while pulling the man out of the now loosened rope. When he was free, she dropped the anchor and came up behind him, put her arms around his chest and dragged him up to the surface. When she got there, Ben was nowhere in sight.

Ben had picked up the woman and one of the men in his claws and flown into the air with them. There was land close by on both sides of the narrows, but he wanted to put them somewhere that would make rescue easy or where they could walk out on their own if they had to. On the Vancouver Island side, he spotted a trail that came out of the woods so that hikers could look out over the narrows. He followed that to a place where the trail was close to a small cove and put the two boaters down before flying back to rescue the others.

When Ben got back, he discovered that Charla was waiting for him with a man that appeared unresponsive in her arms. He hovered over Charla and picked up the man she held, and then snagged the man who floated nearby by his life jacket. He carried these two to where he left the others. This time, he landed and transformed into a human boy.

All of the boaters were shivering with cold. He doubted that any of them would be able to act to save their friend's life. "Please collect some firewood, if you can," he said.

"Who are you? What are you?" they asked through chattering teeth.

"That's not important. You get the wood, and I'll see if I can save your friend's life." Ben began to perform life-saving maneuvers on the unconscious man. He pinched his nose and breathed air into his lungs. He continued on for about five minutes, and then the man coughed and started breathing on his own.

"A lot of good this wood is going to do when we have nothing to start a fire with, and even if we did, this wood is not dry enough," one of the men pointed out.

Ben grabbed a few more pieces of wood and threw them down where the others had put theirs— "Step back," he said.

Ben transformed into a dragon and let out a mighty blast of dragon fire. His dragon fire dried out and ignited the wood. "I have to leave now. Someone will likely see this fire and come to your rescue, but if they don't, you're only a couple of miles from the road. Please do me a favor and don't tell anyone what you've seen."

"Who are you? Where do you come from?"

Ben ignored their questions and leapt into the air. He plucked Charla out of the ocean and took her to the shore where she could transform into a human and climb onto his back, and they were soon winging their way over to the other side of the island.

Chapter Nine: Endings and Beginnings

Ben landed on the dock at the fishing lodge. A dog barked from within the house and Kevin's wife told it to be quiet.

Charla sat and transformed her legs into a tail.

"Are you going through the portal tonight?" Ben asked quietly as he sat down beside her.

"Yes. Hopefully, no one will be there when I get back. They are normally only watching when a Chosen from another world is expected, so if I'm lucky, no one will see me."

"I hope neither of us are expelled," Ben said.

"You should never have agreed to take me." Charla slapped the water with her tail as she said that.

"I didn't want to." Ben could feel himself getting angry. "But you said you'd go on your own if I didn't. You said I owed you. You appealed to our friendship." Ben's voice had gotten loud. A dog barked from within the house. Charla slipped into the water and Ben climbed into the kayak, and they moved away from the dock before speaking again.

"We might have done something really bad when we saved that man's life," Charla said.

"What can be bad about saving someone's life? That's the work of the Guardian, and Chosen go to other worlds to save lives all the time."

"Yes, but we go because the Guardian sends us. The Guardian didn't send me, and I don't know if what I did has brought good or evil to your world. How have we changed the timeline of Earth by saving the life of a man who otherwise would have died? Perhaps he will do some terrible things or give birth to a monster who will kill a lot of people."

Ben stared at Charla. He could tell that she was serious, and he wondered if she was right. Yet, he knew that if he came upon someone in trouble again, he wouldn't hesitate to save their life. And yet, how was the future changed because of what they did?

"Yes," he said hesitantly, "but perhaps he'll do something that will save a lot of lives instead."

"And maybe one of the lives he saves will create a weapon that destroys your world."

"Charla, we were there and those people were in trouble. We couldn't have just flown away and left them, because that's not who either one of us is. We are chosen heroes of the Guardian for a reason."

"You're right, but from now on, when I come through a portal, it will be because the Guardian has sent me."

They had reached the place where the Portal to Lushaka was located. "Goodbye, Ben, I hope we meet again," Charla said as she swam toward the spot between three rocks.

Ben was surprised to find himself hoping that he would see Charla again. But one thing for sure, he would never let Charla or anyone else talk him into doing something he knew he ought not to do again. More than ever, he knew that being a Chosen of the Guardian meant a commitment to what was right and true. It meant using your gifts as a Chosen not for your own pleasure, but to work for peace and justice on one of the Six Worlds.

With their two wayward Chosen returning, the Watchers on Earth and Lushaka breathed a sigh of relief. Miss Templeton was thinking about the conversation she would have tomorrow with Ben and wondering how long to make his detention.

Dianne has always wanted to be a dragon. When it appeared that was impossible she got a dog and started to write books with dragons in them. "Charla Visits Earth" continues the story begun in Ben the Dragonborn.
astled@telus.net

Cry of the Cave Lion

E. Kaiser Writes

Our leader squatted on the sandbar, studying the track. The rest of us hung back, leaning on our spears or hunching down to rest. There was no need for more than one opinion here, and we all knew it.

He tipped his head and then lifted narrowed eyes to slide over the near landscape, scanning for any faint sign that would influence his decision. Then he stood, and we all raised ourselves to readiness once more. He jumped back over the small spit of wind-worn sand to the roughened rock where the rest of us stood, and then he paused a minute.

I liked him, our leader. He was cautious. A thinker. He was the best among us and had seen many hunts, many hundreds of them. A scar twisted its ugly way over the smooth plane of his back; the worst of many, a sign of a meeting with a cave lion. The most fearsome creature of our acquaintance, it was something few of us had seen...but nearly all of us feared.

Some, like I, from the bottom of our hearts.

And some not at all, like Be'gorn.

He tossed his curling hair back out of his eyes and his barrel chest expanded for a deeper breath. That one knew no fear. "He's young," our leader had laughed, when it was talked about. "He has not yet had reason for it."

But no younger than I.

I had scars, true, but they were from stick fighting as a child. If Be'gorn had no reason for fear, then neither ought I. But it lived in me, and Be'gorn's heedless bravery burned my eyes with the reminder.

There was, perhaps, one reason I had. When we both were much younger, right after we had gone on our first hunt as "new men," a fear-cat had come to our homeland. It had roamed our gullies and ravines, left franticly scraped ground where it killed its thrashing prey, its huge tracks at the edge of nearby water holes.

I saw the tracks for the first time when it was our streambed that it crossed, and in that instant, my blood stilled at the knowledge that it knew of our place. The little children that chased shrieking after each other, the women going slowly down to fetch water.

It knew of us and was not afraid.

Then my eyes had lifted from the tracks at my feet. My ears caught a faint sound, the whisper of a rasping panting only a little distance up the ridge.

I stared across the small space of rippling water for several frozen minutes. Then a dusty-leaved bush shivered, and the panting silenced.

The next day, the more experienced men went hunting, and three did not return. The peace in the eyes of the victors knew that it was a price meant to be paid...and the widows held up their heads for the bravery of their men. But it was a bitter courage.

We had no more of the creatures for a long while afterward; snows and suns piled upon themselves...until this time.

Now, another had been driven out from the blue mountains where the sun slept and had come down into this dry land, where no other creature lived who could challenge us, where no other men lived to envy us.

But now I was a man of experience, now I would follow the track of the fear-cat. We took our javelins down and put our water flasks around our necks, and we left our homes.

We had been very near upon it four days ago. While the others wakened after my dawn watch, I had gone to the nearby stream bank in the coming day. But I did not fill my flask. There on the opposite bank was another track, new and fresh.

I turned, the sounds across the stream causing that sickening cold wind to waft along my spine, across my shoulders, and down to my heels. Fear. I hated it...and the lion.

I knew that we would hunt in earnest tomorrow, hunting the beast that could kill us. To wait for it was folly. It was there, and we needed to kill it before it found us. It was simple and so hard.

Then Be'gorn was beside me, empty flask in hand and in an instant forgotten, also. But he did not stand on the water's edge, like I. He leaped into the stream and then next onto the bank. His eyes scanned the terrain, and then he was off, dashing through the scattered rocks, dodging the thorny brush.

And there I was following him, because I could not face being left behind.

Suddenly, he doubled back so fast that I barely had time to get out of the way, and then he pushed aside a wilted branch. There in the soft dust lay the impression of a resting hunter, the long legs lounging out to make little scuffs which made my throat tighten. I looked around us quickly to be certain it had left...but there was no movement anywhere.

"Stay here," he said. "I'll bring them." Then he grinned, that reckless, wild grin that had made me hate it. And then he was gone.

Perhaps he would be the leader one day. I knew he reckoned on it. He certainly had the prowess. Taller than I, stronger than most, he had shown himself to be an eager and reckless hunter. He had never known fear. And his boldness was born of that. I knew from the way his eyes raked the field before every dangerous hunt that he had no knowledge of the kind of feeling that swept up my back at the very thought of it.

And stayed there.

Late in the fourth day after that, we found it. It had been lying under the shade cast by a rift in the rugged sandstone outcropping, the massive lion's tawny hide blending seamlessly with the color of the stone. It was one of those lucky accidents that we spotted it, that I caught the twitch of a tail that let us know the creature was lying in wait for us.

It was on the side of a hill, a series of rocky outcroppings and ledges that gave the hunter easy view of the prey and everything else. We halted momentarily, and our leader outlined the plan, one of many we knew by heart.

He pointed to Be'gorn and I, and we slipped away through the dust-dry trees and smoothly, quickly along the tip of the crest, disappearing from view with only the soft sounds of leather-clad feet against stone.

We waited for their warbled signal and then went forward.

The air was parched and the footing was dry; a single misstep would alert the beast and send it off for another day's try at us, but Be'gorn ran like a deer, hardly taking a second glance at his footing.

How could he be so silent? I was pressed to stay up with his pace, and only kept the stillness by blindly following his footsteps, trusting his earlier passage to assure my own safe footfalls.

We heard the snarl before we broke over the knob of rock, the sounds quickly telling us that the cat had come out to face his foes and was in no good mood about it. I noticed the shoulders in front of me spasm in the fear that the fight would be over before he got there, and then Be'gorn threw caution to the wind with a redoubled pace, leading us tearing over the rocks, ducking under the bristly limbs of parched and tortured pines.

We broke out onto the overhang above where the lion was, slapping at the javelin heads of our clansmen, the careless, angry roar telling of the big cat's irritation more than anything else.

It was a bad position we were in. That was easy to see.

There was no real hold on the beast; at any moment, it could leap up to the shelf where we stood and be away. The men below could not get close enough for a killing blow, and we above were just a little too prominent. If the creature caught sight of us, it would likely fly straight out of our grasp.

There was only one way: if they could keep it focused on them while we got into a side position to hurl our javelins into one of the few fatal spots such beasts had.

I re-gripped the handle of my weapon and slid swiftly sideways over the dusty surface of rock.

But Be'gorn leaped straight from the rock.

I wanted to cry out to him, "Stay back!" when he leaped, but it was already too late, and the cry would only draw the beast's attack toward him the more.

Like a twisting flame, the lion turned, with all his fierceness collected into a single move, and Be'gorn was there to face him. He stood against the golden fury like a rock against the ocean, and the wave of animal madness broke over him.

I saw him go down and knew that the full force of the lion's power could kill any man...and that for an instant, the huge cat saw nothing else but his kill.

With a will that brooked no discussion with my heart, I ran to the edge of the rock and jumped with my spear point first, sinking it deep into the tawny hide behind the protruding ridge of the shoulder blade. It slid cleanly in past the decorative wrappings I'd so carefully plaited around the shaft, burying the tassels I had left to swing in the breeze when it was at rest above our door.

I leaped back from the exploding creature and, by some miracle, felt no ripping fangs or crushing claws. The others were all around me, their spears also sinking deep into the body of our foe, their long knives out and ready for any reply.

But there was none. The beast lay writhing on the ground in the last throes after life has fled, his last victim crumpled on the dry ground where the creature had roared a few minutes ago.

And then it was still.

Two others gently approached the form of Be'gorn, and I crept up to see.

He lay on his back with his hands gripping a gaping mass in his chest, of bone and distorted muscle smothered in rich, sickly blood. His eyes were wide with the pain and his breath came in gulps between clenched teeth, his face twitching in reaction.

They raised their eyes and looked at me, my own meeting theirs. There was no word, but we knew as clearly as if a voice had shouted from the sky.

As one, we bent and gathered him up, and the others joined us. Someone took better hold than I and I dropped away, back from the beaten hunter. They carried him up the hill, and his gasps could be heard plainly as they went.

I and another returned to the place where we had left our belongings; the water in the flasks would be needed. We gathered them all and rejoined our comrades in a dry cave along the hillside. One had begun a fire in the entrance.

They had laid him in the back recess, where the sun was less bright and the air was cool, and as I brought the water flasks in, I could hear that he was still alive.

"We will need more water," someone said beside me, and I turned and followed him out to search for the spring that was said to sometimes flow here.

But when we found it, there was only a damp smear against the lowest part of sandstone, and there was nothing to do but return empty-handed.

A sickening curiosity drew us to see if Be'gorn still lived, and a trembling emptiness made us not want to know. The shadows cut dark swathes close over the bright sunbaked rocks, and the red sun nestled in its fiery bed of clouds against the horizon. The night would soon descend like a raptor, and there was no more excuse to stay away.

In the back of the cave, the most knowledgeable among us in the way of healing bent over the form of the wounded man. The others had made a meal at the small fire at the entrance, and they gave us our portions as we all hunched on the sand-rock and tried to think of home and other things far away.

When I was finished, I went to take a turn at the fallen man's side, in the flickering light of a small pine taper. Our healer looked up as I approached, and no word was exchanged between us. He rose and went to the cave's mouth and I sat near Be'gorn.

The fire from the entrance cast dancing shadows on the uneven faces of the cave's walls, and our own small flame illumined the beaded sweat on Be'gorn's tense brow.

The men at the front of the cave spoke only in low tones, their voices indistinguishable to us here.

He lay with his eyes staring at the ceiling, though I knew it was not the rough stone that he saw. His breathing was low and even, with the forced calm of acceptance.

When he spoke, his tone was feelingless; the only sign of emotion that I could hear was that his tongue was dry. His words were low and distanced.

"They think I'm going to die."

An unexpected tightness constricted my throat.

"They think so," I replied evenly.

I tipped the flask to his lips. He set his mouth. He would not drink.

I lowered my hand. If he was going to die, he would not waste water that the living might need.

Suddenly, I wanted to protest it, to disallow him the sacrifice I myself would have made if it were me.

"We will find water somewhere else," I told him.

He did not acknowledge my words.

The air was silent again for a while.

"Do you think so?" He returned to his first statement.

It was a question I wished he had not asked. This afternoon, I had certainly thought so, without a doubt. Sometimes, the scale of living tipped in an unexpected balance, but it was rare, nearly unheard of. Such injuries as he had sustained were enough to take the stomach out of any man. And I was never a raving optimist.

To tell him "no" would be lying. To tell him "yes" was more than I could bear to do. I never expected to feel my heart so strangled on account of a man who had been at odds with me my entire life.

"I think you are stronger than they estimate. I think if you see the sunrise, you will live."

My words were halting and half-faced in my mind, but they came out well and seemed so assured of themselves that I was afraid if I breathed, the trembling would betray me.

He did not move, yet I felt somehow that what I had said comforted him, taking away a little of the fear. For we all fear, when faced with the long night into the ever sleep. Those who have never felt it...have never been there.

And then I wanted to cry, like a child, for the change in him now, and for the anger I had felt toward him before. I was covered in shame for myself, as if my longing had brought this about. I had hurt over the fear that held me back, guarded over the chance it might betray me to cowardice. And I had envied his ignorance of fear and silently wished he could know it as well as I.

Now that he did...now, I could weep with the heartache of it.

I stayed there beside him, as the fire burned low in the entrance, and the others came not near. To die alone in the night was not a good way, not a way I would allow. I could not take back the lion's paw, could not take back my envy, could not change the days that lay between that first hunt and this night. When he had been lauded for his outstanding courage and I had felt the first sharp sting of what I knew.

These were written into the stone face of our life, but these hours now between the darkening and the sun were mine to choose, and I would wait with him. In atonement? No. There can be no atonement for what is past. There can only be change, for what is to come.

And I hoped that when I again saw a strong, young man, fully brave with the hardheadedness of inexperience, that I would look upon him kindly and in my deep heart be glad of what he did not yet know.

Far above us, the stars swam their courses, and as the hush of morning filled the air, I looked down at his closed eyes. Stilled. I rose and walked past the shapes of my sleeping comrades at the cave's mouth to where the sun was painting a new day in bright golds.

We had done what we had come for. The creature was dead, and the children and the women at the watering holes were safe again. The young ones would grow up, and I knew that they would hear of Be'gorn the mighty.

I would tell them.

And perhaps he would be a little wiser in the telling, a little more careful of himself and others. Perhaps that is what legends do best...improve upon the truth. There is nothing amiss with bravery and strength, but add a little wisdom to it, if you can.

Just a little wisdom...if you can.

This tale delves into the complicated relationship between fear and the shame it so often links with...especially compared to the bluster of those who are without that fear. I think it's safe to say that the older hunters carry fear with them, yet do not allow it to dictate their actions; as our main character learns is his destiny as well.

Sometimes fear is a good thing, and can keep us safe. Sometimes those without it actually create the circumstances that deserve being feared... and sometimes the intersections between all the angles leaves a more nuanced picture than first inexperience can envision. There's nothing like having lived through something to make insight so much deeper.

I know. I have been there.

And may my tellings pass on a little wisdom, if they can.

Online everywhere as E. Kaiser Writes

Save The Day

Page Zaplendam

"Wow. Did you seriously think you could make the team?" Alice asked.

Jenny looked over at her. Alice's salon-perfect blonde hair and pink, perpetually-manicured nails gave her away as the senator's daughter she was. Varsity Volleyball for three years, Alice didn't take kindly to untalented plebs from the wrong side of the tracks. Once again, Jenny felt a bout of shame and nausea swirl up from her stomach. She would always be the outcast—not only because she didn't come from an elite, moneyed family, but also because her abilities were pretty uninspiring. They certainly wouldn't be much help on a volleyball team.

She almost wished that she went to a normal school, for normal kids. She winced inside, cringing at how ungrateful she sounded. Despite how annoying most of the kids that she went to school with were, she knew she should try harder to ignore it, considering that her parents were scraping the bottom of the proverbial barrel to get her into a private school for children with abilities. Her older sister, Becca, was due to graduate soon and, in typical fashion, had outshone Jenny in just about everything, including popularity. If Becca saw this entire exchange, she'd be having fits at Jenny's inability to stand up for herself.

On the other hand, what in the world could she say? Her ability wasn't showy and loud, unlike Alice and her troupe of fans. She had...wait for it...super senses, and even then they weren't particularly bang up to the mark. In fact, whether or not they would work at all seemed hit or miss. If she was honest, she could probably use some intense training on focusing her ability. The problem was, it was not only a mental ability, which meant it didn't manifest in a way that was easily apparent, it was so rare there wasn't an instructor who could guide her in learning to control it, unless her parents paid for a private tutor, which wasn't going to happen.

Alice smirked before she turned and walked away, leaving a cloud of her signature lilac perfume behind. Jenny could swear Alice was preening, purposely ruffling and flexing the white wings which hung on her back. Next to her, her two hangers-on girlfriends linked their arms through hers and strutted away.

Jenny turned back to the roster, blinking back tears; Alice was right. Why did she ever try out in the first place? She never should have taken Becca's advice, no matter how hopelessly and unrealistically optimistic her older sister was. If Jenny's abilities were reliable, she would actually be an asset to the team. As it was, she was just a clumsy, fumbling dork who had the nerve to aim higher than she should have. Like Icarus. She snorted back another tear.

An arm slung around her shoulder. Jenny turned to see Becca's smiling face.

"Hey, li'l sis. Did you make the cut?!" Becca asked brightly.

"As if," Jenny said, rolling her eyes. Becca's face fell, but after a moment lit up again like a beacon.

"That's okay. You're an awesome volleyball player. If I can do it, you can do it!"

"Yeah, right. It's not like a senator's daughter just made you look like a complete idiot in front of the whole school," Jenny said.

"Aw, come on, it's not that bad," Becca said.

"Whatever." Jenny walked away in a huff, slinging her backpack over her shoulder. Okay, granted, even though there was an audience, it wasn't the whole school. But why couldn't Becca ever understand? Not everyone was a ray of sunshine. Not everyone excelled at their abilities. Heck, not everyone had flashy abilities. As she walked away, she could feel the need for a really good, deep cry coming on. Her solitude was guaranteed an interruption though, as behind her the squeak of sneakers told her Colin was coming up at a run.

"Hey, how'd it go?" he asked, matching his long stride to her own.

"Don't even ask." Jenny kept walking, headed for the double doors on the abandoned side of the school. She didn't want to have to face Alice's snubs again, and she for sure didn't want Colin, who seemed invariably cool and impervious to the slights of their wealthier peers, seeing her all weepy. It wasn't easy having a sister who was so popular *and* a best friend who was universally recognized as the class hunk.

It was kind of amazing that all the popularity had never gone to his head, that they were still the same friends they had been since they met in first grade. It just made her realize that she had all the more reason to feel grateful to Mom and Dad. If her and Becca's education hadn't been so important to them, odds were she never would have been friends with Colin in the first place. She would have ended up in a public school instead of the prestigious private school they had attended through eighth grade.

Still, it wasn't easy. She had to ignore a lot of cracks from other girls about her being so undeserving of his friendship. Sometimes, they weren't so easy to ignore, because honestly, she didn't really know what it was Colin saw in her.

"Is Becca coming with us?" he asked, interrupting her reverie as they left the building.

"Not if I can help it. I've had about as much as I can take of the senior class at the moment," Jenny said. She huffed out a sigh, trying her hardest to let go of her disappointment in herself. "Where'd you park?"

Colin grabbed her arm, bringing her to a stop. Concern flared in his eyes.

"Come on, Jenny. What's wrong?" he asked.

For just a second, Jenny was reminded again how good-looking he was. Considering his strength abilities, his boy-next-door good looks, and his sincere interest in people, there were more than a few girls in school who would be more than happy to be "friends" with him.

"It's Becca. It's Alice. Just... Everyone. Or, whatever. I guess it's just me," Jenny said. She sighed and hesitated, not wanting to appear petty or jealous, but wanting to be honest. "You all have really cool abilities. You are invincible and crazy strong, Becca's fast, and Alice—" Jenny paused to expel an exasperated breath. "Alice is a gorgeous, fabulously wealthy senator's daughter with wings. White wings."

"And?" he asked flatly.

"What do you mean, 'and'? Isn't that enough? What do I have? *Super senses.* Big. Whoop."

"Popularity isn't everything." Colin's green eyes filled with frustration. Frustration at her? The situation?

"Easy for you to say, you aren't a complete reject. And at least she's given you a white feather."

"Jenny, do you want a white feather?" He arched a brow at her, disbelieving.

"No...yes...no." Jenny shrugged her shoulders and shook her head. It wasn't that she put much stock into Alice's stupid signs of favor. "I just want an ability that isn't completely lame."

Colin rolled his eyes and whacked her on the shoulder. "Whatever," he said, and Jenny tried not to feel hurt that he brushed it off so lightly.

Colin started walking toward his car. "You comin'?"

Jenny turned to follow him, determined to shrug off her dejection. She had never been a fan of Eeyore anyway. The least she could do is be grateful for the many blessings she had in her life, like her parents, Becca, and Colin. In the grand scheme of things, Alice—and all her perfections—really didn't matter. At least, that's what Jenny told herself.

"When are you going to get rid of your outdated clunker?" she asked.

"This baby is classic, I'll have you know," he said, stroking its paint-chipped hood. "Just wait until you see what she looks like when I finish her."

"Yeah, I don't think it's going to matter. You won't even be able to buy gas for it once they get rid of fossil fuels," Jenny said. Her voice trailed away as she looked across the parking lot. Movement at the other end of it caught her attention, and she stopped, transfixed by what she was seeing.

Alice struggled with a man, her white wings flapping wildly as he manhandled her toward a black van. Jenny looked around, but the parking lot was empty except for Colin's beat-up Impala and the black van.

"Uh, Colin, you seeing what I'm seeing?" she asked, stuttering.

"No. What?" Colin looked up from trying to find the right key for his car, his body tensing at the sight. "Oh-my-gosh."

As they watched, the man slammed the back doors of the van shut and jumped into the driver's seat. Suddenly, Jenny's brain kicked into overdrive and out of the frozen horror that had stolen over her.

"Colin! Do something!" Jenny screamed.

Colin broke into a sprint after the van, but the van's wheels screeched out as it peeled off down the road, leaving Colin in a cloud of dust.

"Alice just got kidnapped!" Jenny said to herself and covered her mouth with her hand. Colin ran back to his car.

"C'mon, get in. We have to follow them," he said, a hard line of tension evident in his clenched jaw.

Jenny slid into the passenger's seat and Colin threw the car into drive.

"Wait, shouldn't we call somebody? Like, the cops or something?" Jenny asked, clutching her fingers together to keep them from trembling.

"Here." Colin reached out a hand. "Gimme your phone. I'll call. See if you can use your senses to keep track of Alice."

Jenny tossed him her phone, but quailed at his request to track Alice. It was a lot of pressure and she couldn't screw this up. After all, it was quite possible Alice's life might depend on her ability to track them. Fear-induced nausea—the fear of failure—threatened to overwhelm her.

She didn't like Alice, sure, and if Jenny had a colder heart, she could easily see herself thinking, "good riddance to bad rubbish," but that just wasn't her. Whether she liked Alice or not, Jenny and Colin were the only two people in the world capable of doing something to help Alice at this moment. She took several deep, calming breaths, swallowed down her nerves, and closed her eyes, determined to do whatever it took to focus her ability.

She forced herself to relax, opening her mind in the peculiar way her ability required. A myriad of sensations began to flood in, razor-sharp in their clarity, but also overlapping and muddled, like really good stereo tracks played too loud and at the same time: the sounds of the wheels going over the highway, the roaring engine, the smells of the restaurants they were passing by, Colin's rugged body spray, the sensation of hot leather against her back, and the vibrations of the car. Everything swirled together in a massive sensate vacuum in her head, blocking her ability to pick up the trace.

She pressed her fingers to her temples, fear of failure overtaking her again and splitting her attention. Her breaths started coming faster and faster.

"Come on, Jenny, I need you," Colin said, driving with one hand and dialing 911 with the other.

Jenny's eyes popped open and she stared at him aghast. "I-I can't do it!"

Colin thumped the steering wheel with his hand.

"Yes, you can," he shouted, and then he dropped his voice. "Focus! This is what you do. Remember, focus and calm. You can do this."

Jenny took a calming breath, squeezed her eyes shut again, and bent her head down onto her knees. The sensations came flooding in once more. At first, she tried to pluck out what she needed from the stream—the occasional whiff of Alice's lilac perfume—but her mind was inevitably overwhelmed with everything else, especially the visceral thrum of Colin's blasted Impala. Desperate, she ripped the rumbling sensation aside and mentally tossed it.

To her surprise, it didn't reappear. Slowly, and then faster and faster, she began identifying and discarding anything that wasn't helping her locate Alice until, at last, she had filtered out all the extra sensations one by one and only the smell of Alice's lilac perfume dominated her senses.

In her mind's eye, she could see the route the van took, like a hazy, purple, floating path—without picture or vision and yet perfectly directional. She wouldn't be able to draw a map or provide street names, but she could "see" the route they took and knew exactly where to turn. Her eyes flew open as she realized they were about to miss their turn.

"Turn left," she shouted.

The car's rear end fishtailed as Colin spun the steering wheel, shouting into the cellphone meanwhile. Thankfully, oncoming traffic was a good hundred feet away, so Jenny's retroactive fears were relieved. It would have been beyond disastrous to end up in a deadly car accident while trying to track their classmate.

After five minutes, the road cleared of businesses and Colin stomped on the gas. On either side of them, open fields gave way to forests. Their quarry came into view as a black blip at the end of the road.

"Jenny, the cops are telling us to stop following them," Colin said softly.

"What?! No! How are they going to know where he goes? I can do this!"

"I know that," he said, again making sure not to raise his voice above a low pitch.

It was sweet of him to be considerate of her concentration, but truth be told, now that she had learned how to filter the sensations, the practice of doing so became easier and easier, to the point that she was surprised there was ever a time—much less twenty minutes ago—when she wasn't able to do it. Hopefully, *all* aspects of her abilities would come as easily and strongly.

And then, just as she was congratulating herself on finally getting a handle on her abilities, a deer darted onto the road. Time seemed to slow to milliseconds. The startled creature whipped its head around, freezing mid-leap at the sight of the vehicle, which was impossibly weird, but something she chalked up to her mind playing tricks on her.

She couldn't tell how long the car, in her distorted sense of time, drifted toward the animal, who had not yet managed to do more than plant all four of its hooves on the ground. But she didn't want to hit the deer, so everything in her shouted at the stupid animal to move on. Fortunately, a moment later (could she call it a moment? Was it more like a nanosecond?) the deer ran into the brush on the other side of the road. She heaved a sigh of relief and then suddenly, time caught up with her and resumed its normal pace.

Colin, in what felt like a woefully belated move, slammed on the brakes, tossed the phone, and twisted the steering wheel with both hands. Jenny screamed, bracing herself against the dash and door, and shut her eyes. The car began spinning one hundred and eighty degrees, skewing off the road and onto the easement. With a jolt, the right rear end slammed into something on the easement and the other three wheels lifted up off the ground. For a split second, a spasm of terror went through Jenny that the car was going to roll, but then it pounded back onto the grass with a creaking thump, rattling her teeth.

Pain lanced through her head, and she lost sight of the mental pathway to Alice. Her body flushed hot and then cold, and her teeth began chattering involuntarily as her brain began to accustom itself to the loss of the vibrant sensation overload.

Colin dropped his head onto the steering wheel, breathing hard. He turned off the engine and then turned to look at Jenny, who was still gripping the dash and door as if her life depended on it.

"We're still alive," she panted, cracking open an eye and wincing at the pain that accompanied the light.

"Guardian angels," Colin said.

Jenny sighed and dropped her head back against the seat, closing her eyes again, because she suddenly felt too weak to even open them.

"You okay?" Colin asked. "You are looking...pale."

"I think I just need a minute," she murmured.

"You sure? I mean, you look, like, death pale."

Jenny cracked open an eye at him. His gaze was intense, skeptical, and concerned.

"Mapping withdrawals, I think," she said. "I'm not really used to this whole thing."

He nodded knowingly, satisfied and relieved. "That'll pass. Everyone goes through that. I mean, not as late as you're going through it—"

"What? When did you go through it?" she asked.

He looked abashed, or maybe just embarrassed for her?

"Um, around twelve years old, when my abilities started coming in."

"What? You never told me that," she said, smacking his shoulder with the back of her hand. "You suck at this best friend thing."

"I didn't want to look like a wimp. And I had to kind of learn how to control them pretty fast, unless Mom and Dad were going to have to constantly fix the house."

She laughed softly, but it was short-lived given how epically they had failed.

"We better see how bad it is." Colin got out of the car and went around to the back. He whistled low. The right rear end was crumpled into a fallen tree trunk, the tire punctured and deflating.

"How bad?" Jenny asked.

"Bad. We'll have to call a tow truck."

Jenny sighed, her thoughts going back to Alice and the sickly sweet smell of fear that had permeated her enemy's lilac perfume. She groaned at herself in frustration. Her abilities hadn't helped her avoid that deer in time. If they had, maybe she and Colin would still be on their way.

"Looks like the cops got what they wanted after all," Jenny said.

The next morning, Jenny sat at the table, absentmindedly nibbling on toast and sipping orange juice. Mom and Dad were still visiting Grandma Benson in Wisconsin, but they'd be back tomorrow night. She didn't know whether to be grateful or upset that they weren't there right then.

Behind her came the droning noise of the morning news. Becca sat on the sofa, eating a bowl of cereal.

"Can you believe she was kidnapped?" Jenny asked her sister.

"Crazy," Becca replied in between bites, her attention fixed on the TV.

Jenny was about to ask if any of Alice's friends had mentioned anything about it to Becca, but then her attention was caught by the newscaster's announcement.

"Turn it up! It's about Alice," Jenny said, abandoning her toast and sliding onto the sofa next to her sister.

"The kidnapper released a ransom note a short time ago. It was emailed to three different news agencies and appeared on the internet, where it spread within a matter of minutes. Fair warning: viewers may find the following video disturbing," the newscaster reported. A video came on, showing a trembling and bound Alice, her eyes covered and mouth gagged. A male voice came through on the audio.

"People of America, you are pawns. Pawns in a game of political and economic powers. These powers are our politicians and huge corporations. To them, your families mean nothing. Your children mean nothing. You mean nothing. Until we fight back, they will continue to pay each other off, cover each other's backs, and use all of us for their own gain. This is a call to arms. To fund the Green Militia, we are asking Senator Livingston to pay a ransom for his daughter, the same senator who, among other payoffs, received campaign contributions in exchange for his silence about toxins dumped along the Columbia River. This is not for personal gain. I repeat, this is not for personal gain."

The camera pulled in closer to Alice. She was trembling with fear, her head swinging from side to side in agitation. Despite Jenny's aversion to Alice's attitude, she wouldn't wish this on her worst enemy.

The voice continued, *"This is his daughter, Alice. She drives an expensive sports car and wears designer clothes, all of which is paid for with the labor of our backs. She attends an exclusive prep school in order to further her understanding of you and me as objects to be used and discarded. Like father, like daughter. We are going to turn the tide against political corruption. The war starts now."*

The video cut back to the newscaster, who went on to report the amount of the ransom and the foreign bank account it was to be routed to.

"Police are still searching the area but have little information to go on and no communication with the kidnappers. Moments ago, Senator Livingston made a statement to the press concerning the disappearance."

The image of Senator Livingston holding a press conference outside his multimillion dollar mansion came on.

"Alice, I won't give up—" the senator began, just before Jenny's phone rang. She picked it up and answered it, not bothering to look at the screen.

"Are you watching this?" Colin asked, his voice tinny and a delayed echo of the senator's speech coming through over the line.

"Yeah," she said. Too stunned and horrified to express her feelings, she listened in silence while Senator Livingston promised dire retribution if any harm befell Alice, denied the allegations about the campaign funds, promised the full amount of the ransom, and pleaded for more time.

"He's not going to let her go," Colin said.

Jenny's eyes drifted over to Becca. She got up and went outside to sit on the old swing that hung from an oak tree.

"You think he'll just kill her when he gets the money?" Jenny asked.

"No, I don't think he'll just kill her. I think he'll kill her in a way that will be attention-getting."

"Like, bomb a building?"

"Yeah, but not where other people could get hurt. He wouldn't want to alienate the public."

Becca opened the door to the house.

"Hey, they just canceled school," Becca hollered. "They're afraid he might have planted a bomb."

"Thanks." Jenny turned her attention back to Colin on the other end of the phone and snorted. "Speaking of bombing buildings, did you hear that?"

"Yeah, just saw it on the news."

They were silent, contemplating everything. Jenny couldn't help it; she still felt like she had to do something. Admittedly, the cops were looking everywhere for Alice, especially up north toward Two Rivers, where the road led.

"They are flying people in from out of state. Specialists, but it will take another day or so before they're here," Colin said, updating her.

"This is stupid," Jenny said. "They have a whole group of 'specialists' that went to the same school Alice did, why don't they use us?"

"We're kids, what do we know? And they wouldn't want us to get hurt. Plus, you think any of *our* parents would want us anywhere near this thing? Everyone's parents are probably all worried their kids are next. All hunkered down in their safe rooms and waiting for this to blow over."

"And you, what about your parents?" Jenny asked. "You know my parents aren't rich enough for Becca and me to be targeted, but we *do* go to school there."

"My parents are just rich. They're not politicians. But, yeah, like you said, maybe that doesn't matter to someone who's obviously so mentally derailed. It's a rich kids' school."

Jenny chewed her lip, thinking. The specialists wouldn't be here for another day, and that day could mean the difference between life and death for Alice—especially considering the kidnapper would know when those specialists were going to get here. It wasn't as if the local media was going to hide when they arrived in town.

"Jenny, you there?" Colin asked.

"Yeah. I was just thinking, the kidnapper knows when those specialists are going to get here, won't he kill her before that happens?"

"Probably, especially if he doesn't get the money."

"I just—" She swallowed, unsure of how receptive Colin was going to be to her thoughts. "We have to do something."

Colin was silent for a moment.

"You want to try and hunt them down again?" Colin asked.

"Well...if the cops aren't doing it."

"You know we can't ask for their help. If they caught a whiff of what we were doing, they would make sure you stayed out of the way." He paused before resuming. "I'm not even sure about it. Of course, I'll be there, but if anything happened to you..."

"What? You'll die of a broken heart?" Jenny rolled her eyes. "Puuullease, Colin. I'll be fine. You'll be there. I won't do anything stupid and heroic. I just want to find her. Have a little faith. Once we know where she is, we can call it in."

Jenny waited, listening to his breathing over the phone.

"Say you'll come with me. You know you don't want me going by myself," Jenny prodded.

Colin groaned.

"All right. But we do it my way," he said.

"You mean *my* way, because I'm the one with the super senses."

She could almost hear him rolling his eyes.

"Whatever. I'll use my brother's Razor and pick you up in fifteen. Down by the main road. Don't be late," Colin said.

"'K," Jenny said and then hung up.

She ran up to her room, slipped into some hiking clothes, and prepared a daypack with water, a few granola bars, and a basic survival kit. At the last moment, she threw her father's hunting knife in as well. Who knew what they might find themselves up against.

"You headed out?" Becca asked, poking her head out of her bedroom. Jenny held back a wince. Becca was in charge whenever Mom and Dad were gone, and there was a 99.9% chance she'd say Jenny couldn't go if she knew what she was up to.

"Yeah, you need anything?" Jenny asked, playing it cool.

"No, but you should probably stay away from any public places, y'know, because of the bomb threat."

"That was at the school, though," Jenny said. "Anyway, Colin is picking me up, and we were going to go for a drive in his brother's Razor, so I'll be fine."

Becca pursed her lips and Jenny was afraid her older sister was going to say she couldn't go, but then Becca nodded—probably agreeing to let her go because Colin was such a titan. "Okay. Have fun. But be careful."

"I will," Jenny said. She snatched up her bag then ran down the stairs and down the driveway.

Colin floated up the street in his brother's sleek new Razor. Hovercraft were all the rage for the wealthy, and Colin's brother, Jim, a gadget nerd if ever there was one, wasn't going to pass on something like that. Despite her grumpy twinge of annoyance at the ostentation, Jenny had to admit that she was looking forward to the ride. It was way more luxe than Colin's hobby clunker. And then she gave herself a good smack inside for thinking something so frivolous when someone's life was on the line.

She climbed in under the pneumatic door and settled into the seat.

"Sweet ride, huh?" Colin said, voicing what she had thought only moments before.

"Let's just hope your brother doesn't kill you for taking off with his car."

"I asked permission...sort of." Colin thumbed the drive panel and the Razor moved forward smoothly, navigating the twists and turns of the suburban neighborhood.

"What does that even mean?" Jenny asked.

"I left him a note. Told him he'd get it back without a scratch before tonight."

"Let's hope so," Jenny said. "How long do you think it will take to get out there?"

Colin pulled onto the highway, merging into traffic and receiving honks from the other vehicles on the road—a motley assortment of older gas cars, newer electric ones, and the rare hovercraft.

"I'm hoping it won't take more than a half hour. If I drive fast."

"I just want to get there in one piece," Jenny said. "Hopefully, I'll be able to pick up the scent again if they are within a five-mile radius."

Colin looked over at her, impressed.

"Wow, you can smell five miles away? I don't even want to know what that means about smelling someone right next to you. I think I'd be dying. How do you stand it?"

Jenny rummaged around in her backpack, searching for a granola bar. She hadn't finished breakfast, and even though she should save them for later, she was starving.

"My intense senses only kick in when I choose to make them."

Colin looked relieved.

"But let's just say, I'm glad you showered this morning," Jenny added around a bite of granola bar.

"Hey!" Colin protested, but then grew serious again. "What about if the trail is old? It's been almost a full day."

"Half, but it won't really be like a trail this time. It'll be more like a wide-range homing beacon. And time shouldn't matter, as long as we're within five miles. Fear sends out a strong pheromone."

"You know what Alice's fear smells like?" Colin was obviously grossed out.

"Yeah, it's...uh, not good. Makes me afraid too, like I can kind of feel what she's feeling." Jenny took a swig out of one of the water bottles and then put everything away. "What did you bring? Come prepared?"

"For what?" Colin glanced over at her and then stomped on the brakes as someone unexpectedly changed lanes. They kept moving. "Did I bring my 'bomb defuser kit? No. Left it back at the ranch."

"So, sarcasm aside, you brought nothing?"

"Nothing but my lovely self. Honestly, Jenny, think about it. We aren't doing anything crazy here—just figure out exactly where they are so we can call it in to the police."

"Our cellphones won't work out there."

"Which is why—" Colin reached behind her seat and dumped something in her lap. "I brought the sat phone."

"Okay. One, you told me you didn't bring anything. Two, you have a sat phone? Why?"

"Technically, I didn't bring it, it was already in the car," Colin said. He pulled off the highway and turned onto the street that led from the school. "Secondly, Jim likes to take off into the boonies—base-jumping, spelunking...he always keeps a sat phone in the car."

"Huh, guess he would need to," Jenny muttered, trying to hold back her disgust at Colin's brother's lifestyle. The fields started to be replaced by thick stands of trees until finally the trees came together to form unbroken walls of forest on both sides.

Jenny suddenly noticed that the now-familiar smell of Alice's fear-tainted lilac perfume had begun to steal over her senses. It was a huge relief, considering she had feared placing the scent would require as much concentration as it did yesterday. Maybe once a scent was identified, it was easier to distinguish again?

"Yeah, I know," she said, touching her nose.

"All right. Guess that means we're close enough." Colin pulled off the road behind some low brush. "Just as well, considering they'll probably have the cops down at that other scene."

"We can't just leave the car here, Colin. Someone will steal it. And then your brother really will kill you."

"Not to worry." Colin keyed some buttons on the panel. "One of the coolest features about this vehicle is its stealth mode."

"You're kidding. That's ridiculous."

"Come on, let's go." Colin climbed out of the car and Jenny followed. She surveyed the abandoned field and then the empty road. The cherry red Razor would be hidden by some scrub, but if its stealth mode wasn't top notch, there wasn't a chance it would be missed by passersby. Was Colin really going to just leave it here?

She turned around to ask him, but her mouth sagged open. The car was gone.

"Wha—?"

"Put out your hand," Colin said with a smirk.

She put out her hand and her fingers smashed into the cold, smooth, and now invisible sides of the Razor.

"Okay," Jenny said. "Invisible vehicle. Check. Good to have around when one must escape."

"Got your bag of goodies?"

Jenny nodded.

"'K, then. Lead on."

Jenny closed her eyes and took a deep, long whiff. In her mind's eye, a mist of purple sprouted before her; the other scents of deer, raccoon, and wildcat were mere shadows in comparison. It was dimmer closer to her and stronger, deeper, and more profuse farther away in a northeasterly direction.

"Come on, this way." Jenny began walking into the forest at a diagonal from the road. It was impossible to tell just how far away Alice was. She couldn't see the specific point where the trail ended yet, but she was starting to realize that one of the peripheral scents overlapped Alice's. She feared it smelled like triumph.

"Come on, Jenny, we have to be close," Colin said. "We've been hiking for four hours, crossed two streams, three embankments, and more hills than I can count. And, worst of all, we're down to one granola bar."

"Aw, you getting worn out, big boy?" Jenny looked over at him. He wasn't even breaking a sweat, even after jumping the twenty-foot creek he had just cleared with her on his back. He didn't bother to respond to her completely undeserved dig but sent her a scathing look over his shoulder.

A twinge of guilt came with her teasing. Truth be told, she was the one slowing them down. He had shortened his ever sure-footed stride in order to help her keep up.

"We're close," Jenny reassured him. "I can see where she is now, or at least where the trail ends."

They continued walking for another mile before she hissed at him to stop.

"What?" he asked.

"Shhh...just there, up ahead. Do you see the clearing?" She couldn't say what it was, but all her senses were suddenly buzzing in a strange way, every instinct of fear sending an unsettling feeling into her gut that yelled at her to run away. But she wasn't about to abandon Alice, especially not when it seemed they were so close to their goal. She was pretty sure that if Colin had any idea of how bad a feeling she was having right now, he'd insist on their returning.

"Uh, no. I don't see anything," Colin said.

"Well, there's a clearing about a quarter mile up ahead. We'll have to go quietly."

"What do you mean, go quietly? I'm just going to call it in. If the trail ends there, that's probably where they are."

"Oh. Right." Jenny shrugged the backpack off her shoulder and handed him the sat phone.

Colin thumbed the button to turn it on. Nothing.

"You've got to be kidding me. It's not charged." Colin shook it and held it to his ear. Was he expecting it to buzz or something?

"What? You didn't check it?!" Jenny asked, her high-pitched whisper breaking in disbelief.

"No, I assumed he kept it charged." Colin looked in the bag for batteries but didn't find anything but the vehicle charger cord. "I could run back to the Razor."

Jenny slapped her forehead. "I just realized, assuming you didn't get lost in the woods on the trek back, what were we going to tell the cops anyway? 'She's over that way somewhere?'"

"What else are we supposed to do?" His jaw clamped down hard. "I knew this wasn't a good idea."

Jenny looked at him and raised her eyebrows.

"You're not thinking of—no. Uh, huh. I'm not getting myself killed for Miss Priss," Colin said.

"Please, don't overwhelm me with your chivalry," Jenny snapped. "Honestly, Colin, you could probably crush rocks with your bare hands if you wanted to."

"Doesn't mean I'm impervious to bombs," he mumbled. "Come on, Jenny, we're in over our heads. Let's just go back and call it in from the car."

Jenny shuffled her feet, disappointed. She couldn't just leave Alice out here to die while the police scrambled to find her and waited on specialists to drop in. Nor would they let her show them where she had tracked Alice to. It wasn't as if her ability was hugely reliable or well-understood by those at school, much less appreciated and lauded. She could either risk leaving Alice and calling it in, which might make the difference between life and death for Alice (could she live with that kind of guilt if it did happen that way?) or she could take a stand here and now.

"I'm going," she said. "You can go—and probably get lost in the woods trying to get back to your Razor without me—or you can come and help me save Alice."

Tense seconds passed before Colin heaved a sigh of annoyance and handed over the useless sat phone. With a nod, Jenny stuffed it into her backpack and began leading the way.

The quarter mile felt like it went quickly, even though they were all but creeping through the trees and brush, but maybe that was just her dread and worry skewing her sense of time. The clearing came into view and they stood inside the tree line, watching for anyone to come out of the abandoned utility building that sat in the clearing's center, surrounded by old power line supports. The black van sat outside, backed up near the door.

Jenny closed her eyes and tuned out the sound of Colin breathing next to her, the rustle of the breeze through the trees. Just barely, she could hear the murmur of a voice, a male voice. She sharpened her hearing that much more, straining to isolate the sound.

"I think they're underground," she whispered. "His voice is really muffled. I can't hear Alice at all."

Colin looked at her, admiration in his eyes. "You are sooo cool."

Jenny smirked at him, before the seriousness of the moment hit her again. They were about to lay it all on the line...and all for someone she didn't even like. Alice was going to owe her big time. "You ready for this?" she asked.

"What's the plan?" he asked.

"Charge the building? Hope he doesn't have a gun?" Why hadn't she thought this far ahead?

"It'll take more than a few bullets to bring me down," Colin said. He sounded cocksure, which had Jenny drawing back, blanching. The thought of losing Colin smacked her with a wave of horror. He could be killed. She could be killed. What was she thinking? This was a horrible, stupid plan!

"No, we can't do this. What if you die? What if I die?" Jenny whispered in a panic.

"Jenny, what are you doing? You can't stop now. That's what I was saying back there. *Now* you change your mind?" Colin shook his head.

The sound of muffled screams pierced through her worry and her eyes settled on the building again.

"Did you hear that?" Jenny whimpered, biting into a finger to keep from crying out.

"No. What was it?" His eyes met hers, concern reflected in their depths.

"Alice. Sounds like she's screaming through a gag."

"That's it. I'm going in," Colin said.

Before she could stop him (because, again, this was a horrible, stupid plan), Colin took off at a run for the door of the utility building. She screamed at him in a whisper to stop—which Colin completely ignored. She was still whisper-screaming at him when she was surprised to see him stumble to a stop and then have difficulty getting up. It was an oddly timed fall, considering Colin was typically as sure-footed as a mountain goat and he was running over level ground.

He attempted getting to his feet again and then shot her a dirty look as if she was stopping him from moving forward. She shrugged her shoulders in innocence and shook her head. Whatever it was that had him stumbling, it was hardly a good idea to linger in the open ground. What was wrong with him?

Get up, Colin! she thought in her head, and then gasped in relief when he regained his feet. She waved her hands at him to come back; he hesitated and then shook his head and moved again, racing for the door to the building. She groaned, watching his progress through her fingers. What if he got himself killed? And he wouldn't even be here if she hadn't been so insistent!

Jenny sprang into action, sprinting up the road toward the building and ignoring every instinct that told her this was the worst idea she had had yet. But second thoughts or no, there wasn't a chance she'd let him face that psycho kidnapper alone.

The door was unlocked. A dust-covered desk stood in one corner next to a file cabinet with its empty drawers pulled out. The interior looked like no one had been inside for years, except for the footprints that led to a closet door. Colin stood off to one side of the room, arms crossed over his chest.

"There," Jenny whispered and pointed at the footprints.

"I see it."

"They're underground, so there must be steps going down."

Colin nodded his head. He released his arms and shook himself, danced back and forth on his toes, and then clenched his fists. "Ready?"

"Whenever you are, Rocky...I guess."

Colin nodded at her and Jenny threw the door open. It screeched, announcing their presence, and Colin ran down the steps. She followed and saw a light on in the room at the bottom.

Colin was already out of sight in the room when the shots rang out, two in succession. Jenny gasped and cowered against the wall in the stairwell. Frozen. Fear pulled her between running out and staying put, hoping the gunman wouldn't know she was there and that she could somehow get away.

Before she could decide, a man stepped into view, a pistol trained on her.

He didn't look particularly threatening. Other than the fact that he was holding a gun, and the knowledge that he was keeping Alice tied up, he might have been any one of the long, lanky, middle-aged men she came across when she went shopping or visited the library. His length of paternal, meticulously combed, salt-and-pepper beard was an innocuous and strange contrast to the light in his eyes that declared he was a zealot. Nevertheless, was it too much to hope that he could reasoned with?

"Of all the *stupid* ideas," he said. He waved the gun, indicating that she was to go into the room. Jenny raised her hands defensively and complied. As soon as she rounded the corner, she saw Colin standing against the wall, hands raised. Blood was starting to seep through one shoulder and a line of blood welled up on his cheek. Jenny ran over to him, her hands shaking. What had they got themselves into?

"Jenny." Colin tilted his head toward the corner. A monitor displayed a video feed with Alice wearing a bomb vest. Jenny felt herself collapse inside. Alice wasn't even in this room. She was close, but not here. Jenny had got it completely wrong.

"I almost took your friend's head off. Now, that would not have been a pretty sight to see." The man walked in front of them, keeping the gun trained in one hand. Jenny noticed a detonator in his other hand. The man's eyes followed her glance. "That's right. Your girlfriend goes boom if either of you move an inch."

"You'll never get away with this!" Jenny said. It sounded really lame and pathetic just then, like an elementary school kid standing up to a high school bully.

"Oh, but I will." He smiled. The chirping of a phone interrupted him. He holstered the gun on his hip and pulled a sat phone out of his pocket. He looked at it, his smile broadening. "In fact, the money came in just now."

What does that mean? Jenny thought, anxiety causing her heart to race. They had to get out of here.

"Y-you have your money, so let us go. All of us. Alice too. That's what you wanted, right? The money?" Jenny swallowed, knowing what his response would be before he said it. They had seen his face.

"I don't think so." The man pulled the gun from his holster and raised the detonator. "She wasn't ever going to go free anyway. And now, sadly, neither are you."

Jenny's blood boiled over with dread. She felt her fingers go cold as sweat broke out on her brow. She wasn't going to die like this. Alice wasn't going to die like this. Not like this.

Time slowed into milliseconds as Jenny's senses kicked into overdrive. Her eyes registered the movement of his arms in slow motion as the man brought up the detonator and the gun. *Do something! Somebody, do something!* Jenny screamed inside. *Make him stop!*

"No!" she screamed, reaching out her hands as if she could make him stop the motion of his thumbs by the sheer force of her will alone. She waited for the boom of the gun to announce the shots, but nothing happened. He stood there, his eyes fixed on her, a triumphant grin frozen on his face.

Seconds passed. What was he waiting for?

Jenny licked her lips and glanced over at Colin.

"Are you—are you going to shoot us?" she asked the man.

No response.

More seconds ticked by.

"Hello?"

Colin took a tentative step forward. The man didn't respond or bat an eyelash. In fact, he didn't move at all. What was going on?

Jenny, her hands shaking, took a step forward, ready to jump back in case he moved. But he didn't. Colin moved to stand in front of him and waved a hand in front of his face. Still no response.

"Wha-what happened?" Jenny asked.

"I don't know. But he seems...unable to move." Colin tested the theory, gently pushing down on the man's arm. It tilted down a bit, but sprung back up when Colin released it.

"What'd you do?" Colin asked.

"Me? Nothing." Jenny felt her mouth go dry as she realized that she *had* done it. She had willed with every part of her that he stop. And he had. He couldn't move and they could get away. Even while she was collapsing inside with relief, nausea rolled through her at the realization that she could do that to someone. She shook her head. Now was not the time to be thinking about these things. She had to be strong, because who knew how long they had before the effect wore off.

"Maybe—maybe we should get the detonator and the gun?" Jenny asked.

"Yeah, you find something to tie him up with," Colin agreed, carefully prying the detonator and the gun out of the man's stiff fingers. "This is creepy."

In a matter of minutes, the man was bound as best they could with his mannequin-like posture. They called the cops with the man's sat phone and then commenced a hunt for Alice, who they discovered outside in a cellar some hundred feet away. Alice sobbed and shook with relief when they released her. Her wings had been clipped so deeply that the white, short-feathered arms were little more than ungainly, bloodied appendages on her back. They would grow back, of course, but until they healed, they would be painful and unsightly. Jenny couldn't help but feel pity for her.

A bevy of cops and EMTs swarmed the premises not long after, and then a few minutes after that, as if the cosmos sensed her attention was no longer on him, or that she didn't require him to remain frozen, the kidnapper "unfroze." Jenny and Colin watched as he was taken away, raving insensibly about how those with abilities were abominations that shouldn't be allowed to enter the world.

While the cops were taking statements and treating both Alice and Colin, Jenny tried her best not to think about how exactly she had managed to stop the guy. She also did her best not to think about how much trouble she was going to be in when Mom and Dad got home. Talk about having the grounding of the century.

Nevertheless, the thought percolated at the back of her mind that a terrifying, incredibly splashy, and dangerous ability had manifested itself. Telekinesis was no joking matter. It far and away trumped wings, super speed, strength, or just about any other ability that was considered enviable at school. What would Colin say?

"Miss," a blue-uniformed cop snagged her on the shoulder. "We're going to need you to speak with Detective Marks, give us a full explanation on your telekinetic ability."

Jenny looked up at him, confused, and then over to Colin for help in explaining. How in the world was she supposed to explain this? She didn't even really understand how it had happened in the first place.

"I—uh, I don't really—" Jenny stammered.

"We'll be right there, officer," Colin called out. The officer turned away and Colin came up to her, grasping both her arms in his hands. For a moment, he just stared down at her, an unreadable expression in his eyes. "You saved my life. Our lives."

Jenny blew air out through her mouth and dropped her gaze to his chest. One of her hands settled on his bound shoulder.

"By accident," she said. "I still don't even understand what happened."

"Don't you?" he asked, lifting her chin with a finger. "I felt what you did when I was running toward the building."

Her brows came together in confusion.

"When I fell down?" he prompted. "You didn't want me to keep running, did you?"

"I—" She frowned, the realization dawning on her. "No, I didn't. You felt that?"

"Oh, yeah," he said. Amusement settled in the corners of his eyes before he nodded in the direction of the waiting detective. "Just tell him that this is all new to you and what happened, what you were thinking when it happened."

"You don't..." She swallowed and looked away from him, afraid to see his expression when she finished her question. "You don't think I'm a freak?"

"No." He chuckled and wrapped his arms around her, bringing her in close against his chest. "If anything, I'm kinda in awe of you right now, like, in all the best ways. And really happy for you, of course. And I do not mind at all being the first to take credit for having said you are special, long before this ability ever manifested itself."

Jenny smiled, her eyes watering. For a moment, Jenny laid her head against him, feeling like here was the safest, most reliable place in the world to be. And then she almost dropped to the floor as he bent his head and kissed her lightly just on the outside of her mouth. He stepped back, still holding her arms, and she blushed.

"What was that for?" she asked.

"You saved the day. Least I could do." He winked and then turned her around and gave her a gentle push toward the detective.

She moved away from him, biting the inside of her cheek to keep down the sudden giddy elation that filled her. Not only did she have a great best friend (and dare she hope, possibly more someday?), she also had the coolest ability of anyone she knew. Alice had nothin' on her.

Page Zaplendam is a longtime fan of science fiction everything, dystopian novels, folk lore, fairy tales, and Regency romance. She has been a contributor to several science fiction anthologies, owns a novel editing service, and occasionally blogs.

An engaging and humorous entertainer, she loves doing live interviews, public speaking, and sharing about writing and marketing craft both on her blog and on 10 Minute Novelists, the Catholic Writer's Guild, and the Clean Indie Reads group. Interested parties may find her on Twitter (@pagezaplendam), Facebook, or Goodreads, when she's not working on becoming the next bestseller or changing diapers.

Boy Of Sand And Sky

Laura Matthias Bendoly

The one child born in the village of Sommêt-les-Rochers that year was Gabriel deLuce, named for both the miracle of birth during a plague year and for the angel's breath that filled his lungs ten minutes after pronouncement of his death.

His mother knew immediately the child was special.

Unlike his broad-shouldered brothers, Gabriel was a spindly child with greenish skin like the bronze St. Christopher that stood in the village fountain. Gabriel's eyes were pale and wide like he was perpetually in shock. He was smart, though, and shrewd, knowing at age six every trapdoor on the village square and never finding himself seized in the vice grip of the baker whose leftovers he was prone to swipe from market.

Though he hiked and climbed like any boy raised among mountains, Gabriel was not a talker. It was established by age four that he was mute. Or mostly. He declared a few words on occasion that he found in the Bible. Usually complex words uttered suddenly and in a ferocious voice.

"Lamentation."

"Seraphim."

At ten, the boy made letters. Lads were needed in the scriptorium after the last of the adult scribes perished from plague. Relying only on imitation, Gabriel's writing was as fine as a bishop's. As the ink left his brush, it glowed, spreading particles of light to the parchment edge.

His neighbor, Eric, who shared Gabriel's bench in the copy room, stared at Gabriel's calligraphy. It appeared to have a halo, not just on the letters but all around the paper's edges, above, below, and on all sides of his written passage.

"Let me see that!" Eric snatched Gabriel's work. His own page was neat but slanted like most novices'. A finished page of scripture, though worked on by fifteen individuals, should look like it was made by a single pair of hands. All the boys had learned just so much on the down stroke, a swish of the hand to the right, a flourish over the top. Too much ink on the curve of a P or too little on an I, and one had to begin the page anew.

Gabriel laid his stylus aside. He watched how Eric raised and lowered his parchment and ran his hand along the edges, trying to gather up its halo.

"How ya do that, Gabriel? Ya tryin' to make me look bad? It ain't real gold, that's for sure."

The rector shouted from the front of the copying room, "Why do I hear voices!"

Eric shoved the manuscript back at Gabriel. "He's doing it again, master. Glowing his pages. It ain't natural." The lad glared. "Nothin' natural about ya, witch-boy."

Gabriel slunk home faster than usual from the monastery. Not that the other boys beat him. But they followed him sometimes, calling names that stuck like meat gristle that you can't work down.

"What's wrong with you, Gabriel?" came a voice from a tree branch—one of his classmates goading him from his hiding place. "Why ya all green and bandy-legged?"

Another voice answered, "It's cuz he's from a bog. That's why he's green. His father weren't no plague victim. He were a bogman! Careful you don't touch him or you'll catch it."

"We should run 'im out of town."

Gabriel didn't believe the bogman stories, but the threats of being chased from town were frightening. Didn't they see his gold touch only worked on scripture passages? What fear had they from that? Soon, however, Gabriel developed another supernatural skill. He woke hovering above his bed. His mother told him it would pass when he'd grown to full height. But he wondered: could he drift off the Earth completely? Wind up adrift in the night sky?

Though his mother worried, she believed her son must have a mission like young David in the Bible. She stayed late after mass to look at Gabriel's letters with their swirls and arabesques. She never learned to write, herself. *He is blessed. Never mind that he was the child of violence.* Indeed, Gabriel was a child created when the plague was at its height and men took leave of their senses. *Great things will come. After all, he was delivered by angels.*

At his birth, the villagers had been kinder. Indeed, it was neighbors who wrapped Gabriel in linen and whispered prayers. But eventually, they took their leave, hope having vanished from the birthing room.

Seeing the lad about the village in early spring his eleventh year, making faces at a cat, writing letters in the dirt, and, yes, setting parchments aglow, made folks cross themselves. He had too many gifts. Why should he be blessed when so many others in Sommêt had lost their entire families? Fortune at that extreme wasn't natural. He and his mother weren't to be trusted.

Gabriel left the scribe's cellar at seven bells, his hands black with ink. Arriving at his cottage for the evening meal, he leaned over the basin to wash, scrubbing at his fingers with ash and soda. They pinked a little but were hardly clean.

The boy and his mother bent to their soup—cabbage and carrot—which they ate nightly from winter stores.

The mother frowned. "Did you wash your hands?"

Gabriel lifted his spoon and nodded.

She indicated a large purple-black smear on his index finger, like a pirate's death mark. "You should ask the master what he uses. Beeswax, perhaps."

Gabriel shrugged.

"Well, so you know, Denis and Luc are both installed at the village stable. Your brothers will make good at that apprenticeship. Do you think you'd like to join them? Learn to tend fine horses?"

Does Mother wish me to leave scribe's work? Unsure how to answer her, Gabriel held out his right hand.

She bent to look. "What is it, son?" She put down her spoon. "I don't see anything."

But on his ink-stained skin, there *was* something. It took shape gradually, the smears merging into an elongated bell shape.

She gasped. "Is that...a horn?"

"Judgment's cornet," he whispered.

She closed her son's fingers and pushed his hand away. Gabriel hadn't spoken a word in years, and now "Judgement's cornet?" How was she to manage him?

She cleared their bowls in agitation and put them in the wash bucket for later. Best to clear the hearth of the tenebrous feeling she got when hearing her boy's voice produce the words of a prophet.

"I'll get you to the monastery early tomorrow." She dried her hands. "If I speak to your master, he might let you work with the animals. There's fewer questions asked at a stable. Think about it, Gabriel. Stable work is peaceful. I've heard the names the other copyists call you. It's cruel what they say. They could roust a mob if they wanted."

Gabriel just moved his chair by the fire and took up his Bible. Though he knew what his mother said was right, he didn't want to consider threats from the villagers. It was such splendid work he did. Surely the other boys wouldn't harm him.

"I don't know, Madam deLuce." The scribes' master clasped his hands the next day. "Without a father or uncle's guidance, I'm not sure he'll take to livestock. He's bookish, as you know, and so gifted with the stylus. I was thinking of finding him a place with the illuminators in Arles. They might not mind his...gold...rays."

"But, Monseigneur." She called every member of the clergy by that title, never mind that it was reserved for cardinals. "Gabriel isn't normal. Casting halos is peculiar. And levitating in bed! He's more an angel than a boy! It's from being too in love with his work."

"Isn't that a blessing, though? Few villagers are so devoted to a calling, especially if they toil in a stony field."

"What I mean, sir, is he gets strange ideas from those pages. Mystic ideas. I think he..." She hesitated. "He believes himself a prophet."

"A prophet?"

"Or a saint."

"A young man's excess." The master smiled. "It is his age, madam. Adolescent boys all think they're kings. Perhaps he wishes to impress a sweetheart. With that gold touch of his. Show it off, so to speak."

"I suppose." But she knew it wasn't so. Gabriel had no interest in girls. He seemed to have no urges and almost no awareness of his body. He'd left the house completely naked last year in the thick of winter. Not once did he seem to feel cold or heat. As many as three days could pass for him without food or water, and he had several times been burned on the cook pot but came away unmarked. Not once had Gabriel become sick, overslept, suffered boredom or melancholy. His brothers teased him for it, tried to tickle and torture him, but he didn't seem to notice. Normal boys were incapable of causing him discomfort even though at fourteen and fifteen his brothers were as big as mules.

At his mother's insistence, Gabriel took work alongside Dennis and Luc at the stable. He was sent to shovel manure but upended a cart of it in the water trough. Next, he fed the horses straw instead of hay, gave them holy water to drink, and tried to make the goat stable with the donkey, which resulted in a black-eyed doe and a bite taken from the rump of a horse. Without telling anyone, Gabriel spent the night with an old pony that he took for lonely. When his eldest brother, Luc, found him curled around the old mare, he carried the boy back to his cottage. "Find something else, Mother."

Next, Gabriel tried carpentry. The village carpenter, Poulard, was replacing timbers in the vestry at the east arm of the church. Gabriel watched the work but didn't feel called by it. Poulard seemed to spend ages doing exactly the same thing—stuffing a new wedge into a slot where a previous one had been. No invention. No variation. Why would anyone choose this profession? A carpenter was alone all day in a cold room with nothing to read or draw on.

His mother made him carry Poulard's tool chest every day, just the same. "To get you accustomed to new materials. There's got to be a trade that doesn't glow or discomfort people. You're going to have to work to find it. Be patient."

Gabriel tried. For two weeks, he sorted and cleaned Poulard's chisels. They didn't glow, nor did the timbers that went into the vestry.

When Poulard wasn't looking, Gabriel snuck into the scriptorium and snatched discarded parchment from the scribes. No longer having ink or stylus, he entertained himself by folding the paper into birds. After four tries, he was good at it. He set his best bird on the prayer rail to admire and was just about to put a slightly better angle on the tail when it peeped at him.

Did you tweet! Gabriel gaped.

It hopped a tiny step toward him and cocked its head. "The carpenter will swat you if you aren't careful!"

You can talk? He was astonished. *Is it because you're made from holy verses?*

"Your hands bring life," the bird peeped. "Carpentry is not your calling. Your true profession will be shown to you by another. Listen for a call of urgent need."

When he mustered the courage, Gabriel plucked the paper bird up and hid it in his lunch pail. After that, voices seemed to come from everywhere. When he woke early, music came to Gabriel on the first sun rays, like harp strings or a finger circling a lead goblet. Were angels made of music? In illuminations, they were composed of feathers and gold leaf with the skin of mortals. It was hard to say what matter made an angel. They all held human attributes. A flute, a bow, a lily, a standard, a sword. His namesake angel was a messenger, and he blew a horn. This, Gabriel believed, was the cornet that had appeared on his hand that day. The sound of the cornet was the noise we would all hear on Judgment Day. That made it the most sacred instrument. The one he most wished he could play if he ever laid eyes on one.

It was no surprise when Poulard told Gabriel he wasn't made for carpentry. He went back to the scribes' master. Asked to clean ink wells the following week, Gabriel set off with a set of glassware to the church well. He swirled clean water around the inside of each ink well to draw out clumps of pigment. But as he finished cleaning the sixth container, he knocked the finished clean ones down the well shaft.

He clenched his teeth. *Don't cry! What would Saint Paul do? Or Nicolas the Stylite?*

Gabriel reached for the rope. He had earlier drawn up water on this cord. What if he'd knocked the ink wells into this very pail and they were waiting for him at the bottom? It was unlikely, but why not check?

Angels, help me.

He pulled.

Faster and faster, hand over hand. It was a long rope, like the rigging on a schooner, but with every pull, the bucket felt lighter. So light, that at a point he stopped pulling, and, Lord, if the rope didn't glide upward by itself. As the final section slid miraculously through its pulley, the church bell began to toll. Not the slow tone of the hour, but the carillon of a feast day.

The miller, working nearby with a pile of flour sacks, ran to see what was the matter, the carillon only being used on special Sundays or times of disaster.

"No fire, lad?" The miller looked about. "Why the bell peal?" He leaned over Gabriel. "Did someone poison the well?"

Gabriel shook his head vigorously and, with trembling hands, pointed to the bucket that was still rising on its own from the depths of the shaft. It crested the edge of the well and set itself in Gabriel's lap. At its center lay five unblemished ink wells, spotless and still stoppered.

Gabriel didn't tell his mother about what happened. He knew it was extraordinary. If she heard, she would tell him to leave the scriptorium altogether. Or go into hiding. She was losing sleep with worry. Secrecy did little good in Sommêt. The miller was out in no time, crowing about the mute boy's "flying pail."

A rock came through their cottage window late that night. Calligraphy covered the stone's flat surface: *Satan Flies through* Sommêt *in Your Bucket.*

A few days afterward, Sommêt's chickens became lethargic. They were no one's special pets, but they had been reliable layers. Quite suddenly, they stopped producing eggs and the rooster wouldn't crow. They gathered on straw bales and sulked. No kicking dust, no pecking fleas. They'd become the bird equivalent of waterlogged worms.

Known, now, as a kind of wizard, Gabriel was called to help. "Bring those ink wells," the fowler muttered. "Their magic might cure 'em."

Perhaps the villagers were coming around. It was hard to tell. Neighbors wanted his help, now. But they also put three pews between themselves and his family at mass. What would a saint do? Help the neighbors despite their unfriendliness? Doing the right thing despite thrown rocks might be better than doing nothing.

Gabriel walked up to those hens and studied them. How did you discover what made a hen lethargic? He stroked the feathers of one and examined the wing of another. They smelled awful, but that wasn't unusual.

Holding up two fingers, he motioned that he'd need two nights to think about the fowler's dilemma. On the second night, he had a dream. In it, an egg appeared in the bedroll of the stablemaster's serving girl, a fourteen-year-old named Filene. He went to his brothers the next morning and led them to the unmade bed of their master's servant. He gestured for the lads to look through her bedding.

They did so.

Sixteen eggs lay nestled under Filene's pillow. Six of them had hatched and ten were still whole. The hens had been laying. Filene had simply gotten to them first.

"Yeah, I stole 'em." She lowered her head when they confronted her. "To raise 'em for my family. We's poor as rats in them hills. Nothing growing in all those rocks!"

Her employer let her take three chicks to raise but held back wages in punishment.

"Go on an' gloat!" Filene shouted at Gabriel as she packed up to leave.

And later, she caught up to him on the footpath. "I'm done for in this village. No one will hire me thanks to you. Whatchoo have to go proph-seeing for? It ain't Christian. An' I'm tellin' the constable when I sees him next to take a look at your mother's house. Yeah. She's got more linen there than I ever saw any housewife put up on laundry day. She profited from the plague, I'll wager. Helped herself to empty houses."

It was horrible what Filene was saying and yet she could say what she pleased. Her voice functioned, though her words were lies. Gabriel ran from Filene into the woods then wound his way back to St. Christopher's fountain. The saint was from the parable where an old man carries Christ across a river. Sommêt's Christopher stood at the center of a wide, cool fountain and reached some seven feet in height. His gold-green skin was the same color as Gabriel's. While washing his hands in the water, something extraordinary happened. Christopher's reflection smiled and lifted his hand. Then he pointed his index finger at the lad and spoke, "Gabriel, do not fear the calling God has given you. You have a gift."

He stared at the reflection, astonished. He looked up at the bronze statue, still as death but with a reflection as mobile as a dancer.

"Just as you see me, Gabriel," the reflection continued, "you will work mysteries."

Gabriel replied as best he could, *I will work mysteries? How?*

"You are special, lad. Your writing makes light and your dreams bring justice. You will now try your hand at healing."

Gabriel wanted to argue, to refuse. But a breeze came and stippled the fountain pool. When the water stilled, the reflection had gone quiet. Gabriel ran home to ponder what to do. Was miraculous healing really a profession? Would it endanger his mother? Would the villagers cast them out? He had solved the problem with the hens. He was something of a finder of lost things. And yet, Filene's fury. The rock through the cottage window. There were slurs, still, in the copy room and cruel remarks to his mother at market. Embittered words could lead to worse. His mother still talked of riots over oil during the plague. How no one had light enough to sit vigil for the dying.

A week later, an accident called Gabriel to Poulard the carpenter's house.

It was the Sabbath. No one labored, so the boy was surprised to hear the neighbors shouting through the village about a work injury.

It happened at the rear of Poulard's cottage on a scaffold he built to repair the battlements. Sommêt was circled with medieval fortifications that had once been mighty but had crumbled under bombardment during battle with the Caliphate. Certain of the houses, including Poulard's, were set into the fortified wall. The rear of his house joined the cliff's sheer drop into the valley. A fall from this part of the village meant certain death.

Has Poulard fallen from his window?

Gabriel scampered through the village past the fountain and through a flock of sheep that were on the move to summer pasture, knocking into Guy the shepherd.

Sorry! he mouthed.

He arrived at the Poulards' to see the door ajar with three neighbor women wringing their hands. From deeper inside, there came moaning.

Gabriel entered slowly, inquiring silently of the gathered faces.

"He was building a balcony," his wife blubbered. "So we could have a view, of all things, from our table. I never needed a view! I see the square just fine from the doorstep. But Pierre thought we should look out over the crevasse."

Gabriel made a gesture to approach the injured man.

"Don't come near me, lad. I was seized by a...creature...while working on my ledge. He grabbed me by the collar and shook me 'til my teeth cracked. See?"

Gabriel leaned in to look in the fellow's mouth, but he couldn't find any injury. Some misshapen molars, but nothing that looked out of place.

The carpenter ranted on, "Down he cast me to the flagstones. I feared for my life! And then, Gabriel, he...he...blew air in my mouth. When he left, I tasted metal, like my lips were made of bronze. The noise from his mouth still rings like a trumpet. I might have died from shock, only my dear wife came shouting and the creature vanished."

Gabriel trembled at these words. Could the account be true? The almond-sized lump on Poulard's forehead made it clear he had knocked himself a blow. But maybe there *had* been an angel in his home. Gabriel's own life was the result of heaven's intervention.

He gently touched the carpenter's face. The old man was damp and agitated. Gabriel felt the pulse as he'd read you should do in a pamphlet from an itinerant apothecary. Poulard's heart rate was high but not racing. He did have a mark on his neck. Just above one shoulder, the skin was indented and red—what could be the imprint of a hand. Gabriel leaned his head in the direction of a tankard that lay on its side on the night table.

"No, lad. I haven't been drinking." Poulard wiped his face with the back of his hand. "Some soup at dawn and a tisane with honey. I haven't lost my head from drink in fifteen years."

Poulard's wife, who approached from the kitchen, nodded. "C'est vrai. He prefers tea to ale. I fear…" She knit her hands together. "I fear he will have the *touch*"—she whispered the word—"…like you, son, from wrestling with angels. Do you think it possible that angels are invading? Will more of us be thrown about the house? Maybe my husband is being punished for toiling on the Lord's day."

Gabriel considered. All kinds of Bible men had visitations. They fell down, got knocked off horses, and the like. He had just last month copied a page where Jacob fought with angels.

"…he touched the socket of Jacob's hip so that his hip was wrenched…"

Still, miracles seemed to come in single events. Gabriel doubted that an entire legion of seraphs was taking over Sommêt. But he didn't know how to explain this to the Poulards nor whether there'd be lasting injury to monsieur's head and neck. With all these faces looking at him, he, the unnatural boy, had become the authority. At age eleven. In a peasant jerkin. He tried to sit up straight and hold his shoulders square. St. Christopher had signaled him. Picked *him*, not one of his brothers, not the scribes' master, to make a difference. There had been meaning in the gold of his lettering and the music he heard at dawn. He was saved at birth to make miracles.

The neighbor women in the kitchen looked impatient. They would have an answer.

The stable girl, Filene, stepped through the door where she'd apparently been skulking. "Surely, he must have a cure. You was delivered by angels, Gabriel. You found those eggs in my bed. Can't you say how you know these things? It would be wicked to keep God's secrets to yourself."

The others nodded. Six or seven of them now. They closed in on Gabriel where he dithered in the Poulards' kitchen.

"It's true what Filene says," another said.

"You know things other folks don't."

"Readin' and letterin' and how to glow a parchment."

"Withholding cures would be devilry, boy."

"Maybe he spies on us at night." The shepherd's wife shouldered her way forward. "So's to use our secrets against us!"

Madame Poulard put a hand on the woman's wrist then looked calmly at Gabriel. "I believe in you, lad. I don't expect anything from your visions. But if the angels have advice, tell us how to help my husband. If he's in danger of losing *his* speech…" She patted her neck. "Oh, it's hot today. Filene, ladies, let the lad alone. There's nothing else for you to see today. I'll send news if there's a change with the mister. Bring him a cure, Gabriel, if you have one. If not, we're in God's good hands."

Gabriel trembled at those demanding faces. He rose to his feet, staggered, and charged for the door.

St. Christopher's fountain was just around the corner, so he made quick for its serene shade and practically threw himself at the water as he approached. But on extending his hand to the surface, a tremor rippled through both arms. The statue of Christopher was alive again and staring at him. It shook its crinkly, jointed hair but then looked up at the Christ child on its shoulder. Christ, Himself, spoke next. Not moving His lips but in the trembling of the air and the sound of water as it fell from the fountain to the basin below.

"Gabriel, you can heal the carpenter. Take a measure of water from this fountain. His wounds will be cured. Once you do this, you will be a healer and will tend thousands like the Lady at Lourdes. Do you want that, Gabriel—boy whom angels brought to life?"

I don't know, Lord! Tears streamed from Gabriel's eyes. This was his Savior speaking. Could he refuse? *I'll be called a sorcerer. A false prophet.*

"Play this for them if they doubt you." Suddenly floating on the water was a shiny instrument. A cornet. Like the one still marked on his hand. The very trumpet he'd seen the angels play in Judgment's illumination.

Thank you, Lord. He bowed his head. *But I don't know how to play.*

"It will show you. Keep it safe. Use my holy water for the sick but only when every mortal cure has failed. It will not work to make large ears small or fill a banker's chest."

I understand. I will do this. But I fear I might be cast from the village.

"You may be, but it is your calling. It is how you'll join the angels. That's what you wanted, isn't it?"

It was what Gabriel had been waiting for, what dawn's music had foretold, and what the paper bird had sung about. He would join the illuminations. *Does it mean I will wander all my life?*

But the Savior was returning to bronze. The movement in St. Christopher's hair solidified. Their proclamation was over.

Gabriel needed to think over what the Lord had said. He walked home slowly. Should he do this? Would accepting the calling make him a hero? The idea was both magnificent and terrible. If he accepted, he'd have to leave his family. The church would name him a heretic. The priests already hated the village midwife, never mind that she had brought six villagers back from death during his lifetime. A philosopher in Toulouse was burned three years ago for using something called a telescope to look at heaven. Knowledge in a village was preferred in small amounts and only when delivered by the clergy.

Gabriel considered his future deep into the night as his mother breathed peacefully in her sleep. He decided to become itinerant. A wandering mystic wasn't as suspicious as a gifted child. A traveling healer wouldn't have to demonstrate the making of cures. He'd carry supplies of St. Christopher's water in plentiful supply.

Gabriel packed a small bag the next morning with the bronze cornet, a few apples, a pair of boots, and a traveling cloak. Then he returned to the Poulards with a vial of fountain water. After drinking it, the ringing in Monsieur's ears left, the pain departed, but the handprint on his shoulder remained. When he asked if God meant for him to suffer, Gabriel shook his head.

You've been touched, he wrote on a piece of parchment. *Don't worry, it doesn't hurt.* It was several days before Poulard got those words read to him by the scriptorium master. The water from Gabriel's vial cured his concussion, but he kept the handprint on his shoulder the rest of his life.

Filene was at the market square when Gabriel left the carpenter's house. Her station had sunk dramatically. She was now the village hogwoman.

"I see you, mute boy, and I knows what youze doin'. Twisting that old couple with dream speakin'. You're a spy and a liar, I say. You been spyin' on me in bed. That's how you knew about them eggs. I tole everyone what I think a' your miracles. Snake oil's what you're sellin'. Snake oil and hexes. You'll be run outta the village! If not this 'un, then the next!"

She stared at Gabriel across the square as her hog blundered around her legs, rooting for forage. "I don't care that you make cures! Youze a fraud and a...a...a sinner like the rest of us!" She screamed and yanked her hair. And then she struck the hog as hard as she could with her whip.

A crowd had gathered by that time. They stared at Filene.

"Get along, mad girl."

"I've seen some fits in my day, but goodness!"

They shook their heads at the spectacle. Gabriel hoped this meant he had his neighbors' understanding, that he might visit Sommêt peacefully in the future and that his family would be left in peace. One day, St. Christopher might help another villager.

Perhaps Filene. I hope so. It would be awful to spend a lifetime tearing your hair.

Gabriel said goodbye to the scribes' master and his mother at church. He plucked three words from deep in his heart, more than he had ever said at one time.

"I will heal."

With that, he pressed his cornet-marked hand into his mother's palm and smiled at his teacher.

"Since the church fathers may come for you," his master said, "take a new name. Don't keep deLuce. I know you're blessed by God but not all people will believe. People you've known all your life might turn on you. So, don't be here when the next plague comes. Keep to the road where you'll be safest."

And so the silent scribe became the healer Brian duSable, a dusty mountain man who was in fact a child. He lived many years as a traveler, healing with a calf skin of holy water that never drained. He came back to Sommêt-les-Rochers to see his mother and to pray at St. Christopher's fountain. The statues never spoke to him again, but he didn't need the voices anymore. When he arrived in a town, he blew the cornet which he wore on a cord. With the notes of that trumpet, people knew hope was coming. Gabriel carried music through the mountains for the rest of his life, until he was an old man and one day died peacefully at the edge of a spring, his cornet held lovingly in his arms.

I am a writer of fantasy and fairy tale and I love to use specific historic locations, like Medieval France, as I have in this story. The longer work I am busy with, The Peddler of Wisdom, *urged me to create a side story, "Boy of Sand and Fog," which treats the subject of miracles and superstition in small-town Europe during the mid-16th century. The Inquisition had just ended, France saw its last plague, and the Age of Reason was on the horizon. But not quite yet. Read how a disabled child with a special gift runs into life-threatening danger and surprising deliverance in the heart of his small mountain village.*

http://laurambendoly.wordpress.com

Teamwork

Laura VanArendonk Baugh

D*anger.*

I know it even before I am awake enough to register the noise. The floor is warm beneath me, and the sound is coming from the window at the far side of the room. It is similar to the sound a tree-rat makes when it plays at the windowsill, but not quite the same. I lift my head and I can just make out a silhouette through the frosted glass.

I know the silhouette, know its movement. I rise from the floor and cross to just below the frosted window, where he is working at the frame where the tiny latch connects. I growl, letting the sound swell from my deep chest and fill the room.

The silhouette recoils. Another shape comes into view, but an arm's length back from the glass. I hear them exchange heated whispers. "Doberman," says a voice I know, but I already know it is Stinkface. "I guess she left him home."

Doberman always means me, even if it is not my name. Anyway, I am glad Stinkface knows I am here.

"She keeps him locked in the bathroom," says Stinkface. "It's okay."

This is not really true. Lady put me in the bathroom only when Stinkface came to visit, and only the last few times. Stinkface was afraid of me after the night he tried to hit Lady.

He wanted to mate with her, and she did not want to mate with him. He got angry, and then he got very angry, and that is when Lady and I each saw what he intended. He later tried to pretend he wasn't going to, that he wasn't thinking of it, but Lady and I both knew differently. I jumped up from my chair and growled, and Lady made body language which told him if he were going to hit her, he had better make his first strike count, because it would be the only one he would get.

He was a coward and he could not admit he was afraid. "That dog is vicious!" he snapped the next time he came to visit. "I don't want him in here."

They argued over that too, but Lady tried to make nice with him and locked me in the bathroom. This was not fair at all, and especially not since Stinkface was the one who had done wrong and not me. Lady is very smart and good at many things, but she needs me to help with the men.

Stinkface did not come over many more times. Each time, I did not have to stay in the bathroom long, because he did not stay long. Then Stinkface did not come anymore, and I was pleased.

A new man has been coming to visit Lady. She is out with him right now, in fact. She seems to like him, but I know better. He smells of rubbing alcohol and cotton balls and metal tools and needles, and while he hides his white coat before he comes to our house, I know he is a white-coat man. I have tried to show Lady that I do not like him, refusing to greet him or allow him to rub my ears no matter how he coaxes, but he only laughs and says it is the price he has to pay. Lady laughs too.

Lady is smart at many things, but she needs me for the men.

Anyway, this is Stinkface here at the window. He takes his partner—Stinkface is a coward, and he had to bring someone with him—around the corner to the bedroom window.

I nudge open the bathroom door and go into the bedroom. I was in the bathroom for the heated floor, a luxury Lady likes to leave for me when she goes out on winter nights. I was not locked in. I will not be in the bathroom when Stinkface comes to the next window.

Lady has been talking lately about Stinkface on the phone, with one of her girl friends. She calls him Jamie, and she has a worried tone when she speaks of him. I didn't bother to listen to all of the words, because most of them weren't important words like *leash* or *dinner* or *come*, but I knew the gist of what she was saying. She was worried about Jamie, even though he hasn't been here in weeks. She had heard from him, or of him, or something. I didn't think much about it then, because he wasn't here and I wouldn't let him come back.

But now he is back.

I am glad Lady is not here to put me in the bathroom. I will inform Stinkface he is not welcome here, not even if he tries to come in the bedroom window instead of the front door.

Something smashes through the glass, and I leap back, startled. Bits of broken glass litter the carpet, and a hand reaches through the opening to work the bigger window latch.

I can smell them now, all testosterone and adrenaline and nervous sweat. They are about to do something stupid. More, they know they are about to do something stupid and they are working themselves up to do it anyway.

"The closet is straight across the room," Stinkface says. "We hide in there until she comes home, then we jump out and take her both at once. You hold her while I do it, and—"

"And then you hold her for me," says Stinkface's partner.

"Sure."

I am irritated that Stinkface has brought a partner. Teamwork is good, but Stinkface is not for teamwork. He is a predator, which is all right, but not for food, which is not. This is not good. Because he is a cowardly predator, he has brought a partner to help him, but they are not a team.

Still, there are two of them. But they have only thirty-two teeth each. I have forty-two teeth.

I give them proper warning: I curl the very front of my lips and I go up on my toes with my weight forward to show I am serious. I lift what tail the humans have left me straight in the air, flagging my intent. If they come into this space, I will hurt them.

They do not so much as hesitate in their actions, and I realize they cannot see my slick dark coat in the unlit room. Nor can they scent me with their clumsy human noses. They are indeed foolish predators, not only to hunt on another's territory, but to hunt where their limited senses are useless.

And they are very foolish to hunt my Lady.

Still, it is always best to warn away a threat than to engage it unnecessarily. I rumble out a formidable snarl, deep and full of promise.

Stinkface curses and jerks back the leg he has started over the windowsill. His partner, who has never actually seen me properly and thus is probably ill-informed, abruptly heaves a backpack at me. It strikes me in the face and chest, and while it does no real harm, I instinctively move back and duck away from it. In that moment, the partner-man is through the window and coming at me.

I snarl at him again, a final warning to retreat, but he swings a booted foot at me and catches me in the shoulder hard.

Oh, it is *on*.

I move with the kick and then go in low, slashing with my forward teeth at his calf. I tear cloth but only barely touch skin. It is enough to alarm him, however, and he shifts backward.

But now Stinkface is inside the window and there are two of them. He puts something into his hand and circles the bed, trying to flank me as I engage his partner. Perhaps they have some teamwork after all.

I whip toward Stinkface and snap at his forward arm, and his other hand comes up and cuts me. Cuts me! He has a knife, a human hand-tooth. It hurts, but mostly I am angry that they have come to hunt Lady on our own territory and with a hand-tooth.

"I've wanted to do that forever," laughs Stinkface, a brag which cannot cover the fear-smell rolling off him and choking the room. "Now I—ow!"

I have the hand-tooth arm in my mouth and I am shaking and pulling back, just as I have practiced, and Stinkface drops it as I crush muscle and nerve. He pulls back, tearing his own flesh further, and when I release, he flees backward.

Stinkface's partner yells something and comes for me again, and as I turn to bite him, he punches me in the mouth.

In the mouth. He put his hand in the weapon-hole.

I am certain he thought this a good idea when he did it. Perhaps he thought he would choke me with his fist. I do not know. But I also know that when I bite down, and not with the slashing front teeth but with the crushing, grinding molars between the bulk of my jaw muscles, he stops thinking it is a good plan. He screams and pulls his hand back, uncurling his fist to try to slide it out of my mouth, but that only gives me more surface area to grasp. He slaps and punches at my head with his good hand, trying for my eyes, but every blow he strikes me hurts himself as well and he is still screaming.

I bite down and wrench side to side with my full body, so hard my forefeet skip along the ground. It is the powerful kill-shake to snap the spine of prey, and I feel something move in my grip. Partner-man wails.

Stinkface comes at me from the side with the hand-tooth, and it slashes down the hard muscle of my back. I clench and whirl toward him, tearing chunks of meat from his partner's hand, and the two of them stumble backward. The partner is clutching his hand to his torso, eyes popping wide. They want to flee, I can tell, but now I am between them and the window, and they instinctively move farther into the bedroom, trapping themselves. The closet is behind them.

They are afraid, and now I can drive them out. I will circle and chase them out the window. I roar and lunge forward, opening my mouth.

They yelp like puppies and dash into the closet, pulling one another in as they slam the door in my face.

But something catches in my throat, and I realize it is the meat of his hand, severed fingers slipping back in my mouth as I whirled and leaped. I cough and it shifts, and then it lodges in my windpipe.

I can't breathe.

I try to cough, but I have no air to use. I drop my head and hack, but there is no sound. I push my weight onto my hind legs and claw at my mouth with my forepaws, but of course I cannot reach it. There is a whistling in my throat, but it is not enough air to make a breath.

I cannot breathe.

The edges of my vision are darkening. I need air. I drop to the floor and scrape more furiously at my mouth. My claws tear at my gums, raking blood from them, but it does not bring me air. My flailing feet scrape at the base of the closet door, and I hear the men inside gasp and kick against the door to brace it, as if I am coming through instead of dying.

They will kill me even as they cower in the closet.

I am wheezing, kicking, clawing. Not enough air. Not enough air.

Distantly, I hear the sounds every dog knows above all others—the engine, the walk, the keys in the lock.

"Titan! We're back! Where are you?"

Lady! But there are danger-men in the closet, and she does not know. But she will help me. Somehow, she will help me.

"Titan?"

Lady.

I hear her in the hallway. White-Coat is somewhere behind her, saying something. I can't hear him over the growing pounding in my ears.

"Titan?"

She comes into the bedroom, and she cries my name. I struggle weakly, trying to claw the fingers from my throat and dig at the closet door in warning. She rushes to me. "Jack! He's having some sort of seizure!"

White-Coat rushes to the bedroom after her. I have nothing left to warn him away.

"Look at all this blood from his mouth. Oh, God, please. Titan, what's wrong? Is he dying?"

White-Coat runs his hands over the bloody streaks on my shoulders. "This isn't a seizure. He was attacked and injured."

She looks up at the shattered window. I gag uselessly.

"I think he's choking," says Jack. "Let me in."

He leans over me, and I would resist if I could, but I am dying. He glides his hands along my ribs, tracing two lines, and then hits me hard. Something leaps in my throat. He does it again, and the fingers shift upward. I hack and gasp and spit them forward, trying to work them out of my mouth as I gulp for air.

I miss their exact words as I am busy breathing and struggling to my feet, but it is mostly the usual assortment of human epithets and blasphemy. They stare at the fingers I have spit up on the carpet and say nothing but their short words. I lean shakily against Lady's leg, steadying both of us, and she kneels to embrace me.

"We'd better call the police," says White-Coat. He reaches for the phone at his waist.

I hear the sound, but I cannot turn fast enough with Lady's arms around me. The closet door bursts open and Stinkface lunges at Lady, hand-tooth extended.

She surges upward, deflecting the hand-tooth with a sharp blow and then moving into his close range to grapple. I launch myself at his leg and sink my teeth into his inner thigh, getting a good grip around the muscle and pulling it away from the bone. I pull backward, shaking, and Lady delivers a devastating kick to his small ribs. I hear the satisfying pop of cartilage even over his high-pitched shout. I keep him in place for her, and she snaps his face down into her upraised knee. Stunned, he sags, and I release and move aside to keep from beneath him, and she places a final stomp-kick into his face. He falls loosely backward against the wall, staring at us.

"Don't you ever—*ever*—hurt my dog!"

I show him my teeth. Lady and I are a good team.

White-Coat is holding a phone but not talking into it, just staring at Lady. "Wow," he manages.

In the closet, Stinkface's partner is crying in the corner, cradling his mangled hand and saying something about needing an ambulance. Lady gives him a hard look and tells him to stay where he is. White-Coat gets some supplies from the bathroom and does something for his hand while Lady calls the police.

The police officers come and take Stinkface and his partner and a lot of photos, of the room and the closet and even me. They take photos of the fingers—there are two of them, slick with spit and phlegm and blood—and then put them in a baggie and take them with the partner-man. That is okay, because I don't really want them.

Then White-Coat takes Lady and me to a clinic—I knew, I *knew* he was a clinic man—and they use rubbing alcohol and needles, but then my shoulder and back don't hurt so much, and he shaves and stitches me.

Lady cries a little, which makes me feel bad, even though I know she isn't afraid of White-Coat. She is crying about Stinkface, which is weird because he is already gone and, besides, we have beaten him, both of us together, but humans are weird sometimes.

After I have been stitched and my torn mouth treated, White-Coat holds Lady for a while. She sniffs and laughs and apologizes for talking about an ex on their date. This makes him laugh too. Then he kisses her, and she kisses him back. He kisses her more, and it isn't fair: when I kiss with my tongue she laughs and protests and holds me back, but when he does it now she kisses back with her tongue. I am annoyed, and I go to push between them, and because I am still on the table where White-Coat treated me, I can reach their faces, and I start kissing them both with great vigor.

They break apart, laughing and pushing me back—but not on my sore shoulder—and then Lady hugs both White-Coat and me. And I think that maybe this is okay, because White-Coat helped as best he could. He is not good at the teamwork Lady and I have, not yet, but he might learn.

The urban legend of the Choking Doberman has folkloric roots centuries old. Despite even occasionally being mistakenly reported as news, it is generally presented in an implausible context. Here we can enjoy an accurate retelling from a more knowledgable source.

Laura VanArendonk Baugh writes fiction in a variety of flavors, from epic and urban fantasy to mystery, as well as non-fiction about animal behavior. Find her at www.LauraVAB.com.

The Ungifted Twin

Tamie Dearen

Deria rubbed the sleep from her eyes, blinking until the thatched ceiling came into focus an armspan above her face. She shifted, trying to smooth out a lump in the straw mat atop her sleeping loft. Dim morning light filtered through the cloth-covered window beside her, and she could hear her parents' soft murmurings and her father's heavy boots tromping on the wood floor below.

Squeezing her eyes shut, she tried to feel inside her consciousness, hoping to find something that hadn't been there the previous day.

Nothing. She felt no different. Even though today was her seventeenth birthingday.

Her throat tightened and tears stung her eyes. Her minor giftings with animals and direction would provide little help to her family and her clan. She must be the only person in the entire territory who hadn't manifested at least one major gift during the seventeenth year. It was so unfair that her twin brother Korporan had received not one, but two major gifts—weapons and strength—on his sixteenth birthingday. Yet, she couldn't possibly begrudge her brother his gifts. For though she bantered with him and he tormented her relentlessly, they were so close they almost read one another's minds.

Blinking fast, she forced her tears to recede. She didn't wish to see the pity on her parents' faces when she confessed there was still no indication of a major gift. She had to escape before they could question her. After finger-combing her waist-long black hair into sleek strands, she bound it into a braid and changed into her well-worn pants and everyday tunic. She crept down the ladder and dashed toward the door, shouting over her shoulder.

"I'm going to fetch the day's water!"

She slammed the door behind her, shutting out the sound of her parents calling after her. She found the buckets and shoulder pole and set off on the trail that wound through the trees toward the river.

"Halt!" a voice shouted from above her head.

Startled, she lost her hold on the pole, and the buckets tumbled and clanked to the ground.

"I have solved the mystery of your missing gift!" Korporan declared, swinging from a tree branch and thumping to the ground, where he towered over her. He seemed to grow taller by the day, having passed her diminutive stature several years ago.

"Get out of my way." She retrieved an empty bucket and swung it at her brother, but he sidestepped easily, smiling at the game. His dark hair, still damp from an early morning washing, was tied back with a strip of leather. His emerging beard was beginning to fill in the sparse areas around his chin, while blue-green eyes—the same as hers—twinkled beneath thick brows. His shoulder muscles bulged, already stretching the confines of the tunic that had hung loose on his frame before his strength manifested. He looked so like their father, she wondered if people might mistake them when Korporan was a grown man.

If their family actually survived long enough for them to grow up. *If* Water Clan warriors didn't raid their small farming community of Essenshire as they had the neighboring Abershire, only a moon ago.

But for Deria's sudden bout of odd stomach sickness, she and her family might have been killed in the raid along with all the other Abershire residents. Delaying their trading trip for a day until her unexplained nausea dissipated, they arrived in Abershire with a wagonload of pelts and grain, only to discover a massacre that made her stomach give up its contents as readily as the day before.

"Do you not wish to hear my idea?" Korporan probed.

"I have no time for your nonsense." In truth, a small spark of hope emerged as she wondered if he might have discovered a legitimate explanation for her missing gift.

He stepped to the side, bowing and swiping his arm in a gesture for her to pass. "I will walk with you then, so you won't waste a precious moment."

"Even better, you can carry the buckets for me." She shoved one into his chest, and he doubled over with an exaggerated guttural groan.

"Such strength all of a sudden, Deria! That must be your gift!" He cackled with laughter as he gathered the other fallen bucket and pole.

"I wish there were a gift of patience." She struggled to keep her countenance severe, fighting the twitch at the corners of her mouth. "For I need it to bear such a contrary brother."

"Truly, I have the matter of your gift sorted out." He fell in step beside her with one arm looped through the bucket handles, using the pole in the other hand as a walking stick. "You are clumsy as ever, so your gift could not be agility. And how could you be gifted in weapons when you cannot even wield a table knife? Nothing is left, but you must be a shaman."

A shaman? She'd never considered she might have such a rare gifting. It would be incredible. Did Korporan seriously believe she might have the gift?

When he chortled with laughter, she had her answer. He ducked as she swatted at him. Extending his arm with the pole in hand, he mimed pulling back a bowstring, two buckets dangling from his arm as he aimed an invisible arrow at her chest. "Be quick, Deria. Conjure a shield to thwart my arrow."

"There is no need," she retorted, crossing her arms and lifting her chin in defiance. "For you would miss your target from an armspan's distance."

He chuckled, arranging the pails to hang on either end of the pole on his shoulder, and led the way down the trail. "At least I brought a smile to your face. I propose your gift may be an entirely new one—*grumpiness.*"

"You would be grumpy too, if you had no major gift. As I suggested before, since you have two, you should let me have one of yours."

"Why do you worry so much?" He glanced back and frowned. "Mother says you have your gift, but it simply hasn't manifested. She says it will show itself when it is needed."

"If it hasn't manifested in a year, it may not be there."

"Has it been a whole year?" His voice lifted in feigned surprise. "Do you mean that *today* is our birthingday? I had totally forgotten."

"Ha! And now that we have seventeen years, you need to act with more maturity. No more jumping down from trees to scare me. You should be nice and respectful."

"How can you say I am not nice?" His exclamation dripped with indignation. "Am I not carrying your buckets for you? And did I not help you gather berries yesterday?"

A suspicious thought occurred, and she grabbed his arm, pulling him to a stop and rounding to face him with her hands planted on her hips. "In truth, you have been stuck to me like a shadow for the past moon or so. I believe you have been following me around ever since I had that sudden stomach illness. Have Mother and Father decided I am so frail I cannot be left unattended?"

"They said nothing of the sort." The slightest of nervous twitches passed over his lips as he pronounced the vehement denial. Or was it her overactive imagination?

"Then why do I find you on my every path? And why are you suddenly interested in helping me with my chores?"

His dimples danced under his scruffy beard. "You insult me, Sister, after all I do to make you happy. Because of your gifting with animals, you make me travel a day's distance to hunt, lest I accidentally stumble upon one of your friends."

"Of course I don't want you to hunt close by. You might kill Hopper or one of her children."

"What does that rabbit say to you, anyway? She and her many, many children think nothing of eating all the best vegetables from our garden, and yet you protect her. Perhaps someday I will catch the sneaky critter, and she will be in your stew without your knowledge."

Deria gasped. "No, Korporan! You can't do that! Promise me you'll never do such a thing!"

"Very well—I promise not to put her in your stew. But perhaps in a meat pie, instead..."

"Korporan!" She balled her fist and slammed it into the solid muscle on his arm.

"What was that? I think I felt a feather tickle my arm?" He winked at her. "Come, Sister... What must I do to coax a smile from you this morning? Must I swear to forgo my portion of vegetables to feed your friends? Consider it done. But I beg you; don't ask me to kiss a furry creature on the nose as you do. It is more than my dignity can bear."

A smile fought its way onto her lips, despite her efforts to remain stern.

"I believe I must give up my quest to make you mature."

"I am glad of it." He punctuated his words with a sharp nod. "We must have fun while we have opportunity. Trouble will come in time and bring seriousness without any effort on our part."

When they reached the river, Korporan scrambled down the rocky bank to the water's edge, quickly filling both buckets. As he returned with the sloshing buckets hanging from the pole on his shoulders, Deria's belly rumbled with hunger, a loud racket that caught her brother's amused attention.

"We should hurry home—it sounds as if you missed your breakfast. Why did you leave in such a rush?"

She hesitated, her cheeks burning with embarrassment, but when she turned to look at him, genuine sympathy shone in his eyes, with no mockery.

Her words came out in a hoarse whisper. "I simply couldn't handle seeing the pity on their faces, knowing I still have no gift."

He chewed on his lower lip, a deep crease between his brows. "Deria, I'm not supposed to tell you this, but—"

"Ughh!" A wave of nausea swept through her, churning her gut. She clapped her hand over her mouth, suppressing the urge to throw up—not that there was anything inside her stomach since she had foregone breakfast.

"What's wrong, Deria?" His eyebrows knotted over his eyes. "Do you feel sick? Like before? Like when you were ill a moon ago?"

"I don't know. Yes, I suppose it feels the same, but—"

Korporan shoved the pole off his shoulders, sending the pails splashing to the ground. In a breath, he had her scooped into his arms, and they were hurtling up the path toward their home, crashing through tree branches as he cut the corners in his haste.

"Korporan! What are you doing? It's nothing serious—just a little nausea."

Even as she shouted her objection, saliva flooded her mouth and her stomach convulsed.

"I was about to tell you," he huffed without breaking stride. "Mother believes you have the gift of discernment. She says you felt the presence of evil in Abershire a moon ago when Water Clan attacked. She said a second occurrence would confirm it."

If she weren't so queasy, she might have been ecstatic at the news. *I have a major gift! I am not a useless aberration!*

"But if I feel sick now..." Her heart pounded inside her chest, the import of her newly discovered gift suddenly clear.

"Yes," came his breathless answer as he plunged into the clearing. "Water Clan warriors must be close by. And with no other village remaining near us, they must be coming *here*."

Two

"You don't have to carry me all the way down to the hidden cave," Deria protested, clamping her mouth tight, her head lolling against her brother's chest as he ran.

Mother ran up beside Korporan on the mad dash to their refuge. "You didn't eat breakfast, Deria, and your gift is depleting your energy."

Indeed, Deria felt like she could barely keep her eyes open, and she wondered if there was some way to turn off her gift before it drained her to the point of passing out.

Their family had practiced this escape many times—down to the river, wading upstream, trekking up the side gully to the narrow, vine-covered cave entrance. Korporan carried Deria inside and deposited her gently on the floor. As her eyes adjusted to the dim light, she pushed up on her elbows to survey the space. The stone ceiling arched high enough in the center for Korporan to stand without stooping. The cavern stretched about ten armspans wide and equally deep.

But Deria knew her family would not remain in this comfortable open space. She turned her head, eyeing the long, low fissure that ran all the way across the back of the cave, just deep enough for a person to lie down and wedge sideways under the rock ledge. There was room for all four of them to hide, stretching head-to-toe in the dark crevice. No one seemed eager to squeeze into the shadowy hiding place, waiting instead for Father, who had delayed to set fire to the rags in the smoke pot, a warning signal to neighboring farms.

"You need to eat something." Korporan offered a piece of dried meat from his pocket. Her sensitized gut roiled against the pungent smell of the meat, and she pushed his hand away. "Thank you, Korporan, but I can't eat it."

"I have some bread for you." Her mother handed her a thick slice of bread, wrapped in a cloth. "You must eat something to replenish your energy, even though you feel sick."

As Deria nibbled on the crust, her mother paced back and forth, glancing toward the cave entrance.

"Why didn't you tell me, Mother? Why did you let me believe I had no gift?"

With a sigh, her mother approached, leaning her back against the cave wall and sliding to the floor beside Deria. "I always said your gift would manifest someday, did I not?"

"Yes," she admitted. "But you were as worried as I."

"I was only worried that you were so disconsolate while waiting. I never doubted your gift would come. As we had eliminated the common major gifts, I suspected you were gifted in farsight or discernment. Your coincidental illness on the day of the Abershire attack indicated discernment, but I wanted to be certain before I told you."

Deria nodded, scanning the large hollow as her eyes adjusted to the faint light filtering through the entrance.

"I'm sorry, Mother. I should have trusted you all along."

She shook her head, squeezing her eyes shut. "No, the fault is mine, Deria. I chose to live with your father in this tiny community to avoid Stone Clan purists, who would mistreat you because of your father's Water Clan heritage. But growing up here, you lacked the confidence gained from watching child after child receive their major gifts after their sixteenth birthingdays. It is hard to trust what you haven't experienced for yourself."

The room darkened as her father pushed his way through the vines into the cave. "You should speak softly—your voices carry outside."

"Father." Korporan drew a short blade and gestured with wild frustration. "I want to fight, not hide like a coward. I'm gifted in strength and weapons, as are you. Why do we not kill those Water Clan warriors who reek of such evil that my sister retches when they are in close proximity?"

"Choosing to fight when we will be greatly outnumbered is not an indication of bravery," he replied. "It is a sign of folly. Those warriors are not only gifted, they are also well-trained. With only twelve families in all of Essenshire, we would stand no chance in battle."

"I am not afraid to die." Korporan hissed through gritted teeth, his hand fisted on his raised short sword.

Though she remained sitting on the cave floor, in her heart Deria stood beside her brother. She had prayed to receive her major gift—any gift at all. She thought she would be overjoyed if that happened. But her gift of discernment had only led them into hiding, prolonging the inevitable and offering no real defense. She couldn't help thinking they might have stood a fighting chance if she were gifted in weapons or strength or agility. Anything seemed better than hiding and waiting for Water Clan warriors to find and slaughter them.

"Death is not the worst possible outcome of battle." Father held Korporan's gaze, the muscles in his throat seizing with emotion. "I watched my father and mother submit to the bloodbond to save my life. I pray none of us will be faced with such a vile choice."

Dropping the blade to his side, Korporan sagged in defeat. "I hate hiding, Father. It feels wrong."

"It is never wrong to avoid violence." With unshed tears glistening in his eyes, Father grasped Korporan's shoulders. "Evil men provoke us to actions as vile as their own, but we shall resist. We show our courage when we control our emotions and refuse to be baited into foolishness."

"What if they find our cave?" Deria wondered aloud.

"Even if they come inside, they will not find us in the deep shadows under the ledge. We will be safe in our hiding place." The tremble in Mother's voice belied the confidence in her words, but her jaw hardened as she lay facedown on the ground and edged sideways into the crevice until she disappeared from view.

"If we are discovered, then we will all fight," said her father. "I have small blades for Mother and Deria. God willing, it will not happen, but each of us may have an opportunity to die this day. And if we do, let it be with honor."

No one spoke after Father's declaration. Strengthened by the bread, Deria stretched out onto her stomach and scooted under the low, rocky outcropping to her right, leaving her left arm toward the outside. She shifted and edged until her right side was against the back of the cave, leaving her left side only a few handspans out of sight. As she wiggled to get a sharp stone from under her hip, the thought of creepy insects, which might soon be crawling on her skin, sent a disgusted shiver down her spine. Her gifting with animals did not extend to conversing with creatures of the six- and eight-legged varieties. The side of her face rested on the smooth, damp rock, and the scent of moss invaded her nose. From the blackness of her cramped hiding place, the thin strands of light filtering into the cave entrance seemed bright.

Her father peered under the rock and slid a small knife into her left hand. She heard scraping noises as he wedged into the crack farther down.

Korporan squeezed under the ledge on the end near Deria, stretching his feet the opposite direction so that their heads were close together. He grunted as he worked his way beneath the protective rock. "Don't be afraid," he whispered. "Give me your hand."

She left the blade on the ground by her hip and slid her trembling hand past her head toward Korporan. His warm hand covered hers and squeezed, the comforting gesture saying more of his concerned affection than any words. Deria sent up a prayer for protection.

Please, don't let them find us. Let us survive this day. But if one of us must die, let it be me.

Her mother's soft voice floated across the cave. "Deria... Korporan... Always remember...no matter what happens...we love you—your father and I— with all our hearts."

"We love you, too," Deria replied, almost in unison with her twin.

Quiet descended like a heavy blanket, and the waiting began.

Three

Deria's neck grew stiff and her hips ached where they pressed against the rocky ground. She couldn't say how long she lay unmoving, wedged under the ledge. Gradually, the churning in her stomach increased until the meager contents rolled about like liquid in a barrel tumbling downhill. Though unaccustomed to her discernment gift, Deria had no doubt about the meaning of the nausea.

"They are getting closer." She whispered the words, the first spoken since her family had settled into their dark hiding place. She pulled her hand away from Korporan's, reaching down to her knife and closing her clammy fingers around the smooth handle.

She heard a voice—deep and scratchy—like that of the craggy old man who once came peddling his wares while speaking around a stained reed pipe that dangled from the corner of his mouth.

"We are at the end and there is naught here but a mass of vines. They must have doubled back."

"Look closer," said another man, his tone ripe with impatience. "The plant stems are bent this direction, and none the other way."

"It was probably an animal," said another.

"We are wasting time," said a woman, who spoke with an air of command. "Raenter—climb out and see if the trail continues. We have no footprints on this rock to show whether we are following a person or an animal. Smaede— look behind the foliage. Do not let a leaf go unturned. Everyone else, stand on alert lest another clansman take us by surprise and we have to kill him. Vindrake gave orders to bring them back alive—at least, as many as possible. And I, for one, do not wish to anger our leader."

Grumbles followed, along with rustling vines. Though the cave entrance wasn't visible from her vantage point, Deria saw filtered strands of light dancing across the floor.

"Hie!" yelled the rough voice. "There's a hole here. It's dark—I need a torch!"

We've been found!

Deria's heart pounded against her rib cage, drumming in time with the blood pulsing in her ears. From her hiding place, she saw a flickering light sweep across the ground as thick boots clomped into the cave.

"What do you see, Smaede?"

"It's empty. I see no sign of people. Simply a large hollow. Wait...perhaps down here..."

The boots trudged closer, the torchlight growing brighter. Deria's racing heart seemed to flip over inside her chest. To make matters worse, her stomach boiled with nausea as he approached.

Breathing slowly in an attempt to control the queasiness, Deria tightened her grip on the blade, swallowing her frustration. She had longed for a major gift for an entire year, believing it would bring happiness and fulfillment. Yet, her bittersweet gift of discernment only *warned* her of evil, providing no means to fight against it. She could only pray.

Keep us hidden. Don't let him see us.

Closer and closer, the boots stepped, until she could clearly make out chunks of mud caked on the soles. The boots stopped an arm's length away, just outside the rocky ledge. Rustling and grunting sounds echoed in the cave as he bent to the ground. The hand holding the fiery torch dipped to the cave floor, so near she felt its heat on her face.

Keep us hidden. Don't let him see us.

The air grew thick as mud, and Deria struggled to breathe. Her lips moved, repeating the silent words—a desperate prayer. And as she prayed, she felt her energy seeping from her body, drop by drop, as if she were bleeding.

A face appeared—a pair of stark blue eyes peering under the ledge, a bent nose, and a dark wiry beard, sprinkled with gray. So close was he that she gagged on his foul breath and quaked at the evil emanating from his pores.

Her prayer had failed—she had been seen. But perhaps he had not seen the rest of her family.

I accept I must die this day. Don't let my sacrifice be for naught. Spare my brother and parents.

She waited for him to grab at her. To drag her out of the gap. To call out for the other Water Clan warriors standing outside the cave.

Struggling to remain conscious, she forced her drooping eyelids open, staring at the sneering, bearded face, his sapphire eyes boring into her. So weak she no longer felt the urge to vomit from his proximity, she watched his image wobble through puddled tears. Her entire body shivered, anticipating the pain to come.

"Smaede!" called a voice from outside. "Did you find something?"

Deep in his throat, a grunt sounded. The burly face disappeared, as did the hands and the knees. The light from the torch receded as the boots turned and strode away. "Nay! I found nothing but an empty cave. There is no one here."

Some dim part of her foggy mind wondered if her prayers had worked after all. She labored to stay awake and continue her desperate supplication to keep her family hidden. Gritting her teeth with effort, she kept her eyes focused on the retreating boots until the last of her energy bled away. Then she let the darkness take her.

Four

Dark dreams swirled in Deria's mind. A merciless gaze from squinted eyes, so cold it froze her soul. A grinding voice that rang in her ears. A rocky ledge pressing down to squeeze the air from her lungs.

At times, voices pierced her consciousness and her mind struggled to organize its thoughts. Then she would pray again that no one would find her family, though she wondered if they had already been caught and killed. Perhaps the enemy warriors were waiting for her to awaken so they could force her to accept the bloodbond that would tie her to the evil Water Clan leader. Or perhaps they would be merciful and take her life quickly.

She no longer lay on the ground inside the cave, of that much she was certain. However, she couldn't force her eyes to open and survey her surroundings. Her body refused to respond to her commands. She couldn't even persuade a single finger to twitch.

Deria knew she wasn't dead, but surely she must be dying. Her head swam while every part of her body ached, like a wet cloth someone had twisted to wring out the last drop of water.

Abruptly, the fog lifted from her mind. A hand gripped her arm while a man's voice mumbled strange words into her ear. A peculiar clarity sharpened her senses, though her body lay motionless as if it belonged to another.

"I have stopped it," said the strange man. "Now, if you want her to live, you must get her to eat."

"I have been forcing her to swallow some broth, at least a little every day," said Korporan from some place near her head, and Deria rejoiced that her twin was alive.

"Every day?" the man repeated, his tone incredulous. "How long has she been in this state?"

"Since the attack occurred, three days ago," said Deria's father. "As we hid in the cave, the Water Clan warrior came within a few handspans of her, yet announced to his companions he saw no one. Is it possible he poisoned her?"

Deria would have danced if she could move. Her brother and father were both alive! What of her mother?

Korporan whispered in her ear. "Drink some broth, Deria. Come back to us."

Though she couldn't help him with his job, her head was soon lifted, her lips pried open, and warm broth spooned into her mouth. Fingers massaged her neck, and she swallowed by reflex, warmth spreading down her throat.

"Her state was not a result of poison," the man replied. "The damage came from prolonged use of her gift, beyond what her body had strength to support."

"Your tale is amazing," said another man, his voice commanding, yet encouraging. "You are blessed to have survived the Water Clan attack."

"No thanks to you, Graely. I suppose you expect us to feel grateful that you—the leader of all Stone Clan—have come to Essenshire, even if you arrived too late to be of aid." Her mother's tone was tight and fuming with anger. But Deria exulted. Her prayers had been answered—her whole family lived! She didn't care if her body never worked again.

"Swallow some more," Korporan murmured. "I tire of doing all your chores while you laze about."

She wanted to laugh or voice a snappy response, but she lay frozen and frustrated as he coaxed the broth down her throat.

"We came as soon as we received the signal," Graely defended. "As I warned before, Stone Clan cannot protect all the small communities bordering the river. Yet when we learned of the attack, I came myself with a band of warriors and my chief shaman. Does that not demonstrate my concern for all Stone Clan citizens? Even those who refuse to move to Laegenshire's safety?"

"You know well we would never be accepted in Laegenshire," her mother retorted. "I will not subject my family to ill treatment by ignorant Stone Clan purists who would regard a person as evil by virtue of birth alone. I have seen both of you regard my husband with fear and distrust, based solely on his blue eye color."

"My fear was based on his raised sword, not his blue eyes," Nordamen spat back.

"I will admit I am not without prejudice." Graely's tone was more apologetic. "However, of late I am learning not to judge a person by the color of their eyes. Return with us to Laegenshire, and you will see that attitudes are beginning to change. Surely, you have heard of our new bearer, Alora. Her eyes are similar in color to your own son's."

Deria heard her mother huff. It was the sound she made when she didn't believe what you were saying. Graely was going to have a hard time convincing Mother, but Deria couldn't help being excited. Word of Stone Clan's young bearer had spread throughout the land. They had *not* heard, however, of Alora's mixed heritage.

"Keep drinking." Korporan spooned more broth into Deria's mouth. This time, it almost felt as if she swallowed on purpose.

"You must move your family, no matter your feelings about Laegenshire," said Nordamen. "Your daughter almost lost her life because she overreached her gift. Her teacher has been irresponsible with her training."

"We will not be criticized for how we raise our own children!" Her father was almost growling. "Deria's gift had only manifested one other time, so she had no time to train. And her gift is so rare, we were unaware of its dangers."

"You didn't know it was dangerous?" Nordamen sputtered. "How could you not? And why do you pretend she has no teacher? Has she been training with a shaman from Water Clan? Is that the reason the warriors spared your family when everyone else in Essenshire lost their lives?"

"No!" Korporan's sudden shout startled Deria. "My sister has not trained with any shaman, Water Clan or otherwise! Until the day of the attack, Deria did not know of her gift. I told her she was gifted in discernment that very morning."

"You told her she was gifted in discernment?" Nordamen's pitch lifted on the last word, as if he were confused.

"Yes," Korporan confirmed, in an indignant tone Deria had heard on numerous occasions when her twin was feeling defensive. It warmed her to hear him speak out on her behalf. *Maybe I'll forgive him for teasing me about killing Hopper and putting her in my stew.*

"She had been waiting for most of a year for her major gift to manifest," her mother interjected. "Her twin received his giftings on their birthingday. Deria's gift only revealed itself for the first time a moon ago, and even then we were uncertain discernment was the cause of her illness."

"I cannot believe what I am hearing." Nordamen's mumbled words came from nearby, as if he were bending close to stare at her. "You are saying she had no training whatsoever?"

Deria fumed. What right did this rude man have to ridicule her for her lack of training? Or to criticize her mother for protecting her feelings? That her gift delayed so long in manifesting was no one's fault.

She strained against her frozen body, determined to open her eyes and speak for herself. She forced one finger to bend. And then another. Concentrating, she squeezed her hand into a fist, wishing she could swing it at the insulting shaman.

"We were not negligent," her father boomed from somewhere near her feet, closer than before. "Once we knew of her gift, we would have sought a mentor."

"She will train with me and none other," Nordamen declared in a tone that brooked no argument.

"*No!*" The word exploded from Deria's own lips. Her eyes opened and, at last, her tongue obeyed her will. Her family's gasps mirrored her own shock, yet she kept her glare fixed on Nordamen's deep green eyes, wide with surprise. "No, I won't! I refuse to train with one so arrogant. I will find another to mentor me with my discernment. Have no fear—never again will I utilize my gift without awareness of its dangers."

"Child, I hope you will reconsider." Nordamen had the audacity to bestow an indulgent smile as he held up his palms in mock surrender. "For there is no other in all of Stone Clan better gifted to train you. And your discernment, though obviously powerful in its reach, is not the danger you believe it to be."

"Do you think to trick me with your speech? For I listened to every word you spoke to my family, though it seemed I was sleeping. I heard you say I almost lost my life from misuse of my gift."

"Forgive me for my lack of clarity and let me rectify this misunderstanding." Nordamen cleared his throat. "From the moment I found you lying unconscious, still projecting remnants of an invisibility cloak that is difficult to produce for one with experience and heretofore impossible for one without training, I knew you were extraordinarily gifted—" he paused, leaning in close, his last words a sibilant whisper, "—as a *shaman.*"

Five

Deria sat cross-legged on the ground, stroking the pile of soft brown fur in her lap.

"I will miss you, Hopper. I wish I could take you with me."

The bunny burrowed closer.

"Yes, I know you cannot leave when you have babies to take care of," Deria continued. "But I worry you will not be safe after I am gone. You've grown bold around us, because I have protected you. You must remember, people are not safe. Always run and hide when you see one."

"Ha!" The shout from behind Deria's back came with a simultaneous grab on either side of her ribs.

"Akkk! Korporan! Stop doing that—you scared poor Hopper almost to death." She lifted the rabbit up, kissing her nose. "I apologize for my brother—there is no excuse for him."

"I cannot help myself, dear sister. The temptation to startle you is simply too great to resist. It is far too entertaining to watch you jump out of your skin. And as for Hopper...had I succeeded in frightening that greedy rabbit to death, she would have made a substantial contribution to our evening stew, fat as she is from eating all our vegetables."

"Hush, Korporan." She put a protective hand across Hopper's long ears. "She can hear you."

Her twin rolled his eyes. "It is time to go, Deria. Mother and Father are waiting at the wagon. Unless you've changed your mind and wish to stay here at Essenshire alone."

"No, I'm ready to go." She blinked hard and fast, hoping Korporan wouldn't notice the tears in her eyes as she set Hopper on the ground and watched her disappear into her burrow.

Strong hands reached under Deria's arms, lifting her to her feet.

"I am certain there will be at least one gluttonous rabbit for you to befriend when we arrive. I certainly hope so, for I shall need one for target practice."

She sent an ineffectual elbow into his side while using her sleeve to wipe her damp eyes. "Be quiet, or I will send a family of mice to share your blanket when you are sleeping tonight."

"Though they gnaw my feet completely away, I will likely sleep through it, so tired will I be from walking alongside the wagon all day."

"Mother says she and I will take our turns walking as well. But just think..." Deria bounced on her toes. "In two days, we will be in Laegenshire!"

"I have thought of little else. In fact, I have a plan for us to explore the town unseen, utilizing your very convenient gift." Korporan's eyebrows waggled up and down.

"You know I cannot do that. Nordamen says I must not use my gift in a frivolous manner."

"Deria, you waited an entire year to discover your gift, and you have the rest of your life to use it properly. Why can you not have a bit of fun with it now?"

Deria felt her willpower slipping. Korporan knew her weaknesses, and his twinkling eyes were difficult to resist.

"Even if I wished to, I have not learned how to cloak us without depleting my energy. I could not walk a single step while using my gift, much less go all about the town."

"Ah, yes, but I have a solution. You see, Deria...you are a gifted shaman, while I..."

She squealed when he hefted her up high, as if she weighed nothing, and lowered her onto his shoulders.

He continued his argument. "You are a gifted shaman, while I am gifted in strength. Together..."

"Together, we can do anything!" Deria shouted from her high perch, already imagining the possibilities.

"Together..." A deep voice spoke behind them, and Korporan turned slowly to face their father, who stood with his fists planted on his hips, his muscles flexing along his gritted jaw. Deria's mouth went dry as she absorbed his ice-blue glare. "Together, you may send your mother and me to an early death."

Craning his head, Korporan grinned up at her. "Now would be a good time to practice, Sister."

Deria bit back a smile.

Why not?

She watched her father's eyes go wide as she and her brother disappeared.

Deria and Korporan, introduced in this story, are major characters in the upcoming fourth book of The Alora Series. *In this epic young adult fantasy, Alora, a teen from rural Montana, begins to have visions of a handsome boy with unusual deep green eyes. Her hallucinations become reality when he appears before her in the flesh. As her true hidden identity unfolds, Alora's safe world turns upside-down, thrusting her into a dangerous realm of magic and beauty, where a powerful and evil man seeks to use her ability for his own abhorrent purposes.*

http://www.tamiedearen.com/alora/

Not Quite A Hero

Arthur Daigle

D ana Illwind waited at the forest crossroads north of her town, not happy with her current situation. That was unfortunate given she was responsible for ninety percent of what was happening to her. Maybe eighty-five percent responsible.

It was getting dark and cold, and she pulled her cloak tight over her shoulders. She'd worn her extra thick dress and fur-lined boots and a fur cap over her brown hair. It was still early in the year where winter's cold and spring's warmth traded places nearly every day. Dana had brought a backpack loaded with two days of food, a lamp and extra oil, a knife (never leave home without one), and a purse with her life savings. Granted, fourteen copper pieces and three silver coins didn't go far, but her father was fond of pointing out most people didn't have two coins to rub together and got by on barter. Barter was also harder for the king to tax.

The thick growth of pine trees would make it hard to see her guest when he arrived. He'd said he'd come today, but they were rapidly running out of today. Maybe he was delayed and wouldn't arrive until tomorrow. That would be bad. She'd used every excuse she had to get out of today's chores. Her parents wouldn't tolerate her missing another day.

An owl hooted to the north. Maybe he wouldn't come at all. But then why bother writing to say he would? Paper cost money, and the scruffy-looking man who delivered his letter must have been paid. If he had no intention of coming, then he could have saved time and money by ignoring her request.

"Ms. Illwind, I presume?"

Dana screamed and leaped off the road, landing on a thick carpet of dead pine needles. She scrambled behind a tree and drew her knife. It took her half a minute to stop hyperventilating, and another ten seconds to get angry with the smirking man standing off to the side of the road.

"That was not nice!"

"I'm not a nice person."

Dana sheathed her knife and returned to the road. The man who'd scared the daylights out of her (and nearly several other things) was in his thirties. His long, blond hair was a mess, even if it was clean. His clothes were, well, odd. He favored black with silver highlights, and she'd never seen the style before. The cape flowed like there was a wind, his black gloves ended in silver tips, his boots came up to his knees, and his belt was segmented black metal that reminded her of a centipede.

He was attractive and doubtlessly drew attention wherever he went. Part of that was how confident he looked, like victory was assured by nothing more than his presence. Maybe there was magic at work here? It wouldn't surprise her. He carried no weapon, a rare move when traveling in the wilderness, and more so for a man of his fierce reputation. Then again, if he was half as powerful as the stories claimed, he wouldn't need a sword or bow.

"Um, Sorcerer Lord Jayden?"

"A pleasure, Ms. Illwind." Jayden walked onto the road. She curtsied, and to her surprise Jayden circled her. "I must admit I thought you'd be a tad older. I also expected the town mayor to come in person rather than send his daughter unescorted. It speaks poorly of him."

Dana put her hands on her hips. "I'm fifteen, a grown woman. I'm sorry my father couldn't come. He's a very busy man, sir."

"Busy?" Jayden reached into a pocket and pulled out a letter. "He wasn't too busy to send a letter begging for my help. He gushed his admiration in flowery language, yet after I came a great distance, he decides not to meet me? Instead, he sends a slip of a girl. I take offense at that."

Oh dear. Dana waved her hands in front of her. "No, no, it's not like that! He, uh, he wanted to come, but he's sick! He's drunk! The horse kicked him! The sheriff bit him! I mean, the dog bit him!"

Jayden tilted his head to one side. "You're sure the horse didn't bite him?"

"Very sure! Definitely the dog."

The Sorcerer Lord stared at her a few moments before turning his attention to the letter he'd taken out. "I can't help but notice a level of flattery seldom employed by men. Most are too proud to ask for help, and the more authority they wield, the less willing they are to admit weakness. It makes me wonder."

"Wonder what, sir?"

"I wonder if I were to track down your father the mayor, would he know anything about this letter? It has his seal of office on it. That normally proves a letter's authenticity, except such a seal can be borrowed, especially by someone living in his house."

Dana blushed and looked at her feet. Jayden walked up to her and put a finger under her chin. He pressed up gently until she was looking him in the eyes.

Terrified, she managed to say, "My father...doesn't know you're here. He doesn't know about the monster, either. I couldn't tell him."

"Pray tell, why not?"

"Because he's mayor." She took a deep breath and tried to keep from shaking. "If a town is in danger, the mayor has to lead its defense. He's an old man, and these monsters have killed before. If we still had the town militia, we'd stand a chance, but they were called up for military service by the king. That leaves the men still left in town, none of whom know how to fight, and my father leading them.

"They'd be killed! But, but my father knows his duty, and he'd go anyway. Maybe he'd win. His father killed one of these monsters, but others tried and never came back. So, when I saw one of the fiends in the woods, I didn't tell him. I wrote the letter asking for help, and I hired a traveling peddler to deliver it. He said he knew where to find you. I'd heard you saved another town from a manticore. I have money. It, ah, should cover your expenses."

Dana closed her eyes and braced for the fallout of her lies. She trembled, wondering if he'd burn her alive, cut her into pieces, or maybe turn her into a newt. Getting Jayden here had been a long shot, but she'd been desperate and, now she was willing to admit, overconfident. But lives were at stake, every one a person she loved. She had to do something, even if it was risky! It was, at most, eighty percent her fault.

Jayden threw his head back and laughed. "You have got to be the most conniving, devious, manipulative woman in the entire kingdom! I'm glad we met."

She opened one eye. "You're not going to rip my liver out and feed it to ravens?"

"That would limit your usefulness. After all, you're the only one who's seen this monster and can lead me to it."

"Wait, what?" Both her eyes were open and her jaw dropped. "I, uh, you can't find it with your magic?"

"No." Jayden reread the letter she'd sent him. "Your letter describes the beast as a spider made of dead branches and animal bones, big as a wagon, with holes in it wide enough you could reach a hand inside. It's called an estate guard, brutes I'm familiar with and have killed twice before. Your accurate description made me believe this was a legitimate call for help and not a trap or hoax."

"It was very scary, and I really would rather not meet it again."

Looking up from the letter, he asked, "What was it doing?"

"It was pulling a dead tree deeper into the forest. There's a place in the woods we're not supposed to go. That's where the monsters live. They come out once a generation, maybe twice, and our people have to kill them. Some of our men said the monsters come from ruins the old Sorcerer Lords made."

Jayden folded up the letter. "With due respect to your menfolk, there's only one monster, a blessing indeed. May I borrow your lantern for a moment?"

Dana handed it over. "You know about them?"

"Yes. I was being quite literal when I said there was only one. The others your ancestors killed over the years? It was the same monster. You destroyed its body and nothing more."

"How is that possible? Hey, what are you doing?"

Jayden opened her lantern and put her letter to him inside. He watched it burn before returning the lantern. "Your father's name and seal are on that letter. He would be in considerable trouble if someone should find it. The king and queen wouldn't understand, especially after I poached their deer, robbed two of their storehouses, and looted a caravan bringing them wine."

Dana backed up until she hit a tree. "You did what?"

He smiled at her. "I told you I'm not a nice man. Without going into excessive details, I don't like them and they don't like me. Be honest, do they stir feelings of love and loyalty in your heart, or do their names churn up fear?"

"Fear." Dana was ashamed to say it. Her father had warned her to watch what she said, but there seemed little risk of saying the truth with no witnesses. "Taxes are still high to pay for the civil war twenty years ago. We're struggling to get by, and the king's calling up men to start a new war. So many people have been exiled. My brother Owen, he, um, they took him and said he has to stay in the capital."

"As a hostage, insurance that your father does as he's told. All mayors were required to surrender their eldest sons last year. It's barbaric behavior that the queen takes a fair share of the blame for. Trust me, I've met her and she leaves much to be desired. But that is neither here nor there, and we have a monster to kill. So, if you'll take me to where you saw it last, we can finish this business, and make sure no member of your fair town need face this threat again."

It was totally dark as they walked through the forest, Dana's lantern their only source of light. There was no undergrowth beneath the trees. She saw patches of snow where the trees shaded the ground so completely that the sun never touched it. Dana saw several fresh stumps where lumberjacks had taken trees last winter, but there were no houses or farms. The earth was too sour to support crops except blueberries, and even goblins weren't foolish enough to live here.

"You said there's only one monster, but we've killed many," she said.

"Destroyed, yes. Killed, no. The monster of bones and branches you saw was a temporary body the estate guard built. It can lose that to rot, fire, or damage in battle."

"Then how do you kill it?"

Jayden climbed over a fallen tree lying across the road and stopped to help her over. "Estate guards are actually gold talismans three inches long and shaped like a scarab beetle. It had to be attached somewhere on the body you saw. You need to find that and smash it. Stop at burning or crushing the body, and the talisman will crawl off to make another."

They'd reached the spot where Dana had seen the monster weeks ago. Several pines had died, leaving an opening to the sky above. That provided enough light to support blueberry bushes that were leafing out. Not far from the clearing was a narrow trench six inches deep and running hundreds of feet, and to either side of it were potholes a foot across and just as deep.

"That's where it was," Dana told Jayden. "I was checking rabbit snares when I saw the monster grab a dead tree and pull it away. I hid in that hollow over there until it left."

She shivered at the horror of that night. She'd been having a good day when the stuff of nightmares had come within feet of her. She'd hidden as best she could, held her breath, and prayed that the beast would pass. The sound it had made, a rasping, scratching sound, would stay with her until she died.

Jayden bent down to study the tracks. "Most estate guards were destroyed long ago along with the original Sorcerer Lords. No loss there. The Sorcerer Lords were greedy, vicious, and thoroughly detestable. Most of them died when they turned on one another, and the rest fell in battle with the ancient Elf Empire."

"Are you one of their descendants?"

That made him laugh. "Heavens, no, and a fact I'm proud of. I simply took their name and as much of their magic as I could find. Quite a few others have done so over the years."

Dana perked up. "I'd never heard that. Where are they?"

"Dead," he explained.

"Dead?"

He nodded. "Extremely dead."

"I didn't know there were degrees of being dead."

"Oh yes." He spoke casually on the grisly subject, as if it was no different than discussing the weather. "Most people end up extremely dead. Some end up sort of dead. Vampires, ghouls, ghosts, barrow-wights; it's surprisingly common. Nearly all of them wish they were extremely dead. I've met a few vampires and none were happy."

"Oh. Uh, why was the monster taking a tree?"

"That's something we have to worry about. Estate guards need to make bodies for themselves. If they come across dead material, fallen trees and dry bones, they can pull them together and become a threat to others. But stumbling across enough materials by chance is harder than it sounds, especially bones. Those normally decompose or are eaten by predators and scavengers."

Dana peered over Jayden's shoulder at the tracks. "It was gathering parts for a body?"

"Clever girl! That's exactly what it was doing. Most estate guards aren't too bright, but this one has been active for centuries, long enough to learn. It's had bodies destroyed before, so it's collecting what it needs to make a new body if it loses this one."

Worried, she asked, "How many bodies does it have?"

He shrugged. "There's no way to tell. If the estate guard hasn't been seen in a generation, then it's had plenty of time to prepare. There could be enough branches and bones hidden for it to jump from one body to the next a dozen times."

Dana looked down. "The stories said people fought these monsters for days. That's why, isn't it? They'd kill it but not the talisman, and it made a new body to attack again. Why does it come after us?"

Jayden got up and followed the tracks deeper into the woods. "Estate guards protected the property of the old Sorcerer Lords. I'd guess this one is doing just that. A Sorcerer Lord once claimed this land, and this estate guard survived its maker. As far as it's concerned, your townspeople are trespassers."

"But we've lived here for three hundred years!"

"And the old Sorcerer Lords died out eighteen hundred years ago. Common sense and good manners demand it accepts the situation. Unfortunately, estate guards were built to obey, and while they can think and learn, they can't change their orders. This state of affairs will go on until it's killed."

Dana ran ahead of him and smiled. "You're a Sorcerer Lord, not like the old ones. Can you make it stop being a jerk?"

"I've mastered some of the old Sorcerer Lords' magic, but not enough to make an estate guard or seize control of one. Regretfully, this must end in violence."

"Um, exactly how much magic can you do?"

Jayden bared his teeth. "There are three things you never ask: a woman's age, a miser's wealth, or a wizard's power."

"Sorry! Sorry, sorry, sorry—"

"You're sorry, yes, we established that," he interrupted. "Apology accepted. Now if you don't mind, we...we have a problem."

The tracks ended abruptly, for the estate guard had dragged the fallen tree across stony ground. Jayden marched over to where the tracks ended. He muttered strange words Dana didn't understand, and a glowing orb appeared in his hands. The orb floated high into the sky before winking out, long enough to illuminate the forest for half a mile in all directions. Jayden scowled at what he saw. The rocky ground went on beyond the light of his orb.

"I'd hoped to send you home and finish this alone, but I've little chance to find the monster's lair with the trail gone."

Worried, she asked, "What do you mean?"

"You spoke of ruins the monster uses as its lair. Do you know where to find them?"

Dana frowned. Where was he going with this? "Sort of. I mean, I heard the same stories as everyone else in town."

"That will have to do. Take me there or as close as you can."

Worry quickly turned to panic. "Wait a minute, I can't go there! You're a Sorcerer Lord, a new one, anyway. You can fight scary things like this. I can't!"

"I don't need you to fight, only guide me to it. You can leave once I'm there."

"Can't someone else in the village do that?"

"That would require them to meet me. You don't want your father to know I'm here, difficult enough when only you know of my presence. Do you want a friend or neighbor to know your secret? Can they keep it?" He kept speaking as he walked back to her, his words remorseless. "Will you place them in danger you'd avoid? I thought you braver than that."

"But, but—"

"You summoned me here. You want the estate guard dead and your town forever free from its menace. I'm placing my life at risk for your neighbors, your friends, *your family*. If you respect nothing else about me, respect that and reciprocate."

Dana gulped. Sweat poured off her regardless of the cold. Bringing Jayden here had been the most terrifying thing she'd done, hoping and praying he'd come and that no one would learn about it. She'd done as much as anyone could expect. This wasn't fair!

Fair or not, dangerous or not, Jayden was right. He had to find the monster's hideout. Without help, he could spend weeks searching for it, every day risking discovery. People who saw him might inform the authorities. Or Jayden might leave if she didn't help. Her town would be in the same mess it had been in for hundreds of years. How many more people would the monster kill? If even one person died and Dana could prevent it, the loss would be on her head.

Taking a deep breath, she steeled her nerves and pointed west. "It's supposed to be at the base of the largest mountain."

Dana had never intended to stay out this late. She'd originally hoped to meet Jayden in the early morning and point him in the right direction, then return home. Her parents would be furious. Her sisters would be scared. Her little brother would be digging through her belongings like a deranged raccoon, looking for and probably finding her hidden bag of chocolates. Those goodies had cost her two copper pieces! This was now officially only seventy percent her fault.

The land grew progressively more mountainous. There were still pine trees growing where rock gave way to soil, and they were giants over a hundred feet tall. Lumberjacks would drool at the sight of such beautiful trees, or weep, knowing they couldn't harvest them without being attacked.

"What's that up ahead?" Jayden asked.

Before them was a clearing with three destroyed houses. Their doors had long ago rotted away, but the damage to the brick walls wasn't caused by the ravages of time. One had the front wall caved in, a second was missing two walls, and the third was little more than a pile of bricks. A pine tree fifty feet tall grew from the rubble of the second house, proof of how long ago the damage was done.

"This is from the first time the monster attacked my people," Dana explained. "Our baron's great-great-grandfather built this as a hunting lodge. His workers had just finished it when the monster attacked. You can see what it did. The baron escaped in his underwear but lost all his hounds. His family, ah, they don't come here anymore."

"Even to fight monsters that humiliated their ancestor?" Jayden asked sarcastically.

"Especially to fight monsters. The last time the monster attacked, my grandfather asked for their help. We were told the baron was indisposed and so were all his men."

"Hunting's less fun when the quarry fights back." Jayden studied the ruined buildings and surroundings. "I see a footprint between those stones that could only have come from our foe. There don't seem to be more. It came this way, but I can't tell its direction from one footprint. How far are we from the beast's lair?"

Dana stopped and took a flask of oil from her backpack. She topped off her lantern's reserve and put the flask away. "It's supposed to be a few miles from here. We'll reach it by midnight."

"An inauspicious hour, but it will have the benefit of being dramatic." He smiled when Dana gave him a confused look. "I'm told I have a tendency for being overly theatrical. Allow me my weaknesses."

She hesitated before going farther. "You're positive there's only one monster?"

"If there were two, your town would be little more than a memory."

Dana led him on, her lantern their only light. Jayden made no move to summon another of his light spheres, but it had burned out so fast there was little reason to bother. That was the only spell she'd seen Jayden cast. It worried her. Were all his spells so weak, so limited? He certainly seemed confident, smug even, so maybe he had better magic he was saving for the battle.

"Um, I have a question," she began. "Why did you come alone? This would be easier if you'd brought your men."

Jayden laughed. "That implies I have men. I don't."

Dana stopped and stared at him. "No one follows you? But you're famous, or infamous, maybe both. People should be knocking each other over to work for you."

"Followers are expensive. You have to feed them, arm them, house them, and don't get me started on pensions and medical care. If they have families, I'm expected to support them as well! Studying magic costs an appalling amount of gold, and I have precious little. My choice was learn magic or hire incompetent, smelly, barely educated, and possibly disloyal followers."

"That's kind of harsh."

He smiled at her. "If you only knew."

Jayden's reasonable (albeit rude) response gave her the courage to ask a question that had been bothering her. "You don't like the old Sorcerer Lords much, but you call yourself one. Why?"

Jayden walked on in silence for so long Dana thought he was ignoring her or, worse, angry with her again.

"It's a fair question. The old Sorcerer Lords performed incredible deeds rivaling those of the ancient Elf Empire. I recognize their achievements but curse their name for how they accomplished them. No deed was too foul if the act advanced their power and position in society. They went down in history as monsters, and deservedly so.

"But, and this may seem strange, their name has great allure. If I called myself a hero, a revolutionary, a scholar, or a wizard, few would notice me. Calling myself a Sorcerer Lord draws men's attention. They recall the glory of those days and not the blood. My claim is fair to a point, given all my spells were learned from ruins of the old Sorcerer Lords. I use their tools if not their methods, so I feel using their title is justified."

Struggling to make a point without making an enemy of him, Dana said, "But you get the bad part of their reputation along with the good. If they did bad things, people will think you might, too. They'll be afraid of you."

"There are people I want to be afraid of me. I want them to tremble at my name and the passing of my shadow. I want them to be afraid because they live off fear, they use it as a tool, and it's high time they felt what it was like."

Without thinking, Dana said, "Someone hurt you badly, didn't they?"

She instantly regretted her words and flinched from whatever magic Jayden was sure to throw at her for speaking to him that way. To her amazement, Jayden didn't even look at her. The confidence seemed to drain out of him, just for a moment, and he said, "It's not a tale for children to hear."

People in her town liked Dana, and that had little to do with being the mayor's daughter. She helped those in need, nursed those who were sick, and fed those who were hungry. Following her father's example, she also knew when to ignore minor crimes done from desperation or ignorance. They loved her and she wanted it to be that way.

What sort of person wanted to be feared? It boggled the mind. Jayden's personality seemed to shift as often as a clock's pendulum, kindness changing to anger. Dana wondered what had led him to this point. Whatever it was, it had left him scarred in ways that were hard to heal. Was there anything that could lead him away from giving in to his anger?

It didn't help that Jayden was alone most of the time with no followers or friends. People get weird when they were alone too long. She'd seen it in Anton Carothers, who lived outside town and swore gnomes were after him. Admittedly, they might be, given how foul-tempered most gnomes were, but that was beside the point. Loneliness could eat away at a man until he was left bitter.

They stopped where the forest gave way to mountains that towered high above them, wreathed in clouds and capped with snow. Technically, this was still part of the kingdom, but no one came here. You couldn't grow crops, raise livestock, or even gather wood, and these mountains held no metals or gemstones. It was worthless to all, a property abandoned to the monster because there was nothing here worth fighting for.

"I'm told the Kingdom of the Goblins is nearly this desolate," Jayden said. "Mind you, I think that's just bad press. And unless my eyes deceive me, our goal is at hand."

The ruins at the base of the mountains were in terrible shape. There were five buildings made to massive proportions, three or even four stories high. Two were little more than outer walls with the ceilings and interior gone. Another was an architectural wonder on one side and a rubble pile on the other. The last two had holes in the walls big enough to ride a wagon through them. There were seven piles of rubble so large they must have been buildings at one point. Moss grew across the ground to form a thick carpet that muffled their footsteps.

Jayden walked fearlessly to the edge of the ruins. "This was certainly built by the old Sorcerer Lords. I've visited ruins like this often enough in the far north to recognize their style. I believe it was the private residence of one of their wealthier members, and by the look of things, he went down fighting."

"A Sorcerer Lord lived here?"

He nodded and pointed to the buildings one after another. "Oh yes. That was his mansion, that was a storehouse, the third one was a workshop, that was the slave pen, and—"

"Slave pen?" Dana's hand reflexively went to her knife.

"Few people know this, but the Sorcerer Lords made up less than one percent of the population in lands they ruled. The rest of the people were property, owned from the day they were born until they breathed their last breath. Men, elves, ogres, minotaurs, gnomes; they'd put anyone in chains except goblins, who were too hard to control and could do too little work to bother breaking their will."

Pointing at the ruins, he added, "And somewhere in that mess is our enemy, guarding rubble for a master long since dead. I'd feel sorry for it living such a pointless existence, save for the fact it will kill for a cause lost long ago and never worth fighting for."

"It could be hiding in a dozen places waiting in ambush. How are we going to find it?"

Jayden stretched his arms over his head. "*We* aren't going to do anything of the sort. Your job was to get me here and you succeeded, a deed to be proud of. The rest is up to me. Find a safe place to wait and let me dispose of the estate guard."

Worried, she asked, "You're just going to walk in there?"

He let his arms fall to his side and smirked. "Hardly. The estate guard is bound by ancient commands to defend this slovenly hole in the ground. I need only cause some property damage and it will come to save its home. Once it's in the open, the fight will be short and exceptionally loud."

"Sounds like throwing rocks at a hornet nest." Dana was glad to let Jayden do the hard part. This was so dangerous it was at best fifty percent her responsibility. But she hesitated before looking for cover. "Um, Jayden, the first time I met the monster was miles away."

"And?"

She waved her hands at the distant forest. "How do we know it's here? It could be in the woods looking for parts to make more bodies or patrolling for invaders."

A rasping, scraping sound came from behind them, the sound of dry branches rubbing against each other. Dana and Jayden turned to find the estate guard cresting a hill not thirty feet from where they stood. Its front legs carried a load of deer antlers that must have been shed by their owners a few weeks ago.

The monster was as terrifying as the last time she'd seen it. It was a mishmash of pine branches and animals bones woven together to form a hideous spider. The body and legs weren't solid, instead having holes where the parts didn't fully come together. Scattered across that horrible body were skulls of deer and elk, bears and wolves, their empty eye sockets staring out in all directions. The spider's abdomen was mostly empty space, a net of curving branches and ribs that reminded Dana of a cage.

Surprise froze all three as still as statues. The estate guard acted first and threw down the pile of antlers. It raised its front legs high in the air and howled as it charged them.

"Go left!" Jayden shouted. He went right and spoke strange words she'd never heard before. Dana ran left toward the largest wrecked building. To her horror, she heard the howls and rasping growing closer. It was coming after her!

Dana screamed and ran. She nearly slipped on the mossy ground, recovering just fast enough to keep from tripping. She looked behind her to see the estate guard closing the distance between them while Jayden finished his spell. With a final unpronounceable word, he formed a purplish lash in his hands. He drew back his arm and swung it, the lash stretching farther and farther until it wrapped around the monster. It burned like acid where it touched, but the estate guard raced after Dana regardless of the injury. It ran so fast the lash couldn't stretch quickly enough, and Jayden was pulled off his feet.

Dana kept screaming, the monster kept howling, and Jayden cried out in surprise as he was dragged behind it. Every breath Dana took stank of wood smoke and smoldering bones as the magic lash continued burning through the monster. Dana heard the monster only feet behind her. She planted a foot on a large rock jutting up from the ground and pushed left. That was enough to throw her to the left, and she rolled as she hit the ground. The monster tried to follow her, but it was so large it couldn't stop in time and skidded to a halt twenty feet away.

Facing the very real possibility of dying, she was sure this was at most ten percent her responsibility.

Dana scrambled to her feet and saw the monster wheel about to face her. Jayden came to a halt as well, but he'd never let go of his magic lash. He braced himself against the same rock Dana had jumped off. Pushing back hard, he pulled the lash and it tightened across the monster. The lash had already eaten through much of the beast, but now it looped around it, pinning legs together until the beast fell as helpless as a roped calf.

The monster rocked back and forth in a vain attempt to escape. The lash kept burning through it, taking off one leg and then another. The abdomen was cut in half. One leg got loose only to be hacked off at the base. In seconds, the entire monster fell apart into a pile of smoking branches and cut bones.

"That was, I, oh, God," Dana gasped.

"Find the talisman!" Jayden ordered. He kicked through the debris as the lash dissolved. "Don't let it escape!"

Dana ran to the monster's body. She held her lantern high with her left hand and dug through the remains with her right. The remains smelled horrible and were hot to the touch, but nothing looked like the gold bug Jayden had described. Suddenly, something glinted off the light of her lantern. It tried to scurry under loose branches, but she dug through them until she saw it.

The talisman managed to be both pretty and revolting at the same time. It was only three inches across and looked like a beetle. Whoever had made it had put a lot of effort into the job, and it looked gorgeous. But then the eye on its abdomen blinked, an eye so very much like a person's eye, and it was watching her.

"There!" she shouted. She tried to grab it, but the talisman scuttled away as fast as a racehorse. Jayden cast another spell and formed a magic sword pure black and edged with white. He swung at it and missed, the blade burning through the mossy ground and rocks beneath it. The talisman went right then left, dodging both Jayden and Dana, and ran for the nearest ruined building. It made a mad dash and climbed into a crack in the wall.

"Run before it assembles another body," Jayden ordered. He headed for the nearest hole in the building large enough for him to fit through. Dana looked for a place to hide before the monster returned. Going into the forest was a bad bet when the monster ran faster than she did. The other buildings were close and intact enough for her to hide in. She ran to the one Jayden claimed was a slave pen.

She'd nearly reached it when the estate guard marched out with a new body. This time it was an enormous hound, just as large as the spider but with terrifying jaws big enough to fit a grown man inside. It came out the main entrance with Jayden following a step behind. The hound raced away before Jayden could stab it and was so quick soon it was a hundred feet from him.

Dana ducked into the slave pen, a foul structure that looked like a brick barn three hundred feet long and fifty feet wide. There were rusted gates across wide stalls, some open and others crushed shut. It disgusted Dana to even be here, to see how people had once been treated. She turned away and stayed by the entrance.

Outside, the fight was back on. The estate guard in its new body turned and charged Jayden, and he ran right for it. The hound leaped at him, and Jayden slid onto his back and raised his magic blade. The hound went over him, and the blade split it in half down the middle. He got up and dug through the bones and branches. Dana didn't see the talisman from this distance, but Jayden must have because he ran after something on the ground. It escaped into the old mansion. Jayden gave chase and the sounds of battle came from inside the crumbling structure.

Dana saw a wall bulge on the mansion until the bricks crumbled away. Jayden came out with the estate guard after him. This time, it had the shape of a man ten feet tall but without a head. It had bear skulls on its shoulders and hands ending in long claws that tried to impale Jayden. He dodged the monster's swing and hacked off one of its arms.

"This is insane," Dana said. Jayden was taking the monster apart again and again, but his victories were as hollow as the ones her people had won against it so long ago. It kept fleeing and returning as good as new. Jayden would tire sooner or later. Could he run out of spells? That would be just as bad.

The estate guard lost another body when Jayden impaled it with his magic sword. He pulled left and the sword sliced through it until the upper part tumbled to the ground. Again, he scrambled after the escaping talisman, and again, it found enough materials to rebuild itself, this time as a huge lizard. Battle was joined again, and it knocked him down with a swing of its tail. He recovered fast and lopped off the tail.

Dana backed away from the entrance. She'd brought Jayden here and he was going to get killed. She should have gotten more people so they could catch the talisman between battles and break the stupid thing! Wait. The estate guard had hidden branches and bones for new bodies in the other buildings. Had it left more here?

Dana hurried back inside the slave pens. Some of the pens were open, and sure enough, one had a heaping pile of pine branches and animal bones. She checked the rest of the building and found one, two, three, four pens loaded with wood and bones. Dead pine needles from those branches were thick on the floor. Each pile looked like it was big enough to make a new body.

She went through her possessions for something that could destroy these spare bodies before the estate guard could use them. Her knife couldn't cut through the thick branches fast enough. She dug through her backpack. Food? No. Money? No. Oil?

Oil! Dana smiled. She had extra oil for her lantern, but there wasn't much left. The estate guard had stashed the wood here so it wouldn't get rained on and rot before it could be used. That made sense, but it also meant the branches were dry, and dry pine burned fast.

Dana poured the flask of oil onto the piles of branches. She had so little, she could only lightly lace each pile. Once she was out, she used her lantern to ignite each pile in turn. Whoosh! Flames raced across the piles and the dead needles on the floor. Dana ran outside when the building started to fill with smoke.

She returned to see Jayden dispatch the huge lizard by decapitating it. The rest of it fell apart and the talisman fled. Jayden's sword flickered and went out, and he made a lash to replace it. He swung at the talisman, but the thing was incredibly fast. It went one way and then another, skittering under bricks and into cracks whenever he got close.

The talisman reached the slave pen Dana had just left. It ducked inside then hurried back out to find her waiting for it. She grabbed at it, but it scuttled back inside.

Jayden caught up with her and saw smoke billowing from the slave pen. "What did you do?"

"I torched four spare bodies," she explained. He looked shocked, and she added, "I got bored."

To Dana's amazement, the estate guard left the slave pen with a new body. It resembled a giant stag beetle with huge jaws as long as its body and human skulls for eyes. But this body was built from burning pine, a walking bonfire that lit up the ruins. It lunged forward and tried to catch them in its jaws. Jayden and Dana ran for their lives as the animated inferno chased them. Dana's neck and back felt hot as embers fell around her.

Two of the beetle's legs burned through, and it struggled along on the other four. It hobbled along a few more paces until another leg gave out and the beetle crashed to the ground. The talisman was forced to abandon the body as it burned away, but this time, Jayden and Dana were right on top of it. It circled around the burning pine, trying to use it as a shield, but Dana caught up with it when it made a run for the mansion. She grabbed a loose brick off the ground and swung it like a hammer.

Crack! She smashed off three gold legs from the talisman. It kept running, but slower than before. Jayden swung his magic lash and struck it. Snap! The talisman broke in half under the blow. Its remaining legs curled up and the eye on its back twitched and closed.

Jayden stared hard at the broken talisman. "That was incredibly satisfying."

Dana woke up the next morning in what had once been a mansion. It was spacious, but the place felt wrong. The angles of the walls were odd and the doorframes tilted to one side. It was jarring to look at, and she didn't see how anyone could feel comfortable living here.

Her brief stay was unpleasant but necessary. She'd been too exhausted to go home after the fight. She'd also used all her oil, and it had been so dark she'd have hurt herself stumbling about at night. Chances were the whole town would be looking for her by now, and she could only imagine the punishment waiting for her.

Jayden joined her from another part of the mansion. He carried an armful of loot and smiled like the cat who'd caught the canary. "Good morning, and a glorious morning at that."

"What did you find?"

"This, madam, is a prize beyond all others." He held up a black granite tablet a foot across and two feet long, with markings in white marble on one side. The markings looked like letters, but not in any language she could read.

Dana needed only seconds to guess what it was.

"That was written by the old Sorcerer Lords, wasn't it? It's a spell!"

Jayden smiled. "You are clever. The old Sorcerer Lords wrote their spells on granite tablets. It's not very portable, but they last far longer than spellbooks written on paper or velum. I don't recognize this incantation. It looks promising, and I'm sure it will be a good addition to my repertoire once I've translated it."

Her heart sank at the sight of it. "Is that why you came? I mean, is that what you were after?"

He shrugged. "It was part of the reason. I told you I recognized what you described in your letter as an estate guard. If it was here, then at some point there had been treasure worth guarding. Any riches might have been carried off or destroyed long ago, so there was no guarantee of a reward for my efforts, but thankfully, I won't leave empty-handed. There's also a bit of gold I'm happy to share. You went beyond expectations yesterday, and a reward is owed."

Jayden saw her crestfallen expression and frowned. He sat down next to her and set aside his treasures. "Don't be like that. Saving your people is important. Lord knows the king wouldn't lift a finger for you. But good deeds don't pay the rent, and I've spent all the gold I got for those stolen horses."

Dana put her hands on her hips. "You didn't mention that when you listed your crimes yesterday."

"Please, I'd need a day and a night to tell you everything I'd done against the king. I'm sure those knights won't mind going to war on foot. If I'm successful, they won't go to war at all, but we're a long way from that day."

With that, he bent over and kissed her on the forehead. Dana blushed, in large part because her father did the same thing. "Cut that out! I'm not a little girl!"

Jayden smiled and stood up before helping her to her feet. "Now, we need to come up with a story for you, young lady, one that leaves me out. When you get home, tell your parents you were attacked by the monster. That's true enough. You ran from it when a stranger appeared and defeated the beast. It was too dark to see the stranger's features clearly, but you're sure he's dashingly handsome."

Dana folded her arms across her chest. "Oh, am I?"

"You're positive of it!" Jayden held out the broken pieces of the estate guard and pressed them into her hand. "He gave you this and swore the monster is gone, never to return. Your people may enter these woods without fear."

"You're not taking the credit?"

"The king and queen don't think highly of me. If they learn I helped your town, they'd punish your family, at the very least exiling you and more likely executing you. Better for all concerned if someone else gets blamed for this."

Jayden left the mansion and Dana followed. It was hard to say whether he was a good man or not. He had done good things and others that were questionable. Her father often said flawed men could work wonders if someone gave them a chance. What would Jayden do next? What would he become if left alone with no one to help him should he go off course?

She ran in front of him and stood in his way. "I can help you."

Jayden raised an eyebrow. "You, child, are going home."

"You want more magic. I know a place where you might find it. There's a castle by the sea, abandoned before the kingdom was founded. It might date to the old Sorcerer Lords. There could be treasure in it or even those tablets. No one ever looted it because they say there's a monster there called The Walking Graveyard."

"I'm sure it's done much to earn that charming nickname." Jayden studied his fingers as if he'd never noticed them before. "I've spent very little time in that part of the kingdom and know little of it. I don't relish wandering across a desolate coastline for weeks in search of this castle."

Dana took a deep breath. When you made a choice, you have to take responsibility, all of it. "That's why you need a guide."

Arthur Daigle is the author (no jokes, please, he's heard them all) of five books set on the world of Other Place. These include William Bradshaw King of the Goblins, William Bradshaw and a Faint Hope, William Bradshaw and War Unending, William Bradshaw and Fool's Gold, and Goblin Stories. Expect serious issues drowning in a sea of silliness, mayhem and outright madness. See goblins, the perennial losers of fantasy novels and games, be put into positions of importance no matter how hard they try to avoid it. Feel free to come visit, but watch your step for trip lines and pie traps.

Want more? Buy stories and books from these authors! Or get another collection of short stories to sample in the first Fellowship of Fantasy anthology, *Fantastic Creatures*.

Find more stories from these authors and others
at www.FellowshipOfFantasy.com.

Made in the
USA
Middletown, DE